QUO VADIS

A Classic Story of Love and Adventure

To my dearest Margaret,
who, like Lygia, pointed
the way during hard times.

Copyright © 1992 by James S. Bell, Jr.
Adapted and abridged from Quo Vadis: A Narrative of
the Time of Nero by Henryk Sienkiewicz

Translated from the Polish by Jeremiah Curtin

Copyright © 1896, 1897 Jeremiah Curtin
© 1923, 1925 Alma Mary Curtin

This book was first published in the United States by Moody Press
Reprinted by Hodder and Stoughton by permission

Spire is an imprint of Hodder and Stoughton *Publishers*

British Library Cataloguing in Publication Data

A catalogue record for this book is
available from the British Library

ISBN 0-340-59163-3

*Reproduced from the original setting by arrangement with
Northfield Publishing, Chicago*

*Printed in Great Britain for Hodder and Stoughton Limited, Mill Road, Dunton Green,
Sevenoaks, Kent by Clays Ltd, St Ives plc.*

Hodder and Stoughton Editorial Office: 47 Befrod Square, London WC1B 3DP.

QUO VADIS

A Classic Story of Love and Adventure

Henryk Sienkiewicz

*Edited and Abridged
by James S. Bell, Jr.*

Acknowledgments

To Chris Criel, who stayed one step ahead of me in typing the manuscript for revision; and to those at Moody Press who had the original vision for the Christian Epic series.

Preface

"Quo vadis, Domine?" Or as the apostle Peter would say in common parlance, "Where do we go from here, Lord?" Legend has it that Peter sought to flee Rome after the seeming destruction of the Christian church there, resulting from persecution under Nero. He was supposedly not afraid, but rather wished to preserve the rest of the church in light of the victory of Antichrist (Nero) in the new Babylon (Rome). But the Lord's response to "Quo vadis?" was for Peter to return and die with his brethren, not in defeat, but as a sign of victory over the powers of darkness. Whether this legend is true or not, we all know the outcome. Christianity triumphed, and the blood of the martyrs became the seed of the church. Rome became the center of a new Christian civilization that conquered the world. The early Christians conquered not through the worldly power and human strength of the pagan Romans, but through submission to their Lord, forgiveness, virtue, suffering, and love.

Quo Vadis is an epic spectacle of stark contrasts. We see the lavish excesses and opulence connected with a world empire. Yet it is an empire in decline, grossly immoral and decadent, increasingly lacking in civic virtue and discipline. In contrast to its materialism, outmoded mythology, and abandoned philosophy lies the pristine beauty, purity, and truth of the Christian faith wholeheartedly believed and practiced by its followers.

The characters in this book are unforgettable: gladiators, giant supermen, Jewish philosophers, Roman noblemen, foreign princesses, slaves, centurions, grave-diggers, zealous Christians, super-apostles, beautiful maidens, and Caesar himself.

The authenticity of the descriptions makes this world come alive. There are sumptuous feasts filled with sensual delights, candle-bearing Christians chanting hymns on moonlit nights, roaring flames seen consuming Rome from a hilltop, and heroic martyrs lighting Caesar's gardens and filling the amphitheater with a forest of crosses.

Yet all this pales in comparison to the book's central theme: the ardent and undying love of a headstrong Roman tribune of a prominent pagan family for a beautiful, demure, foreign Christian princess. Vinicius will relinquish all for the holy spark of beauty and truth he perceives in his precious Lygia, who seeks only to please Christ. Their devotion to each other against all odds impresses and illuminates the entire plot and characters. He does not understand this new religion, these "enemies of mankind" who are taking the empire by storm. Nor does his uncle Petronius, the cultivated, urbane, and cynical friend of Nero. But Petronius is not evil, rather he seeks only to enjoy the sublime aspects of life, as would the elite of cultured, pagan Rome.

This is a timeless tale of all that matters to the human heart and soul. Spiritual ideals and romantic love are pitted against greed, lust, and materialism. So it is today, and every reader will recognize this struggle in his own heart and life.

1

Petronius woke only about midday, and as usual he was greatly wearied. The evening before he had been at one of Nero's feasts, which was prolonged until late at night. For some time his health had been failing. He woke up groggy, without the power to think clearly. But the morning bath and careful massaging of the body by trained slaves gradually hastened the course of his sluggish blood flow, roused him, and restored his strength, so that he proceeded from the last division of the bath as if he had risen from the dead, eyes gleaming with gladness, rejuvenated, filled with life, so unapproachable that Otho himself could not compare with him. He was truly a refined and elegant judge of the people, an "Arbiter Elegantiarum."

He visited the public baths rarely, only when some orator appeared there who caused admiration and was spoken of in the city, or when in the ranks of youths there were combats of exceptional interest. Also, in his own insula he had private baths that Celer, the famous contemporary of Severus, had extended for him, reconstructed and arranged with such uncommon taste that Nero himself acknowledged their excellence over those of the emperor, though the imperial baths were more extensive and finished with incomparably greater luxury.

After that feast, at which he was bored by the jesting of Vatinius with Nero, Lucan, and Seneca, he took part in a debate as to whether women have a soul. Rising late, he used the baths, as was his custom. Two enormous balneatores, bath attendants, laid him on a cypress table covered with snow-white Egyptian byssus, and with hands dipped in perfumed olive oil began to rub his shapely body; and he waited with closed eyes until the heat of the laconicum, or steam bath, and the heat of their hands passed through him and put him in a relaxed state.

After a certain time he spoke and opened his eyes; he in-

11

quired about the weather and then about gems the jeweler Idomeneus had promised to send him for examination that day. It
appeared that the weather was beautiful, with a light breeze from
the Alban hills, and that the gems had not been brought. Petronius had closed his eyes again and ordered the slaves to carry him
to the tepidarium, a warm pool, when from behind the curtain the
announcer looked in, telling him that young Marcus Vinicius, recently returned from Asia Minor, had come to visit him.

Petronius ordered them to admit the guest to the tepidarium.
Vinicius was the son of Petronius's oldest sister, who years before
had married Marcus Vinicius, a man of consul position from the
time of Tiberius. The young man Marcus was serving then under
Corbulo against the Parthians and at the close of the war had returned to the city. Petronius had for him a certain weakness bor-
dering on attachment, for Marcus was handsome and athletic, a
young man who knew how to preserve a certain temperance in his
extravagance. Petronius prized that above everything.

"A greeting to Petronius," the young man said, entering the
pool with a springy step. "May all the gods grant you success, but
especially Asklepios and Kypris, for under their double protection
you can meet nothing evil."

"I greet you in Rome, and may your rest be sweet after war,"
replied Petronius, extending his hand from between the folds of
karbas stuff in which he was wrapped. "What's the news in Armenia; or since you were in Asia, did you stumble into Bithynia?"

Petronius once had been proconsul in Bithynia and, further-
more, had governed with energy and justice. That was a marvelous contrast in the character of a man noted for certain feminine
qualities and love of luxury; thus he was fond of mentioning those
times because they were a proof of his manly valor and of what he
might have become had he intended to do so.

"I happened to visit Heraklea," Vinicius answered. "Corbulo
sent me there with an order to assemble reinforcements."

"Ah, Heraklea! At Heraklea I knew a certain maiden from Col-
chis, for whom I would have given all the divorced women of this
city, not excluding Poppaea. But these are old stories. Tell me
now, rather, what is to be heard from the Parthian border? It is
true that every Vologeses wearies me, as do Tiridates and Ti-

granes—those barbarians who, as young Arulenus insists, walk on all fours at home and pretend to be human only when in our presence. But now people in Rome speak well of them, if only for the reason that it is dangerous to speak of anything else."

"The war is going badly and except for Corbulo's efforts might end in defeat."

"Corbulo! By Bacchus! A real god of war, a genuine Mars, a great leader, at the same time quick-tempered, honest, and dull. I love him, even for this—that Nero is afraid of him."

"Corbulo is not an ignorant or stupid man."

"Perhaps you are right, but it's all the same. Foolishness, as Pyrrho says, is in no way worse than wisdom and has many of the same characteristics."

Vinicius began to talk of the war; but when Petronius closed his eyes again, the young man, seeing his uncle's tired and somewhat gaunt face, changed the conversation and inquired with a certain interest about his health.

Petronius opened his eyes again.

Health! No. He did not feel well. He had not gone so far yet, it is true, as young Sissena, who had lost sensation to such a degree that when he was brought to the bath in the morning he inquired, "Am I sitting?" But, nevertheless, he was not well. Vinicius had just committed him to the care of Asklepios and Kypris. But he, Petronius, did not believe in Asklepios. It was not known even whose son this Asklepios was, the son of Arsinoe or Koronis; and if the mother was doubtful, what was to be said of the father? Who, in that time, could be sure who his own father was?

Petronius began to laugh; then he continued: "Two years ago, it is true, I sent three dozen live blackbirds and a goblet of gold to Epidaurus; but do you know why? I said to myself, 'Whether this helps or not, it will do me no harm.' Though people still make offerings to the gods, I believe all people think as I do—with the exception, perhaps, of mule-drivers hired at the Porta Capena by travelers. Besides Asklepios, I have had dealings with sons of Asklepios. When I was troubled a little last year in the bladder, they performed an incubation for me. I saw that they were tricksters, but I said to myself: 'What harm! The world stands on deceit, and life is an illusion. The soul is an illusion too. But one

13

must have reason enough to distinguish pleasant from painful il-lusions.' I shall command that they burn cedarwood sprinkled with ambergris in my hypocaustum [sweat bath], for during life I prefer perfumes to stenches. As to Kypris, to whom you have also committed me, I have known her guardianship to the extent that I have twinges in my right foot. But as to the rest she is a good goddess! I suppose that you will bring white doves to her altar sooner or later."

"True," Vinicius answered. "The arrows of the Parthians have not reached my body, but a dart of love has struck me—unexpect-edly, a few stadia from a gate of this city."

"By the white knees of the Graces! You will tell me of this at a leisure hour I hope."

"I have come for the express purpose of getting your advice," answered Marcus.

But at that moment the epilatores came and occupied them-selves with Petronius. Marcus, throwing aside his tunic, entered the pool of tepid water, for Petronius invited him to a plunge bath.

"Ah, I have not even asked whether your romantic feelings are reciprocated," Petronius said, looking at the youthful body of Marcus, which was as if cut out of marble. "Had Lysippos seen you, you would be adorning the gate leading to the Palatine, as a statue of Hercules in youth."

The young man smiled with satisfaction and began to sink in the pool, splashing warm water abundantly on the mosaic that represented Hera at the moment when she was imploring Sleep to lull Zeus to rest. Petronius looked at him with the satisfied eye of an artist.

When Vinicius had finished and yielded himself in turn to the epilatores, a reader came in with a bronze tube at his chest and rolls of paper in the tube.

"Do you wish to listen?" asked Petronius.

"If it is your written work, gladly!" answered the young trib-une. "If not, I prefer conversation. Poets seize people at present on every street corner."

"Of course they do. You will not pass any basilica, bath, li-brary, or bookshop without seeing a poet making gestures and sounds like a monkey. Agrippa, on coming here from the East,

14

mistook them for madmen. And it is just such a time now. Caesar writes verses; thus everyone follows in his steps. Only it is not permitted to write better verses than Caesar, and for that reason I fear a little for Lucan. But I write prose, with which I do not honor myself or others. What the reader has to share are works of that poor Fabricius Veiento."

"Why 'poor'?"

"Because it has been communicated to him that he must live in Odyssa and not return to his home until he receives a new command. That odyssey will be easier for him than for Ulysses, since his wife is no Penelope. I need not tell you, for that matter, that he acted stupidly. But here no one takes things otherwise than superficially. His is rather a wretched and dull little book, which people have begun to read passionately only when the author is banished. Now one hears on every side, 'Scandal! Scandal!' and it may be that Veiento invented some things; but I who know the city, know our men and our women, assure you that it is all less than substantial. Meanwhile, every man is searching in the book —for himself with alarm, for his acquaintances with delight. A hundred copyists are busy at the bookshop of Avirnus, and its success is assured."

"Are not your doings in it as well?"

"They are, but the author is mistaken, for I am at once worse and yet better in some ways than he represents me. We have long since lost the feeling of what is worthy or unworthy—and it seems to me that there is no difference between them, though Seneca, Musonius, and Trasca pretend that they see it. To me it is all one! By Hercules, I say what I think! I have preserved loftiness, however, because I know what is deformed and what is beautiful; but our poet Bronzebeard, who is the charioteer, the singer, and the actor, does not understand this."

"I am sorry, however, for Fabricius! He is a good companion."

"Vanity ruined the man. Everyone suspected him, no one knew certainly; but he could not restrain himself and told the secret to everyone in confidence. Have you heard the history of Rufinus?"

"No."

"Then come to the frigidarium to cool; there I will tell you."

They went to the cooling room, in the middle of which bub-
bled a fountain of bright rose color, producing the odor of violets.
There they sat in booths that were covered with velvet and began
to cool themselves. Silence reigned for a time. Vinicius looked
thoughtfully at a bronze faun that, bending over the arm of a
nymph, was seeking her lips eagerly with his lips.

"He is right," said the young man. "That is what is best in
life."

"More or less! But besides love itself you love war, for which
I have no liking, since under tents your fingernails break and
cease to be rosy. For that matter, every man has his preferences.
Bronzebeard loves song, especially his own, and old Scaurus his
Corinthian vase, which stands near his bed at night and which he
kisses when he cannot sleep. He has kissed the edge off already.
Tell me, do you write verses?"

"No, I have never composed a single hexameter."

"And do you not play on the lute and sing?"

"No."

"And do you drive a chariot?"

"I tried once in Antioch, but unsuccessfully."

"Then I am satisfied. And to what party in the hippodrome do
you belong?"

"To the Greens."

"Now I am perfectly content, especially since you own a
large property indeed, though you are not so rich as Pallas or Seneca. For it is fine to write poetry, to sing to a lute, to make speeches, and to compete in the Circus; but better, and especially safer,
is it not to write verses, play, sing, or compete in the Circus. Best
of all, it is important to know how to admire when Bronzebeard
admires. You are a handsome young man; so Poppaea may fall in
love with you. This is your only danger. No, she is too experienced; she cares for something else. She has had enough of love
with her two husbands; with the third she has other opinions. Do
you know that stupid Otho loves her yet to distraction? He walks
on the cliffs of Spain and sighs. He has so lost his former habits
and so ceased to take care of himself, that it takes him three hours
each day to dress his hair. Who could have expected this of
Otho?"

"I understand him," Vinicius answered, "but I should have done something else."

"What, exactly?"

"I should have enrolled faithful legions of mountaineers of that country. They are good soldiers—those Iberians."

"Vinicius! Vinicius! I am tempted to tell you that you would not have been capable of that task. Do you know why? Such things are done, but they are not mentioned even in passing. As to me, in Othos's place I should have laughed at Poppaea, laughed at Bronze-beard, and formed my own legions, not of Iberian men, but Iberian women. I would also have written epigrams for no one in particular—not like that poor Rufinus."

"You were going to tell me his history."

"I will tell it in the unctorium."

But in the unctorium the attention of Vinicius was turned to other objects, namely, to the wonderful slave women who were waiting for the bathers. Two of them, Africans, resembling noble statues of ebony, began to anoint their bodies with delicate perfumes from Arabia; others, Phrygians, skilled in hairdressing, held in their hands, which were bending and flexible as serpents, combs and mirrors of polished steel; two Grecian maidens from Kos, who closely resembled deities, waited as vestiplicae until the moment should come to put statuesque folds in the togas of the lords.

"By the cloud-scattering Zeus!" Marcus Vinicius said, "what a choice you have!"

"I prefer choice to numbers," Petronius answered. "My household servants in Rome do not exceed four hundred, and I judge that for personal attendance only upstarts need a greater number of people."

"Even Bronzebeard does not possess more beautiful bodies," Vinicius said, flaring his nostrils.

"You are my relative," Petronius answered, with a certain friendly indifference, "and I am neither so distrustful as Barsus nor such a narrow-minded teacher as Aulus Plautius."

When Vinicius heard this last name, he forgot the maidens from Kos for a moment and, raising his head energetically, inquired, "When did Aulus Plautius come to your mind? Do you know that after I had dislocated my arm outside the city I spent some time in his house? Plautius came up at the moment when the accident happened and, seeing that I was suffering greatly, took me to his house. There a slave of his, the physician Merion, restored me to health. I wished to speak with you on this very matter."

"Why? Is it because you have fallen in love with Pomponia perchance? In that case I pity you; she is not young, and she is virtuous! I cannot imagine a worse combination. Brr!"

"Not with Pomponia—in no way!" Vinicius answered.

"With whom, then?"

"I don't know. I do not even know her name—Lygia or Callina? They call her Lygia in the house, for she comes from the Lygian nation; but she has her own barbarian name, Callina. It is a wonderful house—the Plautiuses'. There are many people in it, but it is as quiet there as in the groves of Subiacum. For a number of days I did not know that a divinity lived in the house. Once about daybreak I saw her bathing in the garden fountain; and I swear to you by that foam from which Aphrodite rose, that the rays of the dawn passed right through her body. I thought that when the sun rose she would vanish before me in the light, as the twilight of morning does. Since then, I have seen her twice; and since then, too, I do not know what rest is, or other desires. I have no wish to know the life of the city. I want neither women, nor gold, nor Corinthian bronze, nor amber, nor pearls, nor wine, nor feasts; I want only Lygia. I am yearning for her, in sincerity I tell you, Petronius, as that dream who is imaged on the mosaic of your bath yearned for Paisythea—whole days and nights I yearn for Lygia."

"If she is a slave, then purchase her."

"She is not a slave."

"What is she? A freed woman of Plautius?"

"She could not be a freed woman never having been a slave."

"Who is she?"

"I don't know—a king's daughter, or something of that sort."

"You arouse my curiosity, Vinicius."

"But if you wish to listen, I will satisfy your curiosity right away. Her story is not a long one. You are acquainted, perhaps

18

personally, with Vannius, king of the Suevi, who, expelled from his country, spent a long time here in Rome and became even famous for his skillful play with dice and his skilled driving of chariots. Drusus put him on the throne again. Vannius, who was quite a strong man, ruled well at first but couldn't handle success. Later he began to seriously harm not only his neighbors, but his own Suevi. Then Vangio and Sido, two nephews of his, and the sons of Vibilius, king of the Hermunduri, determined to force him to Rome again—to try his luck there at gambling."

"I remember; that was in the recent reign of Claudius."

"Yes! War broke out. Vannius sought the aid of the Yazgi people; his dear nephews called in the Lygians, who, hearing of the riches of Vannius and enticed by the hope of booty, came in such great numbers that Claudius Caesar began to fear for the safety of the national boundaries. Claudius did not wish to interfere in a war among barbarians, but he wrote to Atelius Hister, who commanded legions of the Danube, to turn a watchful eye on the progress of the war and not permit them to disturb our peace. Hister required the Lygians to promise not to cross the boundary; they not only agreed to this but gave him hostages, among whom were the wife and daughter of their leader. You know that barbarians take their wives and children to war with them. My Lygia is the daughter of that leader."

"How do you know all this?"

"Aulus Plautius told me himself. The Lygians indeed did not cross the boundary, but barbarians come and go like a tempest. So the Lygians vanished with their wild ox horns on their heads. They killed Vannius's Suevi and Yazgi; but their own king fell. They disappeared with their booty then, and the hostages remained in Hister's hands. The mother died soon after, and Hister, not knowing what to do with the daughter, sent her to Pomponius, the governor of all Germany. At the close of the war with the Catti, Pomponius returned to Rome, where Claudius, as you know, permitted him to demonstrate victory. On that occasion the young woman followed the procession of the conqueror; but at the end of the solemnity—since hostages cannot be considered captives, and since Pomponius did not know what to do with her—he gave her to his sister Pomponia Graecina, the wife of Plautius. In that house where all—beginning with the men and ending with the poultry in the henhouse—are virtuous, that young woman grew up as virtuous as Graecina herself and so beautiful that even Poppaea, if near her, would seem like an autumn fig near an apple of the Hesperides."

"And then?"

"The moment when I saw how the rays of the sun at that fountain passed through her body, I fell in love to the point of distraction."

"She is as transparent as a lamprey eel, or a youthful sardine?"

"Do not jest, Petronius; but if the freedom with which I speak of my desire startles you, know this—that bright garments frequently cover deep wounds. I must tell you that when I was returning from Asia I slept one night in the temple of Mopsus to have a prophetic dream. Well, Mopsus appeared in a dream to me, and declared that, through love, a great change in my life would take place."

"Pliny declares, as I hear, that he does not believe in the gods but he believes in dreams; and perhaps he is right. My jests do not prevent me from thinking at times that in truth there is only one deity—eternal, creative, all-powerful—Venus Genetrix. She brings souls together; she unites bodies and things. Eros called the world out of chaos. Whether he did it well is another question; but, since he did it, we should recognize his might, though we are free not to approve it."

"Petronius, it is easier to find philosophy in the world than wise counsel."

"Tell me, what is your particular wish?"

"I wish to have Lygia. I wish that these arms of mine that now embrace only air might embrace Lygia and press her to my chest. I wish to breathe with her breath. Were she a slave, I would buy her from Aulus with one hundred maidens with feet whitened with lime as a sign that they were exhibited on sale for the first time. I wish to have her in my house until my head is as white as the top of Soracte in winter."

"She is not a slave, but she belongs to the household of Plautius; and since she is a deserted maiden, she may be considered a foster daughter. Plautius might give her to you if he wished."

"Then it seems that you don't know Pomponia Graecina. Both have become as much attached to her as if she were their own daughter."

"Pomponia I know—a real cypress. If she were not the wife of Aulus, she might be employed as a mourner. Since the death of Julius she has not thrown aside dark robes; and in general she looks as if, though still alive, she were walking on a meadow of asphodels. She is, moreover, a 'one-man woman'; so among our ladies of four and five divorces, she is clearly a phoenix. But have you heard that in Upper Egypt the phoenix has just been hatched out, as it is said? An event that doesn't happen more than once in five centuries."

"Petronius! Petronius! Let us talk of the phoenix some other time."

"What shall I tell you, my Marcus? I know Aulus Plautius, who, though he blames my way of life, has a certain weakness for me, and even respects me, perhaps, more than others, for he knows that I have never been an informer like Domitius Afer, Tigellinus, and a whole rabble of Ahenobarbus's [Nero's] intimates. Without pretending to be a stoic, I have been offended more than once at acts of Nero, which Seneca and Burrus looked at through their fingers. If it is your thought that I might do something for you with Aulus, I am at your command."

"I judge that you have the power. You have influence over him, and, besides, your mind possesses inexhaustible resources, if you were to survey the position and speak with Plautius."

"You have too great an opinion of my influence and wit; but if that is the only question, I will talk with Plautius as soon as they return to the city."

"They returned two days ago."

"In that case let us go to the triclinium, where a meal is now ready, and when we have refreshed ourselves, let us give command to bear us to Plautius."

"You have always been kind to me," Vinicius answered with gusto. "But now I shall command that they put your statue among my household gods—just such a beauty as this one—and I will place offerings before it."

21

Then he turned toward the statues that ornamented one entire wall of the perfumed chamber, and, pointing to the one that represented Petronius as Hermes with a staff in his hand, he added, "By the light of Helios! If the 'godlike' Alexander resembled you, I do not wonder at Helen."

And in that exclamation there was as much sincerity as flattery; for Petronius, though older and less athletic, was more beautiful than even Vinicius. The women of Rome admired not only his versatile mind and his aesthetic taste, which gained for him the title Arbiter Elegantiarum, but also his body. This admiration was evident even on the faces of those maidens from Kos who were arranging the folds of his toga; and one, whose name was Eunice, loving him in secret, looked him in the eyes with submission and rapture. But he did not even notice this; and, smiling at Vinicius, he quoted in answer an expression of Seneca about women—*animal impudens*, or "shameless creatures." Then, placing an arm on the shoulders of his nephew, he conducted him to the triclinium.

In the unctorium the two Grecian maidens, the Phrygians, and the two Ethiopians began to put away the perfume vessels. But at that moment, and beyond the curtain of the frigidarium, the heads of the balneatores appeared and a low "Psst!" was heard. At that call one of the Grecians, the Phrygians, and the Ethiopians sprang up quickly and vanished in an instant behind the curtain. In the pools a moment of license began that the inspector did not stop, for he took frequent part in such frolics himself. Petronius suspected that they took place, but, as a prudent man and one who did not like to punish, he winked at them.

In the unctorium only Eunice remained. She listened for a short time to the voices and laughter that retreated in the direction of the laconicum. At last she took the stool inlaid with amber and ivory, on which Petronius had been sitting a short time before, and put it carefully at his statue. The unctorium was full of sunlight and the hues that came from the multicolored marbles that covered the surface of the wall. Eunice stood on the stool and, finding herself at the level of the statue, cast her arms suddenly around its neck; then, throwing back her golden hair and pressing her rosy body to the white marble, she pressed her lips with ecstasy to the cold lips of Petronius.

22

2

After a refreshment, which was called the morning meal and to which the two friends sat down at an hour when common mortals were already long past their midday lunch, Petronius proposed a light doze. According to him, it was too early for visits yet. "There are, it is true," he said, "people who begin to visit their acquaintances about sunrise, thinking that custom an old Roman one, but I look on this as barbarous. The afternoon hours are most proper—not earlier, however, than that one when the sun passes to the side of Jove's temple on the Capitol and begins to appear slantwise on the Forum. In the autumn it is still hot, and people are glad to sleep after eating. At the same time it is pleasant to hear the noise of the fountain in the atrium and, after the obligatory thousand steps, to doze in the red light that filters in through the purple, half-drawn velarium."

Vinicius recognized the justice of these words, and the two men began to walk, speaking in a free manner of what was to be heard on the Palatine and in the city, and philosophizing a little about life. Petronius then withdrew to his cubiculum, or bedroom, but did not sleep long. In half an hour he came out, and, having commanded his slaves to bring verbena, he inhaled the perfume and rubbed his hands and temples with it.

"You will not believe," he said, "how it enlivens and freshens me. Now I am ready."

The litter was waiting long since; so they took their places, and Petronius commanded them to bear them to the Vicus Patricius, to the house of Aulus. Petronius's insula lay on the southern slope of the Palatine, near the so-called Carinae; their nearest way, therefore, was below the Forum; but since Petronius wished to step in on the way to see the jeweller Idomeneus, he directed the slaves to carry them along the Vicus Apollinis and the Forum in the direction of the Vicus Sceleratus, on the corner of which were many shops of every kind.

Gigantic Africans bore the litter and moved on, preceded by slaves called pedisequii. After some time Petronius silently raised his palm, odorous with verbena, to his nostrils and seemed to be meditating on something.

"It occurs to me," said he after a while, "that if your forest goddess is not a slave she might leave the house of Plautius and transfer herself to yours. You would surround her with love and cover her with wealth, as I do my adored Chrysothemis, of whom, speaking between us, I've had quite as nearly enough as she has had of me."

Marcus shook his head in disagreement.

"No?" asked Petronius. "In the worst event, the case would be left with Caesar, and you may be certain that, thanks even to my influence, our Bronzebeard would be on your side."

"You do not know Lygia," Vinicius replied.

"Do you know her other than by sight? Have you spoken with her? Have you confessed your love to her?"

"I saw her first at the fountain; since then I have met her twice. Remember that during my stay in the house of Aulus I stayed in a separate villa intended for guests, and, having a dislocated arm, I could not sit at the common table. Only on the eve of the day I announced my departure did I meet Lygia at supper, but I could not say a word to her. I had to listen to Aulus and his account of victories gained by him in Britain, and then of the fall of small states in Italy, which Licinius Stolo strove to prevent. In general I do not know whether Aulus will be able to speak of anything else, and do not think that we shall escape this history unless it be your wish to hear about the lack of manhood during these days. They have pheasants in their preserves, but they do not eat them, setting out from the principle that every pheasant eaten brings nearer the end of Roman power.

"I met her a second time at the garden cistern, with a freshly plucked reed in her hand. She dipped the top in the water and sprinkled the irises growing around. Look at my knees. By the shield of Hercules, I tell you that they did not tremble when clouds of Parthians advanced on our divisions with howls, but they trembled before the cistern. And, confused as a youth who still wears a bulla on his neck, I merely begged pity with my eyes, not being able to utter a word for a long time."

Petronius looked at him with a certain envy. "Happy man,"

he said. "Though the world and life were the worst possible, one thing in them will remain eternally good—youth!"

After a while he asked, "And have you not spoken to her?"

"When I had recovered somewhat, I told her that I was returning from Asia, that I had dislocated my arm near the city and had suffered severely, but at the moment of leaving that hospitable house I saw that suffering in it was more to be wished than health somewhere else. Confused too on her part, she listened to my words with bent head while drawing something with the reed on the saffron-colored sand. Afterward she raised her eyes, then looked down at the marks drawn already; again she looked at me, as if to ask about something, and then fled on suddenly like a wood nymph before a dull faun."

"She must have beautiful eyes."

"As the sea—and I was drowned in them in the same way. Believe me that the ocean is less blue. After a while a little son of Plautius ran up with a question. But I did not understand what he wanted."

"O Athene!" exclaimed Petronius, "remove from the eyes of this youth the bandage with which Eros has bound them; if not, he will break his head against the columns of Venus's temple.

"O you spring bud on the tree of life," he said, turning to Vinicius, "you first green shoot of the vine! Instead of taking you to the Plautiuses, I ought to command the slaves to bear you to the house of Gelocius, where there is a school for young people unacquainted with the realities of life."

"What do you wish in particular?"

"But what did she write on the sand? Was it the name of Amore, or a heart pierced with his dart, or something of such sort, that one might know from it that the satyrs had whispered to the ear of that nymph various secrets of life? How could you avoid looking at those marks?"

"It has been a longer time since I put on the toga than you realize," Vinicius said, "and before little Aulus ran up, I looked carefully at those marks, for I know that frequently young women in Greece and in Rome draw on the sand a confession they will not speak with their lips. But guess what she drew!"

"If it is not some man's name, I shall not guess."

"A fish."

"What did you say?"

"I said, a fish. What did that mean—that cold blood is flowing in her veins? So far I do not know; but you, who have called me a spring bud on the tree of life, will certainly be able to understand the sign."

"Carissime! Ask such a thing of Pliny the philosopher. He knows fish. If old Apicius were alive, he could tell you something, for in the course of his life he ate more fish than could be found at one time in the bay of Naples."

Further conversation was interrupted, since they entered crowded streets where the noise of people hindered them.

From the Vicus Apollinis they turned to the Boarium, and then entered the Forum Romanum, where on clear days, before sunset, crowds of idle people assembled to stroll among the columns, to exchange news, to see noted people carried past in litters, and finally to look in at the jewelry shops, the bookshops, the arches where coins were changed, and shops for silk, bronze, and all other articles found in the marketplace opposite the Capitol.

One-half of the Forum, immediately under the rock of the Capitol, was buried already in shade; but the columns of the temples, placed higher, seemed golden in the sunshine and the blue sky. Those lying lower cast long shadows on the marble slabs. The place was so filled with columns everywhere that one became lost in them as in a forest.

The buildings and columns seemed huddled together. They towered and stretched toward right and left, they climbed toward the height and clung to the wall of the Capitol. Some clung to others, like greater and smaller, thicker and thinner, white or gold colored tree trunks, buildings now blooming under architraves or flowers of the acanthus, now surrounded with Ionic corners, now finished with a simple Doric quadrangle. Above that forest gleamed colored triglyphs; from tympans the sculptured forms of gods. From the summits winged, golden, four-horse chariots seemed ready to fly away through space into the blue dome, fixed serenely above that crowded place of temples.

Through the middle of the market and along the edges of it flowed a river of people; crowds passed under the arches of the basilica of Julius Caesar; crowds were sitting on the steps of Castor and Pollux, or walking around the temple of Vesta, resembling multicolored swarms of butterflies or beetles on that great marble background. Down immense steps, from the side of the temple on the Capitol dedicated to Jupiter Optimus Maximus, came new waves of people; at the speaker's platform people listened to random orators; here and there rose the shouts of hawkers selling fruit, wine, or water mixed with fig juice; of tricksters; of vendors of marvelous medicines; of soothsayers; of discoverers of hidden treasures; of interpreters of dreams. In the tumult of conversations and cries were mingled sounds of the Egyptian sistra, of the sambuke, or of Grecian flutes. In various places the sick, the pious, or the afflicted were bearing offerings to the temples. In the midst of the people, on the stone flags, gathered flocks of doves, eager for the grain given them, and like movable, many-colored dark spots, now rising for a moment with a loud sound of wings, now dropping down again to places left vacant by people. From time to time the crowds made way for litters to behold the proud faces of women, or the heads of senators and knights, with features that were rigid and exhausted from living. The many-tongued population repeated aloud their names, with the addition of some term of praise or ridicule. Among the unordered groups from time to time, advancing with measured tread, were parties of soldiers, or watchers, preserving order on the streets. Throughout the city, the Greek language was heard as often as Latin.

Vinicius, who had not been in the city for a long time, looked with a certain curiosity on that swarm of people and on that Forum Romanum, which both dominated the sea of the world and was flooded by it, so that Petronius, who guessed the thoughts of his companion, called it "the nest of the Quirites—without the Quirites." In fact, the local element—the Quirites—was practically lost in that crowd, composed of all races and nations. There were Ethiopians, gigantic light-haired people from the distant north, Britons, Gauls, Germans, sloping-eyed dwellers of Lericum; people from the Euphrates and from the Indus, with beards dyed brick color; Syrians from the banks of the Orontes, with black, mild eyes; dwellers in the deserts of Arabia, dried up as a bone; Jews, with their flat breasts; Egyptians, with the eternal, indifferent

27

smile on their faces; Numidians and Africans; Greeks from Hellas, who commanded the city equally with the Romans—but commanded through science, art, wisdom, and deceit; Greeks from the islands, from Asia Minor, from Egypt, from Italy, from Narbonic Gaul. In the throng of slaves, with pierced ears, there was no lack of freemen—an idle population, which Caesar amused, supported, even clothed—and free visitors enticed to the gigantic city by the ease of life and the prospects of fortune; there was no lack of corrupt characters.

There were priests of Serapis, with palm branches in their hands; priests of Isis, to whose altar more offerings were brought than to the temple of the Capitoline Jove; priests of Cybele, bearing in their hands golden ears of rice; and priests of nomad divinities; and dancers of the East with bright headdresses, and dealers in amulets, and snake tamers, and Chaldean seers; and, finally, people without any occupation whatever, who applied for grain every week at the storehouses on the Tiber, who fought for lottery tickets to the Circus, who spent their nights in rickety houses of districts beyond the Tiber, and sunny and warm days under covered porticos, and in foul restaurants of the Subura, on the Milvian bridge, or before the insulae of the great, where from time to time crumbs from the tables of slaves were thrown out to them.

Petronius was well known to those crowds. Vinicius's ears were struck continually by "*Hic est!* [Here he is!]." They loved him for his liberality; and his peculiar popularity increased from the time when they learned that he had spoken before Caesar in opposition to the sentence of death issued against all the slaves of the prefect Pedanius Secundus—without distinction of sex or age —because one of them had killed that monster in a moment of despair. Petronius repeated in public, it is true, that it didn't matter to him, and that he had spoken to Caesar only privately, as the refined eyewitness whose aesthetic taste was offended by a barbarous slaughter befitting Scythians and not Romans. Nevertheless, people who were indignant because of the slaughter loved Petronius from that moment on. But he did not care for their love. He remembered that that crowd of people had also loved Britannicus, poisoned by Nero; and Agrippina, killed at his command; and Octavia, smothered in hot steam at the Pandataria, after her veins had already been cut open; and Rubelius Plautus, who had been banished; and Thrasea, to whom any morning might bring a death sentence. The love of the mob might be considered a bad sign; and the skeptical Petronius was superstitious also. He had a double contempt for the multitude—as an aristocrat and an aesthetic person. Men with the odor of roast beans and who were continually hoarse and sweating from playing mora on the street corners and columned inner courtyards did not in his eyes deserve the term *human*. Hence he gave no answer whatever to the applause or the kisses sent from lips here and there to him. He was relating to Marcus the case of Pedanius, complaining of the fickleness of that rabble which, next morning after the terrible butchery, applauded Nero on his way to the temple of Jupiter Stator. But he stopped before the bookshop of Avirnus and, getting down from the litter, purchased an ornamented manuscript, which he gave to Vinicius.

"Here is a gift for you," he said.

"Thanks!" answered Vinicius. Then, looking at the title, he inquired, *"The Satyricon?* Is this something new? Whose is it?"

"Mine. But I do not wish to go in the road of Rufinus, whose history I will tell you, nor of Fabricius Veiento; so no one knows of this, and do not mention it to anyone."

"You have said that you are no writer of verses," said Vinicius, looking at the middle of the manuscript, "but I see prose closely connected with them."

"When you are reading, turn attention to Trimalchion's feast. As to verses, they have disgusted me, since Nero is writing an epic. Vitelius, when he wishes to relieve himself, uses ivory fingers to thrust down his throat; others serve themselves with flamingo feathers steeped in olive oil or in a decoction of wild thyme. I read Nero's poetry, and the result is immediate. I am able to praise it immediately, if not with a clear conscience, at least with a clear stomach."

When he had said this, he had the litter stopped again before the shop of Idomeneus the goldsmith and, having settled the affair of the gems, commanded the slaves to bear the litter directly to Aulus's mansion.

"On the road I will tell you the story of Rufinus," he said, "as proof of what vanity in an author may be."

But before he had begun, they turned in to the Vicus Patricius and soon found themselves before the dwelling of Aulus. A young and sturdy doorkeeper opened the door leading to the ostium, or entrance hall, over which a magpie confined in a cage greeted them noisily with the word "*Salve!*"

On the way from the ostium to the atrium itself, Vinicius said, "Have you noticed that the doorkeepers are without chains?"

"This is a wonderful house," answered Petronius, in an undertone. "Of course it is known to you that Pomponia Graecina is suspected of entertaining that Eastern superstition which consists in honoring a certain Christus. It seems that Crispinilla rendered her this service—she who cannot forgive Pomponia because one husband has sufficed her for a lifetime. A one-man woman! Today in Rome it is easier to get a half-plate of fresh mushrooms from Noricum than to accomplish this. They tried her before a domestic court—"

"This is a wonderful house," Vinicius interrupted. "Later on I will tell you what I heard and saw in it."

Meanwhile, they had entered the atrium. The butler appointed to it sent an announcer to present the guests. Petronius, who, imagining that perpetual sadness reigned in this severe house, had never been in it, now looked around with astonishment and, as it were, with a feeling of disappointment, for the atrium produced an impression of cheerfulness. A shaft of bright light falling from above through a large opening broke into a thousand sparks on a fountain in a square little basin, the impluvium, which was in the middle of the atrium to receive rain falling through the opening during bad weather; this was surrounded by anemones and lilies. In that house a special love for lilies was evident, for there were whole clumps of them, both white and red; and, finally, sapphire irises, whose delicate leaves seemed silvered from the spray of the fountain. Among the moist mosses, in which lily pots were hidden, and among the bunches of lilies were little bronze statues representing children and water birds. In one corner a bronze fawn, wishing to drink, was bending its greenish head, grizzled by dampness. The floor of the atrium was of mosaic. The walls, which were faced partly with red marble and partly with wood, and were painted with fish, birds, and griffins, attracted the eye by the play of colors. From the door to the side chamber the walls were decorated with tortoiseshell or even ivory; statues of Aulus's ancestors stood against the walls between the doors. Calm was evident everywhere.

Petronius, who lived with incomparably greater pomp and elegance, could find nothing that offended his taste. He had just turned to Vinicius with that remark when the slave in charge of the awning pushed aside the curtain separating the atrium from tablinum, an inner room immediately following the atrium, and in the depths of the building Aulus Plautius appeared, approaching hurriedly.

He was a man nearing the evening of life, with a head whitened by frost, but fresh, with an energetic face, a trifle too short, but still somewhat eaglelike. This time a certain astonishment, and even alarm, was expressed on it because of the unexpected arrival of Nero's friend, companion, and adviser.

Petronius was too much a man of the world and too perceptive not to notice this; therefore, after the first greetings, he announced with all the eloquence and ease at his command that he had come to give thanks for the care his sister's son had found in that house. He stated that gratitude alone was the cause of the visit, to which, also, he was encouraged by his old acquaintance with Aulus.

Aulus assured him that he was a welcome guest; and as to gratitude, he declared that he shared the feeling himself, though surely Petronius did not discover the cause of it.

In fact, Petronius did not comprehend it. In vain he raised his hazel eyes, trying to remember the least service he had rendered to Aulus or to anyone. He recalled none, unless it might be the favor he intended to show Vinicius. Some such thing, it is true, might have happened, but only involuntarily.

"I have great love and esteem for Vespasian, whose life you saved," Aulus said, "when he had the misfortune to doze while listening to Nero's verses."

"He was fortunate," Petronius replied, "for he did not hear them; but I will not deny that the matter might have ended with misfortune. Bronzebeard wished absolutely to send a centurion to him with the friendly advice to cut his veins open."

"But you, Petronius, laughed him out of it."

"That is true, or rather it is not so true. I told Nero that if Orpheus put wild beasts to sleep with song, his triumph was equal, since he had put Vespasian to sleep. Ahenobarbus may be blamed on condition that to a small criticism a great flattery can be added. Our gracious Augusta, Poppaea, understands this perfectly."

"Such are the times," Aulus answered. "I lack two front teeth, knocked out by a stone from the hand of a Briton, and so I speak with a hiss. Still my happiest days were passed in Britain."

"Because they were days of victory," added Vinicius.

But Petronius, alarmed lest the old general might begin a narrative of his former wars, changed the conversation.

"See," he said, "in the neighborhood of Praeneste country people found a dead wolf whelp with two heads; and during a storm about that time lightening struck off a corner of the temple of Luna—a unique event, because of the late autumn. A certain Cotta, too, who had told this, added, while telling it, that the priests of the temple prophesied the fall of the city or, at least, the ruin of a great house—ruin to be averted only by unusual sacrifices."

When Aulus had heard the narrative he said that such signs should not be neglected; that the gods might be angered by too much wickedness. In this there was nothing out of the ordinary, and in such an event atoning sacrifices were perfectly in order.

"Your house, Plautius, is not too large," answered Petronius, "though a great man lives in it. Mine is indeed too large for such a wretched owner, though equally small. But if it is a question of the ruin of something as great, for example, as the Domus Transitoria, would it be worthwhile for us to bring offerings to avert that ruin?"

Plautius did not answer that question—a cautiousness that even Petronius noticed somewhat, for, with all his inability to discern the difference between good and evil, he had never been an informer; and it was possible to talk with him in perfect safety. He changed the conversation again, therefore, and began to praise Plautius's dwelling and the good taste which reigned in the house.

"It is an ancient seat," said Plautius, "in which nothing has been changed since I inherited it."

When the slaves had pushed aside the the curtain dividing the atrium from the tablinum, that opened the house from end to end, so that through the tablinum and the following peristyle (an inner courtyard lined with rows of columns) and the hall lying beyond it, the oecus, one's view extended to the garden, which seemed from a distance like a bright image set in a dark frame. Joyous, childlike laughter came from it to the atrium.

"Oh, General!" Petronius said, "permit us to listen from nearby to that glad laughter which is of a variety heard so rarely these days."

"Willingly," Plautius answered, rising. "That is my little Aulus and Lygia, playing ball. But as to laughter, I think, Petronius, that our whole life is spent in it."

"Life deserves laughter, so people laugh at it," Petronius answered, "but laughter here has a better sound."

"Petronius does not laugh for days in succession," Vinicius said, "but then he laughs entire nights."

Thus conversing, they passed through the length of the house and reached the garden, where Lygia and little Aulus were playing with balls, which slaves, appointed to that game exclusively, picked up and placed in their hands. Petronius cast a quick glance at Lygia. Little Aulus, seeing Vinicius, ran to greet him; but the young tribune, going forward, bent his head before the beautiful maiden, who stood with a ball in her hand, her hair blown apart a little. She was somewhat out of breath, and flushed.

In the garden dining area, shaded by ivy, grapes, and woodbine, sat Pomponia Graecina, and they went to greet her. She was known to Petronius, though he did not visit Plautius, for he had seen her at the house of Antistia, the daughter of Rubelius Plautus, and besides at the house of Seneca and Polion. He could not resist a certain admiration as he looked at her face, pensive but mild, from the dignity of her bearing, her movements, and her words. Pomponia disturbed his understanding of women to such a degree that he, corrupted to the marrow of his bones, and self-confident as no one else in Rome, not only felt a kind of esteem for her, but even lost his previous self-confidence. And now, thanking her for her care of Vinicius, he added, almost involuntarily, "lady," which never occurred to him when speaking, for example, to Calvia Crispinilla, Scribonia, Veleria, Solina, and other women of high society. After he had greeted her and returned thanks, he began to complain that he saw her so rarely, that it was not possible to meet her either in the Circus or the amphitheatre; to which she answered calmly, laying her hand on the hand of her husband: "We are growing old, and love our domestic quiet more and more, both of us."

Petronius wished to object; but Aulus Plautius added in his hissing voice, "And we feel uncomfortable among people who give Greek names to our Roman divinities."

"The gods recently have been given only lip service," Petronius replied carelessly. "But since Greek philosophers taught us, it is easier for even me to say Hera than Juno."

He turned his eyes to Pomponia, as if to signify that in her presence no other divinity could come to his mind; and then he began to contradict what she had said regarding old age.

"People grow old quickly, it is true; but there are some who live another life entirely, and there are faces also that Saturn seems to forget."

Petronius said this with a certain sincerity even, for Pomponia Graecina, though going beyond middle age, had preserved an uncommon freshness of face; and since she had a small head and delicate features, she produced at times, despite her dark robes, solemnity, and sadness, the impression of a quite young woman.

Meanwhile, little Aulus, who had become unusually friendly with Vinicius during his former stay in the house, approached the young man and invited him to play ball. Lygia herself entered the dining area after the little boy. Under the climbing ivy, with the light quivering on her face, she seemed to Petronius more beautiful than at the first glance, and really like a nymph. As he had not spoken to her thus far, he rose, bent his head, and, instead of the usual expressions of greeting, quoted the words with which Ulysses greeted Nausikaa:

"I supplicate you, O queen, whether you are some goddess or a
    mortal!
  If you are one of the daughters of men who dwell on earth,

> Three times blessed are your father and your lady mother,
> And three times blessed your brethren."

The exquisite politeness of this man of the world pleased even Pomponia. As to Lygia, she listened, confused and flushed, without the courage to raise her eyes. But a wayward smile began to quiver at the corners of her lips, and on her face a struggle was evident between the timidity of a maiden and the wish to answer; but clearly the wish was victorious, for, looking quickly at Petronius, she answered him all at once with the words of that same Nausikaa, quoting them in one breath, in the way of reciting a lesson:

> "Stranger, you seem no evil man nor foolish."

Then she turned and ran out as a frightened bird runs.

This time the turn for astonishment came to Petronius, for he had not expected to hear verses of Homer from the lips of a young woman whose barbarian roots he had heard of from Vinicius. Then he looked with a questioning glance at Pomponia; but she could not give him an answer, for she was looking at that moment, with a smile, at the pride reflected on the face of her husband.

He was not able to conceal that pride. First, he had become attached to Lygia as to his own daughter; and second, in spite of his old Roman prejudices, which commanded him to thunder against Greek and the spread of the language, he considered it as the summit of social polish. He himself had never been able to learn it well; he suffered over this in secret. He was glad, therefore, that an answer was given in the language and poetry of Homer to this exquisite man both of fashion and letters, who was ready to consider Plautius's house as barbarian.

"We have a tutor in the house, a Greek," he said, turning to Petronius, "who teaches our boy, and the maiden overhears the lessons. She is a slender bird yet, but a dear one, to which we have both grown attached."

Petronius looked through the branches of woodbine into the garden, and at the three persons who were playing there. Vinicius had thrown aside his toga and, wearing only his tunic, was striking the ball, which Lygia, standing opposite with raised arms, was trying to catch. The young woman did not make a great impression on Petronius at the first glance; she seemed too slender. But from the moment when he saw her more nearly in the dining area he thought to himself that Aurora might look like her; and as a judge he understood everything and estimated everything; considering her face, rosy and clear, her fresh lips, as if set for a kiss, her eyes blue as the azure of the sea, the alabaster whiteness of her forehead, the wealth of her dark hair, with the reflection of amber or Corinthian bronze gleaming in its folds, her slender neck, the divine slope of her shoulders, the whole posture, flexible, slender, young with the youth of May and of freshly opened flowers. The artist was roused in him, and the worshiper of beauty, who felt that beneath a statue of that maiden one might write "Spring." All at once he remembered Chrysothemis, and pure laughter seized him. Chrysothemis seemed to him, with golden powder on her hair and darkened brows, to be fabulously faded—something in the nature of a yellowed rose tree shedding its leaves. But still Rome envied him regarding that same Chrysothemis. Then he recalled Poppaea; and that the most famous Poppaea also seemed to him soulless, a waxen mask. In that maiden with Tanagrian outlines there was not only spring, but a radiant soul, which shone through her rosy body as a flame through a lamp.

Vinicius is right, he thought, *and my Chrysothemis is old, old—as Troy!*

Then he turned to Pomponia Graecina, and, pointing to the garden, said, "I understand now, lady, why you and your husband prefer this house to the Circus and to feasts on the Palatine."

"Yes," she answered, turning her eyes in the direction of little Aulus and Lygia.

But the old general began to relate the history of the young woman, and what he had heard years before from Atelius Hister about the Lygian people who lived in the gloom of the North.

The three outside had finished playing ball, and for some time had been walking along the sand in the garden. They appeared against the dark background of myrtles and cypresses like three white statues. Lygia held little Aulus by the hand. After they had walked a while they sat on a bench near the fish pond, which occupied the middle of the garden. After a time Aulus sprang up to frighten the fish in the transparent water, but Vinicius continued the conversation begun during the walk.

"Yes," he said, in a low, quivering voice, scarcely audible, "I had barely cast aside the pretexta [the toga worn by freeborn boys] when I was sent to the legions in Asia. I had not become acquainted with the city, nor with life, nor with love. I know a small bit of Anacreon by heart, and Horace, but I cannot quote verses like Petronius, when reason is overcome by admiration and unable to find its own words. When I was a youth I studied under Musonius, who told me that happiness is found in agreeing with what the gods wish, and therefore is up to us. I think, however, that there is something else—something greater and more precious, which depends not on our will, for only love can give it. The gods themselves seek that happiness; also I, too, Lygia, who have not known love so far, follow in their footsteps. I also seek her who would give me happiness—"

He was silent—and for a time there was nothing to be heard except the light splash of water into which little Aulus was throwing pebbles to frighten the fish. After a while Vinicius began again in a voice still softer and lower. "But do you know of Vespasian's son Titus? They say that he had scarcely ceased to be a youth when he so loved Berenice that grief almost overcame him. I wanted to love this way, Lygia! Riches, glory, power are mere smoke, vanity! The rich man will find someone richer than himself; the greater glory of one man will overshadow a man who is famous; a strong man will be conquered by a stronger still. But can Caesar himself, can any god even, experience greater delight or be happier than a simple mortal at the moment when at his breast there is breathing another dear breast, or when he kisses beloved lips? I believe love makes us equal to the gods, Lygia."

She listened with alarm, with astonishment, and at the same time as if she were listening to the sound of a Grecian flute or a cithara. It seemed to her at moments that Vinicius was singing a kind of wonderful song, which was penetrating into her ears, moving the blood in her, and entering her heart with a faintness, a fear, and a kind of uncomprehended delight. It seemed to her also that he was reciting something that was contained in her being before but of which she could not give account to herself. She felt that he was rousing in her something that had been sleeping up to this moment, and that in this very moment a hazy dream was being transformed into a reality more and more definite, pleasing, and beautiful than ever before.

Meanwhile, the sun had passed the Tiber long since and had sunk low over the Janiculum. A ruddy light was falling on the motionless cypresses, and the whole atmosphere was filled with this illumination. Lygia raised her blue eyes on Vinicius as if roused from sleep; and he, bending over her with an imploring prayer in his eyes, seemed suddenly, in the reflections of evening, more beautiful than all men, than all Greek and Roman gods whose statues she had seen on the facades of the temples. His fingers clasped her arm lightly just above the wrist, and he asked, "Do you not understand what I say to you, Lygia?"

"No," she in answer whispered, in a voice so low that Vinicius barely heard it.

But he did not believe her, and, drawing her hand toward him more vigorously, he would have drawn it to his heart, which, under the influence of the desire roused by the marvelous maiden, was beating like a hammer, and would have addressed burning words to her directly had not old Aulus appeared on a path set in a frame of myrtles. He said, while approaching them, "The sun is setting, so beware of the evening coolness, and do not trifle with Libitina."

"No," Vinicius answered, "I have not put on my toga yet, and I do not feel the cold."

"But see, barely half the sun's shield is looking from behind the hill. That is a sweet climate of Sicily, where people gather on the square before sunset and say farewell to disappearing Phoebus with a choral song."

And, forgetting that a moment earlier he had warned them against Libitina, he began to tell about Sicily, where he had estates and large cultivated fields he loved. He stated also that it had come to his mind more than once to move permanently to Sicily and live out his life there in quietness. "He whose head winters have whitened has had enough of frost in this climate. Leaves are not falling from the trees yet, and the sky smiles on the city loving-ly; but when the grapevines grow yellow-leaved, when snow falls on the Alban hills, and the gods visit the Campania with piercing wind, who knows? I may transport my entire household to my qui-et country seat."

"Would you leave Rome?" Vinicius asked with sudden alarm.

"I have wished to do so for a long time, for it is quieter in Sicily and safer."

And again he continued to praise his gardens, his herds, his house hidden in green, and the hills grown over with thyme and savory, covered with swarms of buzzing bees. But Vinicius paid no heed to that pastoral note; and thinking that he might lose Ly-gia, he looked toward Petronius as if expecting deliverance from him completely.

Meanwhile, Petronius, sitting near Pomponia, was admiring the view of the setting sun, the garden, and the people standing near the fish pond. Their white garments on the dark background of the myrtles gleamed like gold from the evening rays. The sky's evening light had taken purple and violet hues, and had begun to change and look like an opal. A strip of the sky became lily col-ored. The dark silhouettes of the cypresses grew still more pro-nounced than during bright daylight. In the people, in the trees, in the whole garden an evening calm reigned.

That calm struck Petronius, and it struck him especially in the people. In the faces of Pomponia, old Aulus, their son, and Lygia there was something he did not see in other faces that sur-rounded him every day, or rather every night. There was a certain light, a certain serenity, flowing directly from the life they lived in this house. And with a new level of astonishment he thought that a beauty and sweetness might exist that he, who chased after beauty and sweetness continually, had not known. He could not hide the thought in himself, and said, turning to Pomponia, "I am considering in my soul how different this world of yours is from the world our Nero rules."

She raised her delicate face toward the evening light and said with simplicity, "Not Nero, but God, rules the world."

A moment of silence followed. Near the dining area the steps of the old general, Vinicius, Lygia, and little Aulus were heard; but before they arrived, Petronius had put another question, "But do you believe in the gods, then, Pomponia?"

"I believe in God, who is one, just, and all-powerful," answered the wife of Aulus Plautius.

3

"She believes in God who is one, all-powerful, and just," Petronius said, when he found himself again in the litter with Vinicius. "If her God is all-powerful, He controls life and death; and if He is just, He sends death justly. Why, then, does Pomponia dress in mourning for Julius? By mourning for Julius she is blaming her God. I must repeat this reasoning to our Bronzebeard, the monkey, since I consider that in logical argument I am the equal of Socrates. As to women, I agree that each has three or four souls, but none of them a reasoning one. Let Pomponia meditate with Seneca or Cornutus over the question of what their great Logos is. Let them summon at once the shades of Xenophanes, Parmenides, Zeno, and Plato, who are as much wearied there in Cimerian regions as a finch in a cage. I wished to talk with her and with Plautius about something else. By the holy stomach of the Egyptian Isis! If I had told them blatantly why we came, I suppose that their virtue would have made as much noise as a bronze shield under the blow of a club. But I did not dare to tell them! Will you believe, Vinicius, I did not dare! Peacocks are beautiful birds, but they have too shrill a cry. I feared an outburst. But I must praise your choice. A real 'rosy-fingered Aurora.' And you know what she reminded me of too? Spring! Not our spring in Italy, where an apple tree merely puts forth a blossom here and there and olive groves grow gray, just as they were gray before, but the spring I saw once in Helvetia—young, fresh, bright green. By that pale moon, I do not disagree with you, Marcus; but know that you are loving Diana, because Aulus and Pomponia are ready to tear you

40

to pieces, as the dogs once tore Actaeon."

Vinicius was silent a time without raising his head; then he began to speak with a voice filled with passion. "I desired her before, but now I desire her still more. When I caught her arm, a flame embraced me. I must have her. Were I Zeus, I would surround her with a cloud, as he surrounded Io, or I would fall on her in rain, as he fell on Danae; I would kiss her lips till it was painful! I would hear her scream in my arms. I would kill Aulus and Pomponia and bear her home in my arms. I will not sleep tonight. I will give a command to flog one of my slaves, and listen to his groans—"

"Calm yourself," Petronius said. "You have the longing of a carpenter from the Subura."

"It is all the same to me what you say. I must have her. I have turned to you for aid; but if you will not accomplish it, I will do so myself. Aulus considers Lygia to be a daughter; why should I look on her as a slave? And since there is no other way, let her adorn the door of my house, let her anoint it with wolf's fat, and let her sit at my hearth as my wife."

"Calm yourself, mad descendant of consuls. We do not lead in barbarians bound behind our chariots to make wives of their daughters. We are going to Chrysothemis."

"You are happy in possessing the one you love."

"I? Do you know what amuses me in Chrysothemis? She is unfaithful to me with my freedman Theokles and thinks that I do not notice it. Once I loved her, but now she amuses me with her lying and stupidity. Come with me to her. Should she begin to flirt with you and write letters on the table with her fingers steeped in wine, I shall not be jealous."

And he ordered them both on to Chrysothemis.

But in the entrance Petronius put his hand on Vinicius's shoulder and said, "Wait; I have discovered a plan."

"May all the gods reward you!"

"I have it! I believe this plan is infallible. Do you know what, Marcus?"

"I am listening to you, my wise one."

"Well, in a few days the divine Lygia will eat of Demeter's grain in your house."

"You are greater than Caesar!" Vinicius exclaimed with enthusiasm.

4

In fact, Petronius kept his promise. He slept all the day following his visit to Chrysothemis, it is true; but in the evening he summoned slaves to bear him to the Palatine, where he had a confidential conversation with Nero; as a result, on the third day a centurion, an officer at the head of tens of praetorian soldiers, appeared before the house of Plautius.

A time like this was uncertain and terrible. Messengers of this kind were more frequently heralds of death. So when the centurion struck the hammer at Aulus's door, and when the guard of the atrium announced that there were soldiers in the anteroom, terror rose through the whole house. The family surrounded the old general at once, for no one doubted that danger hung over him above all. Pomponia, embracing his neck with her arms, clung to him with all her strength and her blue lips moved quickly while uttering some whispered phrase. Lygia, with a face pale as linen, kissed his hand; little Aulus clung to his toga. From the corridor, from chambers in the lower story intended for servant women and attendants, from the bath, from the arches of lower dwellings, from the whole house, crowds of slaves began to hurry out, and the cries of "Heu! heu, me miserum!" were heard. The women broke into great weeping; some scratched their cheeks or covered their heads with kerchiefs.

Only the old general himself, accustomed for years to look death straight in the face, remained calm, and his short eagle face became as rigid as if chiseled from stone. After a while, when he had silenced the uproar and commanded the attendants to disappear, he said, "Let me go, Pomponia. If my end has come, we shall have time to say good-bye."

And he pushed her aside gently; but she said, "God grant your fate and mine to be one, Aulus!"

Then, falling on her knees, she began to pray with the intensity that only fear for some loved one alone can give.

Aulus went out to the atrium, where the centurion was waiting for him. It was old Caius Hasta, his former subordinate and companion in British wars.

"I greet you, General," he said. "I bring a command, and the greetings of Caesar; here are the tablets and the signet to show that I come in his name."

"I am thankful to Caesar for the greeting, and I shall obey the command," Aulus answered. "Welcome, Hasta, and give me the news you have brought."

"Aulus Plautius," Hasta began, "Caesar has learned that in your house is dwelling the daughter of the king of the Lygians, whom that king during the life of the divine Claudius gave to the Romans as a pledge that the boundaries of the empire would never be violated by the Lygians. The divine Nero is grateful to you, O General, because you have given her hospitality in your house for so many years; but, not wishing to burden you longer, and considering also that the maiden as a hostage should be under the guardianship of Caesar and the Senate, he commands you to give her into my hands."

Aulus was too much a soldier and too much a veteran to permit himself to display regret in view of an order. A slight wrinkle of sudden anger and pain, however, appeared on his forehead. Before that frown legions in Britain had trembled at one time, and even at that moment fear was evident on the face of Hasta. But in light of the order, Aulus Plautius felt defenseless. He looked for some time at the tablets and the signet; then raising his eyes to the old centurion, he said calmly, "Wait, Hasta, in the atrium till the hostage is delivered to you."

After these words he passed to the other end of the house, to the hall called oecus, where Pomponia Graecina, Lygia, and little Aulus were waiting for him in fear and alarm.

"We are not in danger of death or banishment to distant islands," he said, "but still Caesar's messenger is a herald of misfortune. It is regarding you, Lygia."

43

"Lygia?" exclaimed Pomponia with astonishment.

"Yes," answered Aulus.

And turning to the young woman, he began: "Lygia, you were reared in our house as our own child; Pomponia and I love you as our daughter. But know this, that you are not our daughter. You are a hostage, given by your people to Rome, and guardianship over you belongs to Caesar. Now Caesar will take you from our house."

The general spoke calmly, but with a strange and unusual voice. Lygia listened to his words, puzzled, as if not understanding the question. Pomponia's cheeks became pale. In the doors leading from the corridor to the oecus, terrified faces of slaves began to appear a second time.

"The will of Caesar must be accomplished," Aulus said.

"Aulus!" Pomponia exclaimed, embracing the young girl in her arms, as if wishing to defend her. "It would be better for her to die."

Lygia, burying her head in her breast, cried out, "Mother, Mother!" unable in her sobbing to speak her mind.

On Aulus's face anger and pain were reflected again. "If I were alone in the world," said he, gloomily, "I would not surrender her alive, and my relatives might give offerings this day to 'Jupiter Liberator.' But I do not have the right to kill you and our child, who may live to see happier times. I will go to Caesar today and implore him to change his order. I do not know whether he will hear me. Meanwhile, farewell, Lygia, and know that Pomponia and I always bless the day in which you took your place at our hearth."

After saying this, he placed his hand on her head; but though he tried to keep calm, when Lygia's eyes filled with tears and she put his hand to her lips, his voice was filled with deep, fatherly sorrow.

"Farewell, our joy and the light of our eyes," he said.

And he went to the atrium quickly, so that he would not be conquered by an emotion unworthy of a Roman and a general.

Meanwhile, Pomponia, when she had led Lygia to the cubiculum, began to comfort and encourage her, uttering words that sounded strange in that house where near them, in an adjoining chamber, the household gods remained, as did the hearth on which Aulus Plautius, faithful to ancient usage, had made offerings to the household divinities. The hour of trial has come, Pomponia told Lygia. Once Virginius stabbed the breast of his own daughter to save her from the hands of Appius; still earlier Lucretia dealt with her shame by taking her own life. The house of Caesar is a den of infamy, of evil, of crime. But we, Lygia, know why we do not have the right to raise our hands against ourselves. Yes! The law under which we live is another, greater, and holier law, but it does give permission to defend oneself from evil and shame, even though you must pay for that defense with continued life and torment. Whoever remains pure after living in a house of corruption has the greater reward eventually. The earth is that dwelling; but fortunately life is only a twinkle of an eye, and resurrection is from a powerless grave; beyond that not Nero, but Mercy rules. Instead of pain there is delight; instead of tears there is rejoicing.

Next Pomponia began to speak of her true feelings. She was calm, but in her heart were painful wounds. Aulus darkened her vision; the fountain of light had not flowed to him yet. He did not permit her to raise her son in the Truth. When she thought, therefore, that it might be this way to the end of her life, and that for the two of them a moment of separation might come that would be a hundred times more grievous and terrible than that temporary one over which they were both suffering then, she could not understand how she might be happy even in heaven without them. And she had wept through many nights already; she had passed many nights in prayer, imploring grace and mercy. But she offered her suffering to God, and waited and trusted. And now, when a new blow struck her, when the tyrant's command removed her dear one—the one whom Aulus had called the light of their eyes—she trusted yet, believing that there was a power greater than Nero's and a mercy mightier than his anger.

And she pressed the young girl's head to her heart even more firmly. Lygia dropped to her knees soon after, and, covering her eyes in the folds of Pomponia's peplus, she remained like that a long while in silence; but when she stood up again, calmness was evident on her face.

"I grieve for you, Mother, and for Father and for my brother; but I know that resistance is useless and would destroy all of us. I promise you that in the house of Caesar I will never forget your words."

Once more she threw her arms around Pomponia's neck; then both went out to the oecus, and she said farewell to little Aulus, to their old Greek teacher, to the dressing maid who had been her nurse, and to all the slaves.

One of these, a tall and broad-shouldered Lygian, called Ursus, who with other servants had previously gone with Lygia's mother and her to the camp of the Romans, fell at her feet and then bent down to the knees of Pomponia, saying, "O domina! Allow me to go with my lady, to serve her and watch over her in the house of Caesar."

"You are not our servant, but Lygia's," Pomponia answered, "but if they admit you through Caesar's doors, in what way will you be able to watch over her?"

"I do not know, domina. I know only that iron breaks in my hands just as wood does."

When Aulus, who approached them up at that moment, had heard what the question was, not only did he not oppose the wishes of Ursus, but he stated that he did not have the right to detain him. They were sending away Lygia as a hostage whom Caesar had claimed, and they were obliged in the same way to send her slaves, which also came under the control of Caesar. He then whispered to Pomponia that acting in the role of an escort she could add as many slaves as she thought proper, for the centurion could not refuse to receive them.

This was a comfort to Lygia. Pomponia also was glad that she could surround her child with familiar servants. Therefore, along with Ursus, she added the old dressing woman, two maidens from Cyprus well skilled in hairdressing, and two German maidens for all her bath needs. She exclusively chose adherents of the new faith; Ursus, too, had professed it for a number of years. Pomponia could count on the faithfulness of those servants, and at the same time she consoled herself with the thought that soon grains of truth would be in Caesar's house.

She wrote a few words also, giving oversight for Lygia to Nero's freedwoman, Acte. Pomponia had not seen her, it is true, at meetings of confessors of the new faith; but she had heard from them that Acte had never refused them service and that she read the letters of Paul of Tarsus eagerly. It was known to her also that the young freedwoman was self-controlled, that she was a person different from all other women of Nero's house, and that in general she was the good spirit of the palace.

Hasta agreed to deliver the letter himself to Acte. Considering it natural that the daughter of a king should have a train of her own servants, he did not raise the least difficulty in taking them to the palace, but wondered rather that there should be so few. He asked them to hurry, however, fearing in case he might be suspected of apathy in carrying out orders.

The moment of parting came. The eyes of Pomponia and Lygia were filled with fresh tears; Aulus placed his hand on her head again, and after a while the soldiers, followed by the cry of little Aulus, who in defense of his sister threatened the centurion with his small fists, conducted Lygia to Caesar's house.

The old general commanded his slaves to prepare his litter at once; meanwhile, shutting himself up with Pomponia in the pinacotheca, or picture gallery, adjoining the oecus, he said to her, "Listen to me, Pomponia. I will go to Caesar, though I judge that my visit will be useless; and though Seneca's word means nothing with Nero now, I will go also to Seneca. Today Sophonius, Tigellinus, Petronius, or Vatinius has more influence. As to Caesar, perhaps he has never even heard of the Lygian people; and if he has demanded the delivery of Lygia, the hostage, he has done so because someone persuaded him to do it—it is easy to guess who could do that."

She gave him an inquiring look.

"Is it Petronius?"

"Yes."

A moment of silence followed, and then the general continued. "We should not have allowed into our house those who have no conscience or honor. I curse the moment in which Vinicius entered our house, because he brought Petronius. Lygia is in serious danger, since those men are not seeking a hostage, but a concubine." He felt only helpless rage and sorrow for his adopted

47

daughter. He struggled for a while, and only his clenched fists showed how severe was the conflict within him.

"I have revered the gods so far," he said, "but at this moment I think that they do not rule the world, but one mad, malicious monster named Nero rules."

"Aulus," said Pomponia, "Nero is only a handful of rotten dust before God."

But Aulus began to walk with long steps over the mosaic of the pinacotheca. In his life there had been great deeds, but no great misfortunes; so he could not handle them. The old soldier had grown very attached to Lygia, and now he could not be reconciled to the thought that he had lost her. Besides, he felt humiliated. A hand that he despised was pressing on him, and at the same time he felt that before its power his power was meaningless.

But when at last he stifled the anger that disturbed his thoughts, he said, "I believe that Petronius has not taken her from us for Caesar, since he would not offend Poppaea. Therefore, he took her either for himself or Vinicius. Today I will find out."

Later the litter took him in the direction of the Palatine. Pomponia, when left alone, went to little Aulus, who did not cease crying for his sister, or threatening Caesar.

5

Aulus correctly assumed that he would not be admitted to Nero's presence. They told him that Caesar was busy singing with the lute player, Terpnos, and that in general he did not receive those whom he himself had not summoned. In other words, Aulus must not attempt in the future to see him.

Seneca, though ill with a fever, received the old general with due honor; but when he had heard what the question was, he laughed bitterly and said, "I can render you only one service, noble Plautius, not to show Caesar at any time that my heart feels your pain, or that I should want to help you; for should Caesar have the least suspicion of this, know that he would not give you back Lygia, though for no other reason than to spite me."

He did not advise him, either, to go to Tigellinus or Vatinius or Vitelius. It might be possible to bribe them; perhaps, also, they would like to do harm to Petronius, whose influence they were trying to undermine, but most likely they would disclose before Nero how dear Lygia was to Plautius, and then Nero would all the more resolve not to return her to him.

Here the old sage began to speak with a biting sarcasm, which he turned against himself. "You have been silent, Plautius, you have been silent for whole years, and Caesar does not like those who are silent. How could you help being carried away by his beauty, his virtue, his singing, his chariot driving, and his verses? Why did you not glorify the death of Britannius and repeat flattering poetry in honor of the mother-slayer Nero, and not offer congratulations after the stifling of Octavia? You are lacking in foresight, Aulus, which we who live happily at the court possess in abundance."

He then raised a goblet that he carried at his belt, took water from a fountain at the small pool in the atrium, the impluvium, quenched his burning lips, and continued. "Ah, Nero has a grateful heart. He loves you because you have served Rome and glorified its name to the ends of the earth; he loves me because I was his master in his youth. Therefore, I know that this water is not poisoned, and I drink it in peace. Wine in my own house would be less reliable. If you are thirsty, drink boldly of this water. The aqueducts bring it from beyond the Alban hills, and anyone wishing to poison it would have to poison every fountain in Rome. As you see, it is possible to be safe in this world and to have a quiet old age. I am sick, it is true, but rather in soul than in body."

That was true. Seneca lacked the strength of soul that Cornutus possessed, for example, or Thrasea; so his life was a series of concessions to crime. He felt this himself; he understood that an adherent of the principles of Zeno, of Citium, should go by another road, and he suffered more from that cause than from the fear of death itself.

But the general interrupted these reflections.

"Noble Annaeus," he said, "I know how Caesar rewarded you for the care you gave him in his youthful years. But the instigator of the removal of Lygia is Petronius. Show me how to reach him, make clear the influences that sway him, and alongside this use all the eloquence with which friendship of long-standing for me would inspire you."

"Petronius and I," Seneca answered, "are men of two opposite camps; I know of no way to influence him; he yields to no man's persuasion. Perhaps with all his corruption he is worthier than those scoundrels with whom Nero surrounds himself at present. But to show him that he has done an evil deed is to lose time. Petronius has lost long since that faculty which distinguishes good from evil. Show him that his act is ugly, he will be ashamed of it. When I see him, I will say, 'Your act is worthy of a freedman.' If that will not help you, nothing can."

"Thanks for that, at least," the general answered.

Then Aulus's slaves carried him to the house of Vinicius, whom he found at sword practice with his domestic trainer. Aulus was terribly angry at the sight of the young man occupied calmly with fencing during the attack on Lygia; and barely had the curtain dropped behind the trainer when this anger burst forth in a torrent of bitter accusations and insults. But when Vinicius learned that Lygia had been carried away, he grew so terribly pale that Aulus could not for even an instant suspect him of sharing in the deed. The young man's forehead was covered with sweat; the blood, which had rushed to his heart for a moment, returned to his face in a burning wave; his eyes began to shoot sparks, his mouth to hurl disconnected questions. Jealousy and rage tossed him in turn, like a tempest. It seemed to him that Lygia, once she had crossed the threshold of Caesar's house, was lost to him absolutely. When Aulus pronounced the name of Petronius, suspicion flew like a lightning flash through the young soldier's mind, thinking that Petronius had made sport of him, and either he wanted to win new favor from Nero by the gift of Lygia, or keep her for himself. That anyone who had seen Lygia would not desire her at once did not find a place in his head. Impetuousness, inherited from his family, carried him away like a wild horse and destroyed his clearheadedness.

"General," he said with a broken voice, "return home and wait for me. Know that if Petronius were my own father, I would avenge on him the wrong done to Lygia. Return home and wait for me. Neither Petronius nor Caesar will have her."

Then he went with clenched fists to the waxed masks standing clothed in the atrium and burst out,"By those mortal masks! I would rather kill her and myself!"

When he had said this, he sent another "Wait for me" after Aulus, then ran forth like a madman from the atrium and flew to Petronius's house, pushing pedestrians aside on the way.

Aulus returned home somewhat encouraged. He judged that if Petronius had persuaded Caesar to take Lygia to give her to Vinicius, Vinicius would bring her to their house. Finally—the thought was no consolation to him—that should Lygia not be rescued she would be avenged and protected by death from disgrace. He believed that Vinicius would do everything that he had promised. He had seen his rage, and he knew excitability to be part of the whole family. He himself, though he loved Lygia as her own father, would rather kill her than give her to Caesar; and had he not regarded his son, the last descendant of his stock, he would doubtless have done so. Aulus was a soldier; he had hardly heard of the Stoics, but in character he was not far from their ideas—death was more acceptable to his pride than disgrace.

When he returned home, he pacified Pomponia, shared with her the consolation that he had received, and both began to await news from Vinicius. At moments when the steps of some of the slaves were heard in the atrium they thought that perhaps Vinicius was bringing their beloved child to them, and they were ready in the depth of their souls to bless them both. Time passed, however, and no news came. Only in the evening was the hammer heard on the gate.

After a while a slave entered and handed Aulus a letter. The old general, though he liked to appear in control of himself, took it with a somewhat trembling hand and began to read as hastily as if it were the future destiny of his whole house.

All at once his face darkened, as if a shadow from a passing cloud had fallen on it.

"Read," he said, turning to Pomponia.

Pomponia took the letter and read as follows: "Marcus Vinicius to Aulus Plautius, greeting. What has happened, has happened by the will of Caesar. You must accept this decision as Petronius and I have accepted it."

A long silence followed.

6

Petronius was at home. The doorkeeper did not dare to stop Vinicius, who burst into the atrium like a storm, and, learning that the master of the house was in the library, he rushed into the library with the same impetus. Finding Petronius writing, he snatched the reed from his hand, broke it, trampled the reed on the floor, then poked his fingers into his shoulder and, putting his face directly in front of his uncle, asked, with a hoarse voice, "What have you done with her? Where is she?"

Suddenly an amazing thing happened. The slender and effeminate Petronius seized the hand of the youthful athlete, which was grasping his shoulder, then seized the other, and, holding them both in his one hand with a grip like an iron vice, he said, "I am weak only in the morning; in the evening I regain my former strength. Try to escape. A weaver must have taught you gymnastics, and a blacksmith your manners."

On his face not even anger was evident, but in his eyes there was a certain pale reflection of energy and daring. After a while he let the hands of Vinicius drop. Vinicius stood before him shamefaced and enraged.

"You have a steel hand," he said, "but if you have betrayed me, I swear, by all the infernal gods, that I will thrust a knife into your body, though you be in the chambers of Caesar."

"Let us talk calmly," Petronius said. "Steel is stronger, as you see, than iron; so although out of one of your arms two as large as mine might be made, I have no need to fear you. On the contrary, I grieve over your rudeness, and if the ingratitude of men could astonish me yet, I should be astonished at your ingratitude."

"Where is Lygia?"

"In a brothel—that is, in the house of Caesar."

"Petronius!"

"Calm yourself, and be seated. I asked Caesar for two things, which he promised me—first, to take Lygia from the house of Aulus, and second, to give her to you. Have you not a knife there under the folds of your toga? Perhaps you will stab me! But I advise you to wait a couple of days, for you would be taken to prison, and meanwhile Lygia would be wearied in your house."

Silence followed. Vinicius looked for some time with astonished eyes at Petronius. Then he said, "Pardon me; I love her, and love is disturbing my faculties."

"Look at me, Marcus. The day before yesterday I spoke to Caesar as follows: 'My sister's son, Vinicius, has so fallen in love with a lean little girl who is being reared with the Plautiuses that his house is turned into a steam bath from sighs. Neither you, Caesar, nor I—we who know, each of us, what true beauty is—would give a thousand sesterces for her; but that lad has ever been as dull as a tripod, and now he has lost all the faculties that are in him.'"

"Petronius!"

"If you do not understand that I said this to insure Lygia's safety, I am ready to believe that I told the truth. I persuaded Bronzebeard that a man of his aesthetic nature could not consider such a girl beautiful; and Nero, who so far has not dared to look through other than my eyes, will not find in her beauty, and, not finding it, will not desire her. It was necessary to insure ourselves against the monkey and take him on a rope. Not he, but Poppaea, will value Lygia now; and Poppaea will strive, of course, to send the girl out of the palace at the earliest.

"I said further to Bronzebeard, in passing: 'Take Lygia and give her to Vinicius! You have the right to do so, for she is a hostage; and if you take her, you will inflict pain on Aulus.' He agreed; he had not the least reason not to agree, all the more since I gave him a chance to annoy decent people. They will make you official guardian of the hostage and give that Lygian treasure

53

into your hands; you, as a friend of the valiant Lygians and also a faithful servant of Caesar, will not waste any of the treasure, but will strive to increase it. Caesar, to preserve appearances, will keep her a few days in his house and then send her to your insula. Lucky man!"

"Is this true? Does nothing threaten her there in Caesar's house?"

"If she had to live there permanently, Poppaea would talk about her to Locusta, but for a few days there is no danger. Ten thousand people live in it. Nero will not see her, perhaps, all the more since he left everything to me, to the degree that just now the centurion was here with information that he had conducted the maiden to the palace and committed her to Acte. She is a good soul, that Acte; so I ordered them to deliver Lygia to her. Clearly Pomponia Graecina is of that opinion, too, for she wrote to Acte. Tomorrow there is a feast at Nero's. I have requested a place for you at the side of Lygia."

"Pardon me, Caius, my hastiness. I judged that you had ordered to take her for yourself or for Caesar."

"I can forgive your hastiness; but it is more difficult to forgive rude gestures, vulgar shouts, and a voice reminding one of players at mora. I do not like that style, Marcus, and do guard against it. Know that Tigellinus is Caesar's pimp; but know also that if I wanted the girl for myself now, looking you straight in the eyes, I would say, 'Vinicius! I take Lygia from you, and I will keep her till I am tired of her.'"

He began to look with his hazel eyes straight into the eyes of Vinicius with a cold and insolent stare. The young man lost his composure completely.

"The fault is mine," he said. "You are kind and worthy. I thank you from my whole soul. Permit me only to ask one more question. Why did you not have Lygia sent directly to my house?"

"Because Caesar wishes to preserve appearances. People in Rome will talk about this—that we removed Lygia as a hostage. While they are talking, she will remain in Caesar's palace. Afterward, she will be removed quietly to your house, and there will be no more discussion. Bronzebeard is a cowardly snake. He knows that his power is unlimited, and still he tries to give genuine appearances to every act. Have you recovered to the degree of being able to philosophize a little? More than once have I thought, 'Why does crime, even when it is as powerful as Caesar, and assured of being beyond punishment, strive always for the appearances of truth, justice, and virtue? Why does it take the trouble?' I consider that to murder a brother, a mother, or a wife is an act worthy of some petty Asiatic king, not a Roman Caesar; but if that position were mine, I should not write justifying letters to the Senate. But Nero writes. Nero is looking for appearances, for Nero is a coward.

"But Tiberius was not a coward; still he justified every step he took. Why is this? What a marvelous, involuntary homage is paid to virtue by evil! And do you know what strikes me? That it is done because transgression is ugly and virtue is beautiful. Therefore, a man of genuine aesthetic feeling is also a virtuous man. Hence I am virtuous. Today I must pour out a little wine to the shades of Protagoras, Prodicus, and Gorgias. It seems that sophists, too, can be of service. Listen, for I am still speaking. I took Lygia from Aulus to give her to you. But Lysippus would have made wonderful groups of her and you. You are both beautiful; therefore my act is beautiful, and being beautiful it cannot be bad. Marcus, here sitting before you is virtue incarnate in Caius Petronius! If Aristides were living, it would be his duty to come to me and offer a hundred minae for a short treatise on virtue."

But Vinicius, as a man more concerned with reality than with treatises on virtue, replied, "Tomorrow I shall see Lygia and then have her in my house daily, always, and until death."

"You will have Lygia, and I shall have Aulus after my head. He will summon the vengeance of all the infernal gods against me. And if the beast would take at least a preliminary lesson in good speech! He will blame he, however, as my former door-keeper blamed my clients, but I sent him to prison in the country."

"Aulus has been at my house. I promised to give him news of Lygia."

"Write to him that the will of the 'divine' Caesar is the highest law, and that your first son will bear the name Aulus. It is necessary that the old man should have some consolation. I am ready to petition Bronzebeard to invite him tomorrow to the feast. Let him see you in the triclinium next to Lygia."

"Do not do that. I am sorry for them, especially for Pomponia."

And he sat down to write the aforementioned letter, which removed from the old general the last ray of his hope.

7

Once the highest heads in Rome inclined before Acte, the former favorite of Nero. But even at that period she showed no desire to interfere in public questions, and if on any occasion she used her influence over the young ruler, it was only to implore mercy for someone. Quiet and unassuming, she won the gratitude of many and made no one her enemy. Even Octavia was unable to hate her. To those who envied her she seemed exceedingly harmless. It was known that she continued to love Nero with a sad and pained love, which lived not in hope, but only in memories of a time when Nero was not only younger and loving but of better character. It was known that she could not tear her thoughts and soul from those memories, but expected no improvement. Since there was no real fear that Nero would return to her, she was looked upon as a person wholly harmless, and so was left in peace. Poppaea considered her merely as a quiet servant, so harmless that she did not even try to drive her from the palace.

But since Caesar had loved her once and dropped her without offense in a quiet and friendly manner, a certain respect was retained for her. Nero, when he had freed her, let her live in the palace and gave her special apartments with a few servants. And as in their time Pallas and Narcissus, though freedmen of Claudius, not only sat at feasts with Claudius but also held places of honor as powerful ministers, so she, too, was invited at times to Caesar's table. This was done perhaps because her beautiful form was a true ornament to a feast. Caesar, for that matter, had long since ceased to worry about appearances in his choice of company. At his table the most varied assortment of people of every position and calling found places. Among them were senators, but mainly those who were content to be jesters as well. There were patricians, old and young, eager for luxury, excess, and enjoyment. There were women with great names, who did not hesitate to put on a yellow wig in the evening and seek adventures on dark streets for amusement's sake. There were also high officials and priests who, drinking their fill of wine goblets, were willing to jeer at their own gods. Next to these leaders of society was a rabble of every sort: singers, mimes, musicians, dancers of both sexes; poets who, while uttering their own verses, were thinking of the sesterces that might fall to them for praise of Caesar's verses; hungry philosophers following the dishes with eager eyes; finally, noted charioteers, tricksters, miracle workers, storytellers, jesters, and the most varied adventurers brought through fashion or folly to a few days' notoriety. Even slaves were present, who covered their pierced ears with hair so as not to be detected.

The most well-known people sat directly at the tables; the lesser folk provided amusement while the others ate and waited for the moment when the servants would permit them to rush at the remnants of food and drink. The luxury of the court gilded everything and covered all things with glitter. High and low, the descendants of great families and the needy from the pavements of the city, great artists and vile scrapings of talent, thronged to the palace to fill their dazzled eyes with a splendor almost surpassing human estimate, and to approach the giver of every favor, wealth, and property—whose single glance might bring one to ruin, it is true, but might also exalt one beyond measure.

That day Lygia, too, had to take part in such a feast. Fear, uncertainty, and a dazed feeling after the sudden change were all combined with a wish to resist her fate. She feared Nero, the people, and the palace whose uproar deprived her of presence of mind; she feared the feasts of whose shamelessness she had heard from Aulus, Pomponia Graecina, and their friends. Though young, she was not without knowledge, for knowledge of evil in those times reached even children's ears early. She knew, therefore, that ruin was threatening her in the palace. Pomponia, moreover, had warned her of this when she left. But having a youthful spirit, unacquainted with corruption, and confessing a lofty faith implanted in her by her foster mother, she had promised to defend herself against moral destruction. She had promised her mother, herself, and also that Divine Teacher in whom she believed and whom she had had come to love with her half-childlike heart for the sweetness of His doctrine, the bitterness of His death, and the glory of His resurrection.

She was confident, too, that now neither Aulus nor Pomponia would be answerable for her actions. She was now thinking whether it would be better to resist and not go to the feast. On the one hand, fear and alarm spoke audibly in her soul; on the other, the wish rose in her to show courage in suffering, in exposure to torture and death. The Divine Teacher had commanded to act thus. He had given the example Himself. Pomponia had told her that the most earnest among the adherents of the faith desire with all their souls such a test, and pray for it. And Lygia, when still in the house of Aulus, had been mastered at moments by a similar desire. She had seen herself as a martyr, with wounds on her feet and hands, white as snow, with a beauty not of earth, and borne by equally white angels into the azure sky; and her imagination admired such a vision. It resembled childish brooding, but there was also something of delight in herself, which Pomponia had reprimanded.

But now, when opposition to Caesar's will might incur some terrible punishment, and this martyrdom become a reality, there was added to the beautiful visions and the delight a kind of curiosity mingled with dread. She wondered how they would punish her and what kind of torments they would provide. Her soul, half-childish yet, was hesitating on two sides. But Acte, hearing of these hesitations, looked at her with astonishment as if the young woman were delirious. To oppose Caesar's will, expose oneself immediately to his anger? To act like that one would need to be an ignorant child. From Lygia's own words it appears that she is not really a hostage, but a maiden forgotten by her own people. No law of nations protects her; and even if it did, Caesar is powerful enough to trample on it in a moment of anger. It has pleased Caesar to take her, and he will deal with her as he wishes. From here on she is at his will, above which there is not another on earth.

"So it is," Acte continued, "that I too have read the letters of Paul of Tarsus and know that above the earth is God, and the Son of God, who rose from the dead; but on the earth there is only Caesar. Think of this, Lygia. I, too, know that your doctrine does not permit you to be what I was, and that as to the Stoics—of whom Epiceteus has told me—when it comes to a choice between shame and death, it is permitted to choose only death. But can you say that death awaits you and not moral shame as well? Have you heard of the daughter of Sejanus, a young girl, who at the command of Tiberius had to lose her virginity before her death, to keep to the letter of a law that prohibits the punishment of virgins with death? Lygia, do not irritate Caesar. If the decisive moment comes when you must choose between disgrace and death, you will act as your faith commands; but do not seek destruction yourself, and do not irritate an earthly and cruel divinity for a trivial reason."

Acte spoke with great compassion, and even enthusiasm; and being a little shortsighted, she pushed her sweet face up to Lygia's as if wishing to see the effect of her words.

But Lygia threw her arms around Acte's neck with childish trustfulness and said, "You are kind, Acte."

Acte, pleased by the praise and confidence, pressed her to her heart; and then releasing herself from the arms of the girl, answered, "My happiness has passed and my joy is gone, but I am not wicked."

Then she began to walk with quick steps through the room and to talk to herself, in despair.

"No! And he was not wicked. He thought he was good at that time, and he wished to be good. I know that well. The change in him came later, when he ceased to love. Others made him what he is—yes, others—and Poppaea."

Her eyes filled with tears. Lygia followed her for some time with her blue eyes and asked at last, "Are you sorry for him, Acte?"

"I am sorry for him!" the Grecian answered, with a low voice.

Again she began to walk, her hands clinched as if in pain, and her face without hope.

"Do you love him yet, Acte?" Lygia asked timidly.

"I love him."

And after a while she added, "No one loves him but me."

Silence followed, during which Acte strove to recover her calmness, disturbed by memories; and when at length her face resumed its usual look of calm sorrow, she said, "Lygia, do not even think of opposing Caesar; that would be madness. And be calm. I know this house well, and I judge that on Caesar's part nothing threatens you. If Nero had wanted to take you away for himself, he would not have brought you to the Palatine. Here Poppaea rules; and Nero, since she bore him a daughter, is more than ever under her influence. No, Nero desired, it is true, that you should be at the feast, but he has not seen you yet; he has not inquired about you, so he does not yet care. Maybe he took you from Aulus and Pomponia only through anger at them. Petronius wrote me to have care of you; and since Pomponia also wrote, as you know, maybe they had an understanding. Maybe he did that at her request. If this is true, if he at the request of Pomponia will become acquainted with you, nothing threatens you; and who knows if Nero may not send you back to Aulus at his persuasion? I do not know whether Nero loves him much, but I know that he rarely has the courage to take an opposing viewpoint to Nero."

"Ah, Acte!" Lygia answered, "Petronius was with us before they took me, and my mother was convinced that Nero demanded my surrender at his instigation."

"That would not be a good sign," Acte said. But she stopped for a while and then said, "Perhaps Petronius only said, in Nero's presence at some supper, that he saw a hostage of the Lygians at Aulus's, and Nero, who is jealous of his own power, demanded you only because hostages belong to Caesar. But he does not like Aulus and Pomponia. It does not seem to me that if Petronius wished to take you from Aulus he would use this method. I do not know whether Petronius is more clever than others of Caesar's court, but he is not like the others. Maybe you will find someone else who would be willing to intercede for you. Have you not seen at Aulus's place someone who is close to Caesar?"

"I have seen Vespasian and Titus."

"Caesar does not like them."

"And Seneca."

"If Seneca advised one thing, that would be enough to make Nero do the opposite."

The bright face of Lygia was covered with a blush.

"And Vinicius—"

"I do not know him."

"He is a relative of Petronius and returned not long since from Armenia."

"Do you think that Nero likes him?"

"Everyone likes Vinicius."

"And would he support you?"

"Yes."

Acte smiled tenderly and said, "Then you will surely see him at the feast. You must be there. Only such a child as you could think otherwise. Second, if you wish to return to Aulus's house, you will find ways of petitioning Petronius and Vinicius to gain this favor for you by their influence. If they were here, both would tell you, as I do, that it would be madness and ruin to try resistance. Caesar might not notice your absence, it is true; but if he noticed it and thought that you had the daring to oppose his will, there would be no future hope for you. Go, Lygia! Do you hear the noise in the palace? The sun is nearly setting; guests will begin to arrive soon."

"You are right," Lygia answered. "I will follow your advice."

How much desire to see Vinicius and Petronius there was in this resolve, how much of woman's curiosity there was to see such a feast once in life, and to see Caesar, the court, the renowned Poppaea and other beauties, and all that magnificent splendor of which wonders were narrated in Rome, Lygia could not say for certain. But Acte was right, and Lygia agreed with this wholeheartedly.

Acte conducted her to her own unctorium to anoint and dress her; and though there was no lack of slave women in Caesar's house, and Acte had enough of them for her personal service, still, through sympathy for the girl whose beauty and innocence had captured her heart, she decided to dress her herself. It became clear at once that in the young Grecian, in spite of her sadness and her studying of the letters of Paul of Tarsus, there was much of the ancient Hellenic spirit, to which physical beauty spoke with more eloquence than anything else on earth. When she had undressed Lygia, she could not restrain an exclamation of wonder at the sight of her figure, at once slender and full, created from pearl and roses. Stepping back a few paces, she looked with delight on that matchless, springlike form.

"Lygia," she exclaimed at last, "you are a hundred times more beautiful than Poppaea!"

But, reared in the strict house of Pomponia, where modesty was observed, even when women were by themselves, the girl, wonderful as a dream, harmonious as a word of Praxiteles or as a song, stood alarmed, blushing, with knees pressed together, with her hands on her bosom, and downcast eyes. At last, raising her arms suddenly, she removed the pins that held her hair and with one shake of her head covered herself with it as with a mantel.

Acte, approaching her and touching her dark tresses, said, "Oh what hair you have! I will not sprinkle golden powder on it; it gleams of itself all over with gold, where it waves. I will add, perhaps, barely a sprinkle here and there, as if a sun-ray had freshened it. Your Lygian country must be wonderful where such young women are born!"

"I do not remember it," Lygia answered, "but Ursus has told me that with us it is largely forests."

"But flowers bloom in those forests," Acte said, dipping her hand in a basin filled with verbena and moistening Lygia's hair with it. When she had finished this work, Acte anointed her body lightly with strongly fragrant oils from Arabia and then dressed her in a soft, gold-colored tunic without sleeves, over which she put on a snow-white peplus. But before that, since she had to dress Lygia's hair first, she put a kind of loose fitting dress on Lygia and, seating her in an armchair, put her into the care of slave women, so that she could observe the hairdressing from a distance. Two other slave women put white sandals embroidered with purple on Lygia's feet, fastening them to her alabaster ankles with golden lacings drawn crosswise. When at last the hairdressing was finished, they put the peplus on Lygia in very beautiful, light folds; then Acte fastened pearls to her neck and sprinkled her hair at the folds with gold dust.

She was soon ready, and when the first litters began to appear before the main gate, both entered the side portico; from there the chief entrance, the interior galleries, and the courtyard surrounded by a colonnade of Numidian marble were visible.

Gradually people passed in greater and greater numbers under the lofty arch of the entrance, over which the splendid chariot of Lysias seemed to lift Apollo and Diana into space. Lygia's eyes were struck by that magnificence, to which the modest house of Aulus could not have come close. It was sunset; the last rays were falling on the yellow Numidian marble of the columns, which shone like gold in the gleaming light and changed into rose color. Among the columns, at the side of white statues of the Danaides and others, representing gods or heroes, crowds of people flowed past—men and women, also resembling statues, for they were draped in togas, pepluses, and robes falling with grace and beauty in soft folds, illumined by the rays of the setting sun. A gigantic Hercules, with head in the light, from the breast down sunk in shadow cast by the columns, looked from above on that throng. Acte showed Lygia senators in wide-bordered togas, colored tunics, sandals with crescents on them; and knights, and famed artists; she showed her Roman ladies, in Roman, Grecian, and fantastic oriental costume, with hair dressed in towers or pyramids, or dressed like that of the statues of goddesses and adorned with flowers. Acte mentioned many men and women by name, adding to their names brief and sometimes terrible histories that pierced Lygia with fear, amazement, and wonder. For her this was a strange world, whose beauty intoxicated her eyes, but whose contrasts her young mind could not grasp.

In that twilight, in those rows of motionless columns vanishing in the distance, and in those statuesque people, there was a certain lofty serenity. It seemed that demigods might live free of care in the midst of those marbles, at peace and in happiness. Meanwhile, the low voice of Acte continually disclosed a new and dreadful secret of the palace and people. There at a distance is the covered portico on whose columns and floor are still visible red stains from the blood with which Caligula sprinkled the white marble when he fell beneath the knife of Cassius Chaerea; there his wife was slain; there his child was dashed against a stone. Under that wing is the dungeon in which the younger Drusus gnawed his hands from hunger; there the elder Drusus was poisoned; there Gemellus quivered in terror, and Claudius in convulsions; there Germanicus suffered—everywhere those walls had heard the groans and death-rattle of the dying. Those people hurrying now to the feast in togas, colored tunics, flowers, and jewels may be the condemned of tomorrow. On more than one face a smile conceals terror, alarm, and the uncertainty of the next day. Perhaps feverishness, greed, and envy are gnawing into the hearts of these crowned demigods, who appear free of care.

Lygia's frightened thoughts could not keep pace with Acte's words; and when that wonderful world attracted her eyes with increasing force, her heart contracted within her from fear. In her soul she struggled with an immense, inexpressible yearning for the beloved Pomponia Graecina and the calm house of Aulus, in which love, and not evil, was the ruling power.

Meanwhile, new waves of guests were flowing in from the Vicus Apollinis. From beyond the gates came the uproar and shouts of clients escorting their patrons. The courtyard and the colonnades were swarming with the multitude of Caesar's male and female slaves, small boys, and the praetorian soldiers who kept guard in the palace. Here and there among dark or swarthy faces was the black face of a Numidian in a feathered helmet and with large gold rings in his ears. Some were carrying lutes and citharas, hand lamps of gold, silver, and bronze, and bunches of flowers, grown artificially despite the late autumn season. Louder conversation was mingled with the splashing, rosy streams of the fountain.

Acte had stopped her commentary, but Lygia gazed at the throng, as if searching for someone. All at once she blushed, as Vinicius and Petronius emerged from among the columns. They appeared so beautiful and calm, like white gods in their togas. It seemed when she saw those two friendly faces among strange people, especially Vinicius, that a great weight lifted from her and she felt less alone. That boundless yearning for Pomponia and Aulus, which had consumed her previously, ceased. The desire to see Vinicius and to talk with him overcame other considerations. She could not think about all the evil practices in the house of Caesar, or the ominous words of Acte, or the warnings of Pomponia. In spite of those words and warnings, she felt she must be at that feast. Soon she would hear that dear and pleasant voice of Vinicius, which had spoken of love to her and of happiness worthy of the gods. It still sounded like a song in her ears, and she was delighted.

But then she feared that delight. She might be false to the pure teaching in which she had been reared, false to Pomponia, and false to herself. She felt guilty and unworthy. Despair overcame her, and she wanted to weep. Acte took her hand and led her through the interior apartments to the grand triclinium, where the feast was to begin. Lygia's mind was dark, and conflicting voices were in her ears. Her heart seemed to stop. As in a dream, she saw thousands of lamps gleaming on the tables and walls and heard the shout with which the guests greeted Caesar. As through a mist, she saw Caesar himself. The shout deafened her, the glitter dazzled, the odors intoxicated; and, losing most of her consciousness, she was barely able to recognize Acte, who seated her at the table and took a place at her side.

But after a while a low and known voice was heard at the other side. "A greeting, most beautiful of maidens on earth and of stars in heaven. A greeting to you, divine Callina!"

Lygia, having recovered somewhat, looked up; at her side was Vinicius.

He was without a toga, for convenience and custom allowed him to cast aside the toga at feasts. His body was covered with only a sleeveless scarlet tunic embroidered in silver palms. His bare arms were ornamented in Eastern fashion with two broad, gold bands fastened above the elbow. His were the smooth and muscular arms of a soldier, made for the sword and shield. On his head was a garland of roses. With brows joining above the nose, with splendid eyes and a dark complexion, he was the personification of youth and strength. To Lygia he seemed so beautiful that though her initial infatuation passed, she was barely able to answer, "Greetings, Marcus."

He said, "Happy are my eyes, which see you; privileged are my ears, which hear your voice, dearer to me than the sound of lutes or citharas. If I had to choose who was to rest here by my side at this feast—you, Lygia, or Venus—I would choose you, divine one!"

He looked at the girl as if to fill himself with her presence, to meld her eyes with his eyes. His glance dropped from her face to her neck and bare arms, took in her shapely outlines, admired her, embraced her, and consumed her. But as well as desire, there was a mixture of happiness, admiration, and ecstasy beyond limit.

"I knew that I should see you in Caesar's house," he continued, "but still, when I saw you, such delight shook my whole soul, as if a degree of happiness entirely unexpected had filled me."

Lygia recovered herself and felt that in that throng he was the only being who was close to her heart. She began to converse with him and ask about everything that she did not understand and that filled her with fear. When did he know that he would find her in Caesar's house? Why is she there? Why did Caesar take her from Pomponia? She is full of fear where she is and wishes to return to Pomponia. She would die from alarm and grief were it not for the hope that Petronius and he will intercede for her before Caesar.

Vinicius explained that he learned from Aulus himself that she had been removed. Why she is there, he knows not. Caesar gives account to no one concerning his orders. But she should not fear. He, Vinicius, will stay near her. He would rather lose his eyes than not see her; he would rather lose his life than desert her. She is his very soul, and so he will guard her as such. In his house he will build to her, as to a divinity, an altar on which he will offer myrrh and aloes, and in spring saffron and apple blossoms. And since she has a dread of Caesar's house, he promises that she shall depart soon.

And though he spoke in an evasive and exaggerated way, his words seemed true because his feelings were genuine. Heartfelt pity possessed him, too, and her words went to his soul so thoroughly that when she began to thank him and assure him that Pomponia would love him for his goodness, and that she herself would be grateful to him all her life, he could not master his emotions, and it seemed to him that he would never be able in life to resist her desire. His heart began to melt in him. Her beauty intoxicated his senses. He desired her, but at the same time she was very dear to him, so that in truth he might do homage to her, as to a divinity. He also felt an irresistible impulse to speak of her beauty and of his own homage to it. As the noise at the feast increased, he drew nearer to her, whispering kind, sweet words flowing from the depth of his soul, words as resonant as music and intoxicating as wine.

And he did intoxicate her. Amid those strange people he seemed to her ever nearer and dearer, altogether true, and devoted with his whole soul. He pacified her; he promised to rescue her from the house of Caesar; he promised not to desert her and said that he would serve her. Besides, he had spoken before at Aulus's only in general about love and the happiness it can give; but now he said directly that he loved her, and that she was dear and most precious to him. Lygia heard such words from a man's lips for the first time; and as she heard them it seemed to her that something was wakening in her as from sleep, that some type of happiness was embracing her in which immense delight was mingled with disturbing alarm. Her cheeks began to burn, her heart to beat, her mouth opened as if in wonder. She was seized with fear because she was listening to such things; still, she did not wish for any reason on earth to lose one word. At moments she dropped her eyes; then again she clearly glanced at Vinicius, timid and also inquiring, as if she wished to say to him, "Speak on!" The sound of the music and the odor of flowers and Arabian perfumes began to daze her. In Rome it was the custom to recline at banquets, but at home Lygia held a place between Pomponia and little Aulus. Now Vinicius was reclining near her, youthful, immense, burning with love; and she, sensing the heat that issued from him, felt both delight and shame. A kind of sweet weakness, a kind of faintness and forgetfulness, seized her. Drowsiness tortured her.

But her nearness to him began to act on Vinicius also. His nostrils dilated, like those of an Eastern steed. The beating of his heart with a powerful throb was evident under his scarlet tunic. His breathing grew short, and the expressions that fell from his lips were broken. For the first time he, too, was very close to her. His thoughts became disturbed; he felt a flame in his veins that he tried in vain to quench with wine. Not wine, but her marvelous face, her bare arms, her maiden breast heaving under the golden tunic, and her form hidden in the white folds of the peplus intoxicated him increasingly. Finally, he seized her arm above the wrist, as he had done once at Aulus's, and drawing her toward him whispered, with trembling lips, "I love you, Callina—divine one."

"Let me go, Marcus," Lygia said.

But he continued, his eyes mist covered. "Love me, my goddess!"

But at that moment he heard the voice of Acte, who was reclining on the other side of Lygia.

"Caesar is looking at you both."

Vinicius was carried away by sudden anger at Caesar and at Acte. Her words had broken the charm of his intoxication. To the young man even a friendly voice would have seemed repulsive at such a moment, but he realized that Acte wished purposely to interrupt his conversation with Lygia. So, raising his head and looking over the shoulder of Lygia at the young freedwoman, he said with annoyance, "The hour has passed, Acte, when you reclined near Caesar's side at banquets, and they say that blindness is threatening you; how then can you see him?"

But she answered as if in sadness, "Still, I see him. He, too, has short sight and is looking at you through an emerald."

Everything that Nero did aroused attention, even in those nearest him, so Vinicius was alarmed. He regained self-control and began imperceptibly to look toward Caesar. Lygia was embarrassed at the beginning of the banquet and had seen Nero as in a mist. Afterward, occupied by the presence and conversation of Vinicius, she had not looked at him at all. Now she turned to him with curious and terrified eyes.

Acte spoke correctly. Caesar had bent over the table, half-closed one eye, and, holding before the other a round, polished emerald, was looking at them. For a moment his glance met Lygia's eyes, and the heart of the maiden was stricken with terror. When she was still a child on Aulus's Sicilian estate, an old Egyptian slave had told her of dragons that occupied dens in the mountains, and it seemed to her now that all at once the greenish eye of such a monster was gazing at her. She caught Vinicius's hand as a frightened child would, and disconnected, hasty impressions formed in her head. Was he not terrible and all-powerful? She had not seen him until now, and she thought that he looked different. She had imagined some kind of ghastly face, with malignity petrified in its features; now she saw a great head, sitting on a thick neck, terrible, it is true, but almost ridiculous, for from a distance it resembled the head of a child. A tunic of amethyst color, forbidden to ordinary mortals, cast a bluish glow on his broad and short face. He had dark hair, dressed, in the fashion introduced by Otho, in four curls. He had no beard because he had sacrificed it recently to Jove—for which all Rome gave him thanks, though people whispered to each other that he had sacrificed it because his beard, like that of his whole family, was red. In his forehead, projecting strongly above his brows, there remained something Olympian. In his contracted brows the consciousness of supreme power was evident; but under that forehead of a demigod was the face of a monkey, a drunkard, and a comedian. It was vain, full of changing desires, swollen with fat, even in his youth; it was also sickly and foul. To Lygia he seemed ominous, but above all repulsive.

After a while he laid down the emerald and ceased to look at her. Then she saw his prominent blue eyes, blinking before the excess of light, glassy, without thought, resembling the eyes of the dead.

"Is that the hostage with whom Vinicius is in love?" he asked, turning to Petronius.

"Yes," Petronius answered.

"What are her people called?"

"The Lygians."

"Does Vinicius think she is beautiful?"

"Array a rotten olive trunk in the peplus of a woman, and Vinicius will declare it beautiful. But on your face, incomparable judge, I read her sentence already. You have no need to pronounce it! The sentence is true: she is too dry, thin, a mere blossom on a slender stalk; and you, O divine lover of beauty, esteem the stalk of a woman. Three and four times are you right! The face alone does not tell it all. I have learned much in your company, but even now I am not a perfect judge. But I am ready to lay a wager with Tullius Senecio concerning his mistress, that, although at a feast, when all are reclining, it is difficult to judge the whole form, you have said in your mind already, 'Too narrow in the hips.'"

"Too narrow in the hips," Nero answered, blinking.

A scarcely perceptible smile appeared on Petronius's lips; but Tullius Senecio, who until that moment was occupied in conversing with Vestinius, or rather in reviling dreams, whereas Vestinius believed in them, turned to Petronius and, though he had not the least idea of what they were talking about, said, "You are mistaken! I agree with Caesar."

"Very well," Petronius answered. "I have just maintained that you have a glimmer of understanding, but Caesar insists that you are an ass pure and simple."

"*Habet!*" Caesar said, laughing and turning down his thumb, as was done in the Circus, signifying that the gladiator had received a final blow and was to be finished off.

But Vestinius, thinking that the question was of dreams, exclaimed, "But I believe in dreams, and Seneca told me once that he believes too."

"Last night I dreamed I had become a vestal virgin," Calvia Crispinilla said, bending over the table.

At this Nero clapped his hands; others followed, and in a moment clapping of hands was heard all around—for Crispinilla had been divorced a number of times and was known throughout Rome for her fabulous debauchery.

But she, not upset in the least, said, "Well! They are all old and ugly. Rubria alone has a human resemblance, and so there would be two of us, though Rubria gets freckles in summer."

"But admit, purest Calvia," Petronius said, "that you could become a vestal virgin only in dreams."

"But if Caesar commanded it?"

"I should believe that even the most impossible dreams might come true."

"But they do come true," Vestinius said. "I understand those who do not believe in the gods, but how is it possible not to believe in dreams?"

"But predictions?" Nero asked. "It was predicted to me once that Rome would cease to exist and I would rule the whole Orient."

"Predictions and dreams are connected," Vestinius said. "Once a certain proconsul, a great unbeliever, sent a slave to the temple of Mopsus with a sealed letter he would not let anyone open; he did this to see if the god could answer the question contained in the letter. The slave slept a night in the temple in order to have a prophetic dream. He returned then and said: 'I saw a youth in my dreams; he was as bright as the sun and spoke only one word, 'Black.' When the proconsul heard this he grew pale and, turning to his guests, unbelievers like himself, said: 'Do you know what was in the letter?'" Here Vestinius stopped and, raising his wine-filled goblet, began to drink.

"What was in the letter?" Senecio asked.

"In the letter was the question: 'What is the color of the bull I am to sacrifice: white or black?'"

But the interest roused by the narrative was interrupted by Vitelius, who, drunk when he came to the feast, burst forth suddenly in senseless laughter.

"What is that keg of tallow laughing at?" Nero asked.

"Laughter distinguishes men from animals," Petronius said, "and he has no other proof that he is not a wild boar."

Vitelius stopped halfway in his laughter, and smacking his lips, shining from fat and sauces, looked at those present with as much astonishment as if he had never seen them before; then he raised his two hands, which were like cushions, and said in a hoarse voice, "The ring of a knight has fallen from my finger, and it was inherited from my father."

"Who was a tailor," Nero added.

But Vitelius burst forth again in unexpected laughter and began to search for his ring in the gown of Calvia Crispinilla.

Then Vestinius fell to imitating the cries of a frightened woman. Nigidia, a friend of Calvia—a young widow with the face of a child and the eyes of a loose woman—said aloud, "He is seeking what he has not lost."

"And it will be useless to him if he finds it," finished the poet Lucan.

The feast grew more animated. Crowds of slaves presented successive courses; from great vases filled with snow and garlanded with ivy, smaller vessels with various kinds of wine were introduced continually. Everyone drank freely. Roses regularly fell from the ceiling onto the guests.

Petronius asked Nero to dignify the feast with his song before the guests drank too deeply. A chorus of voices supported his words, but Nero refused at first. It was not a question of courage alone, he said, though that always failed him. The gods knew what efforts every success cost him. He did not avoid them, however, for it was important to perform for art; and besides, if Apollo had gifted him with a good voice, it was not proper to let divine gifts be wasted. He understood, even, that it was his duty to the state not to let the gift be wasted. But that day he was really hoarse. In the night he had placed lead weights on his chest, but that had not helped at all. He was thinking about going to Antium, to breathe the sea air.

Lucan implored him in the name of art and humanity. All knew that the divine poet and singer had composed a new hymn to Venus, compared with which Lucretius's hymn was as the howl of a yearling wolf. Let that feast be a genuine feast. So kind a ruler should not cause such torture to his subjects. "Be not cruel, O Caesar!"

"Be not cruel!" repeated all who were sitting near.

Nero spread his hands in sign that he had to yield. All faces assumed then an expression of gratitude, and all eyes were turned to him, but he wished first to announce to Poppaea that he would sing. He informed those present that she had not come to the feast because she did not feel healthy; but since no medicine gave her such relief as his singing, he would be sorry to deprive her of this opportunity.

In fact, Poppaea came soon. Up to recently she had ruled Nero as if he had been her subject, but she knew that when his vanity as a singer, a charioteer, or a poet was involved, there was danger in provoking it. She thus came in, beautiful as a divinity, arrayed, like Nero, in robes of amethyst color, and wearing a necklace of immense pearls, stolen in the past from Massinissa. She was golden-haired and sweet; and though divorced from two husbands she had the face and the look of a virgin.

She was greeted with shouts and the label of "Divine Augusta." Lygia had never seen anyone so beautiful, and she could not believe her own eyes, for she knew that Poppaea Sabina was one of the vilest women on earth. She knew from Pomponia that she had brought Caesar to murder his mother and his wife. She knew her from accounts given by Aulus's guests and the servants, and she had heard that statues to her had been thrown down at night in the city. She had heard of inscriptions of which the writers had been condemned to severest punishment, but which still appeared on the city walls every morning. Yet at the sight of the notorious Poppaea, considered by the confessors of Christ as crime and evil incarnate, it seemed to her that angels or spirits of heaven might look like her. She was unable simply to take her eyes from Poppaea; and she questioned, "Ah, Marcus, can it be possible?"

But he, roused by wine, and impatient that so many things had scattered her attention and taken her from him and his words, said, "Yes, she is beautiful, but you are a hundred times more beautiful. You do not know yourself, or you would be in love with yourself, as Narcissus was. She bathes in donkeys' milk, but Venus bathed you in her own milk. You do not know yourself! Look not at her. Turn your eyes to me! Touch this goblet of wine with your lips, and I will put mine on the same place."

And he pushed up nearer and nearer, and she began to withdraw toward Acte. But at that moment silence was demanded because Caesar had risen. The singer Diodorus had given him a lute of the kind called delta; another singer named Terpnos, who had to accompany him in playing, approached with an instrument called the nablium. Nero, resting the delta on the table, raised his eyes; and for a moment silence reigned in the triclinium, broken only by a rustle, as roses fell from the ceiling.

Then he began to chant rhythmically, to the accompaniment of the two lutes, his own hymn to Venus. Neither the voice, though somewhat impaired, nor the verses were bad, so that questions of conscience possessed Lygia again. For the hymn, though glorifying the impure pagan Venus, seemed more than beautiful, and Caesar himself, with a laurel crown on his head and uplifted eyes, seemed nobler, much less terrible, and less repulsive than at the beginning of the feast.

The guests answered with a thunder of applause. Cries of "Oh heavenly voice!" were heard round about; some of the women raised their hands and held them, as a sign of delight, even after the end of the hymn; others wiped their tearful eyes. The whole hall was seething as in a beehive. Poppaea, bending her golden-haired head, raised Nero's hand to her lips and held it in silence. Pythagoras, a young Greek of marvelous beauty—the same to whom later the half-insane Nero commanded the flamens (priests) to marry him—knelt now at his feet.

But Nero looked carefully at Petronius, whose praises were desired by him always before every other and who said, "If it is a question of music, Orpheus must at this moment be as yellow from envy as Lucan, who is here present; and as to the verses, I am sorry that they are not worse; if they were I might find proper words to praise them."

Lucan did not take the mention of envy as an insult; on the contrary, he looked at Petronius with gratitude and, pretending to be annoyed, began to murmur, "Cursed fate, which commanded me to live at the same time as such a poet. I will be quenched, as a candle in sunlight."

Petronius, who had an amazing memory, began to repeat extracts from the hymn and cite single verses, exalt, and analyze the more beautiful expressions. Lucan, forgetting his envy before the charm of the poetry, joined his ecstasy to Petronius's words. On Nero's face were reflected delight and fathomless vanity, not only nearing stupidity, but reaching it perfectly. He indicated to them the verses he considered the most beautiful; and finally he began to comfort Lucan and tell him not to lose heart, for though whatever a man is born to be, that he is; nonetheless, the honor that people give Jove does not exclude respect for other divinities.

Then he rose to conduct Poppaea, who, truly being in ill health, wished to withdraw. But he commanded the guests who remained to occupy their places again and promised to return. In fact, he returned a little later, to numb himself with the smoke of incense and gaze at further spectacles he himself, Petronius, or Tigellinus had prepared for the feast.

Again verses were read or dialogues listened to in which extravagance took the place of wit. After that, Paris, the celebrated mime, represented the adventures of Io, the daughter of Inachus. To the guests, and especially to Lygia, unaccustomed to such scenes, it seemed that they were gazing at miracles and enchant-

74

ment. Paris, with motions of his hands and body, was able to express things apparently impossible in a dance. His hands sliced the air, creating a bright, quivering, and voluptuous cloud, surrounding the half-fainting form of a maiden shaken by a spasm of delight. That was a picture, not a dance; an expressive picture, disclosing the secrets of love, bewitching and shameless; and when at the end of it Corybantes rushed in and began a bacchic dance with girls of Syria to the sounds of cithara, lutes, drums, and cymbals—a dance filled with wild shouts and still wilder license—it seemed to Lygia that living fire was burning within her and that a thunderbolt of judgment ought to strike that house, or the ceiling fall on the heads of those feasting there.

But from the golden net fastened to the ceiling only roses fell, and the now half-drunken Vinicius said to her, "I saw you in the house of Aulus, at the fountain. It was daylight, and you thought no one saw you; but I saw you. And I see you this way yet, though that gown hides you. Cast aside the gown, like Crispinilla. See, gods and men make love. There is nothing in the world but love. Lay your head on my breast and close your eyes."

The pulse beat oppressively in Lygia's hands and temples. A feeling seized her that she was flying into some abyss, and that Vinicius, who before had seemed so near and so trustworthy, instead of saving her was drawing her toward it. And she felt sorry for him. She began again to dread the feast and him and herself. Some voice, like that of Pomponia, was calling yet in her soul, "Lygia, save yourself!" But something told her also that it was too late; that the one whom such a flame had embraced as that which had embraced her, the one who had seen what was done at that feast and whose heart had beaten as hers had on hearing the words of Vinicius, the one through whom such a shiver had passed as had passed through her when he approached—that person was lost beyond recovery. She grew weak. It seemed to her at moments that she would faint, and then something terrible would happen. She knew that, under penalty of Caesar's anger, no one was permitted to rise until Caesar rose; but even if that were not the case, she had no strength to rise now.

Meanwhile, it was far from the end of the feast. Slaves brought new courses and filled the goblets repeatedly with wine.

Before the table, on a platform open at one side, appeared two athletes to give the guests a spectacle of wrestling.

They began the struggle at once, and the powerful bodies, shining from olive oil, formed one mass; bones cracked in their iron arms, and from their set jaws came an ominous gritting of teeth. At moments the quick, dull thump of their feet was heard on the platform strewn with saffron; again, they were motionless, and it seemed to the spectators that they had before them a group chiseled out of stone. Roman eyes followed with delight the movement of tremendously exerted backs, thighs, and arms. But the struggle was not too prolonged; for Croton, a master, and the founder of a school of gladiators, was known as the strongest man in the empire. His opponent began to breathe very quickly: next a rattle was heard in his throat; then his face grew blue; finally, he threw blood from his mouth and fell.

A thunder of applause greeted the end of the struggle, and Croton, resting his foot on the breast of his opponent, crossed his gigantic arms on his breast and gave the impression of the victor around the hall.

Next appeared men who mimicked beasts and their voices, ballplayers, and buffoons. Only a few persons looked at them, however, since wine had darkened the eyes of the audience. The feast passed by degrees into a drunken revel and a lewd orgy. The Syrian damsels, who appeared at first in the bacchic dance, mingled now with the guests. The music changed into a disordered and wild outburst of citharas, lutes, Armenian cymbals, Egyptian sistra, trumpets, and horns. As some of the guests wished to talk, they shouted at the musicians to disappear. The air, filled with the odor of flowers and the perfume of oils, with which beautiful boys had sprinkled the feet of the guests during the feast, and permeated with saffron and the exhalations of people, became stifling; lamps burned with a dim flame; the wreaths dropped sideways on the heads of guests; faces grew pale and were covered with sweat. Vitelius rolled under the table. Nigidia removed more clothing and dropped her drunken childlike head on the breast of Lucan, who, drunk in like degree, could only blow the golden powder from her hair and raise his eyes with immense delight. Vestinius, with the stubbornness of intoxication, repeated for the tenth time the answer of Mopsus to the sealed letter of the proconsul. Tullius, who reviled the gods, said, with a drawling voice broken by hiccups, "If the spheros of Xenophanes is round, then consider, such a god might be pushed along before one with the foot, like a barrel."

But Domitius Afer, a hardened criminal and informer, was indignant at the former statement and through indignation spilled Falernian wine over his whole tunic. He had always believed in the gods. People say that Rome will perish, and there are some even who contend that it is perishing already. Surely it would! But if that should come, it is because the youth are without faith, and without faith there can be no virtue. People have also abandoned the strict habits of former days, and it never occurs to them that Epicureans will not stand against barbarians. As for him, he was sorry that he had lived in such times and must seek pleasures as a refuge against griefs that, if not met, would soon kill him.

When he had said this, he drew a Syrian dancer toward himself and kissed her neck and shoulders with his toothless mouth. Seeing this, the consul Memmius Regulus laughed and, raising his bald head with a lopsided wreath, exclaimed, "Who says that Rome is perishing? What folly! I, a consul, know better. *Videant consules!* Thirty legions are guarding our *pax romana!*"

Here he put his fists to his temples and shouted, in a voice heard throughout the triclinium, "Thirty legions! Thirty legions! From Britain to the Parthian boundaries!"

But he stopped suddenly and, putting a finger to his forehead, said, "As I live, I think there are thirty-two."

He rolled under the table and soon began to send forth flamingo tongues, roast and chilled mushrooms, locusts in honey, fish, meat, and everything he had eaten or drunk.

But the number of the legions guarding Roman peace did not pacify Domitius.

No, no! Rome must perish; for faith in the gods was lost, and so were strict habits! Rome must perish; and it was a pity, for life was still pleasant there. Caesar was gracious; wine was good! Oh, what a pity!

And, hiding his head on the arm of a Syrian bacchic dancer, he burst into tears.

"What is a future life! Achilles was right—better be a slave in the world beneath the sun than a king in Cimmerian regions. And still the question whether there are any gods—since it is unbelief—is destroying the youth."

Lucan, meanwhile, had blown all the gold powder from Nigidia's hair, and she, being drunk, had fallen asleep. Next he took wreaths of ivy from the vase before him and put them on the sleeping woman; when he had finished he looked at those present with a delighted and inquiring glance. He arrayed himself in ivy, too, repeating, in a voice of deep conviction, "I am not a man at all, but a faun."

Petronius was not drunk; but Nero, who drank little at first out of regard for his "heavenly" voice, emptied goblet after goblet toward the end. He wanted even to sing more of his verses—this time in Greek—but he had forgotten them and by mistake sang an ode of Anacreon. Pythagoras, Diodorus, and Terpnos accompanied him; but failing to keep time, they stopped. Nero as a judge and a critic was enchanted with the beauty of Pythagoras and was reduced to kissing his hands in ecstasy. "Such beautiful hands I have seen only once, and whose were they?" Then, placing his palm on his moist forehead, he tried to remember. After a while terror was mirrored on his face.

Ah! His mother's—Agrippina's!

And a gloomy vision took hold of him immediately.

"They say," he said, "that she wanders by moonlight on the sea around Baiae and Bauli. She merely walks—walks as if seeking for something. When she approaches a boat, she looks at it and goes away; but the fisherman on whom she has set her eye dies."

"Not a bad theme," Petronius said.

But Vestinius, stretching his neck like a stork, whispered mysteriously, "I do not believe in the gods; but I believe in spirits!"

Nero paid no attention to their words and continued: "I celebrated the Lemuria and have no wish to see her. This is the fifth year—I had to condemn her, for she sent assassins against me; and had I not been quicker than she, you would not be listening tonight to my song."

78

"Thanks be to Caesar, in the name of the city and the world!" Domitius Afer cried.

"Wine! And let them strike the tambourines!"

The uproar began anew. Lucan, all in ivy, wishing to out-shout him, rose and cried, "I am not a man, but a faun; and I dwell in the forest. Eho-o-o-oo!"

Caesar drank himself drunk at last; men were drunk, and so were women. Vinicius was not less drunk than others; and in addition there was aroused in him, besides desire, a wish to quarrel, which happened always when he became intoxicated. His dark face became paler, and his tongue stuttered when he spoke, in a voice now loud and commanding, "Give me your lips! Today, tomorrow, it is all one! Enough of this! Caesar took you from Aulus to give you to me, do you understand? Tomorrow, about dusk, I will send for you. Caesar promised you to me before he took you. You must be mine! Give me your lips! I will not wait for tomorrow —give me your kiss quickly."

And he moved to embrace her; but Acte began to defend her, and she defended herself with the remnant of her strength, for she felt that she was perishing. But she struggled in vain with both hands to remove his arm. In a voice in which terror and grief were quivering she implored him in vain not to act this way and to have pity on her. Filled with wine, he was no longer the former kind Vinicius, almost dear to her soul. He was a drunken, wicked satyr, who filled her with repulsion and terror. But her strength began to desert her. She bent in vain and turned her face to escape his kisses. He rose to his feet, caught her in both arms, and, drawing her head to his breast, began, panting, to press her pale lips with his.

But at this instant a tremendous power removed his arms from her neck with as much ease as if they had been the arms of a child and pushed him aside, like a dried limb or a withered leaf. What had happened? Vinicius rubbed his astonished eyes and saw before him the gigantic figure of the Lygian, called Ursus, whom he had seen at the house of Aulus.

Ursus stood calmly but looked at Vinicius so strangely with his blue eyes that the blood stiffened in the veins of the young man; then the giant took his queen on his arm and walked calmly out of the triclinium.

Acte in that moment went after him.

Vinicius sat for the twinkle of an eye as if petrified; then he sprang up and ran toward the entrance crying, "Lygia! Lygia!"

But desire, astonishment, rage, and wine cut the legs from under him. He staggered once and a second time, seized the naked arm of one of the bacchic dancers, and began to ask, with blinking eyes, what had happened. She, taking a goblet of wine, gave it to him with a smile in her mist-covered eyes.

"Drink!" said she.

Vinicius drank and fell to the floor.

Most of guests were lying under the table; others were staggering through the banquet hall, while others were sleeping on couches at the table, snoring. Meanwhile, from the golden net, roses were dropping on those drunken consuls and senators, knights, philosophers, poets; on those drunken, dancing damsels and patrician ladies; on that society still dominant so far but with the soul gone from it; on that society garlanded and ungirdled but perishing.

Dawn had arrived.

8

No one stopped Ursus; no one even asked what he was doing. Those guests who were not under the table had not kept their own places; so the servants, seeing a giant carrying a guest on his arm, thought he was some slave escorting his intoxicated mistress. Moreover, Acte was with them, and her presence removed all suspicion.

They went from the triclinium to the adjoining chamber and then to the gallery leading to Acte's apartments. Lygia's strength deserted her, and she hung as if dead on the arm of Ursus. But when the cool, pure breeze of morning swirled around her, she opened her eyes. Her head was growing clearer in the open air. After they had passed along the colonnade a while, they came out of a side portico, not in the courtyard but the palace gardens, where the tops of the pines and cypresses were growing reddish from the light of morning. That part of the building was empty, so that echoes of music and sounds of the feast were decreasing. It seemed to Lygia that she had been rescued from hell and deposited into God's bright world outside. There was something, then, besides that disgusting banquet. There was the sky, the dawn, light, and peace. Suddenly weeping overcame her, and, resting on the arm of the giant, she repeated, with sobbing, "Let us go home, Ursus! Home to the house of Aulus."

"Let us go!" Ursus answered.

They found themselves now in the small atrium of Acte's apartments. Ursus placed Lygia on a marble bench at a distance from the fountain. Acte tried to pacify her; she urged her to sleep and told her that for the moment there was no danger—after the feast the drunken guests would sleep until evening. For a long time Lygia could not calm herself, and she repeated like a child, "Let us go home, to the house of Aulus!"

Ursus was ready. At the gates stood praetorians, it is true, but he would pass them. The soldiers would not stop outgoing people. The space before the arch was crowded with litters. Guests were beginning to go forth in throngs. No one would detain them. They would pass through with the crowd and go directly home. For that matter, what does Ursus care? As the queen commands, so must it be. He is there to carry out her orders.

"Yes, Ursus," Lygia said. "Let us go."

Acte was forced to find reason for both. They would pass through, true; no one would stop them. But it is not permitted to flee from the house of Caesar; whoever does that offends Caesar's majesty. They may go; but in the evening a centurion at the head of many soldiers will take a death sentence to Aulus and Pomponia Graecina; they will bring Lygia to the palace again, and then there will be no rescue for her. Should Aulus and his wife receive her under their roof, death awaits them to a certainty.

Lygia's heart sank. There was no acceptable outcome. She must choose her own ruin or that of Plautius Aulus. In going to the feast, she had hoped that Vinicius and Petronius would win her from Caesar and return her to Pomponia; now she knew that it

81

was they who had brought Caesar to remove her from the house of Aulus. There was no hope. Only a miracle could save her from the abyss—a miracle and the sovereignty of God.

"Acte," she said in despair, "did you hear Vinicius say that Caesar had given me to him, and that he will send slaves here this evening to take me to his house?"

"I did," Acte answered; and, raising her arms from her side, she was silent. The despair with which Lygia spoke found in her no reply. She herself had been Nero's favorite. Her heart, though good, could not clearly feel the shame of such a relationship. A former slave, she had grown too much inured to the law of slavery; and, besides, she still loved Nero. If he returned to her, she would stretch her arms to him, as to happiness. Comprehending clearly that Lygia must become the mistress of the youthful and stately Vinicius, or expose Aulus and Pomponia to ruin, she failed to understand how the girl could hesitate.

"In Caesar's house," she said, "it would not be safer for you than in that of Vinicius."

And it did not occur to her that, though she told the truth, her words meant, "Be resigned to fate and become the concubine of Vinicius."

As to Lygia, who yet felt on her lips his kisses, burning as coals and full of beastly desire, the blood rushed to her face with shame at the mere thought of them.

"Never," she cried, with an outburst, "will I remain here, or at the house of Vinicius—never!"

"But," Acte asked, "is Vinicius hateful to you?"

Lygia was unable to answer, for weeping overtook her again. Acte embraced her and tried to calm her excitement. Ursus breathed heavily and balled his giant fists; for, loving his queen with the devotion of a dog, he could not bear the sight of her tears. In his half-wild Lygian heart was the wish to return to the triclinium, choke Vinicius, and, should the need come, Caesar himself; but he feared to thus sacrifice his mistress and was not certain that such an act, which to him seemed very simple, would befit a confessor of the Crucified Lamb.

But Acte, while caressing Lygia, asked again, "Is he so repulsive to you?"

"No," Lygia said. "I am not permitted to hate, for I am a Christian."

"I know, Lygia. I know also from the letters of Paul of Tarsus that it is not permitted to defile yourself, nor to fear death more than sin; but tell me if your teaching permits you to cause the death of others?"

"No."

"Then how can you bring Caesar's vengeance on the house of Aulus?"

A moment of silence followed. A bottomless abyss yawned before Lygia again.

"I ask," continued the young freedwoman, "for I have compassion on you—and I have compassion on the good Pomponia and Aulus, and on their child. It is a long time since I began to live in this house, and I know what Caesar's anger is like. No, you are not at liberty to flee from here! One way remains to you: implore Vinicius to return you to Pomponia."

But Lygia dropped on her knees to implore God. Ursus knelt down after a while, too, and both began to pray in Caesar's house at the morning dawn.

Acte witnessed such a prayer for the first time and could not take her eyes from Lygia, who, seen by Acte in profile, with raised hands, and face turned heavenward, seemed to ask for rescue. The dawn, casting light on Lygia's dark hair and white gown, was reflected in her eyes. Entirely in the light, she herself seemed like light. In that pale face, in those parted lips, in those raised hands and eyes, a kind of superhuman exaltation was evident. Acte understood then why Lygia could not become the concubine of any man. Before Acte a veil was drawn aside that hides a world altogether different from that to which she was accustomed. She was astonished by prayer in that abode of crime and infamy. A moment earlier it had seemed to her that there was no rescue for Lygia; now she began to think that something uncommon would happen, that some aid would come—aid so mighty that Caesar himself would be powerless to resist it; that some winged army would descend from the sky to help the girl, or that the sun would spread its rays beneath her feet and draw her up to itself. She had heard of many miracles among Christians, and she thought now that everything said of them was true, since Lygia was praying.

Lygia rose at last, with a face serene with hope. Ursus rose, too, and, remaining on the bench, looked at his mistress, waiting for her words.

But it grew dark in her eyes, and two great tears rolled down her cheeks slowly.

"May God bless Pomponia and Aulus," she said. "It is not permitted for me to bring them ruin; therefore, I shall never see them again."

Then, turning to Ursus, she said that he alone remained faithful to her; that he must be a protector and father. They could not seek refuge with Aulus, for they would anger Caesar. But she could not remain in the house of Caesar, or of Vinicius either. Let Ursus take her; let him lead her out of the city and conceal her in a place where neither Vinicius nor his servants could find her. She would follow Ursus anywhere, even beyond the sea to the barbarians, where the Roman name was not heard and where the power of Caesar did not exist.

The Lygian was ready and knelt before her feet and embraced them. But Acte, who had been expecting a miracle, was disappointed. Had the prayer accomplished only this much? To flee from the house of Caesar is to commit an offense against his majesty that will be avenged; and even if Lygia succeeded in hiding, Caesar would avenge himself on Aulus and Pomponia. If Lygia wishes to escape, she should try to escape from the house of Vinicius. Then Caesar, who does not like to concern himself with the affairs of others, may not wish to aid Vinicius in the pursuit; regardless, it will not be a crime against his majesty.

But Lygia believed that Aulus would not even know where she was; Pomponia herself would not know. She would not escape from the house of Vinicius, but rather on the way to it. When drunk, Vinicius had said that he would send his slaves for her in the evening. Beyond doubt he had told the truth, his tongue unguarded since he had not been sober. Evidently he, himself, or perhaps he and Petronius, had seen Caesar before the feast and had extracted a promise to give her to them the following evening. And if they forgot, they would send for her on the next day. But Ursus will save her. He will come; he will bring her out of the litter as he bore her out of the triclinium, and they will flee from Rome. No one could resist Ursus, not even that terrible athlete who wrestled at the feast yesterday. But even though Vinicius would send a great number of slaves, Ursus would go at once to Bishop Linus for aid and counsel. The bishop will take compassion on her and will not leave her in the hands of Vinicius. He will command fellow Christians to go with Ursus to rescue her. They will seize her and take her away; then Ursus can remove her from the city and hide her from the power of Rome.

And her face began to flush, and she smiled. She was consoled as the hope of rescue became real. She threw herself on Acte suddenly, and, putting her beautiful lips to Acte's cheek, she whispered: "You will not betray me, Acte, will you?"

"By the soul of my mother," the freedwoman answered, "I will not; but pray to your God that Ursus will be able to take you away."

The blue, childlike eyes of the giant were gleaming with happiness. He had not been able to frame any plan, although he had been trying very hard; but he could do this—whether day or night was all one! He would go to the bishop, for the bishop can divine what is needed. Besides, he could assemble Christians himself. He knew many slaves, gladiators, and free people, both in the Subura and beyond the bridges. He can collect a couple of thousand of them. He will rescue his lady and take her outside the city. They will go to the ends of the earth, even to that place where they originated, where no one has heard of Rome.

Here he began to look into the distance, as if to see things in the future.

"To the forest?" he asked. "Ah, what a forest!"

Then he shook himself out of his visions. Well, he will go to the bishop at once and in the evening will wait with a hundred men. And let not slaves, or even praetorians, take her from him! When he strikes iron earnestly with his fist, the head underneath will not survive.

But Lygia raised her finger with great seriousness.

"Ursus, you should not kill," she said.

Ursus put his fist, which was like a maul, to the back of his head and, rubbing his neck with great seriousness, began to mutter.

He must rescue "his light." She herself had said that his turn had come to help her. In any case, he must save her. But should anything bad happen, he will repent and seek mercy from the Crucified Lamb. He has no wish to offend the Lamb; but then his fists are so willing.

He expressed great tenderness on his face; but wishing to hide it, he bowed and said, "Now I will go to the holy bishop."

Acte put her arms around Lygia's neck and began to weep. Once more the freedwoman understood that there was a world in which greater happiness existed, even in suffering, than in all the excesses and luxury of Caesar's house. Once more a door to the Light was slightly opened before her, but she felt that she was unworthy to pass through it.

9

Lygia grieved for the household of Aulus; still, her despair passed away. She experienced a certain delight in the thought that she was sacrificing luxury and comfort for her Truth and was embarking on an uncertain and wayfaring existence. There was innocent curiosity as to what that life would be, off somewhere in remote regions, among wild beasts and barbarians. There was also a deep and trusting faith, that by taking this course she was doing as the Divine Master had commanded and that He Himself would watch over her, as over an obedient and faithful child. In such a case what could harm her? If sufferings come, she will endure them in His name. If sudden death comes, He will take her; and later, when Pomponia dies, they will be together for all eternity. More than once when she was in the house of Aulus she tortured herself because she, a Christian, could do nothing for the Crucified, the One of whom Ursus spoke with such tenderness. But now her wish might come true. Lygia was almost joyful and began to speak of this to Acte, who could not understand it. To leave everything—to leave house, wealth, the city, everything that is beautiful; leave a sunny land and people close to you—and for the purpose of hiding from the love of a young and stately noble? In Acte's head these things could not make sense. At times she believed Lygia's action was right, that there must be some immense mysterious happiness in it; but it was not clear, especially since an adventure was before Lygia that might have an evil ending, in which she might lose her very life. Acte was timid, and she thought with dread of what the coming evening might bring. But she was afraid to mention her fears to Lygia; meanwhile, the day was clear and the sun beamed into the atrium, and she began to persuade her to rest after a night without sleep. Lygia did not refuse; and they both went to the cubiculum, which was spacious and furnished with luxury because of Acte's former relations with Caesar. There they lay down, but in spite of her weariness Acte could not sleep. For a long time she had been sad, but now she felt a certain uneasiness as well. So far life had seemed to her simply grievous and deprived of hope; now it seemed perplexing.

Chaotic thoughts increased. Again the door to light began to open and close. But in the moment when it opened, that light so dazzled her that she could see nothing distinctly. She perceived vaguely that in that light there was happiness beyond measure, to such a degree that if Caesar, for example, were to set aside Poppaea and love her, Acte, again, it would be mere emptiness. Suddenly the thought came to her that the Caesar whom she loved, whom she held involuntarily as a kind of demigod, was as pitiful as any slave, and that palace, with columns of Numidian marble, no better than a heap of stones. At last she wanted to sleep, but being preoccupied by alarm she could not.

Thinking that Lygia, threatened by so many perils and uncertainties, was not sleeping either, she turned to her to speak of her flight in the evening.

But Lygia was sleeping calmly. Into the dark cubiculum came a few bright rays, in which golden dust particles were dancing. By the light of those rays Acte saw her delicate face resting on her bare arm, her closed eyes, and her mouth slightly open.

She is able to sleep, Acte thought. *She is a child yet.*

After a while she realized that child chose to flee rather than remain the beloved of Vinicius. She preferred want to shame, wandering to a lordly house, robes, jewels, and feasts.

Why?

Acte looked at Lygia's clear forehead, at the calm arch of her brows, her dark tresses, her parted lips, her virgin bosom moved by calm breathing. *How different from me!* she thought.

Lygia seemed to her a miracle, a sort of divine vision, something beloved of the gods, a hundred times more beautiful than all the flowers in Caesar's garden, than all the statues in his palace. But in the Greek woman's heart there was no envy. On the contrary, thinking of the dangers that threatened the girl, great pity overcame her and a certain motherly feeling rose in the woman. Lygia seemed to her not only a beautiful vision, but also very dear. She kissed her dark hair.

Lygia slept on calmly, as if at home, under the care of Pomponia Graecina. Midday had passed when she opened her blue eyes and looked around the cubiculum in astonishment. She seemed to wonder that she was not in the house of Aulus.

"Is that you, Acte?" she said at last, seeing the face of the Greek in the darkness.

"Yes."

"Is it evening?"

"No, child; but midday has passed."

"And has Ursus not returned?"

"Ursus did not say that he would return; he said that he would watch for the litter in the evening, with other Christians."

"True."

Then they left the cubiculum and went to the bath, where Acte bathed Lygia; then she took her to breakfast and afterward to the gardens of the palace, in which no dangerous meeting might be feared, since Caesar and his principal courtiers were still sleeping. For the first time in her life Lygia saw those magnificent gardens, full of cypresses, olives, and myrtles, among which appeared a whole population of statues. The mirrorlike ponds gleamed quietly; groves of roses were blooming, watered with the spray of fountains; entrances to charming grottos were circled with a growth of ivy or woodbine; silver-colored swans were sailing on the water; amid statues and trees tame gazelles from the deserts of Africa and rich-colored birds from all known countries on earth wandered.

The gardens were empty of all but slaves. Some were working, spades in hand, singing in an undertone; others, who were resting, were sitting by ponds or in the shade of groves, in trembling light produced by sun-rays breaking in between leaves; others were watering roses or the pale lily-colored blossoms of the saffron. Acte and Lygia walked for a while, looking at all the wonders of the gardens; and though Lygia's mind was not at rest, she was too young yet to temper her curiosity and wonder. It occurred to her that if Caesar were good, he might be very happy in such a palace and gardens.

But at last, somewhat tired, the two women sat down on a bench hidden almost entirely by dense cypresses and began to talk of that which weighed on their hearts most—Lygia's escape in the evening. Acte was far less certain than Lygia of success. At times it seemed to her even a foolish project that would fail totally. She had a growing pity for Lygia. It would be a hundred times safer to agree with Vinicius. After a while Acte asked how long Lygia had known him, and whether she did not think that he would let himself be persuaded to return her to Pomponia.

But Lygia shook her dark head in sadness. No. Vinicius had been different in Aulus's house; he had been very kind. But since yesterday's feast she feared him and would rather flee to the Lygians.

"But in Aulus's house," Acte asked, "he was dear to you, was he not?"

"He was," Lygia answered.

"And you were not a slave, as I was," Acte said, after a moment's thought. "Vinicius might marry you. You are a hostage and a daughter of the Lygian king. Aulus and Pomponia love you as their own child; I am sure that they are ready to adopt you. Vinicius might marry you, Lygia."

But Lygia answered calmly and with great sadness, "I would rather flee to the Lygians."

"Lygia, do you wish me to go directly to Vinicius, rouse him, if he is sleeping, and tell him what I have told you? I will go to him and say, 'Vinicius, this is a king's daughter and a dear child of the famous Aulus; if you love her, return her to Aulus and Pomponia and take her as wife from their house.'"

But Lygia answered with a voice so low that Acte could barely hear it. "I would rather flee to the Lygians." And two tears were hanging on her drooping lids.

Further conversation was stopped by the rustle of approaching steps, and, before Acte had time to see who was coming, Poppaea Sabina appeared in front of the bench with a small group of slave women. Two of them held over her head bunches of ostrich feathers fixed to golden wires; with these, they fanned her lightly and at the same time protected her from the autumn sun, which was still hot. A woman from Egypt, black as ebony, and with breasts swollen as if from milk, held in her arms an infant wrapped in purple fringed with gold. Acte and Lygia rose, thinking that Poppaea would pass the bench without turning attention to either; but she halted before them and said, "Acte, the bells sent by you for the doll were badly fastened; the child tore off one and put it to her mouth; luckily Lilith saw it."

"Pardon, divinity," Acte answered, crossing her arms on her breast and bending her head.

But Poppaea began to gaze at Lygia.

"What slave is this?" she asked.

"She is not a slave, divine Augusta, but a foster child of Pomponia Graecina and a daughter of the Lygian king given by him as hostage to Rome."

"And has she come to visit you?"

"No, Augusta. She is dwelling in the palace since the day before yesterday."

"Was she at the feast last night?"

"She was, Augusta."

"At whose command?"

"At Caesar's command."

Poppaea looked still more attentively at Lygia, who stood with bowed head, now raising her bright eyes to her with curiosity, now covering them with their lids. Suddenly a frown appeared between the brows of the Augusta. Jealous of her own beauty and power, she lived in continual alarm in case a fortunate rival might ruin her, as she had ruined Octavia. So every beautiful face in the palace roused her suspicion. With the eye of a critic she took in at once every part of Lygia's form, judged every detail of her face, and was frightened. *That is simply a nymph*, she thought, *and it was Venus who gave birth to her.* Suddenly she realized that she herself had grown notably older! Wounded vanity quivered in Poppaea, alarm clutched her, and various fears attacked her. She thought, *Perhaps Nero has not seen the girl, or, seeing her through the emerald, has not appreciated her. But what would happen should he meet such a marvel in sunlight? Also, she is not a slave; she is the daughter of a king—a king of barbarians, it is true, but a king. Immortal gods! She is as beautiful as I, but younger!* The wrinkle between her brows increased, and her eyes began to shine under their golden lashes with a cold gleam.

"Have you spoken with Caesar?"

"No, Augusta."

"Why do you choose to be here rather than in the house of Aulus?"

"I do not choose, lady. Petronius persuaded Caesar to take me from Pomponia. I am here against my will."

"And would you return to Pomponia?"

This last question Poppaea gave with a softer and milder voice, and a sudden hope rose in Lygia's heart.

"Lady," she said, extending her hand to her, "Caesar promised to give me as a slave to Vinicius. Please intercede and return me to Pomponia."

"Then Petronius persuaded Caesar to take you from Aulus and give you to Vinicius?"

"True, lady. Vinicius is to send for me today, but you are good; have compassion on me." When she had said this, she bent down and, seizing the border of Poppaea's robe, waited for her word with beating heart. Poppaea looked at her for a while, with a face lighted by an evil smile, and said, "Then I promise that you will become the slave of Vinicius this day."

And she walked away, beautiful as a vision, but evil. Lygia and Acte heard only the wail of the infant, who began to cry.

Lygia's eyes were red with tears; but after a while she took Acte's hand and said, "Let us return. Help is to be looked for from God only."

And they returned to the atrium, which they did not leave until evening. When darkness had come and slaves brought in candles with great flames, both women were very pale. Their conversation failed. Both were listening to sense if someone were coming. Acte collected feverishly whatever jewels she could and, fastening them in a corner of Lygia's gown, begged her not to reject that gift and means of escape. It seemed to both that they heard at one time a whisper beyond the curtain, at another the distant weeping of a child, at another the barking of dogs.

Suddenly the curtain of the entrance was cast aside and a tall, dark man, his face marked with smallpox, appeared like a spirit in the atrium. Lygia recognized Atacinus, a freedman of Vinicius, who had visited the house of Aulus.

Acte screamed; but Atacinus bent low and said, "A greeting, divine Lygia, from Marcus Vinicius, who awaits you with a feast in his house, which is decked in green."

The lips of the girl grew pale.

"I will go," she said.

Then she threw her arms around Acte's neck in farewell.

10

The house of Vinicius was indeed decked in the green of myrtle and ivy, which had been hung on the walls and over the doors. The columns were wreathed with grapevine. In the atrium, which was closed above by a purple woolen cloth as protection from the night cold, it was as clear as in daylight. Eight and twelve flaming lamps were burning; these were in the shape of vessels, trees, animals, birds, or statues, holding cups filled with perfumed olive oil, lamps of alabaster, marble, or gilded Corinthian bronze. They were not as wonderful as that famed candlestick used by Nero and taken from the temple of Apollo, but beautifully made by famous masters. Some of the lights were shaded by Alexandrian glass or transparent materials from the Indus, of red, blue, yellow, or violet color, so that the whole atrium was filled with multicolored rays. The odor of nard was everywhere, to which Vinicius was accustomed and which he had learned to love in the Orient. The depths of the house, in which male and female slaves were moving, gleamed also with light. In the dining room a table was laid for four persons. At the feast were expected, besides Vinicius and Lygia, Petronius and Chrysothemis. Vinicius listened to Petronius, who advised him not to go for Lygia but to send Atacinus with the permission obtained from Caesar, to receive her himself in the house with friendliness and honor.

"You were drunk yesterday," Petronius said. "I saw you. You acted like a quarryman from the Alban Hills. Do not be overinsistent, and remember that you should drink good wine slowly. Also know that it is sweet to desire, but sweeter to be desired."

Chrysothemis had her own different opinion on this point; but Petronius, calling her his vestal and his dove, began to explain the difference that must exist between a trained charioteer of the Circus and the youth who sits on the chariot for the first time. Then, turning to Vinicius, he continued, "Win her confidence, make her joyful, be magnanimous. I have no wish to see a gloomy feast. Swear to her, by Hades even, that you will return her to Pomponia, and it will be up to her that tomorrow she prefers to stay with you."

Then, pointing to Chrysothemis, he added, "For five years I have acted more or less the same with this timid dove, and I cannot complain of her harshness."

Chrysothemis struck him with her fan of peacock feathers and said, "But I did not resist, you satyr!"

"Out of consideration for my predecessor—"

"But were you not at my feet?"

"Yes, to put rings on your toes."

Chrysothemis looked involuntarily at her feet, on the toes of which diamonds were really glittering, and she and Petronius began to laugh. But Vinicius did not give ear to their bantering. His heart was beating quietly under the Syrian priestly robes in which he had arrayed himself to receive Lygia.

"They must have left the palace," he said, as if speaking to himself.

"They must," Petronius answered. "Meanwhile, I may mention the predictions of Apollonius of Tyana, or that history of Rufinus which I have not finished, I do not remember why."

But Vinicius cared no more for Apollonius of Tyana than for the history of Rufinus. His mind was on Lygia; and though he thought that it was more appropriate to entertain her at home than to go in the role of a loyal subordinate to the palace, he was sorry that he had not gone, for the single reason that he might have seen her sooner and sat near her in the dark, in the double litter.

Meanwhile, slaves brought in a tripod ornamented with rams' heads, bronze dishes with coals, on which they sprinkled bits of myrrh and nard.

"Now they are turning toward the Carinae," Vinicius said again.

"He cannot wait; he will run to meet the litter and is likely to miss them!" Chrysothemis exclaimed.

Vinicius smiled without thinking and said, "On the contrary, I will wait."

But he panted, seeing which, Petronius shrugged his shoulders and said, "He is no philosopher, and I shall never make a man of that son of Mars."

"They are now in the Carinae."

In fact, they were turning toward the Carinae. The slaves were on both sides of the litter. Atacinus was right behind, overseeing the advance. But they moved slowly, for lamps showed the way badly in a place not lighted at all. The streets near the palace were empty; here and there someone moved forward with a lantern, but farther on the place was uncommonly crowded. From almost every alley people were pushing out in threes and fours, all without lamps, all in dark mantles. Some walked on with the procession, mingling with the slaves; others in greater numbers came from the opposite direction. Some staggered as if drunk. At moments the advance grew so difficult that the torchbearers cried, "Give way to the noble tribune, Marcus Vinicius!"

Lygia saw those dark crowds through the curtains, which were pushed aside, and trembled with emotion. She was carried away at one moment by hope, at another by fear.

"There he is! That is Ursus and the Christians! Now it will happen quickly," she said with trembling lips. "O Christ, aid! O Christ, save!"

Atacinus himself, who at first did not notice the uncommon animation of the street, began at last to be alarmed. There was something strange in this. The slaves had to cry oftener and oftener, "Give way to the litter of the noble tribune!" From the sides unknown people crowded up to the litter so much that Atacinus commanded the slaves to beat them back with clubs.

Suddenly a cry was heard in front of the procession. In one instant all the lights were extinguished. Around the litter came an uproar and a struggle.

Atacinus saw that this was simply an attack, and when he saw it he was frightened. It was known to all that Caesar, with a crowd of attendants, frequently made attacks for amusement in the Subura and in other parts of the city. It was known that even at times he came away from those night adventures with black and blue spots; but whoever defended himself went to his death, even if a senator. The house of the guards, whose duty it was to watch over the city, was not very far; but during such attacks the guards pretended to be deaf and blind.

Meanwhile, there was an uproar around the litter; people struck, struggled, threw, and trampled one another. The thought flashed on Atacinus to save Lygia and himself, above all, and leave the rest to their fate. So, drawing her out of the litter, he took her in his arms and tried to escape in the darkness.

But Lygia called, "Ursus! Ursus!"

She was dressed in white, so it was easy to see her. Atacinus, with his other arm, was throwing his own mantle over her hastily when terrible claws seized his neck and a gigantic, crushing mass fell on his head like a stone.

He dropped in one instant, as an ox felled by the back of an axe before the altar of Jove.

The slaves for the greater part were either lying on the ground or had saved themselves by scattering in the thick darkness, around the corners of the walls. On the spot only the litter remained, broken in the rush. Ursus carried Lygia to the Subura; his comrades followed him, dispersing gradually along the way.

Vinicius's slaves assembled before his house. They did not have the courage to enter. After a short discussion they returned to the place of conflict, where they found a few corpses, among them Atacinus. He was quivering yet; but after a moment of violent convulsion, he stretched and was motionless.

They took him and, returning, stopped before the gate a second time. But they must declare to their lord what had happened.

"Let Gulo declare it," whispered some voices. "Blood is flowing from his face as from ours, and the master loves him. It is safer for Gulo than for others."

Gulo, a German, an old slave who had nursed Vinicius and was inherited by him from his mother, the sister of Petronius, said, "I will tell him; but you all come. Do not let his anger fall on my head alone."

Vinicius was growing thoroughly impatient. Petronius and Chrysothemis were laughing; but he walked quickly up and down the atrium.

"They ought to be here!"

He wished to go out to meet the litter, but Petronius and Chrysothemis detained him.

Steps were heard suddenly in the entrance; the slaves rushed into the atrium in a crowd and, halting quickly at the wall, raised their hands and began to groan.

Vinicius sprang toward them.

"Where is Lygia?" he cried, with a terrible and changed voice.

They groaned louder.

Then Gulo pushed his bloody face forward and exclaimed, in haste and a pitiful tone, "See our blood, lord! We fought! See our blood! See our blood!"

But he had not finished when Vinicius seized a bronze lamp and with one blow shattered the skull of the slave; then, seizing his own head with both hands, he drove his fingers into his hair, repeating hoarsely, *"Me miserum! Me miserum!"*

His face became blue, his eyes rolled in his head, and foam came out on his lips.

"Whips!" roared he at last, with an unearthly voice.

"Lord! *Aaaa!* Take pity!" groaned the slaves.

Petronius stood up with an expression of disgust on his face.

"Come, Chrysothemis!" he said. "If it is your wish to look on raw flesh, I will open a butcher's stall on the Carinae!"

And he walked out of the atrium. But through the whole house, ornamented in the green of ivy and prepared for a feast, were heard, from moment to moment, groans and the whistling of whips, which lasted almost until morning.

11

Vinicius did not lie down that night. Some time after the departure of Petronius, when the groans of his flogged slaves could allay neither his rage nor his pain, he collected a crowd of other servants and, though the night was far spent, rushed forth at the head of these to look for Lygia. He visited the district of the Esquiline, then the Subura, Vicus Sceleratus, and all the adjoining alleys. Passing next around the Capitol, he went to the island over the bridge of Fabricius; after that he passed through a part of the Trans-Tiber. But that was a pursuit without purpose, for he himself had no hope of finding Lygia, and if he sought her it was mainly to fill in a terrible night. In fact he returned home about daybreak, when the carts and mules of dealers in vegetables began to appear in the city, and when bakers were opening their shops.

On returning he commanded the slaves to put away Gulo's corpse, which no one had dared to touch. The slaves from whom Lygia had been taken he sent to rural prisons—a punishment almost more dreadful than death. Throwing himself at last on a couch in the atrium, he began to think confusedly of how he was to find and seize Lygia.

To resign her, to lose her, not to see her again, seemed to him impossible; and at this thought alone frenzy took hold of him. For the first time in his life the stubborn nature of the youthful soldier met resistance, met another unbending will, and he simply could not understand how anyone could dare to thwart his wishes. Vinicius would have chosen to see the world and the city sink in ruins rather than fail in his purpose. The cup of delight had been snatched from before his lips almost; so it seemed to him that something impossible had happened, something crying to divine and human laws for vengeance.

But, first of all, he was unwilling and unable to be reconciled with fate, for never in his life had he so desired anything as Lygia. It seemed to him that he could not exist without her. He could not tell himself what he was to do without her the next day, how he was to survive in the future. At moments he was overcome by rage against her, which approached madness. He wanted to have her, to beat her, to drag her by the hair to the cubiculum and gloat over her; then again he was carried away by a terrible yearning for her voice, her form, her eyes, and he thought that he would be ready to lie at her feet. He called to her, gnawed his fingers, clasped his head with his hands. He strove with all his might to think calmly about searching for her—and was unable. A thousand methods and means flew through his head, one wilder than another. At last the thought flashed on him that no one else had intercepted her but Aulus, that in every case Aulus must know where she was hiding. And he sprang up to run to the house of Aulus.

If they will not yield her to him, if they have no fear of his threats, he will go to Caesar, accuse the old general of disobedience and obtain a sentence of death against him. But before that, he will gain a confession of where Lygia is. If they give her to him, even willingly, he will be revenged. They received him, it is true, in their house and nursed him—but that is nothing! With this one injustice they have freed him from every debt of gratitude. Here his vengeful and stubborn soul began to take pleasure at the despair of Pomponia Graecina when the centurion would bring the death sentence to old Aulus. He was almost certain that he would get it. Petronius would assist him. Moreover, Caesar never denies anything to his intimates, the Augustians, unless personal dislike or desire makes him refuse.

Suddenly his heart almost died within him under the influence of this terrible supposition, *But if Caesar himself has taken Lygia?*

All knew that Nero sought relief from boredom by carrying out night attacks. Even Petronius took part in these amusements. Their main object was to seize women and toss each on a soldier's mantle until she fainted. Even Nero himself on occasions called these expeditions "pearl hunts," for it happened that in the depth of districts occupied by a numerous and needy population they sometimes caught a real pearl of youth and beauty. Then the "sagatio," as they termed the tossing, was changed into a genuine carrying away, and the pearl was sent either to the Palatine or to one of Caesar's numberless villas, or finally Caesar yielded her to one of his intimates. So might it happen also with Lygia. Caesar had seen her during the feast; and Vinicius did not doubt for an instant that she must have seemed to him the most beautiful woman he had yet seen. How could it be otherwise? It is true that Lygia had been in Nero's own house on the Palatine, and he might have kept her openly. But, as Petronius said truly, Caesar had no courage in crime, and, with power to act openly, he chose to act always in secret. This time fear of Poppaea might incline him also to secrecy. It occurred now to the young soldier that Aulus would not have dared, perhaps, to carry off forcibly a girl given him, Vinicius, by Caesar. Besides, who would dare? Would that gigantic blue-eyed Lygian, who had the courage to enter the triclinium and carry her from the feast on his arm? But where could he hide with her; where could he take her? No! A slave would not have been that bold. So no one had done the deed except Caesar.

At this thought it grew dark in his eyes, and drops of sweat covered his forehead. In that case Lygia was lost to him forever. It was possible to wrest her from the hands of anyone else, but not from the hands of Caesar. Now, with greater truth than ever, he could exclaim, *"Vae misere mihi!"* His imagination represented Lygia in Nero's arms, and, for the first time in life, he understood that there are thoughts that are simply beyond man's endurance. He knew then, for the first time, how he loved her. As a whole life flashes through the memory of a drowning man, so Lygia began to pass through his. He saw her, heard every word of hers—saw her at the fountain, at the house of Aulus, and at the feast; felt her near him, felt the odor of her hair, the warmth of her body, the delight of the kisses that at the feast he had pressed on her innocent lips. She seemed to him a hundred times sweeter, more beautiful, more desired than ever—a hundred times more the only one, the one chosen from among all mortals and divinities.

And when he thought that all this which had become so fixed in his heart, which had become his blood and life, might be possessed by Nero, a pain seized him that was purely physical and so piercing that he wanted to beat his head against the wall of the atrium until he broke it. He thought that he might go insane; and he would have gone insane beyond doubt had not vengeance remained to him. But as hitherto he had thought that he could not live unless he got Lygia, he thought now that he would not die until he had avenged her. This gave him a certain kind of comfort. *I will be your Cassiuis Chaerea!* (the slayer of Caligula) he said to himself in thinking of Nero. After a while, seizing earth in his hands from the flower vases surrounding the impluvium, he made a dreadful vow to Erebus, Hecate, and his own household gods that he would have vengeance.

And he received a sort of consolation. He had at least something to live for and something with which to fill his nights and days. Then, dropping the idea of visiting Aulus, he commanded the slaves to bear him to the Palatine. Along the way he concluded that if they would not admit him to Caesar, or if they should try to find weapons on his person, it would be a proof that Caesar had taken Lygia. He had no weapons with him. He had lost presence of mind in general; but as is usual with persons possessed by a single idea, he focused on revenge. He did not wish his desire for revenge to leave prematurely. He wished above all to see Acte, for he expected to learn the truth from her. At moments the hope flashed on him that he might see Lygia also, and at that thought he began to tremble. For if Caesar had carried her away without knowledge of whom he was taking, he might return her that day. But after a while he cast aside this supposition. Had there been a wish to return her to him, she would have been sent yesterday. Acte was the only person who could explain everything, and it was important to see her before others.

Convinced of this, he commanded the slaves to hurry; and along the road he thought now of Lygia, now of revenge. He had heard that Egyptian priests of the goddess Pasht could bring disease on whomever they wished, and he determined to learn the means of doing this. In the Orient they had told him, too, that Jews have certain invocations by which they cover their enemies' bodies with ulcers. He had a number of Jews among his domestic slaves; hence he promised himself to torture them on his return until they divulged the secret. He found most delight, however, in thinking of the short Roman sword that lets out a stream of blood such as had gushed from Caius Caligula and made permanent stains on the columns of the portico. He was ready to exterminate all of Rome; and had vengeful gods promised that all people should die except him and Lygia, he would have accepted the promise.

In front of the arch he regained composure and thought when he saw the praetorian guard, *If they make the least difficulty in admitting me, that will prove that Lygia is in the palace by the will of Caesar.*

But the chief centurion smiled at him in a friendly manner, then advanced a number of steps, and said, "A greeting, noble tribune. If you desire to give a tribute to Caesar, you have found an unfortunate moment. I do not think that you will be able to see him."

"What has happened?" Vinicius asked.

"The infant Augusta suddenly fell ill yesterday. Caesar and Poppaea are attending her, with physicians whom they have summoned from the whole city."

This was an important event. When that daughter was born to him, Caesar was simply wild from delight and received her with great enthusiasm. Previously the Senate had committed the womb of Poppaea to the gods with the utmost solemnity. A votive offering was made at Antium, where the delivery took place; splendid games were celebrated and a temple was erected to the two Fortunes. Nero, unable to be moderate in anything, loved the infant excessively. The child was dear to Poppaea also. It strengthened her position and made her influence irresistible.

The fate of the whole empire might depend on the health and life of the infant Augusta; but Vinicius was so occupied with himself, his own case, and his love, that without paying attention to the news of the centurion he answered, "I only wish to see Acte." And he went in.

But Acte was occupied also with the child, and he had to wait a long time to see her. She came only about midday, with a pale and wearied face, which grew paler still at sight of Vinicius.

"Acte!" Vinicius cried, seizing her hand and drawing her to the middle of the atrium. "Where is Lygia?"

"I wanted to ask you about that," she answered, looking him in the eyes with scorn.

But though he had promised himself to ask about Lygia calmly, he pressed his head with his hands again and said, with a face distorted by pain and anger, "She is gone. She was taken from me on the way!"

After a while he recovered and, thrusting his face up to Acte's, said through his gritted teeth, "Acte! If life is dear to you, if you do not wish to cause misfortunes that you are unable even to imagine, answer me truly. Did Caesar take her?"

"Caesar did not leave the palace yesterday."

"By the ghost of your mother, by all the gods, is she not in the palace?"

"By the ghost of my mother, Marcus, she is not in the palace, and Caesar did not kidnap her. The infant Augusta has been ill since yesterday, and Nero has not left her cradle."

Vinicius drew a breath.

"Ah, then," he said, sitting on the bench and clenching his fists, "Aulus intercepted her, and in that case woe to him!"

"Aulus Plautius was here this morning. He could not see me, for I was occupied with the child; but he asked Epaphroditus and others of Caesar's servants about Lygia and told them he would come again to see me."

"He wished to turn suspicion from himself. If he did not know what happened, he would have come to seek Lygia in my house."

"He left a few words on a tablet, from which you will see that, knowing Lygia to have been taken from his house by Caesar at your request and that of Petronius, he expected that she would be sent to you, and he was at your house early this morning, where they told him what had happened."

When she had said this, she went to the cubiculum and returned shortly with the tablet Aulus had left.

Vinicius read the tablet and was silent; Acte seemed to read the thoughts on his gloomy face, for she said, "Lygia herself wished this to happen."

"You knew she wished to flee!"

"I knew that she would not become your concubine."

And she looked almost sternly at him with her misty eyes.

"And you—what have you been all your life?"

"I was a slave, first of all."

But Vinicius was still enraged. Caesar had given him Lygia; so he had no need to inquire what she had been before. He would find her, even under the earth, and he would do what he liked with her. She would be his concubine. He would command his slaves to flog her as often as he pleased. If she grew distasteful to him, he would give her to the lowest of his slaves, or he would command her to turn a handmill on his lands in Africa. He would seek her out now and find her only to bend her, trample on her, and conquer her.

And, growing more and more excited, he lost every sense of measure, to the degree that even Acte saw that he was promising more than he could execute; that he was speaking because of pain and anger. She might have had compassion on him, but his extravagant words exhausted her patience, and at last she asked why he had come to her.

Vinicius did not answer immediately. He had come to her because he wished to come, because he believed that she would give him information. But really he had come to Caesar, and, not being able to see him, he came to her. Lygia, by fleeing, opposed the will of Caesar; so he would implore him to give an order to search for her throughout the city and the empire, even if it came to using all the legions and to ransacking in turn every house within Roman dominion. Petronius would support his plea, and the search would begin from that day.

"Take care," Acte answered, "unless you lose her forever the moment she is found, at the command of Caesar."

Vinicius wrinkled his brows. "What does that mean?"

"Listen to me, Marcus. Yesterday Lygia and I were in the gardens here, and we met Poppaea, with the infant Augusta, carried by an African woman, Lilith. In the evening the child fell ill, and

Lilith insists that she was bewitched, that the foreign woman whom they met in the garden bewitched her. Should the child recover, they will forget this, but if not, Poppaea will be the first to accuse Lygia of witchcraft, and wherever she is found she will not be rescued."

A moment of silence followed. Then Vinicius said, "But perhaps she did bewitch Augusta and has bewitched me."

"Lilith repeats that the child began to cry the moment she carried her past us. And that is true. It is certain that she was sick when they took her out of the garden. Marcus, seek for Lygia whenever it may please you, but until the infant Augusta recovers, do not speak of her to Caesar, or you will bring Poppaea's vengeance on her. Her eyes have wept enough because of you already, and may all the gods guard her poor head."

"Do you love her, Acte?" Vinicius asked gloomily.

"Yes, I love her." And tears glittered in the eyes of the freedwoman.

"You love her because she has not repaid you with hatred, as she has me."

Acte looked at him for a time as if hesitating, or as if wishing to learn if he spoke sincerely. Then she said, "Oh, blind and passionate man—she loved you."

Vinicius revived under the influence of those words, as if possessed. "It is not true." She hated him. How could Acte know? Would Lygia make a confession to her after one day's acquaintance? What love would prefer wandering, the disgrace of poverty, the uncertainty of tomorrow, or a shameful death even, to a wreath-bedecked house, in which a lover is waiting with a feast? It is better for him not to hear such things, for he is ready to go insane. He would not have given away that girl for all Caesar's treasures, and she fled. What kind of love dreads delight and gives pain? Who can fathom it? Except for the hope that he should find her, he would sink a sword in himself. Love surrenders; it does not take away. There were moments at the house of Aulus when he himself nearly believed in happiness, but now he knows that she will die with hatred in her heart.

But Acte, usually mild and timid, was indignant. How had he tried to win Lygia? Instead of bowing before Aulus and Pomponia to get her, he took the child away from her parents by clever strategy. He wanted to make not a wife but a concubine of her, the foster daughter of an honorable house and the daughter of a king. He had her brought to this house of crime and infamy; he defiled her innocent eyes with the sight of a shameful feast; he acted with her as with a prostitute. Had he forgotten the house of Aulus and Pomponia Graecina, who had reared Lygia? Had he not sense enough to understand that there are women different from Nigidia or Calvia Crispinilla or Poppaea, and from all those who he meets in Caesar's house? Did he not understand at once that she is an honest maiden who prefers death to shame? From where does he know what kind of gods she worships, and whether they are not purer and better than the wanton Venus, or than Isis, worshiped by the lawless women of Rome?

No! Lygia had made no confession to her, but she had said that she looked for rescue from Vinicius; she had hoped that he would obtain permission from Caesar to return home, that he would restore her to Pomponia. And while speaking of this, Lygia blushed like a woman who loves and trusts. Lygia's heart beat for him; but he, Vinicius, had terrified and offended her, had made her indignant. Let him seek her now with the aid of Caesar's soldiers, but let him know that should Poppaea's child die, suspicion will fall on Lygia, whose destruction will then be inevitable.

Emotion began to force its way through the anger and pain of Vinicius. The information that he was loved by Lygia shook him to the depth of his soul. He remembered her in Aulus's garden, when she was listening to his words with blushes on her face and her eyes full of light. It seemed to him then that she had begun to love him; and all at once, at that thought, a feeling of profound joy embraced him, a hundred times greater than he expected. He thought that he might have won her gradually. She would have wreathed his door, rubbed it with wolf's fat, and then sat as his wife by his hearth on the sheepskin. He would have heard from her mouth the saying, "Where you are, Caius, there I am, Caia." And she would have been his forever.

Why did he not act like this? True, he had been ready to do so. But now she is gone, and it may be impossible to find her; and should he find her, perhaps he will cause her death. Then neither she nor Aulus nor Pomponia Graecina will favor him. His anger turned now, not against the house of Aulus, or Lygia, but against Petronius. Petronius was to blame for everything. Had it not been for him Lygia would not have been forced to wander; she would be his betrothed, and no danger would be hanging over her dear head. But now all is past, and it is too late to correct this evil.

"Too late!" And it seemed to him that a gulf had opened before his feet. Acte repeated as an echo the words, "Too late," which from another's mouth sounded like a death sentence. He understood one thing, however, that he must find Lygia, or something evil would happen to him.

And, wrapping himself mechanically in his toga, he was about to depart without taking farewell even of Acte, when suddenly the curtain separating the entrance from the atrium was pushed aside, and he saw the serene figure of Pomponia Graecina.

Evidently she too had heard of the disappearance of Lygia and, judging that she could see Acte more easily than Aulus, had come for news to her.

But, seeing Vinicius, she turned her pale, delicate face to him and said, after a pause, "May God forgive you the wrong, Marcus, you have done to us and to Lygia."

He stood with a drooping head, with a feeling of misfortune and guilt, not understanding what God was to forgive him for or could forgive him. Pomponia should not have mentioned forgiveness; she ought to have spoken of revenge.

At last he went out, full of grievous thoughts, immense care, and amazement.

In the court and under the gallery were crowds of anxious people. Among the slaves of the palace were nobles and senators who had come to ask about the health of the infant and at the same time to present themselves in the palace and show proof of their anxiety, even in the presence of Nero's slaves. News of the illness of the "divine" had spread quickly, for new persons appeared in the gateway every moment, and through the opening of the arcade whole crowds were visible. Some of the newly arrived, seeing that Vinicius was coming from the palace, approached him for news, but he hurried on without answering their questions, until Petronius, who had come for news too, stopped him.

Beyond doubt Vinicius would have become enraged at the sight of Petronius and done some lawless act in Caesar's palace had it not been that when he had left Acte he was so crushed, so weighed down and exhausted, that for the moment even his innate aggressiveness had left him. He pushed Petronius aside and wished to pass; but the other detained him, almost by force.

"How is the divine infant?" he asked.

But this constraint angered Vinicius a second time.

"May Hades swallow her and all this house!" he said, gritting his teeth.

"Silence, foolish man!" Petronius said, and, looking around, he added hurriedly, "If you wish to know something of Lygia, come with me; I will tell nothing here! Come with me; I will tell my thoughts in the litter."

Putting his arm around the young tribune, he conducted him from the palace as quickly as possible. That was his main concern, for he had no news whatever; but being a man of resources, and having, in spite of his indignation of yesterday, much sympathy for Vinicius, and finally feeling responsible for all that had happened, he had planned something already. When they entered the litter, he said, "I have commanded my slaves to watch at every gate. I gave them an accurate description of the girl and that giant who carried her from the feast at Caesar's—for he is the man, beyond doubt, who intercepted her. Listen to me; perhaps Aulus and Pomponia wish to hide her in some estate of theirs; in that case we shall learn the direction in which they took her. If my slaves do not see her at some gate, we shall know that she is in the city and shall begin this very day to search in Rome for her."

"Aulus does not know where she is," Vinicius answered.

"Are you sure of that?"

"I saw Pomponia. She, too, is looking for her."

"She could not leave the city yesterday, for the gates are closed at night. Two of my people are watching at each gate. One is to follow Lygia and the giant, the other is returning at once to inform me. If she is in the city, we shall find her, for that Lygian is easily recognized, even by his stature and his shoulders. You are lucky that it was not Caesar who took her, and I can assure you that he did not, for there are no secrets from me on the Palatine."

Vinicius told Petronius in a voice broken by emotion what he had heard from Acte and what new dangers were threatening Lygia—dangers so dreadful that because of them there would be need to hide her from Poppaea very carefully, in case they discovered her. Then he scolded Petronius bitterly for his advice. Had it not been for him, everything would have gone differently. Lygia would have been at the house of Aulus, and he, Vinicius, might have seen her every day, and he would have been happier at that moment than Caesar.

Petronius, who had not even thought that the young man could love and desire to such a degree, when he saw the tears of despair from Vinicius, said to himself, with a certain astonishment, *O mighty Lady of Cyprus, you alone are ruler of gods and men!*

12

When they arrived in front of the judge's house, the chief of the atrium answered that no slaves sent to the gates had yet returned. He had given orders to take food to them and had commanded, under penalty of whips, that they were to watch carefully all who left the city.

"You see," Petronius said, "that they are in Rome, beyond doubt, and in that case we shall find them. But command your people also to watch at the gates—those, namely, who were sent for Lygia, as they will recognize her easily."

"I have given orders to send them to rural prisons," Vinicius said, "but I will recall the orders at once and let them go to the gates."

And writing a few words on a wax-covered tablet, he handed it to Petronius, who gave directions to send it at once to the house of Vinicius. Then they passed into the interior portico and, sitting on a marble bench, began to talk. The golden-haired Eunice and

Iras pushed bronze footstools under their feet and poured wine for them into goblets, out of wonderful narrow-necked pitchers from Volaterrae and Caecina.

"Does anyone among your people know that giant Lygian?" Petronius asked.

"Atacinus and Gulo knew him; but Atacinus fell yesterday at the litter, and I killed Gulo."

"I am sorry for him," Petronius said. "He carried not only you, but me, in his arms."

"I intended to free him," Vinicius answered. "But do not mention him. Let us speak of Lygia. Rome is a sea—"

"A sea is just the place where men fish for pearls. Of course we shall not find her today, or tomorrow, but we shall certainly find her. You have heard from Aulus himself, that he intends to go to Sicily with his whole family. In that case the girl would be far from you."

"I should follow them," Vinicius said. "In any event, she would be out of danger; but now, if that child dies, Poppaea will believe, and will persuade Caesar, that she died because of Lygia."

"True; that alarmed me, too. But that little doll may recover. Should she die, we shall find some way of escape."

Here Petronius meditated a while and added, "Poppaea, it is said, follows the religion of the Jews and believes in evil spirits. Caesar is superstitious. If we spread the report that evil spirits carried off Lygia, the news will be believed, especially as neither Caesar nor Aulus Plautius intercepted her; her escape was really mysterious. The Lygian could not have accomplished it alone; he must have had help. And where could a slave find so many people in the course of one day?"

"Slaves help one another in Rome."

"Some person pays for that with blood at times. True, they support one another, but not some against others. In this case it was known that responsibility and punishment would fall on your people. If you give your people the idea of evil spirits, they will say at once that they saw them with their own eyes because that will justify them in your sight. Ask one of them, as a test, if he did not see spirits carrying off Lygia through the air; he will swear at once by the aegis of Zeus that he saw them."

Vinicius, who was superstitious also, looked at Petronius with sudden and great fear.

"If Ursus could not have men to help him and was unable to take her alone, who could take her?"

Petronius began to laugh.

"See?" he said. "They will believe, since you are half a believer yourself. Our society ridicules the gods. They, too, will believe in spirits, and they will not look for her. Meanwhile, we shall put her away somewhere far off from the city, in some villa of mine or yours."

"But who could help her?"

"Her fellow religious believers," Petronius answered.

"Who are they? What deity does she worship? I ought to know that better than you."

"Nearly every woman in Rome honors a different one. It is almost beyond doubt that Pomponia reared her in the religion of that deity she herself worships; what one she worships I do not know. One thing is certain, that no person has seen her make an offering to our gods in any temple. They have accused her even of being a Christian, but that is not possible; a domestic tribunal cleared her of the charge. They say that Christians not only worship an ass's head, but are enemies of the human race and permit the foulest crimes. Pomponia cannot be a Christian, as her virtue is known, and an enemy of the human race could not treat slaves as she does."

"They are treated well at Aulus's," Vinicius interrupted.

"Ah! Pomponia mentioned to me some god, who must be powerful and merciful. Where she has put away all the others is her affair; it is enough that that Logos of hers cannot be very mighty, since he has had only two adherents—Pomponia and Lygia—and Ursus in addition. It must be that there are more of those adherents, and that they assisted Lygia."

"That faith commands forgiveness," Vinicius said. "At Acte's I met Pomponia, who said to me: 'May God forgive you the evil you have done to us and to Lygia.'"

"Evidently their God is some caretaker who is very mild. Ha! Let him forgive you and in sign of forgiveness return you the girl."

"I have no wish for food, or the bath, or sleep. I will take a dark lantern and wander through the city. Perhaps I shall find her in disguise. I am sick."

Petronius looked at him with compassion. In fact, there was blue under his eyes, his pupils were gleaming with fever, his un-shaven beard indicated a dark strip on his firmly outlined jaws, his hair was in disorder, and he really was like a sick man. Iras and the golden-haired Eunice looked at him also with sympathy; but he seemed not to see them, and he and Petronius took no notice whatever of the slave women, just as they would not have noticed dogs moving around them.

"Fever is tormenting you," Petronius said.

"It is."

"Then listen to me. I do not know what the doctor has pre-scribed to you, but I know how I should act in your place. Until this lost one is found I should seek in another that quality that has gone away with her. I saw splendid forms at your villa. Do not contradict me. I know what love is; and I know that when one is desired another cannot take her place. But in a beautiful slave it is possible to find even momentary distraction."

"I do not need it." Vinicius said.

But Petronius, who had for him a real weakness, and who wished to soften his pain, began to meditate how he could bring this about.

"Perhaps yours have not the charm of novelty," he said—and here he began to look in turn at Iras and Eunice; and finally he placed his palm on the hip of the golden-haired Eunice. "Look at this grace! For whom some days since Fonteius Capiton the younger offered three wonderful boys from Clazomene. A more beautiful figure than hers even Skopas himself has not chiseled. I myself cannot tell why I have remained indifferent to her thus far, since thoughts of Chrysothemis have not restrained me. Well, I give her to you; take her for yourself!"

When the golden-haired Eunice heard this, she grew pale and, looking with frightened eyes on Vinicius, seemed to wait for his answer holding her breath.

But he sprang up suddenly and, pressing his temples with his hands, said quickly, like a man who is tortured by disease and will not hear anything, "No, no! I do not care for her! I do not care for others! I thank you, but I do not want her. I will seek Lygia through the city. Bring me a Gallic cloak with a hood. I will go beyond the Tiber—to see even Ursus."

And he hurried away. Petronius, seeing that Vinicius could not remain, did not try to detain him. Taking, however, his refusal as a temporary dislike for all women save Lygia, he said, turning to the slave, "Eunice, you will bathe and anoint yourself, then dress. After that you will go to the house of Vinicius."

But she dropped before him on her knees and with joined palms implored him not to remove her from the house. She would not go to Vinicius, she said. She would rather carry fuel to the hypocaustum (sweat bath) in his house than be chief servant in that of Vinicius. She would not, she could not go; and she begged him to have pity on her. Let her be flogged daily, only do not send her away.

And, trembling like a leaf with fear, she stretched her hands to him, while he listened with amazement. A slave who begged relief from the fulfillment of a command, who said "I will not and I cannot," was something so unheard of in Rome that at first Petronius could not believe his own ears. Finally, he frowned. He was too refined to be cruel. His slaves, especially in the department of pleasure, were freer than others, on condition of performing their service in an exemplary manner and honoring the will of their master like that of a god. In case they failed in those two respects, he was not able to spare punishment, to which, according to general custom, they were subject. Since, besides this, he could not endure opposition, nor anything that ruffled his calmness, he looked for a while at the kneeling girl and then said, "Call Tiresias, and return with him."

Eunice rose, trembling, with tears in her eyes, and went out. She returned with the chief of the atrium, Tiresias, a Cretan.

"You will take Eunice," Petronius said, "and give her twenty-five lashes. Do not, however, harm her skin."

When he had said this, he went into the library and, sitting down at a table of rose-colored marble, began to work on his "Feast of Trimalchion." But the flight of Lygia and the illness of the infant Augusta had disturbed his mind so much that he could not work long. That illness, above all, was important. It occurred

112

to Petronius that were Caesar to believe that Lygia had cast spells on the infant the responsibility might fall on him also, for the girl had been brought at his request to the palace. But he could count on this, that at the first interview with Caesar he would be able in some way to show the utter absurdity of such an idea; he counted a little, too, on a certain weakness Poppaea had for him—a weakness hidden carefully, it is true, but not so carefully that he could not see it. After a while he shrugged his shoulders at these fears and decided to go to the triclinium to strengthen himself, and then order the litter to bear him once more to the palace, after that to the Campus Martius, and then to Chrysothemis.

But on the way to the triclinium at the entrance to the corridor assigned to servants, he unexpectedly saw the slender form of Eunice standing among other slaves at the wall; and, forgetting that he had given Tiresias no order beyond flogging her, he wrinkled his brow again and looked around for the chief of the atrium. Not seeing him among the servants, he turned to Eunice.

"Have you received the lashes?"

She cast herself at his feet a second time, pressed the border of his toga to her lips, and said, "Oh, yes, lord. I have received them. Oh, yes, lord!"

In her voice were heard, as it were, joy and gratitude. It was clear that she looked on the lashes as a substitute for her removal from the house, and that now she would stay. Petronius, who understood this, wondered at the passionate resistance of the girl; but he was too deeply versed in human nature not to know that love alone could call forth such resistance.

"Do you love someone in this house?" he asked.

She raised her blue, tearful eyes to him and answered, in a voice so low that it was hardly possible to hear her, "Yes, lord."

And with those eyes, with that golden hair thrown back, with fear and hope in her face, she was so beautiful, she looked at him so entreatingly, that Petronius, who, as a philosopher, had proclaimed the might of love and, as a man of aesthetic nature, had given homage to all beauty, felt for her a certain type of compassion.

"Whom do you love?" he asked, indicating the servants with his head.

There was no answer to that question. Eunice inclined her head to his feet and remained motionless.

Petronius looked at the slaves, among whom were beautiful and stately youths. He could read nothing on any face; on the contrary all had certain strange smiles. He looked, then, for a while on Eunice lying at his feet and went in silence to the triclinium.

After he had eaten, he commanded his slaves to bear him to the palace and then to Chrysothemis, with whom he remained until late at night. But when he returned, he called Tiresias.

"Did Eunice receive the flogging?" he asked.

"She did, lord. You did not let the skin be cut, however."

"Did I give no other command touching her?"

"No, lord," answered the foreman with alarm.

"That is well. Whom of the slaves does she love?"

"No one, lord."

"What do you know of her?"

Tiresias began to speak in a somewhat uncertain voice. "At night Eunice never leaves the cubiculum in which she lives with old Acrisiona and Ifida; after you are dressed she never goes to the baths. Other slaves ridicule her and call her Diana."

"Enough," Petronius said. "My relative, Vinicius, to whom I offered her today, did not accept her; so she may stay in the house. You are free to go."

"Am I permitted to speak more of Eunice, lord?"

"I have commanded you to say all you know."

"The whole household is speaking of the flight of the girl who was to dwell in the house of the noble Vinicius. After your departure, Eunice came to me and said that she knew a man who could find her."

"Ah! What kind of man is he?"

"I do not know, lord; but I thought that I ought to inform you of this matter."

"That is well. Let that man wait tomorrow in my house for the arrival of the tribune, whom you will request in my name to meet me here."

The foreman of the slaves bowed and went out. But Petronius began to think of Eunice. At first it seemed clear to him that the young slave wished Vinicius to find Lygia for this reason only, that she would not be forced from his house. Afterward, however, it occurred to him that the man whom Eunice was pushing forward might be her lover, and all at once that thought seemed to him disagreeable. There was, it is true, a simple way of learning the truth, for it was enough to summon Eunice; but the hour was late, and Petronius felt tired after his long visit with Chrysothemis and was in a hurry to sleep. But on the way to the cubiculum he remembered—it is unknown why—that he had noticed wrinkles that day in the corners of Chrysothemis's eyes. He thought, also, that her beauty was more celebrated in Rome than it deserved; and that Fonteius Capiton, who had offered him three boys from Clazomene for Eunice, wanted to buy her too cheaply.

13

Next morning, Petronius had barely finished dressing in the unctorium when Vinicius came, called by Tiresias. He knew that no news had come from the gates. This information, instead of comforting him that Lygia was still in Rome, weighted him down still more, for he began to think that Ursus might have conducted her out of the city immediately after her seizure, and thus before Petronius's slaves had begun to keep watch at the gates. It is true that in autumn, when the days become shorter, the gates are closed rather early; but they are opened for persons leaving, and the number of these is considerable. It was possible, also, to pass the walls by other ways, well known, for instance, to slaves who wish to escape from the city. Vinicius had sent out his people to all roads leading to the provinces, to watchmen in the smaller towns, proclaiming a pair of fugitive slaves, with a detailed description of Ursus and Lygia, coupled with the offer of a reward for seizing them. But it was doubtful whether that pursuit would reach the fugitives, and even should it reach them, whether the local authorities would think themselves justified in making the arrest at the private insistence of Vinicius, without the support of a praetor. Indeed, there had not been time to obtain such support. Vinicius himself, disguised as a slave, had sought Lygia the whole day before, through every corner of the city, but had been unable to find the least trace of her. He had seen Aulus's servants, but they seemed to be seeking something also, and that confirmed him in the belief that it was not Aulus who had intercepted the girl, and that the old general did not know what had happened to her.

When Tiresias announced to him, then, that there was a man who would undertake to find Lygia, he hurried to the house of Petronius; and he just finished saluting his uncle, when he sought for the man.

"We shall see him at once. Eunice knows him," Petronius said. "She will come this moment to fold my toga and will give clearer information concerning him."

"Oh! The one you wished to give me yesterday?"

"The one you rejected; for which I am grateful, for she is the best vestiplica in the whole city."

In fact, the vestiplica came in before he had finished speaking; and taking the toga, laid on a chair inlaid with pearl, Eunice opened the garment to throw it on Petronius's shoulder. Her face was clear and calm; joy was in her eyes.

Petronius looked at her. She seemed to him very beautiful. After a while, when she had covered him with the toga, she began to arrange it, bending at times to lengthen the folds. He noticed that her arms had a marvelous, pale rose-color and that her bosom and shoulders bore the transparent reflections of pearl or alabaster.

"Eunice," he said, "has the man come to Tiresias whom you mentioned yesterday?"

"He has, lord."

"What is his name?"

"Chilo Chilonides."

"Who is he?"

"A physician, sage, and soothsayer who knows how to read people's fates and predict the future."

116

"Has he predicted the future to you?"

Eunice was covered with a blush that gave a rosy color to her ears and even to her neck.

"Yes, lord."

"What has he predicted?"

"That pain and happiness would meet me."

"Pain met you yesterday at the hands of Tiresias; so happiness also should come."

"It has come, lord, already."

"What?"

"I am here," said she in a whisper.

Petronius put his hand on her golden head.

"You have arranged the folds well today, and I am satisfied with you, Eunice."

Under that touch her eyes were mist-covered in one instant from happiness, and her bosom began to heave with joy.

Petronius and Vinicius went into the atrium, where Chilo Chilonides was waiting. When he saw them, he made a low bow. A smile came to the lips of Petronius at the thought of his suspicion of yesterday, that this man might be Eunice's lover. The man who was standing before him could not be anyone's lover. In that marvelous figure there was something both foul and ridiculous. He was not old; in his dirty beard and curly locks a gray hair shone here and there. He had a lank stomach and stooping shoulders, so that at the first cast of the eye he appeared to be hunchbacked; above that hump rose a large head, with the face of a monkey and also of a fox; the eye was penetrating. His yellowish complexion was varied with pimples; and his nose, covered with them completely, might indicate too great a love for the bottle. His neglected clothing, composed of a dark tunic of goat's wool and a mantle of similar material with holes in it, showed real or pretended poverty. At the sight of him, Homer's Thersites came to the mind of Petronius. Thus answering with a wave of the hand to his bow, he said, "A greeting, divine Thersites! How are the lumps which Ulysses gave you at Troy, and what is he doing himself in the Elysian Fields?"

"Noble lord," answered Chilo Chilonides, "Ulysses, the wisest of the dead, sends a greeting through me to Petronius, the wisest of the living, and the request to cover my lumps with a new mantle."

"By Hecate Trifomis!" Petronius exclaimed. "The answer deserves a new mantle."

But further conversation was interrupted by the impatient Vinicius, who asked immediately, "Do you know clearly what you are undertaking?"

"When two households in two lordly mansions speak of nothing else, and when half Rome is repeating the news, it is not difficult to know," Chilo answered. "The night before last a young woman named Lygia, but specially Callina, and reared in the house of Aulus Plautius, was intercepted. Your slaves were conducting her, my lord, from Caesar's palace to your mansion, and I try to find her in the city, or, if she has left the city—which is not likely—to indicate to you, noble tribune, where she has fled, and where she has hidden."

"That is well," Vinicius said, who was pleased with the precision of the answer. "What means have you to do this?"

Chilo smiled cunningly. "You have the means, lord; I have the wit only."

Petronius smiled also, for he was perfectly satisfied with his guest.

That man can find the girl, he thought.

Meanwhile, Vinicius wrinkled his joined brows and said, "Wretch, in case you deceive me for gain, I will give orders to beat you with clubs."

"I am a philosopher, lord, and a philosopher cannot be greedy of gain, especially of such as you have just offered generously."

"Oh, are you a philosopher?" Petronius asked. "Eunice told me that you are a physician and a prophet. How do you know Eunice?"

"She came to me for aid, for my fame reached her ears."

"What aid did she want?"

"Aid in love, lord. She wanted to be cured of dying love."

"Did you cure her?"

"I did more, lord. I gave her an amulet that secures mutuality. In Paphos, on the island of Cyprus, is a temple, my lord, in which

118

is preserved a belt of Venus. I gave her two threads from that belt, enclosed in an almond shell."

"And did you make her pay well for them?"

"One can never pay enough for mutuality, and I, who lack two fingers on my right hand, am collecting money to buy a slave copyist to write down my thoughts and preserve my wisdom for mankind."

"Of what philosophical party are you, divine sage?"

"I am a Cynic, lord, because I keep a tattered mantle; I am a Stoic, because I bear poverty patiently; I am a Peripatetic, for, not owning a litter, I go on foot from one wineshop to another and on the way teach those who promise to pay for a pitcher of wine."

"And drinking the pitcher you become a great speaker?"

"Heraclitus declares that 'all is fluid'; and can you deny, my lord, that wine is fluid?"

"And he declared that fire is a divinity; divinity, therefore, is blushing in your nose."

"But the divine Diogenes from Apollonia declared that air is the essence of things, and the warmer the air the more perfect the beings it makes, and from the warmest come the souls of sages. And since the autumns are cold, a genuine sage should warm his soul with wine; and would you hinder, my lord, a pitcher of even the stuff produced in Capua or Telesia from bearing heat to all the bones of a perishable human body?"

"Chilo Chilonides, where is your birthplace?"

"On the Euxine Pontus. I come from Mesembria."

"Oh, Chilo, you are great!"

"And unrecognized," said the sage, pensively.

But Vinicius was impatient again. In view of the hope that had gleamed before him, he wished Chilo to begin his work at once. So the whole conversation seemed to him simply a vain loss of time, and he was peeved at Petronius.

"When will you begin the search?" he asked, turning to the Greek.

"I have begun it already," Chilo answered. "And since I am here and answering your astute question, I am searching yet. Only have confidence, honored tribune, and know that if you were to lose the string of your sandal I should find it."

"Have you been employed in similar services?" Petronius asked.

The Greek raised his eyes. "Today men esteem virtue and wisdom too low for a philosopher not to be forced to seek other means of living."

"What are your means?"

"To know everything, and to serve those with news who are in need of it."

"And who will pay for it?"

"Ah, lord, I need to buy a copyist. Otherwise my wisdom will perish with me."

"If you have not collected enough yet to buy a sound mantle, your services cannot be very important."

"Modesty hinders me. But remember, lord, that today there are not such numerous benefactors as were formerly and for whom it was as pleasant to cover service with gold as to swallow an oyster from Puteoli. No; my services are not small, but the gratitude of mankind is small. At times, when a valued slave escapes, who will find him, if not the only son of my father? When on the walls there are inscriptions against the divine Poppaea, who will indicate those who composed them? Who will discover at the bookstalls verses against Caesar? Who will declare what is said in the houses of nobles and senators? Who will carry letters that the writers will not entrust to slaves? Who will listen to news at the doors of barbers? For whom have wineshops and bakeshops no secret? In whom do slaves trust? Who can see through every house, from the atrium to the garden? Who knows every street, every alley and hiding place? Who knows what they say in the baths, in the Circus, in the markets, in the fencing schools, and in slave-dealers' sheds?"

"By the gods! Enough, noble sage!" Petronius cried. "We are drowning in your services, your virtue, your wisdom, your eloquence. We wanted to know who you are, and we know!"

But Vinicius was glad, for he thought that this man, like a hound, once put on the trail, would not stop until he had found out the hiding-place.

"Well," he said, "do you need directions?"

"I need arms."

"Of what kind?" Vinicius asked, with astonishment.

The Greek stretched out one hand; with the other he made the gesture of counting money.

"Such are the times, lord," he said, with a sigh.

"You will be the ass, then," Petronius said, "to win the fortress with bags of gold?"

"I am only a poor philosopher," Chilo answered, with humility. "You have the gold."

Vinicius tossed him a purse, which the Greek caught in the air, though two fingers were lacking on his right hand.

He raised his head, then, and said, "I know more than you think. I have not come empty-handed. I know that Aulus did not intercept the girl, for I have spoken with his slaves. I know that she is not on the Palatine, for all are occupied with the infant Augusta; and perhaps I may even know why you prefer to search for her with my help rather than that of the city guards and Caesar's soldiers. I know that her escape was made possible by a servant—a slave coming from the same country as she. He could not find assistance among slaves, for slaves all stand together and would not act against your slaves. Only a fellow religious believer would help him."

"Do you hear, Vinicius?" broke in Petronius. "Have I not said the same, word for word, to you?"

"That is an honor for me," Chilo said. "The woman, sir," he continued, turning again to Vinicius, "worships beyond a doubt the same divinity as that most virtuous of Roman ladies, the matron Pomponia. I have heard that Pomponia was tried in her own house for worshiping some kind of foreign god, but I could not learn from her slaves what god, or what his worshipers are called. If I could learn that, I should go to them, become the most devoted among them, and gain their confidence. But you, lord, who have spent a number of days in the house of the noble Aulus, can you not give me some information?"

"I cannot," Vinicius said.

"You have asked me about various things, noble lords, and I have answered the questions; permit me now to give one. Have you not seen some statuette, some offering, some token, some amulet on Pomponia or your divine Lygia? Have you not even

121

seen them making signs to each other, intelligible to them alone?"

"Signs? Wait! Yes, once I saw Lygia make a fish in the sand."

"A fish? And are you certain, lord, that she outlined a fish?"

"Yes," Vinicius answered, with roused curiosity. "Do you know what that means?"

"Do I know!" Chilo exclaimed. And bowing in sign of farewell, he added: "May Fortune scatter on both equally all gifts, worthy lords!"

"Get a mantle," Petronius said to him as he left.

"What will you say of that noble sage?" Petronius asked Vinicius.

"This, that he will find Lygia," Vinicius answered with delight. "But I will say, too, that were there a kingdom of rogues he might be the king of it."

"Most certainly. I shall make a clearer acquaintance with this Stoic; meanwhile, I will perfume the atrium."

But Chilo Chilonides, wrapping his new mantle about him, threw upon his palm the purse received from Vinicius and admired both its weight and its jingle. Walking on slowly and looking around to see if they were not looking at him from the house, he passed the portico of Livia and, reaching the corner of the Clivus Virbius, turned toward the Subura.

I must go the Sporus, he said to himself, *and pour out a little wine to Fortuna. I have found what I have been seeking this long time. He is young, bounteous as mines in Cyprus, and ready to give half his fortune for that Lygian linnet. I have been seeking just such a man for a long time. I need, however, to be on my guard with him, for the wrinkling of his brow forebodes no good. I should fear that Petronius less. O gods! She drew a fish on the sand! If I know what that means, may I choke myself with a piece of goat's cheese! But I shall know. Fish live underwater, and searching underwater is more difficult than on land, so he will pay me separately for this fish. Another such purse and I might cast aside the beggar's wallet and buy myself a slave. But what would you say, Chilo, were I to advise you to buy not a male but a female slave? I know you; I know that you would consent. If she were beautiful, like Eunice, for instance, you yourself would grow young near her and at the same time would receive a good and certain income. I sold to that poor Eunice two threads from my old mantle. She is ignorant; but if Petronius were to give her to me, I would take her. Chilo Chilonides, you have lost father and mother, you are an orphan; so buy a female slave. She must indeed live somewhere; therefore Vinicius will hire her a home in which you, too, may find shelter; she must dress, hence Vinicius will pay for the dress; and must eat, so he will support her.*

He entered the wineshop and ordered a pitcher of "dark" for himself. Seeing the skeptical look of the shopkeeper, he took a gold coin from his purse and, putting it on the table, said, "Sporus, I toiled today with Seneca from dawn till midday, and this is what my friend gave me at parting."

The plump eyes of Sporus became plumper still at this sight, and the wine was soon before Chilo. Moistening his fingers in it, he drew a fish on the table and said, "Do you know what that means?"

"A fish? Well, a fish—yes, that's a fish."

"You are stupid; though you add so much water to the wine that you might find a fish in it. This is a symbol that, in the language of philosophers, means 'the smile of fortune.' If you had known it, you too might have made a fortune. Listen to philosophy, I tell you, or I shall change my wineshop—an act to which Petronius, my personal friend, has been urging me to do this long time."

14

For a number of days after the interview, Chilo did not show himself anywhere. Vinicius, since he had learned from Acte that Lygia loved him, was a hundred times more eager to find her and began himself to search. He was unwilling, and also unable, to ask aid of Caesar, who was in great fear because of the illness of the infant Augusta.

Sacrifices in the temples did not help, neither did prayers

and offerings, nor the art of physicians, nor all the means of enchantment to which they turned finally. In a week the child died. Mourning fell upon the court and Rome. Caesar, who at the birth of the infant was wild with delight, was wild now from despair and, confining himself in his apartments, refused food for two days; and though the palace was swarming with senators and Augustians, who hastened with signs of sorrow and sympathy, he denied audience to everyone. The Senate assembled in an extraordinary session, at which the dead child was pronounced divine. It was decided to build a temple and appoint a special priest to her service. New sacrifices were offered in other temples in honor of the deceased; statues of her were cast from precious metals; and her funeral was one of immense solemnity, during which the people wondered at the unrestrained show of grief Caesar exhibited; they wept with him, stretched out their hands for gifts, and above all amused themselves with the unparalleled spectacle.

That death alarmed Petronius. All knew in Rome that Poppaea ascribed it to enchantment. The physicians, who were thus enabled to explain the inability of their efforts, supported her. The priests, whose sacrifices proved powerless, did the same, as well as the sorcerers, who were trembling for their lives, and also the people. Petronius was glad now that Lygia had fled; for he wished no evil to Aulus and Pomponia, and he wished good to himself and Vinicius; therefore, when the cypress, set out before the Palatine as a sign of mourning, was removed, he went to the reception for the senators to learn how far Nero had lent ear to reports of spells and to neutralize results that might come from his belief.

Knowing Nero, he thought that though he did not believe in charms, he would feign belief, so as to magnify his own suffering and take vengeance on someone. Finally, he hoped to escape the suspicion that the gods had begun to punish him for crimes. Petronius did not think that Caesar could deeply love even his own child. Though Nero loved her passionately, Petronius was certain, however, that he would exaggerate his sufferings.

He was not mistaken. Nero listened, with stony face and fixed eyes, to the consolation offered by nobles and senators. It was evident that, even if he suffered, he was thinking of this: What impression would his suffering make upon others? He was posing as a Niobe and giving an exhibition of parental sorrow as an actor would give it on the stage. At moments he made a gesture as if to cast the dust of the earth on his head, and at moments he groaned deeply; but seeing Petronius, he sprang up and cried in a tragic voice, so that all present could hear him, "You are guilty of her death! At your advice the evil spirit entered these walls—the evil spirit that, with one look, drew the life from her breast! Woe is me! Would that my eyes had not seen the light of Helios!"

And, raising his voice still more, he gave a despairing shout; but Petronius resolved at that moment to lay everything on one cast of the dice; so, stretching out his hand, he seized the silk kerchief Nero always wore around his neck and, placing it on the mouth of the emperor, said solemnly, "Lord, Rome and the world are benumbed with pain; but preserve your voice for us!"

Those present were amazed; Nero himself was amazed for a moment. Petronius alone was unmoved; he knew too well what he was doing. He remembered, besides, that Terpnos and Diodorus had a direct order to close Caesar's mouth whenever he raised his voice too much and exposed it to danger.

"O Caesar!" he continued, with the same seriousness and sorrow, "we have suffered an immeasurable loss; let only this treasure of consolation remain to us!"

Nero's face quivered, and after a while tears came from his eyes. All at once he rested his hands on Petronius's shoulders and, dropping his head on his breast, began to repeat, amid sobs, "You alone of all thought of this—you alone, O Petronius! You alone!"

Tigellinus grew red with envy, but Petronius continued, "Go to Antium! There she came to the world, there joy flowed in on you, there comfort will come again. Let the sea air freshen your divine throat; let your breast breathe the salt dampness. We, your devoted ones, will follow you everywhere; and when we assuage your pain with friendship, you will comfort us with song."

"True!" Nero answered sadly, "I will write a hymn in her honor and compose music for it."

"And then you will find the warm sun in Baiae."

"And afterward—forgetfulness in Greece."

"In the birthplace of poetry and song."

And his stony, gloomy state of mind passed away gradually, as clouds pass that are covering the sun; and then a conversation began that, though full of sadness, yet was full of plans for the future—touching a journey, artistic exhibitions, and even the receptions required at the promised coming of Tiridates, King of Armenia. Tigellinus tried, it is true, to bring the enchantment forward again; but Petronius, sure now of victory, took up the challenge directly.

"Tigellinus," he said, "do you think that enchantments can injure the gods?"

"Caesar himself has mentioned them," the courtier answered.

"Pain was speaking, not Caesar; but you—what is your opinion of the matter?"

"The gods are too mighty to be subject to charms."

"Then would you deny divinity to Caesar and his family?"

"Peractum est!" muttered Eprius Marcellus, standing near, repeating that shout the people always gave when a gladiator in the arena received such a blow that he needed no other.

Tigellinus gnawed his own anger. Between him and Petronius there had long existed a rivalry touching Nero. Tigellinus had this superiority, that Nero acted with less ceremony, or rather with none whatever, in his presence; whereas thus far Petronius overcame Tigellinus at every encounter with wit and intellect.

So it happened now. Tigellinus was silent and simply recorded in his memory those senators and nobles who, when Petronius withdrew to the depth of the chamber, surrounded him, supposing that after this incident he would surely be Caesar's first favorite.

Petronius, on leaving the palace, went to Vinicius and described his encounter with Caesar and Tigellinus.

"Not only have I turned away danger," he said, "from Aulus Plautius, Pomponia, and us, but even from Lygia, whom they will not seek, for this reason, that I have persuaded Bronzebeard, the monkey, to go to Antium, and then to Naples or Baiae; and he will go. I know that he has not tried yet to appear in the theater publicly; I have known for a long time that he intends to do so at Naples. He is dreaming, also, of Greece, where he wants to sing in all the more prominent cities and then make a triumphal entry into Rome, with all the crowns the Graeculi will bestow on him. During that time we shall be able to seek Lygia unhindered and remove her in safety. But has not our noble philosopher been here yet?"

"Your noble philosopher is a cheat. No, he has not shown himself, and he will not show himself again!"

"But I have a better understanding, if not of his honesty, of his wit. He has drawn blood once from your purse and will come to draw it a second time."

"Let him beware lest I draw his own blood."

"Have patience until you are convinced of his deceit. Do not give him more money but promise a liberal reward if he brings you certain information. Will you undertake something?"

"My two freedmen, Nymphidius and Demas, are searching for her with sixty men. Freedom is promised to the slave who finds her. Besides, I have sent out special persons by all roads leading from Rome to inquire at every inn for the Lygian and the girl. I roam through the city myself day and night, hoping for a chance meeting."

"Whenever you have tidings let me know, for I must go to Antium."

"I will."

"And if you wake up some morning and say, 'It is not worth-while to torment myself for one girl and take so much trouble because of her,' come to Antium. There will be no lack of women there, or amusement."

Vinicius began to walk quickly. Petronius said, "Tell me sincerely, not as a madman, who puts something into his brain and excites himself, but as a man of judgment who is answering a friend: Are you concerned as much as ever about this Lygia?"

Vinicius stopped a moment and looked at Petronius as if he had not seen him before; then he began to walk again. It was evident that he was restraining an outburst. At last, from a feeling of sorrow, anger, and invincible yearning, two tears gathered in his eyes, which spoke with greater power to Petronius than the most eloquent words.

Then, meditating for a moment, he said, "It is not Atlas who carries the world on his shoulders, but woman; and sometimes she plays with it as with a ball."

"True," Vinicius said.

And they began to say farewell to each other. But at that moment a slave announced that Chilo Chilonides was waiting in the antechamber and begged to be admitted to the presence of the lord.

Petronius said, "Ha! Have I not told you? By Hercules! Keep your calmness; or he will command you, not you him."

"A greeting and honor to the noble tribune of the army, and to you, lord," Chilo said, entering. "May your happiness be equal to your fame, and may your fame course through the world from the pillars of Hercules to the boundaries of the Arsacidae."

"A greeting, O lawgiver of virtue and wisdom," Petronius answered.

But Vinicius asked with affected calmness, "What do you bring?"

"The first time I came I brought you hope, my lord; at present, I bring certainty that the girl will be found."

"That means that you have not found her yet?"

"Yes, lord; but I have found what that sign means that she made. I know who the people are who rescued her, and I know the God among whose worshipers to seek her."

Vinicius wished to spring from the chair in which he was sitting; but Petronius placed his hand on his shoulder and, turning to Chilo, said, "Speak on!"

"Are you perfectly certain, lord, that she drew a fish on the sand?"

"Yes," burst out Vinicius.

"Then she is a Christian, and Christians carried her away."

A moment of silence followed.

"Listen, Chilo," Petronius said, "my relative has advanced you a considerable sum of money for finding the girl, but no less considerable number of whips if you deceive him. In the first case you will purchase not one, but three scribes; in the second, the philosophy of all the seven sages, with the addition of your own, will not suffice to get you ointment."

"The girl is a Christian, lord," the Greek cried.

"Stop, Chilo. You are not a dull man. We know that Junia and Calvia Crispinilla accused Pomponia Graecina of confessing the Christian superstition; but we know, too, that a domestic court acquitted her. Would you raise this again? Would you persuade us that Pomponia, and with her Lygia, could belong to the enemies of the human race, to the poisoners of wells and fountains, to the worshipers of an ass's head, to people who murder infants and give themselves up to the foulest license? Think, Chilo, if that thesis you are announcing to us will not rebound as a repayment on your own back."

Chilo spread out his arms in sign that that was not his fault and then said, "Lord, utter in Greek the following sentence: Jesus Christ, Son of God, Savior."

"Well, I have uttered it. What comes of that?"

"Now take the first letters of each of those words and put them into one word."

"Fish!" Petronius said, with astonishment.

"There, that is why the fish has become the watchword of the Christians," Chilo answered proudly.

A moment of silence followed. But there was something so striking in the conclusions of the Greek that the two friends could not keep themselves from amazement.

"Vinicius, are you not mistaken?" Petronius asked. "Did Lygia really draw a fish for you?"

"By all the infernal gods, one might go mad!" the young man cried with excitement. "If she had drawn a bird for me, I should have said a bird!"

"Therefore she is a Christian," repeated Chilo.

"This signifies," said Petronius, "that Pomponia and Lygia poison wells, murder children caught on the street, and give themselves up to dissoluteness! You, Vinicius, were at their house for a time, and I was there a little while; but I know Pomponia and Aulus enough, I know even Lygia enough, to say monstrous and foolish! If a fish is the symbol of the Christians, which it is difficult really to deny, and if those women are Christians, then, by Proserpina! Evidently Christians are not what we hold them to be."

"You speak like Socrates, lord," Chilo answered. "Who has ever examined a Christian? Who has learned their religion? When I was traveling three years ago from Naples to Rome a man named Glaucus joined me, of whom people said that he was a Christian; but in spite of that I convinced myself that he was a good and virtuous man."

"Was it not from that virtuous man that you have learned now what the fish means?"

"Unfortunately, lord, on the way, at an inn, someone thrust a knife into that honorable old man; and his wife and child were carried away by slave-dealers. I lost in their defense these two fingers; since, as people say, there is no lack among Christians of miracles, I hope that the fingers will grow out on my hand again."

"How is that? Have you become a Christian?"

"Since yesterday, lord, since yesterday! The fish made me a Christian. But see what power there is in it. For some days I shall be the most zealous so that they may admit me to all their secrets; and then I shall know where the girl is hiding. Perhaps, then, my Christianity will pay me better than my philosophy. I have made a vow also to Mercury, that if he helps me to find the girl, I will sacrifice to him two heifers of the same size and color and will gild their horns."

"Then your Christianity of yesterday and your philosophy of long-standing permit you to believe in Mercury?"

"I believe always in that in which I need to believe; that is my philosophy, which ought to please Mercury. Unfortunately—you know, worthy lords, what a suspicious god he is—he does not trust the promises even of blameless philosophers and prefers the heifers in advance; meanwhile, this outlay is immense. Not everyone is a Seneca, and I cannot afford the sacrifice; should the noble Vinicius, however, wish to give something, because of that sum he promised—"

"Not an obolus, Chilo!" Petronius said, "not an obolus. The bounty of Vinicius will surpass your expectations, but only when Lygia is found—that is, when you shall indicate to us her hiding place. Mercury must trust you for the two heifers, though I am not astonished at him for not wishing to do so; in this I recognize his intelligence."

"Listen to me, worthy lords. The discovery I have made is great; for though I have not found the girl yet, I have found the way in which I must seek her. You have sent freedmen and slaves throughout the city and into the country; has anyone given you a clue? No! I alone have given one. I will tell you more. Among your slaves there may be Christians, of whom you have no knowledge, for this superstition has spread everywhere; and they, instead of aiding, will betray you. It is unfortunate that they see me here; therefore, noble Petronius, demand silence from Eunice; and you, too, noble Vinicius, spread a report that I am selling you an ointment that insures victory in the Circus to horses rubbed with it. I alone will search for her, and single-handed I will find the fugitives; and trust in me, and know that whatever I receive in advance will be simply an encouragement for me.

"As a philosopher I despise money, though neither Seneca, nor even Musonius, nor Cornutus despises it, though they have not lost fingers in anyone's defense and are able themselves to write and leave their names to posterity. But, aside from the slave, whom I intend to buy, and besides Mercury, to whom I have promised the heifers—and you know how dear cattle have become in these times—the searching itself involves much expense. Only listen to me patiently.

"For the last few days my feet have been wounded from continual walking. I have gone to wineshops to talk with people, to bakeries, butcher shops, dealers in olive oil, and to fishermen. I have run through every street and alley; I have been in the hiding places of fugitive slaves; I have lost money; I have been in laundries, in drying-sheds, in cheap kitchens; I have seen mule drivers and carvers; I have seen people who cure bladder complaints and pull teeth; I have talked with dealers in dried figs; I have been to cemeteries; and do you know why? This is why: to outline a fish everywhere, look people in the eyes, and hear what they say of that sign. For a long time I was unable to learn anything, until at last I saw an old slave at a fountain. He was drawing water with a bucket, and weeping. Approaching him, I asked the cause of his tears. When we had sat down on the steps of the fountain, he answered that all his life he had been collecting sestertium after sestertium, to redeem his beloved son; but when the money was delivered to his master, a certain Pansa, he took it but kept the son in slavery. 'And so I am weeping,' the old man said, 'for though I repeat, Let the will of God be done, I, poor sinner, am not able to keep down my tears.'

"Then I moistened my finger in the water and drew a fish for him. To this he answered, 'My hope, too, is in Christ.' I asked him

131

then, 'Have you confessed to me by that sign?' 'I have,' he said, 'and peace be with you.' I began to draw him out, then, and the honest old man told me everything. His master, that Pansa, is himself a freedman of the great Pansa; and he brings stones by the Tiber to Rome, where slaves and hired persons unload them from the boats and carry them to buildings at night, so as not to obstruct movement in the streets during daylight. Among these people many Christians work, and also his son; as the work is beyond his son's strength, he wished to redeem him. But Pansa preferred to keep both the money and the slave.

"While telling me this, he began again to weep; and I mingled my tears with his—tears came to me easily because of my kind heart and the pain in my feet, which I got from walking excessively. I began also to lament that as I had come from Naples only a few days since, I knew no one of the brotherhood and did not know where they assembled for prayer. He wondered that Christians in Naples had not given me letters to their brethren in Rome, but I explained that the letters were stolen from me on the road. Then he told me to come to the river at night, and he would acquaint me with brethren who would conduct me to houses of prayer and to elders who govern the Christian community. When I heard this, I was so delighted that I gave him the sum needed to redeem his son, in the hope that the lordly Vinicius would return it to me twofold."

"Chilo," Petronius interrupted, "in your narrative falsehood appears on the surface of truth, as oil does on water. You have brought important information; I do not deny that. I assert, even, that a great step is made toward finding Lygia; but do not cover your news with falsehood. What is the name of that old man from whom you have learned that the Christians recognize each other through the sign of a fish?"

"Euricius. A poor, unfortunate old man! He reminded me of Glaucus, whom I defended from murderers, and he touched me mainly by this."

"I believe that you did discover him and will be able to make use of the acquaintance; but you have given him no money."

"But I helped him to lift the bucket, and I spoke of his son with the greatest sympathy. Yes, lord, what can hide before the penetration of Petronius? Well, I did not give him money, or rather, I gave it to him, but only in spirit, in intention, which, had he been a real philosopher, should have sufficed him. I gave it to him because I saw that such an act was indispensable and useful; for think, lord, how this act has won all the Christians at once to me, what access to them it has opened, and what confidence it has roused in them."

"True," Petronius said, "and it was your duty to do it."

"For this very reason I have come to get the means to do it."

Petronius turned to Vinicius. "Order them to count out to him five thousand sesteria, but in spirit, in intention."

"I will give you a young man," Vinicius said, "who will take the sum necessary; you will say to Euricius that the youth is your slave, and you will count out to the old man, in the youth's presence, this money. Since you have brought important tidings, you will receive the same amount for yourself. Come for the youth and the money this evening."

"You are a true Caesar!" Chilo said. "Permit me, lord, to dedicate my work to you; but permit also that this evening I come only for the money, since Euricius told me that all the boats had been unloaded and that new ones would come from Ostia only after some days. Peace be with you! Christians take farewell of one another this way. I will buy myself a slave woman—that is, I wanted to say a slave man. Fish are caught with a bait, and Christians with fish. *Pax vobiscum!*"

15

Petronius to Vinicius:

"I send this letter to you from Antium by a trusty slave. Though your hand is more accustomed to the sword and the javelin than the pen, I think that you will answer through the same messenger without needless delay. I left you on a good trail, and full of hope. I trust that you have either satisfied your pleasant desires in the embraces of Lygia, or will satisfy them before the wintry wind from the summits of Soracte shall blow on the Campania. Oh, my Vinicius! May your patron be the golden goddess of Cyprus. Lygian Aurora flees before the sun of love. And remember always that marble, though most precious, is nothing of itself and acquires real value only when the sculptor's hand turns it into a masterpiece. You are such a sculptor, carissime! To love is not sufficient; one must know how to love; one must know how to teach love. Though the common people, too, and even animals, experience pleasure, a genuine man differs from them in this especially, that he makes love in some way a noble art, and, admiring it, knows all its divine value and makes it present in his mind, thus satisfying not only his body but his soul. More than once, when I think here of the emptiness, uncertainty, and dreariness of life, it occurs to me that perhaps you have chosen better, and that not Caesar's court, but war and love, are the only objects for which it is worthwhile to be born.

"You were fortunate in war; be fortunate also in love; and if you are curious as to what men are doing at the court of Caesar, I will inform you. Caesar and I are living here at Antium and nursing our heavenly voice; we continue to cherish the same hatred of Rome and think of taking ourselves to Baiae for the winter, to appear in public at Naples, whose inhabitants, being Greeks, will appreciate us better than that wolf-brood on the banks of the Tiber. People will hasten to Naples from Baiae, Pompeii, Puteoli, Cumae, and Stabia; neither applause nor crowns will be lacking, and that will be an encouragement for the proposed expedition to Achaea.

"But the memory of the infant Augusta? We are bewailing her yet. We are singing hymns of our own composition, so wonderful that the nymphs have been hiding from envy in Amphitrite's deepest caves. But the dolphins would listen to us, were they not prevented by the sound of the sea. Our suffering is not allayed yet; hence we will exhibit it to the world in every form that sculpture can employ and observe carefully if we are beautiful in our suffering and if people recognize this beauty. Oh, my friend! We shall die buffoons and comedians!

"All the Augustians are here, male and female, not counting ten thousand servants, and five hundred female asses, in whose milk Poppaea bathes. At times it is even cheerful here. Calvia Crispinilla is growing old. It is said that she has begged Poppaea to let her take the bath immediately after herself. Lucan slapped Nigidia on the face because he suspected her of relations with a gladiator. Sporus lost his wife at dice to Senecio. Torquatus Silanus has offered me for Eunice four chestnut horses that this year will win the prize beyond doubt. I would not accept! Thank you that you did not take her. As to Torquatus Silanus, the poor man does not even suspect that he is already more a ghost than a man. His death is decided. And do you know what his crime is? He is the great-grandson of the deified Augustus. There is no rescue for him. Such is our world.

"As is known to you, we have been expecting Tiridates here; meanwhile, Vologeses has written an offensive letter. Because he has conquered Armenia, he asks that it be left to him for Tiridates; if not, he will not yield it in any case. Pure comedy! So we have decided on war. Corbulo will receive power such as Pompeius Magnus received in the war with pirates. There was a moment, however, when Nero hesitated. He seems afraid of the glory Corbulo will win in case of victory. It was even thought to offer the chief command to our Aulus. This was opposed by Poppaea, for whom evidently Pomponia's virtue is as salt in her eye.

"Vatinius described to us a remarkable fight of gladiators, which is to take place in Beneventum. See to what cobblers rise in our time, in spite of the saying 'Ne sutor ultra crepidam!' Vitelius is the descendant of a cobbler; but Vatinius is the son of one! The actor Aliturus represented Oedipus yesterday wonderfully. I asked him, by the way, as a Jew, if Christians and Jews were the same. He answered that the Jews have an eternal religion, but that Christians are a new sect risen recently in Judea; that in the time of Tiberius the Jews crucified a certain man, whose adherents increase daily, and that the Christians consider him as God. They refuse, it seems, to recognize other gods, ours especially. I cannot understand what harm it would do them to recognize these gods.

"Tigellinus shows open hostility now. So far he is unequal to me; but he is superior in this, that he cares more for life, and is at the same time a greater scoundrel, which brings him nearer Ahen-obarbus. These two will understand each other sooner or later, and then my turn will come. I do not know when it will come. Meanwhile, we must amuse ourselves. Life in itself would not be bad were it not for Bronzebeard. Thanks to him, a man at times is disgusted with himself. It is not correct to consider the struggle for his favor as a kind of rivalry in a circus—as a kind of game, as a struggle, in which victory flatters vanity. True, I explain it to myself in that way frequently; but still it seems to me sometimes that I am like Chilo and better in nothing than he. When he ceases to be needful to you, send him to me. I have taken a fancy to his edifying conversation. A greeting from me to your divine Christian, or rather beg her in my name not to be a fish to you. Inform me of your health, inform me of your love, learn how to love, teach how to love, and farewell."

Vinicius to Petronius:

"Lygia is not found yet! Were it not for the hope that I shall find her soon, you would not receive an answer; for when a man is disgusted with life, he has no wish to write letters. I wanted to learn whether Chilo was not deceiving me; and at night when he came to get the money for Euricius, I threw on a military mantle and, unobserved, followed him and the slave I sent with him. When they reached the place, I watched from a distance, hidden behind a portico pillar, and convinced myself that Euricius was not invented. Below, a number of tens of people were unloading stones from a spacious barge and piling them up on the bank. I saw Chilo approach them and begin to talk with some old man, who after a while fell at his feet. Others surrounded them with shouts of admiration. Before my eyes the boy gave a purse to Euricius, who, seizing it, began to pray with upraised hands, while at his side some second person was kneeling, evidently his son. Chilo said something I could not hear and blessed the two who were kneeling, as well as others, making in the air signs in the form of a cross, which they honor apparently, for all bent their knees. The desire seized me to go among them and promise three such purses to him who would deliver to me Lygia; but I was afraid to spoil Chilo's work, and after hesitating a moment, went home.

"This happened at least twelve days after your departure. Since then Chilo has been with me a number of times. He says that he has gained great significance among the Christians; that if he has not found Lygia so far, it is because the Christians in Rome are innumerable, so all are not acquainted with each person in their community and cannot know everything. They are cautious, too, and in general reserved. He gives assurance, however, that when he reaches the elders, who are called presbyters, he will learn every secret. He has made the acquaintance of a number of these already and has begun to ask questions, though carefully, so as not to rouse suspicion by haste and not to make the work still more difficult. Though it is hard to wait, though patience fails, I believe that he is right.

"He learned, too, that they have places of meeting for prayer, frequently outside the city, in empty houses and even in sand pits. There they worship Christ, sing hymns, and have feasts. There are many such places. Chilo supposes that Lygia goes purposely to different ones from Pomponia, so that the latter, in case of legal proceedings or an examination, might swear boldly that she knew nothing of Lygia's hiding-place. It may be that the presbyters have advised caution. When Chilo discovers those places, I will go with him; and if the gods let me see Lygia, I swear to you by Jupiter that she will not escape my hands this time.

"I am thinking continually of these places of prayer. Chilo is unwilling that I should go with him, because he is afraid. But I cannot stay at home. I would know her at once, even in disguise or if veiled. They assemble in the night, but I would recognize her even in the night. I would know her voice and motions anywhere. I will go myself in disguise and look at every person who goes in or out. I am thinking of her always and shall recognize her. Chilo is to come tomorrow, and we shall go. I will bring weapons. Some of my slaves sent to the provinces have returned empty-handed. But I am certain now that she is in the city—perhaps not far away. I myself have visited many houses under pretext of renting them. She will fare better with me a hundred times. Where she is, whole legions of poor people dwell. Besides, I shall spare nothing for her sake.

"You write that I have chosen well. I have chosen suffering

137

and sorrow. We shall go first to those houses that are in the city, then to those beyond the gates. Hope looks for the answer every morning, otherwise life would be impossible. You say that one should know how to love. I knew how to talk of love to Lygia. But now I only yearn; I do nothing but wait for Chilo. Life to me is unendurable in my own house. Farewell!"

16

But Chilo did not appear for some time, and Vinicius did not know what to think of his absence. He repeated to himself that searching, if continued to a certain and successful issue, must be gradual. To do nothing was repulsive to him. To search the alleys of the city in the dark garb of a slave could give him no complete satisfaction. His freedmen, persons of experience, whom he commanded to search independently, turned out less expert than Chilo. Besides his love for Lygia, there was the stubbornness of a player resolved to win. From earliest youth Vinicius had accomplished what he desired with the passion of one who does not understand failure. For a time military discipline had put his self-will within bounds, but also it had instilled a conviction that every command of his to subordinates must be fulfilled. His prolonged stay in the Orient among submissive people used to slavish obedience confirmed in him the faith that for his "I wish" there were no limits.

At present his vanity was wounded painfully. There was in Lygia's resistance and flight a kind of riddle. In trying to solve this riddle he racked his brain. He believed that Acte had told the truth and that Lygia was not indifferent. But if that were true, why had she preferred wandering and misery to his love, his tenderness, and a residence in his splendid mansion? He found no answer to this question and arrived only at a kind of dim understanding that between him and Lygia, between their ideas, between the world that belonged to him and Petronius and the world of Lygia and Pomponia, there existed some sort of difference, some kind of misunderstanding as deep as an abyss, which nothing could fill up.

There were moments in which he did not know whether he loved Lygia or hated her; he understood only that he must find her, and he would rather that the earth swallowed her than that he should not possess her. He felt her near; felt her on his bosom, in his arms; and then desire embraced him like a flame. He loved her and called to her. Sore and endless sorrow seized him, and a kind of deep tenderness flooded his heart like a mighty wave. But there were moments, too, in which he grew pale from rage and delighted in thoughts of the humiliation he would inflict on Lygia when he found her. He wanted not only to have her, but to have her as a trampled slave. At the same time he felt that if the choice were left him, to be her slave or not to see her in life again, he would rather be her slave. Yet he also felt he would be happy if he could kill her.

In this torment he lost health and even beauty. He became a cruel and incomprehensible master. His slaves, and even his freedmen, approached him with trembling; and when punishments fell on them without cause—punishments as merciless as undeserved—they began to hate him in secret; while he, feeling this, took revenge all the more on them. He restrained himself with Chilo alone, fearing that he might cease his searches. The Greek, noting this, began to gain control of him and grew more and more exacting. At first he assured Vinicius at each visit that the affair would proceed quickly; now he began to discover difficulties and, without ceasing to guarantee the undoubted success of the searches, stressed that they must continue for a good while.

At last he came, after long days of waiting, with a face so gloomy that the young man grew pale at sight of him.

"Is she not among the Christians?"

"She is, lord," Chilo answered, "but I found Glaucus among them."

"What are you speaking of, and who is Glaucus?"

"You have forgotten, lord, that old man with whom I journeyed from Naples to Rome and in whose defense I lost these two fingers. Robbers, who bore away his wife and child, stabbed him with a knife. I left him dying at an inn in Minturna and bewailed him long. I have convinced myself that he is alive yet and belongs in Rome to the Christian community."

Vinicius, who could not understand what the question was, understood only that Glaucus was becoming a hindrance to the discovery of Lygia. He suppressed his rising anger and said, "If you defended him, he should be thankful and help you."

"Worthy tribune, even gods are not always grateful; then what must the case be with men? True, he should be thankful. But he is an old man, with a mind weak and darkened by age and disappointment. I learned from his fellow believer that he accuses me of having conspired with the robbers and says that I am the cause of his misfortunes. That is the recompense for my fingers!"

"Scoundrel! I am positive that he is right," Vinicius replied.

"Then you know more than he does, lord, for he only guesses that it was so; that, however, would not prevent him from summoning the Christians and revenging himself on me cruelly. He would have done that, and others would have helped him; but fortunately he does not know my name and did not notice me in the house of prayer where we met. I knew him at once, however, and at the first moment wished to approach him. Wisdom restrained me, though. Therefore, when I left the house of prayer I asked about him, and those who knew him declared that he was the man who had been betrayed by his comrade on the journey from Naples. Otherwise, I should not have known that he tells such a story."

"How does this concern me? Tell me what you saw in the house of prayer."

"It does not concern you, lord, but it concerns me and my fate. Since I wish wisdom to survive me, I would rather renounce the reward you have offered than expose my life for filthy cash, without which I, as a true philosopher, shall still be able to survive and seek divine wisdom."

But Vinicius approached him with a threatening look and said in suppressed voice, "Who told you that death would meet you sooner at the hands of Glaucus than at mine? How do you know, you dog, that I will not have you buried right away in my garden?"

Chilo, who was a coward, looked at Vinicius, and in the twinkle of an eye understood that one more unguarded word and he was lost beyond hope.

"I will search for her, lord, and I will find her!" he cried hurriedly.

After a while, when he noticed that the young patrician was somewhat pacified, the Greek resumed his speech. "Death passed me, but I looked on it with the calmness of Socrates. No, lord, I have not said that I refuse to search for the girl; I desired merely to tell you that searching for her is perilous. You once doubted that there was a certain Euricius in the world, and though you were convinced by your own eyes that the son of my father told the truth to you, you have suspicions now that I have invented Glaucus. Ah? I wish that he were only a fiction, that I might go among the Christians with perfect safety, as I did before. I would give that up for the poor old slave woman I bought three days ago to care for my advanced age and maimed condition. But Glaucus is living, lord; and if he had seen me once, you would not have seen me again, and who would find the girl?"

Here he was silent again and began to dry his tears.

"But while Glaucus lives," he continued, "how can I search for her? For I may meet him anywhere; and if I meet him I shall perish."

"What are you aiming at? What do you wish me to do?" Vinicius asked.

"Aristotle teaches us, lord, that less things should be sacrificed for greater; and King Priam frequently said that old age was a grievous burden. Indeed, the burden of old age and misfortune weighs upon Glaucus this long time and so heavily that death would be a benefit. For what is death, according to Seneca, but liberation?"

"Play the fool with Petronius, not with me! What do you want?"

"If virtue is folly, may the gods permit me to be a fool all my life. I want Glaucus to be set aside, for while he is living my life and searches are in continual peril."

"Hire men to beat him to death with clubs. I will pay them."

"They will rob you, lord, and afterward make profit from the secret. There are as many ruffians in Rome as grains of sand in the arena, but you will not believe how expensive they are when an honest man needs to employ their villainy. No, worthy tribune! But if watchmen catch the murderers in the act? They would tell, beyond doubt, who hired them, and then you would have trouble. They will not point to me, for I shall not give my name. You are wrong in not trusting me, for apart from my keenness, remember that there is a question of my life and the reward you have promised me."

"How much do you need?"

"A thousand sestertia, that I may find honest ruffians, men who when they have received earnest money will not disappear without a trace. For good work there must be good pay! Something might be added, too, for my sake, to wipe away the tears I shall shed out of pity for Glaucus. I take the gods to witness how I love him. If I receive a thousand sestertia today, two days from now his soul will be in hades, and then, if souls preserve memory and the gift of thought, he will know for the first time how I loved him. I will find people this very day and tell them that for each day of the life of Glaucus I will withhold one hundred sestertia."

Once more Vinicius promised him the desired sum. He asked where he had been all the time, what he had seen, and what he had discovered. But Chilo was not able to tell much. He had been in two more houses of prayer—had observed each person carefully, especially the women—but had seen no one who resembled Lygia. The Christians, however, looked on him as one of their own sect, and, since he redeemed the son of Euricius, they honored him as a man following in the steps of "Christ." He had learned from them, also, that a great lawgiver of theirs, a certain Paul of Tarsus, was in Rome, imprisoned because of charges made by the Jews, and he had resolved to become acquainted with this man. But most of all, he was pleased by this—that the supreme priest of the whole sect, who had been Christ's disciple, and to whom Christ had bestowed rulership over the whole world of Christians, might arrive in Rome any moment. All the Christians wanted to see him and hear his teachings. Some great meetings would follow, at which he, Chilo, would be present; and since it is easy to hide in the crowd, he would take Vinicius to those meetings. Then they would certainly find Lygia. If Glaucus were dealt with, there would be no danger. The Christians might seek revenge; but in general they were peaceful people.

Chilo said with a certain surprise that he had never seen them give themselves up to debauchery or poison wells or fountains; they were not enemies of the human race, nor did they worship an ass or eat the flesh of children. No, he had seen nothing of that sort. Certainly he would find among them even people who would hide away Glaucus for money; but their religion, as far as he knew, did not incite to crime—on the contrary, it taught forgiveness of offenses.

Vinicius remembered what Pomponia had said to him at Acte's, and in general he listened to Chilo's words with pleasure. He felt a relief when he heard that the religion which Lygia and Pomponia confessed was neither criminal nor repulsive. But a species of undefined feeling rose in him that it was just that reverence for Christ, unknown and mysterious, that created the difference between himself and Lygia; so he began to fear that religion and to dislike it.

17

For Chilo, it was really important to eradicate Glaucus, who, though advanced in years, was by no means decrepit. There was considerable truth in what Chilo had narrated to Vinicius. He had known Glaucus once; he had betrayed him, sold him to robbers, deprived him of family and of property, and delivered him to murderers. He had thrown the man aside dying, not at an inn, but in a field near Minturna. The one thing he had not foreseen was that Glaucus would be cured of his wounds and come to Rome. When he saw him, therefore, in the house of prayer, he was terrified and immediately wished to discontinue the search for Lygia. But on the other hand, Vinicius terrified him still more. He understood that he must choose between the fear of Glaucus and the pursuit and vengeance of a powerful patrician, to whose aid would come the still greater Petronius. In view of this, he thought it better to have small enemies than great ones, and, though his cowardly nature trembled somewhat at bloody methods, he saw the need of killing Glaucus through the aid of other hands.

At present the only question was the choice of people. Spending his nights in wineshops most frequently and lodging in them among men without a roof, without faith or honor, he could find persons easily to undertake any task. If they sniffed a coin, they would begin; but when they had received earnest money, they would extort the whole sum by threatening to deliver Chilo to justice. Chilo had a repulsion for those disgusting and terrible figures lurking about suspected houses in the Subura or in the Trans-Tiber. Not having fathomed sufficiently the Christians or their religion, he judged that among them, too, he could find willing tools. Since they seemed more reliable than others, he resolved to have them undertake it, not for money's sake merely, but through devotion.

In view of this, he went in the evening to Euricius, who was devoted to him and would do all he could to assist him. Chilo did not even dream of revealing his real intentions, which would be in clear opposition to the faith the old man had in his piety and virtue. He wished to find people who were ready for anything and who would out of self-interest guard it as an eternal secret.

The old man Euricius, after the redemption of his son, hired one of those little shops so numerous near the Circus Maximus, in which were sold olives, beans, unleavened paste, and water sweetened with honey to spectators coming to the Circus. Chilo found him at home arranging his shop; and when he had greeted him in Christ's name, he began to speak of the affair that had brought him. Since he had rendered them a service, he thought that they would pay him with gratitude. He needed two or three strong and courageous men to ward off danger threatening not only him, but all Christians. He was poor, it was true, since he had given to Euricius almost all that he owned. Still, he would pay such men for their services if they would trust him and perform faithfully what he commanded.

Almost on their knees, Euricius and his son Quartus listened to him as their benefactor. Both declared that they were ready themselves to do all that he asked of them, believing that a man so holy could not ask for deeds inconsistent with the teaching of Christ.

Chilo assured them that was true, and, raising his eyes to heaven, he seemed to be praying; in fact, he was thinking whether it would not be well to accept their proposal, which might save him a thousand sestertia. But after a moment of thought he rejected it. Euricius was an old man, perhaps not so much weighted by years as weakened by care and disease. Quartus was sixteen years of age. Chilo needed skilled and, above all, stalwart men. As to the thousand sestertia, he believed that he would be able in any case to spare a large part of it.

They insisted for some time, but when he refused decisively they yielded.

"I know the baker Demas," said Quartus, "in whose mills slaves and hired men are employed. One of those hired men is so strong that he would take the place, not of two, but of four. I myself have seen him lift stones from the ground that four men could not stir."

"If that is a God-fearing man who can sacrifice himself for the brotherhood, make me acquainted with him," Chilo said.

"He is a Christian, lord." Quartus answered. "Nearly all who work for Demas are Christians. He has night as well as day laborers; this man is of the night laborers. Were we to go now to the mill, we should find them at supper, and you might speak to him freely. Demas lives near the Emporium."

Chilo consented most willingly. The Emporium was at the foot of the Aventine, not very far from the Circus Maximus. It was possible, without going around the hill, to pass along the river through the Porticus Aemilia, which would shorten the road considerably.

"I am old," Chilo said, when they went under the Colonnade. "At times I suffer loss of memory. Yes, though our Christ was betrayed by one of His disciples, I cannot recall the name of the traitor—"

"Judas, lord, who hanged himself," Quartus answered, wondering a little in his soul how it was possible to forget that name.

"Oh, yes—Judas! I thank you," Chilo said.

When they came to the Emporium, which was closed, they passed it, and going around the storehouse, from which grain was distributed to the people, they turned toward the left, to houses that stretched along the Via Ostiensis. There they halted before a wooden building, from within which came the noise of millstones. Quartus went in; but Chilo, who did not like to show himself to large numbers of people, and who was in continual dread that he might meet Glaucus, remained outside.

I am curious about that Hercules who serves in a mill, he said to himself, looking at the brightly shining moon. *If he is a scoundrel and a wise man, he will cost me something; if he is a virtuous Christian and dull, he will do what I want without money.*

Further thought was interrupted by the return of Quartus, who walked from the the building with a second man who wore a tunic called "exomis," cut so that the right arm and right breast were exposed. Such garments, since they left perfect freedom of movement, were used especially by laborers. When Chilo saw the man coming, he drew a breath of satisfaction, for he had never seen such an arm and such a breast.

"May the peace of Christ be with you!" Chilo answered. "Quartus, tell this brother whether I deserve faith and trust and then return in the name of God; for there is no need that your gray-haired father should be left in loneliness."

"This is a holy man," Quartus said, "who gave all his property to redeem me from slavery—me, a man unknown to him. May our Lord the Savior prepare him a heavenly reward, therefore!"

The gigantic laborer, hearing this, bent down and kissed Chilo's hand.

"What is your name, brother?" the Greek inquired.

"At holy baptism, father, the name Urban was given to me."

"Urban, my brother, have you time to talk with me freely?"

"Our work begins at midnight, and only now are they preparing our supper."

"Then there is sufficient time. Let us go to the river; there you will hear my words."

They went, and sat on the embankment, in a silence broken only by the distant sound of the millstones and the splash of the onflowing river. Chilo looked into the face of the laborer, which, except for a somewhat severe and sad expression, such as was usual on faces of barbarians living in Rome, seemed to him kind and honest.

This is a good-natured, dull man who will kill Glaucus for nothing, Chilo thought.

"Urban," he then inquired, "do you love Christ?"

"I love Him from the soul of my heart," the laborer said.

"And your brothers and sisters, and those who taught you truth and faith in Christ?"

"I love them, too, father."

"Then may peace be with you!"

"And with you, father!"

Chilo looked with fixed gaze into the clear moonlight and with a slow, restrained voice began to speak of Christ's death. He seemed not as speaking to Urban, but as if recalling to himself that death, or some secret he was confiding to the drowsy city. There was in this, too, something touching as well as impressive. The laborer wept; and when Chilo began to groan and complain that in the moment of the Savior's passion there was no one to defend Him, if not from crucifixion, at least from the insults of Jews and soldiers, the gigantic fists of the barbarian began to squeeze from pity and suppressed rage. The death only moved him, but at thought of the rabble reviling the Lamb nailed to the cross the simple soul in him was indignant and a wild desire of vengeance seized the man.

"Urban, do you know who Judas was?" Chilo asked suddenly.

"I know, I know! But he hanged himself!" the laborer exclaimed.

And in his voice there was a kind of sorrow that the traitor had meted out punishment to himself, and that Judas could not fall into his hands.

"But if he had not hanged himself," Chilo continued, "and if some Christian were to meet him on land or on sea, would it not be the duty of that Christian to take revenge for the torment, the blood, and the death of the Savior?"

"Who is there who would not take revenge, father?"

"Peace be with you, faithful servant of the Lamb! True, it is

147

permitted to forgive wrongs done ourselves; but who has the right to forgive a wrong done to God? But as a serpent breeds a serpent, as malice breeds malice, and treason breeds treason, so from the poison of Judas another traitor has come; and as that one delivered to Jews and Roman soldiers the Savior, so this man who lives among us intends to give Christ's sheep to the wolves; and if no one will anticipate the treason, if no one will crush the head of the serpent in time, destruction is waiting for us all, and with us will perish the honor of the Lamb."

The laborer looked at Chilo with immense alarm, as if not understanding what he had heard. But the Greek, covering his head with a corner of his mantle, began to repeat, with a voice coming as if from beneath the earth, "Woe to you, servants of the true God! Woe to you, Christian men and Christian women!"

And again came silence, again were heard only the roar of the millstones, the deep song of the millers, and the sound of the river.

"Father," the laborer asked at last, "what kind of traitor is that?"

Chilo dropped his head. "What kind of traitor? A son of Judas, a son of his poison, a man who pretends to be a Christian and goes to houses of prayer only to complain of the brotherhood to Caesar—declaring that they will not recognize Caesar as a god; that they poison fountains, murder children, and wish to destroy the city, so that one stone may not remain on another. In a few days a command will be given to the praetorian guards to cast old men, women, and children into prison and lead them to death, just as they led to death the slaves of Pedanius Secundus. All this has been done by that second Judas. But if no one punished the first Judas, if no one took vengeance on him, if no one defended Christ in the hour of torment, who will punish this one, who will destroy the serpent before Caesar hears him, who will defend from destruction our brothers in the faith of Christ?"

Urban, who had been sitting thus far on a stone, stood up suddenly and said, "I will, father."

Chilo also rose. He looked for a while on the face of the laborer, lighted up by the shining moon; then, stretching his arm, he put his hand slowly on his head.

"Go among Christians," he said solemnly. "Go to the houses of prayer, and ask the brethren about Glaucus; and when they show him to you, slay him at once in Christ's name."

"About Glaucus?" the laborer repeated, as if wishing to fix that name in his memory.

"Do you know him?"

"No, I do not. There are thousands of Christians in Rome, and they are not all known to one another. But tomorrow, in Ostrianum, every brother and sister will assemble in the night because a great apostle of Christ has come, who will teach them, and the brethren will point out Glaucus to me."

"In Ostrianum?" Chilo asked. "But that is outside the city gates! The brethren and all the sisters—at night? Outside the city gates, in Ostrianum?"

"Yes, father; that is our cemetery, between the Viae Salaria and Nomentana. Is it not known to you that the great apostle will teach there?"

"I have been two days from home, so I did not receive his letter; and I do not know where Ostrianum is, for I came here not long since from Corinth, where I govern a Christian community. But it is as you say—there you will find Glaucus among the brethren, and you will slay him on the way home to the city. For this all your sins will be forgiven. And now peace be with you—"

"Father—"

"I listen to you, servant of the Lamb."

On the laborer's face perplexity was evident. Not long before he had killed a man, and perhaps two, but the teaching of Christ forbids killing. He had not killed them in his own defense, for even that is not permitted. He had not killed them, Christ preserve, for profit. The bishop himself had given him brethren to help, but he had not permitted him to kill; he had killed inadvertently, for God had punished him with too much strength. And now he was doing grievous penance. Others sing when the millstones are grinding; but he, hapless man, is thinking of his sin, of his offense against the Lamb. He has prayed and wept and implored the Lamb and believes that he has not done enough penance yet! But now he has promised again to kill a traitor—and done well! He is permitted to pardon only offenses against him-

149

self; so he will kill Glaucus, even before the eyes of all the brethren and sisters, in Ostrianum tomorrow. But let Glaucus be condemned previously by the elders among the brethren, by the bishop, or by the apostle. To kill is not a great thing; to kill a traitor is even as pleasant as to kill a bear or a wolf. But suppose Glaucus was to perish innocently? Could he take on his conscience a new murder, a new sin, a new offense against the Lamb?

"There is no time for a trial, my son," Chilo said. "The traitor will hurry from Ostrianum immediately to Caesar in Antium, or hide in the house of a certain patrician whom he is serving. I will give you a sign; if you show it after the death of Glaucus, the bishop and the great apostle will bless your deed."

Saying this, he took out a small coin and began to search for a knife at his belt. Having found it, he scratched the sign of the cross on the coin and gave it to the laborer.

"Here is the sentence of Glaucus and a sign for you. If you show this to the bishop after the death of Glaucus, he will forgive you for that killing you did without wishing it."

The laborer stretched out his hand involuntarily for the coin; but having the first murder too freshly in his memory just then, he experienced a feeling of terror.

"Father," he said with a voice of almost entreaty, "do you take this deed on your conscience, and have you yourself heard Glaucus betraying his brethren?"

Chilo understood that he must give proofs, mention names; otherwise, doubt might creep into the heart of the giant. All at once a happy thought flashed through his head.

"Listen, Urban," he said. "I live in Corinth, but I came from Kos; and here in Rome I instruct in the religion of Christ a certain serving girl named Eunice. She serves in the house of a friend of Caesar, a certain Petronius. In that house I have heard how Glaucus has undertaken to betray all the Christians; and, besides, he has promised another informer of Caesar's, Vinicius, to find a certain girl for him among the Christians."

Here he stopped and looked with amazement at the laborer, whose eyes blazed suddenly like the eyes of a wild beast and whose face took on an expression of mad rage.

"What is the matter with you?" Chilo asked, almost in fear.

150

"Nothing, father; tomorrow I will kill Glaucus."

The Greek was silent. After a while he took the arm of the laborer, turned him so that the light of the moon struck his face squarely, and examined him with care. It was evident that he was wavering in spirit whether to inquire further and bring everything out clearly, or for the moment to stop with what he had learned or guessed.

At last, however, his innate caution prevailed. He breathed deeply once and a second time; then, placing his hand again on the laborer's head, he asked, in an emphatic and solemn voice, "But in holy baptism the name Urban was given to you?"

"It was, father."

"Then peace be with you, Urban!"

18

Petronius to Vinicius:

"Your case is a bad one, carissime. It is clear that Venus has disturbed your mind, deprived you of reason and memory, as well as the power to think of anything but love. Read your answer to my letter, and you will see how indifferent your mind is to all except Lygia; how it always returns to her and circles above her, as a falcon above a choice prey. By Pollux! Find her quickly, or that which fire has not turned into ashes will become an Egyptian sphinx, which, enamored, as is said, of pale Isis, grew deaf and indifferent to all things, waiting only for night, so as to gaze with stony eyes at the loved one.

"Run disguised through the city in the evening, even honor Christian houses of prayer in your philosopher's company. Whatever excites hope and kills time is praiseworthy. But for my friendship's sake do this one thing: Ursus, Lygia's slave, is a man of uncommon strength. Hire Croton, and go out all three together; that will be safer and wiser. The Christians, since Pomponia and

Lygia belong to them, are surely not such scoundrels as most people imagine. But when a lamb of their flock is in question they are no triflers, as they have shown by carrying away Lygia. When you see Lygia you will not restrain yourself, I am sure, and will try to take her away on the spot. But how will you and Chilo do it? Croton would take care of himself, even though ten like Ursus defended the girl. Do not let Chilo plunder you, but do not spare money on Croton. This is the best counsel.

"Here they have ceased to speak of the infant Augusta or to say that she perished through witchcraft. Poppaea mentions her at times; but Caesar's mind is stuffed with something else. Also, if it be true that the divine Augusta is in a changed state again, the memory of the infant Augusta will be blown away without a trace.

"We have been in Naples for some days, or rather in Baiae. We went directly to Baiae, where at first memories of his mother attacked us, and reproaches of conscience. But do you know what Ahenobarbus has done already? Even the murder of his mother is a mere theme for verses and a reason for buffoonish, tragic scenes. Formerly, he felt guilt only insofar as he was a coward; now, when he is convinced that the earth is under his feet as before, and that no god is taking vengeance, he pretends guilt only to impress people with his fate. He springs up at night sometimes declaring that the Furies are hunting him; he rouses us, looks around, assumes the posture of an actor playing the role of Orestes, and the posture of a bad actor too; he recites Greek verses and looks to see if we are admiring him. We admire him apparently; and instead of saying to him, 'Go to sleep, you buffoon!' we bring ourselves also to the tone of tragedy and protect the great artist from the Furies. By Castor! This news at least must have reached you, that he has appeared in public at Naples. They drove in from the city and the surrounding towns Greek ruffians, who filled the arena with such a vile odor of sweat and garlic that I thank the gods that, instead of sitting in the first rows with the Augustians, I was behind the scenes with Ahenobarbus.

"And will you believe it, he was truly afraid! He took my hand and put it to his heart, which was beating with increased pulsation; his breath was short; and at the moment when he had to appear he grew as pale as a parchment, and his forehead was covered with drops of sweat. Still, he saw that in every row of seats were praetorian guards armed with clubs to rouse enthusiasm if the need came. But there was no need. No herd of monkeys from the environs of Carthage could howl as did this rabble. I tell you that the smell of garlic came to the stage; but Nero bowed, pressed his hand to his heart, sent kisses from his lips, and shed tears. Then, like a drunken man, he rushed in among us who were waiting behind the scenes and cried, 'What were the triumphs of Julius compared with this triumph of mine?' But the rabble was still howling and applauding, knowing that it would applaud itself favors, gifts, banquets, lottery tickets, and a fresh exhibition by the imperial buffoon. I do not wonder that they applauded, for such a sight had not been seen until that evening. And every moment he repeated: 'See what the Greeks are! See what the Greeks are!' From that evening it has seemed to me that his hatred for Rome is increasing. Meanwhile, special couriers were hurried to Rome announcing the triumph, and we expect thanks from the Senate one of these days.

"Immediately after Nero's first exhibition, a strange event happened here. The theater caved in suddenly, but just after the audience had gone. I was there and did not see even one corpse taken from the ruins. Many, even among the Greeks, see in this event the anger of the gods, because the dignity of Caesar was disgraced; he, on the contrary, finds in it favor of the gods, who have his song, and those who listen to it, under their evident protection. So there are offerings in all the temples, and great thanks. For Nero it is a great encouragement to make the journey to Achaea. A few days before he told me, however, that he had doubts as to what the Roman people might say; that they might revolt out of love for him, and fear concerning the distribution of grain and touching the games, which might fail them because of his prolonged absence.

"We are going, however, to Beneventum to look at the cobbler magnificence that Vatinius will exhibit, and then to Greece, under the protection of the divine brothers of Helen. As for me, I have noted one thing, that when a man is among the mad he grows mad himself and, what is more, finds a certain charm in mad pranks. Greece and the journey in a thousand ships; a kind of triumphal advance of Bacchus among nymphs and bacchic dancers crowned with myrtle, vine, and honeysuckle. There will be women in tiger skins harnessed to chariots, flowers, thyrses, garlands, shouts of 'Evoe!' music, poetry, and applauding Hellas. All this is well; but we cherish more daring projects. We wish to create a species of Oriental Imperium—an empire of palm trees, sunshine, poetry, and reality turned into a dream.

"We want to forget Rome; to fix the balancing point of the world somewhere between Greece, Asia, and Egypt; to live the life not of men but of gods; to wander in golden galleys under the shadow of purple sails along the archipelago; to be Apollo, Osiris, and Baal in one person; to be rosy with the dawn, golden with the sun, silver with the moon; to command, to sing, to dream. And will you believe that I, who still have sound judgment regarding the value of a sestertium and can sense the value of an ass, let myself be borne away by these fantasies; and I do this because if they are not possible, they are at least grandiose and uncommon? Such a fabulous empire would be a thing that, after long ages, would seem a dream to mankind. Except when Venus takes the form of Lygia, or even of the slave Eunice, or when art beautifies it, life itself is empty and many times' has the face of a monkey.

"But Bronzebeard will not realize his plans, because in his fabulous kingdom of poetry and the Orient no place is given to treason, meanness, and death; and because in him, in the disguise of a poet, sits a wretched comedian, a poor charioteer, and a frivolous tyrant. Meanwhile, we are killing people whenever they displease us in any way. Poor Torquatus Silanus is now a ghost; he opened his veins a few days ago. Lecanius and Licinus will enter the consulate with terror. Old Thrasea will not escape death, for he dares to be honest. Tigellinus is not able yet to frame a command for me to open my veins. I am still needed not only as a wise man, but as a man without whose counsel and taste the expedition to Achaea might fail. More than once, however, I think that sooner or later it must end in opening my veins; and do you know what the question will be? That Bronzebeard should not get my goblet, which you know and admire. Should you be near at the moment of my death, I will give it to you; should you be at a distance, I will break it. But meanwhile, I still have before me Beneventum

154

of the cobblers and Olympian Greece; I have Fate, too, which, unknown and unforeseen, points out the road to everyone.

"Be well, and engage Croton; otherwise they will snatch Lygia from you a second time. When Chilo ceases to be needful, send him to me wherever I may be. Perhaps I shall make him a second Vatinius, and consuls and senators may tremble before him yet, as they trembled before that knight Dratevka. It would be worthwhile to live to see such a spectacle. When you have found Lygia, let me know, so that I may offer for you both a pair of swans and a pair of doves in the round temple of Venus here. Once I saw Lygia in a dream, sitting on your knee, seeking your kisses. Try to make that dream prophetic. May there be no clouds in your sky; or if there be, let them have the color and the odor of roses! Be in good health, and farewell!"

19

Vinicius had barely finished reading the letter when Chilo moved quietly into his library, unannounced by anyone, for the servants had the order to admit him at any hour of the day or night.

"May the divine mother of your magnanimous ancestor Aeneas be full of favor to you, as the son of Maia was kind to me."

"What do you mean?" Vinicius asked, springing from the table at which he was sitting.

Chilo raised his head and said, "Eureka!"

The young patrician was so excited that for a long time he could not utter a word.

"Have you seen her?" he asked at last.

"I have seen Ursus, lord, and have spoken with him."

"Do you know where they are hidden?"

"No, lord. Another, through boastfulness, would have let the Lygian know that he perceived who he was; another would have tried to extort from him the knowledge of where he lived and would have received either a stroke of the fist—after which all earthly affairs would have become indifferent to him—or would have roused the suspicion of the giant. Then a new hiding place would be found for the girl, this very night, perhaps. I did not act this way. It is enough for me to know that Ursus works near the Emporium, for a miller named Demas, the same name as that of your freedman. Now any trusted slave of yours may go in the morning on his way and discover their hiding place. I bring you merely the assurance that, since Ursus is here, the divine Lygia also is in Rome, and more news, that she will be in Ostrianum tonight, almost certainly—"

"In Ostrianum? Where is that?" Vinicius interrupted, wishing to run to the place.

"An old hypogeum [catacomb] between the Viae Salaria and Nomentana. That great leader of the Christians, of whom I spoke to you and whom they expected somewhat later, has come; and tonight he will teach and baptize in that cemetery. They hide their religion, for though there are no edicts to prohibit it as yet, the people hate them, so they must be careful. Ursus himself told me that all, to the last soul, would be in Ostrianum tonight, for everyone wishes to see and hear the foremost disciple of Christ, whom they call apostle. Since women as well as men will hear instruction from him, Pomponia alone, perhaps, will not be there; she could not explain to Aulus, a worshiper of the ancient gods, her absence from home at night. But Lygia, lord, who is under the care of Ursus and the Christian elders, will go undoubtedly with other women."

Vinicius had lived in a fever; now that his hope seemed fulfilled he felt all at once the weakness that a man feels after a journey that is beyond his strength. Chilo noticed this and resolved to make use of it.

"The gates are watched by your people, and the Christians must know that. But they do not need gates. The Tiber, too, does not need them; and though it is far from the river to those roads, it is worthwhile to walk one road more to see the 'great apostle.' Also, they may have a thousand ways of going beyond the walls. You will find Lygia in Ostrianum; and even should she not be there, which I will not admit, Ursus will be there, for he has promised to kill Glaucus. He told me himself that he would be there and that he would kill him.

"Do you hear, noble tribune? Either you will follow Ursus and learn where Lygia lives, or you will command your people to seize him as a murderer and, having him in your hand, make him confess where he has hidden Lygia. I have done my best. Another would have told you that he had drunk ten cantars of the best wine with Ursus before he wormed the secret out of him; another would have told you that he had lost a thousand sestertia to him or that he had bought the intelligence for two thousand; I know that you would repay me doubly, but in spite of that, once in my life—I mean, as always in my life—I shall be honest, for I think, as the magnanimous Petronius says, that your bounty exceeds all my hopes and expectations."

Vinicius, who was a shrewd and calculating soldier, was overcome by a momentary weakness and said, "You will not deceive yourself as to my liberality, but first you will go with me to Ostrianum."

"I, to Ostrianum?" Chilo asked, who had not the least wish to go there. "I, noble tribune, promised you to point out Lygia, but I did not promise to take her away for you. Think, lord, what would happen to me if that Lygian bear, when he had torn Glaucus to pieces, should convince himself that he had torn him apart unjustly? Would he not look on me (of course without reason) as the cause of the murder? Remember, lord, that the greater a philosopher a man is, the more difficult it is for him to answer the foolish questions of common people. What should I tell him if he were to ask me why I had Glaucus killed? But if you suspect that I deceive you, pay me only when I point out the house where Lygia lives. Show me today only a part of your generosity, so that if you, lord, have an accident, I shall not be entirely without recompense. Your heart could not endure that."

Vinicius went to a box, called an arca, standing on a marble pedestal, and, taking out a purse, threw it to Chilo.

"You are Jove!" Chilo exclaimed.

But Vinicius frowned.

"You will receive food here," he said. "Then you may rest. You will not leave this house until evening, and when night falls you will go with me to Ostrianum."

Fear and hesitation were reflected on the Greek's face, but he grew calm in a moment and said, "Who can oppose you, lord! Receive my words as a good omen. As to me, these 'scruples'" —here he shook the purse—"have outweighed mine, not to mention your society, which for me is delight and happiness."

Vinicius interrupted him impatiently and asked for details of his conversation with Ursus. It seemed clear that either Lygia's hiding place would be discovered that night or he would be able to seize her on the road back from Ostrianum. At this thought, Vinicius was borne away by wild delight. Now, when he felt sure of finding Lygia, his anger against her almost vanished. In return for that delight he forgave her every fault. He thought of her only as dear and desired, and he had the same impression as if she were returning after a long journey. He wished to summon his slaves and command them to deck the house with garlands. In that hour he did not even have a complaint against Ursus. He was ready to forgive all people everything. Chilo, for whom he had a certain revulsion, in spite of his services, seemed to him for the first time an amusing and uncommon person. His house grew radiant; his eyes and his face became bright. He began again to feel youth and the pleasure of life. His former gloomy suffering could not compare with how he loved Lygia. He understood this now for the first time, when he hoped to possess her. His desires woke in him as the earth, warmed by the sun, wakes in spring; but his desires this time were less blind and wild and more joyous and tender. He felt also limitless energy and was convinced that should he but see Lygia with his own eyes, all the Christians on earth could not take her from him, nor could Caesar himself.

Chilo, emboldened by the young tribune's delight, began to give advice. It is important for Vinicius not to look on the affair as won and to observe the greatest caution, without which all their work might end in nothing. He implored Vinicius not to carry off Lygia from Ostrianum. They ought to go there with hoods on their heads, with their faces hidden, and restrict themselves to looking from some dark corner at all who were present. When they saw

Lygia, it would be safest to follow her at a distance, see what house she entered, surround it the next morning at daybreak, and take her away in open daylight. Since she was a hostage and belonged particularly to Caesar, they might do that without fear of law. In the event of not finding her in Ostrianum they could follow Ursus, and the result would be the same. To go to the cemetery with a crowd of attendants was not practical. That might draw attention to them easily; then the Christians need only put out the lights, as they did when she was intercepted, and scatter in the darkness, or take themselves to places known only to them. But Vinicius and he should arm, and, still better, take a couple of strong, trusty men to defend them in case of need.

Vinicius saw the perfect truth of what he said and, recalling Petronius's counsel, commanded his slaves to bring Croton. Chilo, who knew everyone in Rome, relaxed notably when he heard the name of the famous athlete, whose superhuman strength in the arena he had wondered at more than once, and declared that he would go to Ostrianum. The purse filled with many coins seemed to him more easily acquired through the aid of Croton.

So he sat down in good spirits at the table to which he was called by the chief of the atrium.

While eating, he told the slaves that he had obtained a miraculous ointment for their master. The worst horse, if rubbed on the hoofs with it, would leave every other far behind. A certain Christian had taught him how to prepare that ointment, for the Christian elders were far more skilled in enchantment and miracles than even the Thessalians, though Thessaly was renowned for its witches. The Christians had immense confidence in him—why, anyone easily understands who knows what a fish means. While speaking, he looked sharply at the eyes of the slaves in the hope of discovering a Christian among them and informing Vinicius. But when that hope failed him, he resigned to eating and drinking uncommon quantities, not sparing praises on the cook and declaring that he would try to buy him from Vinicius. His joyfulness was dimmed only by the thought that at night he must go to Ostrianum. He comforted himself, however, because he would go in disguise, in darkness, and in the company of two men, one of whom was so strong that he was the idol of Rome, the other a patrician, a man of high dignity in the army. *Even if they discover Vinicius, said he to himself, they will not dare to raise a hand to him; as to me, they will be wise if they see even the tip of my nose.*

He recalled his conversation with the laborer, and the recollection of that filled him again with delight. He had not the least doubt that that laborer was Ursus. He knew of the uncommon strength of the man, from the narratives of Vinicius and those who had brought Lygia from Caesar's palace. When he inquired of Euricius concerning men of exceptional strength, there was nothing remarkable in this that they pointed out Ursus. Then the confusion and rage of the laborer at the mention of Vinicius and Lygia left him no doubt that those persons concerned him particularly. The laborer had mentioned also his penance for killing a man— Ursus had killed Atacinus. Finally, the appearance of the laborer answered perfectly to the account Vinicius had given of the Lygian. The change of name was all that could provoke doubt, but Chilo knew that frequently Christians took new names at baptism.

Should Ursus kill Glaucus, Chilo said to himself, that will be better still; but should he not kill him, that will be a good sign, for it will show how difficult it is for Christians to murder. I described Glaucus as a real son of Judas and a traitor to all Christians. I was so eloquent that a stone would have been moved and would have promised to fall on the head of Glaucus. Still, I hardly moved that Lygian bear to put his paw on him. He hesitated, was unwilling, spoke of his penance and sorrow. Evidently murder is not common among them. Offenses against oneself must be forgiven, and there is not much freedom in taking revenge for others. Glaucus is not free to avenge himself on you. If Ursus will not kill Glaucus for such a great crime as the betrayal of all Christians, so much the more will he not kill you, Chilo, for the small offense of betraying one Christian. Moreover, when I have once pointed out to this ardent wood pigeon the nest of that turtledove, I will wash my hands of everything and move to Naples.

The Christians talk, also, of a kind of washing of the hands; that is evidently a method by which, if a man has had dealings with them, he may finish it decisively. What good people these Christians are, and how ill men speak of them! Such is the justice of this world. But I love that religion, since it does not permit killing; it certainly does not permit stealing, deceit, or false testimony; so I will not say that it is easy. It teaches, evidently, not only to die honestly, as the Stoics teach, but to live honestly, also. If I ever have property and a house like this, and slaves in such number as Vinicius, perhaps I shall be a Christian as long as may be convenient. For a rich man can permit himself everything, even virtue. This is a religion for the rich; so I do not understand how there are so many poor among its adherents. What good is it for them, and why do they let virtue tie their hands? I must think this over sometime.

Meanwhile, praise to you, Hermes, for helping me discover this badger. Be ashamed, O slayer of Argos! Such a wise god as you, and not foresee that you will get nothing! I will offer you my gratitude; and if you prefer two beasts to it—you are the third beast yourself, and in the best event you should be a shepherd, not a god. Take care, too, unless I, as a philosopher, prove to men that you are nonexistent, and then all will cease to bring you offerings. It is safer to be on good terms with philosophers.

Speaking to himself and to Hermes, he stretched on the sofa, put his mantle under his head, and was sleeping when the slave removed the dishes. He woke—or rather they roused him—only at the coming of Croton. He went to the atrium, then, and began to examine with pleasure the form of the trainer, an ex-gladiator, who seemed to fill the whole place with his immensity. Croton had stipulated as to the price of the trip and was just speaking to Vinicius.

"By Hercules! It is well, lord," he said, "that you have sent today for me, since I shall start tomorrow for Beneventum, where the noble Vatinius has summoned me to make a trial, in the presence of Caesar, of a certain Syphax, the most powerful African alive. Do you imagine, lord, how his spinal column will crack in my arms, or how besides I shall break his jaw with my fist?"

"By Pollux! Croton, I am sure that you will do that," Vinicius answered.

161

"And you will act excellently," added Chilo. "Yes, to break his jaw, besides. That's a good idea and a deed that fits you. But rub your limbs with olive oil today, my Hercules, and gird yourself, for know this, you may meet a real Cacus. The man who is guarding that girl in whom the worthy Vinicius takes interest has exceptional strength very likely."

Chilo spoke only to arouse Croton's ambition.

"That is true," Vinicius said. "I have not seen him, but they tell me that he can take a bull by the horns and drag him wherever he pleases."

"Oi!" Chilo exclaimed, who had not imagined that Ursus was so strong.

But Croton laughed contemptuously. "I undertake, worthy lord," he said, "to bear away with this hand whomever you shalt point out to me, and with this other defend myself against seven such Lygians, and bring the girl to your house though all the Christians in Rome were pursuing me like Calabrian wolves. If not, I will let myself be beaten with clubs in this place."

"Do not permit that, lord," Chilo cried. "They will hurl stones at us, and how could his strength help? Is it not better to take the girl from the house—not expose yourself or her to destruction?"

"This is true, Croton," Vinicius said.

"I receive your money, I do your will! But remember, lord, that tomorrow I go to Beneventum."

"I have five hundred slaves in the city," Vinicius answered.

He gave them a sign to withdraw, went to the library himself, and, sitting down, wrote the following words to Petronius:

"The Lygian has been found by Chilo. I go this evening with him and Croton to Ostrianum and shall carry her off from the house tonight or tomorrow. May the gods pour down on you everything favorable. Be well, O carissime! For joy will not let me write further."

Laying aside the reed, he began to walk quickly, for besides delight, which was overflowing his soul, he was tormented with fever. He said to himself that tomorrow Lygia would be in that house. He did not know how to act with her but thought that if she would love him he would be her servant. He recalled Acte's assurance that he had been loved, and that moved him to the utter-

162

most. So it would be merely a question of conquering a certain womanly modesty, and a question of certain ceremonies that Christian teaching evidently commanded. But if that were true, Lygia, when once in his house, would yield to persuasion of superior force; she would have to say to herself, "It has happened!" and then she would be amiable and loving.

But Chilo appeared and interrupted these pleasant thoughts.

"Lord," said the Greek, "this has occurred to me. Have not the Christians signs, 'passwords,' without which no one will be admitted to Ostrianum? I know that it is so in houses of prayer, and I have received those passwords from Euricius. Permit me then to go to him, lord, to ask precisely and receive the correct signs."

"Well, noble sage," Vinicius answered gladly, "you speak as a man of forethought, and for that praise belongs to you. You will go, then, to Euricius, or wherever it may please you; but as security you will leave on this table here that purse you have received from me."

Chilo, who always parted with money unwillingly, squirmed; still, he obeyed the command and went out. From the Carinae to the Circus, near which was the little shop of Euricius, it was not very far; so he returned well before evening.

"Here are the signs, lord. Without them they would not admit us. I have inquired carefully about the road. I told Euricius that I needed the signs only for my friends; that I would not go myself, since it was too far for my advanced age; that I should see the great apostle myself tomorrow, and he would repeat to me the choicest parts of his sermon."

"How! You will not be there? You must go!" Vinicius said.

"I know that I must; but I will go well hooded, and I advise you to go in like manner."

In fact, they began soon to prepare, for darkness had come. They put on Gallic cloaks with hoods and took lanterns. Vinicius, besides, armed himself and his companions with short, curved knives. Chilo put on a wig, which he had obtained on the way from the old man's shop, and they went out, hurrying so as to reach the distant Nomentan Gate before it was closed.

20

They reached the Via Nomentana; there, turning to the left, toward the Via Salaria, they found themselves among hills full of sandpits, and here and there they found graveyards.

Meanwhile, it had grown completely dark, and since the moon had not risen yet, it would have been rather difficult for them to find the road were it not that the Christians themselves indicated it, as Chilo foresaw.

In fact, dark forms were evident, making their way carefully toward sandy hollows. Some of these people carried lanterns— covering them, however, as far as possible with mantles; others, knowing the road better, went in the dark. The trained military eye of Vinicius distinguished, by their movements, younger men from old ones, who walked with canes, and from women, wrapped carefully in long mantles. The highway police, and villagers leaving the city, took those night wanderers, evidently, for laborers going to sandpits, or gravediggers, who at times celebrated ceremonies of their own at night. In proportion, however, as the young patrician and his attendants pushed forward, more and more lanterns gleamed, and the number of persons grew greater. Some of them sang songs in low voices, which to Vinicius seemed filled with sadness. At moments a separate word or a phrase of the song struck his ear, as, for instance, "Awake, thou that sleepest," or "Rise from the dead"; at times, again, the name of Christ was repeated by men and women.

But Vinicius paid slight attention to the words, for it came to his mind that one of those dark forms might be Lygia. Some, passing near, said, "Peace be with you!" or, "Glory be to Christ!" but unrest took hold of him, and his heart began to beat with more life, for it seemed to him that he heard Lygia's voice. Forms or movements like hers deceived him in the darkness every moment, and only later did he begin to distrust his own eyes.

The way seemed long to him. He knew the neighborhood exactly but could not fix places in the darkness. Every moment they came to some narrow passage, or piece of wall, that he did not remember. Finally, the edge of the moon appeared from behind a mass of clouds and lighted the place better than dim lanterns. Something from afar began at last to glimmer like a fire, or the flame of a torch. Vinicius turned to Chilo.

"Is that Ostrianum?" he asked.

Chilo, on whom night, distance from the city, and those ghostlike forms made a deep impression, replied in a voice somewhat uncertain, "I know not, lord; I have never been in Ostrianum. But they might praise God in some spot nearer the city."

After a while, feeling the need of conversation and of strengthening his courage, he added, "They come together like murderers; still they are not permitted to murder, unless that Lygian has deceived me shamefully."

Vinicius, who was thinking of Lygia, was astonished also by the caution and mysteriousness with which her fellow believers assembled to hear their highest priest; so he said, "Like all religions, this has its adherents in the midst of us; but the Christians are a Jewish sect. Why do they assemble here, when in the Trans-Tiber there are temples to which the Jews take their offerings in daylight?"

"The Jews, lord, are their bitterest enemies. I have heard that, before the present Caesar's time, it came to war, almost, between Jews and Christians. Those outbreaks forced Claudius Caesar to expel all the Jews, but at present that edict is abolished. The Christians, however, hide themselves from Jews, and from the populace, who, as is known to you, accuse them of crimes and hate them."

They walked on some time in silence, until Chilo, whose fear increased as he was farther from the gates, said, "When returning from the shop of Euricius, I borrowed a wig from a barber and have put two beans in my nostrils. They must not recognize me; but if they do, they will not kill me. They are not malignant! They are even very honest. I esteem and love them."

"Do not win them to yourself by premature praise," Vinicius retorted.

They went now into a narrow ditch, closed, as it were, by two ditches on the side, over which an aqueduct was built in one place. The moon came out from behind clouds, and at the end of the ditch they saw a wall, covered thickly with ivy, which looked silvery in the moonlight. That was Ostrianum.

Vinicius's heart began to beat now with more vigor. At the gate two quarrymen took the signs from them. In a moment Vinicius and his attendants were in a rather spacious place enclosed on all sides by a wall. Here and there were separate monuments, and in the center was the entrance to the crypt. In the lower part of the crypt, beneath the earth, were graves; before the entrance a fountain was playing. But it was evident that no very large number of persons could find room in the crypt; so Vinicius concluded without difficulty that the ceremony would take place outside, where a very large crowd gathered.

As far as the eye could see, lanterns gleamed, but many of those who came had no light whatever. With the exception of a few uncovered heads, all were hooded, from fear of treason or the cold; and the young patrician thought with alarm that, if they would remain this way, he would not be able to recognize Lygia in that crowd and in the dim light.

But all at once, near the crypt, some torches were ignited and put into a little pile. After a while the crowd began to sing an unusual hymn, at first in a low voice, and then louder. Vinicius had never heard such a hymn before. The same yearning that had struck him in the hymns murmured by separate persons on the way to the cemetery was heard now, but with far more distinctness and power; and at last it became as penetrating and immense, as if, together with the people, the hills, the pits, and the region about had begun to yearn. It might seem, also, that there was a certain calling in the night, a certain humble prayer for rescue in wandering and darkness.

They seemed to see someone far above, there on high, and outstretched hands seemed to implore him to descend. When the hymn ceased, there followed a moment of suspense—so impressive that Vinicius and his companions looked unwittingly toward the stars, as if in dread that something uncommon would happen and that someone would really descend to them.

Vinicius had seen a multitude of temples of various structures in Asia Minor, in Egypt, and in Rome itself; he had become acquainted with a multitude of varied religions and had heard many hymns. But here, for the first time, he saw people calling on a divinity with hymns—not to carry out a fixed ritual, but calling from the bottom of the heart, with the genuine yearning that children might feel for a father or a mother. One had to be blind not to see that these people loved their God with the whole soul. Vinicius had not seen this in any land, during any ceremony, or in any sanctuary; for in Rome and in Greece those who still rendered honor to the gods did so to gain aid for themselves or through fear. But it had not even entered anyone's head to love these divinities.

Though his mind was occupied with Lygia, and his attention with seeking her in the crowd, he could not avoid seeing the uncommon and wonderful things that were happening around him. Meanwhile, a few more torches were thrown on the fire, which filled the cemetery with ruddy light and darkened the gleam of the lanterns. That moment an old man, wearing a hooded mantle but with a bare head, came from out of the crypt. This man mounted a stone that lay near the fire.

The crowd swayed before him. Voices near Vinicius whispered, "Peter! Peter!" Some knelt, others extended their hands toward him. There followed a silence so deep that one heard every charred particle that dropped from the torches, the distant rattle of wheels on the Via Nomentana, and the sound of wind through the few pines that grew close to the cemetery.

Chilo bent toward Vinicius and whispered, "This is he! The foremost disciple of Christ—a fisherman!"

The old man raised his hand and blessed those present, who fell on their knees simultaneously. Vinicius and his attendants, not wishing to betray themselves, followed the example of others. The young man could not judge his impressions immediately, for it seemed to him that the form he saw there before him was both simple and uncommon, and, what was more, the uncommonness flowed directly from the simplicity. The old man had no mitre on his head, no garland of oak leaves on his temples, no palm in his hand, no golden tablet on his breast. He wore no white robe embroidered with stars. In a word, he bore no insignia of the kind worn by oriental, Egyptian, or Greek priests—or by Roman priests. And Vinicius was struck by that same difference again that he felt when listening to the Christian hymns. For that "fisherman," too, seemed to him not like some high priest skilled in ceremony, but a witness—simple, aged, and immensely venerable—who had journeyed from afar to relate a truth that he had seen, that he had touched, that he believed as he believed in existence; and he had come to love this truth precisely because he believed it. There was in his face a convincing power leading to truth. And Vinicius, who had been a skeptic, who did not wish to yield to the charm of the old man, yielded, however, to a certain feverish curiosity to know what would flow from the lips of that companion of the mysterious "Christus," and what that teaching was of which Lygia and Pomponia Graecina were followers.

Meanwhile, Peter began to speak, and he spoke from the beginning like a father instructing his children and teaching them how to live. He implored them to renounce excess and luxury, to love poverty, purity of life, and truth, to endure wrongs and persecutions patiently, to obey the government and those placed above them; to guard against treason, deceit, and calumny; finally, to give an example in their own society to each other, and even to pagans.

Vinicius, for whom good was only that which could bring him back to Lygia, and evil everything that stood as a barrier between them, was touched and threatened by certain of these counsels. It seemed to him that by pursuing purity and a struggle with desires the old man dared not only to condemn his love but to rouse Lygia against him and confirm her in opposition. He understood that if she were in the assembly listening to those words, and if she took them to heart, she must think of him as an enemy of that teaching and an outcast.

Anger seized him at this thought. *What have I heard that is new? he thought. Is this the new religion? Everyone knows this, every one has heard it. The Cynics prescribed poverty and a restriction of necessities; Socrates preached virtue as an old thing and a good one. The first Stoic one meets, even such a one as Seneca, who has five hundred tables of lemonwood, praises moderation, promotes truth, patience in adversity, endurance in misfortune—and all that is like stale, mouse-eaten grain; but people do not wish to eat it because it smells of age.*

And besides anger, he had a feeling of disappointment, for

he expected the discovery of unknown, magic secrets of some kind and thought that at least he would hear a speech astonishing by its eloquence; meanwhile, he heard only words that were immensely simple, lacking every ornament. He was astonished only by the mute attention with which the crowd listened.

But the old man spoke on to those people lost in listening—told them to be kind, poor, peaceful, just, and pure; not that they might have peace during life, but that they might live eternally with Christ after death, in such joy and such glory, in such health and delight, as no one on earth had attained at any time. And here Vinicius, though predisposed unfavorably, could not but notice that still there was a difference between the teaching of the old man and that of the Cynics, Stoics, and other philosophers; for they show good and virtue as reasonable and the only thing practical in life, whereas the old man promised immortality, and that not some kind of unsatisfying immortality beneath the earth, in wretchedness, emptiness, and want, but a magnificent life, equal almost to that of the gods. He spoke meanwhile of it as of a thing perfectly certain. So, in view of such a faith, virtue acquired a measureless value, and the misfortunes of this life became incomparably trivial. To suffer temporally for inexhaustible happiness is a thing absolutely different from suffering because such is the order of nature. But the old man said further that virtue and truth should be loved for themselves, since the highest eternal good and the virtue existing before ages is God; whoever loves them loves God and becomes a cherished child of His.

Vinicius did not understand this well, but he knew previously, from words spoken by Pomponia Graecina to Petronius, that, according to the belief of Christians, God was one and almighty; when, therefore, he heard now again that He is all good and all just, he thought involuntarily that, in presence of such a demigod, Jupiter, Saturn, Apollo, Juno, Vesta, and Venus would seem like some vain and noisy rabble, in which all were interfering at once, and each for his or her own purpose.

But the greatest astonishment occurred when the old man declared that God was universal love also; hence he who loves men and women fulfills God's supreme command. But it is not enough to love people of one's own nation, for the God-Man shed

169

His blood for all and found among pagans such elect of His as Cornelius the centurion; it is not enough, either, to love those who do good to us, for Christ forgave the Jews who delivered Him to death and the Roman soldiers who nailed Him to the cross; we should not only forgive but love those who injure us, and return them good for evil; it is not enough to love the good, we must love the wicked, also, since by love alone it is possible to overcome evil.

At these words Chilo thought to himself that his work had amounted to nothing, that never in the world would Ursus dare to kill Glaucus, either that night or any other night. But he comforted himself at once by another inference from the teaching of the old man; namely, that neither would Glaucus kill him, though he should discover and recognize him.

Vinicius did not think now that there was nothing new in the words of the old man, but with amazement he asked himself, *What kind of God is this, what kind of religion is this, and what kind of people are these?* All that he had just heard could not fit well into his mind. For him all was an unheard of medley of ideas. He felt that if he wished, for example, to follow that teaching, he would have to place on a burning pile all his thoughts, habits, and character, his whole nature up to that moment, burn them into ashes, and then fill himself with a life altogether different and an entirely new soul. To him the science or the religion that commanded a Roman to love Parthians, Syrians, Greeks, Egyptians, Gauls, and Britons; to forgive enemies, to return them good for evil, and to love them, seemed madness. At the same time he had a feeling that in that madness itself there was something mightier than all philosophies so far. He thought that because of its madness it was impractical, but because of its impossibility it was divine. In his soul he rejected it; but it seemed to him that he was parting as if from a field full of spikenard, a kind of intoxicating incense; when a man has once breathed of this he must, as in the land of the lotus-eaters, forget all other things ever after and yearn for it only.

It seemed to him that there was nothing real in that religion, but that reality in the presence of it was so pale that it did not deserve attention. Expanses of some kind, of which he had no suspicion, surrounded him—certain immensities, certain clouds.

That cemetery began to produce on him the impression of a meeting place for madmen, but also of a place mysterious and awful, in which, as on a mystic bed, something was in a birthing process. He thought of all that the old man had said touching life, truth, love, and God; and his thoughts were dazed from the brightness, as the eyes are blinded from lightning flashes that follow each other.

As is usual with people for whom life has been turned into one single passion, Vinicius thought of all this through the medium of his love for Lygia; and in the light of those flashes he saw one thing distinctly, that if Lygia was in the cemetery, if she confessed that religion, obeyed and felt it, she never could and never would be his mistress.

For the first time, then, since he had made her acquaintance at Aulus's, Vinicius believed that though now he had found her he would not get her. Nothing similar had come to his head so far, for that was not so much a direct understanding as a dim feeling of irreparable loss and misfortune. There rose in him an alarm that turned soon into a storm of anger against the Christians in general and against the old man in particular. That fisherman, whom at the first glance of the eye he considered a peasant, now filled him with almost fear, and it seemed some mysterious power was tragically deciding his fate.

The quarrymen again, unobserved, added torches to the fire; the wind ceased to sound in the pines; the flame rose evenly toward the stars, which were twinkling in a clear sky. Having mentioned the death of Christ, the old man talked now of Him only. All held the breath in their breasts, and a silence set in that was deeper than the preceding one, so that it was possible almost to hear the beating of hearts. That man had seen, and he narrated as one in whose memory every moment had been fixed in such a way that were he to close his eyes he would see yet. He told, therefore, how on their return from the cross he and John had sat two days and nights in the supper chamber, neither sleeping nor eating; in suffering, doubt, and alarm; holding their heads in their hands and thinking that He had died. Oh, how grievous that was! The third day had dawned, and the light whitened the walls, but he and John were sitting in the chamber, without hope or comfort.

How desire for sleep tortured them (for they had spent the night before the Passion without sleep)! They roused themselves then, and began again to lament. But barely had the sun risen when Mary of Magdala, panting, her hair disheveled, rushed in with the cry "They have taken away the Lord!" When they heard this, he and John sprang up and ran toward the sepulcher. But John, being younger, arrived first; he saw the place empty and dared not enter. Only when there were three at the entrance did he, the person now speaking to them, enter and find on the stone a shirt with a winding sheet; but he did not find the body.

Fear fell on them then, because they thought that the Jewish leaders had taken Christ away, and both returned home in greater grief still. Other disciples came later and raised a cry, now in company, so that the Lord of Hosts might hear them more easily. The spirit died within them, for they had hoped that the Master would redeem Israel, and it was now the third day since His death; so they did not understand why the Father had deserted the Son, and they preferred not to look at the daylight, but to die, so grievous was the burden.

The remembrance of those terrible moments pressed even then from the eyes of the old man two tears, which were visible by the light of the fire, trickling down his gray beard. His hairless and aged head was shaking, and his voice died in his breast.

That man is speaking the truth and is weeping over it, Vinicius said in his soul. Sorrow seized the simple-hearted listeners also. They had heard more than once of Christ's sufferings, and it was known to them that joy succeeded sorrow; but since an apostle who had seen it told this, they sobbed or beat their breasts.

But they calmed themselves gradually, for they wished to hear more. The old man closed his eyes, as if to see distant things more distinctly in his soul, and continued. "When the disciples had lamented in this way, Mary of Magdala rushed in a second time, crying that she had seen the Lord. Unable to recognize Him, she thought He was the gardener; but He said, 'Mary!' She cried, 'Rabboni!' and fell at His feet. He commanded her to go to the disciples and vanished. But the disciples did not believe her; and when she wept for joy, some scolded her and some thought that sorrow had overwhelmed her mind, for she said, too, that she had seen angels at the grave; but they, running there a second time, saw the grave empty. Later in the evening Cleopas appeared, who had come with another from Emmaus, and they returned quickly, saying: "The Lord has indeed risen!" And they talked behind closed doors, out of fear of the Jews. Meanwhile, He stood among them, though the doors had not opened, and when they were frightened, He said, 'Peace be with you!'

"And I saw Him, as did all, and He was like light, and was the happiness of our hearts, for we saw that He had risen from the dead, and that the seas will dry and the mountains turn to dust, but His glory will not pass.

"After eight days Thomas Didymus put his finger in the Lord's wounds and touched His side; Thomas fell at His feet, then, and cried, 'My Lord and my God!' 'Because you have seen me you have believed; blessed are they who have not seen and have believed!' the Lord said. And we heard those words, and our eyes looked at Him, for He was among us."

Vinicius listened, and something wonderful took place in him. He forgot for a moment where he was; he began to lose the feeling of reality. He stood in the midst of two impossibilities. He could not believe what the old man said; and he thought that it would be necessary either to be blind or to renounce one's own reason, to admit that that man who said "I saw" was lying. There was something in his movements, in his tears, in his whole figure, and in the details of the events he narrated that made every suspicion impossible. To Vinicius it seemed at moments that he was dreaming. But round about he saw the silent throng; the odor of lanterns came to his nostrils; at a distance the torches were blazing; and before him on the stone stood an aged man near the grave, with a head trembling somewhat, who, while bearing witness, repeated, "I saw!"

And he narrated to them everything up to the ascension into heaven. At moments he rested, but each minute detail had fixed itself in his memory, as a thing is fixed in a stone into which it has been engraved. Those who listened to him were seized by ecstasy. They threw back their hoods to hear him better and not lose a word of those which for them were priceless. It seemed to them that some superhuman power had borne them to Galilee; that

173

they were walking with the disciples through those groves and on those waters; that the cemetery was turned into the lake of Tiberius; that on the bank, in the mist of morning, stood Christ, as He stood when John, looking from the boat, said, "It is the Lord," and Peter threw himself into the water to swim to shore, so as to fall the more quickly at His beloved feet. In the faces of those present were evident enthusiasm beyond bounds, oblivion to life, happiness, and love immeasurable. When he began to tell how, at the moment of ascension, the clouds closed in under the feet of the Savior, covered Him, and hid Him from the eyes of the apostles, all heads were raised toward the sky unconsciously, and a moment followed as it were of expectation, as if those people hoped to see Him there, or as if they hoped that He would descend again from the fields of heaven and see how the old apostle was feeding the sheep confided to him, and bless both the flock and him.

Rome did not exist for these people, nor did the man Caesar; there were no temples of pagan gods; there was only Christ, who filled the land, the sea, the heavens, and the world.

At the houses scattered here and there along the Via Nomentana, the cocks began to crow, announcing midnight. At that moment Chilo pulled the edge of Vinicius's mantle and whispered, "Lord, I see Urban over there, not far from the old man, and with him is a girl."

Vinicius shook himself, as if out of a dream, and, turning in the direction indicated by the Greek, he saw Lygia.

21

Every drop of blood quivered in the young patrician at sight of her. He forgot the crowd, the old man, his own astonishment at the incomprehensible things he had heard—he saw only her. At last, after all his efforts, he had found her! For the first time he realized that joy might rush at the heart, like a wild beast, and squeeze it until breath was lost. He tried to convince himself that he was not dreaming. But there was no doubt—he saw Lygia, and only a few steps divided them. She stood in perfect light, so that he could rejoice in the sight of her as much as he liked. The hood had fallen from her head and disheveled her hair; her mouth was open slightly, her eyes raised toward the apostle, her face fixed in rapture and delight. She was dressed in a dark wool mantle, like a daughter of the people, but never had Vinicius seen her more beautiful; and even with all the confusion that had risen in him, he was struck by the nobility of that wonderful patrician head in distinction to the dress, almost that of a slave. Love flew over him like a flame, immense, mixed with a marvelous feeling of yearning and homage. He felt the delight that the sight of her caused him; he drank of her as of life-giving water after long thirst. Standing near the gigantic Lygian, she seemed to him smaller than before, almost a child; he noticed, too, that she had grown more slender. Her complexion had become almost transparent; she was like a flower, and a spirit. But all the more did he desire to possess that woman, so different from all women whom he had seen or possessed in Rome or the Orient. He thought that for her he would have given them all, and with them Rome and the world.

He would have lost himself in gazing had it not been for Chilo, who pulled the edge of his mantle, out of fear that he might do something to expose them to danger. Meanwhile, the Christians began to pray and sing. After a while the benediction "Maranatha" thundered forth, and then the great apostle baptized with water from the fountain those whom the presbyters presented as ready. It seemed to Vinicius that night would never end. He wished now to follow Lygia as soon as possible and seize her on the road or at her house.

At last some began to leave the cemetery, and Chilo whispered, "Let us go out before the gate, lord. We have not removed our hoods, and people may look at us."

Such was the case, for during the preaching of the apostle all had cast aside their hoods so as to hear better, and they had not followed the general example. Chilo's advice seemed wise. Standing before the gate, they could look at all who passed; Ursus was easily recognizable by his form and size.

"Let us follow them," Chilo said. "We shall see where they go. Today you will surround the entrances with slaves and take her."

"No!" Vinicius said.

"What do you wish to do, lord?"

"We will follow her to the house and take her now, if you will undertake that task, Croton?"

"I will," Croton replied, "and I will give myself to you as a slave if I do not break the back of that bison who is guarding her."

But Chilo began to dissuade and plead with them by all the gods not to do so. Croton was taken only for defense against attack in case they were recognized, not to carry off the girl. To take her when there were only two of them was to expose themselves to death, and, what was worse, they might let her out of their hands, and then she would hide in another place, or leave Rome. And what could they do? Why not act with certainty? Why expose themselves to destruction and the whole undertaking to failure?

Though Vinicius restrained himself with the greatest effort from seizing Lygia in his arms at once, right there in the cemetery, he believed the Greek was right and would have listened, perhaps, to his counsels, had it not been for Croton, to whom reward was the issue.

"Lord, command that old goat to be silent," he said, "or let me drop my fist on his head. Once in Buxentum, where Lucius Saturnius took me to a play, seven drunken gladiators fell on me at an inn, and none of them escaped with sound ribs. I do not agree to take the girl now from the crowd, for they might throw stones before our feet, but once she is at home I will seize her, carry her away, and take her wherever you indicate."

Vinicius was pleased to hear those words and answered, "That is fine, by Hercules! Tomorrow we may not find her at home. If we surprise them they will surely remove the girl."

"This Lygian seems tremendously strong!" Chilo groaned.

"No one will ask you to hold his hands," Croton answered.

But they had to wait a long time, and the cocks had begun to crow before dawn when they saw Ursus coming through the gate, and with him Lygia. They were accompanied by a number of other persons. It seemed to Chilo that he recognized among them the great apostle; next to him walked another old man, considerably lower in stature, two women who were not young, and a boy, who lighted the way with a lantern. After that handful followed a crowd, about two hundred in number; Vinicius, Chilo, and Croton walked with these people.

"Yes, lord," Chilo said, "your maiden is under powerful protection. That is the great apostle with her."

Vinicius did not look at the people with Lygia. He did not lose her from his eyes for a moment; he thought only of taking her away, and, accustomed as he had been in wars to stratagems of all sorts, he mentally arranged the whole plan of seizure with soldierly precision. He felt that the step on which he had decided would work.

The way was long; so at moments he thought, too, of the gulf that wonderful religion had dug between him and Lygia. Now he understood everything that had happened in the past and had insight into why it had happened. He knew now that Lygia's religion made her different from other women; and he knew as well that his hope that desire, wealth, and luxury would attract her was a vain illusion. Finally, he understood what he and Petronius had not known, that the new religion grafted into the soul something unknown to that world in which he lived, and that Lygia, even if she loved him, would not sacrifice any of her Christian truths for his sake. If pleasure existed for her, it was a pleasure different altogether from that which he and Petronius and Caesar's court and all Rome were pursuing. Every other woman he knew might become his mistress, but that Christian would become only his victim.

When he thought of this, he felt anger and burning pain, for he felt that he was powerless. To carry off Lygia seemed to him possible—he was almost sure that he could take her; but he was equally sure that, in view of her religion, he himself with his bravery was nothing, that his power was nothing, and that through it he could accomplish nothing. That Roman military tribune, convinced that the power of the sword and the fist that had conquered the world and would command it forever, saw for the first time that beyond that power there might be something else. So he asked himself with amazement what it was, and he could not answer distinctly. Through his head flew merely pictures of the cemetery, the assembled crowd, and Lygia, listening with her whole soul to the words of the old man as he narrated the passion, death, and resurrection of the God-Man, who had redeemed the world and promised it happiness on the other shore of the Styx.

When he thought of this, chaos filled him. But he was brought out of this chaos by Chilo, who began lamenting his own fate. He had agreed to find Lygia. He had sought for her at the peril of his life, and he had pointed her out. But what more do they want? Had he offered to carry the girl away? Who could ask anything like this of a maimed man deprived of two fingers, an old man, devoted to meditation, to science, and to virtue? Would that happen were a lord of such dignity as Vinicius to meet some mishap while taking the girl away? It is true that the gods are bound to watch over their chosen ones—but have not such things happened more than once, as if the gods were playing games instead of watching what was happening in the world? Fortune is blindfolded, as is well known, and does not see even in daylight; what must the case be at night? Let something happen—let that Lygian bear hurl a millstone at the noble Vinicius—and who will give assurance that instead of a reward blame will not fall on poor Chilo? He, the unfortunate sage, has attached himself to the noble Vinicius as Aristotle to Alexander of Macedon. If the noble lord should give him at least that purse he had thrust into his cloak before leaving home, there would be something with which to invoke aid in case of need, or to influence the Christians. Oh, why not listen to the counsels of an old man, counsels dictated by experience and prudence?

Vinicius, hearing this, took the purse from his belt and threw it to the fingers of Chilo.

"You have it; be silent!"

The Greek noticed that it was unusually heavy and gained confidence.

"My whole hope is in this," he said, "that Hercules or Theseus performed deeds still more arduous; what is my personal, nearest friend, Croton, if not Hercules? You, worthy lord, I will not call a demigod, for you are a full god, and in future you will not forget a poor, faithful servant, whose needs it will be necessary to provide for from time to time, for once he is sunk in books, he

178

thinks of nothing else; some few acres of garden land and a little house, even with the smallest portico, for coolness in summer, would befit such a donor. Meanwhile, I shall admire your heroic deeds from afar, and invoke Jove to befriend you, and if need be I will make such an outcry that half Rome will be roused to your assistance. What a wretched, rough road! The olive oil is burned out in the lantern; and if Croton, who is as noble as he is strong, would bear me to the gate in his arms, he would learn, to begin with, whether he will carry the girl easily. Second, he would act like Aeneas and win all the good gods to such a degree that I should be thoroughly satisfied."

"I should rather carry a sheep that died of disease a month ago," the gladiator answered. "But give me the purse the worthy tribune gave you, and I will carry you to the gate."

"May you knock the great toe from your foot," the Greek replied. "What profit have you from the teachings of that worthy old man, who described poverty and charity as the two foremost virtues? Has he not commanded you to love me? Never shall I make you, I see, even a poor Christian; it would be easier for the sun to pierce the walls of the Mamertine prison that for truth to penetrate your skull of a hippopotamus."

"Never fear!" Croton said, who with the strength of a beast had no human feeling. "I shall not be a Christian! I have no wish to lose my bread."

"But if you knew even the rudiments of philosophy, you would know that gold is vanity."

"Come to me with your philosophy. I will give you one blow of my head in the stomach. We shall see then who wins."

"An ox might have said the same to Aristotle," Chilo retorted.

It was growing lighter. The dawn covered the outlines of the walls with pale light. The trees along the wayside, the buildings, and the gravestones scattered here and there began to be visible from the shade. The road was no longer quite empty. Marketmen were moving toward the gates, leading donkeys and mules laden with vegetables; here and there moved creaking carts in which meat was carried. On the road and along both sides of it was a light mist at the very earth, which promised good weather. People at some distance seemed like apparitions in that mist. Vinicius stared at the slender form of Lygia, which became more silvery as the light increased.

"Lord," Chilo said, "When you have learned in what house the divine Lygia dwells, I advise you once more to go home for slaves and a litter; do not listen to that elephant trunk, Croton, who tries to carry off the girl only to squeeze your purse as if it were a bag of curds."

"I have a blow of the fist to be struck between the shoulders, which means that you will perish," Croton said.

"I have a cask of Cephalonian wine, which means that I shall be well," Chilo replied.

Vinicius made no answer, for he approached the gate, at which a wonderful sight struck his eyes. Two soldiers nodded when the apostle was passing. Peter placed his hand on their iron helmets for a moment and then blessed them. It had never occurred to the patrician before that there could be Christians in the army; with astonishment he thought that as fire in a burning city takes in more and more houses, so to all appearances that doctrine embraces new souls every day, and extends itself over all humankind. This struck him also with reference to Lygia, for he was convinced that, had she wished to flee from the city, there would be guards willing to help her flight. He thanked the gods then that this had not happened.

After they had passed vacant places beyond the wall, the Christians began to scatter. It was necessary to follow Lygia more from a distance, and more carefully, so as not to rouse attention. Chilo fell to complaining of wounds, of pains in his legs, and dropped more and more to the rear. Vinicius did not oppose this, judging that the cowardly and incompetent Greek would not be needed. He would even have permitted him to depart, had he wished. But curiosity consumed Chilo, since he continued behind and at moments even approached with his previous counsels; he thought, too, that the old man accompanying the apostle might be Glaucus, were it not for his rather low stature.

They walked a good while before reaching the Trans-Tiber, and the sun was nearly rising when the group surrounding Lygia dispersed. The apostle, an old woman, and a boy went up the river. The old man of lower stature, Ursus, and Lygia entered a narrow alley and went about a hundred yards, then turned into a house in which were two shops—one for the sale of olives, the other for poultry.

Chilo, who walked about fifty yards behind Vinicius and Croton, halted all at once, as if fixed to the earth and, squeezing up to the wall, began to hiss at them to turn.

"Go, Chilo," said Vinicius, "and see if this house fronts on another street."

Chilo, though he had complained of wounds in his feet, sprang away as quickly as if he had had the wings of Mercury on his ankles and returned in a moment.

"No," he said, "there is only one entrance."

Then, putting his hands together, he said, "I implore you, lord, by all the gods of the Orient and the Occident to drop this plan. Listen to me—"

But he stopped suddenly, for he saw that Vinicius's face was pale from emotion and that his eyes were glittering like the eyes of a wolf. It was enough to look at him to understand that nothing in the world would restrain him from the undertaking. Croton began to draw air into his Herculean breast and to sway his undeveloped skull from side to side as bears do when confined in a cage. Not the least fear was evident on his face.

"I will go in first," he said.

"You will follow me," Vinicius said in commanding tones.

And after a while both vanished in the dark entrance.

Chilo sprang to the corner of the nearest alley and watched from behind it, waiting for what would happen.

22

Only inside the entrance did Vinicius understand the difficulty. The house was large, several stories high, of the kind of which thousands were built in Rome. In view of profit from rent, as a rule they were built hurriedly and badly. Scarcely a year passed in which numbers of them did not fall on the heads of tenants. These were real hives, too high and too narrow, full of chambers and little dens, in which numerous poor people lived. In a city where many streets had no names, these houses had no numbers; the owners committed the collection of rent to slaves, who, not obliged by the city government to give names of occupants, were ignorant themselves of them. To find someone by inquiry in such a house was often very difficult, especially when there was no gatekeeper.

Vinicius and Croton came to a narrow, corridorlike passage walled in on four sides and forming a kind of common atrium for the whole house, with a fountain in the middle whose stream fell into a stone basin fixed in the ground. All the walls had internal stairways, some of stone, some of wood, leading to galleries that were entrances to lodgings. There were lodgings on the ground, also; some had wooden doors, others were separated from the yard only by wool screens. These, for the greater part, were worn or patched.

"What shall we do, lord?" Croton asked, halting.

"Let us wait here; someone may appear," Vinicius replied. "We should not be seen in the yard."

At this moment, he thought Chilo's counsel was practical. If there were some slaves present, it would be easy to occupy the gate, which seemed the only exit, search all the lodgings simultaneously, and thus come to Lygia's. Otherwise Christians, who surely were not lacking in that house, might give notice that people were seeking her. In view of this, there was risk in inquiring of strangers. Vinicius stopped to think whether it would not be better to go for his slaves. Just then, from behind a screen hiding a more remote lodging, a man with a sieve in his hand came out and approached the fountain.

At the first glance the young tribune recognized Ursus.

"That is the Lygian!" Vinicius whispered.

"Am I to break his bones now?"

"Wait a while!"

Ursus did not notice the two men, as they were in the shadow of the entrance, and he began quietly to sink in water the vegetables that filled the sieve. Croton and Vinicius followed him to a

182

little garden containing a few cypresses, some myrtle bushes, and a small house fixed to the windowless stone wall of another stone building.

Both understood at once that this was a favorable circumstance for them. In the courtyard all the tenants might assemble; the seclusion of the little house helped. They would quickly throw aside defenders, or rather Ursus, and would reach the street just as quickly with the captured Lygia. It was likely that no one would attack them, but if attacked, they would say that they were coming for a hostage fleeing from Caesar. Vinicius would then declare himself to the guards and seek their assistance.

Ursus was almost entering the little house, when the sound of steps attracted his attention. He stopped and, seeing two persons, put his sieve on the balustrade and turned to them.

"What do you want here?" he asked.

"You!" Vinicius said.

Then, turning to Croton, he said in a low, hurried voice, "Kill!"

Croton rushed at him like a tiger, and in one moment, before the Lygian was able to think or to recognize his enemies, Croton had caught him in his arms of steel.

Vinicius was too confident in the man's supernatural strength to wait for the end of the struggle. He passed the two, sprang to the door of the little house, pushed it open, and found himself in a somewhat dark room. It was lighted, however, by a fire burning in the chimney. A gleam of this fire fell on Lygia's face directly. A second person, sitting at the fire, was that old man who had accompanied the young girl and Ursus on the road from Ostrianum.

Vinicius rushed in so suddenly that before Lygia could recognize him he had seized her by the waist and, raising her, rushed toward the door again. The old man barred the way, but pressing the girl with one arm to his chest, Vinicius pushed him aside with the other, which was free. The hood fell from his head, and at sight of that face, which was known to her and which at that moment was frightening, the blood grew cold in Lygia from fear and the voice died in her throat. She wished to seek help but had not the power. Equally vain was her wish to grasp the door, to resist. Her fingers slipped along the stone, and she would have fainted but for the terrible picture that struck her eyes when Vinicius rushed into the garden.

Ursus was holding in his arms some man doubled back completely, with hanging head and mouth filled with blood. When Ursus saw them, he struck the head once more with his fist, and in an instant sprang toward Vinicius like a raging wild beast.

Death! thought the young patrician.

Then he heard, as through a dream, the scream of Lygia, "Do not kill!" He felt that something, as it were a thunderbolt, opened the arms with which he held Lygia; then the earth turned round with him, and the light of day died in his eyes.

Chilo, hidden behind the angle of the corner house, was waiting, since curiosity was struggling with fear. He thought that if they succeeded in carrying off Lygia, he would fare well near Vinicius. He feared Urban no longer, for he also felt certain that Croton would kill him. And he calculated that in case a gathering should begin on the streets, which so far were empty—if Christians, or people of any kind, should offer resistance—he, Chilo, would speak to them as one representing authority, as an executor of Caesar's will, and if need came, call the guards to aid the young patrician against the street rabble—thus winning to himself fresh favor. In his soul he judged yet that the young tribune's method was unwise. Considering, however, Croton's terrible strength, he admitted that it might succeed, and thought, *Vinicius can carry the girl, and Croton clear the way.* Delay grew wearisome, however. *If they do not find her hiding place and make an uproar, they will frighten her.* But this thought was not disagreeable; for Chilo understood that in that event he would be necessary again to Vinicius and could squeeze afresh a goodly number of coins from the tribune.

Whatever they do, said he to himself, *they will work for me, though no one senses that. O gods! O gods! Only permit me—*

And he stopped suddenly, for it seemed to him that someone was bending forward through the entrance; then, squeezing up to the wall, he began to look, holding the breath in his chest.

That is Vinicius, or Croton, Chilo thought, *but if they have taken the girl, why does she not scream, and why are they looking out to the street? They must meet people anyhow, for before they reach the Carinae there will be movement in the city. What is that? By the immortal gods!*

And suddenly his hair stood on end.

In the door Urusus appeared with the body of Croton hanging on his arm, and looking around once more, he began to run, bearing the body along the empty street toward the river.

Chilo made himself as flat against the wall as a bit of mud.

I am lost if he sees me!

But Ursus ran past the corner quickly and disappeared beyond the neighboring house. Chilo, without further waiting, his teeth chattering from terror, ran along the cross street with a speed that even in a young man might have aroused admiration.

If he sees me from a distance when he is returning, he will catch and kill me, he said to himself. *Save me, Zeus; save me, Apollo; save me, Hermes; save me, O God of the Christians! I will leave Rome, I will return to Mesembria, but save me from the hands of that demon!*

And that Lygian who had killed Croton seemed to him at that moment some superhuman being. While running, he thought that he might be some god who had taken the form of a barbarian. He believed in all the gods of the world, and in all myths, at which he usually jeered. It flew through his head, too, that it might be the God of the Christians who had killed Croton; and his hair stood on end again at the thought that he was in conflict with such a power.

Only when he had run through a number of alleys and saw some workmen coming toward him from a distance was he calmed somewhat. Breath failed him, so he sat on the threshold of a house and began to wipe, with a corner of his mantle, his sweat-covered forehead.

"I am old and need calm," he said.

The people coming toward him turned into a little side street. The city was sleeping yet. In the morning movement began earlier in the wealthier parts of the city, where the slaves of rich houses were forced to rise before daylight. After Chilo had sat some time on the threshold he felt a piercing cold; so he rose and, convincing himself that he had not lost the purse received from Vinicius, turned slowly toward the river.

I may see Croton's body somewhere, he said to himself.

O gods! That Lygian, if he is a man, might make millions of sestertia in the course of one year; for if he choked Croton like a whelp, who can resist him? They would give for his every appearance in the arena as much gold as he himself weighs. He guards that maiden better than Cerberus does hades. But may hades swallow him, for all that! A dreadful thing has happened. If he has broken the bones of such a man as Croton, beyond a doubt the soul of Vinicius is near that cursed house now, awaiting his burial. By Castor! But he is a patrician, a friend of Caesar, a relative of Petronius, a man known in all Rome, a military tribune. His death cannot pass without punishment. Suppose I were to go to the praetorian camp, or the guards of the city, for instance?

Here he stopped and began to think, but said to himself after a while, *Woe is me! Who took him to that house if not I? His freedmen and his slaves know that I came to his house, and some of them know with what object. What will happen if they suspect me of having pointed out to him purposely the house where he died? Though it appear afterward, in the court, that I did not wish his death, they will say that I was the cause of it. Besides, he is a patrician, so in no case can I avoid punishment. But if I leave Rome in silence, and go far away somewhere, I shall place myself under still greater suspicion.*

It was bad in every case. The only question was to choose the less evil. Rome was immense; still Chilo thought that it might become too small for him. Any other man might go directly to the prefect of the city guards and tell what had happened and, though some suspicion might fall on him, await the issue calmly. But Chilo's whole past was of such nature that every closer acquaintance with the prefect of the city must cause him very serious trouble and confirm also every suspicion.

On the other hand, to flee would be to confirm Petronius's opinion that Vinicius had been betrayed and murdered through conspiracy. Petronius was a powerful man who could command the police of the whole empire, and who beyond doubt would pursue the guilty parties even to the ends of the earth. Still, Chilo thought to go straight to him and tell what had happened. Yes, that was the best plan. Petronius was calm, and Chilo might be sure of this, at least, that he would hear him out. Petronius, who knew the affair from its inception, would believe in Chilo's innocence more easily than would the prefects.

But if he were to go to Petronius, Croton needed to know with certainty what had happened to Vinicius. He had seen, it is true, the Lygian fleeing with Croton's body to the river, but nothing more. Vinicius might be killed; but he might be wounded or detained. Now it occurred to Chilo for the first time that surely the Christians would not dare to kill a man so powerful—a friend of Caesar, and a high military official—for that kind of act might draw on them a general persecution. It was more likely that they had detained him by superior force, to give Lygia ways to hide herself a second time.

This thought filled Chilo with hope.

If that Lygian dragon has not torn him to pieces at the first attack, he is alive, and if he is alive he himself will testify that I have not betrayed him. I can inform one of the freedmen where to seek his lord; and whether he goes to the prefect or not is his affair, the only point being that I should not go. Also, I can go to Petronius and count on a reward. It is needful to know first whether Vinicius is dead or living.

Here it occurred to him that he might go in the night to the baker Demas and inquire about Ursus. But he rejected that thought immediately. He preferred to have nothing to do with Ursus. He might suppose, justly, that if Ursus had not killed Glaucus he had been warned, evidently, by the Christian elder to whom he had confessed his design—warned that the affair was an evil one, to which some traitor had persuaded him. In every case, at the mere recollection of Ursus, a shiver ran through Chilo's whole body. But he thought that in the evening he would send Euricius for news to that house in which the thing had happened. Meanwhile, he needed refreshment, a bath, and rest. The sleepless night, the journey to Ostrianum, and the flight from the Trans-Tiber had wearied him exceedingly.

One thing gave him permanent comfort: he had on his person two purses—that which Vinicius had given him at home, and that which he had thrown him on the way from the cemetery. In view of this happy circumstance, and of all the excitement through which he had passed, he resolved to eat abundantly and drink better wine than he usually drank.

When the hour for opening the wineshop came at last, he wished to sleep, above all. Drowsiness overcame his strength, so that he returned with tottering step to his dwelling in the Subura, where a slave woman, purchased with money obtained from Vinicius, was waiting for him.

When he had entered a sleeping-room, he threw himself on the bed and fell asleep in one instant. He woke only in the evening, or rather he was roused by the slave woman, who called him to rise, for someone was inquiring and wished to see him on urgent business.

And he was shocked! For he saw before the door of the bedroom the gigantic form of Ursus.

At that sight he felt his feet and head grow ice-cold, his heart ceased to beat in his bosom, and shivers crept along his back. For a time he was unable to speak. Then, with chattering teeth, he said, or rather groaned, "Syra—I am not at home—I don't know that—good man—"

"I told him that you were at home, but asleep, lord," answered the girl. "He asked to awaken you."

"O gods! I will command that you—"

But Ursus, as if impatient of delay, approached the door of the sleeping-room and, bending, thrust in his head.

"O Chilo Chilonides!" he said.

"Pax! Pax!" Chilo answered. "O best of Christians! Yes, I am Chilo; but this is a mistake—I do not know you!"

"Chilo Chilonides," Ursus repeated, "your lord, Vinicius, summons you to go with me to him."

23

A piercing pain woke Vinicius. He could not understand where he was, nor what was happening. He felt a roaring in his head, and his eyes were covered with a mist. Gradually, however, his consciousness returned, and at last he saw through that mist three persons bending over him. Two he recognized. One was Ursus, the other the old man whom he had pushed aside when carrying off Lygia. The third, an utter stranger, was holding his left arm. This caused so terrible a pain that Vinicius, thinking it a kind of revenge they were taking, said through his set teeth, "Kill me!" But they paid no apparent heed to his words, just as though they did not hear them or considered them the usual groans of suffering. Ursus, with his anxious and also threatening face of a barbarian, held a bundle of white cloth torn in long strips. The old man spoke to the person who was pressing the arm of Vinicius. "Glaucus, are you certain that the wound in the head is not mortal?"

"Yes, worthy Crispus," Glaucus answered. "While serving in the fleet as a slave, and afterward while living at Naples, I cured many wounds, and with the pay that came to me from that occupation I freed myself and my relatives at last. The wound in the head is slight. When this one"—here he pointed to Ursus with his head—"took the girl from the young man, he pushed him against the wall; the young man put out his arm when he was falling, evidently to save himself. He broke and disjointed it, but by so doing saved his head and his life."

"You have had more than one of the brotherhood in your care," Crispus added, "and have the reputation of a skillful physician; therefore, I sent Ursus to bring you."

"Ursus, who on the road confessed that yesterday he was ready to kill me!"

"He confessed his intention earlier to me than to you; but I, who know you and your love for Christ, explained to him that the traitor is not you, but the unknown, who tried to persuade him to murder."

"That was an evil spirit, but I took him for an angel," Ursus said with a sigh.

"You will tell me some other time. But now we must think of this wounded man." He then began to set the arm. Though Crispus sprinkled water on his face, Vinicius fainted repeatedly from suffering; that was, however, a fortunate circumstance, since he did not feel the pain of putting his arm into joint, nor of setting it.

Glaucus fixed the limb between two strips of wood, which he bound quickly and firmly, so as to keep the arm motionless. When the operation was over, Vinicius recovered consciousness again and saw Lygia above him. She stood there at the bed holding a brass basin with water, in which from time to time Glaucus dipped a sponge and moistened the head of his patient.

Vinicius gazed and could not believe his eyes. What he saw seemed a dream, or the pleasant vision brought by a fever, and only after a long time could he whisper, "Lygia!"

The basin trembled in her hand at that sound, but she gazed at him full of sadness.

"Peace be with you!" she answered, in a low voice.

She stood there with extended arms, her face full of pity and sorrow. But he gazed, as if to fill his vision with her, so that after his lids were closed he might remember her exactly. He looked at her face, paler and smaller than it had been, at the tresses of dark hair, at the poor dress of a laboring woman; he looked so intently that her snowy forehead began to grow rose-colored under his influence. And first he thought that he would love her always; and second, that that paleness of hers and that poverty were his work —that it was he who had driven her from a house where she was loved and surrounded with plenty and comfort and thrust her into that squalid room and clothed her in that poor robe of dark wool.

He would have arrayed her in the costliest brocade, in all the jewels of the earth. Therefore, astonishment, alarm, and pity seized him, and sorrow so great that he would have fallen at her feet had he been able to move.

"Lygia," he said, "you did not permit my death."

"May God return health to you," she answered with sweetness.

For Vinicius, who knew well the wrongs he had inflicted, there was a real balm in Lygia's words. He forgot at the moment that through her mouth Christian teaching might speak; he felt only that a beloved woman was speaking, and that in her answer there was a special tenderness, a goodness simply superhuman, which shook him to the depth of his soul. As just before he had grown weak from pain, so now he grew weak from emotion. A certain faintness came on him, at once immense and agreeable.

He felt as if he were falling into some abyss, but he felt that fall to be pleasant, and that he was happy. He thought at that moment of weakness that a divinity was standing above him.

Meanwhile, Glaucus had finished washing the wound on his head and had applied a healing ointment. Ursus took the brass basin from Lygia's hands; she brought a cup of water and wine, which stood ready on the table, and put it to the wounded man's lips. Vinicius drank eagerly and felt great relief. After the operation the pain had almost passed; the wound began to grow firm; perfect consciousness returned to him.

"Give me another drink," he said.

Lygia took the empty cup to the next room; meanwhile, Crispus, after a few words with Glaucus, approached the bed, saying, "God has not permitted you, Vinicius, to accomplish an evil deed and has preserved your life so that you should come to your mind. He, before whom man is but dust, delivered you defenseless into our hands; but Christ, in whom we believe, commanded us to love even our enemies. Therefore, we have dressed your wounds, and, as Lygia has said, we will implore God to restore your health, but we cannot watch over you longer. Be in peace, and think whether you should continue your pursuit of Lygia. You have deprived her of guardians, and us of a roof, though we return you good for evil."

"Do you wish to leave me?" Vinicius asked.

"We wish to leave this house, in which prosecution by the prefect of the city may reach us. Your companion was killed; you, who are powerful among your own people, are wounded. This did not happen through our fault, but the anger of the law might fall on us."

"Have no fear of persecution," Vinicius replied. "I will protect you."

Crispus did not like to tell him that with them it was not only a question of the prefect and the police, but of him; they wished to keep Lygia from his further pursuit.

"Lord," he said, "your right arm is well. Here are tablets and a stylus; write to your servants to bring a litter this evening and bear you to your own house, where you will have more comfort than in our poverty. We dwell here with a poor widow, who will return soon with her son, and this youth will take your letter; as to us, we must all find another hiding place."

Vinicius grew pale, for he understood that they wished to separate him from Lygia and that if he lost her now he might never see her in life again. He knew indeed that things of great importance had come between him and her, in light of which, if he wished to possess her, he must seek new methods that he had not had time yet to think over. He understood, too, that whatever he might tell these people, though he should swear that he would return Lygia to Pomponia Graecina, they would not believe him and were justified in refusing belief. Instead of hunting for Lygia, he might have gone to Pomponia and sworn to her that he re-nounced pursuit, and in that case Pomponia herself would have found Lygia and brought her home. No; he felt that such promises would not restrain them and no solemn oath would be accepted, the more since, not being a Christian, he could swear only by the immortal gods, in whom he did not himself believe greatly and whom they considered to be evil spirits.

He desired desperately to influence Lygia and her guardians, but he needed time. As every fragment of a plank or an oar seems salvation to a drowning man, so it seemed to him that during those few days he might say something to bring himself nearer to her, that something favorable might happen. So he said, "Listen to me, Christians. Yesterday I was with you in Ostrianum, and I heard your teaching; but though I did not know it, your deeds have convinced me that you are honest and good people. Tell that widow who occupies this house to stay in it, stay in it yourselves, and let me stay. Let this man"—here he turned to Glaucus—"who is a physician, or at least understands the care of wounds, tell me whether it is possible to carry me from here today. I am sick and have a broken arm, which must remain immovable for a few days. I declare to you that I will not leave this house unless you remove me by force!"

Here he stopped, for breath failed him, and Crispus said, "We will use no force against you, lord; we will leave ourselves."

At this the young man, unused to resistance, frowned and said, "Permit me to recover breath," and after a while began again to speak. "Of Croton, whom Ursus killed, no one will seek. He

192

had to go today to Beneventum, where he was summoned by Vatinius; therefore, all will think that he has gone there. When I entered this house with Croton no one saw us except a Greek who was with us in Ostrainum. I will indicate to you his lodgings; bring that man to me. I will demand silence; he is paid by me. I will send a letter to my own house stating that I, too, went to Beneventum. If the Greek has informed the prefect already, I will declare that I myself killed Croton and that it was he who broke my arm. I will do this, by my father's ghost! You may remain in safety here; not a hair will fall from the head of one of you. Bring here quickly the Greek whose name is Chilo Chilonides!"

"Then Glaucus will remain with you," Crispus said, "and the widow will nurse you."

"Consider, old man, what I say," Vinicius said, frowning still more. "I owe you gratitude, and you seem good and honest; but you are not telling me what you have in the bottom of your soul. You are afraid lest I summon my slaves and command them to take Lygia. Is this true?"

"It is," Crispus said sternly.

"Then remember this: I shall speak before all to Chilo and write a letter home that I have gone to Beneventum. I shall have no messengers but you. Remember this, and do not irritate me longer."

Here he was indignant, and his face was contorted with anger. Afterward he began to speak excitedly. "Have you thought that I would deny that I wish to stay here to see her? A fool would have thought that, even had I denied it. But I will not try to take her by force any longer. I will tell you more: if she will not stay here, I will tear the bandages from my arm with this sound hand and will take neither food nor drink; let my death fall on you and your brethren. Why have you nursed me? Why have you killed me?"

Lygia, who had heard all from the other room and who was certain that Vinicius would do what he promised, was terrified. She would not have him die for anything. Wounded and defenseless, he roused in her compassion, not fear. Living from the time of her flight among people in continual religious enthusiasm, thinking only of sacrifices, offerings, and boundless charity, she had grown so committed herself to that new inspiration that for her it took the place of house, family, and lost happiness, and made her one of those Christian women who, later on, changed the former soul of the world. Vinicius had been too important in recent events, had been thrust too much upon her, to let her forget him. She had thought of him whole days, and more than once she had begged God for the moment when, following the inspiration of her faith, she might return good for his evil, mercy for his persecution, break him, win him to Christ, save him. And now it seemed to her that precisely that moment had come and that her prayers had been heard.

She approached Crispus, therefore, with a transfixed face and addressed him as though some other voice spoke through her. "Let him stay among us, Crispus, and we will stay with him until Christ gives him health."

The old presbyter, accustomed to seek in all things the inspiration of God, recognizing her exaltation, thought at once that perhaps a higher power was speaking though her, and, fearing in his heart, he bent his gray head, saying, "Let it be as you say."

On Vinicius, who the whole time had not taken his eyes from her, this ready obedience of Crispus produced a wonderful and pervading impression. It seemed to him that among the Christians Lygia was a kind of sibyl, or priestess, whom they surrounded with obedience and honor. To the love was now joined a certain awe, in presence of which love itself became something almost secondary. He could not familiarize himself, however, with the thought that their relations had changed; that now she was not dependent on his will, but he on hers; that he was lying there sick and broken; that he had ceased to be an attacking, conquering force; that he was like a defenseless child in her care. For his proud and commanding nature such relations with any other person would have been humiliating. Now, however, not only did he not feel humiliated, but he was as thankful to her as to his Caesar.

His previous excitement had so exhausted him that he could not speak, and he thanked her only with his eyes, which were gleaming from delight because he remained near her and would be able to see her—tomorrow, next day, perhaps a long time. That delight was diminished only by the dread that he might lose what he had gained. So great was this dread that when Lygia gave him water a second time, and the wish seized him to take her hand, he feared to do so. He feared! He, that Vinicius who at Caesar's feast had kissed her lips in spite of her! He, that Vinicius who after her flight had promised himself to drag her by the hair to the cubiculum.

24

But he began also to fear that some outside force might disturb his delight. Chilo might announce his disappearance to the prefect of the city, or to his freedmen at home; and in such an event an invasion of the house by the city guards was likely. In that event he might order them to seize Lygia and shut her up in his house, but he thought that he ought not to do so, and he was not capable of acting this way. He was tyrannical, insolent, and corrupt enough, but he was not Tigellinus or Nero. Military life had left in him a certain feeling of justice and fairness, and a conscience to understand that such a deed would be monstrously mean. He would have been capable, perhaps, of committing such a deed during a fit of anger and while in possession of his strength, but at that moment he was filled with tenderness and was sick.

He noticed, too, with astonishment, that from the moment when Lygia had been in his favor, neither she herself nor Crispus asked any assistance from him. They were confident that, in case of need, some superhuman power would defend them. The young tribune, since hearing the discourse of the apostle in Ostrianum, was also not too far from supposing that miracles might take place. Then he remembered what he had said of the Greek and asked again that Chilo be brought to him.

Crispus agreed, and they decided to send Ursus. Venicius said, turning to Crispus, "I give a tablet, for this man is suspicious and cunning. Frequently when summoned by me, he gave directions to answer my people that he was not at home; he did so always when he had no good news for me and feared my anger."

"If I find him, I will bring him, willing or unwilling," Ursus said. Then, taking his mantle, he went out hurriedly.

To find anyone in Rome was not easy, even with the most accurate directions; but in those cases the instinct of a hunter aided Ursus, and also his great knowledge of the city. He found himself at Chilo's lodgings, but he did not recognize Chilo, however. He had seen him but once in his life before, and in the night. Besides, that lofty and confident old man who had persuaded him to murder Glaucus was so unlike the Greek, bent double from terror, that no one could suppose the two to be one person. Chilo, noticing that Ursus looked at him as a perfect stranger, recovered from his first fear. The sight of the tablet, with the writing of Vinicius, calmed him still more. At least the suspicion that he would take him into an ambush purposely did not trouble him. He thought, besides, that the Christians had not killed Vinicius, evidently because they had not dared to strike so noted a person.

And then Vinicius will protect me in case of need, he thought. *Of course he does not send for me to deliver me to death.*

Summoning some courage, therefore, he said, "My good man, has not my friend the noble Vinicius sent a litter? My feet are swollen; I cannot walk so far."

"He has not," Ursus answered. "We shall go on foot."

"But if I refuse?"

"Do not, for you will have to go."

"And I will go, but of my own will. No one could force me, for I am a free man and a friend of the prefect of the city. As a sage, I have also means to overcome others, and I know how to turn people into trees and wild beasts. I will only put on a mantle somewhat warmer, and a hood, lest the slaves of that quarter might recognize me; they would stop me every moment to kiss my hands."

He put on a new mantle then, and let down a broad Gallic hood, lest Ursus might recognize his features upon clearer light.

"Where will you take me?" he asked on the road.

"To the Trans-Tiber."

"I have not been in Rome a long time, and I have never been to that district, but there, too, of course, men who love virtue live."

But Ursus, who had heard Vinicius say that the Greek had

been with him in Ostrianum and had seen him with Croton enter the house in which Lygia lived, stopped for a moment and said, "Speak no untruth, old man, for today you were with Vinicius in Ostrianum and under our gate."

"Ah!" Chilo said, "then that is your house in the Trans-Tiber? I have not been long in Rome and do not know how the different parts are named. That is true, friend; I was under the gate and implored Vinicius in the name of virtue not to enter. I was in Ostrianum, and do you know why? I am working for a certain time over the conversion of Vinicius and wished him to hear the chief of the apostles. May the light penetrate his soul and yours! But you are a Christian and wish truth to overcome falsehood."

"That is true," Ursus answered humbly.

Courage returned to Chilo completely.

"Vinicius is a powerful lord," he said, "and a friend of Caesar's. He listens often yet to the whisperings of the evil spirit; but if even a hair should fall from his head, Caesar would take vengeance on all the Christians"

"A higher power is protecting us."

"Surely! But what do you intend to do with Vinicius?" Chilo asked, with fresh alarm.

"I do not know. Christ commands mercy."

"You have answered well. Think of this always, or you will fry in hell like a sausage in a frying pan."

Ursus sighed, and Chilo thought that he could always do what he liked with that man, who was terrible at the moment of his first outburst. So, wishing to know what happened at the seizing of Lygia, he asked further, in the voice of a stern judge, "How did you treat Croton? Speak, and do not lie."

Ursus sighed a second time. "Vinicius will tell you."

"That means that you stabbed him with a knife, or killed him with a club."

"I was without a weapon."

The Greek could not resist amazement at the superhuman strength of the barbarian.

"May Pluto—that is to say—may Christ pardon you!"

They went on for some time in silence. Then Chilo said, "I will not betray you, but be careful of the watches."

"I fear Christ, not the guards."

"And that is proper. There is no more grievous crime than murder. I will pray for you, but I know not if even my prayer can be effective, unless you make a vow never to touch anyone else in life with even a finger."

"I have not killed on purpose," Ursus answered.

But Chilo, who desired to secure himself in every case, did not cease to condemn murder and urge Ursus to make the vow. He asked also about Vinicius; but the Lygian answered his inquires unwillingly, repeating that he would hear from Vinicius himself what he needed. They passed at last the long road that separated the lodgings of the Greek from the Trans-Tiber and found themselves before the house. Chilo's heart began to pound again. It seemed to him that Ursus was beginning to look at him with a kind of greedy expression.

It is small consolation to me, he said to himself, *if he kills me unwillingly. I prefer in every case that paralysis should strike him, and with him all Lygians—which you bring about, O Zeus, if you are able.*

Finally, when they had passed the entrance and the first court and found themselves in a corridor leading to the garden of the little house, he halted and said, "Let me draw my breath, or I shall not be able to speak with Vinicius and give him saving advice."

He halted; for though he said to himself that no danger threatened, still his legs trembled under him at the thought that he was among those mysterious people whom he had seen in Ostrianum.

Meanwhile, a hymn came to their ears from the little house.

"What is that?" inquired Chilo.

"You say that you are a Christian, and yet you do not know that among us it is the custom after every meal to glorify our Savior with singing," Ursus answered. "Miriam and her son must have returned, and perhaps the apostle is with them, for he visits the widow and Crispus every day."

"Conduct me directly to Vinicius."

They entered. It was rather dark in the room; the evening was cloudy and cold, and the flames of a few candles did not dispel the darkness altogether. Vinicius sensed rather than recognized

198

Chilo in the hooded man. Chilo, seeing the bed in the corner of the room, and on it Vinicius, moved toward him directly, not looking at the others, as if it would be safest near him.

"Oh lord, why did you not listen to my counsels?" he exclaimed, putting his hands together.

"Silence!" Vinicius said. "And listen!"

Here he looked sharply into Chilo's eyes and spoke slowly with emphasis, as if wishing the Greek to understand every word of his as a command and to keep it forever in memory.

"Croton threw himself on me to kill and rob me, do you understand? I killed him then, and these people dressed the wounds I received in the struggle."

Chilo understood in a moment that if Vinicius spoke in this way it must be in virtue of some agreement with the Christians, and in that case he wished people to believe him. So in one moment, without showing doubt or astonishment, he raised his eyes and exclaimed, "That was a treacherous scoundrel ruffian! But I warned you, lord, not to trust him; my teachings bounce from his thoughts as do peas when thrown against a wall. In all hades there are not torments enough for him. He who cannot be honest must be a rogue; what is more difficult than for a rogue to become honest? But to fall on his benefactor, a lord so generous—O gods!"

Here he remembered that he had represented himself to Ursus on the way as a Christian, and stopped.

"I bless the moment in which I advised you to take a knife."

Vinicius turned and glanced at the Greek, and asked, "What have you done today?"

"How? What! Have I not told you, lord, that I made a vow for your health?"

"Nothing more?"

"I was just preparing to visit you when this good man came and said that you had sent for me."

"Here is a tablet. You will go to my house; you will find my freedman and give it to him. It is written on the tablet that I have gone to Beneventum. You will tell Demas from yourself that I went this morning, summoned by an urgent letter from Petronius." Here he repeated with emphasis: "I have gone to Beneventum, do you understand?"

"You have gone, lord. This morning I took leave of you at the Porta Capena, and from the time of your departure such sadness possessed me that if your goodness will not soften it, I shall cry myself to death, like the unhappy wife of Zethos in grief for Itylos, who turned into a nightingale."

Vinicius, though sick and accustomed to the Greek's cunning, could not repress a smile. He was glad that Chilo understood in a flash; so he said, "Therefore I will write that your tears be wiped away. Give me the candle." Chilo, now pacified perfectly, rose, and, advancing a few steps toward the chimney, took one of the candles that was burning at the wall. But while he was doing this, the hood slipped from his head and the light fell directly on his face. Glaucus sprang from his seat and stood before him.

"Do you not recognize me, Cephas?" he asked. In his voice there was something so terrible that a shiver ran through all present.

Chilo raised the candle and dropped it to the earth almost the same instant; then he bent nearly double and began to groan, "I am not he—I am not he! Mercy!"

Glaucus turned toward the faithful and said, "This is the man who betrayed me—who ruined me and my family!"

That history was known to all the Christians and to Vinicius, who had not guessed who that Glaucus was—for this reason only, that he fainted repeatedly from pain during the dressing of his wound and had not heard his name. But for Ursus that short moment, with the words of Glaucus, was like a lightening flash in darkness. Recognizing Chilo, he was at his side with one spring and, seizing his arm, bent it back, exclaiming, "This is the man who persuaded me to kill Glaucus!"

"Mercy!" Chilo groaned. "I will give you—O lord!" he exclaimed, turning his head toward Vinicius. "Save me! I trusted in you—take my part. Your letter—I will deliver it. O lord, lord!"

But Vinicius, who looked with more indifference than anyone at what was happening, first because all the affairs of the Greek were more or less known to him, and second because his heart did not know what pity was, said, "Bury him in the garden; someone else will take the letter."

It seemed to Chilo that those words were his final sentence. His bones were shaking in the terrible hands of Ursus; his eyes were filed with tears from pain.

"By your God, pity!" he cried. "I am a Christian! *Pax vobiscum!* I am a Christian; and if you do not believe me, baptize me again, baptize me twice, ten times! Glaucus, that is a mistake! Let me speak, make me a slave! Do not kill me! Have mercy!"

His voice, stifled with pain, was growing weaker and weaker, when the apostle Peter rose at the table; for a moment his white head shook, drooping toward his breast, and his eyes were closed; but he opened them then, and said amid silence, "The Savior said this to us: 'If your brother has sinned against you, chastise him, but if he is repentant, forgive him. And if he has offended seven times in the day against you, and has turned to you seven times saying, "Have mercy on me!" forgive him.'"

Then came a still deeper silence. Glaucus remained a long time with his hands covering his face. At last he removed them and said, "Cephas, may God forgive your offenses, as I forgive them in the name of Christ."

Ursus, letting go the arms of the Greek, added at once: "May the Savior be merciful to you as I forgive you."

Chilo dropped to the ground and, supported on it with his hands, turned his head like a wild beast caught in a snare, looking around to see from where death might come. He did not trust his eyes and ears yet and dared not hope for forgiveness. Consciousness returned to him slowly; his blue lips were still trembling from terror.

"Depart in peace!" the apostle said, meanwhile.

Chilo rose but could not speak. He approached the bed of Vinicius, as if seeking protection in it still; for he had not yet had time to think that that man, though he had used his services and was still his accomplice, condemned him, while those against whom he had acted, forgave him. This thought was to come to him later. At present, simple astonishment and disbelief consumed him. Though he had seen that they forgave him, he wished to hide his head at the earliest from among these incomprehensible people, whose kindness terrified him almost as much as their cruelty would have done. It seemed to him that should he remain longer, something unexpected would happen again; so, standing above Vinicius, he said with a broken voice, "Give the letter, lord—give the letter!" And, snatching the tablet Vinicius handed him, he made one bow to the Christians, another to the sick man, pushed along sideways by the wall, and hurried out through the door. In the garden, when darkness surrounded him, fear raised the hair on his head again, for he thought that Ursus would rush out and kill him in the night. He would have run with all his might, but his legs would not move; the next moment they were totally uncontrollable, for Ursus stood very near him.

Chilo fell with his face to the earth and began to groan. "Urban—in Christ's name—"

But Urban said, "Fear not. The apostle commanded me to lead you out beyond the gate, in case you might go astray in the darkness, and, if strength failed you, to conduct you home."

"What do you say?" asked Chilo, raising his face. "What? You will not kill me?"

"No, I will not; and if I seized you too roughly and harmed a bone in you, pardon me."

"Help me to rise," the Greek said. "You will not kill me? You will not? Take me to the street; I will go farther alone."

Ursus raised him as he might a feather and placed him on his feet; then he led him through the dark corridor to the second court. From there was a passage to the entrance and the street. In the corridor Chilo repeated again in his soul, *It is all over with me!* Only when he found himself on the street did he recover and say, "I can go on alone."

"Peace be with you."

"And with you! Let me draw my breath."

And after Ursus had gone, he took a full deep breath. He felt his waist and hips, as if to convince himself that he was living, and then moved forward with hurried step.

"But why did they not kill me?" And in spite of all his talk with Euricius about Christian teaching, in spite of his conversation at the river with Urban, and in spite of all that he had heard in Ostrianum, he could find no answer to that question.

25

Vinicius could not discover the cause of what happened either; and in the depths of his being he was almost as much astonished as Chilo. The fact that these people should dress his wounds carefully instead of avenging his attack he associated with the doctrine they confessed, Lygia, and his great social standing. But their conduct with Chilo simply went beyond the power of forgiveness. Why did they not kill the Greek? They might have justly killed him. Ursus would have buried him in the garden, or taken him in the dark to the Tiber, which during that period of night murders, committed even by Caesar himself, cast up human bodies so frequently in the morning that no one asked where they came from. True, pity was not entirely a stranger to the world in which the young patrician belonged. The Athenians raised an altar to pity and for a long time opposed the introduction of gladiatorial combats into Athens. In Rome itself the conquered received pardon at times. Calicratus, king of the Britons, was taken prisoner in the time of Claudius and was provided for by him bountifully. But vengeance for a personal wrong seemed to Vinicius, and to all, proper and justified. The neglect of vengeance could not be comprehended. True, he had heard in Ostrianum that one should love even enemies; that, however, he considered as a kind of theory without application. Perhaps they had not killed Chilo because the day was among festivals or was in some period of the moon during which it was not proper for Christians to kill a man. He had heard that there are days among various nations during which it is not permitted to begin even war. But why, in such a case, did they not deliver the Greek to justice? Why did the apostle say that if a man offended seven times, it was necessary to forgive him seven times; and why did Glaucus say to Chilo, "May God forgive you, as I forgive you"?

Chilo had done him the most terrible wrong that one man could do another. The thought of how he would act with a man who killed Lygia caused the blood of Vinicius to boil, as does water in a caldron; there were no torments he would not inflict in his vengeance! But Glaucus had forgiven. Ursus, too, had forgiven

—Ursus, who might in fact kill whomever he wished in Rome with perfect ease. There was only one answer to all these questions: they refrained from killing him because of a goodness so great that its power had not been in the world up to that time and because of an unbounded love of neighbor, which commands one to forget one's self, wrongs, happiness, and misfortune, and live for others. What reward these people were to receive for this, Vinicius heard in Ostrianum, but he could not understand it. He thought, however, that the earthly life connected with the duty of renouncing everything good and rich for the benefit of others must be wretched. So his thoughts of the Christians at that moment were a mixture of astonishment, pity, and a shade of contempt. It seemed to him that they were sheep that sooner or later must be eaten by wolves; his Roman nature could yield no recognition to people who let themselves be devoured. He noticed, however, that after Chilo's departure the faces of all were bright with a certain deep joy. The apostle approached Glaucus, placed his hand on his head, and said, "In you Christ has triumphed."

The other raised his eyes, which were full of hope and as bright with joy as if some great, unexpected happiness had been poured on him. Vinicius, who could understand only joy or delight born of vengeance or lust, looked on him with eyes staring from fever, as if he were a madman. He saw, however, with inward scorn, Lygia press her lips of a queen to the hand of that man who had the appearance of a slave; and it seemed to him that the order of the world was utterly turned upside down. Next, Ursus told how he had led Chilo to the street and had asked forgiveness for the harm he might have done to his bones; for this the apostle blessed him also. Crispus declared that it was a day of great victory. Hearing of this victory, Vinicius lost his train of thought altogether.

But when Lygia gave him a cooling drink again, he held her hand for a moment and asked, "Then must you also forgive me?"

"We are Christians. It is not permitted us to keep anger in the heart."

"Lygia," he said, "whoever your God is, I honor Him only because He is yours."

"You will honor Him in your heart when you love Him."

"Only because He is yours," Vinicius repeated, in a fainter voice; and he closed his eyes, for weakness had overcome him again.

Lygia went out but returned later and bent over him to learn if he were sleeping. Vinicius, sensing that she was near, opened his eyes and smiled. She placed her hand over them lightly, as if to cause him to slumber. A great sweetness seized him; but soon he felt more seriously ill than before and was very ill in reality. Night had come, and with it a more violent fever. He could not sleep and followed Lygia with his eyes wherever she went.

He had feverish dreams. In some old, deserted cemetery stood a temple, in the form of a tower, in which Lygia was priestess. He did not take his eyes from her but saw her on the summit of the tower, with a lute in her hands, all in the light, like those priestesses who in the night sing hymns in honor of the moon and whom he had seen in the Orient. He himself was climbing up winding steps, with great effort, to steal her away with him. Chilo was creeping up behind, with teeth chattering from terror, and repeating, "Do not do that, lord; she is a priestess, for whom He will take vengeance." Vinicius did not know who that He was, but he understood that he himself was going to commit some sacrilege, and he felt a boundless fear also. But when he went to the balcony surrounding the summit of the tower, the apostle with his silvery beard suddenly stood at Lygia's side and said, "Do not raise a hand; she belongs to me." Then he moved forward with her, on a path formed by rays from the moon, as if on a path made to heaven. He stretched his hands toward them and begged both to take him into their company.

Here he woke and looked before him. The lamp on the tall staff shone more dimly but still cast a clear light. All were sitting in front of the fire warming themselves, for the night was chilly and the room rather cold. Vinicius saw the breath coming as steam from their lips. In the midst of them sat the apostle. At his knees, on a low footstool, was Lygia. Farther on were Glaucus, Crispus, and Miriam; at the edge, Ursus was on one side, and on the other was Miriam's son Nazarius, a youth with a handsome face and long, dark hair reaching down to his shoulders.

Lygia looked at the apostle, and every head was turned toward him, while he told something in an undertone. Vinicius gazed at Peter with a certain superstitious awe, hardly inferior to that terror he experienced during the feverish dream. The thought passed through his mind that that dream had touched truth; that the gray-haired there, who came from distant shores, would take Lygia from him by unknown paths. He felt sure also that the old man was speaking of him, perhaps telling them how to separate him from Lygia, for it seemed to him impossible that anyone could speak of anything else. So he listened to Peter's words.

But he was mistaken altogether, for the apostle was speaking of Christ again.

They live their lives only through that name, Vinicius thought.

The old man was describing the arrest of Christ. "A company came, and servants of the priest, to seize Him. When the Savior asked whom they were seeking, they answered, 'Jesus of Nazareth.' But when He said to them, 'I am He,' they fell on the ground and dared not raise a hand on Him. Only after the second inquiry did they seize Him."

Here the apostle stopped, stretched out his hands toward the fire, and continued. "The night was cold, like this one, but I was angry; so, drawing a sword to defend Him, I cut an ear from the servant of the high priest. I would have defended Him more than my own life had He not said to me, 'Put your sword into the sheath: the cup which my Father has given me, shall I not drink it?' Then they seized and bound Him."

Peter then placed his palm on his forehead and was silent, wishing before he went further to stop the crowd of his recollections. But Ursus, unable to restrain himself, sprang to his feet and trimmed the light on the staff until the sparks scattered in golden rain and the flame shot up with more strength.

Though he was ready at all times to kiss the feet of the apostle, that act was one he could not accept; if someone in his presence had raised hands on the Redeemer, if he had been with Him on that night—oh! Splinters would have shot from the soldiers, the servants of the priest, and the officials. Tears came to his eyes at the very thought of this, and because of his sorrow and mental struggle; for on the one hand he thought that he would not only have defended the Redeemer but would have called Lygians to his aid—splendid fellows—and on the other, if he had acted this way he would have disobeyed the Redeemer and hindered the salvation of man.

Vinicius was overpowered by a new, feverish, waking dream. He remembered Peter's speech in which Christ appeared on the shore of the sea of Tiberius. He saw a sheet of water and on it a fisherman's boat, with Peter and Lygia. He himself was moving with all his might after that boat, but pain in his broken arm prevented him from reaching it. The wind hurled waves in his eyes, and he began to sink and called for rescue. Lygia knelt down before the apostle, who turned his boat and reached an oar, which Vinicius seized. With their assistance he entered the boat and fell to the bottom.

He saw a multitude of people sailing after them. Waves covered their heads with foam; in the whirl only the hands of a few could be seen; but Peter saved those drowning and gathered them into his boat, which grew larger, as if by a miracle. Soon crowds filled it, more numerous than those that were gathered before Ostrianum. Vinicius wondered how they could find room there, and he was afraid that they would sink to the bottom. But Lygia calmed him by showing him a light on the distant shore toward which they were sailing.

These dream pictures of Vinicius were blended again with descriptions he had heard in Ostrianum, from the lips of the apostle, as to how Christ had appeared on the lake. He saw now in that light on the shore a certain form toward which Peter was steering, and as he approached it the weather grew calmer, the water grew smoother, the light became greater. The crowd began to sing sweet hymns; the air was filled with the odor of nard; the water formed a rainbow, as if from the bottom of the lake lilies and roses were seen; and at last the boat struck its prow safely against the sand. Lygia took his hand and said, "Come, I will lead you!" and she led him to the light.

Vinicius woke again; but his dreaming ceased slowly. For a long time it seemed to him that he was still on the lake and surrounded by crowds, among which he began to look for Petronius and was astonished not to find him. The bright light from the chimney brought him completely to his senses. Olive sticks were burning slowly under the rosy ashes; but the splinters of pine, which evidently had been put there some moments before, shot up a bright flame, and in the light of this, Vinicius saw Lygia.

The sight of her touched him to the depth of his soul. He remembered that she had spent the night before in Ostrianum and had busied herself the whole day in nursing him, and now, when all had gone to rest, she was the only one watching. It was easy to see that she must be wearied, for while sitting motionless her eyes were closed. He looked at her profile, at her drooping lashes, at her hands lying on her knees; and in his pagan head the idea began to awaken with difficulty that beside Greek and Roman beauty and symmetry there is another in the world, new and immensely pure, in which a soul has its dwelling.

He could not bring himself so far as to call it Christian, but, thinking of Lygia, he could not separate her from the religion she confessed. He understood that if all the others had gone to rest, and she alone were watching, she whom he had injured, it was because her religion commanded her to watch. He would rather that Lygia acted thus out of love for him, his face, his eyes, his statuesque form—in a word for reasons because of which more than once snow-white Grecian and Roman arms had been wound around his neck.

She opened her eyes then, and, seeing that Vinicius was gazing at her, she approached him and said, "I am with you."

"I saw your soul in a dream," he replied.

26

The next morning he woke up weak, but with a cool head and free of fever. Ursus, stooping before the chimney, was raking apart the gray ashes, seeking live coals beneath them. When he found some, he began to blow, not with his mouth it seemed, but with the bellows of a blacksmith. Vinicius, remembering how that man had crushed Croton the day before, examined with attention as a lover of the arena his gigantic back, which resembled the back of a Cyclops, and his limbs strong as columns.

Thanks to Mercury that my neck was not broken by him, Vinicius thought. *By Pollux! If the other Lygians are like this one, the Danubian legions will have heavy work!*

But aloud he said, "Hey, slave!"

Ursus drew his head out of the chimney and, smiling in an almost friendly manner, said, "God give you a good day, lord, and good health; but I am a free man, not a slave."

Vinicius wished to question Ursus concerning Lygia's birthplace. So these words produced a pleasant impression; for discussion with a free though common man was less disagreeable to his Roman and patrician pride than with a slave, in whom neither law nor custom recognized human nature.

"Then you do not belong to Aulus?" he asked.

"No, lord, I serve Callina, as I served her mother, of my own will."

Here he hid his head again in the chimney, to blow the coals, on which he had placed some wood. When he had finished, he took it out and said, "With us there are no slaves."

"Where is Lygia?" Vinicius asked.

"She has gone out, and I am to cook food for you. She watched over you the whole night."

"Why did you not take her place?"

"Because she wished to care for you, and I would not refuse."

"Are you sorry for not having killed me?"

"No, lord. Christ has not commanded us to kill."

"But Atacinus and Croton?"

"I could not do otherwise," muttered Ursus. And he looked with regret on his hands, which had remained pagan to a degree, though his soul had accepted the cross. Then he put a pot on the hearth and fixed his thoughtful eyes on the fire.

"That was your fault, lord," he said at last. "Why did you raise your hand against her, a king's daughter?"

Vinicius was indignant because a common man and barbarian had not merely dared to speak to him with familiarity, but to blame him as well. But because he was weak and had no slaves with him, he restrained himself, especially since he wished to learn some details of Lygia's life.

He calmed himself and asked about the war of the Lygians against Vannius and the Suevi. Ursus was glad to talk but could not add much that was new to what Aulus Plautius had told. Ursus had not been in battle, for he had attended the hostages to the camp of Atelius Hister. Immediately after they received news that the Semnones had set fire to forests on their boundaries, they returned in haste to avenge the wrong, and the hostages remained with Atelius, who ordered at first to give them kingly honors. Afterward, Lygia's mother died. The Roman commander did not know what to do with the child. Ursus wished to return with her to their own country, but the road was unsafe because of wild beasts and wild tribes. When the news came that a group of Lygians had visited Pomponius, offering him aid against the Marcomani, Hister sent him with Lygia to Pomponius. When they came to him they learned, however, that no ambassadors had been there, and they remained in the camp. Pomponius took them to Rome, and at the conclusion of his triumph he gave the king's daughter to Pomponia Graecina.

Vinicius had an enormous sense of the pride of family name. He was pleased that an eyewitness had confirmed Lygia's royal descent. As a king's daughter she might occupy a position at Caesar's court equal to the daughters of the very first families of Rome, all the more since the nation whose ruler her father had been had not warred with Rome so far, and, though barbarian, it might become formidable; for, according to Ursus, it possessed an immense force of warriors.

"We live in the woods," he said in answer to Vinicius, "but we have so much land that no man knows where it ends, and there are many people. There are also wooden towns in the forests, in which there is great wealth. When the Semnones, the Marcomani, the Vandals, and the Quadi plunder through the world, we take from them. They dare not come to us; but when the wind blows from their side, they burn our forests. We fear neither them nor the Roman Caesar."

210

"The gods gave Rome dominion over the earth," Vinicius said severely.

"The gods are evil spirits," Ursus replied simply, "and where there are no Romans, there is no supremacy."

Here he fixed the fire and said, "When Caesar took Callina to the palace, and I thought that harm might come, I wanted to go to the forest and bring Lygians to help the king's daughter. And the Lygians would have moved toward the Danube, for they are virtuous people, though pagan. If ever Callina returns to Pomponia Graecina I will bow down to her for permission to go to them; for Christus was born far from them, and they have not even heard of Him. He knew better than I where He should be born; but if He had come to the world with us, in the forests, we would not have tortured Him to death, that is certain. We would have taken care of the Child, and guarded Him, so He would never lack meat, mushrooms, beaver skins, or amber. And what we plundered from the Suevi and the Marcomani we would have given Him, so that He might have comfort and plenty."

He put the vessel with food for Vinicius near the fire and was silent. Then he poured the liquid into a shallow plate and, cooling it properly, said, "Glaucus advises you, lord, to move even your sound arm as little as possible; Callina has asked me to give you food."

But Ursus proved to be an awkward and painstaking nurse; the cup was lost among his Herculean fingers so completely that there was no place left for the mouth of the sick man. After a few fruitless efforts the giant was troubled greatly, and said, "Ei! It would be easier to lead an ox out of a snare."

"Have you tried to take such beasts by the horns?" Vinicius asked.

"Until the twentieth winter passed over me, I was afraid," Ursus answered, "but after that it happened."

And he began to feed Vinicius still more awkwardly than before.

But now Lygia's pale face appeared from behind the curtain.

"I will help you," she said. She came from the cubiculum, in which she had been preparing to sleep, for she was in a single close tunic covering the breast completely, and her hair was unbound. Vinicius, whose heart beat with more quickness at the sight of her, began to scold her for not thinking of sleep; but she answered him cheerfully, "I was just preparing to sleep, but first I will take the place of Ursus."

She took the cup and, sitting on the edge of the bed, began to give food to Vinicius, who felt at once overcome and delighted. The warmth of her body struck him, and her unbound hair fell on his breast. He grew pale from this experience, but in the strong heat of desires he felt also that her head was dear and magnified above all, in comparison with which the whole world was worth nothing. At first he had desired her; now he began to love her with a full heart. Before that, as generally in life and in feeling, he had been, like all people of that time, a blind, unconditional egotist, who thought only of himself. Now he finally began to think of someone else.

After a while he refused further nourishment; and though he found inexhaustible delight in her presence and in looking at her, he said, "Enough! Go to rest, my divine one."

"Do not address me in that way," Lygia answered. "It is not proper for me to hear such words."

She smiled at him, however, and said that she would not go to rest until Glaucus came. Vinicius listened to her words as to music; his heart rose with increasing delight and gratitude.

"Lygia," he said, after a moment of silence, "I did not know you before. But I know now that I wished to gain you falsely; so please return to Pomponia Graecina and be assured that in the future no hand will be raised against you."

She became downcast. "I cannot return to her now."

"Why?" Vinicius asked with surprise.

"We Christians know, through Acte, what is done on the Palatine. Have you not heard that Caesar, soon after my flight and before his departure for Naples, summoned Aulus and Pomponia and, thinking that they had helped me, threatened them with his anger? Fortunately Aulus was able to say to him, 'You know, lord, that a lie has never passed my lips; I swear to you now that we did not help her escape, and we do not know what has happened to her,' and Caesar believed them. By the advice of the elders I have never written to mother from where I am, so that she might take an oath boldly at all times that she has no knowledge of me. You will not understand this, perhaps, Vinicius; but it is not permitted for us to lie, even in a question of survival. This is the heart of our religion. Therefore I have not seen Pomponia from the hour when I left. From time to time distant echoes barely reach her that I am alive and not in danger."

Here a longing filled Lygia, and her eyes were moist with tears; but she calmed herself quickly and said, "I know that Pomponia, too, yearns for me; but we have hope that others do not have."

"Yes," Vinicius answered, "Christ is your consolation, but I do not understand that."

"Look at the Christians! For us there are no lasting sufferings. And death itself, which for you is the end of life, is for us merely its beginning—the exchange of a lower for a higher happiness, a happiness less complete for one that is eternal. Consider a religion that asks us to love even our enemies, forbids falsehood, purifies our souls from hatred, and promises total happiness after death."

"I heard those teachings in Ostrianum through Peter, and I have seen how you acted with me and with Chilo; when I remember your deeds, they are like a marvelous dream, and it seems that I should not believe my ears or eyes. But answer this question: Are you happy?"

"I am," Lygia answered. "One who confesses Christ cannot be unhappy."

"And have you no wish to return to Pomponia?"

"I should like very much to return to her; and shall return, if it be God's will."

"Therefore please do so, and I swear that I will not raise a hand against you."

Lygia thought for a moment, then answered, "No, I cannot expose those near me to danger. Caesar does not like the Plautiuses. If I return—you know how all news is spread throughout Rome by slaves—my return would be spoken about in the city. Nero would hear of it through his slaves and punish Aulus and Pomponia—at least take me from them a second time."

"True," Vinicius answered, frowning, "that would be possible. He would do so, even to show that his will must be obeyed. It is true that he only forgot you because the loss was not his, but mine. Perhaps, if he took you from Aulus and Pomponia, he would send you to me and I could give you back to them."

"Vinicius, would you see me again on the Palatine?" Lygia asked.

He gritted his teeth and answered, "No. You are right. I spoke like a fool! No!"

And all at once he saw before him a cliff without bottom. He was a patrician, a military tribune, a powerful man; but above every power of that world to which he belonged was a madman whose will and evil power it was impossible to control. Only such people as the Christians might cease to reckon with Nero or fear him—people for whom this whole world, with its separations and sufferings, was as nothing; people for whom death itself was as nothing. All others had to tremble before him. The terrors of the time in which they lived were displayed before Vinicius in all their monstrous reality. He could not return Lygia to Aulus and Pomponia through fear that the monster would remember her and turn his anger on her. If he should take her as his wife, he might expose her, himself, and Aulus. Vinicius realized, for the first time in his life, that the world must change and be transformed, or life would become altogether impossible. He understood, also, which only a moment before had been unclear to him, that in such times only Christians could be happy.

He understood, too, that it was he who had so complicated his own life and Lygia's that no positive outcome was possible. And under the influence of that sorrow he began to speak.

"Do you know that you are happier than I am? You are in poverty; and in this one room, among simple people, you have your religion and your Christ; but I have only you, and when I lacked you I was like a beggar without a roof above him and without bread. You are dearer to me than the whole world. I sought you, for I could not live without you. I wished neither feasts nor sleep. Had it not been for the hope of finding you, I should have fallen on a sword. But I fear death, for if I were dead I could not see you. I speak the pure truth in saying that I shall not be able to live without you. I have lived so far only in the hope of finding and beholding you.

"Do you remember our conversation at the house of Aulus? Once you drew a fish for me on the sand, and I did not know its meaning. Do you remember how we played ball? I loved you then above life, and you had begun already to realize that I loved you. Aulus came, frightened us with Libitina, and interrupted our talk. Pomponia, at parting, told Petronius that God is one, almighty, and all-merciful, but it did not even occur to us that Christ was your God and hers. Let Him give you to me, and I will love Him, though He seems to me a god of slaves, foreigners, and beggars. You sit near me and think of Him only. Think of me, too, or I shall hate Him. For me you alone are a divinity. Blessed be your father and mother; blessed the land that produced you! I should wish to embrace your feet and pray to you, give you honor, homage, and offerings, divine one! You do not know how I love you."

He placed his hand on his pale forehead and closed his eyes. His nature never knew limits in either love or anger. He spoke with enthusiasm, like a man who, having lost self-control, has no wish to observe any restraint in words or feelings. But he spoke sincerely from the depth of his soul. The pain, ecstasy, desire, and homage combined in his heart had burst forth at last in an irresistible torrent of words. To Lygia his words appeared blasphemous, but still her heart began to beat as if it would tear the tunic enclosing her bosom. She could not resist pity for him and his suffering. She was moved by the homage with which he spoke to her. She felt beloved and deified without measure. She felt that that unbending and dangerous man belonged to her now, soul and body, like a slave; and that feeling of his submission and her own power filled her with happiness.

Her recollections revived in one moment. He was for her again that splendid Vinicius, beautiful as a pagan god; was again the one who in the house of Aulus had spoken to her of love and roused as if from sleep her half-childlike heart; was again the one from whose embraces Ursus had separated her on the Palatine, as he might have separated her from flames. But at present, with ecstasy and at the same time with pain in his eagle face, with pale forehead and imploring eyes—wounded, broken by love, loving, full of homage and submissive—he seemed to her just as she would have wished him, the way she would have loved him with her whole soul, dearer than he had ever been before.

All at once she understood that a moment might come in which his love would seize her and bear her away, as a whirlwind; and when she felt this, she had the same impression that he had a moment before—that she was standing on the edge of a cliff. Was it for this that she had left the house of Aulus? Was it for this that she had saved herself by flight? Was it for this that she had hidden so long in wretched parts of the city? Who was this Vinicius? An Augustian, a soldier, a courtier of Nero! Moreover, he took part in his excess and madness, as was shown by that feast, which she could not forget; and he went with others to the temples and made offerings to vile gods, in whom he did not believe, perhaps, but still he gave them official honor. Still more he had pursued her to make her his slave and mistress, and at the same time to thrust her into that terrible world of excess, luxury, crime, and dishonor that calls for the anger and vengeance of God. He seemed changed, it is true, but still he had just said to her that if she would think more of Christ than of him, he was ready to hate Christ. It seemed to Lygia that the very idea of any other love than the love of Christ was a sin against Him and against her religion. When she saw, then, that other feelings and desires might be roused in the depth of her soul, she was taken by alarm for her own future.

At this moment of internal struggle Glaucus appeared, who had come to care for the patient and study his health. In the twinkle of an eye, anger and impatience were reflected on the face of Vinicius. He was angry that his conversation with Lygia had been interrupted; and when Glaucus questioned him, he answered with almost contempt. It is true that he shifted his mood quickly; but if Lygia had any illusions as to this—that what he had heard in Ostrianum might have acted on his unyielding nature—those illusions would vanish. He had changed only for her; but beyond that single feeling there remained in his being the former harsh and selfish heart, truly Roman and wolfish, incapable not only of the sweet sentiment of Christian teaching but even of gratitude.

She went away at last filled with internal care and anxiety.

Formerly in her prayers she had offered to Christ a calm heart, and truly pure as a tear. Now that calmness was disturbed. To the interior of the flower a poisonous insect had come and begun to buzz. Even sleep, in spite of the two nights spent without sleep, brought her no relief. She dreamed that at Ostrianum Nero, at the head of a whole band of Augustians, bacchic dancers, Corybants, and gladiators, was trampling crowds of Christians with his chariot wreathed in roses; and Vinicius seized her by the arm, drew her to the chariot, and, pressing her to his bosom, whispered, "Come with us."

27

From that moment Lygia rarely appeared in the common chamber. But peace did not return to her. She saw that Vinicius followed her with an imploring glance; that he was waiting for every word of hers, as for a favor; that he suffered and dared not complain, lest he might turn her away from him; that she alone was his health and delight. And then her heart swelled with compassion. Soon she observed, too, that the more she tried to avoid him, the more compassion she had for him; and by this itself the more tender were the feelings that rose in her. Peace left her. At times she said to herself that it was her special duty to be near him always; first, because the religion of God commands return of good for evil; second, that by conversing with him, she might attract him to the faith. But at the same time conscience told her that she was tempting herself; that only love for him and the charm he exerted were attracting her, nothing else.

She lived in a ceaseless struggle, which was intensified daily. At times it seemed that a kind of net surrounded her, and that in trying to break through it she entangled herself more and more. She had also to confess that for her the sight of him was becoming more desirable, his voice was becoming dearer, and that she had to struggle with all her might against the wish to sit at his bedside. When she approached him, and he grew radiant, delight filled her heart. On a certain day she noticed traces of tears on his eyelids, and for the first time the thought came to her to dry them with kisses. Terrified by that thought, and full of self-contempt, she wept all the following night.

When at moments his eyes flashed with petulance, self-will, and anger, he restrained those flashes promptly and looked with alarm at her, as if to implore pardon. This acted still more on her. Never had she such a feeling of being greatly loved as then; and when she thought of this, she felt at once guilty and happy. Vinicius, too, had changed. In his conversations with Glaucus there was less pride. It occurred to him that even that poor slave physician and that foreign woman, old Miriam, who surrounded him with attention, and Crispus, whom he saw absorbed in continual prayer, were still human. He was astonished at such thoughts, but he had them. After a time he began a liking for Ursus, with whom he talked for entire days; for with him he could talk about Lygia. The giant, on his part, was talkative, and while performing the most simple services for the sick man he began to show him also some attachment. For Vinicius, Lygia had been at all times a being of another order, higher a hundred times than those around her; nevertheless, he began to observe simple and poor people— a thing he had never done before—and he discovered in them various attractive traits.

Nazarius, however, he could not endure, for it seemed to him that the young lad had dared to fall in love with Lygia. He had avoided her for a long time, it is true; but once when he brought her two quails, which he had bought in the market with his own earned money, and heard Lygia's thanks, he grew terribly pale; and when he went out to get water for the birds, Vinicius said, "Lygia, can you accept these gifts? Do you not know that the Greeks call people of his nation Jewish dogs?"

"I do not know what the Greeks call them; but I know that Nazarius is a Christian and my brother."

When she had said this she looked at Vinicius with astonishment and regret, for he had ceased similar outbursts; and he set his teeth, so as not to tell her that he would have commanded them to beat such a brother with sticks, or would have sent him as a man who labors with chained feet to dig earth in his Sicilian vineyards. He restrained himself, however, throttled the anger within him, and said, "Pardon me, Lygia. For me you are the daughter of a king and the adopted child of Plautius." He subdued himself to such a degree that when Nazarius appeared in the room again he promised him, on returning to his villa, the gift of a pair of peacocks or flamingoes, of which he had a garden full.

Lygia understood what such victories over his nature must have cost him; the more often he gained them the more her heart turned to him. Vinicius might be indignant for a moment, but he could not be jealous of Nazarius. In fact the son of Miriam did not, in his eyes, mean much more than a dog. Besides, he was a child yet, who, if he loved Lygia, loved her unconsciously and with infatuation. The young tribune had great struggles with himself in submitting, even in silence, to that degree of character which these people, for the name of Christ and His religion, maintained. A great change took place in Vinicius.

Afterward, when he returned to health, he remembered the whole series of events that had happened since that night at Ostrianum. He was overwhelmed at the superhuman power of that religion which changed the entire souls of men. There was in it something uncommon that had not been on earth before, and he thought that could it embrace the whole world, and could it impart to the world its love and charity, an era would come recalling not Jupiter, but Saturn's rule. He did not dare, either, to doubt the supernatural origin of Christ, or His resurrection, or the other miracles. The eyewitnesses who spoke of them were too trustworthy and despised falsehood too much to let him believe that they were recalling things that did not happen.

Finally, Roman skepticism permitted disbelief in the gods, yet belief in miracles. Vinicius stood before a kind of marvelous puzzle he could not solve. But this religion seemed to him to oppose the existing state of things, impossible to practice, and insane as well. People in Rome and in the whole world might be bad, but the order of things was good. Had Caesar, for example, been an honest man, had the Senate been composed, not of insignificant libertines, but of men like Thrasea, what more could one wish? No, Roman peace and supremacy were good, distinction among people just and proper. But the Christian religion, according to the understanding of Vinicius, would destroy all order, all supremacy, every distinction. What would happen then to the dominion and lordship of Rome? Could the Romans cease to rule, or could they recognize a whole herd of conquered nations as equal to themselves? That thought could find no place in the head of a patrician. Personally, the Christian religion was opposed to all his ideas and habits, his whole character and understanding of life. He was simply unable to imagine how he could exist were he to accept it. He feared and admired it; but as to accepting it, his nature shuddered at that. He understood, finally, that nothing except that religion separated him from Lygia; and when he thought of this, he hated it with all the strength of his soul.

Still, he acknowledged to himself that it had adorned Lygia with that exceptional and unexplained beauty that in his heart had produced love, respect, desire, and homage, a being dear to him beyond all others in the world. And then he wished once again to love Christ. And he understood clearly that he must either love or hate Him; he could not remain indifferent. So two opposing currents drove him: he hesitated in thought and in feeling; he did not know how to choose. He bowed his head, however, to that uncomprehended God and paid silent honor for this sole reason, that He was Lygia's God.

Lygia saw what was happening in him. She saw how he was fracturing himself, how his nature was rejecting that religion. Though this mortified her to the death, a sense of compassion, pity, and gratitude for the silent respect he showed Christ bent her heart to him with irresistible force. She recalled Pomponia Graecina and Aulus. A source of ceaseless sorrow and tears that never dried was the thought that beyond the grave Pomponia would not find Aulus. Lygia began now to understand better that pain, that bitterness. She, too, had found a being dear to her, and she was threatened by eternal separation from this dear one.

At times, it is true, she was self-deceived, thinking that his soul would open itself to Christ's teaching; but these illusions could not remain. She knew and understood him too well. Vinicius a Christian! Those two ideas could find no place together in her unenlightened head. If the thoughtful, discreet Aulus had not become a Christian under the influence of the wise and perfect Pomponia, how could Vinicius become one? To this there was no answer, or rather there was only one—that for him there was neither hope nor salvation.

The sentence of condemnation upon Vinicius made Lygia even more compassionate to him. At times she wished to speak to him of his dark future without Christ. Once when she told him that outside Christian truth there was no life, he, having grown stronger by then, rose on his sound arm and placed his head suddenly on her knees. "You are life!" he said. At that moment her breath failed and presence of mind fled, and a certain quiver of ecstasy rushed over her from head to feet. Seizing his temples with her hands, she tried to raise him, but bent over so that her lips touched his hair; and for a moment both were overcome with delight with themselves and love, which drew them ever closer.

Lygia rose at last and rushed away, with a flame in her veins and giddiness in her head; but here was the drop of desire that overflowed the cup filled already to the brim. Vinicius did not know how dearly he would have to pay for that happy moment, but Lygia understood that now she herself needed rescue. She spent the night without sleep, in tears and in prayer, feeling she was unworthy to pray and could not be heard. The next morning she went from the cubiculum early and, calling Crispus to the garden summerhouse, covered with ivy and withered vines, bared her whole soul to him, imploring him at the same time to let her leave Miriam's house, since she could not trust herself longer and could not overcome her heart's love for Vinicius.

Crispus, a strict, old man, absorbed in endless piety, consented to the plan of leaving Miriam's house, but he had no words of forgiveness for that love. To his thinking it was sinful. His heart swelled with indignation at the very thought of it. He had guarded Lygia since the time of her flight, had loved and confirmed her in the faith. She was a white lily grown up on the field of Christian teaching undefiled by any earthly breath. How could she have found a place in her soul for love other than heavenly? He had believed previously that nowhere in the world did there beat a heart more purely devoted to the glory of Christ. He wanted to offer her to Him as a pearl, a jewel, the precious work of his own hands; so he was disappointed and filled with grief and perplexity.

"Go and beg God to forgive your fault," he said peevishly. "Flee before the evil spirit who influenced you brings you to utter ruin and you oppose the Savior. God died on the cross to redeem your soul with His blood, but you have preferred to love him who wished to make you his mistress. God saved you by a miracle of His own hands, but you have opened your heart to impure desire and have loved this son of darkness. Who is he? The friend and servant of Antichrist, his co-partner in crime and destruction. He will lead you to that abyss and to that Sodom in which he himself is living, but which God will destroy with the flame of His anger. I say to you, if you had only died, the walls of this house would have fallen on your head before that serpent had crept into your bosom and fouled it with the poison of iniquity."

And he carried on in this way, for Lygia's fault filled him not only with anger but with loathing and contempt for sinful nature in general, and in particular for women, whom even, it seemed, Christian truth could not save from Eve's weakness. To him it was of no value that the girl had remained pure, that she wished to flee from that love, that she had confessed it with remorse. Crispus had wished to transform her into an angel, to raise her to heights where love for Christ alone existed, and she had fallen in love with an Augustian Roman! The very thought of that filled his heart with horror. No, he could not forgive her. Words of rebuke burned his lips like glowing coals; he struggled with himself not to utter them, but he shook his emaciated hands over the terrified girl. Lygia felt guilty, but not to that degree. She had judged even that withdrawal from Miriam's house would be her victory over temptation and would lessen her fault. Crispus, however, rubbed her into the dust, showed her all the baseness and insignificance of her soul, which she had not suspected. She had judged even that the old deacon, who from the moment of her flight from the Palatine had been a type of father, would show some compassion and strengthen her.

"I offer my pain and disappointment to God," he said, "but you have deceived the Savior also, for you have gone to a swamp that has poisoned your soul with its stench. You might have offered it to Christ as a precious vessel and said to Him, 'Fill it with grace, O Lord!' but you have preferred to offer it to the servant of the evil one. May God forgive you and have mercy on you; for till you cast out the serpent, I who held you as chosen—"

But he ceased to speak, for he saw that they were not alone. Through the withered vines and the ivy, which was green both in summer and winter, he saw two men, one of whom was Peter the apostle. The other he was unable to recognize at once, for a mantle of coarse wool concealed a part of his face. It seemed to Crispus for a moment that it was Chilo.

They, hearing the loud voice of Crispus, entered the summerhouse and sat on a stone bench. Peter's companion had an emaciated face; his head, which was growing bald, was covered at the sides with curly hair; he had reddened eyelids and a crooked nose; in the face, ugly and at the same time inspired, Crispus recognized the features of Paul of Tarsus.

Lygia fell on her knees, embraced Peter's feet in despair, and, burying her head in the fold of his mantle, remained silent.

"Peace to your spirits!" Peter said.

And, seeing the girl at his feet, he asked what had happened. Crispus began to tell them all that Lygia had confessed to him— her sinful love, her desire to flee from Miriam's house—and his sorrow that a soul he had wanted to offer to Christ as pure as a pearl had defiled itself with earthly feelings for a partaker in all the evil into which the pagan world had indulged, and which called for God's vengeance.

Lygia, during his speech embraced with increasing force the feet of the apostle, as if wishing to seek refuge near them and to beg even a little compassion.

But the apostle, when he had listened to the end, bent down and placed his aged hand on her head; then he raised his eyes to the old deacon and said, "Crispus, have you not heard that our beloved Master was in Cana, at a wedding, and blessed love between man and woman?"

Crispus's hands dropped, and he looked with astonishment on the speaker, without power to utter one word. After a moment's silence Peter asked again, "Crispus, do you think that Christ, who permitted Mary of Magdala to lie at his feet and who forgave the public sinner, would turn from this girl, who is a pure as a lily of the field?"

Lygia remained at the feet of Peter, with sobbing. The apostle raised her face, which was covered with tears, and said to her, "While the eyes of him whom you love are not open to the light of truth, avoid him, lest he bring you to sin, but pray for him, and know that there is no sin in your love. And since it is your wish to avoid temptation, this will be to your benefit. Do not suffer, and do not weep; for I tell you that the grace of the Redeemer has not deserted you, and that your prayers will be heard; after sorrow will come days of gladness."

When he had said this, he placed both hands on her head and, raising his eyes, blessed her. From his face there shone a goodness beyond that of earth.

The penitent Crispus began humbly to explain himself. "I have sinned against mercy," he said, "but I thought that by allowing an earthly love she had denied Christ."

"I denied Him three times," Peter answered, "and still He forgave me and commanded me to feed His sheep."

"And because," concluded Crispus, "Vinicius is an Augustian."

"Christ softened harder hearts than his," replied Peter.

Then Paul of Tarsus, who had been silent so far, placed his finger on his breast, pointing to himself, and said, "I am he who persecuted and hurried servants of Christ to their death; I am he who during the stoning of Stephen kept the garments of those who stoned him; I am he who wished to root out the truth in every part of the inhabited earth; and yet the Lord predestined me to declare it in every land. I have declared it in Judea, in Greece, on the Islands, among the Gentiles, and in this godless city, where first I lived as a prisoner. And now when Peter has summoned me, I enter this house to bend that proud head to the feet of Christ and cast a grain of seed in that man's stony field, which the Lord will fertilize, so that it may bring forth a bountiful harvest."

And he rose. To Crispus that small, bent figure appeared to be a giant, who was to stir the world to its foundations and gather in lands and nations to a great spiritual harvest.

28

Petronius to Vinicius:

"Have pity, my dear one; do not imitate Julius Caesar in your letters! Could you, like Julius, write *'Veni, vidi, vici'* ['I came, I saw, I conquered'], I might understand your brevity. But your letter means absolutely *'Veni, vidi, fugi'* ['I came, I saw, I fled']. Since such a conclusion is directly opposed to your nature, since you are wounded, and since uncommon things are happening to you, your letter needs explanation. I could not believe my eyes when I read that the Lygian giant killed Croton as easily as a Caledonian dog would kill a wolf in the wilds of Hibernia. That man is worth as much gold as he himself weighs, and it depends on him alone to become a favorite of Caesar. When I return to the city, I must get acquainted with that Lygian and have a bronze statue of him made for myself. Ahenobarbus will burst from curiosity when I tell him that it is an actual man. Athletic bodies are becoming rarer in Italy and Greece; and none in the Orient. The Germans, though large, have muscles covered with fat and are greater in bulk than in strength. Learn from the Lygian if he is an exception, or if in his country there are more men like him. If we organize games officially, it would be well to know where to seek for the best bodies.

"But praise to the gods of the Orient and the Occident that you have come out of such hands alive. You have escaped, of course, because you are a patrician and the son of a consul; but everything that has happened amazes me in the highest degree—that cemetery where you were among the Christians, they, their treatment of you, the subsequent flight of Lygia; finally, that peculiar sadness and unrest that breathes from your short letter. Explain, for there are many points that I cannot understand; and if you wish the truth, I will tell you plainly that I understand neither the Christians nor you nor Lygia. Do not wonder that I, who care for few things on earth except my own person, inquire of you so eagerly. I have contributed to all this affair of yours; so it is my affair too. Write soon, for I cannot foresee when we may meet. In Bronzebeard's head plans change, as winds do in autumn. At present, while tarrying in Beneventum, he has the wish to go to

225

Greece without first returning to Rome. Tigellinus, however, advises him to visit the city, since the people are yearning for him (read 'for games and bread') and may revolt. So I cannot tell what will happen. We may want to see Egypt. I should insist upon your coming, for I think that in your state of mind traveling and our amusements would be a medicine, but you might not find us. Consider, then, whether in that case rest in your Sicilian estates would not be preferable to remaining in Rome. Write me in detail of yourself, and farewell. I add no wish except health; for, by Pollux! I do not know what to wish you."

Vinicius, on receiving this letter, felt at first no desire to reply. He thought it was not worthwhile to reply, that an answer would explain nothing. Discontent, and a feeling of the vanity of life, possessed him. He thought, also, that Petronius would not understand him, and that something had happened that would remove them from each other. When he returned from the Trans-Tiber to his splendid home he was exhausted and found for the first days a certain satisfaction in rest and in comfort and abundance. That satisfaction lasted but a short time, however. He felt soon that he was living in vanity, that all that so far had been the passion of his life either had ceased to exist for him or had shrunk to small proportions. He had a feeling as if those ties that had connected him with life had been cut in his soul, and that no new ones had been formed. He had a feeling of emptiness at the thought that he might go to Beneventum and from there to Achaea, to swim in a life of luxury and wild excess. *To what end? What shall I gain from it?* Those were the first questions that passed through his head. And for the first time in his life he thought that if he went the conversation of Petronius, his wit, quickness, and exquisite expression of thought might annoy him.

But solitude, too, had begun to vex him. All his acquaintances were with Caesar in Beneventum; so he had to stay at home alone, with a head full of questions and a heart full of feelings he could not analyze. He had moments, however, in which he felt that if he could discuss with someone about everything that took place inside of him he might be able to grasp it all somehow. After some days of hesitation, he decided to answer Petronius, and he wrote the following words.

226

"It is your wish that I write more specifically; I agree. Whether I shall be able to do it more clearly, I cannot tell, for there are many knots I do not know how to loosen. I described to you my stay among the Christians and their treatment of enemies, myself and Chilo included. I told of the kindness with which they nursed me and of the disappearance of Lygia. No, my dear friend, I was not spared because I was the son of a consul. Such considerations do not exist for them, since they forgave even Chilo, though I urged them to bury him in the garden. These are people which the world has not seen up to now, and their teaching is of a kind that the world has not yet heard. I can say nothing else, and he is mistaken who judges them by our rules. I tell you that if I had been lying with a broken arm in my own house, and if my own people, even my own family, had nursed me, I should have had more comforts, of course, but I should not have received half the care I found among them.

"Know this, too, that Lygia is like the others. Had she been my sister or my wife, she could not have nursed me more tenderly. Delight filled my heart more than once, for I found that love alone could inspire this wonderful tenderness. More than once I saw love in her look, in her face. Among those simple people in that poor dwelling I felt happier than ever before. No; she was not indifferent to me. Still, that same Lygia left Miriam's dwelling in secret because of me. I sit now whole days with my head in my hands and think, *Why did she do this?* Have I written you that I volunteered to give her back to Aulus? True, she stated that was impossible then because Aulus and Pomponia had gone to Sicily and because news of her return, going from house to house, through slaves, would reach the Palatine, and Caesar might take her from Aulus again. But she knew that I would not pursue her any longer; that I had stopped the ways of violence; that, unable to cease loving her or to live without her, I would bring her into my house through a wreathed door and seat her on a sacred skin at my hearth. Still, she fled! Why? Nothing was threatening her. If she did not love me, she might have rejected me.

"The day before her flight, I made the acquaintance of a wonderful man, a certain Paul of Tarsus, who spoke to me of Christ and His teachings, and spoke with such power that every word of his, without his willing it, turns all the foundations of our society into ashes. That same man visited me after her flight and said, 'If God opens your eyes to the light, and takes the beam from them as He took it from mine, you will feel that she acted properly; and then, perhaps, you will find her.' And now I am shaking my head over these words, as if I had heard them from the mouth of the Pythoness at Delphi. I seem to understand this at least. Though they love people, the Christians are enemies of our life, our gods, and our evil deeds; so she fled from me, as from a man who belongs to our society and with whom she would have to share a life judged as ungodly by Christians. You will say that since she might reject me, she had no need to withdraw. But what if she loved me? In that case she desired to flee from love. At the very thought of this I wish to send slaves into every alley in Rome and command them to cry throughout the houses, 'Return, Lygia!' But I fail to understand why she fled. I should not have stopped her from believing in her Christ and would myself have erected an altar to Him in my atrium. What harm could one more god do me? Why might I not believe in Him—I who do not believe much in the old gods?

"I know with full certainty that the Christians do not lie, and they say that He rose from the dead. A man cannot rise from the dead. That Paul of Tarsus, who is a Roman citizen, but who, as a Jew, knows the old Hebrew writings, told me that the coming of Christ was promised by prophets for thousands of years. These are uncommon things, but does not the mysterious surround us on every side? People have not ceased talking yet of Apollonius of Tyana. Paul's statement that there is one God, not a whole assembly of them, seems sound to me. Perhaps Seneca is of this opinion, and before him many others. Christ lived, gave Himself to be crucified for the salvation of the world, and rose from the dead. All this is perfectly certain. I do not see, therefore, a reason why I should insist on an opposite opinion, or why I should not construct an altar to Him, if I am ready to build one to Serapis, for instance. It would not be difficult for me even to renounce other gods, for no reasoning mind believes in them at present. But it seems that all this is not enough yet for the Christians. It is not enough to honor Christ; one must also live according to His teachings; and here you are on the shore of a sea they command you to wade through.

"If I promised to do so, they themselves would feel that the promise was mere words. Paul told me this openly. You know how I love Lygia and know that there is nothing I would not do for her. Still, even at her wish, I cannot raise Soracte or Vesuvius on my shoulders, or place Lake Thrasymene on the palm of my hand, or make my eyes blue, like those of the Lygians. I am not a philosopher, but I am not so dull as I have seemed, perhaps, more than once to you. I do not know how the Christians order their own lives, but I know that where their religion begins, Roman rule ends, our mode of life ends, the distinction between conquered and conqueror, between rich and poor, lord and slave, ends. This government with Caesar ends, law and all the order of the world ends; and in place of these appears Christ, with mercy and kindness, opposed to previous human instincts.

"It is true that Lygia is more to me than all Rome and its lordship; and I would let society vanish could I have her in my house. But agreement in words does not satisfy the Christians; a man must feel that their teaching is truth and not have anything else in his soul. But that (the gods are my witnesses) is beyond me. Do you understand what that means? There is something in my nature that shudders at this religion; and were my lips to glorify it, were I to conform to its precepts, my soul and my reason would say that I do so through love for Lygia. But apart from her there is nothing on earth more repulsive. And strangely, Paul of Tarsus understands this, and so does that old Peter, who in spite of all his simplicity and low origin is the highest among them and was a disciple of Christ. And do you know what they are doing? They are praying for me, and calling down something they call grace. But nothing descends on me now except anxiety and a greater yearning for Lygia.

"I have written to you that she went away secretly; but when going she left me a cross which she put together from twigs of boxwood. When I woke up, I found it near my bed. I have it now in my living quarters, and I observe it. I cannot tell why, as if there were something suggestive in it of a greater truth. I love it because she bound it together, and I hate it because it divides us. At times

229

it seems to me that there are enchantments of some kind in all this affair, and that the apostle Peter, though he declares himself to be a simple shepherd, is greater than Apollonius and all who preceded him, and that he has involved us all—Lygia, Pomponia, and me—with them.

"You have written that in my previous letter anxiety and sadness are visible. Sadness there must be, for I have lost her again, and there is anxiety because something has changed in me. I tell you sincerely, that nothing is more repulsive to my nature than that religion, and still I cannot recognize myself since I met Lygia. Is it enchantment, or love? Circe changed people's bodies by touching them, but my soul has been changed. No one but Lygia could have done that, or rather Lygia through that wonderful religion she professes.

"When I returned to my house from the Christians, no one was waiting for me. The slaves thought I was in Beneventum and would not return soon; so there was disorder in the house. I found my slaves drunk, and they were giving themselves a feast. They had more thought of seeing death than me, and would have been less terrified. You know with what a firm hand I hold my house; all to the last one dropped on their knees, and some fainted from terror. But do you know how I acted? At the first moment I wished to call for rods and hot iron, but immediately a kind of shame seized me, and—will you believe this?—a type of pity for those wretched people emerged. Among them are old slaves whom my grandfather, Marcus Vinicius, brought from the Rhine in the time of Augustus. I shut myself up alone in the library, and there came stranger thoughts still, namely, that after what I had heard and seen among the Christians, it did not become me to act with slaves as I had acted before—that they, too, were people.

"For a number of days they moved about in mortal terror, in the belief that I was delaying so as to invent a more cruel punishment; but I did not punish, and did not punish them because I was not able. Summoning them on the third day, I said, 'I forgive you; strive earnestly to correct your fault!' They fell on their knees, covering their faces with tears, stretching forth their hands with groans, and called me lord and father; but I—shamefully—was equally moved. It seemed to me that at that moment I was looking

230

at the sweet face of Lygia, and her eyes filled with tears, thanking me for that act. I felt that my lips, too, were moist. Do you know what I will confess to you? This—that I cannot do without her, that my sadness is greater than you will admit. But, as to my slaves, one thing kept my attention. The forgiveness they received not only did not make them rebellious, not only did not weaken discipline, but motivated them to ready service and gratitude. Not only do they serve, but they seem to vie with one another to discover my wishes.

"I mention this to you because, on the day before I left the Christians, I told Paul that society would fall apart because of his religion. He answered, 'Love is a stronger hook than fear.' And now I see that in certain cases his opinion may be right. I have verified it also with references to clients, who, learning of my return, hurried to greet me. You know that I have never been stingy with them; but my father acted proudly with clients on principle and taught me to treat them in like manner. But when I saw their worn mantles and hungry faces, I had a compassionate feeling. I ordered food and had conversation with them—called some by name, asked some about their wives and children—and again in the eyes before me I saw tears. Again it seemed to me that Lygia saw what I was doing, that she praised me and was delighted. Is my mind beginning to wander, or is it love that confuses my feelings? I cannot tell. But this I do know: I have a continual feeling that she is looking at me from a distance, and I am afraid to do anything that might trouble or offend her.

"So it is, Caius! But they have changed my soul, and sometimes I feel better for that reason. At times I am tormented with the thought, for I fear that my manhood and energy are taken from me; that, perhaps, I am useless, not only for counsel and judgment, but for feasts and war also. These are undoubted enchantments! And to such a degree am I changed that I thought when I lay wounded, that if Lygia were like Nigidia, Poppaea, Crispinilla, and our divorced women, if she were as vile, as pitiless, and as cheap as they, I should not love her as I do at present. But since I love her for that which divides us, you will see the chaos that is rising in my soul, in what darkness I live, how it is that I cannot see certain roads before me, and how far I am from knowing where to begin. I live through the hope that I shall see her. But what will happen to me in a year or two years, I cannot possibly know. I shall not leave Rome. I could not endure the society of the Augustians; and besides, the one comfort in my sadness and pre-occupation is the thought that I am near Lygia, that through Glaucus the physician, who promised to visit me, or through Paul of Tarsus, I can learn something of her. No, I would not leave Rome, even were you to offer me the government of Egypt.

"Also know that I have ordered the sculptor to make a stone monument for Gulo, whom I killed in anger. It came too late to my mind how he had carried me in his arms and was the first to teach me how to put an arrow on a bow. I do not know why this recollection of him rose in me causing sorrow and despair. If what I write startles you, I reply that it bewilders me no less, but I write pure truth. Farewell."

29

Vinicius received no answer to this letter. Petronius did not write, thinking that Caesar might command a return to Rome any day. In fact, news of it was spread in the city and roused great delight in the hearts of the rabble, eager for games with gifts of grain and olives, great supplies of which had been accumulated in Osia. Helius, Nero's freedman, announced at last his return in the Senate. But Nero, having embarked with his court on ships at Misenum, returned slowly, disembarking at coast towns for rest or exhibitions in theaters. He even thought of returning to Naples and waiting there for spring.

During all this time Vinicius lived shut up in his house, thinking of Lygia and all those new things that occupied his soul and brought to it ideas and feelings foreign to it thus far. He saw, from time to time, only Glaucus the physician, every one of whose visits delighted him, for he could talk with the man about Lygia.

Glaucus did not know where she had found refuge, but he gave assurance that the elders were protecting her with watchful care. Once, when moved by the sadness of Vinicius, he told him that Peter had blamed Crispus for rebuking Lygia for her love for him. The young patrician, hearing this, grew pale. He had thought that Lygia was not indifferent to him, but he was frequently doubtful. Now for the first time he heard the confirmation of his desires and hopes from strange lips, and, besides, those of a Christian.

At the first moment of gratitude he wished to run to Peter. When he learned, however, that he was not in the city, but teaching in the neighborhood, he asked Glaucus to accompany him there, promising to make large gifts to the poor community. It seemed to him, too, that if Lygia loved him, all obstacles were set aside, because he was ready at any moment to honor Christ. Glaucus, though he urged him persistently to receive baptism, would not assure him that he would gain Lygia at once. He said that it was necessary to desire their religion for its own sake, through love of Christ, not for other reasons. "One must have a Christian soul, too," he said. Though every obstacle angered Vinicius, he had begun to understand that Glaucus, as a Christian, said what he should. He had not become clearly conscious of one of the deepest changes in his nature. Formerly he measured people and things only by his own selfishness, but now he was getting accustomed gradually to the thought that other eyes might see differently and that justice did not necessarily equal personal profit.

He wished often to see Paul of Tarsus, whose speeches made him curious and disturbed him. He developed arguments to overcome his teaching, he resisted him in thought; still, he wished to see and hear him. Paul, however, had gone to Aricium, and, since the visits of Glaucus had become rarer, Vinicius was in perfect solitude. He began again to run through back streets adjoining the Subura, and narrow lanes of the Trans-Tiber, in the hope that even from a distance he might see Lygia. When even that hope failed him, he became weary and impatient. At last the time came when his former nature came alive. It seemed to him that he had been a fool to no purpose and filled his mind with futile goals, and that he ought to accept from life what it gives. He resolved to forget Lygia, or at least to seek pleasure apart from her. He felt that this trial, however, was the last, and he threw himself into it with all the blind energy of impulse that characterized him.

The city began to revive with hope of the near coming of Caesar. A solemn reception was waiting for him. Meanwhile, spring was there; the snow from the Alban Hills had vanished under the breath of winds from Africa. Grass-plots in the gardens were covered with violets. The Forums and the Campus Martius were filled with people warmed by the growing heat of the sun. Along the Appian Way, the usual place for drives outside the city, a movement of richly ornamented chariots had begun. Excursions were made to the Alban Hills. Youthful women, under pretext of worshiping Juno in Lanuvium, or Diana in Aricia, left home to seek adventures beyond the city. Here Vinicius saw one day among lordly chariots the splendid car of Chrysothemis, the mistress of Petronius, preceded by two Molossian dogs; it was surrounded by a crowd of young men and by old senators, whose position kept them in the city.

Chrysothemis, driving four Coriscan ponies herself, scattered smiles all about and gave light strokes with her golden whip; but when she saw Vinicius she reined in her horses, took him into her car, and then to a feast at her house, which lasted all night. At that feast Vinicius drank so much that he did not remember when they took him home; he remembered, however, that when Chrysothemis mentioned Lygia he was offended and, being drunk, emptied a goblet of Falernian wine on her head. When he thought of this in soberness, he was angrier still. But a day later Chrysothemis, forgetting evidently the injury, visited him at his house and took him to the Appian Way a second time. Then she dined at his house and confessed that not only Petronius, but his lute-player, had grown boring to her long ago, and that her heart was free now. They appeared together for a week, but the relationship did not promise permanence.

After the wine incident, however, Lygia's name was never mentioned, but Vinicius could not free himself from thoughts of her. He had the feeling always that her eyes were looking at his face. He suffered and could not escape the thought that he was saddening Lygia or the regret which that thought roused in him.

After the first scenes of jealousy Chrysothemis made because of two Syrian damsels he purchased, he let her go in rude fashion. He did not cease at once from pleasure and license, it is true, but he indulged in them out of spite toward Lygia. At last he realized that she was the one cause of his evil activity as well as his good; and that really nothing in the world occupied him except her. Disgust, and then weariness, mastered him. Pleasure had grown loathsome and left mere guilt. It seemed to him that he was wretched, and this last feeling filled him with measureless amazement, for formerly he recognized good as everything that pleased him. Finally, he lost his sense of freedom and self-confidence and fell into total depression. Nothing touched him, and he did not visit Petronius until the latter sent an invitation and his litter.

On seeing his uncle, though greeted with gladness, he replied unwillingly to his questions. Once more he told in detail the search for Lygia, his life among the Christians, everything that had passed through his head and heart; and finally, he complained that his life had fallen into chaos. Nothing, he said, attracted him, nothing was pleasing. He was ready both to honor and persecute Christ. He understood the loftiness of His teaching, but he felt also an irresistible aversion to it. He understood that, even if he possessed Lygia, he would not possess her completely, for he would have to share her with Christ. He was living without hope, happiness, or a future. Around him was darkness in which he was groping for an exit and could not find it.

During this narrative Petronius looked at Vinicius's changed face and hands, which as he spoke he stretched out in a strange way, as if actually seeking a road in the darkness. All at once Petronius rose and, approaching Vinicius, touched the hair above his ear.

"Do you know," he asked, "that you have gray hairs on your temple?"

"Perhaps I have," Vinicius answered. "I should not be surprised if all my hair were to grow white soon."

Silence followed. Petronius was a man of sense, and more than once he meditated on the soul of man and on life. In general, life in the society in which they both lived might be happy or unhappy externally, but internally it was at rest. Just as a thunderbolt or an earthquake might overturn a temple, so might misfortune crush a life. But there was something else in the words of Vinicius, and Petronius stood for the first time before a series of spiritual snarls no one had straightened out before. He was sufficiently a man of reason to judge their importance, but with all his quickness he could not answer the questions put to him. After a long silence, he said at last, "These must be enchantments."

"I, too, have thought so," Vinicius answered. "More than once it seemed to me that we were enchanted, both myself and Lygia."

"And if you were to go, for example, to the priests of Serapis? Among them, as among priests in general, there are many deceivers, but there are others, who have revealed wonderful secrets."

He said this, however, without conviction and with an uncertain voice, for he himself felt how empty and even ridiculous that counsel must seem on his lips.

Vinicius rubbed his forehead and said, "Enchantments! I have seen sorcerers who employed unknown and hidden powers to their personal profit; I have seen those who used them to the harm of their enemies. But these Christians live in poverty, forgive their enemies, preach submission, virtue, and mercy; what profit could they get from enchantments, and why should they use them?"

Petronius was angry that his reasoning could find no reply. Not wishing, however, to acknowledge this, he said, so as to offer an answer of some kind, "This is a new sect." After a while he added, "By the divine dweller in Paphian groves, how all that injures life! You will admire the goodness and virtue of those people; but I tell you that they are bad, for they are enemies of life, as are diseases and death itself. As things are, we have enough of these enemies; we do not need the Christians in addition. Just count them: diseases, Caesar, Tigellinus, Caesar's poetry, freedmen who sit in the Senate. By Castor! There is enough of this already. That is a destructive and disgusting sect. Have you tried to shake yourself out of this sadness and make some little use of life?"

"I have tried," Vinicius answered.

"Ah, traitor!" Petronius said, laughing. "News spreads quickly through slaves; you have seduced Chrysothemis!"

236

Vinicius waved his hand in disgust.

"In every case I thank you," said Petronius. "I will send her a pair of slippers embroidered with pearls. In my language of a lover that means, 'Walk away.' I owe you a double gratitude—first, you did not accept Eunice; second, you have freed me from Chrysothemis. Listen to me! You see before you a man who has risen early, bathed, feasted, possessed Chrysothemis, written satires, and even at times interwoven prose with verses, but who has been as wearied as Caesar from gloomy thoughts. And do you know why that was so? It was because I sought at a distance that which was near. A beautiful woman is worth her weight in gold; but if she loves in addition, she has simply no price. Such a one you will not buy with the riches of Verres. I will fill my life with happiness, as a goblet with the foremost wine the earth has produced, and I will drink until my hand becomes powerless and my lips grow pale. What will come, I do not care; and this is my latest philosophy."

"You have proclaimed it always; there is nothing new in it," Vinicius said.

"There is substance now, which was lacking before," Petronius replied.

When he had said this, he called Eunice, who entered dressed in white drapery—the former slave no longer, but a goddess of love and happiness.

"Come."

At this she ran up to him and, sitting on his knee, surrounded his neck with her arms and placed her head on his breast. Vinicius saw how a reflection of purple began to cover her cheeks, how her eyes melted gradually in mist. They formed a wonderful group of love and happiness. Petronius reached for a flat vase standing at one side on a table and, taking a whole handful of violets, covered the head, bosom, and robe of Eunice; then he pushed the tunic from her arms, and said, "Happy is he who, like me, has found love enclosed in such a form! At times it seems to me that we are a pair of gods. Look yourself! Has Praxiteles or Miron created a more wonderful figure? Or does there exist in Paros or in Pentelicus such marble as this—warm, rosy, and full of love?"

He began to put his lips on her shoulders and neck. She shuddered, her eyes now closed, now opened, with an expression of unspeakable delight. Petronius after a while raised her exquisite head and said, turning to Vinicius, "But now think, what are your gloomy Christians in comparison with this? And if you do not understand the difference, go to them. But this sight will cure you."

Vinicius smelled the odor of violets, which filled the whole chamber, and he grew pale; for he thought that if he could have put his lips along Lygia's shoulders in that way, it would have been a kind of sacrilegious delight so great that the world would vanish afterward!

"Eunice," Petronius said, "you divine one, prepare garlands for our heads and a meal."

When she had gone out he turned to Vinicius.

"I offered to make her free, but do you know what she answered? 'I would rather be your slave than Caesar's wife!' And she would not consent. I freed her then without her knowledge. The judge favored me by not requiring her presence. But she does not know that she is free, as also she does not know that this house and all my jewels, excepting the gems, will belong to her in case of my death." He rose and walked through the room, then said, "Love changes some more, others less, but it has changed even me. Once I loved the odor of verbenas; but as Eunice prefers violets, I like them now beyond all other flowers, and since spring came we breathe only violets. But as to you, do you keep always to nard?"

"Give me peace!" the young man answered.

"I wanted you to see Eunice, and I mentioned her to you, because you, perhaps, are seeking also at a distance that which is near. Maybe there is beating for you, too, somewhere in the chambers of your slaves, a true and simple heart. Apply this balm to your wounds. You say that Lygia loves you? Perhaps she does. But what kind of love is that which flees? Is there another force stronger than love? No, my dear; Lygia is not Eunice."

"It is all torment," Vinicius answered. "I saw you kissing Eunice's shoulders, and I thought then that if Lygia would lay hers bare to me I should not care if the ground opened under us. But a

238

certain dread seized me, as if I had attacked some vestal virgin or wished to defile a divinity. Lygia is not Eunice, but I understand the difference not in your way. Love has changed your heart, and you prefer violets to verbenas; but it has changed my soul. So in spite of my misery and desire, I prefer Lygia to be what she is rather than to be like others."

"I do not understand your position."

"True, true!" Vinicius answered feverishly. "We understand each other no longer."

A tense moment of silence followed.

"May hades swallow your Christians!" Petronius exclaimed. "They have filled you with misery and destroyed your sense of life. May hades devour them! You are mistaken in thinking that their religion is good, for good is what gives people happiness—namely, beauty, love, power; but these they call vanity. You are mistaken in believing they are just! For if we repay good for evil, what shall we pay for good? And besides, if we pay the same for both, why should people be good?"

"No, the pay is not the same; but according to their teaching it begins in a future life, which is without limit."

"I do not enter into that question, for we shall see hereafter if it is possible to see anything without our earthly eyes. Meanwhile, they are simply incompetents. Ursus strangled Croton because he has limbs of bronze; but these are simpletons, and the future cannot belong to simpletons."

"For them life begins with death."

"Which is as if one were to say, 'Day begins with night.' Do you intend to carry off Lygia?"

"No, I cannot pay her evil for good, and I swore that I would not."

"Do you intend to accept the religion of Christ?"

"I wish to do so, but my nature cannot endure it."

"But will you be able to forget Lygia?"

"No."

"Then travel."

At that moment the slaves announced that the meal was ready; but Petronius said, on the way in, "You have traveled over a large part of the world, but only as a soldier hurrying to his place of destination and without halting by the way. Go with us to Achaea. Caesar still plans the journey. He will stop everywhere on the way, sing, receive crowns, plunder temples, and return as a triumphator to Italy. That will resemble a journey of Bacchus and Apollo in one person."

He placed himself on the couch before the table, by the side of Eunice; and when the slaves put a wreath of anemones on his head, he continued. "What have you seen in Corbulo's service? Nothing. Have you seen the Grecian temples thoroughly, as I have—I who was spending more than two years from the hands of one guide to those of another? Have you been in Rhodes to examine the site of the Colossus? Have you seen in Panopeus the clay from which Prometheus shaped man; or in Sparta the eggs laid by Leda; or in Athens the famous Sarmatian armor made of horse hoofs; or in Euboea the ship of Agamemnon? Have you seen Alexandria, Memphis, the Pyramids, the hair that Isis tore from her head in grief for Osiris? I will accompany Caesar, and when he returns I will leave him and go to Cyprus; for it is the wish of this golden-haired goddess of mine that we offer doves together to the divinity in Paphos, and you must know that whatever she wishes must happen."

"I am your slave," Eunice said.

He rested his garlanded head on her chest and said with a smile, "Then I am the slave of a slave. I admire you, divine one, from feet to head!"

Then he said to Vinicius, "Come with us to Cyprus. But first remember that you must see Caesar. It is improper that you have not been with him yet; Tigellinus is ready to use this to your disadvantage. He has no personal hatred for you, it is true; but he cannot love you, even because you are my sister's son. We shall say that you were sick. We must think over what you are to answer should he ask you about Lygia. It will be best to wave your hand and say that she was with you till she wearied you. He will understand that. Tell him also that sickness kept you at home; that your fever increased because of disappointment at not being able to visit Naples and hear his song; that you were returned to health only through the hope of hearing him. Do not worry about exaggeration."

"Do you know," Vinicius said, "that there are people who have no fear of Caesar and who live as calmly as if he were nonexistent?"

"I know whom you have in mind—the Christians."

"Yes; they alone. But our life is unbroken terror."

"Do not mention your Christians. They do not fear Caesar perhaps because he has not even heard of them; and in every case he knows nothing of them, and they concern him as much as withered leaves. But I tell you that they are incompetents. You feel this yourself. If your nature is opposed to their teaching, it is just because you know their failure. You are a man of different stock; so do not trouble yourself or me with them."

These words struck Vinicius; and when he returned home, he began to think that perhaps the goodness and charity of Christians were proof of their weakness of character. It seemed to him that people of strength and temper could not forgive like this. It came to him that this must be the real cause of the repulsion his Roman soul felt toward their teaching. "We shall be able to live and die!" Petronius said. As for them, they know only how to forgive, and understand neither true love nor true hatred.

30

Caesar, on returning to Rome, was angry because he had returned, and after some days wished to visit Achaea. He even issued an edict declaring that his absence would be short, and that public affairs would not suffer. In company with Augustians, among whom was Vinicius, he returned to the Capitol to make offerings to the gods for a profitable journey. But on the second day, when he visited the temple of Vesta, an event took place that altered all his goals. Nero feared the gods, though he did not believe in them. He feared especially the mysterious Vesta, who filled him with such awe that at the sight of the divinity and the

241

sacred fire his hair rose from terror, his teeth chattered, a shiver ran through his limbs, and he dropped into the arms of Vinicius, who happened to be behind him. He was carried out of the temple at once and conveyed to the Palatine, where he recovered soon, though he did not leave the bed for that day. He declared, to the great surprise of those present, that he would postpone his journey, since the divinity had warned him secretly against haste. An hour later it was announced throughout Rome that Caesar, seeing the gloomy faces of the citizens, and moved by love for them, as a father for his children, would remain to share their pleasures.

The people rejoiced at this decision and, certain that they would not miss games and a distribution of wheat, assembled in crowds before the gates of the Palatine and raised shouts in honor of the divine Caesar. He interrupted playing dice, with which he was amusing himself with Augustians, and said, "Yes, there was need to defer the journey. I will give command to cut through the Isthmus of Corinth; I will build such monuments in Egypt that the Pyramids will seem childish toys in comparison. I will have a sphinx built seven times greater than that which is gazing into the desert outside Memphis; but I will command that it have my face. Coming ages will speak only of that monument and of me."

"With your verses you have built a monument to yourself already, not seven, but three times seven, greater than the Pyramid of Cheops," Petronius said.

"But with my song?" Nero asked.

"Ah! If men could only build for you a statue, like that of Memnon, to call with the voice at sunrise! For all ages to come the seas adjoining Egypt would swarm with ships in which crowds from the three parts of the world would be lost in listening to your song."

"Alas! Who can do that?" Nero said.

"But you can give command to cut out of basalt yourself driving a chariot."

"True! I will do that!"

"You will bestow a gift on humanity."

"In Egypt I will marry the Moon, who is now a widow, and I shall be a god really."

"And you will give us stars for wives; we will make a new constellation, which will be called the constellation of Nero. But marry Vitelius to the Nile, so that he may beget hippopotamuses. Give the desert to Tigellinus; he will be king of the jackals."

"And what do you plan for me?" Vatinius asked.

"Apis bless you! You arranged such splendid games in Beneventum that I cannot wish you ill. Make a pair of boots for the Sphinx, whose paws must grow numb during night-dews; after that you will make sandals for the Colossi that form the alleys before the temples. Domitius Afer will be treasurer, since he is known for his honesty. I am glad, Caesar, when you are dreaming of Egypt, and I am saddened because you have delayed your plan for a journey."

"Your mortal eyes saw nothing, for the deity becomes invisible to whomever it wishes," Nero said. "When I was in the temple of Vesta she herself stood near me and whispered in my ear, 'Delay the journey.' That happened so unexpectedly that I was terrified, though for such an obvious care of the gods for me I should be thankful."

"We were all terrified," Tigellinus said, "and the vestal Rubria fainted."

"Rubria!" Nero said. "What a snowy neck she has!"

"But she blushed at sight of the divine Caesar—"

"True! I noticed that myself. That is wonderful. There is something divine in every vestal, and Rubria is very beautiful."

"Tell me," he said, after a moment's meditation, "why people fear Vesta more than other gods? What does this mean? Though I am the chief priest, fear seized me today. I remember only that I was falling back and should have dropped to the ground had not someone supported me. Who was it?"

"I," Vinicius answered.

"Oh, you 'stern Mars'! Why were you not in Beneventum? They told me that you were ill, and indeed your face is changed. But I heard that Croton wished to kill you. Is that true?"

"It is, and he broke my arm; but I defended myself."

"With a broken arm?"

"A certain barbarian helped me; he was stronger than Croton."

Nero looked at him with disbelief. "Stronger than Croton? Are you jesting? Croton was the strongest of men, but now here is Syphax from Ethiopia."

"I tell you, Caesar, what I saw with my own eyes."

"Where is that pearl? Has he not become king of Nemi?"

"I cannot tell, Caesar. I have lost sight of him."

"You know not even of what people he is?"

"I had a broken arm and could not ask for him."

"Seek him, and find him for me."

"I will do that," Tigellinus said.

But Nero spoke further to Vinicius. "I thank you for having supported me; I might have broken my head by a fall. Once you were a good companion, but campaigning and service with Corbulo have made you wild in some ways; I see you rarely.

"How is that maiden too narrow in the hips, with whom you were in love," he asked after a while, "and whom I took from Aulus for you?"

Vinicius was fearful, but Petronius came to his aid at that moment.

"I will lay a wager, lord," he said, "that he has forgotten. Do you see his confusion? Ask him how many of them there were since that time, and I will not give assurance of his power to answer. The Vinicii are good soldiers, but still better lovers. They need whole flocks. Punish him for that, lord, by not inviting him to the feast which Tigellinus promises to arrange in your honor on the pond of Agrippa."

"I will not do that. I trust, Tigellinus, that flocks of beauty will not be lacking there."

"Could the Graces be absent where Amor will be present?" Tigellinus answered.

"Weariness tortures me," Nero said. "I have remained in Rome at the will of the goddess, but I cannot endure the city. I will go to Antium. I am stifled in these narrow streets, amid these tumbledown houses, amid these alleys. Foul air flies even here to my house and my gardens. Oh, if an earthquake would destroy Rome, if some angry god would level it to the earth! I would show how a city should be built, which is the head of the world and my capital."

"Caesar," Tigellinus answered, "you say, 'If some angry god would destroy the city'—is it so?"

"It is! What then?"

"But are you not a god?"

Nero waved his hand with an expression of weariness and said, "We shall see your work on the pond of Agrippa. Afterward I go to Antium."

Then he closed his eyes to indicate that he needed rest. In fact, the Augustians were beginning to depart. Petronius went out with Vinicius and said to him, "You are invited, then, to share in the amusement. Bronzebeard has renounced the journey, but he will be more insane than ever; he has settled himself in the city as in his own house. Try to find in these madnesses amusement and forgetfulness.

"Well! We have conquered the world, and have a right to amuse ourselves. You, Marcus, are a very handsome fellow, and to that I ascribe in part the weakness that I have for you. By the Ephesian Diana! If you could see your joined brows and your face in which the ancient blood of the Quirites is evident! Others near you look like freedmen. True! Were it not for that mad religion, Lygia would be in your house today. Attempt once more to prove to me that they are not enemies of life and mankind. They have acted well toward you, so you may be grateful to them; but in your place I should detest that religion and seek pleasure where I could find it. You are an attractive fellow, I repeat, and Rome is swarming with divorced women."

"I wonder only that all this does not torture you yet?" Vinicius said.

"Who has told you that it does not? I am not of your years. Besides, I have other attachments. I love books, you have no love for them. I love poetry, which annoys you; I love pottery, gems, a multitude of things, at which you do not look; and, finally, I have found Eunice, but you have found nothing similar. For me, it is pleasant in my house, among masterpieces; I can never make you a man of aesthetic feeling. I know that in this life I shall never find anything beyond what I have found; you know not that you are hoping continually and seeking something new. If death were to visit you, with all your courage and sadness, you would die with surprise that it was necessary to leave the world. I will accept death as a necessity, with the conviction that there is no fruit in the world that I have not tasted. I do not hurry, neither shall I delay; I shall try merely to be joyful to the end.

"There are cheerful skeptics in the world. For me, the Stoics are fools; but stoicism tempers men, at least, whereas your Christians bring sadness to the world, which in life is the same as rain in nature. Do you know what I have learned? That during the festivities that Tigellinus will arrange at the pond of Agrippa, there will be women from the first houses of Rome. Will there not be even one sufficiently beautiful to console you? There will be maidens, too, appearing in society for the first time—as nymphs. Such is our Roman Caesardom! The air is mild already; the midday breeze will warm the water. And you, Narcissus, know this, that there will not be one to refuse you—not one, even though she be a vestal virgin."

"I should need luck to find such a one."

"And who made you this way if not the Christians? But people whose standard is a cross cannot be different. Listen to me. Greece was beautiful, and created wisdom; we created power; and what, to your thinking, can this teaching create? If you know, explain; for, by Pollux! I cannot understand it."

"You are afraid, it seems, in case I become a Christian," Vinicius said, shrugging his shoulders.

"I am afraid that you have spoiled life for yourself. If you cannot be a Grecian, be a Roman; possess and enjoy. I despise Bronzebeard because he is a Greek buffoon. If he were a true Roman, I would recognize that he was right in permitting himself madness."

31

Praetorian guards surrounded the groves on the banks of the pond of Agrippa, so that numerous throngs of spectators could not annoy Caesar and his guests. It was said that everyone in Rome distinguished for wealth, beauty, or intellect was present at that feast, which had no equal in the history of the city. Tigellinus wished to recompense Caesar for the deferred journey to Achaea, to surpass all who had ever feasted Nero, and to prove than no man could entertain as he could. With this in view, while with Caesar in Naples, and later in Beneventum, he sent orders to bring from remotest regions of the earth beasts, birds, rare fish, plants, vessels, and cloth, which were to enhance the splendor of the feast. The revenues of whole provinces were spent to satisfy mad projects; but the powerful favorite had no need to hesitate. His influence grew daily.

Tigellinus was not dearer than others to Nero yet, perhaps, but he was becoming more and more indispensable. Petronius surpassed him infinitely in polish, intellect, and wit; in conversation he knew better how to amuse Caesar. But to his misfortune he surpassed in conversation even Caesar himself, and so he aroused jealousy. Also, he could not be an obedient instrument in everything, and Caesar feared his opinion when there were questions in matters of taste. But Nero never felt any restraint before Tigellinus. The very title, Arbiter Elegantiarum, which had been given to Petronius, annoyed Nero's vanity. Who had the right to bear that title but himself?

Tigellinus had sense enough to know his own deficiencies; and, seeing that he could not compete with Petronius, Lucan, or others distinguished by birth, talents, or learning, he resolved to overshadow them by the lavishness of his services. Above all, he strove for such a magnificence that the imagination of Nero himself would be struck by it. He had arranged to give the feast on a gigantic raft made of gilded timbers. The borders of this raft were decked with splendid shells found in the Red Sea and the Indian Ocean, shells brilliant with the colors of pearls and the rainbow. The banks of the pond were covered with groups of palm, groves of lotus, and blooming roses. In the midst of these were hidden fountains of perfumed water, statues of gods and goddesses, and gold or silver cages filled with birds of various colors. In the center of the raft arose the roof of an immense tent made of Syrian purple and resting on silver columns. Under it were gleaming, like suns, tables prepared for the guests, loaded with Alexandrian glass, crystal, and vessels simply beyond price—the plunder of Italy, Greece, and Asia Minor.

The raft, which because of plants accumulated on it had the appearance of an island and a garden, was joined by cords of gold and purple to boats shaped like fish, swans, mews, and flamingoes, in which sat at painted oars rowers of both sexes, with forms and features of marvelous beauty, their hair dressed in oriental fashion, or gathered in golden nets. When Nero arrived at the main raft with Poppaea and the Augustians and sat beneath the purple roof of the tent, the oars struck the water, the boats moved, the golden cords stretched, and the raft with the feast and the guests began to move and make circles on the pond. Other boats surrounded it, and other smaller rafts, filled with women playing on citharae and harps, women whose rosy bodies on the blue background of the sky and the water and in the reflections from golden instruments seemed to absorb that blue and those reflections, and to change and bloom like flowers.

From the groves at the banks, from fantastic buildings arranged for that day and hidden among thickets, were heard music and song. The whole area resounded with noise; echoes bore around the voices of horns and trumpets. Caesar himself, with Poppaea on one side of him, and Pythagoras on the other, was amazed; and more especially, when among the boats young slave maidens appeared as sirens covered with green nets in imitation of scales, he did not spare praises on Tigellinus. But he looked at Petronius from habit, wishing to learn the opinion of the "arbiter," who seemed indifferent for a long time, and only when questioned outright, answered, "I judge, lord, that ten thousand naked maidens make less impression than one."

But the "floating feast" pleased Caesar, for it was something new. Besides, such exquisite dishes were served that the imagination of Apicius would have failed at sight of them, and wines of so many kinds that Otho, who used to serve eighty, would have hidden under water with shame, could he have witnessed the luxury of that feast. Besides women, the Augustians sat down at the table, among whom Vinicius excelled all with his handsome form. Formerly his figure and face indicated too clearly the soldier by profession; now the mental suffering and the physical pain through

248

which he had passed had chiseled his features, as if the delicate hand of a master had passed over them. His complexion had lost its former swarthiness, but the yellowish gleam of Numidian marble remained on it. His eyes had grown larger and more pensive. His body had retained its former powerful outlines, as if created for armor; but above the body of a legionary was seen the head of a Grecian god, or at least of a refined patrician, at once subtle and splendid. Petronius, in saying that none of the ladies of Caesar's court would be able or willing to resist Vinicius, spoke like a man of experience. All gazed at him now, even Poppaea and the vestal virgin Rubria, whom Caesar wished to see at the feast.

Wines, cooled in mountain snow, soon warmed the hearts and heads of the guests. Boats shaped as grasshoppers or butterflies shot forth from the bushes at the shore every moment. The blue surface of the pond seemed occupied by butterflies. Above the boats here and there flew doves and other birds from India and Africa, fastened with silver and blue threads or strings. The sun had passed the greater part of the sky, but the day was warm and even hot, though it was in the beginning of May. The pond heaved from the strokes of oars, which beat the water in time with music; but in the air there was not the least breath of wind. The groves were motionless, as if lost in listening and in gazing at that which was happening on the water. The raft circled continually on the pond, bearing guests who were increasingly drunk and boisterous.

The feast had not run half its course when places changed at the table. Caesar gave the example, who, rising himself, commanded Vinicius, who sat next to Rubria the vestal, to move. Nero occupied the place and began to whisper something in Rubria's ear. Vinicius found himself next to Poppaea, who extended her arm and begged him to fasten her loosened bracelet. When he did so, with hands trembling somewhat, she cast at him from beneath her long lashes a glance as it were of modesty, and shook her golden head as if in resistance.

Meanwhile, the sun, growing larger and ruddier, sank slowly behind the tops of the grove. The guests were for the greater part thoroughly intoxicated. The raft circled now nearer the shore, on which, among bunches of trees and flowers, were seen groups of people, disguised as fauns or satyrs, playing flutes, bagpipes, and drums, with groups of maidens representing nymphs and dryads. Darkness fell at last amid drunken shouts from the tent, shouts raised in honor of Luna. Meanwhile, the groves were lighted with a thousand lamps. From the shores shone swarms of lights; on the terraces appeared new naked groups, formed of the wives and daughters of the first Roman houses. These with voice and unrestrained manner began to lure partners. The raft touched the shore at last. Caesar and the Augustians vanished in the groves, scattered in tents hidden in thickets and in grottos artificially arranged among fountains and springs. Madness possessed everyone; no one knew where Caesar had gone; no one knew who was a senator, who a soldier, dancer, or musician. Satyrs and fauns began to chase nymphs, while shouting. Darkness covered certain parts of the grove. Everywhere, however, laughter and shouts were heard, and whispers and panting breaths. In fact Rome had not seen anything like that before.

Vinicius was not drunk, as he had been at the feast in Nero's palace when Lygia was present; but he was roused and intoxicated by the sight of everything done about him, and at last the fever of pleasure seized him. Rushing into the forest, he ran, with others, examining who of the dryads seemed most beautiful. New flocks of these raced around him every moment with shouts and with songs; these flocks were pursued by fauns, satyrs, senators, soldiers, and by sounds of music. Seeing at last a band of maidens led by one arrayed as Diana, he sprang to it, intending to examine the goddess more closely. All at once his heart sank into his bosom, for he thought that in that goddess, with the moon on her forehead, he recognized Lygia.

They circled him with a mad whirl and, wishing evidently to incline him to follow, rushed away the next moment like a herd of deer. But he stood breathlessly on the spot with beating heart; for though he saw that Diana was not Lygia, and close up was not even like her, this powerful impression removed his enthusiasm. He was gripped by such yearning as he had never felt before, and love for Lygia rushed through his blood in an immense wave. Never had she seemed so dear, pure, and beloved as in that forest of madness and frenzied excess. A moment before, he himself wished to drink of that cup and share in that shameless sensuality; now disgust and revulsion possessed him. He felt that evil was stifling him, that his chest needed air and the stars that were hidden by the thickets of that dreadful grove. He determined to flee; but barely had he moved when a veiled figure stood in front of him, placed its hands on his shoulders, and whispered, flooding his face with burning breath, "I love you! Come! No one will see us, hasten!"

Vinicius was roused, as if from a dream.

"Who are you?"

But she leaned on him and insisted, "Hurry! See how lonely it is here, and I love you! Come!"

"Who are you?" Vinicius repeated.

"Guess!"

As she said this, she pressed her lips to his through the veil, drawing his head toward her at the same time, until at last breath failed the woman and she tore her face from him.

"Night of love! Night of madness!" she said, catching the air quickly. "Tonight is free! You have me!"

But that kiss burned Vinicius; it filled him with panic. His soul and heart were elsewhere; in the whole world nothing existed for him except Lygia. So, pushing back the veiled figure, he said, "Whoever you be, I love another. I do not wish you."

"Remove the veil," she said, lowering her head toward him.

At that moment the leaves of the nearest myrtle began to rustle; the veiled woman vanished like a dream vision, but from a distance her laugh was heard, strange and ominous.

Petronius stood before Vinicius.

"I have heard and seen," he said.

"Let us go from this place," Vinicius replied.

And they went. They passed the grove and the line of mounted praetorian guards and found the litters.

"I will go with you," Petronius said.

They sat down together. On the road both were silent, and only in the atrium of Vinicius's house did Petronius ask, "Do you know who that was?"

"Was it Rubria?" Vinicius asked, repulsed at the very thought that Rubria was a vestal.

"No."

"Who then?"

Petronius lowered his voice.

"The fire of Vesta was defiled, for Rubria was with Caesar. But with you"—and he finished in a still lower voice—"the divine Augusta, the queen."

A moment of silence followed.

"Caesar," Petronius said, "was unable to hide from Poppaea his desire for Rubria; therefore she wished, perhaps, to avenge herself. But I hindered you both. Had you recognized the Augusta and refused her, you would have been ruined beyond rescue—you, Lygia, and I, perhaps."

"I have had enough of Rome, Caesar, feasts, the Augusta, Tigellinus, and all of you!" Vinicius burst out. "I am stifling. I cannot live this way; I cannot. Do you understand me?"

"Vinicius, you are losing sense, judgment, and moderation."

"I love only her in this world."

"What of that?"

"This, that I wish no other love. I have no wish for your life, your feasts, your shamelessness, your crimes!"

"What is taking place in you? Are you a Christian?"

The young man seized his head with both hands, and repeated, as if in despair, "Not yet! Not yet!"

32

Petronius went home shrugging his shoulders and greatly dissatisfied. It was evident to him that he and Vinicius had ceased to understand each other, that their souls had separated entirely. Once Petronius had immense influence over the young soldier. He had been for him a model in everything, and frequently a few ironical words of his sufficed to restrain Vinicius or urge him to something. At present that influence ceased. Petronius felt that his wit and irony would be ineffective alongside the new principles that love and contact with the incomprehensible society of Christians had put in the soul of Vinicius. The veteran skeptic understood that he had lost the key to that soul. This knowledge filled him with dissatisfaction and even fear, which was heightened by the events of that night. *If on the part of the Augusta it is not a passing whim but a strong desire,* Petronius thought, *one of two things will happen—either Vinicius will not resist her, and he may be ruined by any accident, or, that like today, he will resist, and in that event he will certainly be ruined. Perhaps I with him, because I am his relative, and because the Augusta, having included a whole family in her hatred, will throw the weight of her influence on the side of Tigellinus.*

Petronius was a man of courage and had no dread of death; but since he hoped nothing from it, he had no wish to seek it. After long meditation, he decided at last that it would be better and safer to send Vinicius from Rome on a journey. Ah! But if in addition he could give him Lygia for the road, he would do so with pleasure. But he hoped it would not be too difficult to persuade him to the journey without her. He would then spread a report on the Palatine of Vinicius's illness, and remove danger as well from his nephew as himself. The Augusta did not know whether she was recognized by Vinicius; she might suppose that she was not, so her vanity had not suffered much so far. But it might be different in the future, and it was necessary to avoid peril. Petronius wished to gain time, above all; for he understood that once Caesar set out for Achaea, Tigellinus, who comprehended nothing in the domain of art, would descend to the second place and lose his influence. In Greece Petronius was sure of victory over every opponent.

Meanwhile, he determined to watch over Vinicius and urge him to the journey. For a number of days he was always thinking about this. If he obtained an edict from Caesar expelling the Christians from Rome, Lygia would leave it with the other confessors of Christ, and after her Vinicius too. Then there would be no need to persuade him. The thing itself was possible. In fact it was not so long since, when the Jews began disturbances out of hatred for the Christians, Claudius, unable to distinguish one from the other, expelled the Jews. Why should not Nero expel the Christians? There would be more room in Rome without them. After that "floating feast" Petronius saw Nero daily, both on the Palatine and in other houses. To suggest such an idea was easy, for Nero never opposed suggestions that brought harm or ruin to anyone. After thoughtful consideration Petronius framed a whole plan for himself. He would prepare a feast in his own house, and at this feast persuade Caesar to issue an edict. He had even a hope, which was not futile, that Caesar would entrust the execution of the edict to him. He would send out Lygia with all the consideration proper to the mistress of Vinicius to Baiae, for instance, and let them love and amuse themselves there with Christianity as much as they liked.

Meanwhile, he visited Vinicius frequently, first, because he could not, despite all his Roman selfishness, rid himself of attachment to the young tribune, and second, because he wished to persuade him to make the journey. Vinicius pretended sickness and did not show himself on the Palatine, where new plans appeared every day. At last Petronius heard from Caesar's own lips that three days from then he would go to Antium. Next morning he went to inform Vinicius, who showed him a list of persons invited to Antium, which list one of Caesar's freedmen had brought him that morning.

"My name is on it; so is yours," he said. "You will find the same at your house on returning."

"Were I not among the invited," Petronius replied, "it would mean that I must die; I do not expect that to happen before the journey to Achaea. I shall be too useful to Nero. Barely have we come to Rome," he said, on looking at the list, "when we must leave again and drag over the road to Antium. But we must go, for this is not merely an invitation, but a command."

"And if someone would not obey?"

"He would be invited in another style to go on a journey notably longer—one from which people do not return. What a pity that you have not obeyed my counsel and left Rome in season! Now you must go to Antium."

"I must go to Antium. See in what times we live and what vile slaves we are!"

"Have you noticed that only today?"

"No. But you have explained to me that Christian teaching is an enemy of life, since it shackles it. But can their shackles be stronger than those which we carry? You have said, 'Greece created wisdom and beauty; and Rome, power.' Where is our power?"

"Call Chilo and talk with him. I have no desire today to philosophize. By Hercules! I did not create these times, and I do not answer for them. Let us speak of Antium. Know that great danger is awaiting you, and it would be better, perhaps, to measure strength with that Ursus who choked Croton than to go there, but still you cannot refuse."

Vinicius waved his hand carelessly and said, "Danger! We are all wandering in the shadow of death, and every moment some head sinks in its darkness."

"Am I to enumerate all who had a little sense and, therefore, in spite of the times of Tiberius, Caligula, Claudius, and Nero lived eighty and ninety years? Let even such a man as Domitius After serve you as an example. He has grown old quietly, though all his life he has been a criminal and a villain."

"Perhaps for that very reason!" Vinicius answered.

Then he began to glance over the list and read: "Tigellinus, Vatinius, Sextus Africanus, Aquilinus Regulus, Suilius Nerulinus, Eprius Marcellus, and so on! What an assembly of ruffians and scoundrels! And to say that they govern the world! Would it not be better to exhibit an Egyptian or Syrian divinity through villages and earn their bread by telling fortunes or dancing?"

"Or exhibiting learned monkeys, calculating gods, or a flute-playing donkey," Petronius said. "That is true, but let us speak of something more important. Give me your attention and listen. I have said on the Palatine that you are ill, unable to leave the house. Still, your name is on the list, which proves that someone does not credit my stories and has seen to this purposely. Nero cares nothing for the matter, since for him you are a soldier who has no conception of poetry or music and with whom at the very highest he can talk only about races in the Circus. So Poppaea must have put down your name, which means that her desire for you was not a passing whim and that she wants to win you."

"She is a daring Augusta."

"Indeed she is daring, for she may ruin herself beyond redemption. May Venus inspire her, however, with another love as soon as possible; but since she desires you, you must observe the very greatest caution. She has begun to weary Bronzebeard already; he prefers Rubria now, or Pythagoras, but, through consideration of himself, he would wreak the most horrible vengeance on us."

"In the grove I did not know that she was speaking to me; but you were listening. I said that I loved another and did not wish her. You know that."

"I implore you, by all the infernal gods, do not lose the remnant of reason the Christians have left in you. How is it possible to hesitate, having a choice between probable and certain destruction? Have I not said already that if you had wounded the Augusta's vanity, there would have been no rescue for you? By hades! If life has grown hateful to you, better open your veins at once, or cast yourself on a sword, for should you offend Poppaea a less easy death may meet you. It was easier once to reason with you. What concerns you? Would this affair cause you loss, or hinder you from loving your Lygia? Remember, besides, that Poppaea saw her on the Palatine. It will not be difficult for her to guess why you are rejecting such lofty favor, and she will get Lygia even from under the earth. You will ruin not only yourself, but Lygia too. Do you understand?"

Vinicius listened as if thinking of something else, and at last he said, "I must see her."

"Who? Lygia?"

"Lygia."

"Do you know where she is?"

"No."

"Then you will begin anew to search for her in old cemeteries and beyond the Tiber?"

"I do not know, but I must see her."

"Well, though she is a Christian, it may turn out that she has more judgment than you; and she will certainly, unless she wishes your ruin."

Vinicius shrugged his shoulders. "She saved me from the hands of Ursus."

"Then hurry, for Bronzebeard will not postpone his departure. Sentences of death may be issued in Antium also."

But Vinicius did not hear. One thought alone occupied him—a meeting with Lygia.

Meanwhile, Chilo came to his house unexpectedly.

He entered wretched, worn, and in rags, with signs of hunger on his face. But the servants, who were commanded to admit him at all hours of the day or night, did not dare to detain him, so he went straight to the atrium and, standing before Vinicius, said, "May the gods give you immortality and share with you dominion over the world."

Vinicius at first wished to give orders to throw him out, but the thought came to him that the Greek perhaps knew something of Lygia, and curiosity overcame his disgust.

"What has happened to you, Chilo?"

"Evil, O son of Jove," answered Chilo. "Real virtue is a jewel for which no one seeks now, and a genuine sage must even be glad of this, that once in five days he may buy a sheep's head from the butcher to gnaw in a attic, washing it down with his tears. Ah, lord! What coins you gave me I paid Atractus for books, and afterward I was robbed and ruined. The slave who was to write down my wisdom fled, taking the remnant of your generosity. I am in misery, but I thought, To whom can I go, if not to you, O Serapis, whom I love and deify, for whom I have exposed my life?"

"Why have you come, and what do you bring?"

"I come for aid, O Baal, and I bring my misery, my love, and finally the information which through love for you I have collected. I know where the divine Lygia is living; I will show you the house."

"Where is she?"

"With Linus, the elder leader of the Christians. She is there with Ursus, who goes as before to the miller, a namesake of Demas. Yes, Demas! Ursus works in the night; so if you surround the house at night, you will not find him. Linus is old, and there are only two aged women in the house."

"How do you know all this?"

"You remember, lord, that the Christians had me in their grasp and spared me. True, Glaucus was mistaken in thinking that

I was the cause of his misfortunes; but he still believed that I was, poor man. Still they spared me. Of course, lord, gratitude filled my heart. I am a man of former, and better, times. Was I to desert friends and benefactors? I would have been hard-hearted not to ask for them and discover they were living. By the Pessinian Cybele! I am not capable of such conduct. At first I was restrained by fear that they might misunderstand me, but my love for them proved greater than my fear, and the ease with which they forgive every injustice gave me special courage. Our last attempt ended in defeat; but can such a son of Fortune be reconciled with defeat? Their house is unguarded. You may command your slaves to surround it so that not a mouse could escape. It depends on you alone to have that magnanimous king's daughter in your house this very night. But should that happen, remember that the success is due to this very poor and hungry son of my father."

Temptation shook all Vinicius's being again. Yes; this was the right time and method. Once Lygia is in his house, who can remove her? Once he makes Lygia his mistress, she must remain so forever. And let all religions perish! What good will the Christians do to him then, with their mercy and alien faith? He should shake himself free of all that worry. What will Lygia do later, except to reconcile her fate with the religion she professes? That, too, is a question of minor significance. Will this religion remain in her soul against a world opposing it, against luxury and excitements to which she might yield? Today she could be his. He needs only to give an order at dark. And then delight without end! *What has my life been?* Vinicius thought. *Suffering, unsatisfied desire, and endless problems without answer.*

He remembered that he had promised not to raise a hand against her. But by what had he sworn? Not by the gods, for he did not believe in them; not by Christ, for he did not believe in Him yet. Finally, if she feels injured, he will marry her, and thus repair the injury. Yes; to that house he feels bound, for to her he is indebted for life. Here he recalled the day when he and Croton attacked her retreat; he remembered the Lygian's fist raised above him and all that had happened later. He remembered the little cross she left him before going. Will he pay for all that by a new attack? Will he drag her by the hair as a slave to his home? He felt it was not enough to seize her in his arms by superior force; but he needed something more—her consent, her love, and her soul. Blessed be that roof, if she come under it willingly. Then the happiness of both will be as inexhaustible as the ocean and the sun. But to seize her by violence would be to destroy that happiness forever and to defile that which is most precious and beloved in life.

He glanced at Chilo, who, while watching him, pushed his hands under his rags and scratched himself uneasily. That instant, unspeakable disgust took hold of Vinicius and a wish to throttle that former assistant of his as he would a foul worm or venomous serpent. In an instant he knew what to do. Following the impulse of his stern Roman nature, he turned toward Chilo and said, "I will not do what you advise, but in case you go without a just reward, I will order them to give you three hundred stripes in the city prison."

Chilo grew pale. There was so much cold resolution in the handsome face of Vinicius that he could not deceive himself with the hope that the promised reward was no more than a cruel jest.

He threw himself on his knees in one instant and, bending double began to groan in a broken voice, "How, O king of Persia? Why? O pyramid of kindness! Colossus of mercy! For what? I am old, hungry, unfortunate. I have served you—do you repay this way?"

"As you did to the Christians," said Vinicius. And he called the chief slave.

But Chilo sprang toward Vinicius's feet and, embracing them tightly, begged while his face was covered with deathly pallor. "O lord, O lord! I am old! Fifty, not three hundred stripes. Oh, mercy, mercy!"

Vinicius thrust him away with his foot and gave the order. In the twinkle of a eye two powerful Quadi followed the slave and, seizing Chilo by the hair, tied his own rags around his neck and dragged him to the prison.

"In the name of Christ!" the Greek called, at the exit to the corridor.

Vinicius was left alone. The order just issued enlivened him. He tried to collect his scattered thoughts. He felt great relief, and the victory he had gained over himself filled him with comfort. He thought that he had made some great strides toward Lygia, and that some high reward should be given him. At the first moment it did not even occur to him that he had done a grievous wrong to Chilo and had had him flogged for the very acts for which he had rewarded him previously. He was too much of a Roman yet to be pained by another man's suffering or to occupy his attention with one wretched Greek. Had he even thought of Chilo's suffering he would have considered that he had acted properly in ordering punishment for such a villain. But he was thinking of Lygia, and said to her in his mind, *I will not pay you with evil for good; and when you learn how I acted with him who tried to persuade me to raise hands against you, you will be grateful.* But here he stopped at this thought. *Would Lygia praise his treatment of Chilo?* The religion she professed commanded forgiveness; nay, the Christians forgave the villain, though they had greater reasons for revenge. Then he heard in his soul the cry "In the name of Christ!" He remembered then that Chilo had ransomed himself from the hands of Ursus with such a cry, and he determined to redeem the remainder of the punishment.

The slave then asked, "Lord, the old man has fainted, and perhaps he is dead. Am I to command further flogging?"

"Revive him and bring him before me."

The chief of the atrium vanished behind the curtain; but the revival could not have been easy, for Vinicius waited a long time and was growing impatient when slaves brought in Chilo and disappeared at a signal.

Chilo was as pale as linen, and down his legs threads of blood were flowing to the mosaic pavement of the atrium. He was conscious, however, and, falling on his knees, began to speak. "Thanks to you, lord. You are great and merciful."

"Dog," said Vinicius, "know that I forgave you because of that Christ to whom I owe my life."

"O lord, I will serve Him and you."

"Be silent and listen. Rise! You will go and show me the house in which Lygia dwells."

Chilo sprang up; but he was barely on his feet when he said in a falling voice, "Lord, I am really hungry—I will go, lord, I will go! But I have not the strength. Command them to give me even remnants from the plate of your dog, and I will go."

Vinicius command his slaves to give Chilo food, a piece of gold, and a cloak. But Chilo, weakened by the beating and hunger, could not go to take food, though terror raised the hair on his head, lest Vinicius might mistake his weakness for stubbornness and command them to flog him again.

"Only let the wine warm me," he repeated, with chattering teeth. "I shall be able to go at once, even to Magna Graecia."

He regained some strength later, and they went out.

The way was long, for, like the majority of Christians, Linus lived in the Trans-Tiber, and not far from Miriam. At last Chilo showed Vinicius a small house, standing alone, surrounded by a wall covered entirely with ivy, and said, "Here it is, lord."

"Well," Vinicius said, "go your way now, but listen first to what I tell you. Forget that you have served me; forget where Peter and Glaucus live, and all Christians. You will come every month to my house, where Demas, my freedman, will pay you two pieces of gold. But should you spy further after Christians, I will have you flogged, or delivered into the hands of the prefect of the city."

Chilo bowed down and said, "I will forget."

But when Vinicius vanished beyond the corner of the street, he raised his fists and threatened, "By the Furies! I will not forget!"

33

Vinicius went directly to the house in which Miriam lived. Before the gate he met Nazarius, who was confused at sight of him; but giving a friendly greeting to the boy, he asked to be led to his mother's house.

Besides Miriam, Vinicius found Peter, Glaucus, Crispus, and Paul of Tarsus, who had returned recently from Fregellae. They were shocked at the sight of the young tribune, but he said, "I greet you in the name of Christ, whom you honor."

"May His name be glorified forever!" they answered.

"I have seen your virtue and experienced your kindness, so I come as a friend."

"And we greet you as a friend," Peter answered. "Sit down, lord, and enjoy a meal as a guest."

"I will sit down and share your food; but first listen, Peter and Paul of Tarsus, so that you may know my sincerity. I know where Lygia is. I have returned from the house of Linus, which is near. I have a right to take her away, given me by Caesar. I might surround her hiding-place with my five hundred slaves and seize her; but I will not do this."

"For this reason the blessing of the Lord will be upon you, and your heart will be purified," said Peter.

"I thank you. Before I knew you, I would have captured her and held her by force. But your virtue and your religion, though I do not yet profess it, have changed something in my soul, so that I will not resort to violence. I do not know myself why this is so, but you take the place of Lygia's father and mother, so I ask you: Give her to me as my wife, and I promise I will not forbid her to confess Christ, but I will begin myself to learn His religion."

He spoke confidently, but his legs trembled beneath his tunic. He paused and continued, as if anticipating an unfavorable answer, "I know obstacles exist, but I love her more than my own life, and though I am not a Christian yet, I am neither your enemy nor Christ's. I am being sincere. Please trust me. Another might say, 'Baptize me'; I say, 'Enlighten me.' I believe that Christ rose from the dead, for people say so who love the truth and who saw Him after death. I believe, for I have seen myself, that your religion produces virtue, justice, and mercy—not evil. I still do not know much of your religion. I have listened to some teaching from you, observed your works, and watched Lygia.

"I repeat that it has made some positive change in me. Formerly I ruled my servants with an iron hand, but now I show pity. I was fond of pleasure; the other night I fled from the pond of Agrippa out of pure disgust. Formerly I believed in the stronger ruling the weaker, but no longer. I do not even recognize myself. I am disgusted by feasts, wine, singing, garlands, the court of Caesar, naked bodies, and all wrongdoing. When I think that Lygia is like snow in the mountains, I love her the more. When I think that she is what she is through your religion, I love and desire that, too. But since I do not understand fully, or know whether I shall be able to live according to its teachings, or whether my nature can endure it, I am in uncertainty and suffering, as if my soul were in prison."

Here his brows met in a wrinkle of pain, and a flush appeared on his cheeks. Then he spoke on with growing emotion. "As you see, I am tortured both from love and from uncertainty. Men tell me that in your religion there is no place for human joy, order, authority, or Roman dominion. Is this true? Men tell me that you are all madmen; but tell me your viewpoint. Is it a sin to love, a sin to feel joy, a sin to want happiness? I have many questions. Are you enemies of life? Must a Christian be miserable? Must I give up Lygia? In your view, what is the purpose of life? Your deeds and words are like transparent water, but what is beneath it?

"Believe that I am sincere. Remove darkness from me. Men say Greece created beauty and wisdom, and Rome created power; but what do they achieve? If there is light beyond your doors, open them and share it with me."

"We bring you God's love," Peter said.

And Paul of Tarsus added, "If I speak with the tongues of men and of angels, but do not have love, I am like a clanging instrument."

But the heart of the old apostle was moved by that soul in suffering, which, like a bird in a cage, was struggling toward air and the sun. Stretching his hand to Vinicius, he said, "Whoever knocks at the door, to him it will be opened. The favor and grace of God is upon you; for this reason I bless you, and your love, in the name of the Redeemer of mankind."

Vinicius, who had spoken with passion already, sprang toward Peter on hearing this blessing, and did something unheard of. That descendant of Quirites, who until recently had not recognized humanity in a foreigner, seized the hand of the old Galilean and pressed it in gratitude to his lips.

Peter was pleased; for he understood that his sowing had fallen on another field, that his fishing-net had gathered in a new soul.

Those present were also pleased by that visible expression of honor for the apostle of God. They exclaimed in one voice, "Praise to the Lord in the highest!"

Vinicius rose with a radiant face, and said, "I recognize your approval, for I am very grateful, and I think that you can convince me of other parts of your religion in the same way. But I will add that this cannot happen in Rome. Caesar is going to Antium, and I must go with him, for I have the order. You know that not to obey is death. But if I have found favor in your eyes, go with me to teach them your truth. It will be safer for you than for me. Even in that great throng of people, you can announce your truth in the very court of Caesar. They say that Acte is a Christian; and there are Christians among the praetorian guard itself, for I have seen soldiers kneeling before you, Peter, at the Nomentan gate. In Antium I have a villa where we shall assemble to hear your teaching, at Nero's side. Glaucus told me that you are ready to go to the end of the earth for one soul; so do for me what you have done for those for whose sake you have come from Judea—please do this, and do not desert my soul."

Hearing this, they began to deliberate, thinking of the great possibilities and the significance there would be for the pagan world with the conversion of an Augustian and a descendant of one of the oldest Roman families. They were ready, indeed, to wander to the end of the earth for one human soul, and since the death of the Master they had, in fact, done nothing else. Peter was the pastor of a huge multitude, so he could not go; but Paul of Tarsus, who had been in Aricium and Fregellae not long before, and who was preparing for a long journey to the East to visit churches there and enliven them with a new spirit of zeal, consented to accompany the young tribune to Antium.

Vinicius, though sad because Peter, to whom he owed so much, could not visit Antium, thanked him and then turned to the old apostle with his last request. "Knowing Lygia's dwelling," he said, "I might have gone to her and asked, as is proper, whether she would take me as her husband should I become Christian, but

264

I prefer to ask you. Permit me to see her, or take me yourself to her. I do not know how long I shall be in Antium; and remember that those near Caesar cannot be sure of tomorrow. Petronius himself told me that I should not be completely safe there. Let me see her before I go; let me delight my eyes with her presence; and let me ask her if she will forget my evil and return good to me."

Peter smiled kindly and said, "But who could refuse you a proper joy, my son?"

Vinicius stooped again to kiss Peter's hands, for he could not in any way restrain his overflowing heart. The apostle took him by the temples and said, "Have no fear of Caesar, for I tell you that a hair will not fall from your head."

He sent Miriam for Lygia, telling her not to reveal who was present, so that they could surprise with delight.

It was not far, so after a short time those in the room saw among the myrtles of the garden Miriam leading Lygia by the hand.

Vinicius wished to run to meet her, but at the sight of that beloved form happiness overcame his strength. He stood with beating heart, breathless, barely able to keep on his feet, a hundred times more excited than when for the first time in war he heard the Parthian arrows whizzing round his head.

She ran in, unsuspecting; but at sight of him she halted as if rooted in the earth. Her face flushed, and then in turn became very pale; she looked with startled and frightened eyes on those present.

But round about she saw kind glances. The apostle Peter approached her and asked, "Lygia, do you love him as much as ever?"

A moment of tense silence followed. Her lips began to quiver like those of a child who is beginning to cry, who feels guilty, but is ready to confess.

"Please answer," said the apostle.

Then, with humility, obedience, and fear in her voice, she whispered, kneeling at the knees of Peter, "I do."

In one moment Vinicius knelt at her side. Peter placed his hands on their heads, and said, "Love each other in the Lord and to His glory, for there is no sin in your love."

34

While walking with Lygia through the garden, Vinicius described, in words from the depth of his heart, what he had confessed to the apostles—the pain of his soul, the changes that had taken place in him, and, finally, that immense yearning that had taken the joy of life from him. He confessed to Lygia that he had thought for whole days and nights about her. He revered the little cross of boxwood twigs she had given him, and it reminded him of her. Some of his acts had been evil, he knew, but they had their origin in sincere love. He had loved her when she was in the house of Aulus, when she was on the Palatine, when he saw her in Ostrianum listening to Peter's words, when he went with Croton to carry her away, when she watched at his bedside, and when she deserted him. Blessed be the moment when he thought to go to the apostles, for now he is at her side, and she will not flee from him, as the last time she fled from the house of Miriam.

"I did not flee from you," Lygia said.

"Then why did you go?"

She raised her iris-colored eyes to him and, bending her blushing face, said, "You know why," she said shyly.

Vinicius was speechless for a moment from ecstasy, realizing that she was utterly different from Roman women, and resembled Pomponia alone. He could not explain this to her clearly, for he could not define this feeling, recognizing true spiritual beauty. He filled her with delight when he told her that he loved her because she had fled from him, and that she would be sacred to him at his hearth. Then, grasping her hand, he ceased speaking; he merely gazed on her with rapture. He had won his life's happiness, and he now repeated her name, as if to assure himself that he had found her.

"Oh, Lygia, Lygia!"

She confessed also that she had loved him while in the house of Aulus, and that if he had taken her back to them from the Palatine she would have told Aulus and Pomponia of her love and tried to soften their anger against them.

"I swear to you," Vinicius said, "that it had not even occurred to me to take you from Aulus. Petronius will tell you sometime that I told him then how I loved and wished to marry you. 'Let her anoint my door with wolf fat, and let her sit at my hearth,' I said to him. But he ridiculed me and gave Caesar the idea of demanding you as a hostage and giving you to me. How often in my sorrow have I cursed him; but perhaps fate ordained this, for otherwise I should not have known the Christians and should not have understood you."

"Believe me, Marcus," Lygia replied, "it was Christ who led you to Himself by design."

Vinicius considered this carefully.

"True," he answered, with animation. "Everything worked out for the good that in seeking you I met the Christians. In Ostrianum I listened to the apostle with wonder, for I had never heard such words. And did you pray for me there?"

"I did," Lygia answered.

They passed near the summerhouse covered with thick ivy and approached the place where Ursus, after stifling Croton, threw himself upon Vinicius.

"Here," the young man said, "I should have perished but for you."

"Do not remind me," Lygia answered, "and do not speak of it to Ursus."

"Could seek revenge against him for defending you? Had he been a slave, I should have given him freedom immediately."

"Had he been a slave, Aulus would have freed him long ago."

"Do you remember," Vinicius asked, "that I wished to take you back to Aulus, but your answer was that Caesar might hear of it and take revenge on Aulus and Pomponia? You may see them now as often as you wish."

"How, Marcus?"

"I say 'now,' and I think that you will be able to see them without danger when you are mine. For should Caesar hear of this and ask what I did with the hostage whom he gave me, I should say, 'I married her, and she visits the house of Aulus with my consent.' He will not remain long in Antium, for he wishes to go to Achaea; and even if he stays in Antium, I shall not need to see him daily. When Paul of Tarsus teaches me your faith, I will receive baptism at once. I will come here, gain the friendship of Aulus and Pomponia, who will have returned to the city by that time, and there will be no further problem. I will seat you at my hearth. Oh, carissima! Carissima!"

And he stretched forth his hand, as if taking heaven as a witness of his love; and Lygia, raising her clear eyes to him, said, "And then I shall say, 'Wherever you are, Caius, there am I, Caia.'"

"No, Lygia," Vinicius cried, "I swear to you that no woman will be so honored in the house of her husband as you."

For a time they walked on in silence, without being able to comprehend their mutual happiness, in love with each other, like two deities, and as beautiful as if spring had given them to the world with the flowers.

They halted at last under the cypress growing near the entrance of the house. Lygia leaned against his chest, and Vinicius began to ask again with a trembling voice, "Tell Ursus to go to the house of Aulus for your furniture and toys of childhood."

But she, blushing like a rose, answered, "Custom commands otherwise."

"I know that. The matron who accompanies the bride and explains to her the duties of a wife usually brings them behind the bride, but do this for me. I will take them to my villa in Antium, and they will remind me of you."

Here he placed his hands together and repeated, like a child who is begging for something, "It will be some days before Pomponia returns; so do this, diva, do this, carissima."

"But Pomponia will do as she likes," Lygia answered, blushing still more deeply at mention of the matron.

And again they were silent, for love had nearly taken their breath away. Lygia stood with shoulders leaning against the cypress, her face whitening in the shadow, like a flower, her eyes drooping, her bosom heaving with increasing life. Vinicius grew pale. In the silence of the afternoon they heard only the beating of their hearts; and in their mutual ecstasy the cypress, the myrtle bushes, and the ivy of the summerhouse became for them a paradise of love. But soon Miriam appeared in the door and invited them to the afternoon meal. They sat down then with the apostles, who gazed at them with pleasure, as on the young generation that after their death would preserve and sow the seed of the new faith. Peter broke and blessed bread. There was peace on all their faces, and a certain immense contentment seemed to overflow within the house.

"See," Paul said at last, turning to Vinicius, "are we enemies of life and happiness?"

"No, indeed," Vinicius answered, "for never have I been so happy as among all of you."

35

On the evening of that day Vinicius, while returning home through the Forum, saw at the entrance to the Vicus Tuscus the gilded litter of Petronius, carried by eight stalwart Bithynians, and, stopping it with a sign of his hand, he approached the curtains.

"You have had a pleasant dream, I trust, and a happy one!" he cried, laughing at sight of the slumbering Petronius.

"Oh, is it you?" Petronius said, waking up. "Yes, I dropped asleep for a moment, because I passed the night at the Palatine. I have come out to buy something to read on the road to Antium. What is the news?"

"Are you visiting the bookshops?" Vinicius asked.

"Yes, I am collecting a special supply for the journey. It is likely that some new things of Musonius and Seneca have come out. I am looking also for Persius and for a certain edition of the "Eclogues" of Virgil, which I do not possess. When a man is once in a bookshop curiosity seizes him to look here and there. I was at the shop of Avirnus and with the Sozii on Vicus Sandalarius. By Castor! How I want to sleep!"

"You were on the Palatine? Then I would ask you what you heard? Come to my house, and we will talk of Antium and of other things."

"That is fine," Petronius answered, stepping out of the litter. "You must know, besides, that we start for Antium the day after tomorrow."

"How should I know that?"

"In what world are you living? Well, I shall be the first to announce the news to you. Yes; be ready for the day after tomorrow. Peas in olive oil have not helped, a cloth around his thick neck has not helped, and Bronzebeard is hoarse. In view of this, delay is not to be mentioned. He curses Rome and its atmosphere; he would be glad to level it to the earth or to destroy it with fire, and he longs for the sea. He says that the smells the wind brings from the narrow streets are driving him into the grave. Today great sacrifices were offered in all the temples to restore his voice; and woe to Rome, but especially to the Senate, should it not return quickly!"

"Then there would be no reason for his visit to Achaea?"

"But is that the only talent possessed by our divine Caesar?" Petronius asked, smiling. "He would appear in the Olympic games, as a poet, with his 'Burning of Troy'; as a charioteer, as a musician, as an athlete—even as a dancer, and would receive in every case all the crowns intended for victors. Do you know why that monkey grew hoarse? Yesterday he wanted to equal our Paris in dancing, and he danced the adventures of Leda for us, during which he sweat and caught cold. He was as wet and slippery as an eel. He changed masks one after another, whirled like a spindle, waved his hands like a drunken sailor, until disgust filled me while I looked at that great stomach and those thin legs. Paris taught him during two weeks; but imagine Ahenobarbus as Leda or as the divine swan. That was quite a swan! There is no use in denying it. But he wants to appear before the public in that pantomime—first in Antium, and then in Rome."

"People are offended already because he sang in public; but to think that a Roman Caesar will appear as a mime! No; even Rome will not endure that!" Vinicius said.

"My dear friend, Rome will endure anything; the Senate will pass a vote of thanks to the 'Father of his country.' And the rabble will be elated because Caesar is its buffoon," Petronius countered.

"Is it possible to be more debased?"

Petronius shrugged his shoulders. "You are living by yourself at home and meditating, now about Lygia, now about Christians, so you do not know, perhaps, what happened two days ago. Nero married, in public, Pythagoras, who appeared as a bride. That exceeded the ultimate madness, it would seem. The flamens [priests], who were summoned, came and performed the ceremony with solemnity. I was present. I can endure much; still, I thought, I confess, that the gods, if there be any, would give an ominous sign. But Caesar does not believe in the gods, and he is right."

"So he is in one person chief priest, god, and atheist."

"True," Petronius said, beginning to laugh. "That had not entered my head, but the combination is peculiar to the world." Then, stopping a moment, he said, "One should add that this chief priest who does not believe in the gods, and this god who reviles the gods, fears them in his character of atheist."

"The proof of this is what happened in the temple of Vesta."

"What a society!"

"As the society is, so is Caesar. But this will not last long."

They then entered the house of Vinicius, who joyously called for supper. Turning to Petronius, he said, "No, my dear Petronius, society must be renewed."

"We shall not renew it," Petronius answered, "even for the reason that in Nero's time man is like a butterfly—he lives in the sunshine of favor, and at the first cold wind he perishes, even against his will. More than once I have asked: By what miracle has such a man as Lucius Saturninus been able to reach the age of ninety-three, to survive Tiberius, Caligula, and Claudius? But never mind. Will you permit me to send your litter for Eunice? My wish to sleep has gone, somehow, and I should like to be festive. Give an order to cithara players to come to the supper, and afterward we will talk of Antium."

Vinicius gave the order to send for Eunice but declared that he had no thought of worrying about the stay in Antium.

"Let those worry who can only live in the rays of Caesar's favor. The world does not end on the Palatine, especially for those who have something else in their hearts and souls."

He said this so carelessly and with such animation and gladness that his whole manner struck Petronius. Looking for a time at Vinicius, he asked, "What is happening within you? You act today as you did when wearing the golden bulla on your neck."

"I am happy," Vinicius answered. "I have purposely invited you to tell you so."

"What has happened?"

"Something that I would not give for the Roman Empire."

Then he sat down and, leaning on the arm of the chair, asked, "Do remember when we were at the house of Aulus Plautius and there saw for the first time the godlike maiden you called 'the dawn and the spring'? Do you remember that Psyche, that incomparable, that one more beautiful than our maidens and our goddesses?"

Petronius looked at him with bewilderment, as if he wished to make sure that he was in his right mind.

"Of whom are you speaking?" he asked at last. "Evidently I remember Lygia."

"I am her betrothed."

"What!"

Vinicius sprang up and called his chief servant.

"Let the slaves stand before me to the last soul, quickly!"

"Are you her betrothed?" Petronius repeated.

But before he had recovered from his shock the immense atrium was swarming with people. Panting old men ran in, men in the vigor of life, women, boys, and girls. In corridors voices were heard calling in various languages. Finally, all took their places in rows at the walls and among the columns. Vinicius, standing by, turned to Demas, the freedman, and said, "Those who have served twenty years in my house are to appear tomorrow before me, where they will receive three pieces of gold and double rations for a week. Send an order to the village prisons to absolve punishment, remove the fetters from people's feet, and feed them sufficiently. Know that a happy day has come to me, and I wish others to rejoice in the house."

For a moment they stood in silence, as if not believing their ears; then all hands were raised at once, and all mouths cried, "Lord! Lord!"

272

Vinicius dismissed them with a wave of his hand. Though they desired to thank him and to fall at his feet, they went away hurriedly, filling the house with happiness from cellar to roof.

"Tomorrow," said Vinicius, "I will command them to meet again in the garden and to make such signs on the ground as they choose. Lygia will free those who draw a fish."

Petronius, who never wondered long at anything, had grown indifferent, and asked, "A fish, is it? Ah, ha! According to Chilo, that is the sign of a Christian, I remember." Then he extended his hand to Vinicius and said, "Happiness is always where a man sees it. May Flora strew flowers under your feet for long years. I wish you everything that you wish for yourself."

"I thank you, for I thought that you would oppose me, and that, as you see, would be time lost."

"I? Oppose? By no means. On the contrary, I tell you that you are doing well."

"Ha, traitor!" Vinicius answered joyfully. "Have you forgotten what you told me once when we were leaving the house of Pomponia Graecina?"

"No," Petronius answered in a cool manner. "But I have changed my opinion. My dear," he added, "in Rome everything changes. Husbands change wives, wives change husbands; why should not I change opinions? Nero married Acte, whom for his sake they represented as the descendant of a kingly line. Well, he would have had an honest wife, and we an honest Augusta. By Proteus and his barren spaces in the sea! I shall change my opinion as often as I find it appropriate or profitable. As to Lygia, her royal descent is more certain than Acte's. But in Antium be on your guard against Poppaea, who is revengeful."

"A hair will not fall from my head in Antium."

"If you plan to astonish me a second time, you are mistaken; but how do you have certainty?"

"The apostle Peter told me so."

"Ah, the apostle Peter told you! Against that there is no argument; permit me, however, to take certain measures of precaution. If the apostle Peter turns out to be a false prophet, he should then lose your confidence, which certainly will be of use to him in the future."

"Do what may please you, but I believe him. And if you think to turn me against him by repeating his name with sarcasm, you are mistaken."

"But one question more. Have you become a Christian?"

"Not yet; but Paul of Tarsus will travel with me to explain the teachings of Christ, and afterward I will receive baptism; for your statement that they are enemies of life and pleasantness is not true."

"All the better for you and Lygia," Petronius answered. Then, shrugging his shoulders, he said, as if to himself, "But it is astounding how skilled those people are in gaining converts and how that sect is growing."

"Yes," Vinicius answered, with as much warmth as if he had been baptized already. "There are thousands and tens of thousands of them in Rome, in the cities of Italy, in Greece and Asia. There are Christians among the legions and among the praetorian guard. They are in the palace of Caesar itself. Slaves and citizens, poor and rich, plebeian and patrician, confess that faith. Do you know that Pomponia Graecina is a Christian, that likely Octavia was, and Acte is? Yes, that teaching will embrace the world, and it alone is able to renew it. Do not shrug your shoulders, for who knows whether in a month or a year you will not receive it yourself?"

"I?" Petronius said. "No, by the son of Leto! I will not receive it; even if the truth and wisdom of gods and men were contained in it. That would require labor, and I have no fondness for labor. Labor demands self-denial, and I will not deny myself anything. With your nature, which is like fire and boiling water, something like this may happen any time. But I? I have my gems, my cameos, my vases, my Eunice. I do not believe in Olympus, but I arrange it on earth for myself; and I shall flourish until the arrows of the divine archer pierce me, or until Caesar commands me to open my veins. I love the odor of violets too much, and a comfortable hearth. I love even our gods, as mythical figures, and Achaea, to which I am preparing to go with our fat, thin-legged, incomparable, godlike Caesar, the august period-compelling Hercules, Nero."

Then he was joyous at the very thought that he could accept the teaching of Galilean fishermen. But he stopped, for the arrival of Eunice was announced. Immediately after her coming supper was served, during which songs were sung by the cithara players; Vinicius told of Chilo's visit and also how that visit had given him the idea of going to the apostles directly—an idea that came to him while they were flogging Chilo.

At mention of this, Petronius became drowsy and said, "The thought was good, since the object was good. But as to Chilo, I should have given him five pieces of gold; but as it was your will to flog him, it was better to flog him, for who knows but in time senators will bow to him, as today they are bowing to our cobbler-knight, Vatinius. Good night."

And, removing his wreath, he, with Eunice, prepared for home. When they had gone, Vinicius went to his library and wrote to Lygia as follows:

"Caesar will go to Antium the day after tomorrow—and I must go with him. I have told you already that not to obey would be to risk life—and I have no courage to die. But if you do not wish me to go, write one word, and I will stay. Petronius will avert danger with a speech. Today, in the hour of my delight, I gave rewards to all my slaves; those who have served in the house twenty years I shall take tomorrow and free. You, my dear, should be proud of me, since this act I think will be in accord with that merciful religion of yours; second, I do this for your sake. They are to thank you for their freedom. I shall tell them so tomorrow, so that they will be grateful to you. I give myself in bondage to happiness and you. God grant that I never see liberation. May Antium be cursed, as well as the journey of Ahenobarbus! Meanwhile, the period of separation will sweeten my memory of you. Whenever I can tear myself away, I shall sit on a horse and rush back to Rome, to gladden my eyes with your sight and my ears with your voice. When I cannot come I shall send a slave with a letter and an inquiry about you. I salute you, divine one, and embrace your feet. Do not be angry that I call you divine. If you forbid it, I shall obey, but today I cannot call you otherwise."

36

Orders to leave for Antium had been given a number of days earlier. At the Porta Ostiensis, from early morning, crowds made up of the local rabble and of all nations of the earth had gathered to feast their eyes with the sight of Caesar's retinue, with which the Roman population could never become weary. The road to Antium was neither difficult nor long. In the area itself, which was composed of palaces and villas built and furnished in a lordly manner, it was possible to find everything comfortable and the most exquisite luxury of the period. Caesar had the habit, however, of taking with him on a journey every object in which he found delight, beginning with musical instruments and domestic furniture and ending with statues and mosaics, which were taken even when he wished to remain on the road merely a short time for rest or recreation. He was accompanied, therefore, on every expedition by whole legions of servants, as well as divisions of praetorian guards, and Augustians. In terms of the latter, each had a personal retinue of slaves.

Early on the morning of that day, herdsmen from the Campania, with sunburned faces, wearing goatskins on their legs, drove forth five hundred she-asses through the gates, so that Poppaea on the day following her arrival at Antium might have her bath in their milk. After the asses had gone by, crowds of youths rushed forth, swept the road carefully and covered it with flowers and needles from pine trees. In the crowds people whispered to each other, with a certain feeling of pride, that the whole road to Antium would be strewn in that way with flowers taken from private gardens round about or bought at high prices from dealers. The crowds talked of Caesar's present trip and his future journeys. Sailors and old soldiers narrated wonders that, during distant campaigns, they had heard about concerning countries Roman feet had never touched. Home-stayers, who had never gone beyond the Appian Way, listened with amazement to marvelous tales of India, Arabia, and the archipelagos surrounding Britain in which, on a small island inhabited by spirits, Briareus had imprisoned the sleeping Saturn. They heard of hyperborean (extreme northern) regions of glistening seas. Stories of this kind found ready credence among the rabble, stories believed by such men even as Tacitus and Pliny. They spoke also of that ship which Caesar was to look at—a ship that had brought wheat to last for two years, not considering four hundred passengers, an equal number of soldiers, and a multitude of wild beasts to be used during the summer games. This information produced general good feeling toward Caesar, who not only nourished the populace, but amused it. Thus a greeting full of enthusiasm was waiting for him.

A detachment of Numidian cavalry came, which belonged to the praetorian guard. The Numidians wore yellow uniforms, red sashes, and great earrings, which cast a golden gleam on their black faces. The points of their bamboo spears glittered like flames in the sun. After they had passed, a procession began. The throng crowded forward to look at it closely; but divisions of praetorian foot soldiers were there and, forming in line on both sides of the gate, prevented approach to the road. Wagons carrying tents—purple, red, and violet—moved in advance, as well as tents woven from threads as white as snow; oriental carpets, tables of citrus, pieces of mosaic, kitchen utensils, cages with birds from the East whose tongues or brains were to go to Caesar's table, and vessels with wine and baskets with fruit, much of it borne by slaves.

Hundreds of people were seen on foot, carrying vessels and statues of Corinthian bronze. There were companies appointed specially to Etruscan vases, golden or silver vessels, or vessels of Alexandrian glass. These were guarded by small detachments of praetorian infantry and cavalry; over each division of slaves were taskmasters, holding whips armed at the end with lumps of lead or iron. The procession seemed like some solemn religious event, and even more so when the musical instruments of Caesar and the court went by. There were harps, Grecian lutes, lutes of the Hebrews and Egyptians, lyres, formingas, citharas, flutes, buffalo horns, and cymbals. While looking at that sea of instruments, gleaming beneath the sun in gold, bronze, precious stones, and pearls, it might be imagined that Apollo and Bacchus had set out on a journey through the world. After the instruments came rich chariots filled with acrobats, male and female dancers, grouped artistically and carrying wands in their hands.

After them followed slaves who were intended, not for service, but excess; so there were boys and little girls, selected from all Greece and Asia Minor, with long hair, or with winding curls arranged in golden nets, children resembling Cupid, with wonderful faces. Their faces were covered completely with a thick coating of cosmetics, lest the wind of the Campania might tan their delicate complexions.

A praetorian cohort of gigantic Sicambrians appeared, blue-eyed, bearded, blond, and red-haired. In front of them Roman eagles were carried by banner-bearers, tablets with inscriptions, statues of German and Roman gods, and finally, statues and busts of Caesar. From under the skins and armor of the soldier appeared sunburned, mighty limbs, looking like military engines capable of wielding the heavy weapons the guards of that kind were furnished. The earth seemed to tremble beneath their measured and weighty tread. They looked with contempt on the rabble of the street, forgetting, it was evident, that many of themselves had come to that city in manacles. But they were insignificant in numbers, for the praetorian force had remained in camp especially to guard the city and hold it within limits. When they had marched past, Nero's chained lions and tigers were led by, so that, should the wish come to him of imitating Dionysus, he would have them to attach to his chariots. They were led in chains of steel by Arabs and Hindus, but the chains were so entwined with garlands that the beasts seemed led with flowers. The lions and tigers, tamed by skilled trainers, looked at the crowds with green and seemingly sleepy eyes.

Now came Caesar's vehicles and litters, great and small, gold or purple, inlaid with ivory or pearls, or glittering with diamonds; after them came another small cohort of praetorian soldiers in Roman armor, praetorians composed of Italian volunteers only; then crowds of select slaves and boys; and at last came Caesar himself, whose approach was heralded from afar by the shouts of thousands.

In the crowd was the apostle Peter, who wished to see Caesar once in his life. He was accompanied by Lygia, whose face

278

was hidden by a thick veil, and Ursus, whose strength formed the best defense of the young girl in this wild and boisterous crowd. The Lygian seized a stone to be used in building the temple and brought it to the apostle, so that by standing on it he might see better than others.

The crowd muttered when Ursus pushed it apart, as a ship pushes waves; but when he carried the stone, which four of the strongest men could not raise, the muttering was turned into wonderment.

Meanwhile, Caesar appeared. He was sitting in a chariot drawn by six white Idumean stallions shod with gold. The chariot had the form of a tent with its sides purposely open, so that the crowds could see Caesar. A number of persons might have found place in the chariot; but Nero, desiring that attention should be fixed on him exclusively, passed through the city alone, having at his feet merely two deformed dwarfs. He wore a white tunic and a toga of amethyst color, which cast a bluish tinge on his face. On his head was a laurel wreath. Since his departure from Naples he had gained considerable weight. His face had grown wide; under his lower jaw hung a double chin, by which his mouth, always too near his nose, seemed to touch his nostrils. His bulky neck was protected, as usual, by a silk scarf, which he arranged with a white and fat hand grown over with red hair; he would not permit slaves to pluck out this hair, since he had been told that to do so would bring trembling of the fingers and injure his lute playing. Measureless vanity was depicted then, as at all times, on his face, together with boredom and suffering. On the whole, it was a face both terrible and trivial. As he advanced he turned his head from side to side, blinking at times and listening carefully to the manner in which the multitude greeted him. He was met by a storm of shouts and applause. "Hail, divine Caesar! Imperator, hail, conqueror! Hail, incomparable! Son of Apollo, Apollo himself!"

When he heard these words, he smiled; but at moments a cloud passed over his face, for the Roman rabble was satirical and keen in judgment and criticized even great triumphators, even men whom it loved and respected. It was known that once they shouted during the entrance to Rome of Julius Caesar, "Citizens, hide your wives; the old libertine is coming!" But Nero's monstrous vanity could not endure the least blame or criticism; meanwhile, in the throng, amid shouts of applause, were heard cries of "Ahenobarbus, Ahenobarbus! Where have you put your flaming beard? Do you fear that Rome might catch fire from it?" And those who cried out in this way did not know that their jest concealed a dreadful prophecy.

These voices did not anger Caesar much, since he did not wear a beard, for long before he had devoted it in a golden cylinder to Jupiter Capitolinus. But other persons, hidden behind the corners of temples, shouted, "Matricide! Nero! Orestes! Alcmaeon!" Still others cried, "Where is Octavia?" "Surrender the purple!" At Poppaea, who came directly after him, they shouted, "Yellow Hair!" by which name they indicated a streetwalker. Caesar's musical ear caught these exclamations also, and he raised the polished emerald to his eyes as if to see and remember those who uttered them. While looking, his glance rested on the apostle standing on the stone.

For a brief period those two men looked at each other. It did not occur to anyone in that brilliant retinue, nor to anyone in that immense throng, that at that moment the two powers on earth were looking at each other, one of which would vanish quickly as a bloody dream, and the other, dressed in simple garments, would seize in eternal possession the city and the world.

Meanwhile, Caesar had passed; and immediately after him eight Africans bore a magnificent litter, in which sat Poppaea, who was detested by the people. Arrayed, as was Nero, in amethyst color, with a thick application of cosmetics on her face, immovable, she looked like some beautiful and wicked divinity carried in procession. In her wake followed a whole court of servants, next a line of wagons bearing materials of dress and use. The sun had sunk from midday when the parade of Augustians began—a brilliant, glittering line gleaming like an endless serpent. The cynical Petronius, greeted kindly by the multitude, was with his beautiful Eunice in a litter. Tigellinus traveled in a chariot drawn by ponies ornamented with white and purple feathers. He rose in the chariot repeatedly and stretched his neck to see if Caesar was preparing to give him the sign to enter his chariot. Among others, the crowd greeted Licinianus with applause, Vitelius with laughter, Vatinius with hissing.

Caesar's court was innumerable. The wealthiest and the most brilliant and noted in Rome migrated to Antium. The society that accompanied Nero almost always exceeded the number of soldiers in a legion, or twelve thousand men. The decrepit Lucius Saturninus also appeared, as well as Vespasian, who had not gone yet on his expedition to Judea, and a multitude of women renowned for wealth, beauty, luxury, and vice.

The eyes of the multitude were turned to the chariots, the horses, the distinctive dress of the servants, who came from all peoples of the earth. In that procession of pride and grandeur one hardly knew where to look; the eye and the imagination were dazzled by such gleaming of gold, purple, and violet, the flashing of precious stones, the glitter of brocade, pearls, and ivory. It seemed that the very rays of the sun were dissolving in that abyss of brilliancy. And though wretched people were not lacking in that throng, people with empty stomachs and with hunger in their eyes, that spectacle not only inflamed their desire and envy, but filled them with delight and pride, because it conveyed a feeling of the might and invincibility of Rome, before which the world knelt. No one thought that that power would not endure throughout the ages and outlive all nations, or that there was anything in existence that had strength to oppose it.

Vinicius, riding at the end of the retinue, sprang out of his chariot at the sight of the apostle and Lygia, whom he had not expected to see, and, greeting them with a radiant face, spoke like a man who has not time to spare. "I do not know how to thank you for coming, Lygia! God could not have sent me a better omen. I greet you even while departing, but not for long. Farewell!"

"Farewell, Marcus!" Lygia answered. Then she added, in a lower voice, "May Christ go with you and open your soul to Paul's word."

He was gratified that she was concerned about his becoming a Christian soon, so he answered, "*Ocelle mi!* Let it be as you say. Paul is with me and will be my companion and master. Draw aside your veil, my delight, let me see you before my journey. Why are you hidden?"

She raised the veil and showed him her beautiful face and bright, smiling eyes, inquiring, "Is the veil not becoming?"

And her smile had in it a hint of loving resistance, but Vinicius, while looking at her with rapture, answered, "Bad for my eyes, which until death would only look on you."

Then he turned to Ursus and said, "Ursus, guard her with all your mighty strength, for she is my domina as well as yours."

Seizing her hand then, he pressed it to with his lips, to the great amazement of the crowd, who could not understand tokens of such honor from a brilliant Augustian to a maiden arrayed in simple garments more becoming of a slave.

"Farewell!"

Then he departed quickly, for Caesar's whole retinue had pushed forward. The apostle Peter blessed him with a slight sign of the cross; but the kindly Ursus began at once to praise him, glad that his young mistress listened eagerly and was grateful to him for those compliments.

Later, Demas the miller approached, he for whom Ursus worked at night. When he had kissed the apostle's hand, he begged them to enter his house for refreshment, saying that it was near the Emporium, that they must be hungry and wearied since they had spent the greater part of the day at the gate.

They went with him and, after rest and refreshment, returned to the Trans-Tiber toward evening. They passed through the Clivus Publicus, going over the Aventine, between the temples of Diana and Mercury. From that height the apostle looked on the magnificent buildings about him and on those vanishing on the horizon. Sunk in silence, he meditated on the immensity and dominion of the city where he had come to announce the word of God. He had seen the rule of Rome and its legions in various lands, but now he had seen power impersonated in the form of Nero himself. That city—immense, predatory, ravenous, unrestrained, rotten to the marrow of its bones, and unassailable in its superhuman power—that Caesar, a father, mother, and wife slayer. After him dragged a retinue of bloody specters, no fewer than his court.

That rogue, that buffoon, but also lord of thirty legions, and through them lord of the whole earth; those courtiers covered with gold and scarlet, uncertain of the future, but mightier meanwhile than kings—all this together seemed a species of the kingdom of hell itself. In his pure heart he marveled that God could give such inconceivable almightiness to Satan, that He could yield the earth to him to overturn and trample it, to squeeze blood and tears from it, to storm it like a tempest, to consume it like a flame. And his apostle-heart was alarmed by those thoughts, and in spirit he spoke to the Master: "O Lord, how shall I begin in this city where You have sent me? To Rome belong seas and lands, the beasts of the field, and the creatures of the water; it owns other kingdoms and cities, and thirty legions that guard them; but I, O Lord, am a fisherman! How shall I begin, and how shall I conquer its hatred?"

He raised his gray, trembling head toward heaven, praying from the depth of his heart to his divine Master, himself full of sadness and fear.

Meanwhile, his prayer was interrupted by Lygia.

"The whole city seems to be on fire," she said.

In fact the sun went down that day in splendid fashion. Its immense shield had sunk halfway behind the Janiculum, and the whole expanse of heaven was filled with a red gleam. From the place on which they were standing, Peter viewed large expanses. Somewhat to the right they saw the long, extending walls of the Circus Maximus; above it the towering palaces of the Palatine; and directly in front of them, beyond the Forum Boarium and the Velabrum, the summit of the Capitol, with the temple of Jupiter. But the walls and the columns and the summits of the temples were sunk in that golden and purple gleam. The parts of the river visible from afar flowed as if in blood; and as the sun sank quickly behind the mountain, the gleam became redder, like an enormous fire, and it increased and extended until finally it embraced the seven hills, and then on to the whole region about.

"The whole city seems on fire!" Lygia repeated.

Peter shaded his eyes with his hand and said, "The wrath of God is upon it."

37

Vinicius to Lygia:

"The slave Phlegon, by whom I send this letter, is a Christian; so he will receive freedom from your hands, my dearest. He is an old servant of our house; so I can write to you with full confidence. I write from Laurentum, where we have halted because of the heat. Otho owned a lordly villa here, which on a time he presented to Poppaea; and she, though divorced from him, saw fit to retain the magnificent manor.

"I admire and love you from my whole soul and wish to speak only of you; but I must constrain myself to write of our journey, of that which happens to me, and of news of the court. Caesar was the guest of Poppaea, who secretly prepared a magnificent reception for him. She invited only a few of his favorites, but Petronius and I were among them. After dinner we sailed in golden boats over the sea, which was as calm as if it had been sleeping and as blue as your eyes, divine one. We ourselves rowed, for evidently it flattered the Augusta that men of consular dignity were rowing for her. Caesar, sitting at the rudder in a purple toga, sang a hymn in honor of the sea; he had composed this hymn the night before and with Diodorus had arranged music to it. In other boats he was accompanied by slaves from India who knew how to play on seashells, while round about numerous dolphins appeared. Do you know what I was doing? I was thinking of you, and yearning. I wanted to gather in that sea, that calm, that music, and give it all to you.

"Do you wish that we should live someplace by the seashore far from Rome, my Augusta? I have land in Sicily, on which there is an almond forest that has rose-colored blossoms in spring; and this forest goes down near the sea. There I will love you and absorb Paul's teaching, for I know now he is not opposed to love and happiness. Do you agree with this dream?

"Soon the shore was far behind. We saw a sail before us in the distance, and a dispute rose as to whether it was a common fishing boat or a great ship from Ostia. I was the first to discover what it was, and then the Augusta said that from my eyes evidently nothing was hidden, and, dropping a veil over her face, she asked if I could recognize her. Petronius answered immediately that it was not possible to see even the sun behind a cloud. She replied, as if in jest, that love alone could blind a piercing glance such as mine, and, naming various women of the court, she asked which one I loved. I answered calmly, but at last she mentioned your name. Speaking of you, she uncovered her face again, and looked at me with disapproval.

"I am grateful to Petronius, who turned the boat away at that moment, taking away attention from me; for had I heard hostile words regarding you, I would not have been able to hide my anger and would have had to struggle with the wish to break the head of that wicked, malicious woman with my oar. You remember the incident at the pond of Agrippa about which I told you at the house of Linus on the eve of my departure. Petronius is alarmed, and today again he implored me not to offend the Augusta's vanity. But Petronius does not understand me and does not realize that, apart from you, I do not know pleasure or beauty or love, and that for Poppaea I feel only disgust and contempt. You have greatly changed my soul—I do not wish now to return to my former life. But have no fear that harm may reach me here. Poppaea does not love me, for she cannot love anyone, and her desires arise only from anger at Caesar, who is still under her influence and even capable of loving her yet; still, he does not spare her, and does not hide his shamelessness from her.

"I will tell you something that should relieve you. Peter told me in parting not to fear Caesar, since a hair would not fall from my head; and I believe him. Some voice in my soul says that every word of his must be accomplished; that since he blessed our love, neither Caesar, nor all the powers of hades, could take you from me, dear Lygia. When I think of this I am as happy as if I were in heaven, which alone is calm and happy. But what I say of heaven may offend you, a Christian. Christ has not yet washed me, but my heart is like an empty chalice, which Paul of Tarsus is to fill with the sweet doctrine professed by you—the sweeter for me because it is yours. Let me find favor in your eyes.

"In Antium my days and nights will pass in listening to Paul, who gained such influence among my people on the first day that they surround him continually, seeing him not only as a wonder-worker, but as an almost supernatural being. Yesterday I saw gladness on his face, and when I asked what he was doing, he answered, 'I am preaching.' Petronius knows that he is among my people and wishes to see him, as does Seneca also, who heard of him from Gallo.

"But the stars are growing pale, Lygia, and 'Lucifer' of the morning is bright with growing force. Soon the dawn will make the sea ruddy; all is sleeping round about, but I am thinking of you. Be greeted together with the morning dawn, sponsa mea!"

38

Vinicius to Lygia:

"Have you ever been in Antium, my dear one, with Aulus and Pomponia? If not, I shall be happy when I show this place to you. All the way from Laurentum there is a line of villas along the seashore; and Antium itself is an endless succession of palaces and porticos. I have a residence here right over the sea, with an olive garden and a forest of cypresses behind the villa, and when I think that the place will soon be yours, its marble seems whiter to me, its groves more shady, and the sea bluer. Oh, Lygia, how good it is to live and love! Old Menikles, who manages the villa, planted irises on the ground under myrtles, and at sight of them the house of Aulus and the garden in which I sat near you came to my mind. The irises will remind you, too, of your childhood home; therefore, I am certain that you will love Antium and this villa.

"Immediately after our arrival I talked at length with Paul at dinner. We spoke of you, and afterward he taught. I listened, and I say that even if I could write like Petronius, I should not have the power to explain everything that passed through my soul and mind. I had not supposed that there could be such happiness, beauty, and peace of which up to now people had no awareness.

But I will keep all of this for later conversation with you, for at the first free moment I shall be in Rome.

"How could the earth find place at once for the apostle Peter, Paul of Tarsus, and Caesar? I ask because I spent the evening after Paul's teaching with Nero, and do you know what I heard there? He read his poem on the destruction of Troy and complained that he had never seen a burning city. He envied Priam and called him happy just for this, that he saw the burning and ruin of his birthplace. Then Tigellinus said, 'Speak a word, divinity, and I will take a torch, and before the night passes you shall see Antium blazing.' But Caesar called him a fool. 'Where,' he asked, 'should I go to breathe the sea air and preserve the voice with which the gods have gifted me, and which all say I should preserve for the benefit of mankind? It is Rome that injures me; it is the air of the Subura and the Esquiline that add to my hoarseness. Would not the palaces of Rome present a spectacle much more tragic and magnificent than Antium?' They all began to talk and to say what an unheard of tragedy the picture of a city like that would be, a city that had conquered the world turned now into a heap of ashes. Caesar declared that his poem would then surpass the songs of Homer, and he began to describe how he would rebuild the city and how coming ages would admire his achievements, in the presence of which all other human works would be petty. 'Do that! Do that!' exclaimed the drunken company. 'I must have more faithful and more devoted friends,' he answered.

"I admit that I was alarmed at once when I heard this, for you are in Rome, carissima. I laugh now at that alarm, and I think that Caesar and his friends, though mad, would not dare to permit such insanity. Still, see how a man fears for his love; I should prefer that the house of Linus were not in that narrow Trans-Tiber alley, and in a part occupied by common people, who receive less consideration. For me, the very palaces on the Palatine would not be a residence fit for you.

"Go to the house of Aulus, my Lygia. I have thought over this matter. If Caesar were in Rome, news of your return might reach the Palatine through slaves, turn attention to you, and bring persecution because you dared to act against the will of Caesar. But he will remain in Antium for a while, and before he returns slaves

287

will have ceased speaking of you. Linus and Ursus can be with you. Besides, I live in hope that before Palatine sees Caesar, you, my goddess, shall be dwelling in your own house on the Carinae. Blessed be the day, hour, and moment in which you shall cross my threshold; and if Christ, whom I am learning to accept, confirms this, may His name be blessed also. I shall serve Him and give my life and blood for Him. I speak incorrectly; we shall serve Him, both of us, as long as the threads of life hold us.

"I love you and salute you with my whole soul."

39

Ursus was taking water from a cistern and, while drawing it with a rope, was singing a strange Lygian song in an undertone, looking meanwhile with delighted eyes at Lygia and Vinicius, who, among the cypresses in Linus's garden, seemed as white as two statues. Their clothing was not moved by the smallest breeze. A golden, lily-colored twilight was sinking on the world while they were conversing in the calm of evening, each holding the other's hand.

"Will not some evil meet you, Marcus, because you have left Antium without Caesar's knowledge?" asked Lygia.

"No, my dear," Vinicius answered. "Caesar announced that he would shut himself in for two days with Terpnos and compose new songs. He acts this way frequently, and at such times neither knows nor remembers anything else. What is Caesar to me since I am near you? These past few nights sleep has left me. More than once, when I dozed from weariness, I woke suddenly, with a feeling that danger was hanging over you; at times I dreamed that the relays of horses that were to bear me from Antium to Rome were stolen—horses on which I traveled that road more swiftly than any of Caesar's couriers. Besides, I could not live longer without you; I love you too much for that, my dearest."

"I knew that you were coming. Twice Ursus ran out, at my request, to the Carinae and asked for you at your house. Linus laughed at me, and Ursus also."

It was, indeed, evident that she had expected him; for instead of her usual dark dress, she wore a soft white stola, out of whose beautiful folds her arms and head emerged like primroses out of snow. A few ruddy anemones ornamented her hair.

Vinicius pressed his lips to her hands; then they sat on the stone bench amid wild grapevines and, leaning toward each other, were silent, looking at the twilight whose last gleams were reflected in their eyes.

The charm of the quiet evening enveloped them completely.

"How calm it is here, and how beautiful the world is," Vinicius said, in a lowered voice. "The night is wonderfully still. Tell me, Lygia, what is this? I have never thought that there could be such love. I thought that love was merely fire in the blood and desire; but now for the first time I see that it is possible to love with every drop of one's blood and every breath, and feel such sweet and immeasurable calm as if Sleep and Death had put the soul to rest. This is new for me. I look on this calmness of the trees, and it seems to be within me. Now I understand for the first time that there may be joy of which people have not known thus far. Now I begin to understand why you and Pomponia Graecina have such peace. Yes! Christ gives it."

At that moment Lygia placed her beautiful face on his shoulder and said, "My dear Marcus—" But she was unable to continue. Joy, gratitude and the feeling that at last she was free to love deprived her of her voice, and her eyes were filled with tears of emotion.

Vinicius, embracing her slender form with his arm, drew her toward him and said, "Lygia! May the moment be blessed in which I heard His name for the first time."

"I love you, Marcus," she said then in a low voice.

Both were silent again, unable to utter the words that expressed their strong feelings. The last lily reflections had died on the cypresses, and the garden began to be silverlike from the crescent of the moon.

After a while Vinicius said, "I know. I had barely entered

here, I had barely kissed your dear hands, when I read in your eyes the question whether I had received the divine doctrine to which you are attached, and whether I was baptized. No, I am not baptized yet; but do you know, my flower, why? Paul said to me, 'I have convinced you that God came into the world and gave Himself to be crucified for its salvation; but let Peter wash you in the fountain of grace, he who first stretched his hands over you and blessed you.' And I, my dearest, wish you to witness my baptism, and I wish Pomponia to be my godmother. This is why I am not baptized yet, though I believe in the Savior and in His teaching. Paul has convinced me, has converted me; and could it be otherwise? How was I not to believe that Christ came into the world, since he, who was His disciple, says so, and Paul, to whom He appeared? How was I not to believe that He was God, since He rose from the dead? Others saw Him in the city and on the lake and on the mountain; people saw Him whose lips have not known a lie.

"I began to believe this the first time I heard Peter in Ostrianum. Any other man in the whole world might lie rather than this one who says, 'I saw.' But I feared your religion. It seemed to me that your religion would take you from me. But what kind of man should I be were I not to wish truth to rule the world instead of falsehood, love instead of hatred, virtue instead of crime, mercy instead of vengeance? Your religion teaches this. Others desire justice also; but your religion is the only one that makes man's heart just and pure, like yours and Pomponia's. I should be blind if I did not to see this. But if Christ God has promised eternal life, and has promised happiness as immeasurable as the power of God can give, what more can one wish? Were I to ask Seneca why he prefers virtue if wickedness brings more happiness, he would not be able to say anything sensible. But I know now that I ought to be virtuous, because virtue and love flow from Christ, and because, when death closes my eyes, I shall meet Him face to face, I shall find myself and you. Why not love and accept a religion that both speaks the truth and destroys death? Who would not prefer good to evil? O Lygia! Both reason and the heart point to its truth, and who can resist those two forces?"

Lygia listened and gazed at him with her blue eyes, which in the light of the moon were like ethereal flowers.

"Yes, Marcus, that is true!" she said, nestling her head more closely to his shoulder.

At that moment they understood that besides love they were united by another power, at once sweet and irresistible, by which love itself becomes endless, not subject to change, deceit, treason, or even death. Their hearts were filled with perfect certainty that, no matter what might happen, they would not cease to love and belong to each other. Vinicius saw this love as not merely profound and pure, but altogether new—such as the world had not known and could not provide. This love was embodied in Lygia, the teaching of Christ, the light of the moon resting calmly on the cypresses, and the still night—so that the whole universe seemed filled with it.

After a while he said tenderly, "Our hearts will beat together, and we shall have one prayer of gratitude to Christ. Oh my dear! To live together, to honor together the sweet God, and to know that when death comes our eyes will open again, as after a pleasant sleep, to a new light—what better could be imagined? I only marvel that I did not understand this at first. I do not think anyone can resist this religion. In two or three hundred years the whole world will accept it. People will forget Jupiter, and there will be no God except Christ, and only Christian temples. I heard Paul's conversation with Petronius, and do you know what Petronius said at the end? 'That is not for me'; but he could give no other reason."

"Could you tell me Paul's words?" Lygia said.

"One evening at my house Petronius began to speak playfully and to banter, as he usually does. Paul said to him, 'How can you deny, wise Petronius, that Christ existed and rose from the dead, since you were not in that part of the world at that time? But Peter and John saw Him, and I saw Him on the road to Damascus. Let your wisdom show that we are liars, and then you can deny our testimony.' Petronius answered that he could not deny it, for he knew that many incomprehensible things happened, which trustworthy people affirmed. 'But the discovery of some new foreign god is one thing,' he said, 'and the following of his teaching another. I have no wish to know anything that may deform life and mar its beauty. Never mind whether our gods are true or not; they are beautiful, their rule is pleasant for us, and we live with ease.'

"'You are willing to reject the religion of love, justice, and mercy through worry over the cares of life,' Paul replied. 'But think, Petronius, is your life really free from anxieties? No man among the richest and most powerful is certain when he falls asleep that he will not wake to a death sentence. But tell me, if Caesar accepted this religion, which calls for love and justice, would not your future be more assured? You are alarmed about loss of pleasure, but would not life be more joyous then? As to life's beauty and ornaments, if you have erected so many beautiful temples and statues to evil, revengeful, and adulterous divinities, what would you not do to honor the one God of truth and mercy? You are ready to accept your destiny because you are wealthy and live in luxury; but it is possible even in your case to be poor and deserted, though coming from a great fortune; and then in truth it would have been better for you to confess Christ.

"'In Rome even wealthy parents, unwilling to work at raising children, frequently throw them out of the house. Those children are called alumni. Fate may have made you an alumnus, like the others. But if parents follow our religion, that would never happen. Look around and see what happens around you, what vileness, what shame, what bartering in wives! Nay, you yourselves are curious when a woman has only one husband. But I tell you that those women who carry Christ in their hearts will not be unfaithful to their husbands, just as Christian husbands will keep faith with their wives.

"'But you are neither sure of rulers nor fathers nor wives nor children nor servants. The whole world is trembling before you, and you are fearful before your own slaves, for you know that any hour an awful war may begin against your oppression, similar to past wars. Though rich, you are not sure that the command may not come to you tomorrow to leave your wealth; you are not old, but tomorrow it may be necessary for you to die. You love, but treason may spring upon you; you are enamored with villas and statues, but tomorrow power may cast you into the emptiness; you have thousands of servants, but tomorrow those servants may let your blood flow.

"'And if that be the case, how can you be calm, how can you

love in delight? But I proclaim Christ's love and a religion that commands rulers to love their subjects, masters their slaves, slaves to serve with love, to do justice and be merciful; and at last it promises eternal life. How, then, Petronius, can you say this religion spoils life, since it redeems, and since you yourself would be a hundred times happier and more secure were it to embrace the world as Rome's dominion has embraced it?'

"Petronius said, 'That is not for me.' Pretending to be drowsy, he went out, and when going added, 'I prefer my Eunice, O little Jew, but I should not wish to compete with you in a debate.'

"I looked around and saw women such as Poppaea, who cast aside two husbands for Nero, Calvia Crispinilla, Nigidia, and others who were unfaithful, except Pomponia. She and you alone will not desert or deceive their men. In Antium I spoke to you in my heart continually as if you had been at my side. I do not care for Caesar's house any longer; I do not want its luxury and music, only you. Say the word and we will leave Rome to settle somewhere far away."

She said, "Very well, Marcus. You have written to me of Sicily, where Aulus wishes to settle in old age."

"True, my dear! Our lands are adjacent. That has a wonderful coast, where the climate is sweeter and the nights still brighter than in Rome, aromatic and clear."

And he began then to dream of the future.

"There we may forget our cares. In groves, among olive trees, we shall walk and rest in the shade. Oh Lygia! What a life to love and cherish each other, to look at the sea and sky together, to honor together a merciful God, to do in peace what is just and true."

"Will you permit me to see Pomponia?" Lygia asked.

"Yes, dear one. We will invite them to our house, or go there ourselves. If you wish, we can take Peter the apostle. He is bowed down with age and work. Paul will visit us also—he will convert Aulus Plautius; and as soldiers settle colonies in distant lands, so we will start a colony of Christians."

Lygia took his palm and wished to press it to her lips, but he whispered, "No, Lygia, no! It is I who honor you and exalt you; give me your hands."

"I love you."

He pressed his lips to her hands, white as jasmine, and they heard only the beating of their own hearts. There was not the slightest movement in the air; the cypresses stood as motionless as if they too were holding their breath.

All at once the silence was broken by an unexpected, roaring thunder, as if coming from under the earth. A shiver ran through Lygia's body. Vinicius stood up, and said, "Lions are roaring in the stadiums."

Both began to listen. Now the first thunder was answered by a second, and many more, from all sides of the city. In Rome several thousand lions were quartered at times in various arenas, and frequently in the night they approached the bars and, leaning their gigantic heads against them, expressed their yearning for freedom. Answering one another in the stillness of night, they filled the whole city with noise. There was something so indescribably ominous and terrible in those roars that Lygia, whose bright and calm visions of the future were scattered, listened with a certain foreboding.

But Vinicius encircled her with his arm and said, "Fear not, dear one. The games are at hand, and all the stadiums are crowded."

Then both entered the house of Linus, accompanied by the loud thunder of lions.

40

In Antium, meanwhile, Petronius gained new victories almost daily over courtiers vying with him for the favor of Caesar. The influence of Tigellinus had fallen completely. In Rome, when there was occasion to eliminate men who seemed dangerous, to plunder their property or to settle political cases, to give festivals noted for their luxury and bad taste, or finally to satisfy the monstrous whims of Caesar, Tigellinus was an expert and became indispensable. But in Antium, among palaces reflected in the azure of the sea, Caesar led an aesthetic existence. From morning until evening Nero and his attendants read verses, discussed their structure and style, were occupied with music and the theater—in other words, the life of beauty. Petronius, incomparably more refined than Tigellinus and the other courtiers—witty, eloquent, with superb taste, had the upper hand. Caesar sought his company, asked for advice when he composed, and demonstrated a more lively friendship than at any other time.

It seemed to other courtiers that his influence was supreme at last, that close friendship between him and Caesar was cemented and would last for years. Even those who had shown dislike previously to the exquisite Epicurean, began now to crowd around him and vie for his favor. Many were glad that superiority had come to a man who really knew how to judge people, who received with a skeptical smile the flattery of his enemies of yesterday, but who, either through apathy or culture, was not vengeful and did not use his power to the destruction of others. There were moments when he might have destroyed even Tigellinus, but he preferred to ridicule him and expose his lack of refinement. In Rome the Senate was relieved, for no death sentence had been issued for a month and a half. It is true that in Antium and the city people told stories that Caesar had mellowed, but everyone preferred a refined Caesar to one who was brutal in the company of Tigellinus. Tigellinus himself lost his composure and hesitated whether or not to yield as conquered, for Caesar had said repeatedly that in all Rome and in his court there were only two spirits capable of understanding each other, two real Hellenes—he and Petronius.

Because of the amazing dexterity of Petronius the masses did not see how Caesar could dispense with him—with whom could he converse about poetry, music, and philosophy? In whose eyes could he look to learn whether his own words of art were indeed perfect? Petronius, with his habitual indifference, seemed to attach no importance to his position. He gave the impression of a man who made light of them, of himself, of Caesar, and of the whole world. At moments he appeared to criticize Caesar to his face, and when others judged that he was going too far, or simply bringing about his own ruin, he was able to turn the criticism suddenly around in such a way that it profited him. He aroused amazement in those present and the conviction that there was no position from which he could not triumph.

About a week after the return of Vinicius from Rome, Caesar read in a small circle an extract from his Troyad. When he had finished and the shouts of rapture had ended, Petronius, with an imploring glance from Caesar, replied, "Common verses, fit for the fire."

The hearts of those present stopped beating from terror. Since the years of his childhood Nero had never heard such a comment from any man. The face of Tigellinus was radiant with delight. But Vinicius grew pale, thinking that Petronius, who had never been drunk, had drunk to excess.

Nero, however, inquired in a honeyed voice, with deeply wounded vanity, "What defect do you find in them?"

"Do not believe them," said Petronius, pointing to those present. "They understand nothing. You have asked what defect there is in your verses. If you wish the truth, I will tell you. Your verses would be worthy of Virgil, of Ovid, even of Homer, but they are not worthy of you. You are not free to write these. The flames described by you do not blaze enough; your fire is not hot enough. Do not listen to Lucan's flatteries. Had he written those verses, I would admit he was a genius, but your case is different. And do you know why? You are greater, and from him who is gifted by the gods, as you are, more is demanded. But you are lazy—you would rather sleep after dinner than sit and compose. You can create a work such as the world has not heard of to this day; so I tell you to your face, write better!"

And he said this carelessly, as if jesting and also rebuking; but Caesar's eyes were mist-covered from delight.

"The gods have given me a little talent," he said, "but they have given me something greater—a true judge and friend, the only man able to speak the truth to me."

Then he stretched his fat hand, grown over with reddish hair, to a golden candelabrum plundered from Delphi, to burn the verses. But Petronius seized them before the flame touched the paper.

"No, no!" he said. "Even so they belong to mankind. Leave them to me."

"In that case let me send them to you in a cylinder I myself have made," Nero answered, embracing Petronius.

"True; you are right," he said, after a while. "My burning of Troy does not blaze enough; my fire is not hot enough. But I thought it sufficient to equal Homer. A certain hesitation and humility have always held me back. You have opened my eyes. When a sculptor makes the statue of a god, he seeks a model; but I have never had a model. I never have seen a burning city; so there is a lack of truth in my description."

"Then I will say that only a great artist understands this."

Nero grew thoughtful, and after a while he said, "Answer one question, Petronius. Do you regret the burning of Troy?"

"Do I regret? By Venus, not in the least! And I will tell you the reason. Troy would not have been consumed if Prometheus had not given fire to man, and the Greeks made war on Priam. Aeschylus would not have written his Prometheus had there been no fire, just as Homer would not have written the Iliad had there been no Trojan war. I think it is better to have Prometheus and the Iliad than a small and shabby city, which was unclean and wretched, and in which at best there would be now some procurator annoying you through petty quarrels."

"That is sound reasoning," Nero said. "For art and poetry it is permitted, and is right, to sacrifice everything. The Acheaeans were happy when they gave Homer the substance of the Iliad, and Priam was happy who saw the ruin of his birthplace. As for me, I have never seen a burning city."

A period of silence followed, which was broken at last by Tigellinus. "But I have said to you, Caesar, command it and I will burn Antium. If you are are dissatisfied with these villas and palaces, have them burn the ships in Ostia; or I will build a wooden city on the Alban Hills, into which you shall begin the fire yourself. Do you agree?"

"Am I to gaze on the burning of wooden sheds?" Nero asked, casting a look of contempt on him. "Your mind has grown utterly barren, Tigellinus. And I see, besides, that you do not give great value to my talent or my Troyad, since you judge that any sacrifice would be too great for it."

Tigellinus was silenced; but Nero, wishing to change the conversation, added, "Summer is passing. Oh, what stench there must be in Rome now! And still, we must return for the summer games."

"When you dismiss the Augustians, O Caesar, permit me to remain with you a moment," Tigellinus said.

An hour later Vinicius, returning with Petronius from Caesar's villa, said, "I was a little alarmed for you. I thought that while drunk you had ruined yourself beyond all hope. Remember that you are playing with death."

"That is my arena," Petronius answered carelessly, "and the feeling that I am the best gladiator in it amuses me. See how it ended? My influence has increased this evening. He will send me his verses in a cylinder that—do you wish to lay a wager?—will be immensely rich and in extremely bad taste. I shall command my physician to keep medicine in it. I did this for another reason— because Tigellinus, seeing how this succeeded, will imitate me, and I can imagine what will happen. The moment he starts a witty comment, it will be as if a bear of the Pyrenees were rope-walking. I shall laugh like Democritus. If I wished I could destroy Tigellinus, perhaps, and become praetorian prefect in his place, and have Ahenobarbus himself under my control, but I am apathetic; I prefer my present life and even Caesar's verses to trouble."

"What skill to be able to turn even blame into flattery! But are those verses really so bad? I am no judge in those matters."

"The verses are not worse than his others, though Lucan has more talent in one finger. Bronzebeard has, above all, an immense love for poetry and music. We shall be in a small circle— only I, you, Tullius Senecio, and young Nerva. At times Nero's verses are eloquent. Hecuba's words are touching. She complains of the pangs of birth, and Nero was able to find eloquent expressions—that is why, perhaps, he gives birth to every verse in torment. At times I am sorry for him. By Pollux, what a marvelous mixture! Even Caligula never did such strange things."

"Who can foresee where the madness of Ahenobarbus will go?" Vinicius asked.

"No man whatever. Such things may still happen that will make the hair stand on men's heads for whole centuries at the thought of them. But it is precisely that which interests me; and though I am bored, I believe that under another Caesar I should be bored a hundred times more. Paul, your friend from Judea, is eloquent—that I give him; and if people like him proclaim that religion, our gods must defend themselves seriously, or in time they may be led away captive. It is true that if Caesar, for example, were a Christian, all would feel safer. But your prophet of Tarsus, in applying proofs to me, did not realize that for me this uncertainty becomes the charm of life. He who does not play at dice will not lose property, but still people play at dice. There is in it a certain delight and destruction combined. I have known sons of soldiers and senators to become gamblers with their own fate.

"I play with life, you say, and that is true, but I play because it pleases me; whereas Christian virtues would bore me in a day, as does the philosophy of Seneca. Because of this, Paul's eloquence is displayed in vain. He should understand that people like me will never accept his religion. With your temperament you might either hate Christians or become a Christian immediately. I recognize, while yawning, the truth of what they say. We are mad. We are hastening to our doom, something unknown is coming toward us, something is dying around us—agreed! But life exists for itself alone, not for death."

"But I pity you, Petronius."

"Do not pity me more than I pity myself. Formerly you were happy among us; while campaigning in Armenia, you were longing for Rome."

"Even now I am longing for Rome."

"True; for you are in love with a Christian vestal, who sits in the Trans-Tiber. I do not wonder at this, nor do I blame you. I wonder more, that in spite of a religion described by you as the only and final truth, and in spite of a love that is soon to be crowned, sadness has not left your face. Pomponia Graecina is eternally thoughtful; from the time of your becoming a Christian you have ceased to laugh. Do not try to persuade me that this religion is cheerful. You have returned from Rome sadder than ever. If Christians love in this way, by the bright curls of Bacchus! I shall not imitate them!"

"I swear to you," Vinicius answered, "not by the curls of Bacchus, but by the soul of my father, that never in times past have I experienced even a foretaste of such happiness as I breathe today. But I yearn greatly; and what is stranger, when I am far from Lygia, I think that danger is threatening her. I do not know what danger, but I feel it, as one feels a coming tempest."

"In two days I will try to obtain permission for you to leave Antium for as long a time as you wish. Poppaea is quiet, and, as far as I know, no danger from her threatens you or Lygia."

"This very day she asked me what I was doing in Rome, though my departure was secret."

"Perhaps she ordered spies."

"Paul told me," Vinicius said, "that God forewarns us sometimes but does not permit us to believe in omens; so I guard myself against this belief, but I cannot ward it off. I will tell you what happened, to unburden my heart. Lygia and I were sitting together, on a night as calm as this, and planning our future. I cannot tell you how content we were. All at once lions began to roar. That is common in Rome, but since then I have no rest. It seems to me that in that roaring there was a threat, an announcement of misfortune. You know that I am not frightened easily. That night, however, something happened that filled us with darkness and terror. It came so strangely and unexpectedly that I still have those sounds in my ears, as if Lygia were asking my protection from something dreadful—even from those same lions. I would like permission to leave Antium, or I shall go without it. I cannot remain."

"Sons of consuls or their wives are not given to lions in the arena," Petronius said, laughing. "Any other death may meet you but that. How do you know they were lions? German bisons roar with no less gentleness than lions. As to me, I ridicule omens and fates. Last night was warm, and I saw stars falling like rain. Many a man has an evil foreboding at such a sight; but I thought, *If among these is my star too, I can do nothing about it.*" Then Petronius was silent but added after a moment's thought, "If your

Christ has risen from the dead, He may perhaps protect you both from death."

"He may," Vinicius answered, looking at the heavens filled with stars.

41

Nero played and sang, in honor of the "Lady of Cyprus," a hymn he composed himself. That day his voice was good, and he felt that his music really captivated those present. He was so inspired that he grew pale with genuine emotion. This was surely the first time that he had no desire to hear praises from others. He sat for a time with his hands on the cithara and with bowed head; then, rising suddenly, he said, "I am tired and need air. Meanwhile, you will tune the citharae.

"You will go with me," he said, turning to Petronius and Vinicius, who were sitting in a corner of the hall. "Give me your arm, Vinicius, for strength fails me; Petronius will talk to me about music."

They went out on the terrace, which was paved with alabaster and sprinkled with saffron.

"Here I can breathe more freely," Nero said. "My soul is moved and sad, though I see that with what I have sung to you on trial my triumph will be such as no Roman has ever achieved."

"You may appear here, in Rome, in Achaea. I admire you with my whole heart and mind, divinity," Petronius answered.

"I know. You are too unconcerned to force yourself to flattery, and you are sincere. Tell me, what is your judgment on music?"

"When I listen to poetry, when I look at a beautiful statue, temple, or picture, I feel that I comprehend perfectly what I see, that my enthusiasm takes in all that these can give. But when I listen to music, especially your music, new delights and beauties open before me every moment. I pursue them, I try to grasp them; but before I can take them into myself, newer ones flow in, like waves of the sea, which roll in from infinity. Music is like the sea; we stand on one shore and gaze, but we cannot see the other shore."

"Ah, what deep knowledge you have!" Nero said. "You have expressed my thoughts; so in all Rome you are the only man able to understand me. My judgment of music is the same as yours. When I play and sing, I see things I did not know existed in my dominions. I am Caesar, and the world is mine. I can do everything. But music opens new kingdoms to me, new, unknown delights. I cannot name them or grasp them; I only feel them. I feel the gods, I see Olympus. Some kind of breeze from beyond the earth blows in on me; I see, as in a mist, immeasurable greatness, but calm and bright as sunshine. The whole Spheros plays around me; and I declare to you that I, Caesar and god, feel at such times as tiny as dust. Do you believe this?"

"I do. Only great artists have power to feel small in the presence of art."

"I open my soul to you as to a friend, and I will say more: do you consider that I am blind or deprived of reason? Do you think that I am ignorant that people in Rome write insults on the walls against me, call me a mother and wife murderer, consider me a monster and a tyrant because Tigellinus obtained a few sentences of death against my enemies? Yes, my friend, they believe I am a monster, and I know it. They have said cruel things about me to the degree that at times I put the question to myself, 'Am I cruel?' Yet a man's deeds may be cruel at times while he himself is not cruel. Ah, no one will believe, and perhaps even you, my friend, will not believe, that at moments when music caresses my soul I feel as kind as a child in the cradle. People do not know how much goodness lies in this heart and what treasures I see in it when music opens the door to them."

Petronius, who had not the least doubt that Nero was speaking sincerely at that moment, and that music might bring out various noble tendencies of his soul, which were now overwhelmed by mountains of egotism and evildoing, said, "Men should know you as clearly as I do; Rome has never been able to appreciate you."

302

Caesar leaned more heavily on Vinicius's arm, as if he were bending under the weight of injustice, and answered, "Tigellinus has told me that in the Senate they whisper into one another's ears that Diodorus and Terpnos play on the cithara better than I do. They refuse me even that! But tell me, you who are truthful always, do they play better, or as well?"

"By no means. Your touch is finer and has greater power."

"If that is true, let them live. They will never imagine what service you have rendered them in this moment.

"I think that to reach those Olympian worlds I must do something no man has done before—I must surpass the stature of man in both good or evil. I know that people think I am mad, but I am only seeking beauty and truth. If I am going mad, it is out of disgust and impatience that I cannot find them. Therefore, I wish to be greater than man, for only in that way can I be the greatest artist."

Then Nero whispered to Petronius, "Do know that I condemned my mother and wife to death mainly because I wished to lay at the gate of an unknown world the greatest sacrifice that man could put there? I thought that afterward doors would open into the next world. It might be wonderful or awful, surpassing human imagination. But that sacrifice was not sufficient. To open the celestial doors something greater is needed, and let it be given as the Fates desire."

"What do you intend to do?"

"You shall see sooner than you think. Meanwhile, be assured that there are two Neros—the one people know, the other who is an artist, whom you alone know; and if he slays others or is in a frenzy like Bacchus, it is only because the flatness and misery of common life stifle him; and I should like to destroy those conditions, even if I had to use fire or iron. Oh, how flat this world will be when I am gone from it! No man has suspected yet, not you even, what an artist I am. But precisely because of this I suffer, and I tell you that the soul in me is as gloomy as those cypresses that stand dark in front of us. It is difficult for a man to bear at once the weight of supreme power and the highest talents."

"I sympathize with you, Caesar; and with me earth and sea, not counting Vinicius, who deifies you in his soul."

"He, too, has always been dear to me," Caesar said, "though he serves the war-god, Mars, not the artistic Muses."

"He serves Aphrodite first of all," Petronius answered. And suddenly he determined to settle the affair of his nephew at one blow and at the same time to eliminate every danger that might threaten him. "He is in love, as was Troilus with Cressida. Permit him, lord, to visit Rome, for he is perishing in my hands. Do you know that that Lygian hostage whom you gave him has been found, and Vinicius, when leaving for Antium, left her in the care of a certain Linus? I did not mention this to you, for you were composing your hymn, and that was more important than anything. Vinicius wanted her as mistress; but when she turned out to be as virtuous as Lucretia, he fell in love with her virtue, and now his desire is to marry her. She is a king's daughter, so she will cause him no harm. But he is a real soldier; he sighs and withers, but he is waiting for the permission of his Imperator."

"The Imperator does not choose wives for his soldiers. What good is my permission to Vinicius?"

"I have told you, O lord, that he deifies you."

"Then he may be certain of my permission. She is a comely maiden, but too narrow in the hips. The Augusta Poppaea has complained to me that she enchanted our child in the gardens of the Palatine."

"But I told Tigellinus that the gods are not subject to evil charms. You remember this, divinity?'"

"I remember."

Here he turned to Vinicius, "Do you love her, as Petronius says?"

"I love her, lord," replied Vinicius.

"Then I command you to set out for Rome tomorrow and marry her. Do not appear before my eyes without the marriage ring."

"Thanks to you, lord, from my heart and soul."

"Oh, how pleasant it is to make people happy!" Nero said. "I wish to do nothing else all my life!"

"Grant us one more favor, O divinity," said Petronius. "Declare your will in this matter before the Augusta. Vinicius would never venture to wed a woman displeasing to the Augusta; you will overcome her prejudice, O lord, with a word, by declaring that you have commanded this marriage."

"I am willing," Caesar said. "I could refuse nothing to you or Vinicius."

They turned toward the villa. Their hearts were filled with delight over the victory; and Vinicius had to use self-restraint to avoid throwing his arms around the neck of Petronius, for it seemed now that all dangers and obstacles were removed.

Nero entered the atrium of the villa, sat in an armchair inlaid with tortoiseshell, whispered something in the ear of a Greek slave near his side, and waited.

The page soon returned with a golden case. Nero opened it and took out a necklace of great opals.

"These are jewels worthy of this evening," he said.

"The light of Aurora is playing in them," Poppaea answered, convinced that the necklace was for her.

Caesar raised the rosy stones and said, "Vinicius, you will give, from me, this necklace to her whom I command you to marry, the youthful daughter of the Lygian king."

Poppaea's glance, which was filled with anger, passed from Caesar to Vinicius and at last rested on Petronius. But he, leaning carelessly over the arm of the chair, passed his hand along the back of the harp, pretending to put its form firmly in his mind.

Vinicius thanked him for the gift, approached Petronius, and asked, quietly, "How shall I thank you for what you have done this day for me?"

"Sacrifice a pair of swans to Euterpe," Petronius replied. "Praise Caesar's songs, and laugh at omens. The roaring of lions will not disturb your sleep, nor that of your Lygian lily."

"No," Vinicius said. "Now I am perfectly at rest."

"May Fortune favor you! But be prepared, for Caesar is taking his lute again. Hold your breath, listen, and shed tears."

Caesar had taken the lute and raised his eyes. In the hall conversation had stopped and people were as still as if petrified. Terpnos and Diodorus, who had to accompany Caesar, were on the alert, looking first at each other, then at his lips, waiting for the first tones of the song.

Just then a noise began in the entrance; and after a moment

Caesar's freedman, Phaon, appeared from behind the curtain. Close behind him was the consul Lecanius.

Nero frowned.

"Pardon, divine Imperator," Phaon said, with panting voice, "there is a fire in Rome! The greater part of the city is in flames!"

At this news all sprang from their seats.

"O gods! I shall see a burning city and finish the Troyad," Nero said, setting aside his lute.

Then he turned to the consul. "If I go at once, shall I see the fire?"

"Lord," answered Lecanius, as pale as a wall, "the whole city is one sea of flame; smoke is suffocating the inhabitants, and people faint, or cast themselves into the fire from delirium. Rome is perishing, lord."

A moment of silence followed, which was broken by the cry of Vinicius—"All is lost!" And the young man, casting his toga aside, rushed forth in his tunic.

Nero raised his hands and exclaimed, "Woe to you, sacred city of Priam!"

42

Vinicius barely had time to command a few slaves to follow him; then, springing on his horse, he sped into the deep night along the empty streets toward Laurentum. Through the influence of the dreadful news he had fallen into frenzy and despair.

In silence and in that calm night, the rider and the horse, gleaming in the moonlight, seemed like dream visions. The Idumean stallion, dropping his ears and stretching his neck, shot on like an arrow past the motionless cypresses and the white villas hidden among them. The slaves hastening after Vinicius fell behind, as their horses were not as fast. When he had rushed like a storm through sleeping Laurentum, he turned toward Ardea, in which, as in Aricia, Bovillae, and Ustrinum, he had kept relays of horses from the day of his coming to Antium, so as to pass in the shortest time possible the distance between Rome and him. Remembering those relays, he used up all the strength from his horse.

Beyond Ardea it seemed to him that the sky on the northeast was covered with a rosy reflection. That might be the dawn, for the hour was late, and in July daybreak came early. But Vinicius could not hold down a cry of rage and despair, for it seemed to him that it was the glare of a towering inferno. He remembered the consul's words, "The whole city is one sea of flame," and for a while he thought that madness was threatening him, for he utterly lost hope that he could save Lygia, or even reach the city before it was turned into one heap of ashes. His thoughts were quicker now than the rush of the stallion; they flew on ahead like a flock of birds, black, monstrous, and causing pain. He did not know, it is true, in what part of the city the fire had begun; but he supposed that the Trans-Tiber division, because it was packed with tenements, timberyards, storehouses, and wooden sheds serving as slave markets, might have become the first food of the flames.

Fires happened frequently enough in Rome; during those fires deeds of violence and robbery were committed, especially in the parts occupied by a needy and half-barbarous population. What might happen, then, in a place like the Trans-Tiber, which was the retreat of a rabble collected from all parts of the earth? Here the thought of Ursus with his superhuman power flashed into Vinicius's head; but what could be done by one man, even were he a Titan, against the destructive force of fire?

The fear of a slave rebellion was like a nightmare and had stifled Rome for years. Hundreds of thousands of those people were thinking of the times of the slave Spartacus and were merely waiting for a favorable moment to gain arms against their oppressors and Rome. Now the moment had come! Perhaps war and slaughter were raging in the city, together with the fire. It was possible even that the praetorian guard had unleashed themselves on the city and were killing occupants the at command of Caesar.

At that moment the hair rose on his head from terror. He recalled all the conversations about burning cities, which for some time had been repeated at Caesar's court with continued persistence; he recalled Caesar's complaints that he was forced to describe a burning city without having seen a real fire; his contemptuous answer to Tigellinus, who offered to burn Antium or an artificial wooden city; finally, his complaints against Rome, and the disease-ridden alleys of the Subura. Yes; Caesar has commanded the burning of the city! He alone could give such a command, and Tigellinus alone could accomplish it. But if Rome is burning at command of Caesar, who can be sure that the population will not be slaughtered at his command also? The monster is capable even of such a deed. Fire, a slave revolt, and slaughter! What a horrible chaos, what a letting loose of destructive elements and popular frenzy! And in all this is Lygia.

Who will snatch her from the burning city; who can save her? Here Viniciuis, stretching himself out entirely on the horse, thrust his fingers into his own hair, ready to gnaw the beast's neck from pain.

A horseman, rushing also like a whirlwind toward Antium, shouted as he raced past, "Rome is perishing!" To the ears of Vinicius came only one more expression: "Gods!" The rest was drowned by the thunder of hoofs. But that expression sobered him—"Gods!"

Vinicius raised his head suddenly and, stretching his arms toward the sky filled with stars, began to pray.

"Not to you do I call whose temples are burning, but to You! You Yourself have suffered. You alone are merciful! You alone have understood people's pain; You came to this world to teach pity to mankind; so please show it now. If You are what Peter and Paul declare, save Lygia for me, take her in Your arms, remove her from the flames. You have the power to do that! Give her to me, and I will give You my blood. But if You are unwilling to do this for me, do it for her. She loves You and trusts in You. You promise life and happiness after death, but happiness after death will not pass away, and she does not wish to die yet. Let her live. Take her in Your arms, out of Rome. You can do so, unless You are unwilling."

And he stopped, for he thought that further prayer might turn to a threat; he feared to offend Divinity at the moment when he

308

needed favor and mercy most. He was terrified at the very thought of that, and, so as not to admit even a shade of threat, he began to lash his horse again, especially since the white walls of Aricia, which lay midway to Rome, gleamed before him in the moonlight.

He rushed at full speed past the temple of Mercury, which stood in a grove before the city. Evidently people knew of the catastrophe, for there was an unusual movement in front of the temple. While passing, Vinicius saw crowds on the steps and between the columns. People holding torches were hurrying to put themselves under the protection of the deity. The road was not so empty or free as beyond Ardea. Crowds were hurrying to the grove by side roads, and on the main road were groups that pushed aside hurriedly before the onrushing horseman. Vinicius rode into Aricia like a whirlwind, overturning and trampling a number of persons on the way. He was surrounded by shouts of "Rome is burning!" "Rome is on fire!" "May the gods rescue Rome!"

The horse stumbled but, reined in by his powerful hand, rose on his haunches before the inn, where Vinicius had another beast ready. Slaves, as if waiting for the arrival of their master, stood before the inn and at his command ran one before the other to lead out a fresh horse. Vinicius, seeing a detachment of ten mounted praetorians, going evidently with news from the city to Antium, sprang toward them.

"What part of the city is on fire?" he asked.

"Who are you?" asked the decurion.

"Vinicius, a tribune of the army, an Augustian. Answer on your life!"

"The fire broke out in the shops near the Circus Maximus. When we were despatched, the center of the city was on fire."

"And the Trans-Tiber?"

"The fire has not reached the Trans-Tiber yet, but it is reaching new parts every moment with a force nothing can stop. People are perishing from heat and smoke; all rescue is impossible."

At this moment they brought the fresh horse. The young tribune sprang to its back and rushed on. He was riding now toward Albanum, leaving Alba Longa and its splendid lake on the right. The road from Aricia lay at the foot of the mountain, which hid the horizon completely, and Albanum lying on the other side of it. But Vinicius knew that on reaching the top he should see, not only Bovillae and Ustrianum, where fresh horses were ready for him, but Rome as well; for beyond Albanum the Campania stretched on both sides of the Appian Way, along which only the arches of the aqueducts ran toward the city, and nothing obstructed the view.

"From the top I shall see the flames," he said; and he began to lash his horse again. But before he had reached the top of the mountain, the odor of smoke came to his nostrils.

The night had faded long since, the dawn had passed into light, and on all the nearest summits golden and rosy gleams were shining, coming from either burning Rome or the rising daylight. Vinicius touched the summit at last, and a terrible sight struck his eyes.

The whole lower region was covered with smoke, forming as it were one gigantic cloud lying close to the earth. In this cloud towns, aqueducts, villas, and trees disappeared; but beyond this gray, ghastly plain, the city was burning on the hills.

The conflagration did not have the form of a pillar, as happens when a single building is burning. It was a long belt, stretching like the dawn. Above this belt rose a wave of smoke, in places entirely black, in places rose-colored, in places like blood, in others unwinding like a serpent.

To Vinicius it seemed at first glance that not only the city was burning, but the whole world, and that no living being could save itself from that ocean of flame and smoke.

The wind blew with growing strength from the region of the fire, bringing the smell of burning objects and of smoke, which began to obscure even closer objects. Clear daylight had come, and the sun lit up the summits surrounding the Alban Lake. But the bright golden rays of the morning appeared reddish and sickly through the haze. Vinicius, while descending toward Albanum, entered smoke that was denser and less transparent. The town itself was buried in smoke, and the alarmed citizens had fled into the streets. It was terrible to think of what Rome was like, when it was already difficult to breathe in Albanum.

It is impossible, Vinicius thought, *that a city should begin to burn in all places at once. The wind is blowing from the north and brings smoke only in this direction. On the other side there is none. It will be hard for Ursus to go through the Janiculum gate with Lygia, to save himself and her. It is impossible for a whole population to perish and the world's ruling city to be swept from the face of the earth. Even in captured places, where fire and slaughter rage together, some people survive,* he thought. *Perhaps Lygia would not perish of a certainty. God watches over her, He who Himself conquered death.* He began to pray again and made great vows to Christ, with promises of gifts and sacrifices.

After he had hurried through Albanum, where nearly all of the inhabitants were on roofs and trees to look at Rome, he grew somewhat calm and regained his composure. He remembered, too, that Lygia was protected not only by Ursus and Linus, but by the apostle Peter. At the mere remembrance of this, fresh comfort entered his heart. For him, Peter was an incomprehensible, almost superhuman being. From the time he heard him at Ostrianum, a wonderful impression clung to him, which he had described by letter to Lygia at the beginning of his stay in Antium. He believed that every word of the old man was true, or would prove true later. The closer acquaintance that during his illness he had formed with the apostle heightened the impression, which was turned later into a firm faith. Since Peter had blessed his love and promised him Lygia, Lygia could not perish in the flames. The city might burn, but no spark from the fire would fall on her garments.

Under the influence of a sleepless night, mad riding, and impressions, a wonderful exaltation possessed the young tribune; in this hope all things seemed possible. He imagined Peter speaking to the flame, opening it with a word, and Lygia and her companions passing uninjured through an alley of fire. Also, Peter saw future events; so, beyond doubt, he foresaw the fire, and in that case how could he fail to warn and lead the Christians from the city, especially Lygia, whom he loved as his own child? And a hope, strengthening every moment, entered Vinicius. If they were fleeing from the city, he might find them in Bovillae, or meet them on the road. The beloved face might appear any moment from out of the smoke, which was stretching widely over all the Campania.

311

He met increasing numbers of people who had deserted the city and were going to the Alban Hills. They had escaped the fire and wished to go beyond the line of smoke. Before he had reached Ustrinum he had to slacken his pace because of the throng. Besides pedestrians with bundles on their backs, he met horses with packs, mules and vehicles laden with goods, and finally, litters in which slaves were bearing wealthier citizens. At the market square, under temple porticos, and on the streets were swarms of fugitives. Here and there people were erecting tents under which whole families were to find shelter. Others settled down under the naked sky, shouting, calling on the gods or cursing the fates. People to whom Vinicius spoke either did not answer, or, with eyes half-blinded from terror, answered that the city and the world were perishing. New crowds of men, women, and children arrived from the direction of Rome every moment. Some, gone astray in the throng, sought desperately those whom they had lost; others fought for a camping place. Half-wild shepherds from the Campania crowded to the town to hear news or find profit in plunder made easy by the uproar. Gladiators and crowds of slaves of every nationality began to rob houses and villas in the town and to fight with the soldiers who appeared in defense of the citizens.

Junius, a senator, whom Vinicius saw at the inn surrounded by a detachment of Batavian slaves, was the first to give more detailed news of the inferno. The fire had begun at the Circus Maximus but extended rapidly and engulfed the whole center of the city. Never since the time of Brennus had such an awful catastrophe come upon Rome. "The entire Circus has burned, as well as the shops and houses surrounding it," Junius said. "The Aventine and Caelian Hills are on fire. The flames surrounding the Palatine have reached the Carinae."

Here Junius, who possessed on the Carinae a magnificent manor filled with words of art he loved, seized a handful of foul dust and, scattering it on his head, began to groan despairingly.

But Vinicius shook him by the shoulder. "My house, too, is on the Carinae," he said, "but when everything is perishing, let it perish also."

Then remembering that at his advice Lygia might have gone

to the house of Aulus, he asked, "But the Vicus Patricius?"

"On fire!" replied Junius.

"And the Trans-Tiber?"

Junius looked at him with amazement. "Never mind the Trans-Tiber," he said, pressing his aching temples with his palms.

"The Trans-Tiber is more important to me than all other parts of Rome," Vinicius cried vehemently.

"The way is through the Via Portuensis, near the Aventine, but the heat will stifle you. The Trans-Tiber? I do not know. The fire had not reached it; but whether it is there at this moment the gods alone know." Here Junius hesitated a moment, then said in a low voice, "I know that you will not betray me, so I will tell you that this is no common fire. People were not permitted to save the Circus. When houses began to burn in every direction, I myself heard thousands of voices exclaiming, 'Death to those who save it!' Certain people ran through the city and hurled burning torches into buildings. On the other hand, people are revolting and crying that the city is burning at the command of someone. I can say nothing more. Woe to the city, woe to us all, and to me! People are perishing in flames or slaying one another in the mobs. This is the end of Rome!"

Vinicius sprang to his horse and hurried forward along the Appian Way. But now he struggled through a river of people and vehicles, which was flowing from the city. The city, embraced by a monstrous inferno, lay before Vinicius. From the sea of fire and smoke came a terrible heat, and the uproar of people could not drown the roar and hissing of flames.

43

As Vinicius reached Rome he found it difficult to push along the Appian Way because of the mob of people. In the temple of Mars, which stood near the Porta Appia, the crowd had thrown down the doors to find a refuge within during the night. In the cemeteries the larger monuments were seized and battles fought over them to the point of bloodshed. Ustrinum with its disorder was only a slight foretaste what was happening within the walls of the capital. All regard for the dignity of law, for family ties, for class distinction had ceased. Gladiators drunk with wine seized in the Emporium gathered in crowds, ran with wild shouts through the neighboring squares, scattering, trampling, and robbing the people. A crowd of barbarians, displayed for sale in the city, escaped from the booths. For them the burning and ruin of Rome was both the end of slavery and the hour of revenge. When the residents, who had lost all they owned in the fire, stretched their arms to the gods in despair, calling for rescue, these slaves with howls of delight scattered the crowds, dragging clothing from people's backs and taking away the younger women.

Joining the slaves serving in the city were old wretches who had nothing on their bodies except wool garments around their hips, and also dreadful figures from the alleys, who were hardly ever seen on the streets in the daytime, and whose existence in Rome it was difficult to detect. Men of this wild and unrestrained crowd, Asiatics, Africans, Greeks, Germans, Britons, howling in every language of the earth, raged, thinking that the hour had come when they were free to reward themselves for years of misery and suffering. In the midst of that surging throng of humanity, in the glitter of day and of fire, shone the helmets of the praetorian guards, under whose protection the more peaceable population had taken refuge, and who in hand-to-hand battle had to meet the raging multitude in many places.

Vinicius had seen captured cities, but never had his eyes beheld a spectacle in which despair, tears, wild delight, madness, rage, and license were mingled together in such immeasurable chaos. Above this heaving, mad, human multitude roared the fire, surging up to the hilltops of the greatest city on earth, sending into the whirling throng its fiery breath, and covering it with smoke, through which it was impossible to see the blue sky. The young tribune, with supreme effort and risking his life every moment, forced his way at last to the Appian Gate; but there he saw that he could not reach the city through the division of the Porta Capena.

He must turn from the Appian Way, cross the river below the city, and go to the Via Portuensis, which led straight to the Trans-Tiber. That was not easy because of the increasing disorder on the Appian Way. He must open a passage for himself there, even with his sword. Vinicius had no weapons; he had left Antium just as the news of the fire had reached him in Caesar's villa. At the fountain of Mercury, however, he saw a centurion who was known to him. This man, at the head of a few tens of soldiers, was defending the precinct of the temple. Vinicius commanded him to follow. Recognizing a tribune and an Augustian, the centurion did not dare to disobey the order.

Vinicius took command of the detachment himself, and, forgetting for that moment the teaching of Paul concerning love for one's neighbor, he swung at the throng with his sword in a haste that was fatal to many who could not get out of his way. He and his men were followed by curses and a shower of stones, but he paid no attention. People who had set up camp would not move, and they reviled and threatened Caesar and the praetorians. Vinicius heard voices accusing Nero of burning the city. He and Poppaea were threatened with death. Shouts of "Buffoon," "Actor," and "Matricide" were heard throughout. Some wished to drag him to the Tiber; others thought that Rome had shown enough patience. It was clear that were a leader found, these threats could be changed into open rebellion.

Meanwhile, the road was blocked by piles of goods, taken from the fire previously and including barrels of provisions, costly furniture, beds, and carts. The rebels and the praetorians fought hand-to-hand; but the praetorians conquered the weaponless pack of discontents. After they had passed with difficulty around villas, cemeteries, and temples, Vinicius reached at last a village called Vicus Alexandri, where he crossed the Tiber and where there was less smoke. He learned from fugitives that only certain alleys of the Trans-Tiber were burning, but that surely nothing could resist the fury of the blaze, since people were spreading the fire purposely and permitted no one to quench it, declaring that they acted on orders.

The young tribune had not the least doubt then that Caesar had decided to burn Rome; and the vengeance that people demanded seemed to him just and proper. What more could Mithridates or any of Rome's strongest enemies have done? Vinicius believed that Nero's time had come, that those ruins into which the city was falling would overwhelm the monstrous buffoon, together with all his crimes. That might happen in a few hours, should a man be found of sufficient courage to stand at the head of these restless people. Vengeful and daring thoughts began to cross his mind. But if he should try it? The house of Vinicius, which until recent times counted a whole series of consuls, was known throughout Rome. The crowds needed only a name. Once, when four hundred slaves of the prefect Pedanius Secundus were sentenced, Rome reached the verge of rebellion and civil war. What would happen today in view of a dreadful calamity surpassing almost everything Rome had undergone in the course of eight centuries? *Whoever calls the legions to arms,* thought Vinicius, *will overthrow Nero undoubtedly and clothe himself in purple.*

And why should he not do this? He was firmer, more active, younger than other Augustians. True, Nero commanded thirty legions stationed on the borders of the Empire; but would those legions and their leaders rise up at news of the burning of Rome and its temples? And in that case Vinicius might become Caesar. It was even whispered among the Augustians that an enchanter had predicted the purple robe to Otho. In what way was he inferior to Otho? Perhaps Christ Himself would assist him with His divine power; maybe that inspiration was His? *Oh, would that it were!* exclaimed Vinicius in his spirit. He would take vengeance on Nero for the danger of Lygia and his own fear; he would begin the reign of truth and justice; he would extend Christ's religion from the Euphrates to the misty shores of Britain; he would array Lygia in purple and make her mistress of the world.

But these thoughts, which had burst forth in his mind like sparks from a blazing house, died away. First of all was the need to save Lygia. He looked now on the catastrophe from nearby; and before that dreadful reality of flame and smoke his belief that Peter would rescue Lygia died in his heart altogether. Despair seized him a second time when he had come out on the Via Portuensis, which led directly to the Trans-Tiber. He did not recover until he came to the gate, where people repeated what fugitives had said before, that the greater part of that division of the city was not seized by the flames yet, but that fire had crossed the river in a number of places.

The main street itself was in many parts filled completely with goods, and around the Naumachia Augusta great heaps were piled up. Narrow alleys, in which smoke had collected more densely, were simply impassable. The inhabitants were fleeing in thousands. On the way Vinicius saw amazing sights. More than once two rivers of people, flowing in opposite directions, met in a narrow passage, stopped each other, fought hand-to-hand, struck and trampled one another. Families lost one another in the uproar; mothers cried out for their children. The young tribune trembled at the thought of what must be happening nearer the fire.

Amid shouts and howls it was difficult to inquire about anything or understand what was said. At times new columns of smoke from beyond the river rolled toward them, smoke black and so heavy that it moved near the ground, hiding houses and people, as if it were night. But the wind caused by the fire blew it away again, and then Vinicius pushed farther toward the alley in which stood the house of Linus. The impact of a July day, increased by the heat of the burning parts of the city, became unendurable. Smoke pained the eyes; breath failed in men's breasts. The praetorians accompanying Vinicius remained in the rear. In the crush someone wounded his horse with a hammer; the beast threw up its bloody head, reared, and refused obedience. The crowd recognized Vinicius to be an Augustian by his rich tunic, and at once cries were raised all around: "Death to Nero and his followers!" This was a moment of terrible danger; hundreds of hands were stretched toward Vinicius; but his frightened horse sped him away, trampling people as he went, and the next moment a new wave of black smoke rolled in and filled the street with darkness. Vinicius, seeing that he could not ride past, sprang to the earth and rushed forward on foot, creeping along walls, and at times waiting until the fleeing crowd passed him.

He said to himself that these were vain efforts. Lygia might not be in the city; she might have saved herself by flight. It was easier to find a pin on the seashore than her in that crowd and chaos. Still, he wished to reach the house of Linus, even at the cost of his own life. At times he stopped and rubbed his eyes. Tearing off the edge of his tunic, he covered his nose and mouth with it and ran on. As he approached the river, the heat increased terribly. One old man on fleeing crutches, the last whom Vinicius noticed, cried, "Do not go near the bridge of Cestius! The whole island is on fire!" It was, indeed, impossible to be deceived any longer. At the turn toward the Vicus Judaeorum, on which stood the house of Linus, the young tribune saw flames amid clouds of smoke. Not only the island was burning, but the Trans-Tiber, or at least the other end of the street on which Lygia lived.

Vinicius remembered that the house of Linus was surrounded by a garden; between the garden and the Tiber was an unoccupied small field. The fire might stop at the vacant place; and in that hope he ran forward, though every breeze brought not only smoke, but sparks in the thousands that might raise a fire at the other end of the alley and cut off his return.

At last he saw through the smoky curtain the cypresses in Linus's garden. The houses beyond the unoccupied field were burning already like piles of fuel, but Linus's little home stood untouched yet. Vinicius glanced heavenward with thankfulness and sprang toward the house though the very air began to burn him. The door was closed, but he pushed it open and rushed in.

There was not a living soul in the garden, and the house seemed quite empty. *Perhaps they have fainted from smoke and heat,* Vinicius thought. He began to call, "Lygia! Lygia!"

Silence answered him. Nothing could be heard in the stillness there except the roar of the distant fire.

"Lygia!"

Suddenly his ear was struck by that gloomy sound he had heard before in that garden. On the island nearby every kind of wild beast began to roar from fright. A shiver ran through Vinicius from foot to head. Now, a second time, at a moment when his whole being was concentrated in Lygia, those terrible voices answered, as a herald of misfortune and an ominous future.

But this was a brief impression, for the thunder of the flames, more terrible yet that the roaring of wild beasts, commanded him to think of something else. Lygia did not answer his calls; but she could have fainted or stifled in that threatened building. Vinicius sprang to the interior. The little atrium was empty and dark with smoke. Feeling for the door that led to the sleeping rooms, he saw the gleaming flame of a small lamp and, approaching it, saw the room in which was a cross. Under the cross a candle was burning. Through the head of the young catechumen the thought passed with lightening speed that that cross sent him the candle with which he could find Lygia. He took the candle and searched for the sleeping rooms. He found one, pushed aside the curtains, and, holding the candle, looked around.

There was no one there, either. Vinicius was sure that he had found Lygia's sleeping room, for her clothing was on nails in the wall, and on the bed lay a close garment worn by women next to the body. Vinicius seized that, pressed it to his lips, and, taking it on his arm, went farther. The house was small, so that he examined every room, and even the cellar, quickly. Nowhere could he find a living soul. It was evident that Lygia, Linus, and Ursus, with other inhabitants of that part, must have sought safety in flight.

I must seek them among the crowd beyond the gates of the city, he thought.

He saw, it is true, the terrible danger the flight brought about, but he was comforted at the thought of the superhuman strength of Ursus. *I must flee now,* he reasoned, *and reach the gardens of Agrippina through the gardens of Domitius, where I will find them. The smoke is not so terrible there, since the wind blows from the Sabine Hill.*

The hour had come now in which he must think of his own safety, for the river of fire was flowing nearer and nearer from the direction of the island, and rolls of smoke covered the alley almost completely. The candle, which had lighted him in the house, was snuffed out by the current of air. Vinicius rushed to the street and ran at full speed toward the Via Portuensis, from where he had come. The fire seemed to pursue him with burning breath, now covering him with sparks, which fell on his hair and clothing. His tunic began to smolder in places, but he ran forward, fearing he might choke from the smoke. He could taste of soot in his mouth; his throat and lungs were scorched. The blood rushed to his head, and at moments all things, even the smoke, appeared in a red haze to him. Then he thought, *This is living fire!*

Better to fall on the ground and perish. He was streaming with sweat, which scalded like boiling water. Had it not been for Lygia's name in his mind, and her garment, which he wound across his mouth, he would have fallen. Moments later he failed to recognize the street along which he ran. Consciousness was leaving him gradually; he knew only that he must flee, for somewhere in the open field beyond waited Lygia, whom Peter had promised him. All at once he had a deep conviction, half-feverish, like a vision before death, that he must see her, marry her, and then die.

He ran on as if drunk, staggering from one side of the street to the other. Suddenly everything that until then had only glimmered burst forth into one sea of flame. That smoke which had collected in the streets was swept away by a mad whirl of heated air, driving with it millions of sparks, so that Vinicius was running in a glittering cloud. Passing the corner, he found himself in a street that led to the Via Portuensis and the Codetan Field. The sparks ceased to drive him. He understood that if he could run to the Via Portuensis he was safe, even were he to faint on reaching it.

At the end of the street he saw a cloud that blocked the exit. *If that is smoke,* he thought, *I cannot pass.* He ran with the remnant of his strength. On the way he threw off his tunic, which, on fire from the sparks, was burning him like the shirt of Nessus, and kept only Lygia's gown around his head and mouth. When he had run farther, he saw that what he had taken for smoke was dust, from which rose various screams and shouts.

That rabble are plundering houses, he thought. But he ran toward the voices because they might assist him. He shouted for aid with all his might even before he reached them. But this was his last effort. Breath failed his lungs, strength failed his bones, and he collapsed.

They heard him, however, or rather saw him. Two men ran with gourds full of water. Vinicius, who had fallen from exhaustion but had not lost consciousness, seized a gourd with both hands, and emptied one-half of it.

"Thanks," he said. "Place me on my feet. I can walk on alone."

The other laborer poured water on his head. They raised him from the ground and carried him to the others, who surrounded him and asked if he had suffered seriously. Vinicius marveled at this tenderness.

"Who are you?" he asked.

"We are demolishing houses, so that the fire may not reach the Via Portuensis," said one of the laborers.

"You came to my aid when I had fallen. Thanks to you."

"We are not permitted to refuse aid," answered a number of voices.

Vinicius, who from early morning had seen brutal crowds murdering and robbing, looked carefully at the faces around him and said, "May Christ reward you."

"Praise to His name!" exclaimed a whole chorus of voices.

"Linus?" inquired Vinicius.

But he could not finish the question or hear the answer, for he fainted from emotion and exhaustion. He recovered later in a garden, surrounded by a number of men and women. The first words which he uttered were, "Where is Linus?"

For a while there was no answer; then some voice, known to Vinicius, said all at once, "He went out by the Nomentan Gate to Ostrianum two days ago. Peace be with you!"

Vinicius rose to a sitting posture and saw Chilo before him.

"Your house is burned surely, O lord," the Greek said, "for the Carinae is in flames; but you will be always as rich as Midas. Oh, what a misfortune! The Christians, O sun of Serapis, have long predicted that fire would destroy the city. But Linus, with the daughter of Jove, is in Ostrianum. Oh, what a misfortune for the city!"

"Have you seen them?" Vinicius asked.

"I saw them, O lord. May Christ and all the gods be thanked that I am able to pay for your generosity with good news. But, O Cyrus, I shall pay you still more, I swear by this burning of Rome."

It was evening now, but in the garden it appeared to be daylight, for the blaze increased, covering the length and the breadth of the entire city.

44

The moon rose large and full from behind the mountains and, inflamed at once by the smoky glare from the burning city, took on the color of heated brass. It seemed to look with amazement on the world-ruling city that was perishing. In the rose-colored vaults of heaven red-tinged stars were glittering, but this night the earth was brighter than the heavens. In the bloody light were seen distant mountains, towns, villas, temples, and the aqueducts stretching toward the city from all the adjacent hills; on the aqueducts were swarms of people, who had gathered there for safety or to gaze at the fire.

Meanwhile, it was impossible to doubt that criminal hands were spreading the fire, since fresh blazes were breaking out all the time in places remote from the main fire. From the heights on which Rome was founded the flames flowed like waves of the sea into the valleys densely occupied by houses of five and six stories, full of shops, booths, movable wooden amphitheaters, and also storehouses of wood, olives, grain, nuts, pine cones, and clothing, which through Caesar's favor was distributed from time to time among the rabble huddled into narrow alleys. The furious power of the wind carried from the fiery gulf millions of burning shells of walnuts and almonds, which, shooting suddenly into the sky, like countless flocks of bright butterflies, burst with a crackling noise.

All hope of rescue had ceased. Confusion increased by the hour, for on one side the population of the city was fleeing through every gate to places outside; on the other, the fire had lured in thousands of people from small towns, peasants, and half-wild shepherds of the Campania, brought in by hope of plunder. The shout "Rome is perishing!" was heard continually from the crowd. Only the spectacle of the perishing city restrained for the moment an outburst of slaughter, which would begin as soon as the city was turning into ruins. Hundreds of thousands of slaves, forgetting that Rome possessed some tens of legions in all parts of the world, appeared merely waiting for a watchword and a leader. People began to mention the name of Spartacus, but Spartacus was dead. Meanwhile, citizens assembled and armed themselves with what they could find. Some declared that Vulcan, commanded by Jupiter, was destroying the city with fire from beneath the earth. People with these convictions did not wish to save anything, but storming the temples, implored mercy of the gods. It was believed that Caesar had given the command to burn Rome, to be free from the odors that rose from the Subura and to build a new city named Neronia. Rage seized the populace at the thought of this; and if, as Vinicius believed, a leader had taken advantage of that outburst of hatred, Nero's hour would have struck whole years before it did.

It was also said that Caesar had gone mad, that he would command praetorian guards and gladiators to slaughter the people. Others swore by the gods that wild beasts had been let out into the city at Bronzebeard's command. Men had seen lions with burning manes on the streets and mad elephants and bisons trampling down people in crowds. There was some truth in this; for in certain places elephants, seeing the approaching fire, had burst out of the places where they were confined, rushing away from the fire in wild fright, destroying everything before them like a tempest. Public report estimated at tens of thousands the number of persons who had perished. There were people who, losing all their property, or those dearest to their hearts, threw themselves willingly into the flames.

Those who took refuge in the markets and squares of the city, where the Folavian Amphitheater stood afterward, near the temple of the Earth, near the Proticom of Silvia, and higher up, at the temples of Juno and Lucinia, perished from heat, surrounded by a sea of fire. Thousands of bodies were found burned to a crisp, though some unfortunates tore up stones and half buried themselves to defend against the heat. Hardly a family inhabiting the center of the city survived in full; hence along the walls, at the gates, and on all roads the howls of despairing women were heard, calling out the dear names of their lost loved ones.

And so, while some were seeking the gods, others cursed them because of this awful catastrophe. Old men were seen coming from the temple of Jupiter Liberator crying, "If you are a liberator, save your altars and the city!" Anger turned mainly against the old Roman gods, who, in the minds of the populace, were bound to watch over the city more carefully than others. They were now seen as powerless. On the Via Asinaria a company of Egyptian priests was carrying a statue of Isis they had saved from a nearby temple. A crowd of people rushed to the chariot, which they drew to the Appian Gate and, seizing the statue, placed it in the temple of Mars, abusing the priests of that deity who dared to resist them.

In other places people invoked Serapis, Baal, or Jehovah. Some of the citizens joined the chorus and glorified "the Lord of the World"; others, indignant at this glad shouting, tried to repress it by violence. Hymns wonderful and solemn were heard, whose meaning they did not understand but in which were repeated the words "Behold the Judge cometh in the day of wrath and disaster." This deluge of restless and sleepless people encircled the burning city, like a tempest-driven sea.

But neither despair nor blasphemy nor hymn helped. In a few hours parts of the city, beyond which lay the Campus Martius, were lit by bright yellow flames. It seemed to the spectators, only half-conscious from terror, that in the general ruin night and day had been reversed, and that they were looking at sunshine. But later a monstrous bloody gleam extinguished all other colors of flame. Gigantic fountains from the sea of fire shot up to the heated sky as did pillars of flame spreading at their summits into fiery branches and feathers; then the wind blew them away, turned them into golden threads, and swept them over the Campania toward the Alban Hills. The night became brighter with flame and the Tiber flowed on as living fire. The hapless city was turned into total pandemonium. The conflagration took hills by storm, flooded level places, drowned valleys, raged, roared, and thundered.

45

Macrinus, a weaver, carried Vinicius to his house, washed, fed, and clothed him. When the young tribune had recovered his strength, he stated that he would search for Linus that very night. Macrinus, who was a Christian, confirmed Chilo's report that Linus, with Clement the chief priest, had gone to Ostrianum, where Peter was to baptize a whole company of confessors of the new faith. It was known to Christians that Linus had given the care of his house two days before to a certain Gaius. For Vinicius this was a proof that neither Lygia nor Ursus had remained in the house, and that they also must have gone to Ostrianum.

This gave him great comfort. Linus was an old man, for whom it would be difficult to walk daily to the distant Nomentan Gate and back to the Trans-Tiber. It was likely that he lodged with some fellow Christians beyond the walls, and with him also Lygia and Ursus. Thus they would have escaped the fire. Vinicius saw in all this the sovereignty of Christ, whose care he sensed around him, and his heart was filled with even more love. He swore in his soul to give his whole life in return for God's favor.

He hurried to Ostrianum. He would find Lygia, Linus, and Peter and would take them to a distant land, even to Sicily. Let Rome burn; in a few days it would be a mere heap of ashes. Why remain in the face of disaster and a mad crowd? In his lands troops of obedient slaves would protect them, and they would be surrounded by a peaceful country, living in harmony under Christ's wings.

Finding them was no easy thing. Vinicius remembered the difficulty with which he had passed from the Appian Way to the Trans-Tiber, and how he must circle around to reach the Via Portuensis. He decided to go around the city in the opposite direction.

Macrinus provided two mules, which would serve Lygia in a further journey. He wished to give a slave, too; but Vinicius refused, judging that the first detachment of praetorian guards he met on the road would go with him under his orders.

Soon he and Chilo moved on through the Pagus Janiculensis to the Triumphal Way. There were vehicles there, too, in open places; but they pushed between them with less difficulty, because the many inhabitants had fled by the Via Portuensis toward the sea. Beyond the Septimian Gate they rode between the river and the splendid gardens of Domitius; the mighty cypresses were red from the fire, as if from evening sunshine. Vinicius urged his mule forward as much as possible; but Chilo, riding closely in the rear, talked to himself almost the whole way.

He said, "O Zeus! If you will not send torrents of rain on that fire, you have no love for Rome, surely. The power of man will not quench those flames. Such a city—a city that Greece and the whole world was serving! And now the first Greek who comes along may roast beans in its ashes. And now there will be no longer a Rome, nor Roman rulers. Whoever wants to walk on the ashes, when they grow cold, and whistle over them, may whistle without danger. O gods! To whistle over such a world-ruling city! What Greek, or even barbarian, could have hoped for this?"

Talking in this manner, he looked at the waves of flame with a face filled at once with delight and hatred.

"Hurry!" urged Vinicius. "What are you doing there?"

"I am weeping over Rome, lord—Jove's city!"

For a while they rode on in silence, listening to the roar of the burning and the sound of birds. Every kind of field bird from near the sea and the surrounding mountains, mistaking the gleam of the fire for sunlight, were flying, whole flocks of them, blindly into the fire. Vinicius broke the silence first. "Where were you when the fire burst out?"

"I was going to my friend Euricius, lord, who kept a shop near the Circus Maximus, and I was just meditating on the teachings of Christ, when men began to shout: 'Fire!'"

"Did you see people throwing torches into houses?"

"What have I not seen, O grandson of Aeneas! I saw people making a trail through the crowd with swords; I have seen battles, the insides of people trampled on the pavement. Ah, if you had seen that, you would have thought that barbarians had captured the city and were putting it to the sword. Everyone cried that the end of the world had come. Some lost their heads altogether and, forgetting to flee, waited stupidly until the flames seized them. Others howled in both despair and delight. My lord, there are many evil people in the world who do not know how to value the generosity of your mild rule and those just laws in virtue of which you take from all that they have and give it to yourselves. People will not be reconciled to the will of God!"

Vinicius was too occupied with his own thoughts to note the irony stinging in Chilo's words. A shudder of terror seized him at the thought that Lygia might be in the midst of that chaos on those terrible streets where people's body parts were trampled on. "But have you seen them in Ostrianum with your own eyes?" he said.

"I saw them, O son of Venus; I saw the maiden, the good Lygian, holy Linus, and the apostle Peter."

"Before the fire?"

"Before the fire, O Mithra!"

But a doubt rose in the soul of Vinicius whether Chilo was not lying; so, reining his mule in, he looked threateningly at the old Greek and inquired, "What were you doing there?"

Chilo was on guard. True, it seemed to him that with the destruction of Rome would also come the end of Roman dominion. But he was face to face with Vinicius; he remembered that the young soldier had prohibited him, under a terrible threat, from watching the Christians, and especially Linus and Lygia.

"Lord," he said, "why do you not believe that I love them? I do. I was in Ostrianum, for I am half a Christian. Pyrrho has taught me to esteem virtue more than philosophy; so I cling more and more to virtuous people. And, besides, I am poor; and when you, O Jove, were at Antium, I suffered hunger frequently when studying my books; therefore, I sat at the wall of Ostrianum. The Christians, though poor, distribute more alms than all other inhabitants of Rome taken together."

This reason seemed sufficient to Vinicius, and he asked less severely, "And do you not know where Linus is dwelling at this moment?"

"You punished me sharply once for curiosity," replied the Greek.

Vinicius stopped talking and rode on.

"O lord," said Chilo, after a while, "you would not have found the girl but for me, and if we find her now, you will not forget the needy sage?"

"You will receive a house with a vineyard at Ameriola."

"Thanks to you, O Hercules! With a vineyard? Thanks to you!"

They were passing the Vatican Hill now, which was ruddy

327

from the fire; they then passed the Vatican Field, so that they would reach the river and, crossing it, go to the Flamian Gate. Suddenly Chilo reined in his mule and said, "Between the Janiculum and the Vatican Hill, beyond the gardens of Agrippina, are excavations from which stones and sand were taken to build the Circus of Nero. Recently the Jews, of whom there is a multitude in the Trans-Tiber, have begun to persecute Christians cruelly. You remember that in the time of the divine Claudius there were such disturbances that Caesar was forced to expel them from Rome. Now, when they have returned and when, thanks to the protection of the Augusta, they feel safe, they annoy Christians more than ever. I know this; I have seen it. No edict against Christians has been issued; but the Jews complain to the prefect of the city that Christians murder infants, worship an ass, and preach a religion not recognized by the Senate. They beat them and attack their houses of prayer so fiercely that the Christians are forced to hide."

"What does this mean?" Vinicius asked.

"This, lord, that synagogues exist openly in the Trans-Tiber; but that Christians, in their wish to avoid persecution, are forced to pray in secret and assemble in ruined sheds outside the city or in sandpits. Those who dwell in the Trans-Tiber have chosen just that place which was excavated for the building of the Circus and various houses along the Tiber. Now, when the city is perishing, the followers of Christ are praying. Beyond doubt we shall find many of them there, so my advice is to go in there along the road."

"But you said that Linus has gone to Ostrianum," Vinicius said impatiently.

"But you have promised me a house with a vineyard at Ameriola," Chilo answered. "For that reason I wish to seek the girl wherever I may find her. They might have returned to the Trans-Tiber to be nearer his house to see if the fire had taken that part of the city. If they have returned, I swear to you, by Persephone, that we shall find them praying in the excavation; at least we shall get tidings of them."

"You are right; lead on!" the tribune said.

Chilo, without hesitation, turned to the left toward the hill. When they had passed the Circus, they turned still to the left and entered a kind of dark passage. But in that darkness Vinicius saw swarms of gleaming lanterns.

"They are there," Chilo said. "There will be more of them today than ever, for other houses of prayer are burned or are filled with smoke, as is the whole Trans-Tiber."

"True!" Vinicius said. "I hear singing."

The voices of people singing reached the hill from the dark opening, and the lanterns vanished in it one after the other. But from side passages new forms appeared continually, so that after a while Vinicius and Chilo found themselves amid a whole assembly of people.

Chilo slipped from his mule and, calling a youth who sat nearby, said to him, "I am a priest of Christ and a bishop. Hold the mules for us; you will receive my blessing and forgiveness of sins."

Then, without waiting for an answer, he thrust the reins into his hands and, in company with Vinicius, joined the advancing throng.

They entered the excavation and pushed on through the dark passage by the dim light of lanterns until they reached a spacious cave, from which stone had been taken, for the walls were made of fresh fragments.

It was brighter there than in the corridor, for, in addition to candles and lanterns, torches were burning. By the light of these Vinicius saw a whole throng of kneeling people with upraised hands. He could not see Lygia, the apostle Peter, or Linus, but he was surrounded by faces solemn and full of emotion. On some of them expectation or alarm was evident, on some, hope. Some were singing hymns, others were repeating feverishly the name of Jesus, some were beating their breasts. It was apparent that they expected something uncommon at any moment.

Meanwhile, the hymn ceased and, above the assembly, in a niche formed by the removal of an immense stone, Crispus appeared, the acquaintance of Vinicius, with a face half-delirious, pale, and stern. All eyes were turned to him, as though waiting for words of consolation and hope. After he had blessed the assembly, he began to speak in hurried, almost shouting tones. "Bewail your sins, for the hour has come! Behold, the Lord has sent down

329

destroying flames on Babylon, on the city of filth and evil. The hour of judgment has struck, the hour of wrath and destruction. The Lord has promised to come, and soon you will see Him. He will not come as the Lamb, who offered His blood for your sins, but as an awful judge, who in His justice will hurl sinners and unbelievers into the pit. Woe to the world, woe to sinners! There will be no mercy for them. I see You, O Christ! Stars are falling to the earth in showers, the sun is darkened, the earth opens in yawning gulfs, the dead rise from their graves; but You are moving amid the sound of trumpets and legions of angels, amid thunders and lightening. I see You, I hear You, O Christ!"

Then he was silent and, raising his eyes, seemed to gaze into something distant and dreadful. That moment a dull roar was heard in the cave. In the burning city whole streets of partly consumed houses began to fall with a crash. But most Christians took those sounds as a visible sign that the dreadful hour was approaching; belief in the early second coming of Christ and in the end of the world was universal among them, and now the destruction of the city had strengthened it. Terror seized the assembly. Many voices repeated, "The day of judgment! Behold, it is coming!" Some covered their faces with their hands, believing that the earth would be shaken to its foundation, that beasts of hell would rush out through its openings and hurl themselves on sinners. Others cried, "Christ, have mercy on us!" "Redeemer, be pitiful!" Some confessed their sins aloud; others cast themselves into the arms of friends, so as to have some dear heart with them in the hour of dismay.

But there were faces that seemed taken into heaven, faces with smiles not of earth, and these showed no fear. The voices of people in spiritual rapture were heard in some places, crying out unknown words in strange languages. Some person in a dark corner cried, "Wake you that sleep!" Above all rose the shout of Crispus, "Watch! Watch!"

At moments, however, silence came, as if all were holding their breath and waiting for what would come. The thunder was heard of distant parts of the city falling into ruins, and then groans and cries. "Renounce earthly riches, for soon there will be no earth beneath your feet! Renounce earthly loves, for the Lord will condemn those who love wife or child more than Him. Woe to the one who loves the creature more than the Creator! Woe to the rich! Woe to the luxurious!"

Suddenly a roar louder than any preceding shook the quarry. Everyone fell to the earth, stretching their arms in cross form to ward away evil spirits by that gesture. Silence followed, in which was heard only panting breaths, whispers full of terror, "Jesus, Jesus, Jesus!" and the weeping of children. At that moment a calm voice spoke above the prostrate multitude, "Peace be with you!"

It was the voice of Peter the apostle, who had entered the cave a moment earlier. At the sound of his voice terror left at once, as it leaves a flock in which the shepherd has appeared. The flock rose from the ground; those who were nearer gathered at his knees, as if seeking protection from him. He stretched his hands over them and said, "Why are you troubled in heart? Who of you can tell what will happen before the hour comes? The Lord has punished Babylon with fire; but His mercy will be on those whom baptism has purified, and you whose sins are redeemed by the blood of the Lamb will die with His name on your lips. Peace be with you!"

After the terrible and merciless words of Crispus, those of Peter fell like a balm on all present. Instead of fear of God, the love of God took possession of their spirits. Those people found the Christ, whom they had learned to love from the apostle's stories, not a merciless judge but a mild and patient Lamb, whose mercy surpasses man's wickedness a hundredfold. A feeling of comfort possessed the whole assembly, with thankfulness to the apostle. Voices from various sides began to cry, "We are your sheep, feed us!" Those nearer said, "Do not desert us in the day of disaster!" And they knelt at his knees. Vinicius approached, seized the edge of Peter's mantle, and said, "Save me, lord. I have sought her in the smoke of the burning and among the crowds. I could not find her anywhere, but I believe that you can restore her."

Peter placed his hand on the tribune's head.

"Trust in God," he said, "and come with me."

46

The city burned on. The Circus Maximus had fallen in ruins. Entire streets and alleys in the sections of the city that had begun to burn first were falling in turn. At the command of Tigellinus, who had hurried from Antium the third day before, houses on the Esquiline were torn down so that the fire, reaching empty spaces, died out. That was, however, undertaken only to save a remnant of the city. There was need now to guard against further ruin. Incalculable wealth had perished in Rome; all the property of its citizens had vanished; hundreds of thousands of people were wandering in utter want outside the walls. Hunger had begun to pinch this throng the second day, for the immense provisions in the city had burned with it. In the universal disorder and in the destruction of authority, no one had thought of furnishing new supplies. Only after the arrival of Tigellinus were proper orders sent to Ostia; but meanwhile the people had grown more hungry and threatening.

The house at Aqua Appia, in which Tigellinus lodged for the moment, was surrounded by crowds of women, who from morning until late at night cried, "Bread and a roof!" Vainly did praetorian guards, brought from the great camp between the Via Salaria and the Nomentana, strive to maintain order of some kind. Here and there they were met by open, armed resistance. The crowd abused Caesar, the Augustians, the praetorians; excitement rose every moment, so that Tigellinus, looking at night on the thousands of fires around the city, said to himself that those were fires in hostile camps.

When the first installment of baked bread came at night to the Emporium, the people broke the chief gate toward the Aventine, seized all supplies in the blink of an eye, and caused terrible disturbances. In the light of the fires they fought for loaves and trampled many soldiers.

It was rumored that water in the aqueducts had been poisoned; that Nero intended to annihilate the city, destroy the inhabitants to the last person, then move to Greece or to Egypt and rule the world from a new place. Each report ran with lightning speed, and each found belief among the rabble, causing outbursts of hope, terror, or rage. Finally, a kind of fever mastered those noma-dic thousands. The belief of Christians that the end of the world by fire was at hand spread even among adherents of the gods, and extended daily.

In the city incalculable treasures accumulated through centu-ries of conquest, priceless works of art, splendid temples, the most precious monuments of Rome's past were destroyed. Tigel-linus sent courier after courier to Antium, imploring Caesar in each letter to come and calm the despairing people with his pres-ence. But Nero moved only at the last moment, and he hurried so as not to miss the moment in which the great fire of Rome would be at its highest.

Nero wished to come at night so as to view the perishing capital in full contrast. Therefore, he halted in the neighborhood of Aqua Albana and, calling to his tent the tragic actor Aliturus, decided with this aid on his posture and expression and learned proper gestures, stubbornly disputing with the actor whether at the words "O sacred city, which seemed more enduring than Ida" he was to raise both hands or only the one. This question seemed to him more important than all others. Starting at last about night-fall, he asked Petronius whether lines describing the catastrophe might have a few magnificent blasphemies against the gods, and whether, from the standpoint of art, they would not have come spontaneously from the mouth of a man in such a position, a man who was losing his birthplace.

He approached the walls about midnight with his large court, composed of whole detachments of senators, soldiers, freedmen, slaves, women, and children. Sixteen thousand praetorian guards, arranged in line of battle along the road, guarded the peace and safety of his entrance and held the excited populace at a distance. The people cursed and shouted on seeing the parade but dared not attack it. In many places, however, applause was given by the rabble who, owning nothing, had lost nothing in the fire, and who hoped for a more bountiful distribution than usual of wheat, ol-ives, clothing, and money.

Nero, on arriving at the Ostian Gate, halted and said, "House-less ruler of a houseless people, where shall I lay my unfortunate head for the night?"

333

After he had passed the Clivus Delphini, he ascended the Appian aqueduct on steps purposely prepared. After him followed the Augustians and a choir of singers, bearing citharae, lutes, and other musical instruments.

And all held their breath, waiting to learn if he would say some great words, which for their own safety they ought to remember. But he stood solemn, silent, in a purple mantle and a wreath of golden laurels, gazing at the raging might of the flames. When Terpnos gave him a golden lute, he raised his eyes to the sky, filled with the inferno, as if he were waiting for inspiration.

The people pointed at him from afar as he stood in the bloody gleam. The ancient and most sacred edifices were in flames. The past and the spirit of Rome was burning. But he, Caesar, was there with a lute in his hand and a theatrical expression on his face, not thinking of his perishing country but of his posture and the prophetic words with which he might describe best the greatness of the catastrophe, rouse the most admiration, and receive the warmest plaudits. He detested that city and its inhabitants; he loved only his own songs and verses; hence he rejoiced in heart that at last he saw a tragedy like that which he was writing about.

The verse-maker was delighted at the awful sight and thought with rapture that even the destruction of Troy was as nothing if compared with the destruction of this giant city. What more could he desire? There was world-ruling Rome in flames, and he, standing on the arches of the aqueduct with a golden lute, magnificent and poetic. Down below, somewhere in the darkness, the people are cursing with despair. But let them mutter! Ages will pass, but mankind will remember and glorify the poet who in that night sang of the fall and the burning of his own Troy. What was Homer compared with him? What was Apollo himself compared with his hollowed-out lute?

"O nest of my fathers, O dear cradle!" His voice in the open air, with the roar of the fire and the distant murmur of crowding thousands, seemed strikingly weak and uncertain, and the sound of the accompaniment like the buzzing of insects. But dignitaries and Augustians, assembled on the aqueduct, bowed their heads and listened in silent rapture. He sang a long time. Then he cast his robe from his shoulder with a gesture, struck the lute, and sang on. He sought grandiose comparisons in the spectacle unfolded before him. At last he dropped the lute to his feet with a clatter and, wrapping himself in the robe, stood as if petrified, like one of those statues of Niobe which ornamented the courtyard of the Palatine.

Soon a storm of applause broke the silence. But in the distance this was answered by the howling of multitudes. No one doubted then that Caesar had given the command to burn the city, so as to allow himself this spectacle and sing of it. Nero, when he heard that cry from the suffering thousands, turned to the Augustians, with the sad, resigned smile of a man who is suffering from injustice.

"See," he said, "how the people value poetry and me."

"Scoundrels!" Vatinus answered. "Command the praetorian guards, lord, to fall on them."

Nero turned to Tigellinus, "Can I count on the loyalty of the soldiers?"

"Yes, divinity," the prefect answered.

But Petronius shrugged his shoulders and said, "On their loyalty, yes, but not on their numbers. Remain meanwhile where you are, for here it is safest; but there is need to pacify the people."

Seneca was of this opinion also, as was Licinus, the consul. Meanwhile, the excitement below was increasing. The people were arming with stones, tent poles, and various pieces of iron. After a while some of the praetorian leaders came, declaring that the cohorts, pressed by the multitude, kept the line of battle only with extreme difficulty, and, being without orders to attack, they did not know what to do.

"O gods," Nero said, "what a night!" On one side a fire, on the other a raging sea of people. And he began to seek the most splendid expressions to describe the danger of the moment, but, seeing alarmed looks and pale faces around him, he was frightened, with the others.

"Give me my dark mantle with a hood!" he cried. "Must it come really to battle?"

"Lord," Tigellinus said in an uncertain voice, "I have done

what I could, but danger is threatening. Speak, O lord, to the people, and make them promises."

"Shall Caesar speak to the rabble? Let another do that in my name. Who will undertake it?"

"I!" Petronius answered calmly.

"Go, my friend; you are most faithful to me in every necessity. Go, and spare no promises."

Petronius turned to the others with a careless, sarcastic expression. "Senators here present, also Piso, Nerva, and Senecio, follow me."

Then he descended the aqueduct slowly. Those whom he had summoned followed, not without hesitation, but with a certain confidence his calmness had given them. Petronius, halting at the foot of the arches, ordered them to bring him a white horse, and, mounting, he rode on, at the head of the cavalcade, between the deep ranks of praetorian guards, to the black, howling multitude. He was unarmed, having only a slender ivory cane.

When he had ridden up, he pushed his horse into the throng. All around, visible in the light of the burning, were upraised hands, armed with every manner of weapon, inflamed eyes, sweating faces, bellowing and foaming lips.

The outbursts increased and became an unearthly roar; poles, forks, and even swords were brandished about Petronius; grasping hands were stretched toward his horse's reins, but he rode farther, indifferent and contemptuous. At moments he struck heads with his cane, as if clearing a road for himself in an ordinary crowd; and that confidence and calmness amazed the raging rabble. They recognized him finally, and numerous voices began to shout, "Petronius! Arbiter Elegantiarum! Petronius!" As that name was repeated, the faces about became less savage, for that exquisite patrician, though he had never striven for the favor of the populace, was still their favorite. He passed for a humane and magnanimous man; and his popularity had increased, especially since the affair of Pedanius Secundus, when he spoke in favor of shortening the cruel sentences condemning all the slaves of that man to death. The slaves more especially loved him then with that unbounded love that the oppressed are used to giving those who show them even small sympathy. The crowd was curious as to what Caesar's envoy would say, for no one doubted that Caesar had sent him.

He removed his white toga, bordered with scarlet, raised it in the air, and waved it above his head, as a sign that he wished to speak.

"Silence! Silence!" cried the people on all sides.

After a while there was silence. Then he said in a clear, firm voice, "Citizens, let those who hear me repeat my words to those farther away, and conduct yourselves like men, not like beasts in the arena."

"We will, we will!"

"Then listen. The city will be rebuilt. The gardens of Lucullus, Maecenas, Caesar, and Agrippina will be opened to you. Tomorrow will begin the distribution of wheat, wine, and olives, so that every man may be satisfied. Then Caesar will have games for you such as the world has not seen yet; during these games banquets and gifts will be given to you. You will be richer after the fire than before it."

Those nearer repeated his words to those in the distance. There were shouts of both anger and applause.

Petronius wrapped himself in his toga and listened for a time without moving, resembling a marble statue in his white garment. The uproar increased, drowned the roar of the fire, and was answered from ever increasing distances. But evidently the envoy had something to add, for he waited. Finally, commanding silence, he cried, "I promised you bread and circuses; and now shout in honor of Caesar, who feeds and clothes you; then go to sleep, dear people, for the dawn will begin before long."

He turned his horse, then, and, tapping lightly with his cane the heads and faces of those who stood in his way, rode slowly to the praetorian ranks. Soon he was under the aqueduct. He found almost a panic above, where they had not understood the shout "Bread and circuses," and supposed it to be a new outburst of rage. They had not even expected that Petronius would save himself. So Nero, when he saw him, ran to the steps and, with a face pale from emotion, asked, "Well, what are they doing? Is there a battle?"

Petronius breathed deeply and answered, "By Pollux! They

are sweating! And such a stench! Will someone help me? For I am faint." Then he turned to Caesar.

"I promised them," he said, "wheat, olives, the opening of the gardens, and games. They worship you anew and are howling in your honor. Gods, what a foul odor those plebeian commoners have!"

"I had guards ready," Tigellinus cried, "and had you not quieted them, the rabble would have been silenced forever. It is a pity, Caesar, that you did not let me use force."

Petronius looked at him, shrugged his shoulders, and added, "The chance is not lost. You may have to use it tomorrow."

"No, no!" Caesar cried, "I will give open the gardens to them and distribute wheat. Thanks to you, Petronius, I will have games; and that song, which I sang today, I will sing publicly."

Then he placed his hands on the arbiter's shoulder, was silent a moment, and asked, "Tell me sincerely, how did I seem to you while I was singing?"

"You were worthy of the spectacle, and the spectacle was worthy of you," Petronius said.

"But let us look at it again," he said, turning to the fire, "and bid farewell to ancient Rome."

47

The apostle's words put confidence in the souls of the Christians. The end of the world seemed even nearer to them, but they began to think that the day of judgment would not come immediately. They felt that first they would see the end of Nero's reign, which they looked on as the reign of Satan, and the punishment of God for Caesar's crimes, which were crying for vengeance. Strengthened in heart, they departed, after the prayer, to their temporary dwellings, and even to the Trans-Tiber. News had come that the fire, set there in a number of places, had, with the change of wind, turned back toward the river and had ceased to expand.

The apostle, with Vinicius and Chilo, who followed him, left the excavation as well. The young tribune did not venture to interrupt his prayers; so he walked on in silence, trembling from alarm. Many approached to kiss Peter's hands and the hem of his robe. Mothers held out their children to him; some knelt in the dark passage and, holding up candles, begged a blessing. Others, walking alongside, sang, so there was no chance for conversation. When the burning city was in view, the apostle blessed them three times and said, turning to Vinicius, "Fear not. The hut of the quarryman is near; in it we shall find Linus and Lygia, with her faithful servant. Christ, who betrothed her to you, has preserved her."

Vinicius staggered and placed his hand against the cliff. The road from Antium, the events at the wall, the search for Lygia amid burning houses, sleeplessness, and his terrible panic had exhausted him; and the news that the dearest person in the world was nearby, and that soon he would see her, took the remains of his strength from him. He suddenly dropped to the apostle's feet and, embracing his knees, remained without the power to say a word.

"Not to me, not to me, but to Christ," the apostle said, who warded off thanks and honor.

"What a good God!" said the voice of Chilo from behind. "But what shall I do with the mules that are waiting down here?"

"Rise and come with me," Peter said to Vinicius.

Vinicius rose. Visible in the light of the fire, tears were on his face, which was pale from emotion. His lips moved, as if in prayer.

"Let us go," he said.

But Chilo repeated again: "Lord, what shall I do with the mules that are waiting? Perhaps this worthy prophet prefers riding to walking."

Vinicius did not know himself what to answer; but hearing from Peter that the quarryman's hut was nearby, he said, "Take the mules to Macrinus."

"Pardon me, lord, if I mention the house in Ameriola. In view of such an awful fire, it is easy to forget a thing so unimportant."

"You will get it."

"O grandson of Jove, I have always been sure, but now, when this marvelous prophet also has heard the promise, I will not remind you even of this, that you have promised me a vineyard. Peace be with you."

They answered, "And peace with you."

Then both turned to the right toward the hills. Along the road Vinicius said, "Lord, wash me with the water of baptism, so that I may call myself a true confessor of Christ, for I love Him with all the power of my soul. Wash me quickly, for my heart is ready. And what you command I will do; but tell me, so that I may do it as well."

"Love men as your own brothers," the apostle answered, "for only with love may you serve Him."

"Yes, I understand that. When a child I believed in the Roman gods, though I did not love them. But I so love the One God that I would give my life for Him gladly." And he looked toward the sky, repeating with gladness: "For He is one, for He alone is kind and merciful. Let not only this city perish, but the whole world; Him alone will I confess and recognize."

"And He will bless you and your house," concluded the apostle.

Meanwhile, they turned into another ravine, at the end of which a faint light was visible. Peter pointed to it and said, "There is the hut of the quarryman who gave us a refuge when, on the way from Ostrianum with the sick Linus, we could not go to the Trans-Tiber."

The hut was a cave rounded out in an indentation of the hill and was covered outside with a wall made of reeds. The door was closed, but through an opening, which served as a window, the interior was visible, lighted by a fire. A dark, giant figure rose to meet them and asked, "Who are you?"

"Servants of Christ," Peter answered. "Peace be with you, Ursus."

Ursus knelt at the apostle's feet; then, recognizing Vinicius, he seized his hand by the wrist and raised it to his lips.

"And you, lord," he said. "Blessed be the name of the Lamb, for the joy you will bring to Callina."

Linus was lying on a bundle of straw, with an emaciated face and a forehead as yellow as ivory. Near the fire Lygia sat with a string of small fish, intended for supper. Busy with removing the fish from the string, and thinking that it was Ursus who had entered, she did not raise her eyes. But Vinicius approached and pronounced her name. She sprang up quickly; a flash of astonishment and delight shot across her face. Without a word, like a child who after days of fear and sorrow has found her father or mother, she threw herself into his open arms.

He embraced her, pressed her to his bosom for some time with ecstasy. It was as if she had been saved by a miracle. Then, withdrawing his arms, he took her temples between his hands, kissed her forehead and her eyes, embraced her again, repeated her name, bent to her knees, greeted her, and honored her. His delight, love, and happiness had no bounds.

He told her how he had rushed in from Antium; had searched for her at the walls, in the smoke at the house of Linus; how he had suffered and was terrified; how much he had endured before the apostle had shown him her retreat.

"But now that I have found you," he said, "I will not leave you near any fire or raging crowds. People are slaying one another under the walls, and slaves are revolting and plundering. God alone knows what miseries may yet fall on Rome. But I will save you. Oh, my dear, let us go to Antium; we will take a ship there and sail to Sicily. My land is your land; my houses are your houses. Listen to me! In Sicily we shall find Aulus. I will give you back to Pomponia and take you from her hands afterward. But O carissima, have no further fear of me. Christ has not washed me yet, but ask Peter if on the way here I have not told him my wish to be a true confessor of Christ and begged him to baptize me, even in this hut of a quarryman. Believe, and let all believe me."

Lygia heard these words with a radiant face. The Christians formerly, because of Jewish persecutions, and then because of the fire and disturbance caused by the disaster, lived in fear and uncertainty. A journey to quiet Sicily would put an end to all danger and open a new period of happiness in their lives. Had Vinicius wished to take only Lygia, she would have resisted the temptation, since she did not wish to leave Peter and Linus. But

Vinicius said to them, "Come with me; my lands are your lands, my houses your houses." At this Lygia wished to kiss his hand, as a sign of obedience, and said, "Where you are, Caius, there am I, Caia."

Then, embarrassed that she had spoken words that by Roman custom were repeated only at marriage, she blushed deeply and stood in the light of the fire with drooping head, in doubt lest he take them poorly. But in his face boundless homage alone was depicted. He turned then to Peter and continued, "Rome is burning at the command of Caesar. In Antium he complained that he had never seen a great fire. And if he has not hesitated at such a crime, think what may happen yet. Who knows that he may not bring in troops and command a slaughter? Who knows whether after the fire, civil war, murder, and famine may not come? Hide yourselves, therefore, and let us hide Lygia. There you can wait until the storm passes, and when it is over return to sow your grain again."

Outside, from the direction of the Vatican Field, as if to confirm his fears, distant cries full of rage and terror were heard. At that moment the quarryman entered, the master of the hut, and, shutting the door hastily, he cried, "People are killing one another near the Circus of Nero. Slaves and gladiators have attacked the citizens."

"Do you hear that?" Vinicius said.

"The measure is full," the apostle said, "and disasters will come, like a boundless sea." Then he turned and, pointing to Lygia, said, "Take the girl, whom God has ordained for you, and save her, and let Linus, who is sick, and Ursus go with you."

But Vinicius, who had come to love the apostle with all the power of his impetuous soul, exclaimed: "I swear, my teacher, that I will not leave you here to destruction."

"The Lord bless you for your wish," Peter answered, "but have you not heard that Christ repeated three times on the lake to me, 'Feed my lambs'?"

Vinicius was silent.

"When there was a storm on the lake, and we were terrified in heart, He did not desert us; why should I, a servant, not follow my Master's example?"

Then Linus raised his emaciated face and inquired, "O servant of the Lord, why should I not follow your example?"

Vinicius seized Lygia by the hand and said, in a trembling voice, "Hear me, Peter, Linus, and you, Lygia! I spoke as my human reason dictated; but you have another reason, which regards only the commands of the Redeemer. True, I did not understand this, and I failed, for the beam is not taken from my eyes yet, and the former nature remains in me. But since I love Christ, and wish to be His servant, I kneel here before you and swear that I will accomplish the commands of sacrificial love and will not leave my brethren in the day of trouble."

Then he knelt and with enthusiasm raised his hands and cried: "Do I understand You, O Christ? Am I worthy of You?"

His hands trembled; his eyes glistened with tears; his body was filled with faith and love. Peter took an earthen vessel with water and, bringing it near him, said with solemnity, "Behold, I baptize you in the name of the Father, Son, and Holy Ghost. Amen."

Then a spiritual ecstasy filled all present. They thought that some light from beyond this world had filled the hut, that they heard some superhuman music, that the cliffs had opened above their heads, that choirs of angels were floating down from heaven; and far up there they seemed to see a cross and pierced hands blessing them.

Meanwhile, the shouts of fighting were heard outside and the roar of flames in the burning city.

48

Camps of people were found in the lordly gardens of Caesar, Domitius, and Agrippina; on the Campus Martius; and in porticos, tennis courts, splendid summerhouses, and buildings erected for wild beasts. Peacocks, flamingoes, swans, ostriches, gazelles, African antelopes, and deer, which had served as ornaments to those gardens, were hacked down by the rabble. Abundant supplies began to come in now from Ostia. Wheat was sold at the unheard-of low price of three sestertia and was given free to the indigent. Immense supplies of wine, olives, and chestnuts were brought to the city; sheep and cattle were driven in every day from the mountains. Wretches who before the fire had been hiding in alleys of the Subura, and were perishing of hunger in ordinary times, had a more pleasant life now.

The danger of famine was averted completely, but it was more difficult to suppress robbery, murder, and abuses. A nomadic life insured freedom to thieves; the more easily since they proclaimed themselves admirers of Caesar and were unsparing of praise wherever he appeared. Moreover, when there was a lack of armed force to quell an insurrection in a city inhabited by the dregs of mankind, deeds were done that passed human imagination. Every night there were battles and murders; every night boys and women were snatched away. At the Porta Mugionis, where there was a halting-place for herds driven in from the Campania, it came to battles in which people perished by hundreds. Every morning the banks of the Tiber were covered with drowned bodies, which no one collected; these decayed quickly because of heat heightened by fire and filled the air with foul odors. Sickness broke out on the camping-grounds, and many foresaw a great pestilence.

But the city burned on unceasingly. Only on the sixth day, when the fire reached empty spaces on the Esquiline, where an enormous number of houses had been demolished purposely, it finally weakened. But the piles of burning cinders gave such strong light that people would not believe that the end of the catastrophe had come.

Of the fourteen divisions of Rome there remained only four, including the Trans-Tiber. Flames had consumed all the others. When at last the piles of cinders had been turned into ashes, an immense gray space was visible from the Tiber to the Esquiline. In this space stood rows of chimneys, like columns over graves in a cemetery. Among these columns gloomy crowds of people moved about in the daytime, some seeking for precious objects, others for the bones of those dear to them. In the night dogs howled above the ashes and ruins of former dwellings.

People who had lost all their property and their nearest relatives were not won over by the opening of gardens, the distribution of bread, or the promise of games and gifts. The catastrophe had been too great and unparalleled. Others, in whom was hidden yet some spark of love for the city and their birthplace, were brought to despair by news that the old name "Roma" was to vanish, and that from the ashes of the capital Caesar would erect a new city called Neropolis. A flood of hatred rose and swelled every day, despite the flatteries of the Augustians. Nero, more sensitive than any former Caesar to the favor of the populace, thought with alarm that in the mortal struggle he was waging with patricians in the Senate, he might lack support. The Augustians themselves were also alarmed, for any morning might bring them destruction. Tigellinus thought of summoning certain legions from Asia Minor. Vatinius, who laughed even when slapped on the face, lost his humor; Vitelius lost his appetite.

Others were taking counsel among themselves how to stop the danger, for it was no secret that were an outburst to carry off Caesar, not one of the Augustians would escape, except, perhaps, Petronius. They influenced Nero. It was from their influence that all the crimes were committed. Hatred for the Augustians almost surpassed that for Nero. So they began to disclaim responsibility for the burning of the city. But to free themselves they also had to clear Caesar from suspicion, or no one would believe that they had not caused the catastrophe. Tigellinus discussed this subject with Domitius Afer, and even with Seneca, though he hated him. Poppaea, who understood that the ruin of Nero would be her own sentence, listened to her confidants and Hebrew prophets, for it was known for years that she held the faith of Jehovah. Nero was at times fearful, childishly delighted, and full of complaints.

Petronius thought it best to leave these troubles, go to Greece, and then to Egypt and Asia Minor. The journey had been planned long before; why put it off when in Rome there were only sadness and danger?

Caesar accepted the advice eagerly; but Seneca, after thinking it over, said, "It is easy to go, but it would be more difficult to return."

"By Heracles!" Petronius replied. "We may return at the head of Asiatic legions."

"I will do this!" Nero exclaimed.

But Tigellinus opposed the plan. He could discover nothing original himself, and if Petronius's idea had come to his own mind he would have promoted it; but with Tigellinus the question was that Petronius might not be a second time the only man who in difficult moments could rescue all and everyone.

"Hear me, divinity," he said. "This advice is destructive! Before you are at Ostia a civil war will break out; perhaps one of the other surviving descendants of the divine Augustus will declare himself Caesar. What shall we do if the legions take his side?"

"We shall attempt," Nero answered, "to get rid of all descendants of Augustus. There are not many now; so it is easy to rid ourselves of the others."

"Is it a question of them alone? Yesterday my people heard from the crowd that a man like Thrasea should be Caesar."

Nero bit his lips. After a while he raised his eyes and said, "Demanding and thankless. They have enough grain, and they have coal to bake cakes; what more do they want?"

"Vengeance!" Tigellinus replied.

Silence followed. Caesar rose suddenly, raised his hand, and began to declare, "Hearts call for vengeance, and vengeance wants a victim." Then, forgetting everything, he said, with radiant face: "Give me the tablet and stylus to write this line. Never could Lucan have composed one like it. Have you noticed that I found it in an instant?"

"O incomparable!" exclaimed a number of voices.

Nero wrote down the line and said, "Yes, vengeance wants a victim." Then he cast a glance on those around him. "What if we spread the report that Vatinius ordered them to burn the city, and sacrifice him to the anger of the people?"

"O divinity! Who am I?" Vatinus exclaimed.

"True! One more important than you is demanded. Is it Vitelius?"

Vitelius grew pale but began to laugh.

"My fat," he answered, "might start the fire again."

But Nero had something else on his mind; in his soul he was

346

looking for a victim who might really satisfy the people's anger, and he found him.

"Tigellinus," he said after a while, "it was you who burned Rome!"

A shiver ran through those present. They understood that Caesar had ceased to jest this time, and that an ominous moment had come.

The face of Tigellinus was wrinkled, like the lips of a dog about to bite.

"I burned Rome at your command!" he said.

And the two glared at each other like a pair of devils. Such silence followed that the buzzing of flies was heard as they flew through the atrium.

"Tigellinus," Nero said, "do you love me?"

"You know I do, lord."

"Sacrifice yourself for me."

"O divine Caesar," Tigellinus answered, "why present the sweet cup that I may not raise to my lips? The people are cursing and rebelling; do you wish the praetorians also to rise?"

A feeling of terror filled the hearts of those present. Tigellinus was praetorian prefect, and his words had the direct meaning of a threat. Nero himself understood this, and his face became pale.

At that moment Epaphroditus, Caesar's assistant, entered, announcing that the Augusta wished to see Tigellinus, because there were people with her whom the prefect ought to hear.

Tigellinus bowed to Caesar and went out, appearing calm and contemptuous. When Caesar had finally struck him, he had shown his teeth and made them understand his power. Knowing Nero's underlying cowardice, he was confident that this ruler of the world would never dare to raise a hand against him.

Nero sat in silence initially, then, seeing they expected a reply, answered, "I have raised a serpent in my house."

Petronius shrugged his shoulder, as if to say that it was not difficult to cut off the head from this serpent.

"What will you say? Speak, advise me!" Nero exclaimed, noticing this motion. "I trust in you alone, for you have more sense than all of them, and you love me."

Petronius had this in mind: "Make me praetorian prefect; I

347

will deliver Tigellinus to the people and pacify the city in a day."
But his innate slothfulness prevailed. To be prefect meant to perform tasks related to thousands of public affairs. And why should he work hard? It was better to read poetry in his splendid library, look at vases and statues, or hold close the divine body of Eunice, twining her golden hair through his fingers and putting his lips on her coral mouth? So he said, "I suggest the journey to Achaea."

Nero answered, "I looked for something more from you. The Senate hates me. If I go, who will guarantee that it will not revolt and proclaim someone else Caesar? The people have been faithful to me so far, but now they will follow the Senate. By hades! If that Senate and that people had one head!"

"Permit me to say, O divinity, that if you desire to save Rome, there is a need to save even a few Romans," remarked Petronius, with a smile.

"What do I care for Rome and Romans?" Nero complained. "I should be obeyed in Achaea. Only here does treason surround me. Everyone is deserting me, and you are preparing for treason. I know it, I know it. You do not even imagine what future ages will say of you if you desert such an artist as I am."

Then Nero turned to Petronius with a radiant face. "Petronius," he said, "the people murmur; but if I take my lute and go to the Campus Martius, if I sing that song to them which I sang during the fire, do you not think that I will win them over, as Orpheus did with the wild beasts?"

Tullius Senecio, who was impatient to return to his slave women brought in from Antium, and who had been impatient for a long time, replied, "Beyond doubt, O Caesar, if they permit you to begin."

"Let us go to Hellas!" Nero cried, with disgust.

But at that moment Poppaea and Tigellinus appeared. Never had a triumphator ascended the Capitol with pride such as his when he stood before Caesar. He began to speak slowly and with emphasis, in tones through which the bite of iron was heard. "Listen, O Caesar, for I can say: I have found the answer! The people want vengeance—they want not one victim, but thousands. Have you heard, lord, who Christus was—he who was crucified by Pontius Pilate? And do you know who the Christians are? Have I not

348

told you of their crimes and foul ceremonies, of their predictions that fire would cause the end of the world? People hate and suspect them. No one has seen them in a temple at any time, for they consider our gods evil spirits; they are not in the Stadium, for they despise horse races. None of them recognizes you as god. They are enemies of the human race, of the city, and of you. The people murmur against you; but you have given me no order to burn Rome, and I did not burn it. The people want vengeance; let them have it. The people want blood and games; let them have them. The people suspect you; let their suspicion turn in another direction."

Nero listened with amazement at first; but as Tigellinus proceeded, his actor's face changed and assumed in succession expressions of anger, sorrow, sympathy, and indignation. Suddenly he rose and, casting off the toga, which dropped at his feet, he raised both hands and stood silent for a time. At last he said, in the tones of a tragedian, "O Zeus, Apollo, Athene, Persephone, and all you immortals! Why did you not come to aid us? What has this forsaken city done to those cruel wretches that they burned it so inhumanly?"

"They are enemies of mankind and of you," Poppaea said.

"Do justice!" others cried. "Punish the rebels! The gods themselves call for vengeance!"

Nero sat down, dropped his head to his chest, and was silent a second time, as if stunned by the wickedness of what he had heard. But after a while he wrung his hands and said, "What punishments, what tortures fit such a crime? But the gods will inspire me, and, aided by the powers of Tartarus, I will give my poor people such a spectacle that they will remember me for ages with gratitude."

Petronius became alarmed. He thought of the danger hanging over Lygia and over Vinicius, whom he loved, and over all those people whose religion he rejected, but of whose innocence he was certain. He also thought that one of those bloody orgies would begin that his eyes, he being an aesthetic person, could not stand. But above all he thought, *I must save Vinicius, who will go mad if that maiden perishes;* and this consideration outweighed every other, for Petronius understood well that he was beginning a game far more perilous that any in his life. He began, however, to speak freely and carelessly, as usual when criticizing or ridiculing the plans of Caesar and the Augustians that were not sufficiently aesthetic. "You have found victims! That is true. You may send them to the arena. That is true also. But hear me! You have authority, praetorian guards, and power; then be sincere, at least, when no one is listening! Deceive the people, but do not deceive one another. Give the Christians to the populace, condemn them to any torture you like; but have the courage to say to yourselves that it was not they who burned Rome.

"You call me 'Arbiter Elegantiarum,' a refined eyewitness and judge; so I tell to you that I cannot endure wretched comedies! How all this reminds me of the theatrical booths near the Porta Asinaria, in which actors play the parts of gods and kings to amuse the suburban rabble, and when the play is over wash down onions with sour wine. Be gods and kings in reality; for I say that you can permit yourselves the position!

"As to you, O Caesar, you have threatened us with the sentence of coming ages; but think, those ages will utter judgment concerning you also. By the divine Clio! Nero, ruler of the world, Nero, a god, burned Rome because he was as powerful on earth as Zeus on Olympus; Nero the poet loved poetry so much that he sacrificed to it his country! Do not renounce such glory, for songs about you will sound to the end of the ages. What will Priam be when compared with you; or Achilles; or the gods themselves? We do not need to say that the burning of Rome was good, but that it was colossal and uncommon. The people will raise no hand against you! They will not. Have courage; guard yourself against acts unworthy of you—for this alone threatens you, that future ages may say, 'Nero burned Rome; but as a timid Caesar and a timid poet he denied the great deed out of fear and cast the blame on the innocent!'"

The arbiter's words produced the usual deep impression on Nero; but Petronius was not deceived that what he had said was a desperate means that in a fortunate event might save the Christians. He might also destroy himself. He had not hesitated, however, for it was a question at once of Vinicius, whom he loved, and of danger, with which he amused himself. *The dice are thrown,* he said to himself, *and we shall see how far fear for his own life outweighs in the monkey his love of glory.*

And in his soul he had no doubt that fear would outweigh glory.

Silence fell after his words. Poppaea and all present were looking at Nero's eyes as at a rainbow. He began to raise his lips, drawing them to his very nostrils, as was his custom when he did not know what to do. Disgust and perplexity were evident on his features.

"Lord," Tigellinus cried, on noting this, "permit me to go; for when people wish to expose you to destruction and call you, besides, a cowardly Caesar, a cowardly poet, and a comedian, my ears cannot suffer such expressions!"

I have lost, Petronius thought. But, turning to Tigellinus, he measured him with a glance in which was that contempt for a fool that is felt by a great lord who is a connoisseur.

"Tigellinus," he said, "it was you whom I called a comedian; for you are one at this very moment."

"Is it because I will not listen to your insults?"

"It is because you are pretending boundless love for Caesar—you who a short while ago were threatening him with praetorians, which we all understood as did he!"

Tigellinus, who had not thought Petronius sufficiently daring to throw dice such as those on the table, turned pale, lost his head, and was speechless. This was, however, the last victory of Petronius over his rival, for at that moment Poppaea said, "Lord, how can we permit that such a thought should even pass through the head of anyone, and all the more that anyone should venture to express it aloud in your presence!"

"Punish the insolent!" Vitelius exclaimed.

Nero raised his lips again to his nostrils and, turning his nearsighted, glassy eyes on Petronius, said, "Is this the way you pay me for the friendship I had for you?"

"If I am mistaken, show me my error," Petronius said, "but you know that I speak out of love for you."

"Punish the insolent!" Vitelius repeated.

"Punish!" called a number of voices.

In the atrium there was a murmur and a movement, for people

351

began to withdraw from Petronius. Even Tullius Senecio, his constant companion at the court, walked away, as did young Nerva, who had shown him the greatest friendship. After a while Petronius was alone on the left side of the atrium, with a smile on his lips; and, gathering with his hands the folds of his toga, he waited for what Caesar would say or do.

"You wish me to punish him," Caesar said, "but he is my friend and comrade. Though he has wounded my heart, let him know that for friends this heart has nothing but forgiveness."

I have lost and am ruined, Petronius thought.

Meanwhile, Caesar rose, and the meeting was ended.

49

Petronius went home. Nero and Tigellinus went to Poppaea's atrium, where they were expected by people with whom the prefect had spoken already.

There were two Trans-Tiber rabbis in long robes and miters, a young scribe, who was their assistant, together with Chilo. At sight of Caesar the priest grew pale from fear.

"Be greeted, O ruler of the earth, guardian of the chosen people, and Caesar, lion among men, whose reign is like sunlight, like the cedar of Lebanon, like the balm of Jericho."

"Do you refuse to call me god?" Nero asked.

The priest grew still paler. The chief one spoke again. "Your words, O lord, are as sweet as a cluster of grapes, as a ripe fig— for Jehovah filled your heart with goodness! Your father's predecessor, Caesar Caius, was stern; still, our envoys did not call him god, preferring death itself to violation of the law."

"And did not Caligula give command them for to be thrown to the lions?"

"No, lord; Caesar Caius feared Jehovah's anger."

And they raised their heads, for the name of the powerful

Jehovah gave them courage. Confident in His might, they looked into Nero's eyes with more boldness.

"Do you accuse the Christians of burning Rome?" Caesar asked.

"We, lord, accuse them of being enemies of the law, the human race, Rome, and of you. They have long since threatened the city and the world with fire! The rest will be told to you by this man, whose lips are unstained by a lie, for in his mother's veins flowed the blood of the chosen people."

Nero turned to Chilo. "Who are you?"

"One who honors you, O Cyrus; and besides a poor Stoic—"

"I hate Stoics," Nero said. "Their speech is repulsive to me; their contempt for art, their voluntary squalor and filth."

"O lord, I am a Stoic from necessity. Dress my stoicism, O Radiant One, in a garland of roses, put a pitcher of wine before it; it will sing Anacreon in such strains as to deafen every Epicurean."

Nero, who was pleased by the title "Radiant," smiled and said, "You please me."

"This man is worth his weight in gold!" Tigellinus cried.

"Put your generosity together with my weight," answered Chilo, "or the wind will blow my reward away."

"He would not outweigh Vitelius," put in Caesar.

"Silver-bowed, my wit is not of lead."

"I see that your faith does not hinder you from calling me a god," Nero replied.

"O Immortal! My faith is in you; the Christians blaspheme against that faith, and I hate them."

"What do you know of the Christians?"

"Will you permit me to weep, O divinity?"

"No," Nero answered. "Weeping annoys me."

"You are right again, for eyes that have seen you should be free of tears forever. O lord, defend me against my enemies."

"Speak of the Christians," Poppaea said, with a shade of impatience.

"It will be at your command, O Isis," Chilo answered. "From youth I devoted myself to philosophy and sought truth. I sought it among the ancient divine sages, in the Academy at Athens, and in the Serapeuum at Alexandria. When I heard of the Christians, I thought that they formed some new school in which I could find kernels of truth; and to my misfortune I made their acquaintance. The first Christian whom evil fate brought me near was one Glaucus, a physician of Naples. From him I learned in time that they worship a certain Christus, who promised to exterminate all people and destroy every city on earth, but to spare them if they helped him to exterminate the children of Deucalion. For this reason they hate me and poison fountains; for this same reason in their assemblies they shower curses on Rome and on all temples in which our gods are honored. Christus was crucified; but He promised that when Rome was destroyed by fire, He would come again and give Christians dominion over the world."

"People will understand now why Rome was destroyed," Tigellinus interrupted.

"Many understand that already, O lord, for I go about in the gardens, I go to the Campus Martius, and teach. But if you listen to the end, you will know my reasons for vengeance. Glaucus the physician did not reveal to me at first that their religion taught hatred. He told me that Christus was a good divinity, that the basis of their religion was love. My sensitive heart could not resist such a truth, so I loved Glaucus. I trusted him, I shared every morsel of bread with him, every copper coin—and do you know, lady, how he repaid me? On the road from Naples to Rome he thrust a knife into my body, and my wife, the beautiful young Berenice, was sold to a slave-merchant. If Sophocles knew my history—but what am I saying? One better than Sophocles is listening."

"Poor man!" Poppaea said.

"Whoever has seen the face of Aphrodite is not poor, lady; and I see it at this moment. But then I found consolation in philosophy. When I came to Rome, I tried to meet Christian elders to obtain justice against Glaucus. I thought that they would force him to give up my wife. I became acquainted with their chief priest and another man named Paul, who was in prison in this city but was liberated afterward. I became acquainted with the son of Zebedee, with Linus and Clitus and many others. I can point out one excavation in the Vatican Hill and a cemetery beyond the Nomentan Gate where they celebrate their shameless ceremonies. I saw the apostle Peter. I saw how Glaucus killed children, so that the apostle might have something to sprinkle on the heads of those present; I saw Lygia, the foster-child of Pomponia Graecina, who boasted that though unable to bring the blood of an infant, she was able to bring about the death of an infant, for she bewitched the little Augusta, your daughter, O Cyrus, and yours, O Isis!"

"Do you hear, Caesar?" Poppaea asked.

"Can that be!" Nero exclaimed.

"I could forgive wrongs done myself," Chilo continued, "but when I heard of yours, I wanted to stab her. Unfortunately, I was stopped by the noble Vinicius, who loves her."

"Vinicius? But did she not flee from him?"

"She fled, but he searched for her; he could not exist without her. I helped him in the search, and it was I who pointed out to him the house where she lived among the Christians in the Trans-Tiber. We went there together, and with us your wrestler Croton, whom the noble Vinicius hired to protect him. But Ursus, Lygia's slave, crushed Croton. He is a man of dreadful strength, O lord, who can break a bull's neck as easily as another might a poppy stalk. Aulus and Pomponia loved him because of that."

"By Hercules," Nero said, "the mortal who crushed Croton deserves a statue in the Forum. But, old man, you are mistaken and are inventing this, for Vinicius killed Croton with a knife."

"O lord, I myself saw Croton's ribs breaking in the arms of Ursus, who rushed then on Vinicius and would have killed him but for Lygia. Vinicius was ill for a long time after that, but they nursed him in the hope that through love he would become a Christian. In fact, he did became a Christian."

"Vinicius?"

"Yes."

"And perhaps Petronius too?" Tigellinus inquired hurriedly.

Chilo squirmed, rubbed his hands, and said, "I admire your perception, O lord. He may have become one! He may very well have become one."

"Now I understand why he defended the Christians."

Nero laughed. "Petronius a Christian! Petronius an enemy of life and luxury! Do not be foolish, and do not ask me to believe that, since I am not ready to believe anything."

"But the noble Vinicius became a Christian, lord. I swear by that radiance that comes from you that I speak the truth and that nothing pierces me with such disgust as lying. Pomponia Graecina is a Christian, little Aulus is a Christian, Lygia is a Christian, and so is Vinicius. I served him faithfully, and in return, at the desire of Glaucus the physician, he had me flogged, though I am old and sick. And I have sworn by hades that I will not forgive him for that. O lord, avenge my wrongs, and I will deliver you Peter the apostle and Linus and Clitus and Glaucus and Crispus, the highest ones, and Lygia and Ursus. I will point out hundreds of them to you, thousands. I will show you their houses of prayer, the cemeteries—all your prisons will not hold them! Without me you could not find them. In misfortunes I have sought consolation in philosophy; now I will find it in favors that will descend on me. I am old and have not known life; let me begin."

"It is your wish to be a Stoic before a full plate," Nero said.

"Whoever renders service to you will fill it by that same."

"You are not mistaken, O philosopher."

But Poppaea did not forget her enemies. Her fancy for Vinicius was, indeed, a momentary whim that had risen from the influence of jealousy, anger, and wounded vanity. Still, the coolness of the young patrician touched her deeply and filled her heart with a stubborn feeling of offense. This alone, that he had dared to prefer another, seemed to her a crime calling for vengeance. As to Lygia, she hated her from the first moment, when the beauty of that northern lily alarmed her. Petronius, who spoke of the narrow hips of the girl, might persuade Caesar, but not the Augusta. Poppaea the critic understood at one glance that in all Rome Lygia alone could rival and even surpass her, so she vowed her ruin.

"Lord," she said, "avenge our child."

"Hurry!" Chilo cried. "Otherwise Vinicius will hide her. I will point out the house to which she returned after the fire."

"I will give you ten men, and go this moment," Tigellinus said.

"O lord! You have not seen Croton in the arms of Ursus; if you will give us fifty men, I will only point out the house from a distance. But if you will not imprison Vinicius, I am lost."

Tigellinus looked at Nero. "Would it not be well, O divinity, to finish at once with the uncle and nephew?"

Nero thought a moment and answered, "No, not now. People would not believe us if we tried to persuade them that Petronius, Vinicius, or Pomponia Graecina had burned Rome. Their houses were too beautiful. Their turn will come later; today other victims are needed."

"Then, O lord, give me soldiers as a guard," Chilo said.

"See to this, Tigellinus."

"You will stay with me meanwhile," the prefect said to Chilo. The face of the Greek beamed with delight.

"I will give up everything! Only hurry!" he cried, with a hoarse voice.

50

On leaving Caesar, Petronius went to his house on the Carinae. Because it was surrounded on three sides by a garden, it luckily escaped the fire. For this reason other Augustians, who had lost their homes and in them vast wealth and many works of art, thought that Petronius was fortunate. For years it had been said that he was the firstborn of Fortune, and Caesar's growing friendship in recent times seemed to confirm the correctness of it.

But that same firstborn of Fortune would meditate now on the fickleness of Fortune's mother, or rather on her likeness to Chronos (the Greek god of time), who devoured his own children.

Were my house burned, he said to himself, *and with it my gems, Etruscan vases, Alexandrian glass, and Corinthian bronze, Nero might have forgotten the offense. By Pollux! And to think that I could have been praetorian prefect at this moment. I would proclaim Tigellinus the rebel, and I would deliver him to the populace, protect the Christians, and rebuild Rome. Who knows even if a better era would not begin for honest people? I ought to have taken the office, simply out of regard for Vinicius. In case of over-*

work I could have surrendered the details to him, and Nero would not have even tried to resist. Then let Vinicius baptize all the praetorian guards, even Caesar himself; what harm could that be to me? Nero pious, Nero virtuous and merciful—this would even be an amusing spectacle.

Then he began to laugh, but after a while his thoughts turned in another direction. It seemed to him that he was in Antium; that Paul of Tarsus was saying to him, "You call us enemies of life, but answer me, Petronius: If Caesar were a Christian and acted according to our religion, would not life be safer and more certain?"

And remembering these words, he continued: *By Castor! No matter how many Christians they murder here, Paul will find as many new ones; for he is right, unless the world has a foundation of evil. But who knows if this will not be the case soon? I myself, who have learned much, did not learn how to be a great enough scoundrel; so I shall have to open my veins and die. I am sorry to lose Eunice and my Myrrhene vase; but Eunice is free, and the vase will go with me. Ahenobarbus will not get it, anyway! I am also sorry for Vinicius. But, though I was bored less lately, I am ready. Things are beautiful in the world, but people are so vile that life is not worth a single regret. One who knew how to live should know how to die. Though I belong to the Augustians, I was freer than they supposed.*

Here he shrugged his shoulders. *They may think that my knees are trembling at this moment, but on reaching home, I will take a bath in violet water, my golden-haired one herself will anoint me; then after refreshment we will have sung to us that hymn to Apollo composed by Anthemios. I said once to myself that it was not worthwhile to think of death, for death thinks of us without our assistance. It would be a wonder if there are really Elysian fields, and in them souls of people. Eunice would come in time to me, and we should wander together over meadows filled with asphodels. I should find, too, society better than this. What buffoons and cowards, tricksters—a vile herd without taste or polish! Tens of Arbiters Elegantairum could not transform those ignoramuses into decent people. By Persephone! I have had enough!*

But afterward he began to think over his position. Thanks to his keen insight, he knew that destruction was not threatening him directly. Nero had seized this occasion to utter a few select, lofty phrases about friendship and forgiveness, thus keeping their relationship together for the moment. *He will have to seek reasons, and before he finds them he may be distracted. First of all, he will celebrate the games with Christians,* Petronius said to himself. *Only then will he think of me, and if that is true, it is not worthwhile to take trouble or change my course of life. But closer danger threatens Vinicius!*

And from then on he thought only of Vinicius, whom he determined to rescue. Four sturdy Bithynians carried his litter quickly through the ruins and ash-heaps the Carinae was filled with, but he commanded them even to run, so as to be home quickly. Vinicius, whose home had been burned, was living with him and fortunately was at home.

"Have you seen Lygia today?" were Petronius's first words.

"I have just visited her."

"Listen to what I tell you, and lose no time questioning me. It has been decided this morning at Caesar's to lay the blame for the burning of Rome on the Christians. Persecutions and tortures threaten them, and pursuit may begin any moment. Take Lygia and flee at once beyond the Alps, or to Africa. And hurry, for the Palatine is very near the Trans-Tiber."

Vinicius was a trained soldier and did not lose time in useless questions. He listened intently with dismay, but he was fearless. The soldier in him wished to do battle.

"I am leaving," he said.

"One more thought. Take a purse of gold, weapons, and a group of your Christians. If need be, rescue her!"

Vinicius was in the door of the atrium already.

"Send me news by a slave!" Petronius cried.

When left alone, he began to walk by the columns that adorned the atrium, thinking of what had happened. He knew that Lygia and Linus had returned after the fire to the former house, which, like the greater part of the Trans-Tiber, had been saved. That was an unfavorable circumstance, for otherwise it would have been difficult to find them among the large crowd. Petronius hoped, however, that as things stood, no one in the Palatine knew where they lived, and therefore Vinicius would anticipate the praetorians everywhere. It occurred to him that Tigellinus, wishing to seize as many Christians as possible, would extend his net all over Rome. *If they send no more than ten people after her,* he thought, *that giant Lygian will break their bones, and it will make no difference if Vinicius comes with assistance.* Thinking of this he was consoled. True, armed resistance to the praetorians was almost the same as war with Caesar. Petronius knew also that if Vinicius hid from the vengeance of Nero, that vengeance might fall on himself, but he did not care. On the contrary, he rejoiced at the thought of intercepting Nero's plans as well as those of Tigellinus. Since in Antium Paul of Tarsus had converted most of his slaves, he, while defending Christians, might count on their zeal and devotion.

The entrance of Eunice interrupted his thoughts. At sight of her all his cares and troubles vanished without a trace. He forgot Caesar, the disfavor into which he had fallen, the degraded Augustians, the persecution threatening the Christians, and Vinicius and Lygia, and looked only at her with the eyes of an aesthetic man enamored by marvelous forms, and of a lover for whom love originates from those forms. She, in a transparent violet robe through which her maidenlike form appeared, was really as beautiful as a goddess. Feeling herself admired, and loving him with all her soul, ever eager for his caresses, she blushed with delight as if she had been an innocent maiden.

"What will you say to me, Charis?" Petronius asked, stretching his hands to her.

She, leaning her golden head toward him, answered, "Anthemios has come with his choristers and asks if it is your wish to hear him."

"Let him stay; he will sing the hymn to Apollo to us during dinner. By the groves of Paphos! When I see you in that robe, I think that Aphrodite has veiled herself with a piece of sky and is standing before me."

"O lord!"

"Come here, Eunice, embrace me with your arms and give your lips to me. Do you love me?"

"I should not have loved Zeus more."

Then she pressed her lips to his, while melting in his arms

from ecstasy. After a while Petronius asked, "But what if we should have to separate?"

Eunice looked at him with fear in her eyes.

"How is that, lord?"

"Fear not; I ask because I may have to set out on a long journey."

"Take me with you—"

Petronius changed the conversation quickly and said, "Tell me, are there asphodels on the grass plot in the garden?"

"The cypresses and the grass plots are yellow from the fire, the leaves have fallen from the myrtles, and the whole garden seems dead."

"All Rome seems dead, and soon it will be a real graveyard. Do you know that an edict against the Christians is to be issued and a persecution will begin in which thousands will die?"

"Why punish the Christians, lord? They are good and peaceful."

"For that very reason."

"Let us go to the sea. Your beautiful eyes do not like to see blood."

"Yes, but meanwhile I must bathe. Come to the bathhouse to anoint my arms. By the belt of Kypris! Never have you seemed so beautiful to me! I will order a bath for you in the form of a shell; you will be like a costly pearl in it. Come, Golden-haired!"

He went out, and an hour later both, in garlands of roses and with misty eyes, were resting before a golden table. They were served by boys dressed as Cupid, and they drank wine from ivy-wreathed goblets and heard the hymn to Apollo sung to the sound of harps, under direction of Anthemios. What did they care if only the villa chimneys pointed up from the ruins of houses and gusts of wind swept the ashes of burned Rome in every direction? They were happy thinking only of their love, which had made their lives like a divine dream. But before the hymn was finished a slave, the chief of the atrium, entered the hall.

"Lord," he said, in a voice quivering with alarm, "a centurion with a detachment of praetorians is standing at the gate and, at the command of Caesar, wishes to see you."

The song and the sound of lutes ceased. There was alarm,

because Caesar, in communications with friends, did not send these guards usually, and their arrival forbode no good. Petronius did not show the slightest emotion but said, like a man annoyed by intruders, "They might let me dine in peace." Then, turning to the chief of the atrium, he said, "Let him enter."

The slave disappeared behind the curtain; a moment later heavy steps were heard and an acquaintance of Petronius appeared, the centurion Aper, armed and with an iron helmet on his head.

"Noble lord," he said, "here is a letter from Caesar."

Petronius took the tablet and, looking it over, gave it calmly to Eunice.

"He will read a new book of the Troyad this evening and invites me to come."

"I only have the order to deliver the letter," the centurion said.

"Yes, there will be no answer. But, centurion, you should rest a while with us and empty a goblet of wine."

"Thanks to you, noble lord. I will willingly drink a goblet of wine to your health; but I may not rest, for I am on duty."

"Why was the letter given to you and not sent by a slave?"

"I do not know, lord. Perhaps because I was sent in this direction on other duty."

"Against the Christians?"

"Yes, lord."

"When was the pursuit begun?"

"Some divisions were sent to the Trans-Tiber before midday." The centurion then shook a little wine from the goblet in honor of Mars; then he emptied it and said, "May the gods grant you, lord, what you desire."

"Take the goblet too," Petronius said.

Then he told Anthemios to finish the hymn to Apollo.

Bronzebeard is beginning to play with me and Vinicius, he thought, when the harps sounded again. *I foresee his plan! He wanted to terrify me by sending the invitation through a centurion. They will ask the centurion in the evening how I received him. No! You will not amuse yourself too much, cruel and wicked king. I know that you will not forget the offense, I know that my destruc-*

362

tion is inevitable; but if you think that I shall plead with you, that you will see fear and humility on my face, you are mistaken.

"Caesar writes, 'Come if you have the desire.'" Eunice said. "Will you go?"

"I am in excellent health and can listen even to his verses," Petronius answered. "So I shall go, all the more since Vinicius cannot go."

In fact, after the dinner was finished and after the usual walk, he went to the hairdressers and slaves, who arranged his robes. An hour later, handsome as a god, he ordered them to take him to the Palatine.

It was late, and the evening was warm and calm. The moon shone so brightly that the slaves going ahead of the litter put out their torches. On the streets and among the ruins crowds of people were pushing along, drunk with wine, in garlands of ivy and honeysuckle. In their hands were branches of myrtle and laurel taken from Caesar's gardens. Abundance of grain and hopes of exciting games filled the hearts of all with gladness. The slaves were forced repeatedly to demand space for the litter "of the noble Petronius," and then the crowd pushed apart, shouting in honor of their favorite ruler.

He was thinking of Vinicius and wondering why he had no news from him. He was an Epicurean and an egotist, but passing time with Paul of Tarsus and with Vinicius and hearing daily of the Christians, he had changed somewhat without knowing it. A breeze of their spirit had blown on him; this cast new seeds into his soul. Besides himself he thought of others. He had always been attached to Vinicius, for in childhood he had great love for his sister, the mother of Vinicius.

Petronius did not lose hope that Vinicius had anticipated the praetorians and fled with Lygia, or, in the worst case, had at least rescued her. But he would have preferred to be certain, since he realized that he might have to answer a number of questions for which it was better for him to be prepared.

Stopping at the house of Tiberius, he entered the atrium, which was already filled with Augustians. Yesterday's friends, though astonished that he was invited, still remained aloof, but he moved freely among them, carefree, unconcerned, and self-confi-

363

dent, as if he himself had the power to distribute favors. Some, seeing him this way, were afraid lest they had rejected him too soon.

Caesar, however, pretended not to see him and did not return his greeting, pretending to be occupied in conversation. But Tigellinus approached and said, "Good evening, Arbiter Elegantiarum. Do you still assert that it was not the Christians who burned Rome?"

Petronius shrugged his shoulders and, clapping Tigellinus on the back as he would a freedman, answered, "You know as well as I the answer to that question."

"I do not dare to rival you in wisdom."

"And you are right, for when Caesar reads to us a new book from the Troyad, you, instead of crying out like a jackdaw, would have to give an intelligent opinion."

Tigellinus bit his lips. He was not very pleased that Caesar had decided to read a new book, for he entered a field in which he could not rival Petronius. In fact, during the reading, Nero, from habit, turned his eyes involuntarily toward Petronius, looking carefully to see what he could read in his face. The latter listened, raised his brows, agreed at times, at times increased his attention as if to be sure that he heard correctly. Then he praised or criticized, demanded corrections or the refining of certain verses. Nero himself felt that when others gave exaggerated praises it was simply to promote themselves, that Petronius alone was occupied with poetry for its own sake; that he alone understood it, and that if he praised verses one could be sure that the verses deserved it. Gradually, therefore, he began to discuss with him, to dispute; and when at last Petronius brought the fitness of a certain expression into doubt, he said, "You will see in the final book why I used it."

Ah, thought Petronius, *then we shall eagerly wait for the last book.*

Many, upon hearing this, said in their hearts, *Woe to me! With time before him Petronius may return to favor and overturn even Tigellinus.* And they began again to approach him. But the end of the evening was less fortunate; for Caesar, at the moment when Petronius was leaving, inquired suddenly, with blinking eyes and a face at once glad and malicious, "Why did Vinicius not come?"

Had Petronius been sure that Vinicius and Lygia were beyond the gates of the city, he would have answered, "With your permission he has married and gone." But seeing Nero's strange smile, he answered, "Your invitation, divinity, did not find him at home."

"Tell Vinicius that I shall be glad to see him," Nero answered, "and tell him from me not to neglect the games in which Christians will appear."

These words alarmed Petronius. It seemed to him that they related to Lygia directly. Sitting in his litter, he wished to arrive home before morning. That, however, was not easy. A large crowd, noisy and drunk, stood in front of the house of Tiberius, and though they were not singing and dancing, they were certainly agitated. From far away came shouts Petronius could not understand at once, but that rose and grew until at last they were one savage roar: "To the lions with Christians!"

Rich litters carrying couriers pushed through the howling rabble. From the depths of burned streets new crowds rushed forward continually and, hearing the cry from afar, repeated it. News passed by word of mouth that the pursuit had continued from the previous noon, that a multitude of rebels were seized. Immediately along the newly cleared streets, through alleys lying among ruins around the Palatine, over all the hills and gardens were heard through the length and breadth of Rome shouts of swelling rage: "To the lions with Christians!"

"Herd!" repeated Petronius, with contempt. "A people worthy of Caesar!" And he began to think that a society resting on superior force, on cruelty of which even barbarians had no conception, on crimes and decadence, could not endure. Rome ruled the world but was also its ulcer. The odor of a corpse was rising from it. The shadow of death was descending over its decaying life. This had been mentioned more than once even among the Augustians, but never before had Petronius had a clearer view of this truth, that the laureled chariot on which Rome stood in the form of a triumphator, and which dragged behind a chained herd of nations, was careening to the edge of the cliff. The life of that world-ruling city seemed to him a kind of mad dance, an orgy, which must end. He saw, then, that the Christians alone had a new basis of life; but he judged that soon there would not remain a trace of the Christians. And what then?

The mad dance would continue under Nero; and if Nero disappeared, another would be found of the same kind or worse, for with such a people and such patricians there was no reason to find a better leader. There would be a new orgy of death—and probably a fouler and viler one.

Petronius became immensely weary. Was it worthwhile to live in uncertainty, with no purpose but to endure such a society? The value of death was not less beautiful than the value of sleep.

The litter stopped before the arbiter's door, which was opened that instant by the watchful keeper.

"Has the noble Vinicius returned?" Petronius asked.

"Yes, lord, a moment ago," the slave replied.

He has not rescued her, Petronius thought. And, casting aside his toga, he ran into the atrium. Vinicius was sitting on a stool; his head bent almost to his knees and his hands on his head; but at the sound of steps he raised his worn face, in which the eyes alone had a feverish brightness.

"You were too late?" Petronius asked.

"Yes; they seized her before midday."

A moment of tense silence followed.

"Have you seen her?"

"Yes."

"Where is she?"

"In the Mamertine prison."

Petronius trembled and looked at Vinicius with an inquiring glance. The latter understood.

"No," he said. "She was not thrust down to the Tullianuum [the lowest part of the prison, which lies entirely underground, with only a single opening in the ceiling], nor even to the middle prison. I paid the guard to give her his own room. Ursus took his place at the threshold and is guarding her."

"Why did Ursus not defend her?"

"They sent fifty praetorians, and Linus forbade him."

"But what of Linus?"

"Linus is dying; therefore they did not seize him."

"What is your plan?"

"To save her or die with her. I too believe in Christ."

Vinicius spoke with apparent calmness, but there was such despair in his voice that the heart of Petronius beat from pure pity.

"I understand you," he said, "but how do you plan to save her?"

"I paid the guards well, first to protect her from indignity, and second not to hinder her flight."

"When can that happen?"

"They answered that they could not give her to me at once, because they feared being caught. When the prison is filled with a multitude of people and the number of prisoners is confused, they will deliver her. But that will be a desperate attempt! Save her, and me first! You are a friend of Caesar. He himself gave her to me. Go to him and save me!"

Petronius, instead of answering, called a slave and, commanding him to bring two dark cloaks and two swords, turned to Vinicius. "On the way I will tell you," he said. "Meanwhile, take the cloak and weapon, and we will go to the prison. Give the guards there a hundred thousand sestertia; give them twice and five times that amount, if they will free Lygia at once. Otherwise, it will be too late."

"Let us go," Vinicius said.

After a while both were on the street.

"Now listen to me," Petronius said. "I did not wish to lose time. I am in disfavor, beginning with today. My own life is hanging on a hair, so I can do nothing with Caesar. Worse than that, I am sure that he would oppose my request. If that were not the case, would I advise you to flee with Lygia or to rescue her? Besides, if you escape, Caesar's wrath will turn on me. Today he would rather do something at your request than at mine. Do not count on that, however. Get her out of the prison, and flee! Nothing else is left. If that does not succeed, there will be time for other methods.

"Lygia is in prison not only for belief in Christ, but because Poppaea's anger is pursuing her and you. You have offended the Augusta by rejecting her, do you remember? She knows that she was rejected for Lygia, whom she hated from the first look. Nay, she tried to destroy Lygia before by blaming the death of her own infant on Lygia's witchcraft. The hand of Poppaea is in this. How can you explain that Lygia was the first to be imprisoned? Who could point out the house of Linus? I tell you that she has been followed all along. I know that I wrench your soul and take the remnant of hope away from you, but I tell you this purposely, for if you do not free her before they arrive at the idea that you will try to do this, you are both lost."

"Yes. I understand." Vinicius muttered.

The streets were empty because of the late hour. Their further conversation was interrupted, however, by a drunken gladiator who came toward them. He reeled against Petronius, put one hand on his shoulder, covering his face with wine-laden breath, and shouted in a hoarse voice, "To the lions with Christians!"

"Mirmillon," Petronius answered quietly, "listen to good advice; go your way."

With his other hand the drunken man seized him by the arm, "Shout with me, or I'll break your neck: Christians to the lions!"

But the arbiter's nerves had had enough of those shouts. From the time that he had left the Palatine they had been stifling him like a nightmare and piercing his ears. So when he saw the giant above him, his patience was exceeded. "Friend," he said, "you have the smell of wine and are blocking my path."

He then drove a short sword into the man's breast all the way to hilt. Then, taking the arm of Vinicius, he continued as if nothing had happened. "Caesar said today, 'Tell Vinicius from me to be at the games in which Christians will appear.' They wish to make a spectacle of your pain. That is a final decision. Perhaps that is why you and I are not imprisoned yet. If you are not able to get her at once—I do not know—Acte might take your part; but can she accomplish anything? Your Sicilian lands, too, might tempt Tigellinus. Make the attempt."

"I will give him all that I have," Vinicius answered.

It was not very far from the Carinae to the Forum, so they arrived soon. The night had begun to pale, and the walls of the castle were striking in the shadow.

Suddenly, as they turned toward the Mamertine prison, Petronius stopped and said, "Praetorians! Too late!"

In fact the prison was surrounded by a double rank of soldiers. The morning dawn was silvering their helmets and the points of their javelins.

Vinicius grew as pale as marble. "Let us go on," he said.

Finally, they halted before the line. Gifted with an unusual memory, Petronius knew not only the officers, but nearly all the praetorian soldiers. Soon he saw an acquaintance, a leader of a cohort, and nodded to him.

"But what is this, Niger?" he asked. "Are you commanded to watch the prison?"

"Yes, noble Petronius. The prefect feared that they might try to rescue the rebels."

"Have you the order to admit no one?" asked Vinicius.

"No. Friends and relatives may visit the prisoners, and in this way we shall seize more Christians."

"Then let me in," Vinicius said; and, pressing Petronius's hand, he said, "See Acte. I will come to learn her answer."

"Come," Petronius responded.

At that moment under the ground and beyond the thick walls was heard singing. The hymn, at first low and muffled, grew louder. The voices of men, women, and children were mingled in one harmonious chorus. The whole prison began to sound, in the calmness of dawn, like a harp. But those were not voices of sorrow or despair; on the contrary, gladness and triumph were heard in them.

The soldiers looked at one another with amazement. The first golden and rosy gleams of the morning appeared in the sky.

51

The cry "Christians to the lions!" was increasingly heard in every part of the city. No one doubted that they were the true cause of the fire, but no one wished to doubt, since their punishment was to be a splendid amusement for the populace. Still, the opinion spread that the catastrophe would not have assumed such dreadful proportions except for the anger of the gods. For this reason purifying sacrifices were commanded in the temples. By advice of the Sibylline books, the Senate ordained solemnities and public prayer to Vulcan, Ceres, and Proserpina. Matrons made offerings to Juno; a whole procession of them went to the seashore to take water and sprinkle the statue of the goddess with it. Married women prepared feasts to the gods and night watches. All Rome purified itself from sin, made offerings, and placated the Immortals.

Meanwhile, new broad streets were opened among the ruins. In various places foundations were laid for magnificent houses, palaces, and temples. But first of all they very quickly built an enormous wooden amphitheater in which Christians were to die. Immediately after that meeting in the house of Tiberius, orders went to consuls to furnish wild beasts. Tigellinus emptied the cages of all Italian cities. In Africa, at his command, gigantic hunts were organized, in which the entire local population was forced to take part. Elephants and tigers were brought in from Asia, crocodiles and hippopotamuses from the Nile, lions from afar, wolves and bears from the Pyrenees, savage hounds from Hibernia, Molossian dogs from Epirus, bisons and the gigantic wild aurochs from Germany. Because of the number of prisoners, the games were to surpass in greatness anything seen up to that time. Caesar wished to drown in blood all memory of the fire and make Rome drunk with it; so never had there been a greater promise of bloodshed.

The people willingly helped the guards and praetorians in hunting Christians. That was not difficult labor, for whole groups of them camped with the other population in the midst of the gardens. They confessed their faith openly. When surrounded, they knelt, and while singing hymns let themselves be taken away without resistance. But their patience only increased the anger of the populace, who, not understanding its origin, considered it as defiance and persistence. Madness filled the persecutors. The mob began to seize Christians from praetorian guards and tore them to pieces; women were dragged to prison by their hair; children's heads were dashed against stones. Thousands of people rushed, howling, night and day through the streets. Victims were

370

sought in ruins, in chimneys, in cellars. Before the prison, bacchanalian feasts and dances were celebrated at fires, around casks of wine. In the evening, celebrations were heard with delight that was like thunder, and which sounded throughout the city. The prisons were overflowing with thousands of people. Every day the mob and praetorians brought in new victims. Pity had vanished. It seemed that people had forgotten any other words and in their wild frenzy remembered only one shout: "To the lions with Christians!" Extremely hot days followed, and nights more stifling than ever before. The very air seemed filled with blood, evil, and madness.

And that surpassing measure of cruelty was answered by an equal desire for martyrdom—the confessors of Christ went to death willingly, or even sought death until they were restrained by the stern commands of their shepherds. By the order of these elders they began to assemble only outside the city, in excavations near the Appian Way and in vineyards belonging to patrician Christians, none of whom had been imprisoned so far. It was known perfectly well on the Palatine that Flavius, Domitilla, Pomponia Graecina, Cornelius Pudens, and Vinicius belonged to the confessors of Christ. Caesar himself, however, feared that the mob would not believe that such people had burned Rome, and since it was most important to convince the mob, punishment and vengeance were deferred for them until later on. Others were of the false opinion that those patricians were saved by the influence of Acte. Petronius, after parting with Vinicius, turned to Acte, it is true, to gain assistance for Lygia, but she could offer him only tears, for she lived in oblivion and suffering and was tolerated only because she hid herself from Poppaea and Caesar.

But she had visited Lygia in prison and had carried her clothing and food, and above all had saved her from injury on the part of the prison guards, who were already bribed.

Petronius was unable to forget that had it not been for him and his plan of taking Lygia from the house of Aulus, she probably would not be in prison at that moment. Besides, wishing to win the struggle against Tigellinus, he spared neither time nor efforts. Within a few days he saw Seneca, Domitius Afer, Crispinilla, and Diodorus, through whom he wished to reach Poppaea. He also saw Terpnos, and the beautiful Pythagoras, and finally Aliturus and Paris, to whom Caesar usually refused nothing.

But all these efforts were fruitless. Seneca, uncertain of his future, explained to him that the Christians, even if they had not burned Rome, should be exterminated, for the good of the city—in other words, he justified the slaughter for political reasons. Terpnos and Diodorus took the money and did nothing in return for it. Vatinius reported to Caesar that they had been trying to bribe him. Aliturus alone, who at first was hostile to the Christians, took pity on them then and boldly mentioned to Caesar the fate of the imprisoned maiden and implored him on her behalf. Nero answered, "Do you think that I have a soul inferior to that of Brutus, who did not spare his own sons for the good of Rome?"

When this answer was repeated to Petronius, he said, "Since Nero has compared himself to Brutus, there is no hope."

But he was sorry for Vinicius, and he was afraid that he might attempt his own life. *Now,* the arbiter thought, *he is upheld by the efforts he makes to save her, by the sight of her, and by his own suffering; but when all means fail and the last ray of hope is quenched, by Castor! He will not survive, he will throw himself on his sword.* Petronius would not take this path; he would not love and suffer like Vinicius.

Meanwhile, Vinicius did all that he could think of to save Lygia. He visited Augustians; and he, once so proud, now begged their assistance. Through Vitelius he offered Tigellinus all his Sicilian estates and whatever else the man might ask; but Tigellinus, not wishing apparently to offend the Augusta, refused. To go to Caesar himself, fall on his knees and plead, would lead to nothing. Vinicius wished to do this; but Petronius asked, "But should he refuse you, or answer with a jest or a shameless threat, what would you do?"

At this the young tribune's features were distorted with pain and rage.

"Yes," Petronius said, "I advise you against this, because you would close all paths of rescue."

Vinicius restrained himself and, wiping his forehead, which was covered with cold sweat, replied, "No, no! I am a Christian."

"But you will forget this, as you did a moment ago. You have the right to ruin yourself, but not her."

He was not altogether sincere, since he was concerned more for Vinicius than for Lygia. Still, he knew that there was no better way to restrain him from something even more dangerous than to tell him that he would bring complete destruction on Lygia. He was right; for on the Palatine they had counted on the visit of the young tribune and had taken needful precautions.

But the suffering of Vinicius surpassed human endurance. From the moment that Lygia was imprisoned and the glory of coming martyrdom had fallen on her, not only did he love her a hundred times more, but he began to think of her as he would a superhuman being. And now, at the thought that he must lose this being both loved and holy, that besides death torments might be inflicted on her more terrible than death itself, the blood froze in his veins. He ceased to understand the reasons for all that had happened. He ceased to understand why Christ, the Merciful, the Divine, did not come to aid His followers; why the dingy walls of the Palatine did not sink through the earth, and with them Nero, the Augustians, the praetorian camp, and entire city of wickedness. It should not be otherwise; and all the evil he saw, because of which his heart was breaking, was like a bad dream. But the roaring of wild beasts informed him that it was actually reality; the sound of the axes beneath which the arena was constructed told him that it was true; the howling of the people and the overfilled prisons confirmed this. Then his faith in Christ was tested; and that doubt was a new trial, perhaps the most dreadful of all.

"Remember what torture the daughter of Sejanus endured before her death," Petronius reminded him.

52

And everything had failed. Vinicius lowered himself by seeking support from mere freedmen and slaves of Caesar and Poppaea. He overpaid their empty promises and won their useless goodwill with rich gifts. He found the first husband of Poppaea, Rufinus Crispinus, and obtained a letter from him. He gave a villa in Antium to Rufius, but merely angered Caesar, who hated his stepson. By a special courier he sent a letter to Poppaea's second husband, Otho, in Spain. He sacrificed his property and himself, until he saw at last that he was simply the plaything of people and that if he had pretended that the imprisonment of Lygia was not of great concern to him, he might have freed her.

Finally, the amphitheater was finished. Entrance tickets were distributed to the morning games. But this time the morning games, because of the unheard-of number of victims, were to continue for days, weeks, and months. The prisons were crammed with Christians, and fever was raging among them. The common pits in which slaves were kept began to be overfilled. There was fear that disease might spread over the whole city; so they hurried.

The spectacles would soon begin. Lygia might find herself any day in a cell in the circus, where the only exit was to the arena. Vinicius visited all the stadiums, bribed guards and beastkeepers to find her. In time he saw that he was only trying to make death less terrible for her.

He determined to perish at the same time with her. But he feared that his personal pain might burn him out before the dreadful hour came. His friends and Petronius also thought that any day the other world might overtake him. He spent whole nights with Ursus at Lygia's door in the prison; if she told him to go away and rest, he returned to Petronius and walked in the halls all night. The slaves found him frequently kneeling with upraised hands or lying with his face to the ground. He prayed to Christ, for Christ was his last hope. Everything had failed him. Only a miracle could save Lygia; so he beat the stone flagstones with his forehead and prayed for the miracle.

And a certain night he went to seek the apostle. The Christians now concealed him carefully even from other brethren, unless any of the weaker in spirit might betray him. Vinicius, amid the general confusion and disaster, attempting to get Lygia out of prison, had lost sight of Peter. He had barely seen him from the time of his own baptism until the beginning of the persecution. He visited the quarryman in whose hut he was baptized and learned that there would be a meeting outside the Porta Salaria in a nearby vineyard. The quarryman offered to guide him and told him he would find Peter there. They started about dusk and, traveling beyond the wall, through hollows overgrown with reeds, reached the vineyard in a wild and lonely place. The meeting was held in a windshed. As Vinicius drew near, the murmur of prayer reached his ears. On entering, he saw by dim lamplight kneeling figures sunk in prayer. They were saying a kind of litany; a chorus of sorrowful voices, male and female, repeated every moment, "Christ have mercy on us."

Peter was present. He was kneeling in front of the others, before a wooden cross nailed to the wall of the shed, and was praying. From a distance Vinicius recognized his white hair and his upraised hands. The first thought of the young patrician was to pass through the assembly, cast himself at the apostle's feet, and cry, "Help me!" But whether it was the solemnity of the prayer, or because weakness bent his knees, Vinicius said while he groaned and clasped his hands, "Christ have mercy!" and other prayers. Had he been aware of it, he would have understood that his was not the only prayer in which there was a groan; that he was not the only one who had felt pain, fear, and grief. There was not in that assembly one soul that had not lost persons dear to his heart. The most zealous and courageous confessors of Christ were in prison already. Every moment brought new tidings of insults and tortures inflicted on them in the prisons. When the greatness of the calamity exceeded every imagination, when only that handful remained, there was not one heart there that was not terrified even when expressing faith. All asked inwardly, *Where is Christ? And why does He let evil seem to be mightier than God?* Meanwhile, they implored Him for mercy, since in each soul there still smoldered a spark of hope that Christ would come, hurl Nero into the abyss, and rule the world. They looked yet continually toward the sky; they still listened; they trembled as they prayed. Vinicius, too, as he repeated, "Christ have mercy on us!" was filled with the same ecstasy he formerly experienced in the quarryman's hut.

From the depths the worshipers called on Christ in the profoundness of their sorrow; now Peter called on Him; so any moment the heavens may be rent, the earth tremble to its foundations, and He appear in infinite glory, with stars at His feet—merciful, but awful. He will raise up the faithful and command the abyss to swallow the persecutors.

Vinicius covered his face with both hands and bowed to the earth. Silence was around him, as if fear had stopped further breathing on the lips of all present. And it seemed to him that something must happen surely, that a moment of miracle would follow. He felt certain that when he rose and opened his eyes he would see a blinding light and hear a voice that would shake the assembly.

But the silence was unbroken. It was interrupted at last by the sobbing of women. Vinicius rose and looked around in a daze. In the shed, instead of heavenly glories, shone the faint gleam of lanterns and the rays of the moon, entering through an opening in the roof, filling the place with a silvery light.

Peter rose and said, "Children, raise your hearts to the Redeemer and offer Him your tears."

All at once the voice of a woman was heard, full of sorrowful complaint. "I am a widow; I had one son who supported me. Give him back, O Lord!"

Peter was standing before the kneeling audience, old and full of cares. In that moment he seemed to them decrepitude and weakness personified. With that a second voice began to complain, "Executioners insulted my daughter, and Christ permitted them!"

Then a third, "I alone remain with my children, and when I am taken who will give them bread and water?"

Then a fourth, "Linus, whom You spared at first, has been taken and tortured, O Lord!"

Then a fifth. "When we return to our houses, praetorians will seize us. We do not know where to hide."

"Woe to us! Who will protect us?"

And in that silent night complaint after complaint was heard. The old fisherman closed his eyes and shook his white head over that human pain and fear.

Vinicius wondered, *What if the apostle were to confess his own weakness, affirm that the Roman Caesar was stronger than Christ the Nazarene?* At that thought terror raised the hair on his head, for he felt that in such a case not only the remnant of his hope would fall into the abyss, but with it himself, and there would remain only night and death, resembling a shoreless sea.

Peter began to speak in a voice so low at first that it was barely possible to hear him. "My children, on Golgotha I saw them nail God to the cross. I heard the hammers, and I saw them raise the cross on high, so that the rabble might gaze at the death of the Son of Man. I saw them open His side, and I saw Him die. When returning from the cross, I cried in pain, as you are crying, 'Woe! O Lord, You are God! Why have You permitted this? Why have You died, and why have You tormented the hearts of us who believed that Your kingdom would come?'

"But He, our Lord and God, rose from the dead on the third day and was among us until He entered His kingdom in great glory.

"And we, realizing our little faith, became strong in heart, and from that time we are sowing His grain."

Turning toward the place where the first complaint came from, he began in a stronger voice. "Why do you complain? God gave Himself to torture and death, and you wish Him to shield you from the same. People of little faith, have you received His teaching? Has He promised you nothing but life? He comes to you and says, 'Follow in My path.' He raises you up to Himself, and you grasp at this earth with your hands, crying, 'Lord, save us!' I speak to you in the name of Christ. Not death is before you, but life; not tortures, but endless delights; not tears and groans, but singing; not bondage, but rule! I, God's apostle, say this: O widow, your son will not die; he will be born into glory, into eternal life, and you will rejoin him! To you, O father, whose innocent daughter was defiled by executioners, I promise that you shall find her whiter than the lilies of Hebron! To you, mothers, whom they are tearing away from your orphans; to you who will see the death of loved ones; to the careworn, the unfortunate, the timid; to you who must die—in the name of Christ I declare that you will happily wake as if from sleep, as if from night to the light of God. In the name of Christ, let the beam fall from your eyes, and let your hearts be inflamed."

When he had said this, he raised his hand as if pointing onward, and they felt new blood in their veins and strength in their bones; for before them was standing, not a decrepit and careworn old man, but a powerful leader who took their souls and raised them from dust and terror.

"Amen!" called a number of voices.

From the apostle's eyes came an increasing light, and power, majesty, and holiness. Heads bent before him, and, when the "Amens" ceased, he continued. "You sow in tears to reap in joy. Why do you fear the power of evil? Above the earth, Rome, and the walls of cities is the Lord, who has made His dwelling within you. The stones will be wet from tears and sand steeped in blood; the valleys will be filled with your bodies, but I say that you are victorious. The Lord is advancing to the conquest of this wicked city of perversity, oppression, and pride, and you are His legions! He redeemed with His own blood and torture the sins of the world; so He wishes that you should redeem with torture and blood this nest of iniquity. He announced this to you through my lips."

And he opened his arms and fixed his eyes upward; their hearts almost ceased to beat, for they felt that his glance beheld something their mortal sight could not see.

In fact, his face had changed and was covered with serenity; he gazed in silence, as if speechless from ecstasy, but after a while they heard his voice. "You are here, O Lord, and You show Your ways to me. Here, O Christ! Not in Jerusalem, but in this city of Satan will You do a mighty work. You wish to build Your church here out of these tears and this blood. Here, where Nero rules today, Your eternal kingdom will be present. And You command these timid ones to stand firm and help build the foundation of Your holy Zion from their bones. And You are pouring a fountain of strength on the weak, so that they become strong; and now You command me to feed Your sheep and encourage them. Oh, be praised in Your decrees by which You command to conquer. Hosanna! Hosanna!"

Those who were timid rose; streams of faith flowed into

those who doubted. Some voices cried, "Hosanna!" others, *"Pro Christo!"* Then silence followed. Bright summer lightening illuminated the interior of the shed and the pale, excited faces.

Peter, transfixed in a vision, prayed a while; then he turned his illuminated face to the assembly and said, "This is how the Lord has overcome doubt in you; so you will go to victory in His name."

And though he knew that they would conquer, though he knew what would grow out of their tears and blood, still his voice quivered with emotion when he was blessing them, and he said, "Now I bless you, my children, as you go to torture, to death, to eternity."

They gathered round him and wept. "We are ready," they said. "But guard yourself, O holy one, for your are our dear shepherd."

As they spoke, they seized his cloak. He placed his hands on their heads and blessed each one separately, just as a father does children whom he is sending on a long journey.

They went to their houses, and from them to the prisons and arenas. Their thoughts were not related to this earth. Their souls had soared toward eternity and they walked as if in a dream, in confidence opposing the force of cruelty known as the "Beast."

Nereus, the servant of Pudens, took the apostle and led him by a secret path in the vineyard to his house. But Vinicius followed them in the clear night, and when they reached the cottage of Nereus at last, he threw himself at the feet of the apostle.

"What do you wish, my son?" Peter asked, recognizing him.

After what he had heard in the vineyard, Vinicius dared not ask him for anything; but, embracing his feet with both hands, he pressed his forehead to them and wept, and sought compassion.

"I know. They took the young girl whom you love. Pray for her."

"Lord," Vinicius groaned, embracing his feet still more firmly, "lord, I am a wretched worm; but you knew Christ. Implore Him—take her part."

And from pain he trembled like a leaf; and he banged the ground with his forehead, for, knowing the spiritual strength of the apostle, he felt that he could rescue her with his prayers.

Peter was moved by that pain. He remembered how one time Lygia herself, when attacked by Crispus, lay at his feet in the same manner, imploring pity. He remembered that he had comforted her; so now he addressed Vinicius.

"My son," he said, "I will pray for her; but do you remember that I told those doubting ones that God Himself passed through the torment of the cross, and remember that after this life begins another—an eternal one."

"I know; I have heard!" Vinicius answered. "But you see, lord, that I cannot! If blood is required, ask Christ to take mine—I am a soldier. Let Him double, let Him triple, the torment intended for her, I will suffer it; but let Him spare her. She is a child yet, and He is mightier than Caesar, I believe, mightier. You loved her yourself; you blessed us. She is still an innocent child."

Again he bowed, and, putting his face to Peter's knees, he repeated, "You knew Christ. He will give listen to you; intercede for her."

Peter closed his eyes and prayed earnestly. The summer lightening illuminated the sky again. Vinicius, by the light of it, looked at the lips of the apostle, awaiting the sentence of life or death from them. In the silence quail were heard calling in the vineyard, as was the dull, distant sound of treadmills near the Via Salaria.

"Vinicius," asked the apostle at last, "do you believe?"

"Would I have come here if I had not?" he answered.

"Then believe to the end, for faith will remove mountains. Though you were to see Lygia under the sword of the executioner or in the jaws of a lion, believe that Christ can save her. Believe, and pray to Him, and I will pray with you."

Then, raising his face toward heaven, he prayed, "O merciful Christ, look on this aching heart and console it! O merciful Christ, temper the wind to the fleece of the lamb! O merciful Christ, who implored the Father to turn away the bitter cup from Your mouth, turn it from the mouth of this Your servant! Amen."

But Vinicius, stretching his hand toward the stars, said, groaning, "I am Yours; take me instead of her."

The sky began to grow pale in the east.

53

Vinicius, after leaving the apostle, went to the prison with a heart renewed by hope. Somewhere in the depth of his soul despair and terror were still gnawing at him, but he stifled those voices. It seemed impossible to him that the intercession of the apostle of God should be ineffective. He feared to hope; he feared to doubt. *I will believe in His mercy,* he said to himself, *even though I saw her in the jaws of a lion.* And at this thought, even though his soul shook and cold sweat drenched his temples, he believed. Every throb of his heart was a prayer. He began to understand that faith would move mountains, for he felt a wonderful strength in himself that he had not known earlier. It seemed to him that he could do things he had no power to do the day before. At moments he had an impression that the danger had passed. If despair again entered his soul, he recalled that night and that holy, gray face raised to heaven in prayer. "No; Christ will not refuse one of His apostles and a pastor of His flock! Christ will not refuse him! I will not doubt!" And he ran toward the prison as a herald of good news.

But an unexpected thing awaited him there.

All the praetorian guards taking turn before the Mamertine prison knew him, and generally they did not raise the least difficulty; this time, however, the line did not open, but a centurion approached him and said, "Pardon, noble tribune, today we have a command to admit no one."

"A command?" Vinicius repeated, growing pale.

The soldier looked at him with pity and answered, "Yes, lord, a command of Caesar. In the prison there are many sick people, and perhaps it is feared that visitors might spread infection through the city."

"But had you said that the order was for today only?"

"The guards change at noon."

Vinicius was silent and uncovered his head, for it seemed to him that the helmet he wore was of lead.

Meanwhile, the soldier approached him and said in a low

voice, "Be at rest, lord. The guard and Ursus are watching over her." When he had said this, he bent and, in the twinkle of an eye, drew the form of a fish with his long Gallic sword.

Vinicius looked at him quickly.

"And you are a praetorian?"

"Until I shall be there," the soldier answered, pointing to the prison.

"And I, too, worship Christ."

"May His name be praised! I know, lord, I cannot admit you to the prison, but write a letter, I will give it to the guard."

"Thanks to you, brother."

He pressed the soldier's hand and went away. The helmet ceased to weigh like lead. The morning sun rose over the walls of the prison, and with its brightness consolation began to enter his heart again. That Christian soldier was for him a new witness of the power of Christ. After a while he halted, and, fixing his glance on the rosy clouds above the Capitol and the temple of Jupiter Stator, he said, "I have not seen her today, O Lord, but I believe in Your mercy."

At the house he found Petronius, who had stayed up all night as usual and had returned not long before. He had succeeded, however, in taking his bath and anointing himself for sleep.

"I have news for you," he said. "Today I was with Tullius Senecio, whom Caesar also visited. I do not know why it came to the mind of the Augusta to bring little Rufius with her—perhaps to soften the heart of Caesar by his beauty. Unfortunately, the child, wearied by drowsiness, fell asleep during the reading. Seeing this, Ahenobarbus hurled a goblet at his stepson and wounded him seriously. Poppaea fainted; all heard how Caesar said, 'I have enough of this brood!' and that, you know, means death."

"The punishment of God was hanging over the Augusta," Vinicius answered, "but why do you tell me this?"

"I tell you because the anger of Poppaea pursued you and Lygia. Concerned now with her own misfortune, she may leave her vengeance and be more easily influenced. I will see her this evening and talk with her."

"Thank you. You give me good news."

"But you should bathe and rest. Your lips are blue, and there is not a shadow of you left."

"Is not the time of the games to be announced?" Vinicius asked.

"In ten days. But they will take other prisons first. The more time that remains the better. All is not yet lost."

But he did not believe this; for he knew perfectly that because, in response to the request of Aliturus, Caesar had found the splendidly sounding answer in which he compared himself to Brutus, there was no rescue for Lygia. He hid from Vinicius also, through pity, what he had heard at Senecio's, that Caesar and Tigellinus had decided to select for themselves and their friends the most beautiful Christian maidens and defile them before the torture. The others were to be given, on the day of the games, to praetorians and beast-keepers.

Knowing that Vinicius would not survive Lygia in any case, he strengthened hope in his heart, first, through sympathy for him; and second, because he wished that if Vinicius had to die, he should die with dignity, not being tortured by watching Lygia meet her death.

"Today I will say this to Augusta," he said: "'Save Lygia for Vinicius, I will save Rufius for you.' And I will try to spare Rufius. One word spoken to Ahenobarbus at the right moment may save or ruin anyone. In the worst case, we will gain time."

"Thank you again," Vinicius repeated.

"You will thank me best if you eat and sleep. By Athene! In the greatest straits Odysseus had sleep and food in mind. You have spent the whole night in prison?"

"No," Vinicius answered. "I wished to visit the prison today, but there is an order to admit no one. If you could learn, Petronius, whether the order is for today alone, or until the day of the games, I would appreciate it."

"I will find out this evening, and tomorrow morning I will tell you for how long and why the order was issued. But now, even were Helios to go to Cimmerian regions from sorrow, I shall sleep, and you follow my example."

They separated; but Vinicius went to the library and wrote a letter to Lygia. When he had finished, he took it himself to the

Christian centurion, who carried it at once to the prison. After a while he returned with a greeting from Lygia and promised to deliver her answer that day.

Vinicius did not wish to return home but sat on a stone and waited for Lygia's letter. The sun had risen high in the heavens, and crowds of people flowed in, as usual, through the Clivus Argentarius to the Forum. Hucksters called out their wares, fortune-tellers offered their services to passers-by, citizens walked with deliberate steps toward the rostrum to hear orators of the day, or to tell the latest news.

From too much light and the influence of exhaustion and heat, the eyes of Vinicius began to close. The monotonous calls of boys playing their games and the measured tread of soldiers lulled him to sleep.

Soon dreams came. It seemed to him that he was carrying Lygia in his arms at night through a strange vineyard. Before him was Pomponia Graecina lighting the way with a lamp. The voice of Petronius called from afar to him, "Turn back!" but he did not heed the call and followed Pomponia till they reached a cottage; at the threshold stood Peter. He showed Lygia to Peter and said, "We are coming from the arena, lord, but we cannot wake her." "Christ Himself will come to wake her," the apostle answered.

Then the images began to change. He was resting near Lygia; but between the tables walked lions from whose yellow manes trickled blood. Lygia begged him to take her away, but a terrible weakness had seized him and he could not even move.

He was roused from deep sleep at last by the heat of the sun and shouts around the place where he was sitting. Vinicius rubbed his eyes. The street was swarming with people. Two runners, wearing yellow tunics, pushed aside the throng with long staffs, shouting to make room for a splendid litter carried by four stalwart Egyptian slaves.

In the litter was a man in white robes, whose face was not easily seen, for he held a roll of papyrus close to his eyes and was reading something diligently.

"Make way for the noble Augustian!" cried the runners.

But the street was so crowded that the litter had to wait a

while. The Augustian put down his roll of papyrus and bent his head, crying, "Push aside those wretches! Make haste!"

Seeing Vinicius suddenly, he pulled his head in and raised the papyrus quickly.

Vinicius thought he was still dreaming.

Chilo was sitting in the litter.

When the Egyptians were ready to move, the young tribune, who in one moment understood many things that until then had been incomprehensible, approached the litter.

"A greeting to you, O Chilo," he said.

"Young man," answered the Greek, with pride and importance, trying to give his face an expression of calmness that was not in his soul, "I greet you, but do not detain me, for I am hastening to my friend, the noble Tigellinus."

Vinicius, grasping the edge of the litter and looking him straight in the eyes, said with a soft voice, "Did you betray Lygia?"

"Colossus of Memnot!" Chilo cried, with fear.

But there was no threat in the eyes of Vinicius; so the old Greek's alarm vanished quickly. He remembered that he was under the protection of Tigellinus and of Caesar himself—that is, of a power before which everything trembled—that he was surrounded by sturdy slaves, and that Vinicius stood before him unarmed, with an emaciated face and a body bent by suffering.

At this thought his insolence returned to him. He stared at Vinicius and whispered in answer, "But you, when I was dying of hunger, commanded them to flog me."

For a moment both were silent; then the voice of Vinicius was heard, "I wronged you, Chilo."

The Greek raised his head, and, snapping his fingers, which in Rome was a mark of slight and contempt, said so loudly that all could hear him, "Friend, if you have a petition to present, come to my house on the Esquiline in the morning hour, when I receive guests and clients after my bath."

And he waved his hand; at that sign the Egyptians raised the litter, and the slaves, dressed in yellow tunics, began to cry as they waved their staffs, "Make way for the litter of the noble Chilo Chilonides! Make way, make way!"

54

Lygia, in a long letter written hurriedly, said good-bye to Vinicius forever. She knew that no one was permitted to enter the prison and that she could see Vinicius only from the arena. She begged him to discover when the turn of the Mamertine prisoners would come and to be at the games, for she wished to see him once more in this life. There was no fear apparent in her letter. She wrote that she and the others were longing for the arena, where they would find liberation from imprisonment. She hoped for the coming of Pomponia and Aulus; she asked that they too be present. Every word of hers showed contentment and a lack of concern for earthly things that all the prisoners felt, and at the same time an unshaken faith that all promises would be fulfilled beyond the grave.

"Whether Christ," she wrote, "frees me in this life or after death, He has promised me to you by the words of the apostle; therefore I am yours." She asked him not to grieve for her and not to let himself be overcome by suffering. For her death was not a dissolution of marriage. With the faith of a child she assured Vinicius that immediately after her suffering in the arena she would tell Christ that her betrothed Vinicius had remained in Rome, that he was longing for her with his whole heart. And she thought that Christ would permit her soul, perhaps, to return to him for a moment, to tell him that she was living, that she did not remember her torments, and that she was happy. Her whole letter breathed happiness and immense hope. There was only one request in it connected with affairs of earth—that Vinicius should take her body and bury it as that of his wife in the tomb in which he himself would rest later.

He read this letter with a suffering spirit, but at the same time it seemed to him impossible that Lygia should perish under the claws of wild beasts and that Christ would not take compassion on her. When he returned home, he wrote that he would come every day to the walls of the Tullianum to wait until Christ crushed them and restored her. He told her to believe that Christ could give her to him, even in the Circus; that the great apostle was imploring Him to do so, and that the hour of liberation was near. The converted centurion was to bear this letter to her on the next day.

But when Vinicius came to the prison next morning, the centurion left the rank, approached him first, and said, "Listen to me, lord. Christ, who enlightened you, has shown you favor. Last night Caesar's freedman and those of the prefect came to select Christian women for disgrace. They inquired for your betrothed, but our Lord sent her a fever, of which prisoners are dying in the Tullianum, and they left her alone. Last evening she was unconscious; and blessed be the name of the Redeemer, for the sickness that has saved her from shame may save her from death."

Vinicius placed his hand on the soldier's shoulder to guard himself from falling; but the other continued, "Thank the mercy of the Lord! They took and tortured Linus, but, seeing that he was dying, they surrendered him. They may give her to you now, and Christ will give back health to her."

The young tribune said in a whisper, "True, centurion. Christ, who saved her from shame, will save her from death." And sitting at the wall of the prison until evening, he returned home to send people for Linus and have him taken to one of his suburban villas.

But when Petronius had heard everything, he determined to act once again. He had visited the Augusta; now he went to her a second time. He found her at the bed of little Rufius. The child with the broken head was struggling in a fever. His mother, with despair and terror in her heart, was trying to save him, thinking that if she did save him he would only experience a more dreadful death.

Occupied exclusively with her own suffering, she would not even hear of Vinicius and Lygia; but Petronius shocked her.

"You have offended," he said to her, "a new, unknown divinity. You, Augusta, are a worshiper, it seems, of the Hebrew Jehovah; but the Christians believe that Christus is His son. Perhaps the anger of the father is now pursuing you. It may be Jehovah's vengeance that has struck you. The life of Rufius may depend on this—how will you act?"

"What do you wish me to do?" Poppaea asked, with alarm.

"Pacify the offended deities."

"How?"

"Lygia is sick; influence Caesar or Tigellinus to give her to Vinicius."

"Do you think that I can do that?" she asked, in despair.

"You can do something else. If Lygia recovers, she must die. Go to the temple of Vesta, and ask the chief priest to go near the Tullianum at the moment when they are leading prisoners out to death and command them to free that maiden. The chief vestal will not refuse you."

"But if Lygia dies of the fever?"

"The Christians say that Christ is vengeful, but just; maybe you will soften Him by your wish alone."

"Let Him give me some sign that will heal Rufius."

Petronius shrugged his shoulders.

"I have not come as His messenger, O divinity. I merely say to you, Be on better terms with all the gods, Roman and foreign."

"I will go!" Poppaea said with a broken voice.

Petronius drew a deep breath. *At last I have done something,* he thought, and returning to Vinicius he said to him, "Ask your God to heal Lygia of fever, for should she survive, the chief vestal will command her to be free. The Augusta herself will ask her to do so."

"Christ will free her," Vinicius said with a feverish look.

Poppaea, who for the recovery of Rufius was willing to burn sacrifices to all the gods of the world, went that same evening through the Forum to the vestals, leaving care of the sick child to her faithful nurse, Silvia, by whom she herself had been reared.

But on the Palatine a death sentence had been issued against the child already; Poppaea's litter had barely vanished behind the great gate when two freedmen entered the chamber in which her son was resting. One of these threw himself on old Silvia and gagged her. The other, seizing a bronze statue of the Sphinx, stunned the old woman with the first blow.

Then they approached Rufius. The little boy, tormented with fever, not knowing what was happening around him, smiled at them and blinked with his beautiful eyes, as if trying to recognize the men. Stripping her belt from the nurse, they put it around the boy's neck and pulled it. The child called once for his mother, and died easily. Then they wound him in a sheet and, sitting on horses that were waiting, hurried to Ostia, where they threw the body into the sea.

Poppaea, not finding the priest, who with other vestals was at the house of Vatinius, returned soon to the Palatine. Seeing the empty bed and the cold body of Silvia, she fainted, and when they restored her she began to scream. Her wild cries were heard all that night and the day following.

But Caesar commanded her to appear at a feast on the third day; so, arraying herself in an amethyst-colored tunic, she came and sat with stony face, golden-haired and silent, and as ominous as an angel of death.

55

Amphitheaters in Rome were built mainly of wood; for that reason nearly all of them had burned during the fire. But Nero, for the celebration of the promised games, had commanded them to build several, and among them a gigantic one, for which they began, immediately after the fire was extinguished, to bring by sea and the Tiber great trunks, for the games were to surpass all previous ones in splendor and the number of victims.

Large spaces were given for people and for animals. Thousands of carpenters worked at the structure night and day. They built and designed without rest. Wonders were told concerning pillars inlaid with bronze, amber, ivory, mother-of-pearl, and transmarine tortoiseshell. Canals filled with ice-cold water from the mountains and running along the seats were to keep an agreeable coolness in the building, even during the greatest heat. A gigantic purple awning gave shelter from the rays of the sun. Among the rows of seats were vessels for burning Arabian perfumes; above them were instruments to sprinkle the spectators with dew of saffron and verbena. The renowned builders Severus and Celer used all their skill to construct an incomparable amphitheater for thousands.

On the day when the games were to begin, from daylight on, throngs were awaiting the opening of the gates, listening with delight to the roars of lions, the hoarse growls of panthers, and the howls of dogs. The beasts had not been fed for two days, but pieces of bloody flesh had been pushed before them to arouse their rage and hunger all the more. At times such a storm of wild voices was heard that people standing before the Circus could not hear.

Resonant but calm hymns were intoned in the enclosure of the Circus with the rising of the sun. The people heard these with amazement and said one to another, "The Christians!" In fact, many groups of Christians had been brought to the amphitheater that night, and not from one place, as planned at first, but a few from each prison. It was known in the crowd that the spectacles would continue through weeks and months, but they doubted that it would be possible to finish off in a single day those Christians who had been intended for that one occasion. The voices of men, women, and children singing the morning hymn were so numerous that spectators asserted that even if one or two hundred persons were sent out at once, the beasts would grow tired, become full, and not tear all of them to pieces before evening. Others declared that an excessive number of victims in the arena would divert attention and not give them a chance to enjoy the spectacle properly.

As the moment drew near for opening the passages that led to the interior, people grew animated and joyous. Parties were formed praising the greater efficiency of lions or tigers in tearing. Here and there bets were made. Others, however, talked about gladiators who were to appear in the arena earlier than the Christians.

Early in the morning larger or smaller detachments of gladiators began to arrive at the amphitheater under the lead of masters. Not wishing to be wearied too soon, they entered unarmed, often with green boughs in their hands, or crowned with flowers in the light of morning, and full of life. Their bodies, shining from olive oil, were strong as if chiseled from marble; they attempted to delight people who loved shapely forms. Many were known personally, and from moment to moment were heard, "A greeting, Furnius!

A greeting, Leo!" Young maidens gazed upon them with eyes full of admiration. The gladiators, selecting the most beautiful maiden, answered with jests, sending kisses, or exclaiming, "Embrace me before death does!" Then they vanished in the gates, through which many of them were never to come out of again.

New arrivals drew away the attention of the throngs. Behind the gladiators came men armed with scourges, whose duty it was to lash and urge forward combatants. Next mules drew, in the direction of the stadium, whole rows of vehicles on which were piled wooden coffins. People were amazed by this, guessing from the number of coffins the greatness of the spectacle. Then men marched in who were to kill the wounded; these were dressed so that each resembled Charon or Mercury. Next those came who looked after order in the Circus and assigned places; after that slaves to carry around food and refreshments. Finally, praetorian guards, whom every Caesar always had at hand, came into the amphitheater.

At last the gates were opened and crowds rushed to the center. But so many were assembled that they flowed in for hours, until it was a marvel that the Circus could hold such a countless multitude. The roars of wild beasts grew louder. While taking their places, the spectators made an uproar like the sea in time of storm.

Finally, the prefect of the city came, surrounded by guards; and after him, in an unbroken line, appeared the litters of senators, consuls, praetors, ediles, officials of the government and the palace, praetorian officers, patricians, and exquisite ladies. Some litters were preceded by attendants bearing maces in bundles of rods, others by crowds of slaves. The sun shone on the gilding of the litters; on feathers, earrings, and jewels; and on the steel of the maces. From the Circus came shouts with which the people greeted great dignitaries. Small divisions of praetorians arrived from time to time.

The priests of various temples came somewhat later; only after them were brought in the sacred virgins of Vesta.

They were waiting now only for Caesar to begin the spectacle, who, unwilling to expose the people to a long wait, and wishing to win them by promptness, soon came, in company with the Augusta and Augustians.

Petronius arrived among the Augustians, carrying Vinicius in his litter. The latter knew that Lygia was sick and unconscious; but access to the prison had been forbidden during the preceding days. The former guards had been replaced by new ones who were not permitted to speak with the jailers or even to communicate the least information to those who came to inquire about prisoners. He was not even sure that she was not among the victims intended for the first day of spectacles. They might send out even a sick woman for the lions, though she were unconscious. But since the victims were to be sewed up in skins of wild beasts and sent to the arena in crowds, no spectator could be certain of who might be among them, and no one could recognize anyone. The jailers and all the servants of the amphitheater had been bribed, and a bargain had been made with the beast-keepers to hide Lygia in some dark corner and give her at night into the hands of a friend of Vinicius, who would take her at once to the Alban Hills. Petronius, admitted to the secret, advised Vinicius to go with him openly to the amphitheater and, after he had entered, to disappear in the throng and hurry to the vaults, where, to avoid any possible mistake, he was to point out Lygia to the guards personally.

The guards admitted him through a small door by which they came out themselves. One of these, named Cyrus, led him at once to the Christians. On the way he said, "I do not know, lord, that you will find what you are seeking. We sought for a woman named Lygia, but no one gave us an answer; it may be, though, that they do not trust us."

"Are there many?" Vinicius asked.

"Many, lord, had to wait until tomorrow."

"Are there sick ones among them?"

"There were none who could not stand."

Cyrus opened a door and entered as it were an enormous, low, dark chamber, for the light came in only through grated openings that separated it from the arena. At first Vinicius could see nothing; he heard only the murmur of voices in the room and the shouts of people in the amphitheater. But after a while, when his eyes had grown used to the gloom, he saw crowds of strange beings, resembling wolves and bears. They were Christians sewed up in skins of beasts. Some of them were standing; others were kneeling in prayer. Here and there one might realize by the long hair flowing over the skin that the victim was a woman. Women, looking like wolves, carried in their arms children sewed up in equally shaggy coverings. But from beneath the skins appeared bright faces and eyes that in the darkness gleamed with delight and fever.

It was evident that the greater number of these people were mastered by one exclusive thought, which during this time made them indifferent to everything that happened around them. Some, when asked by Vinicius about Lygia, looked at him with eyes as if roused from sleep, without answering his questions; others smiled at him, placing a finger on their lips or pointing to the iron grating through which bright streaks of light entered. But here and there children were crying, frightened by the roaring of beasts, the howling of dogs, the uproar of people, and the forms of their own parents, who looked like wild beasts. As Vinicius walked by the side of Cyrus he looked into faces and at times stumbled against bodies of people who had fainted from the crowd, the stifling air, and the heat; he pushed farther into the depths of the room, which seemed to be as spacious as a whole amphitheater.

But he stopped suddenly, for he seemed to hear near the grating a voice known to him. He listened for a while, turned, and, pushing through the crowd, went near. Light fell on the face of the speaker, and Vinicius recognized under the skin of a wolf the emaciated and stern countenance of Crispus.

"Mourn for your sins!" Crispus exclaimed, "for the moment is near. But whoever thinks by death itself to redeem his sins commits a fresh sin and will be hurled into endless fire. With every sin committed in life you have renewed the Lord's suffering; how dare you think that that life which awaits you will redeem this one? Today the just and the sinner will die the same death; but the Lord will find His own. Woe to you; the claws of the lions will rend your bodies, but not your sins, nor your reckoning with God. The Lord showed mercy sufficient when He let Himself be nailed to the cross; but from now on He will be only the judge, who will leave no fault unpunished. Whoever among you has thought to extinguish his sins by suffering has blasphemed against God's justice and will sink all the deeper. Mercy is at an end, and the hour of God's wrath has come. Soon you will stand before the awful Judge in whose presence the good will hardly be justified. Bewail your sins, for the jaws of hell are open; woe to you, husbands and wives; woe to you, parents and children."

And stretching forth his bony hands, he shook them above the bent heads; he was unafraid and immovable even in the presence of death, to which in a while all those doomed people were to go. After his words were heard voices; "We weep for our sins!" Then came silence, and only the cry of children was audible, and the beating of hands against breasts.

The blood of Vinicius stiffened in his veins. He, who had placed all his hope in the mercy of Christ, heard now that the day of wrath had come, and that even death in the arena would not obtain mercy. Through his mind went the thought, clear and swift as lightning, that Peter would have spoken otherwise to those about to die. Still, those terrible words of Crispus filled that dark chamber with fanaticism, where beyond was the field of torture. The nearness of that torture and the throng of victims arrayed for death filled Vinicius's soul with fear and terror. All this seemed to him dreadful, and a hundred times more ghastly than the bloodiest battle in which he had ever taken part. The odor and heat began to stifle him; cold sweat came out on his forehead. He was seized by fear that he would faint like those against whose bodies he had stumbled while searching in the depths of the cavern; so when he remembered that they might open the grating any moment, he began to call aloud for Lygia and Ursus, in the hope that, if not they, someone knowing them would answer.

In fact, some man, clothed as a bear, pulled his toga, and said, "Lord, they remained in prison. I was the last one brought out; I saw her sick on the couch."

"Who are you?" Vinicius asked.

"The quarryman in whose hut the apostle baptized you, lord. They imprisoned me three days ago, and today I die."

Vinicius was relieved. When entering, he had wished to find Lygia; now he was ready to thank Christ that she was not there and to see in that a sign of mercy. Meanwhile, the quarryman said, "Do you remember, lord, that I led you to the vineyard of Cornelius, when the apostle spoke in the shed?"

"I remember."

"I saw him later, the day before they imprisoned me. He blessed me and said that he would come to the amphitheater to bless those perishing. If I could look at him in the moment of death and see the sign of the cross, it would be easier for me to die. If you know where he is, lord, inform me."

Vinicius lowered his voice and said, "He is among the people of Petronius, disguised as a slave. I do not know where they chose their places, but I will return to the Circus and see. Look at me when you enter the arena. I will rise and turn my face toward them; then you will find him with your eyes."

"Thanks to you, lord, and peace be with you."

"Amen."

Vinicius went out and to the amphitheater, where he had a place near Petronius among the other Augustians.

"Is she there?" Petronius asked.

"No; she remained in prison."

"Hear what has occurred to me, but while listening look at Nigidia, for example, so that we may seem to talk of her hairdressing. Tigellinus and Chilo are looking at us now. Listen then. Let them put Lygia in a coffin at night and carry her out of the prison as a corpse; do you understand the rest?"

"Yes," Vinicius answered.

Their further conversation was interrupted by Tullius Senecio, who, bending toward them, asked, "Do you know whether they will give weapons to the Christians?"

"We do not," Petronius answered.

"I should prefer that arms were given," Tullius said. "If not, the arena will become like butchers' shops too early. But what a splendid amphitheater!"

The sight was, in truth, magnificent. The lower seats, crowded with togas, were as white as snow. In the gilded podium sat Caesar, wearing a diamond collar and a golden crown on his head; next to him sat the beautiful and gloomy Augusta, and on both sides were vestal virgins, great officials, senators with embroidered togas, officers of the army with glittering weapons—in a word, all that was powerful, brilliant, and wealthy in Rome. In the farther rows sat nobles; and higher up darkened in rows a sea of common heads, above which from pillar to pillar hung festoons of roses, lilies, ivy, and grapevines.

People conversed aloud, called to one another, sang; at times they broke into laughter at some witty word that was sent from row to row, and they stamped with impatience to hasten the spectacle.

At last the stamping became like thunder, and unbroken. Then the prefect of the city, who rode around the arena with a brilliant retinue, gave a signal with a handkerchief, which was answered throughout the amphitheater by thousands of voices.

Usually a spectacle was begun by hunts of wild beasts, in which various northern and southern barbarians excelled; but this time they had too many beasts, so they began with men wearing helmets without an opening for the eyes, in other words, fighting blindfolded. A number of these came into the arena together and slashed at random with their swords; with long forks the scourgers pushed some toward others to make them meet. The veterans of the audience looked with contempt and indifference at this spectacle; but the crowds were amused by the awkward motions of the swordsmen. When it happened that they met with their shoulders, they burst out in loud laughter. "To the right!" "To the left!" they cried, misleading the opponents frequently by design.

A number of pairs closed, however, and the struggle began to be bloody. The determined fighters cast aside their shields and, holding their left hands together, so as not to part again, struggled to the death with their right hands. Whoever fell raised his fingers, begging mercy by that sign; but in the beginning of a spectacle the audience usually demanded death for the wounded, especially in the case of men who had their faces covered and were unknown. Gradually the number of combatants decreased; and when at last only two remained, these were pushed together; both fell on the sand and stabbed each other mutually. Then servants carried out the bodies and youths raked away the bloody traces on the sand and sprinkled it with leaves of saffron.

Now a more important contest was to come, where young patricians made enormous bets and lost all they owned. Tablets went from hand to hand on which were written names of favorites and also the number of sestertia each man wagered. Champions who had appeared already in the arena and gained victories were favored by many, but many betters risked considerable sums on gladiators who were new and quite unknown, hoping to win immense rewards should they conquer. Caesar himself bet, as well as priests, vestals, senators, nobles, and the common people. When their money ran out, many in the crowd bet their own freedom. They waited with hearts pounding and even with fear for the combatants, and more than one made audible vows to the gods to gain protection for a favorite competitor.

In fact, when the shrill sound of trumpets was heard, there was a stillness of expectation in the amphitheater. Thousands of eyes were turned to the great gatebolts, which a man approached and, amid the total silence, struck three times with a hammer, as if summoning to their death those who were hidden behind them. Then both halves of the gate opened slowly, out of which gladiators began to appear in the bright arena. They came in divisions of twenty-five, among them Thracians, Mirmillons, Samnites, and Gauls. Each nation came separately, all heavily armed; and last were those holding in one hand a net, in the other a trident spear. At the sight of them, there was applause on the benches, which soon turned into an immense and unbroken storm. From above and below excited faces and clapping hands were seen; thunderous shouts burst forth. The gladiators circled the whole arena with an even and springy tread, gleaming with their weapons and rich outfiting; they halted before Caesar's podium, proud, calm, and brilliant. The shrill sound of a horn stopped the applause and the combatants stretched their right hands upward, raised their eyes and heads toward Caesar, and began to cry, or rather to chant:

> "Hail, Caesar Imperator!
> We who are about to die salute you!"

Then they spread apart quickly, taking their places in the arena. They were to attack one another in whole detachments; but first they allowed the most famous swordsmen to have a series of single combats, in which the strength and skill of opponents were best exhibited. In fact, there appeared a champion from among the Gauls, Lanio, who was well known to lovers of the amphitheater and a victor in many games. A great helmet rested on his head, and he was covered with chain mail, which made him look in the gleam of the golden arena like a giant beetle. The no less famous gladiator Calendio came out against him.

The spectators began to bet.

"Five hundred gold coins on the Gaul!"

"Five hundred on Calendio!"

"By Hercules, one thousand!"

"Two thousand!"

Meanwhile, the great Gaul, reaching the center of the arena, began to withdraw with his pointed sword and, lowering his head, watched his opponent carefully through the opening of his visor; his lighter opponent was stately, statuesque, and wholly naked except for a loincloth. He circled quickly around his heavy antagonist, waving the net with graceful movements, lowering and raising his trident, and singing,

> "I do seek not you, I seek a fish;
> Why flee from me, O Gaul?"

But the Gaul was not fleeing, for after a while he stopped and began to turn with a slight movement, keeping his enemy always in front. There was something terrible about his monstrously large head. The spectators understood perfectly that that heavy body encased in bronze was preparing for a sudden thrust to decide the battle. The lighter man meanwhile sprang up to him and then sprang away, making quick motions with his three-toothed fork. The sound of the trident on the shield was heard repeatedly; but the Gaul did not give way. All his attention seemed fixed, not on the trident, but on the net circling above his head like a bird of prey. The spectators held their breath and followed the masterful play of the gladiators. The Gaul waited, chose the right moment, and rushed at last on his enemy; the latter with equal quickness shot past under his sword, raised himself up, and threw the net.

The Gaul, turning where he stood, caught it on his shield; then both opponents sprang apart. Caesar himself, who at first had been talking with Rubria, and so far had not paid much attention to the spectacle, turned his head toward the arena.

The combatants began to struggle again. The Gaul escaped twice more from the net and moved toward the edge of the arena; those who held bets against him, not wishing the champion to rest, began to cry, "Fight on!" The Gaul obeyed, and attacked. The arm of the lighter gladiator was covered suddenly with blood, and his net dropped. The Gaul sprang forward to give the final blow. That instant, Calendio, who pretended an inability to wield the net, sprang aside, escaped the thrust, ran the trident between the knees of his opponent, and brought him to the earth.

The Gaul tried to rise but in an instant was covered by the fatal meshes, in which he was entangled more and more by every movement of his feet and hands. Meanwhile, stabs from the trident caused him to fall continually. He made one more effort and tried to rise, but in vain. He raised to his head his falling hand, which could hold the sword no longer, and fell on his back. Calendio pressed his neck to the ground with the trident and, resting both hands on the handle of it, turned toward Caesar's box.

The whole Circus was trembling from the roars of the people. For those who had bet on Calendio he was greater than Caesar was at that moment; but for this very reason animosity against the Gaul vanished from their hearts. At the cost of his blood he had filled their purses. The voices of the audience were divided. On the upper seats half the signs were for death, and half for mercy; but Calendio looked only at the box of Caesar, waiting for what he would decide.

Nero did not like the fallen gladiator, for at the last games before the fire he had bet against the Gaul and had lost considerable sums to Licinus; so he put his hand outside of the podium and turned his thumb toward the ground.

The vestals supported the sign at once. Calendio knelt on the breast of the Gaul, drew a short knife from his belt, pushed apart the armor around the neck of his opponent, and drove the three-edged blade into his throat to the handle.

"It is the end!" sounded voices in the amphitheater.

The Gaul shook once more, like a stabbed bullock, dug the sand with his heels, stretched, and was motionless.

After them came a battle of whole detachments. The audience howled, whistled, applauded, laughed, urged on the combatants, and grew wild. The two legions fought with the rage of wild beasts; bodies were intertwined in a death grapple, strong limbs cracked at the joints, swords were buried in chests and stomachs, pale lips threw blood onto the sand. Toward the end such terrible fear seized some novices that they tore themselves from the turmoil and fled. But the scourgers drove them back again quickly to the battle with whips tipped with lead. More and more naked and armed bodies lay stretched like grain sheaves. The living fought atop the corpses; they struck against armor and shield, cut their feet against broken weapons, and fell. The audience became intoxicated with death. They breathed it, sated their eyes with the sight of it, and drew it into their lungs with great pleasure.

The conquered lay dead, almost to a man. Barely a few wounded knelt in the middle of the arena and, trembling, stretched their hands to the audience with a prayer for mercy. To the victors were given crowns and olive wreaths. And a moment of quiet arrived that, at the command of the all-powerful Caesar, was turned into a feast. Perfumes were burned in vases. Sprinklers scattered saffron and violet rain on the people. Cool drinks were served, roasted meats, sweet cakes, wine, olives, and fruits. The people devoured, talked, and shouted in honor of Caesar, to urge him to greater generosity.

When hunger and thirst had been satisfied, hundreds of slaves carried baskets around full of gifts, from which boys, dressed as Cupid, took various objects and threw them with both hands among the seats. When lottery tickets were distributed, a battle began. People crowded and trampled one another, for whoever got a lucky number might possibly win a house with a garden, a slave, a splendid dress, or a wild beast he could sell to the amphitheater afterward. For this reason there were such disorders that frequently the praetorians had to interfere; and after every distribution they carried out people with broken arms or legs, and some were even trampled to death.

But the more wealthy took no part in this fight. The Augustians amused themselves now with the spectacle of Chilo. They made fun of his efforts to show that he could look at fighting and bloodspilling as well as any man. But it was in vain that the unfortunate Greek wrinkled his brow, gnawed his lips, and squeezed his fists until the nails entered his palms. His Greek nature and his personal cowardice were unable to endure such sights. His face grew pale, his forehead was dotted with drops of sweat, his lips were blue, his teeth began to chatter, and he trembled. At the end of the battle he recovered somewhat; but when they attacked him verbally he was angry and desperately defended himself.

"Ha, Greek! The sight of torn skin on a man is beyond your strength!" Vatinus said, taking him by the beard.

Chilo bared his last two yellow teeth at him and answered, "My father was not a cobbler, so I cannot mend it."

"Good! He caught it!" called a number of voices; but others jeered on.

"He cannot help that instead of a heart he has a piece of cheese in his breast," Senecio said.

"You are not to blame that instead of a head you have a bladder," Chilo retorted.

"Maybe you will become a gladiator! You would look well with a net in the arena."

"If I should catch you in it, I should catch a stinking fish."

"And how will it be with the Christians?" asked Festus, from Liguria. "Would you not like to be a dog and bite them?"

"I should not like to be your brother."

After a while Petronius approached and, touching the Greek's shoulder with his carved ivory cane, said coldly, "This is well, philosopher; but in one thing you have blundered; the gods created you to be a pickpocket, and you have become a demon. That is why you cannot endure."

The old man looked at him with his red eyes, but this time somehow he did not find a ready insult. He was silent for a moment, then answered, "I shall endure."

Meanwhile, the trumpets announced the end of the interval. Senators and patricians hastened to their places. On the arena a crowd of people appeared whose work was to dig out lumps of sand formed with stiffened blood.

The Christians' turn was at hand. But since that was a new spectacle for people, and no one knew how the Christians would conduct themselves, all waited with curiosity. The mood of the audience was attentive but unfriendly; they were waiting for unusual events. Those people who were to appear had burned Rome and its ancient treasures. They had drunk the blood of infants and poisoned water. They had cursed the whole human race and committed the vilest crimes. The harshest punishment did not satisfy the strong hatred roused against them; and if any fear possessed people's hearts, it was this: that the torture of the Christians would not equal the guilt of those horrible criminals.

Meanwhile, the sun had risen high; its rays, passing through the purple awning, had filled the amphitheater with blood-colored light. The sand took on a fiery hue, and in those gleams and in the faces of people, as well as in the empty arena, which soon would be filled with the torture of people and the rage of savage beasts, there was evil foreboding. Death and terror seemed to hover in the air. The throng, usually in good humor, became sullen and vengeful.

Now the prefect gave a sign. The same old man appeared who had called the gladiators to death, and, walking slowly across the arena amid silence, he struck three times again on the door.

Throughout the amphitheater was heard the deep murmur, "The Christians! the Christians!"

The iron gratings creaked; through the dark openings were heard the usual cries of the scourgers, "To the sand!" and in one moment the arena was peopled with crowds looking like satyrs covered with skins. All ran quickly, and, reaching the middle of the circle, they knelt close to each other with raised heads. The spectators, judging this to be a prayer for pity, and enraged by such cowardice, began to stamp, whistle, throw empty wine vessels and bones from which the flesh had been eaten, and shout, "The beasts! The beasts!" But all at once something unexpected took place. From out of the shaggy assembly singing voices were raised, and then sounded that hymn heard for the first time in a Roman amphitheater, "Christ reigns! Christ reigns!"

The spectators were astonished. The condemned sang with eyes raised to the sky. The audience saw pale faces, but inspired, nonetheless. They all understood that these people were not asking for mercy, and that they did not seem to see the Circus, the audience, the Senate, or Caesar. "Christ reigns!" rose ever louder, and far up to the highest seat, among the rows of spectators, more than one asked himself the question, *What is happening, and who is that Christ who reigns in the mouths of these people who are about to die?* But meanwhile, a new grating was opened, and into the arena rushed, with mad speed and barking, whole packs of dogs—gigantic, yellow Molossians from the Peloponnesus, pied dogs from the Pyrenees, and wolflike hounds from Hibernia, purposely famished, their sides lank and their eyes bloodshot. Their howls and whines filled the amphitheater.

When the Christians had finished their hymn, they remained kneeling, motionless, as if petrified, merely repeating in one groaning chorus, "We serve Christ!" The dogs, catching the odor of people under the skins of beasts, did not rush on them at once. Some stood against the walls of the boxes, as if wishing to go among the spectators; others ran around barking furiously, as though chasing some unseen beast. The spectators were angry. A thousand voices began to call; some howled like wild beasts; some barked like dogs; others urged them on in every language. The amphitheater itself was trembling from the uproar. The excited dogs began to run to the kneeling people, then to draw back, snapping their teeth, until at last one of the Molossians drove his teeth into the shoulder of a woman kneeling in front and dragged her under him.

Numerous dogs rushed into the crowd now, as if to break through it. The audience ceased to howl. In the arena formed quivering masses of the bodies of dogs and people. Blood flowed in streams from the torn bodies. Dogs dragged from each other the bloody limbs of various Christians. The odor of blood and torn insides was stronger than the Arabian perfumes and filled the whole Circus.

At last only here and there were visible single kneeling forms, which were soon covered by masses of dogs.

Vinicius, at the moment when the Christians ran in, stood up and turned to indicate to the quarryman, as he had promised, the direction in which the apostle was hidden among the people of Petronius. He now sat down again, and with the face of a dead man continued to look with glassy eyes on the ghastly spectacle. At first his fear that the quarryman might have been mistaken, and that perhaps Lygia was among the victims, numbed him completely. But when he heard the voices, "Servants of Christ!" when he saw the torture of so many victims who, in dying, confessed their faith and their God, another feeling possessed him, piercing him like the most dreadful but irresistible pain. That feeling was this— if Christ Himself died in torment, if thousands are perishing for Him now, if a sea of blood is poured out, one drop more achieves nothing, and it is a sin even to ask for mercy. That thought came to him from the arena, penetrated him with the groans of the dying and the odor of their blood. But still he prayed and repeated with parched lips, "O Christ! O Christ! And Your apostle prayed for her!" Then he lost track of everything and lost consciousness. It seemed to him that the blood in the arena was ever rising, that it was coming up and flowing out of the Circus all over Rome. He heard no more, neither the howling of dogs nor the uproar of the people nor the voices of the Augustians, who began to cry, "Chilo has fainted!"

Chilo sat there white as linen, his head fallen back, his mouth wide open, like that of a corpse.

At that same moment they were urging new victims into the arena, sewn up in skins.

They knelt immediately, like those who had gone before; but the weary dogs would not devour them. Only a few threw themselves on those kneeling nearby; but others lay down and, raising their bloody jaws, began to scratch their sides and yawn heavily.

Then the audience, drunk with blood and hatred, began to cry with hoarse voices, "The lions! Let out the lions!"

The lions were to be kept for the next day; but in the amphitheaters the people imposed their will on everyone, even on Caesar. Caligula alone, insolent and stubborn, dared to oppose them, and there were cases when he commanded that the people be beaten with clubs; but even he yielded frequently. Nero, to whom applause was dearer than all else in the world, never resisted. He would not resist now, when it was a question of pacifying the populace, excited after the great fire, and a question of the Christians, on whom he wished to cast the blame for the catastrophe.

He gave the sign, therefore, to open the cages, and the people were calmed in a moment. They heard the creaking of the doors behind which were the lions. At the sight of the lions, the dogs gathered with low whines on the opposite side of the arena. The lions walked into the arena one after another, immense, tawny, with great shaggy heads. Caesar himself turned his wearied face toward them and placed the emerald to his eye to see better. The Augustians greeted them with applause; the crowd counted them on their fingers and eagerly followed the impression that the sight of them would make on the Christians kneeling in the center, who again had begun to repeat the words, without meaning for many, though annoying to all, "In service of Christ!"

But the lions, though hungry, did not hasten to their victims. The ruddy light in the arena dazzled them, and they half closed their eyes as if dazed. Some stretched their yellowish bodies lazily; some, opening their jaws, yawned—one might have said that they wanted to show their terrible teeth to the audience. But then the odor of blood and torn bodies, many of which were lying on the sand, began to have an effect on them. Soon their movements became restless, their manes rose, their nostrils drew in the air with hoarse sound. One fell suddenly on the body of a woman with a torn face, and, lying with his forepaws on the body, licked the stiffened blood; another approached a man who was holding in his arms a child sewed up in a fawn's skin.

The child, trembling from crying, and weeping, clung tightly to the neck of its father. He, to prolong the child's life even for a moment, tried to pull it from his neck, in order to hand it to those kneeling farther on. But the cry and the movement irritated the lion. All at once he gave a short, broken roar, killed the child with one blow of his paw and, seizing the head of the father in his jaws, crushed it in an instant.

All the other lions then fell upon the crowd of Christians. Some women could not restrain cries of terror; but the audience drowned these with applause, which soon ceased, however, for the wish to see the spectacle. They beheld terrible things: heads disappearing entirely in open jaws, breasts torn apart with one blow, hearts and lungs swept away; the crushing of bones under the teeth of lions. Some lions, seizing victims by the ribs or loins, ran with mad springs through the arena, as if seeking hidden places in which to devour them. Others fought, rose on their hind legs, grappled one another like wrestlers, and filled the amphitheater with thunder. People rose from their places. Some left their seats, went down lower through the passages to see better, and trampled one another. It seemed that the excited multitude would throw itself at last into the arena and kill the Christians in company with the lions. At moments unearthly noise was heard; at moments applause; at moments roaring, rumbling, the clashing of teeth, the howling of Molossian dogs; and at times only groans.

Caesar, holding the emerald to his eye, looked now with attention. The face of Petronius assumed an expression of contempt and disgust. Chilo had been taken out of the Circus.

But from the underground cells new victims were driven forth continually.

From the highest row in the amphitheater the apostle Peter looked at them. No one saw him, for all heads were turned to the arena; so he rose as in the vineyard of Cornelius. He had blessed for death and eternity those who were intended for imprisonment; so now he blessed with the cross those who were perishing under the teeth of wild beasts. He blessed their blood, their torture, their dead bodies turned into shapeless masses, and their souls flying away from the bloody sand. Some raised their eyes to him, and their faces grew radiant; they smiled when they saw high above them the sign of the cross. But his heart was torn, and he said, "O Lord! Let Your will be done. These my sheep perish to Your glory in testimony of the truth. You commanded me to feed them; so I give them to You. Count them, Lord, take them, heal their wounds, soften their pain, give them happiness greater than the torments they suffered here."

And he blessed one after another, crowd after crowd, with as much love as if they had been his children whom he was giving directly into the hands of Christ. Then Caesar, whether from madness, or the wish that the exhibition should surpass everything seen in Rome so far, whispered a few words to the prefect of the city. He left the podium and went at once to the underground cell. Even the populace was astonished when, after a while, they saw the gratings open again. Beasts of all kinds were let out this time—tigers from the Euphrates, Numidian panthers, bears, wolves, hyenas, and jackals. The whole arena was covered as with a moving sea of striped, yellow, flax-colored, dark-brown, and spotted skins. A chaos arose in which the eye could tell nothing except a terrible turning and twisting of the backs of wild beasts. The spectacle lost the appearance of reality and became an orgy of blood, a dreadful dream, a gigantic kaleidoscope of mad fancy. Amid roars, howls, and whines, here and there were heard on the seats of the spectators the terrified and spasmodic laughter of women, whose strength had gone at last. The people were terrified. Faces grew dark. Various voices began to cry, "Enough! Enough!"

But it was easier to let the beasts in than drive them back again. Caesar, however, found a way of clearing the arena, and a new amusement for the people. In all the passages between the seats appeared detachments of Numidians, black and stately, in feathers and earrings, with bows in their hands. The people understood what was coming and greeted the archers with a shout of delight. The Numidians approached the railing and, putting their arrows to the strings, began to shoot from their bows into the crowd of beasts. That was truly a new spectacle. Their bodies of the Numidians, shapely as if cut from dark marble, bent backward, stretched the flexible bows, and sent bolt after bolt. The whizzing of the strings and the whistling of the feathered missiles were mingled with the howling of beasts and cries of wonder from the audience. Wolves, bears, panthers, and people yet alive fell side by side. Here and there a lion, feeling a shaft in his ribs, turned with sudden movement, his jaws wrinkled from rage, to seize and break the arrow. Others groaned from pain. The small beasts ran around the arena at random or thrust their heads into the grating; meanwhile, the arrows whizzed on, until all that was living had lain down in the final spasm of death.

Hundreds of slaves rushed into the arena armed with spades, shovels, brooms, wheelbarrows, baskets for carrying out body parts, and bags of sand. The space was soon cleared of bodies, blood, and mire, dug over, made smooth, and sprinkled with a thick layer of fresh sand. That done, Cupids ran in, scattering petals of roses, lilies, and a great variety of flowers. The censers were ignited again, and the awning was removed, for the sun had now sunk considerably. But people inquired what kind of new spectacle was waiting for them after such marvels.

Caesar, who had left the podium previously, appeared all at once in the flowery arena, wearing a purple mantle and a crown of gold. Twelve choristers holding lutes followed him. He had a silver lute and, advanced to the middle, bowed a number of times to the spectators, raised his eyes, and stood as if waiting for inspiration.

In the Circus there was silence. After a while Caesar sang:

> "With the sounds of your heavenly lyre
> You could drown the wailing,
> The lament of hearts.
> At the sad sound of this song
> The eye today is filled with tears,
> As a flower is filled with dew,
> But who can raise from dust and ashes
> That day of fire, disaster, ruin?
> O Smintheus, where were you then?"

Here his voice quivered and his eyes grew moist. Tears appeared among the vestal maidens; the people listened in silence before they burst into a long unbroken storm of applause.

Meanwhile, from outside through the stadium came the sound of creaking carts on which were placed the bloody remnants of Christians—men, women, and children—to be taken to the burial pits.

But the apostle Peter cried in spirit, *O Lord, to whom have You given rule over the earth, and why have You allowed this slaughter to happen in this heathen city?*

56

The sun had begun to set and seemed to dissolve in the red of the evening. The spectacle was finished. Crowds were leaving the amphitheater and pouring out to the city through the stadium passages. Only Augustians delayed, for they were waiting for the stream of people to pass. They had all left their seats and assembled at the podium, in which Caesar appeared again to hear praises. Though the spectators had not spared applause at the end of the song, Nero was not satisfied. He had looked for enthusiasm touching on frenzy. Hymns of praise were not enough; vestals kissing his "divine" hand did not satisfy, and while doing so Rubria bent until her reddish hair touched his breast. Nero was not happy and could not hide the fact. He was astonished and also disturbed because Petronius was silent. Some flattering and pointed word from his mouth would have been a great consolation at that moment. Unable at last to restrain himself, Caesar beckoned him.

"Speak," he said, when Petronius entered the podium.

"I am silent," Petronius answered coldly, "for I cannot find words. You have surpassed yourself."

"So it seems to me too; but still this people—"

"Can you expect mongrels to appreciate poetry?"

"But you too have noticed that they have not thanked me as I deserve."

"Because you have chosen a bad moment."

"How?"

"When men's brains are filled with the odor of blood, they cannot listen attentively."

"Ah, those Christians!" Nero replied, clenching his fists. "They burned Rome and injure me now as well. What new punishment shall I invent for them?"

Petronius saw that he had taken the wrong road, that his words had produced the very opposite effect of what he intended; so, to turn Caesar's mind in another direction, he bent toward him and whispered, "Your song is marvelous, but I will make one remark; in the fourth line of the third strophe the meter leaves something to be desired."

Nero, blushing with shame as if caught in a disgraceful deed, answered in a whisper also, "You see everything. I know, and I will rewrite that. But no one else noticed it, I think. For the love of the gods, mention it to no one—if life is dear to you."

To this Petronius answered, as if in an outburst of vexation and anger, "Condemn me to death, O divinity, if I deceive you. But you will not terrify me, for the gods know best of all if I fear death."

And while speaking he looked straight into Caesar's eyes, who answered after a while, "Be not angry; you know that I love you."

A bad sign! thought Petronius.

"I wanted to invite you today to a feast," Nero continued, "but I prefer to shut myself in and polish that cursed line in the third strophe. Besides you, Seneca may have noticed it, and perhaps Secundus Carinas did; but I will rid myself of them quickly."

Then he summoned Seneca and declared that, with Acratus and Secundus Carinas, he would send him to the Italian cities and all other provinces for money, which he commanded him to obtain from cities, villages, famous temples—in a word, from every place where it was possible to find or force money from the populace. But Seneca, who saw that Caesar was asking him to do a work of plunder, refused straightway.

"I must go to the country, lord," he said, "and await death, for I am old and my nerves are worn."

Seneca's Iberian nerves were stronger than Chilo's. But though his nerves were sound, in general his health was bad, for he seemed like a shadow, and recently his hair had grown totally white.

Nero, too, when he looked at him, thought that he would not have to wait long for the man's death, and answered, "I will not expose you to a journey if you are ill, but through affection I wish to keep you near me. Instead of going to the country, then, you will stay in your own house and not leave it."

Then he looked around and asked, "But what has happened to Chilo?"

Chilo, who had recovered in the open air and returned to the amphitheater for Caesar's song, sat up and said, "I am here, O radiant offspring of the sun and moon. I was ill, but your song has restored me."

"I will send you to Achea," Nero said. "You must know to a copper how much there is in each temple there."

"Do so, O Zeus, and the gods will give you such tribute as they have never given anyone."

"I would, but I do not like to prevent you from seeing the games."

"Baa!" Chilo said.

The Augustians, delighted that Caesar had regained humor, laughed and exclaimed, "No, lord, do not deprive this valiant Greek of a sight of the games."

"But preserve me, O lord, from the sight of these noisy geese of the Capitol, whose brains put together would not fill a nutshell," Chilo retorted. "O firstborn of Apollo, I am writing a Greek hymn in your honor, and I wish to spend a few days in the temple of the Muses to seek inspiration."

"Oh, no!" Nero exclaimed. "It is your wish to escape future games. Nothing will come of that!"

"I swear to you, lord, that I am writing a hymn."

"Then you will write it at night. Beg inspiration of Diana, who, by the way, is a sister of Apollo."

Chilo dropped his head and looked with malice on those present, who began to laugh again. Caesar, turning to Senecio said, "Imagine, of all the Christians appointed for today we have been able to finish hardly half of them!"

At this old Aquilus Regulus, who had great knowledge of everything regarding the amphitheater, said, "Spectacles in which people appear without weapons last almost as long and are less entertaining."

"I will order them to be given weapons," Nero answered.

But the superstitious Vestinius asked in a mysterious voice, "Have you noticed that when dying they see something? They look up and die as almost without pain. I am sure that they see something."

He raised his eyes then to the opening of the amphitheater, over which night had begun to fall and dotted the sky with stars. But others answered with laughter and humorous possibilities as to what the Christians could see at the moment of death. Meanwhile, Caesar gave a signal to the slave torchbearers, and left the Circus; after him followed vestals, senators, dignitaries, and Augustians.

The night was clear and warm. Throngs of people were moving before the Circus, curious to witness the departure of Caesar;

411

but in some way they were gloomy and silent. Here and there applause was heard, but it ended quickly.

Petronius and Vinicius traveled their road in silence. Only when near his villa did Petronius ask, "Have you thought of what I told you?"

"I have," Vinicius answered.

"Do you believe that for me also this is a question of the highest importance? I must liberate her in spite of Caesar and Tigellinus. This is a kind of battle in which I have decided to win, a kind of play in which I wish to be the victor, even at the cost of my life. Today I am more confirmed in my plan."

"May Christ reward you."

"You will see."

Continuing to talk, they stopped at the door of the villa and got out of the litter. At that moment a dark figure approached them and asked, "Is the noble Vinicius here?"

"He is," the tribune answered. "What is your wish?"

"I am Nazarius, the son of Miriam. I come from the prison and bring tidings of Lygia."

Vinicius placed his hand on the young man's shoulder and looked into his eyes by the torchlight, without power to speak a word, but Nazarius understood his question and replied, "She is still living. Ursus sent me to say that she prays in her fever and repeats your name."

"Praise be to Christ, who has power to restore her to me," Vinicius said.

He led Nazarius to the library, and after a while Petronius came in to hear their conversation.

"Sickness saved her from shame, for executioners are timid," the youth said. "Ursus and Glaucus the physician watch over her night and day."

"Are the guards the same?"

"They are, and she is in their chamber. All the prisoners in the lower dungeon died of fever, or were choked from foul air."

"Who are you?" Petronius asked.

"The noble Vinicius knows me. I am the son of that widow with whom Lygia lodged."

"And a Christian?"

The youth looked at Vinicius, but, seeing him in prayer, he raised his head and answered, "I am."

"How can you enter the prison freely?"

"I hired myself to carry out corpses; I did so to assist my brethren and bring them news from the city."

Petronius looked more attentively at the handsome face of the youth, his blue eyes, and dark, abundant hair.

"What country are you from, young man?" he asked.

"I am a Galilean, lord."

"Would you like to see Lygia free?"

The youth raised his eyes. "Yes, even if had I to die afterwards."

Then Vinicius ceased to pray and said, "Tell the guards to place her in a coffin as if she were dead. You will find assistants to carry her out in the night with you. Near the 'Putrid Pits' will be people with a litter waiting for you; give them the coffin. Promise the guards from me as much gold as each can carry in his mantle."

Nazarius flushed with delight and, raising his hands, exclaimed, "May Christ give her health, for she will be free."

"Do you think that the guards will consent?" Petronius asked.

"Yes, if they know that punishment and torture will not come to them."

"If the guards would agree to her escape, all the more will they let us carry her out as a corpse," Vinicius said.

"There is a man, it is true," Nazarius said, "who is very concerned to see if the bodies we carry out are dead. But he will take even a few coins not to touch the face of the dead with a red-hot iron. For one coin he will touch the coffin, not the body."

"Tell him that he will get a capful of coins," Petronius said. "But can you find a reliable assistant?"

"I can find men who would sell their own wives and children for money."

"Where will you find them?"

"In the prison itself or in the city. Once the guards are paid, they will admit whomever I like."

"In that case take me as a hired servant," Vinicius said.

But Petronius earnestly opposed this. "The praetorians might recognize you even in disguise, and all would be lost. Do not go

413

to the prison or the 'Putrid Pits.' All, including Caesar and Tigellinus, should be convinced that she died; otherwise, seek her immediately. We can avoid suspicion only in this way: When she is taken to the Alban Hills or farther, to Sicily, we shall be in Rome. A week or two later you will fall ill and summon Nero's physician; he will tell you to go to the mountains. You and she will meet, and afterward—"

Here he thought a while; then, waving his hand, he said, "Other times may come."

"May Christ have mercy on her," Vinicius said. "You are speaking of Sicily, while she is sick and may die."

"Let us keep her nearer Rome at first. The air alone will restore her, if only we snatch her from the dungeon. Have you no caretaker in the mountains whom you can trust?"

"I have," Vinicius replied hurriedly. "Near Corioli is a reliable man who carried me in his arms when I was a child, and who still is my friend."

"Write to him to come tomorrow," Petronius said, handing Vinicius tablets. "I will send a courier at once."

He called the chief of the atrium, then, and gave the needful orders. A few minutes later, a mounted slave was traveling in the night toward Corioli.

"It would please me if Ursus were to accompany her," Vinicius said. "I would not worry as much."

"Lord," Nazarius said, "that is a man of superhuman strength; he can break steel doors and follow her. There is one window above a steep, high rock where no guard is placed. I will give Ursus a rope, and he will be able to do it himself."

"By Hercules!" Petronius said. "Let him escape as he pleases, but not at the same time with her, and not two or three days later, for they would follow him and discover her hiding place. Do you wish to destroy yourselves and her?"

Both recognized the justice of these words and were silent. Nazarius left, promising to come the next morning at daybreak.

He determined not to seek an assistant in the city, but to find and bribe one from among his fellow corpse-bearers. When leaving, he stopped, and, taking Vinicius aside, whispered, "I will not mention our plan to anyone, but the apostle Peter promised to come from the amphitheater to our house; I will tell him everything."

"Here you can speak openly," Vinicius replied. "The apostle was in the amphitheater with the people of Petronius. But I will go with you myself."

He took a slave's mantle, and they left. Petronius sighed deeply.

"Ah! Ahenobarbus, you wished to turn a lover's pain into a spectacle; you, Augusta, were jealous of the maiden's beauty and wished to devour her alive because your Rufius has perished. You, Tigellinus, wished to destroy her to spite me! We shall see. I tell you that you will not see her on the arena, for she will either die her own death or I shall take her from you as from the jaws of dogs, and take her in such a way that you shall not know it. Later, when I observe you, I shall think, *These are the fools whom Caius Petronius outwitted.*"

And, self-satisfied, he sat down to supper with Eunice. During the meal a slave read to them the Idyls of Thecritus. Out of doors the wind brought clouds, and a sudden storm broke the silence of the calm summer night. Thunder echoed on the seven hills, while they, reclining near each other at the table, listened to the pastoral poet, who in the Doric dialect celebrated the loves of shepherds. Later on, with minds at rest, they prepared for sweet slumber.

But before this Vinicius returned.

"Well? Have you found anything new?" he asked. "Has Nazarius gone to the prison?"

"He has," the young man answered, fixing his hair, wet from the rain. "Nazarius went to alert the guards, and I have seen Peter, who commanded me to pray and believe."

"That is well. If all goes favorably, we can take her away tomorrow night."

"My foreman must be here at daybreak with his men."

"The road is a short one. Go to rest."

But Vinicius knelt in his room and prayed.

At sunrise Niger, the foreman, arrived from Corioli, bringing with him, at the order of Vinicius, mules, a litter, and four trusted men selected among slaves from Britain, whom, for the sake of appearance, he had left at an inn in the Subura. Vinicius, who had waited all night, went to meet him. Niger, moved at sight of his youthful master, kissed his hand, saying, "My friend, you are ill, or else suffering has made you pale, for I hardly knew you at first."

Vinicius took him to the inner colonnade and there told him the secret. Niger listened with rapt attention.

"Then she is a Christian?" He wondered also about Vinicius, who guessed his next question and answered, "I too am a Christian."

Tears glistened in Niger's eyes, and he was silent for a while. Then, raising his hands, he said, "I thank You, O Christ, for having taken the beam from eyes that are the dearest on earth to me."

Then he embraced Vinicius and, weeping from joy, kissed his forehead. A moment later, Petronius appeared, bringing Nazarius.

"Good news!" he cried, while still at a distance.

Indeed, the news was good. First, Glaucus the physician guaranteed that Lygia was alive, though she had the same prison fever of which, in the Tullianum and other dungeons, hundreds of people were dying daily. As to the guards and the man who burned corpses with red-hot irons, there would not be the least difficulty.

"We made openings in the coffin to let the sick woman breathe," said Nazarius. "The only danger is that she may groan or speak as we pass the praetorians. But she is very weak and has had her eyes closed since early morning. Besides, Glaucus will give her a sleeping drug brought purposely by me from the city. The cover will not be nailed to the coffin; you will raise it easily and take the patient to the litter. We will place a long bag of sand in the coffin, which you will provide."

"Will they carry out other bodies from the prison?" Petronius asked.

"About twenty died last night, and before evening more will be dead," the youth said. "We must go with a whole company, but we will delay and drop back. We will pretend my comrade is lame. We shall then fall considerably behind the others. You both will wait for us at the small temple of Libitina. May God give us a dark night!"

"Will you go without torches?" Vinicius asked.

"The torches are carried only in advance. In any event, be near the temple at dark, though usually we carry out the corpses only just before midnight."

They stopped. Nothing was to be heard except the hurried breathing of Vinicius. Petronius turned to him. "I said yesterday that it would be best for us both to stay at home, but now I could not stay. Were it a question of fleeing, we would need to be cautious, but since she will be taken out as a corpse, it seems that no one will be the least suspicious."

"True!" Vinicius answered. "I will take her from the coffin myself."

"Once she is in my house at Corioli, I answer for her," Niger said.

Conversation stopped here. Niger returned to his men at the inn. Nazarius took a purse of gold under his tunic and went to the prison.

"The undertaking ought to succeed, for it is well planned," Petronius said. "You must pretend you are suffering and wear a dark toga. Do not desert the amphitheater. Let people see you. But—are you perfectly sure of your Niger?"

"He is a Christian," Vinicius replied.

Petronius looked at him with amazement, then shrugged his shoulders and said, as if talking to himself, "By Pollux! How it spreads, and rules people's souls. Under such terror as the present, men would immediately renounce all the gods of Rome, Greece, and Egypt. Still, this is wonderful! If I believed that anything depended on our gods, I would sacrifice six white bullocks to each of them, and twelve to Capitoline Jove. Spare no promises to the Christ."

"I have given Him my soul," Vinicius said.

And they parted. Petronius returned to his room, but Vinicius went to look at the prison from a distance and then went to the slope of the Vatican Hill—to that hut of the quarryman where he had received baptism from the apostle. It seemed to him that Christ would more readily hear him there than in any other place. When he found it, he threw himself on the ground and exerted all the strength of his suffering soul in a prayer for mercy, and so

417

forgot himself that he did not remember where he was or what he was doing. In the afternoon he was roused by the sound of trumpets that came from the direction of Nero's Circus. He went out of the hut and gazed around the area.

Vinicius went home. Petronius was waiting for him in the atrium.

"I have been on the Palatine," he said. "I showed myself there purposely, and even sat down and played dice. There is a feast at the house of Anicius this evening. I promised to go, but only after midnight, saying that I must sleep before then. In fact I shall be there, and it would be good for you to go too."

"Are there no messages from Niger or Nazarius?" Vinicius asked.

"No; we shall see them at midnight only. Have you noticed that a storm is threatening?"

"Yes."

"Tomorrow there is to be an exhibition of crucified Christians, but perhaps rain will prevent it."

Then he drew nearer and, touching his nephew's shoulder, said, "But you will not see her on the cross; you will see her only in Corioli. We will free her for all the gems in Rome. The evening is near."

Darkness began to encircle the city earlier than usual, because clouds covered the whole horizon. With the coming of night heavy rain fell, which turned into steam on the stones warmed by the heat of the day and filled the streets of the city with mist. After that came a lull, then brief, violent showers.

"Let us hurry!" Vinicius said at last. "They may carry bodies away from the prison earlier because of the storm."

"It is time!" Petronius said.

And taking Gallic cloaks with hoods, they went through the garden door to the street. Petronius had armed himself, which he always did during night trips.

The city was empty because of the storm. From time to time lightning split the clouds, illuminating with its glare the fresh walls of newly built houses from the fire and the wet flagstones with which the streets were paved. At last a flash came, when they saw, along a road, the mound on which stood the small temple of

Libitina, and at the foot of the mound a group of mules and horses.

"Niger!" Vinicius called in a low voice.

"I am here, lord," said a voice in the rain.

"Is everything ready?"

"It is. We were here at dark. But hide yourselves under the rampart, or you will be drenched. What a storm! Hail will fall, I think."

In fact Niger's fear was justified, for soon hail began to fall, at first fine, then larger and more frequent. While standing under the rampart, sheltered from the wind and icy missiles, they spoke in low voices.

"Even if someone should see us," Niger said, "there will be no suspicion; we look like people waiting for the storm to pass. But I fear that they may not bring the bodies out till morning."

"The hailstorm will not last," Petronius said. "We must wait even till daybreak."

They waited, listening to hear the sound of the procession. The hailstorm passed, but immediately after that a shower began to roar. At times the wind rose and brought from the "Putrid Pits" a dreadful odor of decaying bodies, buried carelessly near the surface.

"I see a light through the mist," Niger said. "Those are torches. See that the mules do not snort," he said, turning to the men.

"They are coming!" said Petronius.

The lights were growing more and more distinct. After a while it was possible to see torches under the glowing flames.

Niger made the sign of the cross and began to pray. Meanwhile, the gloomy procession drew nearer and halted at last in front of the temple of Libitina. Petronius, Vinicius, and Niger pressed against the rampart in silence, not knowing why the procession stopped. But the men had halted only to cover their mouths with cloths to ward off the stifling stench that at the edge of the "Putrid Pits" was simply unendurable. Then they raised the biers with coffins and moved on. Only one coffin stopped before the temple. Vinicius, Petronius, and Niger sprang toward it, and two British slaves with the litter.

But before they had reached it in the darkness, the voice of Nazarius was heard, full of pain, "Lord, they took her with Ursus to the Esquiline prison. We are carrying another body! They removed her before midnight."

Petronius, when he had returned home, was downcast and did not even try to console Vinicius. He understood that to free Lygia from the Esquiline dungeons was not to be dreamed of. He believed that very likely she had been taken from the Tullianum so as not to die of fever and escape the amphitheater assigned to her. But for this very reason she was watched and guarded more carefully than others. From the bottom of his soul Petronius was sorry for her and Vinicius, but he was wounded also by the thought that for the first time in his life he had not succeeded, and for the first time was beaten in a struggle.

Fortune seems to desert me, he said to himself, *but the gods are mistaken if they think that I will accept such a life as his, for example.*

Here he turned toward Vinicius, who stared at him.

"What is the matter? You have a fever," Petronius said.

But Vinicius answered with the broken voice of a sick child, "But I believe that He—can restore her to me."

Above the city the last thunders of the storm had ceased.

57

Meanwhile, beautiful weather returned. The amphitheater was filled at daybreak with thousands of people. Caesar came early with the vestals and the court. The spectacle was to begin with a battle among the Christians, who were arrayed as gladiators and furnished with all kinds of weapons that served gladiators in various struggles. But there was profound disappointment. The Christians threw nets, darts, tridents, and swords in the arena, embraced and encouraged one another to endure in light of torture and death. Deep indignation and resentment filled the hearts of the multitude. Some insulted the Christians as cowards; others said that they refused to fight because of hatred for the people, so as to keep them from seeing brave deeds. Finally, at the command of Caesar, real gladiators were let out, who despatched in one instant the kneeling and defenseless victims.

When these bodies were removed, the spectacle was a series of mythologic pictures—Caesar's own idea. The audience saw Hercules blazing in living fire on Mount Oeta. Vinicius had trembled at the thought that the role of Hercules might be intended for Ursus. But evidently the turn of Lygia's faithful servant had not come, for on the pile some other Christian was burning—a man unknown to Vinicius. In the next picture Chilo, whom Caesar would not excuse from attendance, saw Greek myths. The death of Daedalus and Icarus was represented. Euricius, that old man who had given Chilo the sign of the fish, appeared in the role of Daedalus; the role of Icarus was taken by Euricius's son, Quartus. Both were raised aloft with machinery and then hurled suddenly from an immense height to the arena. Young Quartus fell so near Caesar's podium that he spattered with blood not only the ornaments but the purple covering spread over the front of the podium. Chilo did not see the fall, for he closed his eyes; but he heard the dull thump of the body, and when he saw blood close to him, he nearly fainted a second time.

They saw priestesses of Cybele and Ceres; finally they saw young girls, not mature yet, torn asunder by wild horses. Every moment the crowd applauded new ideas of Nero, who, proud of them, and made happy by praise, did not take the emerald from his eye for one instant while looking at white bodies torn with iron and the convulsions of scores of victims.

Pictures were given from the history of the city. After the maidens they saw Mucius Scaevola, whose hand fastened over a fire to a tripod filled the amphitheater with the odor of burnt flesh; but this man, like the real Scaevola, remained without a groan, his eyes raised and the murmur of prayer on his blackening lips. When he had expired and his body was dragged out of the amphitheater, the usual midday interlude followed. Caesar with the vestals and the Augustians left the amphitheater and withdrew to an immense scarlet tent erected purposely; in this was prepared for him and the guests a magnificent feast. The spectators followed his example and, streaming out, gathered around the tent to rest their weary limbs from long sitting and to enjoy the food that, through Caesar's favor, was served by slaves to them. Only the most curious descended to the arena itself and, touching lumps of sand held together by blood, conversed about what had happened and what would follow. Soon even they went away, lest they be late for the feast. Only those few were left who stayed through sympathy for the coming victims. They concealed themselves behind seats or in the lower areas.

Meanwhile, the arena was leveled and slaves began to dig holes in rows throughout the whole circuit from side to side, so that the last row was only a few paces from Caesar's podium. From outside came the murmur of people, shouts, and applause, while within they were preparing in hot haste for new tortures. The gates were opened simultaneously, and in all passages leading to the arena crowds of Christians were urged forward, naked and carrying crosses on their shoulders. The whole arena was filled with them. Old men, bending under the weight of wooden beams, ran forward; at the side of these went men in the prime of life, women with loosened hair trying to hide their nakedness, and little children. The crosses, for the greater part, as well as the victims, were wreathed with flowers. The servants of the amphitheater beat them with clubs, forcing them to lay down their crosses near the holes prepared and stand themselves there in rows. Black slaves seized the victims, laid them face upward on the wood, and nailed their hands hurriedly to the arms of the crosses, so that people returning after the interlude might find all the crosses standing. The whole amphitheater resounded with the noise of hammers that echoed through all the rows and into the tent where Caesar was entertaining his suite. There he drank wine, bantered with Chilo, and whispered strange words in the ears of the priestess Vesta; but in the arena the work continued—nails were driven into the hands and feet of the Christians; shovels moved quickly, filling the holes in which the crosses had been planted.

Among the new victims whose turn was to come soon was

Crispus. The lions had not had time to devour him; so he was chosen for a cross. He, ready at all times for death, was delighted with the thought that his hour was approaching. He seemed another man, for his emaciated body was wholly naked—only a girdle of ivy encircled his hips, and on his head was a garland of roses. But in his eyes gleamed always that same unending energy; that same fanatical stern face gazed from beneath the crown of roses. His heart had not changed; for, as in the prison he had threatened his brethren sewed up in the skins of wild beasts with the wrath of God, so today he thundered in place of consoling them.

"Thank the Redeemer," Crispus said, "that He permits you to die the same death that He Himself died. Maybe a part of your sins will be remitted for this reason; but tremble, since justice must be satisfied, and there cannot be one reward for the just and the wicked."

His words were accompanied by the sound of hammers nailing the hands and feet of victims. Every moment more crosses were raised on the arena; but he, turning to the crowd standing by their crosses, continued, "I see heaven open, but I also see the yawning abyss. I do not know what account of my life to give the Lord, though I have believed, and hated evil. I fear, not death, but resurrection; I fear, not torture, but judgment, for the day of wrath is at hand."

At that moment was heard a calm and solemn voice from between the nearest rows. "Not the day of wrath, but of mercy, the day of salvation and happiness; for I say that Christ will gather you in, will comfort you and seat you at His right hand. Be confident, for heaven is opening before you."

At these words all eyes were turned to the benches; even those who were hanging on the crosses raised their pale, tortured faces, and looked toward the man who was speaking.

But he went to the barrier surrounding the arena and blessed them with the sign of the cross.

Crispus stretched out his arm as if to thunder at him; but when he saw the man's face, he dropped his arm, the knees bent under him, and his lips whispered, "Paul the apostle!"

Paul turned to Crispus and said, "Do not threaten them, Crispus, for this day they will be with you in paradise. It is your idea that they may be condemned. But who will condemn? Will God, who gave His Son for them? Will Christ, who died for their salvation, condemn them when they die for His name? And how is it possible that He who loves can condemn? Who will accuse the chosen of God? Who will say of this blood, 'It is cursed'?"

"I have hated evil," the old priest said.

"Christ's command to love men was higher than that to hate evil, for His religion is not hatred, but love."

"I have sinned in the hour of death," Crispus answered, beating his breast.

The manager of the seats approached the apostle and asked, "Who are you, speaking to the condemned?"

"A Roman citizen," Paul answered calmly. Then, turning to Crispus, he said, "Be confident, for today is a day of grace; die in peace, O servant of God."

The black men approached Crispus at that moment to place him on the cross, but he looked around once again and cried, "My brethren, pray for me!"

His face had lost its usual sternness; his stony features had taken on an expression of peace and sweetness. He stretched his arms himself along the arms of the cross, to make the work easier and, looking into heaven, began to pray earnestly. He seemed to feel nothing; for when the nails entered his hands, not the least pain shook his body. No wrinkle of pain appeared on his face. He prayed when they raised the cross and trampled the earth around it. When crowds began to fill the amphitheater with shouts and laughter his brows frowned somewhat, as if in anger that a pagan people were disturbing the calm and peace of a sweet death.

But all the crosses had been raised, so that in the arena appeared a forest, with people hanging on the trees. The sun gleamed on the arms of the crosses and on the heads of the martyrs. This was a spectacle in which the whole delight of the audience consisted of looking at a lingering death. Never before had anyone seen such a density of crosses. The arena was packed so closely that the servants squeezed between them only with difficulty. On the edges were many women, but Crispus, as a leader, was raised almost in front of Caesar's podium, on an immense cross, wreathed below with honeysuckle. None of the victims had died yet, but some of those fastened earlier had fainted. No one groaned; no one called for mercy. Some were hanging with their heads resting on one arm, or dropped on their breast; some seemed in meditation; some, looking toward heaven, were moving their lips quietly. In this terrible forest of crosses, among those crucified bodies, in that silence of victims, there was something ominous. The people, who, full from the feast and joyful, had returned to the Circus with shouts, became silent, not knowing on which body to rest their eyes, or what to think of the spectacle. The nakedness of strained female forms roused no feeling. They did not make the usual bets as to who would die first. It seemed that Caesar himself was bored, for he turned lazily and with drowsy expression to arrange his necklace.

At that moment Crispus, who was hanging opposite, and who, like a man in a faint or dying, had kept his eyes closed, opened them and looked at Caesar. His face assumed an expression so pitiless, and his eyes flashed with such fire, that the Augustians whispered to one another, pointing at him with their fingers, and at last Caesar himself turned to that cross and placed the emerald to his eye sluggishly.

Perfect silence followed. The eyes of the spectators were fixed on Crispus, who strove to move his right hand, as if to tear it from the tree.

After a while his breast rose, his ribs were visible, and he cried: "Matricide! Woe to you!"

The Augustians, hearing this mortal insult flung at the lord of the world in the presence of thousands, did not dare to breathe. Chilo was half dead. Caesar trembled and dropped the emerald from his fingers. The people, too, held their breath. The voice of Crispus was heard, as it rose in power, throughout the amphitheater, "Woe to you, murderer of wife and brother! Woe to you, Antichrist. The abyss is opening beneath you, death is stretching its hands to you, the grave is waiting for you. Woe, living corpse, for in terror shall you die and be damned to eternity!"

Unable to tear his hand from the cross, Crispus strained. He was terrible—a living, unbending skeleton; he shook his white beard over Nero's podium, scattering, as he nodded, rose leaves from the garland on his head.

"Woe to you, murderer! Your measure is surpassed, and your hour is at hand!"

Here he made one more effort. It seemed for a moment that he would free his hand from the cross and hold it in menace above Caesar; but all at once his emaciated arms extended still more, his body settled down, his head fell on his breast, and he died.

In that forest of crosses the weakest began the sleep of eternity.

58

"Lord," Chilo said, "the sea is like olive oil, the waves seem to sleep. Let us go to Achaea. There the glory of Apollo is awaiting you, crowns and triumph are awaiting you, the people will deify you, the gods will receive you as a guest, their own equal; but here, O lord—"

"We will go when the games are over," Nero replied.

Then he frowned and looked at Chilo, as if expecting an answer, for he only pretended to be cool. At the last exhibition he himself feared the words of Crispus; and when he had returned to the Palatine he could not sleep.

Then Vestinius, who heard their conversation in silence, looked around and said in a mysterious voice, "Listen, lord, to this old man. There is something strange in those Christians. Their deity gives them an easy death, but he may be vengeful."

"It was not I who arranged the games, but Tigellinus," Nero replied.

"True! It was I," Tigellinus added, who heard Caesar's answer, "and I jeer at all Christian gods. Vestinius is a man full of prejudices, and this valiant Greek is ready to die of terror at sight of a hen with feathers up in defense of her chickens."

"True!" Nero said. "But from now on command them to cut

the tongues out of Christians and stop their mouths."

"Fire will stop them, O divinity."

"Woe is me!" Chilo groaned.

But Caesar, to whom the insolent confidence of Tigellinus gave courage, began to laugh and said, pointing to the old Greek, "See how the descendant of Achilles looks!"

Indeed Chilo looked terrible. The remnant of hair on his head had grown white; on his face was fixed an expression of some immense dread. Often he gave no answer to questions; then again he became so angry the Augustians preferred not to attack him.

"Do what you like with me, but I will not go to the games!" he cried in desperation.

Nero looked on him for a while and, turning to Tigellinus, said, "See that this Stoic is near me in the gardens. I want to see what impression our torches will make on him."

Chilo was afraid of the threat that quivered in Caesar's voice. "O lord," he said, "I shall see nothing, for I cannot see in the nighttime."

"The night will be as bright as day," Caesar replied, with a threatening laugh.

Turning then to the Augustians, Nero talked about races he intended to have when the games were over.

Petronius approached Chilo and said, "Have I not said that you would not survive?"

"I wish to drink," Chilo said, stretching his trembling hand toward a goblet of wine; but he was unable to raise it to his lips. Seeing this, Vestinius took the vessel; but later he came near them and asked with a frightened voice, "Are the Furies pursuing you?"

The old man looked at him with open mouth, as if not understanding what he said. But Vestinius repeated it. "Are the Furies pursuing you?"

"No," Chilo answered, "but night is before me."

"Night? May the gods have mercy on you."

"Night, ghastly and impenetrable, in which something is moving, something coming toward me; but I do not know what it is, and I am terrified."

"Are you sorry for the Christians?"

"Why do you shed so much blood? Have you heard what that one said from the cross? Woe to us!"

427

"I heard," Vestinius answered, in a low voice. "But they are rebels."

"Not true!"

"And enemies of the human race."

"Not true!"

"And poisoners of water."

"Not true!"

"And murderers of children."

"Not true!"

"How?" Vestinius asked, with astonishment. "You have said so yourself, and betrayed them into the hands of Tigellinus."

"Therefore night has surrounded me, and death is coming toward me. At times it seems to me that I am dead already, and you also."

"No! It is they who are dying; we are alive. But tell me, what do they see when they are dying?"

"Christ."

"That is their god. Is he a mighty god?"

But Chilo answered with a question. "What kind of torches are to burn in the gardens? Have you heard what Caesar said?"

"I heard, and I know. They are made by arraying men in painful shirts steeped in tar and binding them to pillars, to which fire is set afterward. May their god not send misfortune on the city. That is a dreadful punishment."

Others also made comments about the Christians. Old Domitius Afer reviled them.

"There is such a large number of them," he said, "that they might begin a civil war; and, remember, there are fears that they might take weapons. But they die like sheep."

"Let them try to die otherwise!" Tigellinus said.

Petronius answered, "You deceive yourselves. They are armed with patience."

"That is a new kind of weapon."

"True. But can you say that they die like common criminals? No! They die as if the criminals were those who condemned them to death—that is, we and the whole Roman people."

"What raving!" Tigellinus said.

"You are the dullest of the dull," Petronius answered.

But others, struck by the justice of his remark, began to look at one another with astonishment and repeat, "True! There is something peculiar and strange in their death."

"I tell you that they see their divinity!" Vestinius cried, from one side.

Thereupon a number of Augustians turned to Chilo, "Old man, you know them well; tell us what they see."

The Greek spat out wine on his tunic and answered. "The resurrection." And he began to tremble so that the guests sitting nearby burst into loud laughter.

59

Vinicius had spent his nights away from home for some time. It occurred to Petronius that perhaps he had formed a new plan and was working to liberate Lygia from the Esquiline dungeon. He did not wish, however, to ask for fear that he might bring misfortune to the work. He had failed to snatch Lygia from the Mamertine prison, so he had ceased to believe in his good fortune.

The Esquiline prison, formed in a hurry from the cellars of houses knocked down to stop the fire, was not, it is true, so terrible as the old Tullianum near the Capitol, but it was a hundred times better guarded. Petronius understood perfectly that Lygia had been taken there only to escape death and not to escape the amphitheater, and that she was guarded carefully.

Evidently, he said to himself, *Caesar and Tigellinus have reserved her for some special spectacle, more dreadful than all others, and Vinicius is more likely to perish than rescue her.*

Vinicius, too, had lost hope of being able to free Lygia. Christ alone could do that. The young tribune now thought only of seeing her in prison.

For some time the knowledge that Nazarius had penetrated the Mamertine prison as a corpse-bearer had given him no peace, so he decided to try that method also.

The overseer of the "Putrid Pits," who had been bribed for an immense sum of money, admitted him at last among servants whom he sent nightly to prisons for corpses. The danger that Vinicius might be recognized was quite small. He went at night, dressed as a slave. Who would think that a patrician, the grandson of a consul and the son of another, could be found among servants, corpse-bearers, exposed to the stench of prisons and the "Putrid Pits"?

When the desired evening came, he dressed as a slave, covered his head with a cloth steeped in turpentine and, with a throbbing heart, went, with a crowd of others, to the Esquiline.

The praetorian guards gave him no trouble, for all had brought proper identification, which the centurion examined by the light of a lantern. The great iron doors opened before them, and they entered.

Vinicius saw an extensive vaulted cellar, from which they passed to a series of others. Dim candles illuminated the interior, which was filled with people. Some were lying by walls, sunk in sleep, or perhaps dead. Others surrounded large vessels of water, which stood in the middle, out of which they drank as people tormented with fever; others were sitting on the ground, their elbows on their knees, their heads on their palms. Here and there children were sleeping, nestled up to their mothers. Groans, the labored breathing of the sick, weeping, whispered prayers, hymns in an undertone, and the curses of overseers were heard round about. The odor of crowds and corpses was everywhere. In its gloomy depths dark figures were swarming; nearer, close to flickering lights, could be seen pale, terrified, and hungry faces. Their eyes were dim, or else flaming with fever, with blue lips and streams of sweat on their foreheads and in their clammy hair. In corners the sick were moaning loudly; some begged for water, others to be led to death. The legs bent under Vinicius when he saw all this. At the thought that Lygia was in the midst of this misery he stifled a cry of despair. The amphitheater, the teeth of wild beasts, the cross—anything was better than these dreadful dungeons filled with the odor of corpses.

"Lead us to death!" they cried.

Vinicius felt that he was growing weak and that his presence of mind was deserting him. All that he had felt until then, all his love and pain, changed in an instant to a single desire for death.

Just then he heard the overseer of the "Putrid Pits." "How many corpses have you today?"

"About a dozen," answered the guardian of the prison, "but there will be more before morning."

He complained of women who concealed dead children in order to keep them close and not release them to the "Putrid Pits." "We discover corpses by the odor first. I would rather be a slave in some rural prison than guard these dogs rotting here while alive."

The overseer of the pits comforted him, saying that his own service was no easier. By this time full consciousness had returned to Vinicius. He began to search the dungeon, but sought in vain for Lygia, fearing meanwhile that he would never see her alive. A number of cellars were connected by newly made passages; the corpse-bearers entered only those from which corpses were to be carried. Vinicius was afraid that the privilege that had cost so much trouble might serve no purpose. Luckily his patron aided him.

"Infection spreads most through corpses," he said. "You must carry out the bodies at once, or die yourselves, along with the prisoners."

"There are only ten of us for all the cellars," the guardian said, "and we must sleep."

"I will leave four men of mine, who will go through the cellars at night to see if there are any dead."

Four men were selected, among them Vinicius. The others put the corpses on the biers.

Vinicius was now certain at least of finding Lygia. The young tribune began by examining the first dungeon carefully; he looked into all the dark corners hard to reach by the light of his torch. He examined figures sleeping at the walls under coarse cloths; he saw that the most grievously ill were drawn apart into a corner. But he did not find Lygia. In a second and third dungeon his search was equally fruitless.

Meanwhile, the hour had grown late and all corpses had been carried out. The guards, positioning themselves in the corridors between cellars, were asleep; the children, wearied with crying, were silent; nothing was heard except breathing and the murmur of prayer.

Vinicius went with his torch to the fourth dungeon, which was considerably smaller. Searching with his light, he began to examine it, and it seemed to him that he saw, near a latticed opening in the wall, the gigantic form of Ursus. Then, blowing out the light, he approached him and asked, "Ursus, are you here?"

"Who are you?" the giant asked, turning his head.

"Do you not know me?"

"You have quenched the torch; how could I know you?"

But at that moment Vinicius saw Lygia lying on a cloak near the wall; so, without speaking further, he knelt near her. Ursus recognized him and said, "Praise be to Christ! But do not wake her, lord."

Vinicius, kneeling down, gazed at her through his tears. In spite of the darkness he could distinguish her face and her emaciated arms, which seemed to him as pale as alabaster. At that sight he was filled with a love that was like a rending pain, a love that shook his soul to its uttermost depth and that at the same time was so full of pity, respect, and homage that he fell on his face and kissed the hem of the cloak on which rested that head dearer to him than everything on earth.

Ursus looked at Vinicius for a long time in silence, but at last he pulled his tunic.

"Lord," he asked, "how did you come, and have you come here to save her?"

Vinicius rose, and struggled with his emotions. "Show me the means for escape," he replied.

"I thought that you would find them, lord. Only one method came to my mind—"

Here he turned toward the grating in the wall and said, "In that way—but there are soldiers outside—"

"A hundred praetorians."

"Then we cannot pass?"

"No!"

The Lygian rubbed his forehead and asked again, "How did you enter?"

"By permission from the overseer of the 'Putrid Pits.'" Then

Vinicius stopped suddenly, because an idea had flashed through his head.

"I will stay here. Let her take my clothing; she can wrap her head in a cloth, cover her shoulders with a mantle, and pass through. Among the slaves who carry out corpses there are several youths not full grown; so the praetorians will not take notice of her, and once she arrives at the house of Petronius she is safe."

But Ursus replied, "She would not consent, for she loves you; besides, she is sick and unable to stand alone. If you and the noble Petronius cannot save her from prison, who can?" he said.

"Christ alone."

Then both were silent.

Christ could save all Christians, the Lygian thought in his simple heart, *but since He does not save them, it is clear that the hour of torture and death has come.*

He accepted it for himself but was grieved to the depth of his soul for Lygia, who had grown up in his arms and whom he loved beyond life.

Vinicius knelt again near Lygia. Through the grating in the wall moonbeams came in and gave better light than the one candle burning over the entrance. Lygia opened her eyes now and said, placing her feverish hand on the arm of Vinicius, "I see you; I knew that you would come."

He took her hands, pressed them to his forehead and his heart, raised her up, and held her to his breast.

"I have come, dearest. May Christ guard and free you, beloved Lygia!"

He could say no more, for his heart ached from pain and love, and he would not show pain in her presence.

"I am sick, Marcus," Lygia said, "and I must die either on the arena or here in prison—I have prayed to see you before death; you have come—Christ has heard me."

Unable to utter a word yet, he pressed her to his chest, and she continued. "I saw you through the window in the Tullianum. I knew that you had the wish to come to me. Now the Redeemer has given me a moment of awareness, so that we may take farewell of each other. I am going to Him, Marcus, but I love you and shall always love you."

Vinicius conquered himself; he stifled his pain to speak in a calm voice. "No, dear Lygia, you will not die. The apostle commanded me to believe, and he promised to pray for you. He knew Christ—Christ loved him and will not refuse him. Had you to die, Peter would not have commanded me to be confident; but he said, 'Have confidence!' No, Lygia! Christ will have mercy. He does not wish your death. He will not permit it. I swear to you by the name of the Redeemer that Peter is praying for you."

Silence followed. The one candle hanging above the entrance went out, but moonlight entered through the whole opening. In the opposite corner of the cellar a child whined and was silent. From outside came the voices of praetorians, who, after their watch, were playing dice under the wall.

"O Marcus," Lygia said, "Christ Himself called to the Father, 'Remove this bitter cup from Me'; still, He drank it. Christ Himself died on the cross, and thousands are perishing for His sake. Why, then, should He spare me alone? Who am I, Marcus? I have heard Peter say that he, too, would die in torture. Who am I, compared with Peter? When the praetorians came to us, I dreaded death and torture, but I dread them no longer. See what a terrible prison this is, but I am going to heaven. Think of it: Caesar is here, but there is the Redeemer, kind and merciful. And there is no death there. You loved me; think, then, how happy I shall be. Oh, dear Marcus, you will come to me there."

Here she stopped to catch her breath and then raised his hand to her lips. "Marcus?"

"What, dear one?"

"Do not weep for me, and remember this—you will come to me. I have lived a short time, but God gave your soul to me; so I shall tell Christ that though I died, and you watched my death, though you were left in grief, you did not blaspheme against His will, and that you loved Him always. You will love Him and endure my death patiently, won't you? For then He will unite us. I love you, and I wish to be with you."

Breath failed her then, and in a barely audible voice she finished, "Promise me this, Marcus!"

Vinicius embraced her with trembling arms and said, "By your sacred head! I promise."

Her pale face became radiant in the sad light of the moon, and once more she raised his hand to her lips and whispered, "I am your wife!"

Beyond the wall the praetorians playing dice loudly disputed; but Vinicius and Lygia forgot the prison, the guards, the world; and, feeling as if they were angels, they began to pray.

60

For three days, or rather three nights, nothing disturbed their peace. When the usual prison work was finished, which consisted of separating the dead from the living and the very sick from those in better health, when the wearied guards had lain down to sleep in the corridors, Vinicius entered Lygia's dungeon and remained there until daylight. She put her head on his breast, and they talked in low voices of love and of death. In thought and speech, in desires and hopes, both were removed more and more from this life, and they lost the awareness of it. Both were like people who, having sailed from land in a ship, saw the shore no more and were sinking gradually into infinity. Both changed by degrees into sad souls in love with each other and with Christ, and ready to fly away. Only at times did pain well up in the heart of Vinicius like a whirlwind; at times there flashed in him like lightning, hope, born of love and faith in the crucified God; but he tore himself away from this earth and yielded to the possibility of death.

In the morning, when he left the prison, he looked on the world, on the city, on acquaintances, on his vital interests, as if they were a dream. Everything seemed to him strange, distant, vain, fleeting. Even torture ceased to terrify him, since one might pass through it while sunk in thought and with eyes fixed on other things. It seemed to both that eternity had begun to receive them. They talked of how they would love and live together, but beyond the grave. If their thoughts returned to the earth at times, these were thoughts of people who, setting out on a long journey, speak of preparations for the road. Their only concern was that Christ should not separate them; and at each moment their conviction was strengthened that He would not. They loved Him as a link uniting them in endless happiness and peace. The soul of each was as pure as a tear. Under terror of death, amid misery and suffering, in that prison den, heaven had begun, for she had taken him by the hand and, as if saved and a saint, had led him to the source of endless life.

Petronius was astonished at seeing in the face of Vinicius increasing peace and a certain wonderful serenity he had not noted before. At times he even supposed that Vinicius had found some mode of rescue, and he was curious because his nephew had not confided his hopes to him. At last, unable to restrain himself, he said, "Now you have a new attitude; do not keep secrets from me, for I wish and am able to aid you. Have you arranged anything?"

"I have," said Vinicius, "but you cannot help me. After her death I will confess that I am a Christian and follow her."

"Then you have no hope?"

"On the contrary, I have. Christ will give her to me, and I shall never be separated from her."

Petronius began to walk in the atrium. Disillusion and impatience were evident on his face.

"Your Christ is not needed for this—our Thanatos [death god] can render the same service."

Vinicius smiled sadly and said, "No, my dear uncle, you are unwilling to understand."

"I am unwilling and unable. It is not the time for discussion, but remember what I said when we failed to free her from the Tullianum. I lost all hope, and on the way home you said, 'But I believe that Christ can restore her to me.' Let Him restore her. If I throw a costly goblet into the sea, no god of ours can give it back to me; if yours is no better, I do not know why I should honor Him beyond the old ones."

"But He will restore her to me."

Petronius shrugged his shoulders. "Do you know," he asked, "that Christians are to illuminate Caesar's gardens tomorrow?"

"Tomorrow?" repeated Vinicius.

And in view of the near and dreadful reality his heart trembled with pain and fear. *This is the last night, perhaps, that I can spend with Lygia,* he thought. So bidding farewell to Petronius, he went hurriedly to the overseer of the "Putrid Pits" for his disguise. But disappointment was in waiting—the overseer would not give it to him.

"Pardon me," he said, "I have done what I could for you, but I cannot risk my life. Tonight they are to conduct the Christians to Caesar's gardens. The prisons will be full of soldiers and officials. Should you be recognized, I and my children would be lost."

Vinicius understood that it would be vain to insist. He hoped, however, that the soldiers who had seen him before would admit him even without a disguise; so, with the coming of night, he disguised himself as usual in the tunic of a corpse-bearer and, winding a cloth around his head, took himself to the prison.

But that day the corpse garments were checked with greater care than usual; and what was more, the centurion Scevinus, a strict soldier, devoted soul and body to Caesar, recognized Vinicius. But evidently in his iron-clad breast there glimmered yet some spark of pity for unfortunates. Instead of striking his spear in token of alarm, he led Vinicius aside and said, "Return to your house, lord. I recognize you; but not wishing your ruin, I am silent. I cannot admit you; go your way, and may the gods send you comfort."

"You cannot admit me," Vinicius said, "but let me stand here and look at those who are led forth."

"My order does not forbid that," Scevinus said.

Vinicius stood before the gate and waited. About midnight the prison gate opened wide and whole ranks of prisoners appeared—men, women, and children, surrounded by armed praetorians. The night was very bright; so it was possible to distinguish not only the forms, but the faces of the prisoners. They went two abreast, in a long, gloomy train, amid stillness broken only by the clatter of weapons. So many were led out that it seemed all the dungeons must be empty. In the rear of the line Vinicius saw Glaucus the physician distinctly, but Lygia and Ursus were not among the condemned.

61

Darkness had not yet arrived when the first waves of people began to flow into Caesar's gardens. The crowds, in holiday costume, crowned with flowers, singing, and some of them drunk, were going to look at the new, magnificent spectacle. Shouts of all sorts were heard on the Via Tecta, from the other side of the Tiber, on the Triumphal Way, around the Circus of Nero, and off towards the Vatican Hill. In Rome people had been seen burned on pillars before, but no one had ever seen such a number of victims.

Caesar and Tigellinus hoped to finish at once with the Christians and avoid general infection, which was spreading from the prisons throughout the city. Caesar commanded them to empty all the dungeons, so that only a few people intended for the close of the spectacles remained. So, when the crowds had passed the gates, they were dumb with amazement. All the main and side alleys, dense groves, lawns, thickets, ponds, fields, and squares filled with flowers were packed with pillars smeared with pitch, to which Christians were fastened. In higher places, where the view was not hindered by trees, one could see whole rows of pillars and bodies decked with flowers, myrtle, and ivy, extending into the distance. Though the nearest victims were like masts of ships, the farthest seemed like colored darts, or staffs thrust into the earth. The huge number of victims surpassed the wildest expectation of the multitude. One might suppose that a whole nation had been lashed to pillars for Rome's and Caesar's amusement. The throng of spectators halted before single masts when their curiosity was roused by the form or the sex of the victim. They looked at the faces, the crowns, the garlands of ivy, and asked, "Could there have been so many criminals, or how could children barely able to walk have set fire to Rome?" and their astonishment contained an element of fear.

Meanwhile, darkness came, and the first stars twinkled in the sky. Near each condemned person a slave took his place, torch in hand. When the sound of trumpets was heard in various parts of the gardens, signaling that the spectacle was to begin, each slave set fire with his torch to the foot of a pillar. The straw, hidden under the flowers and steeped in pitch, burned at once with a bright flame that, increasing every instant, withered the ivy, and rising, burned the feet of the victims. The people were terrified; the gardens resounded with one immense groan and with cries of pain. Some victims, however, raising their faces toward the starry sky, began to sing, praising Christ. The people listened with awe. But the hardest hearts were filled with terror when, on small pillars, children cried with shrill voices, "Mamma! Mamma!" A shiver ran through even spectators who were drunk when they saw little heads and innocent faces distorted with pain, or children fainting in the smoke that began to stifle them.

But the flames rose, and every instant reached new crowns of roses and ivy. The main and side alleys were illuminated; the groups of trees, the lawns, and the flowery squares were bright; the water in pools and ponds was gleaming, the trembling leaves on the trees had grown rose-colored, and all was as visible as in daylight. When the odor of burned bodies filled the gardens, slaves sprinkled myrrh and aloes between the pillars. In the crowds shouts were heard—whether of sympathy or delight and joy was unknown. They increased every moment when the fire, which embraced the pillars, climbed to the breasts of the victims, shriveled with burning breath the hair on their heads, threw veils over their blackened faces, and then shot up higher, as if showing the victory and triumph of the power that had commanded it.

At the very beginning of the spectacle Caesar had appeared among the people in a magnificent square of the Circus, drawn by four white steeds. He was dressed as a charioteer in the color of the Greens, that is, the color of the court party. Other chariots followed, filled with courtiers in brilliant array, senators, priests, revelers, naked and crowned, holding pitchers of wine, and partly drunk, uttering wild shouts. At the side of these were musicians dressed as fauns and satyrs, who played on citharae, formingas, flutes, and horns. In other chariots matrons and maidens of Rome advanced, drunk also and half-naked. Around the chariots ran men who shook tambourines ornamented with ribbons; others beat drums; others scattered flowers.

The brilliant throng moved forward, shouting, on the widest road of the garden, amid smoke and processions of people. Caesar had Tigellinus near him, and also Chilo, in whose terror he hoped to find amusement. He drove the steeds himself and, advancing at a walking pace, looked at the burning bodies and heard the shouts of the multitude. Standing on the lofty gilded chariot, surrounded by a sea of people who bowed to his feet, in the glitter of the fire, in the golden crown of a circus-victor, he was a head above the courtiers and the crowd. He seemed a giant. His immense arms, stretched forward to hold the reins, seemed to bless the multitude. There was a smile on his face and in his blinking eyes; he shone above the throng as a sun or a deity, terrible but commanding and mighty.

At times he stopped to look with more care at some maiden who had begun to shrink in the flames, or at the face of a child distorted by convulsions; and again he drove on, leading behind him a wild, excited retinue. At times he bowed to the people, then again he bent backward, drew in the golden reins, and spoke to Tigellinus. At last, when he had reached the great fountain in the middle of two cross streets, he stepped from the chariot and, nodding to his attendants, mingled with the crowd.

He was greeted with shouts and compliments. The bacchic dancers, nymphs, senators and Augustians, priests, fauns, satyrs, and soldiers surrounded him at once in an excited circle; but he, with Tigellinus on one side and Chilo on the other, walked around the fountain, around which were burning some tens of torches; stopping before each one. He made remarks about the victims, or jeered at the old Greek, on whose face boundless despair was seen.

At last he stood before a lofty mast decked with myrtle and ivy. The red tongues of fire had risen only to the knees of the victim; but it was impossible to see his face, for the green burning twigs had covered it with smoke. After a while, however, the light breeze of night turned away the smoke and uncovered the head of a man with a gray beard falling down to his chest.

At the sight of him Chilo was twisted into a lump like a wounded snake, and from his mouth came a cry more like cawing than a human voice.

"Glaucus! Glaucus!"

In fact, Glaucus the physician looked down from the burning pillar at him.

Glaucus was yet alive. His face expressed pain and was leaning forward, as if to look closely for the last time at his executioner, at the man who had betrayed him, robbed him of wife and
children, set a murderer on him, and who, when all this had been
forgiven in the name of Christ, delivered him to executioners. Never had one person inflicted more dreadful or bloody wrongs on
another. Now the victim was burning on the pitched pillar, and
the executioner was standing at his feet. The eyes of Glaucus did
not leave the face of the Greek. At moments they were hidden by
smoke; but when the breeze blew this away, Chilo saw again
those eyes fixed on him. He rose and tried to flee, but he did not
have the strength. All at once his legs seemed like lead; an invisible hand seemed to hold him at that pillar with superhuman
force. He was petrified. He felt that something was overflowing in
him, something giving way. He felt that he had had an overdose of
blood and torture, that the end of his life was approaching, that
everything was vanishing. Caesar, the court, the multitude was
only a kind of bottomless, dreadful black vacuum with no visible
thing in it, except those eyes of a martyr, which were calling him
to judgment. But Glaucus, bending his head lower, looked at him
intently. Those present realized that something was taking place
between the two men. Laughter died on their lips, however, for in
Chilo's face there was something terrible; such pain and fear had
distorted it as if those tongues of fire were burning his body. Suddenly he staggered and, stretching his arms upward, cried in a
terrible and piercing voice, "Glaucus! In Christ's name! Forgive
me!"

It grew silent around him, a quiver ran through the spectators, and all eyes were raised involuntarily.

The head of the martyr moved slightly, and from the top of
the mast a voice like a groan was heard. "I forgive!"

Chilo threw himself on his face and howled like a wild beast;
grasping earth in both hands, he sprinkled it on his head. Meanwhile, the flames shot up, seizing the breast and face of Glaucus.
They unbound the myrtle crown on his head and grabbed the ribbons on the top of the great, blazing pillar.

Chilo stood up after a while with a face so changed that to
the Augustians he seemed another man. His eyes flashed with a

new light, ecstasy came from his wrinkled forehead. The Greek, incoherent a short time before, looked now like some priest visited by a divinity and ready to reveal unknown truths.

"What is the matter? Has he gone mad?" asked a number of voices.

But he turned to the multitude and, raising his right hand, shouted, in a voice so piercing that not only the Augustians but the entire multitude heard him, "Roman people! I swear by my death that innocent persons are perishing here. That is the cause. Traitor!"

And he pointed his finger at Nero.

Then came a moment of silence. The courtiers were awe-struck. Chilo continued to stand with outstretched, trembling arm, and with his finger pointed at Nero. All at once a tumult arose. The people, like a wave, urged by a sudden whirlwind, rushed toward the old man to look at him more closely. Here and there were heard cries, "Hold him!" In another place, "Woe to us!" In the crowd a hissing and uproar began. "Ahenobarbus! Matricide! Traitor!" Disorder increased every instant. The revelers screamed in heaven-piercing voices and began to hide in the chariots. Then some pillars that were burned through, fell, scattered sparks, and increased the confusion. A blind, dense wave of people swept Chilo away and took him to the depth of the garden.

The pillars began to burn through in every direction and fall across the streets, filling alleys with smoke, sparks, and the odor of burned wood and flesh. The closer lights died out. The gardens began to grow dark. The crowds, alarmed and angry, pressed toward the gates. News of what had happened passed from one to another and became distorted. Some said that Caesar had fainted; others that he had confessed, saying that he had given the order to burn Rome; others said that he had fallen seriously ill; and still others said that he had been carried out, as if dead, in the chariot.

Voices of sympathy for the Christians were heard here and there: "If they had not burned Rome, why so much blood, torture, and injustice? Will not the gods avenge the innocent, and what can mollify them now?" Women expressed their pity aloud for children thrown in such numbers to wild beasts, nailed to crosses, or burned in those cursed gardens! Finally, pity was turned

442

into abuse of Caesar and Tigellinus. There were persons, also, who, stopping suddenly, asked themselves or others the question, "What kind of divinity is that which gives such strength to meet torture and death?" And they returned home in deep thought.

But Chilo was wandering about in the gardens, not knowing where to go or where to turn. Again he felt himself a weak, helpless, sick old man.

Now he stumbled against a party of burned bodies; now he struck a torch, which sent a shower of sparks after him; now he sat down and looked around with a vacant stare. The gardens had become almost dark. The pale moon moving among the trees shone with an uncertain light on the alleys, the dark pillars lying across them, and the partly burned victims turned into shapeless lumps. But the old Greek thought that in the moon he saw the face of Glaucus, whose eyes were looking at him yet persistently, and he hid himself from the light. At last he went out of the shadow, in spite of himself; as if pushed by some hidden power, he turned toward the fountain where Glaucus had yielded up his spirit.

Then a hand touched his shoulder. He turned and saw an unknown person before him.

"Who are you?" he exclaimed, with terror.

"Paul of Tarsus."

"I am cursed! What do you wish?"

"I wish to save you," the apostle answered.

Chilo supported himself against a tree. His legs bent under him, and his arms hung parallel with his body.

"For me there is no salvation," he said in despair.

"Have you heard how God forgave the thief on the cross who pitied Him?" Paul asked.

"Do you know what I have done?"

"I saw your suffering and heard your testimony to the truth."

"O lord!"

"And if a servant of Christ forgave you in the hour of torture and death, why should Christ not forgive you?"

Chilo seized his head with both hands, in bewilderment.

"Forgiveness! For me, forgiveness!"

"Our God is a God of mercy," Paul said.

"For me?" Chilo repeated; and he began to groan like a man

who lacks strength to control his pain and suffering.

"Lean on me," Paul said, "and go with me."

And, taking him, he went to the cross streets, guided by the voice of the fountain, which seemed to weep in the night stillness over the bodies of those who had died in torture.

"Our God is a God of mercy," the apostle repeated. "Were you to stand at the sea and cast pebbles into it, could you fill its depth with them? I tell you that the mercy of Christ is as the sea, and that the sins and faults of men sink in it as pebbles in the abyss; I tell you that it is like the sky that covers mountains, lands, and seas, for it is everywhere and has neither end nor limit. You have suffered at the pillar of Glaucus. Christ saw your suffering. Without reference to what may meet you tomorrow, you did say, 'That is the traitor,' and Christ remembers your words. Your malice and falsehood are gone; in your heart is left only boundless sorrow. Follow me and listen to what I say. I am he who hated Christ and persecuted His chosen ones. I did not want Him, I did not believe in Him until He revealed Himself and called me. Since then He is, for me, mercy. He has visited you with repentance, alarm, and pain to call you to Himself. You hated Him, but He loved you. You delivered His confessors to torture, but He wishes to forgive and save you."

The wretched man sobbed immensely, sobbed to the depths of his soul; but Paul took possession of him, mastered him, led him away as a soldier leads a captive.

After a while the apostle began again to speak. "Come with me; I will lead you to Him. For why else have I come to you? Christ commanded me to gather in souls in the name of love; so I perform His service. You think yourself accursed, but I say: Believe in Him, and salvation awaits you. You think that you are hated, but I repeat that He loves you. Look at me. Before I had Him I had nothing except malice, which dwelt in my heart, and now His love satisfies me instead of father and mother, wealth and power. In Him alone is refuge. He alone will see your sorrow, believe in your misery, remove your alarm, and raise you to Himself."

Thus speaking, he lead him to the fountain, the silver stream gleaming in the moonlight. Round about was silence; the gardens were empty, for slaves had removed the charred pillars and the bodies of the martyrs.

Chilo threw himself on his knees with a groan and, hiding his face in his hands, remained motionless. Paul raised his face to the stars. "O Lord," he prayed, "look on this wretched man, on his sorrow, his tears, and his suffering! O God of mercy, who shed Your blood for our sins, forgive him, through Your torment, Your death, and Your resurrection!"

Then he was silent; but for a long time he looked toward the stars and prayed.

Meanwhile, from under his feet a cry was heard that resembled a groan, "O Christ! O Christ! Forgive me!"

Paul approached the fountain then, and, taking water in his hand, turned to the kneeling wretch. "Chilo!—I baptize you in the name of the Father, Son, and Spirit. Amen!"

Chilo raised his head, opened his arms, and remained in that posture. The moon shone with full light on his white hair and on his equally white face, which was as motionless as if dead or cut out of stone. The moments passed one after another. From the great aviaries in the gardens of Domitian came the crowing of cocks; but Chilo remained kneeling, like a statue on a monument. As last he recovered, spoke to the apostle, and asked, "What am I to do before death?"

Paul was roused also from meditation on the measureless power that even such spirits as that of this Greek could not resist and answered, "Have faith, and bear witness to the truth."

They went out together. At the gate the apostle blessed the old man again, and they parted. Chilo himself insisted that they part, for after what had happened he knew that Caesar and Tigellinus would order that he himself be pursued.

Indeed he was not mistaken. When he returned home, he found the house surrounded by praetorians, who led him away and took him to the Palatine.

Caesar had gone to rest, but Tigellinus was waiting. When he saw the unfortunate Greek, he greeted him with a calm but threatening face.

"You have committed the crime of treason," he said, "and

you will be punished; but tomorrow if you testify in the amphitheater that you were drunk and foolish, and that the originators of the great fire were Christians, your punishment will be limited to stripes and exile."

"I cannot do that," Chilo answered calmly.

Tigellinus approached him with slow step. "How is that?" he asked. "You cannot, Greek dog? Were you not drunk, and do you not understand what is waiting for you? Look there!" And he pointed to a corner of the atrium in which, near a long, wooden bench, stood four Thracian slaves in the shade with ropes, and with pincers in their hands.

But Chilo answered, "I cannot!"

Rage filled Tigellinus, but he still restrained himself.

"Have you seen how Christians die? Do you wish to die in that way?"

The old man raised his pale face; his lips moved in silence, and he answered, "I too believe in Christ."

Tigellinus looked at him with amazement.

"Dog, you have gone mad!"

And suddenly his rage broke its bounds. Springing at Chilo, he caught him by the beard with both hands, hurled him to the floor, trampled him, repeating, with foam on his lips, "You will retract! You will!"

"I cannot!" Chilo answered from the floor.

"To the tortures with him!"

The Thracians seized the old man and placed him on the bench; then, fastening him with ropes to it they began to squeeze his thin shanks with pincers. But when they were tying him he kissed their hands with humility; then he closed his eyes and seemed dead.

He was alive, though; for when Tigellinus bent over him and asked once again, "Will you retract?" his white lips moved slightly and he whispered, "I cannot."

Tigellinus gave the command to stop the torture and began to walk up and down in the atrium, with a face distorted by anger, but helpless. At last a new idea came to his head, for he turned to the Thracians and said, "Tear out his tongue!"

62

The drama "Aureolus" was usually given in theaters so arranged that they could open and present two separate stages. But after the spectacle in the gardens of Caesar the usual method was omitted; for in this case the problem was to let the greatest number of people look at a slave who, in the drama, is devoured by a bear. In the theaters the role of the bear was played by an actor sewed up in a skin, but this time the representation was to be real. This was a new idea of Tigellinus. At first Caesar refused to come, but changed his mind at the persuasion of his favorite courtier. Tigellinus explained that after what had happened in the gardens it was all the more his duty to appear before the people, and he guaranteed that the crucified slave would not insult him as had Crispus. The people were somewhat satisfied and tired of blood-spilling; so a new distribution of lottery tickets and gifts were promised, as well as a feast. The spectacle was to be in the evening, in a brilliantly lighted amphitheater.

About dusk the whole amphitheater was packed; the Augustians came to a man, with Tigellinus at the head of them, not only for the spectacle itself, but to show their devotion to Caesar and their opinion of Chilo, of whom all Rome was then talking.

They whispered to one another that Caesar, when returning from the gardens, had fallen into a frenzy and could not sleep, that terrible visions had attacked him; so he had announced on the following morning his early journey to Achaea. But others denied this, saying that he would be ever more pitiless toward the Christians. Finally, there were those who through compassion begged Tigellinus to stop the persecution.

"See where you are going," Barcus Soranus said. "You wished to slow people's anger and convince them that punishment was falling on the guilty; the result is just the opposite."

"True!" Antistius Verus added. "All whisper to one another now that the Christians were innocent. Chilo was right when he said that your brains could be hid in a nutshell."

Tigellinus turned to them and said, "Barcus Soranus, people whisper also to one another that your daughter Servilia removed her Christian slaves from Caesar's justice; they say the same also of your wife, Antistius."

"That is not true!" Barcus exclaimed with alarm.

"Your divorced women wished to ruin my wife, whose virtue they envy," Antistius Verus said, with no less alarm.

But others spoke of Chilo.

"What has happened to him?" asked Eprilus Marcellus. "He delivered them himself into the hands of Tigellinus; he was beggar, and now he is rich. It was possible for him to live out his days in peace, have a splendid funeral, and a tomb, but no! All at once he preferred to lose everything and destroy himself; he must, in truth, be a maniac."

"Not a maniac, but he has become a Christian," Tigellinus said.

"Impossible!" Vitelius said.

"Have I not said," put in Vestinius, "'Kill Christians if you like; but believe me you cannot conquer their divinity. With Him there is no jesting'? See what is taking place. I have not burned Rome; but if Caesar permitted it I would give a sacrifice at once to their divinity. And all should do the same, for I repeat: With Him there is no jesting! Remember my words to you."

"And I said something else," Petronius added. "Tigellinus laughed when I said that they were arming, but I say more—they are conquering."

"How is that?" said a number of voices.

"By Pollux, they are! For if such a man as Chilo could not resist them, who can? If you think that after every spectacle the Christians do not increase, you should become coppersmiths or go to shaving beards, for then you will know better what people think and what is happening in the city."

"He speaks pure truth, by the sacred peplus of Diana," Vestinius cried.

But Barcus turned to Petronius.

"What is your conclusion?"

"I conclude where you began—there has been enough of bloodshed."

Tigellinus looked at him and jeered. "Ei! A little more!"

"If your head is not sufficient, you have another on your cane," Petronius said.

Further conversation was interrupted by the coming of Caesar. Immediately after, "Aureolus" began, but not much attention was paid, for the minds of the audience were fixed on Chilo. The spectators, familiar with blood and torture, were bored; they hissed at the court and demanded the bear scene, which for them was the only thing of interest. Had it not been for gifts and the hope of seeing Chilo, the spectacle would not have held the audience.

At last the awaited moment came. Servants of the Circus brought a wooden cross in first, so low that a bear standing on his hind feet could reach the martyr's breast. Then two men brought, or rather dragged in, Chilo, for as the bones in his legs were broken, he was unable to walk alone. They laid him down and nailed him to the wood so quickly that the curious Augustians had not even a good look at him, and only after the cross had been fixed in the place prepared for it did all eyes turn to the victim.

But it was a rare person who could recognize in that naked man the former Chilo. As a result of the tortures Tigellinus had commanded, there was not one drop of blood in his face, and only on his white beard was a red trace left by blood after they had torn his tongue out. Through the transparent skin it was quite possible to see his bones. He seemed far older also, almost decrepit. Previously his eyes were filled with unrest and ill will, and his watchful face reflected alarm and uncertainty. Now his face had an expression of pain, but it was as mild and calm as faces of the sleeping or the dead. Perhaps remembrance of that thief on the cross whom Christ had forgiven gave him confidence. Perhaps, also, he said in his soul to the merciful God, *O Lord, I bit like a venomous worm; but all my life I was forsaken. I was famishing from hunger, people trampled on me, beat me, jeered at me. Now they put me to torture and nail me to a cross; but You, O Merciful, will not reject me in this hour!* Peace descended into his crushed heart. No one laughed, for there was in that crucified man something so calm, he seemed so old, so defenseless, so weak, calling so much for pity with his lowliness, that each one asked himself how it was possible to torture and nail to crosses men who would die soon in any case. The crowd was silent. Among the Augustians, Vestinius, bending to the right and left, whispered in a terrified voice, "See how they die!" Others were looking for the bear, wishing the spectacle to end early.

The bear came into the arena at last, and, swaying from side to side, he looked around as if thinking of something or seeking something. At last he saw the cross and the naked body. He approached it and stood on his hind legs; but after a moment he dropped again on his forepaws and, sitting under the cross, began to growl, as if in his heart of a beast there was pity for that remnant of a man.

Cries were heard from the Circus slaves urging on the bear, but the people were silent.

Chilo raised his head with slow motion and moved his eyes over the audience. At last his glance rested somewhere on the highest rows of the amphitheater; his breast moved with more life, and something happened that caused wonder. That face became bright with a smile; a ray of light circled his forehead; his eyes were uplifted before death, and two great tears that had risen between the lids flowed slowly down his face.

And he died.

At that same moment a resonant male voice high up under the theater awning exclaimed, "Peace to the martyrs!"

Deep silence reigned in the amphitheater.

63

After the spectacle in Caesar's gardens the prisons were considerably emptied. It is true that victims suspected of the supposed oriental superstition were still seized and imprisoned, but pursuit brought in fewer and fewer persons—barely enough for coming exhibitions, which were to follow quickly. People showed growing weariness and increasing alarm because of the holy conduct of the condemned. Fears like those of the superstitious Vestinius seized thousands of people. Among the crowds wonderful tales were related of the vengefulness of the Christian God. Prison diseases, which had spread through the city, increased the general dread. The large number of funerals was evident, and offerings were needed to mollify the unknown Christian god. Offerings were made in the temples to Jove and Libitina. Eventually, in spite of every effort of Tigellinus and his assistants, the opinion kept spreading that the city had been burned at the command of Caesar, and that the Christians were suffering innocently.

But for this very reason Nero and Tigellinus were untiring in persecution. To calm the multitude, fresh orders were made to distribute wheat, wine, and olives. To help homeowners, new rules were introduced to aid the building of houses. Caesar himself attended sessions of the Senate and counseled the "fathers" concerning the good of the people and the city; but no favor was shown to the Christians. The ruler of the world was anxious to convince people that such merciless punishment could be given only to the guilty. In the Senate no voice was heard on behalf of the Christians, for no one wished to offend Caesar; and besides, those who looked farther into the future insisted that the foundation of Roman rule could not withstand the new faith.

The dead and dying were given to their relatives, because Roman law took no vengeance on the dead. Vinicius received a certain comfort from the thought that if Lygia died he would bury her in his family tomb and rest near her. At that time he had no hope of rescuing her. Half separated from life, he himself was wholly absorbed in Christ and dreamed no longer of any union with her except an eternal one in heaven. His faith had become boundless, for eternity seemed something incomparably truer and more real than the fleeting life he had lived up to that time.

His heart was overflowing with enthusiasm for Christ. Though yet alive, he had changed into an almost immaterial being, which desiring complete liberation for itself, desired it also for his beloved. He imagined that when free he and Lygia would each take the other's hand and go to heaven, where Christ would bless them and let them live in light as peaceful and boundless as the light of the dawn. He merely begged Christ to spare Lygia the torments of

451

the Circus, and let her fall asleep calmly in prison. He felt with perfect certainty that he himself would die at the same time. In view of the sea of blood that had been shed, he did not even think that she alone would be spared. He had heard from Peter and Paul that they, too, must die as martyrs. The sight of Chilo on the cross had convinced him that even a martyr's death could be sweet; so he wished this for Lygia and himself. He saw this as a transformation of an evil and oppressive fate for a better one.

At times he felt he had a foretaste of life beyond the grave. The sadness that hung over both souls was losing its former burning bitterness and changing gradually into a kind of transterrestrial, calm abandon to the will of God. Vinicius, who formerly had struggled against the current and tortured himself, yielded now to the stream, believing that it would bear him to eternal calm. He sensed, too, that Lygia, as well as he, was preparing for death— that, in spite of the prison walls separating them, they were advancing together; and he smiled at that thought as at happiness.

To Lygia, death was presented not only as liberation from the terrible walls of the prison, from the hands of Caesar and Tigellinus—but as the hour of her marriage to Vinicius. In view of this unshaken certainty, all else lost importance. Her happiness would come after death. She waited for it as a betrothed woman waits for the wedding day.

That immense current of faith, which swept away from this life and took beyond the grave thousands of those first confessors, swept away Ursus also. He had not been resigned to Lygia's death, but when day after day through the prison walls came news of what was happening in the amphitheaters and the gardens, when death seemed the common, inevitable lot of all Christians and also their good, he did not dare to pray to Christ to deprive Lygia of that happiness. In his simple barbarian soul he thought, besides, that more of those heavenly delights would belong to the daughter of the Lygian chief, and that in eternal glory she would sit nearer to the Lamb than would others.

He had heard, it is true, that before God men are equal; but a conviction was lingering at the bottom of his soul that the daughter of the leader of all the Lygians was not the same as the first slave one might meet. He hoped also that Christ would let him continue to serve her. His one secret wish was to die on a cross as the Lamb died. But this seemed a happiness so great that he hardly dared to pray for it, thought he knew that in Rome even the worst criminals were crucified. He thought that surely he would be condemned to die devoured by the teeth of wild beasts; and this was his one sorrow.

From childhood he had lived in dense forests, amid continual hunts, in which, thanks to his superhuman strength, he was famous among the Lygians even before he had grown to manhood. This occupation had become for him so agreeable that later, when in Rome and forced to live without hunting, he went to amphitheaters just to look at beasts known and unknown to him. The sight of these always aroused in the man an irresistible desire for fighting and killing; so now he feared in his soul that on meeting them in the amphitheater he would be attacked by thoughts unworthy of a Christian, whose duty it was to die piously and patiently. But in this he committed himself to Christ. Hearing that the Lamb had declared war against the powers of hell and evil spirits with which the Christian faith connected all pagan divinities, he thought that in this war he might serve the Lamb greatly, for he could not help believing that his soul was stronger than the souls of other martyrs.

Finally, he prayed whole days, rendered service to prisoners, helped overseers, and comforted his queen, who complained at times that in her short life she had not been able to do so many good deeds as the renowned Tabitha, spoken of by Peter the apostle. Even the prison guards, who feared the terrible strength of this giant, since neither bars nor chains could restrain it, came to love him at last for his mildness. Amazed at his good temper, they asked more than once what its cause was. He spoke with such firm certainty of the life waiting after death for him, that they listened with surprise, seeing for the first time that happiness might penetrate a dungeon that sunlight could not reach. He urged them to believe in the Lamb.

Nonetheless, death brought fear at times, while that giant and that maiden, who was like a flower cast on the straw of the prison, went toward it with delight, as toward the gates of happiness.

64

One evening Scevinus, a senator, visited Petronius and began a long conversation about the unpleasant times in which they were living, and also concerning Caesar. He spoke so openly that Petronius, though his friend, began to be cautious. Scevinus complained that the world was living wickedly and unjustly, that all must end in some catastrophe more dreadful still than the burning of Rome. He said that even Augustians were dissatisfied; that Fenius Rufus, second prefect of the praetorians, only endured the vile orders of Tigellinus; and that all Seneca's relatives were opposed to Caesar's conduct. Finally, he began to hint of the dissatisfaction of the people, and even of the praetorians, the greater part of whom had been won by Fenius Rufus.

"Why do you say this?" Petronius asked.

"Out of concern for Caesar," Scevinus said. "I have a distant relative among the praetorians, also Scevinus; through him I know what takes place in the camp. Dissatisfaction is growing there also. Caligula, you know, was mad, too, and see what happened. Cassius Chaerea appeared. That was a dreadful deed, and surely there is no one among us who would praise it; nonetheless, Chaerea freed the world of a monster."

"Do you mean this: 'I do not praise Chaerea, but he was a perfect man, and I wish that the gods had given us as many such as him'?" Petronius asked.

But Scevinus changed the subject and began to praise Piso, exalting his family, nobility of mind, attachment to his wife, and, finally, his intellect, his calmness, and his wonderful gift of winning people.

"Caesar is childless," he said, "and everyone sees his successor in Piso. Everyone would wholeheartedly help him gain power. Fenius Rufus loves him; the relatives of Annaeus are devoted to him altogether. Plautius Lateranus and Tullius Senecio would jump into fire for him; as well as even Vestinius."

"From this last man not much will help Piso," Petronius replied. "Vestinius is afraid of his own shadow."

"Vestinius fears dreams and spirits," Scevinus answered,

"but he is a practical man, whom people wish wisely to make a consul. In his soul he is opposed to persecuting Christians, but you should not think badly of him, for is it not of concern to you too that this madness should end?"

"Not me, but Vinicius," Petronius answered. "Out of concern for Vinicius, I should like to save a certain girl; but I cannot, for I have fallen out of favor with Ahenobarbus."

"How is that? Do you not notice that Caesar is approaching you again and beginning to talk with you? And I will tell you why. He is preparing again for Achaea, where he is to sing songs in Greek of his own composition. He has a burning desire for that journey; but also he trembles at the thought of the cynical genius of the Greeks. He imagines that either the greatest triumph may meet him or the greatest failure. He needs good counsel, and he knows that no one can give it better than you. This is why you are returning to favor."

"Lucan might take my place."

"Bronzebeard hates Lucan, and in his soul has written down death for the poet. He is merely seeking a reason, for he always seeks reasons."

"By Castor!" Petronius said, "that may be. But I might have still another way for a quick return to favor."

"What?"

"To repeat to Bronzebeard what you have told me just now."

"I have said nothing!" Scevinus cried with alarm.

Petronius placed his hand upon the senator's shoulder. "You have called Caesar a madman, you have foreseen the heirship of Piso, and have said, 'Lucan understands that there is need to hurry.' What would you hasten, my friend?"

Scevinus grew pale, and for a moment each looked into the eyes of the other.

"You will not repeat it!"

"By the hips of Kypris, I will not! How well you know me! No, I will not repeat it. I have heard nothing, and, moreover, I wish to hear nothing. Do you understand? Life is too short to make any undertaking worth the while. I beg you only to visit Tigellinus today and talk with him as long as you have with me of whatever may please you."

"Why?"

"So that should Tigellinus ever say to me, 'Scevinus was with you,' I might answer, 'He was with you, too, that very day.'"

When Scevinus heard this, he broke the ivory cane he had in his hand and said, "May the evil fall on this stick! I shall be with Tigellinus today, and later at Nerva's feast. You, too, will be there? Farewell, until we meet in the amphitheater, where the last of the Christians will appear the day after tomorrow."

"After tomorrow!" Petronius repeated when he was alone. "There is not time to lose. Ahenobarbus will really need me in Achaea; so he may stay on my side."

And he determined to try a final means of escape for Lygia.

In fact, at Nerva's feast Caesar himself asked that Petronius recline opposite him, for he wished to speak with the arbiter about Achaea and the cities in which he might appear with hopes of the greatest success. He cared most for the Athenians, whom he feared. Other Augustians listened to this conversation with attention, so as to seize crumbs of the arbiter's opinions and give them out later on as their own.

"It seems to me that I have not lived up to this time," Nero said, "and that my birth will come only in Greece."

"You will be born to new glory and immortality," Petronius answered.

"I trust that this is true and that Apollo will not seem jealous. If I return in triumph, I will offer him such a sacrifice as no god has had so far.

"The ship is ready at Naples," Caesar said. "I should like to go tomorrow."

At this Petronius rose and, looking straight into Nero's eyes, said, "Permit me, O divinity, to celebrate a wedding feast, to which I shall invite you before others."

"What wedding feast?" Nero asked.

"That of Vinicius with your hostage the daughter of the Lygian king. She is in prison at present, it is true; but as a hostage she is not subject to imprisonment, and, secondly, you yourself have permitted Vinicius to marry her; and as your sentences, like those of Zeus, are unchangeable, you will give a command to free her from prison, and I will give her to your favorite."

The cool blood and calm self-possession with which Petronius spoke discomforted Nero, who was disturbed whenever anyone spoke in that fashion to him.

"I know," he said, dropping his eyes. "I have thought of her and of that giant who killed Croton."

"In that case both are saved," Petronius answered calmly.

But Tigellinus came to the aid of his master. "She is in prison by the will of Caesar; you yourself have said, Petronius, that his sentences are unchangeable."

All present, knowing the history of Vinicius and Lygia, understood perfectly what the question was; so they were silent, curious as to the outcome of the conversation.

"She is in prison against the will of Caesar and through your error, through your ignorance of the law of nations," Petronius said, with emphasis. "You are a naive man, Tigellinus; but even you will not assert that she burned Rome, and if you were to do so, Caesar would not believe you."

But Nero had recovered and begun to half close his nearsighted eyes with an expression of indescribable malice.

"Petronius is right," he said, after a while.

Tigellinus looked at him with amazement.

"Petronius is right," Nero repeated. "Tomorrow the gates of the prison will be opened to her, and we will speak of the marriage feast the day after at the amphitheater."

I have lost again, Petronius thought.

When he had returned home, he was so certain that the end of Lygia's life had come that he sent a trusty freedman to the amphitheater to bargain with the chief for the delivery of her body, since he wished to give it to Vinicius.

65

Evening exhibitions, given only exceptionally, became common in Nero's time, both in the Circus and amphitheater. The Augustians liked them, because they were frequently followed by feasts and drinking bouts that lasted until daylight. When the news spread that the end of the games was approaching, and that the last of the Christians were to die at an evening spectacle, a countless audience assembled in the amphitheater. The Augustians came to a man, for they understood that it would not be a common spectacle; they knew that Caesar had determined to create a tragedy out of the suffering of Vinicius. Tigellinus had kept secret the kind of punishment intended for the betrothed of the young tribune; but that merely aroused general curiosity. Those who had seen Lygia at the house of Plautus told wonders of her beauty. Others were occupied above all with the question, Would they really see her in the arena that day? For many of those who had heard the answer given to Petronius and Nerva by Caesar explained it in two ways. Some supposed simply that Nero would give the maiden to Vinicius. They remembered that she was a hostage, and thus free to worship whatever divinities she liked, and that the law of nations did not permit her punishment.

Uncertainty and curiosity had consumed all spectators. Caesar arrived earlier than usual; and immediately at his coming people whispered that something uncommon would happen, for besides Tigellinus and Vatinius, Caesar had with him Cassius, a centurion of enormous size and gigantic strength, whom he summoned only when he wished to have a defender at his side—for example, when he desired night expeditions to the Subura, where he arranged for an amusement that consisted of tossing on a soldier's mantle maidens met on the way. It was noted also that certain precautions had been taken in the amphitheater itself. Caesar wished in every case to guard himself against an outburst of despair from Vinicius, and so curiosity rose all the more.

Every eye strained to gaze at the place where the unfortunate lover was sitting. He was exceedingly pale, and his forehead was covered with drops of sweat; he was in as much doubt as were other spectators, but alarmed to the depth of his soul. Petronius did not know what would happen; he was silent, except that he asked Vinicius whether he was ready for everything, and next, whether he would remain at the spectacle. Vinicius answered "Yes" to both questions, but a shudder passed through his whole body; he realized that Petronius did not ask without reason.

For some time he had reconciled himself to Lygia's death, since for both it was to be liberation and marriage; but he learned now that it was one thing to think of the last moment when it was distant and another to look at the torment of a person dearer to one than life. All sufferings formerly endured rose in him again. Despair began again to wail in his soul; the former desire to save Lygia at any price seized him again. In the morning, he had tried to go to the prison to be sure that she was there; but the praetorian guards watched every entrance, and orders were so strict that the soldiers, even those whom he knew, would not be softened by prayers or gold.

It seemed to the tribune that uncertainty would kill him before he saw the spectacle. Somewhere at the bottom of his heart the hope was still throbbing that perhaps Lygia was not in the amphitheater, that his fears were groundless. He believed in his soul that Christ might take her to Himself from the prison but would not permit her torture in the Circus. He was resigned before to the divine will in everything; now, when not admitted to the doors of the prison, he returned to his place in the amphitheater. When he understood, from the curious glances turned on him, that his most dreadful fears might be true, he began to call on Christ with a passionateness that almost approached a threat. "You can!" he repeated, clenching his fists convulsively.

He had the feeling that if he should see Lygia tortured, his love for God would be turned to hatred, and his faith to despair. But he was frightened of the feeling, for he did not wish to offend Christ, whom he was imploring for mercy and miracles. He only wished that she would die before they brought her to the arena, and from the abyss of his pain he repeated in his spirit, *Do not refuse even this, and I will love You still more than now.* A desire for blood and vengeance filled him. He had a foolish wish to rush at Nero and overwhelm him there in presence of all the spectators; but he felt that desire to be another offense against Christ. He hoped all would be turned aside by an almighty and merciful hand; he feared that He who could destroy that Circus with one word and save Lygia had abandoned her, though she trusted in Him and loved Him with all the strength of her pure heart.

He also thought of her lying there in that dark place, weak, defenseless, abandoned to the whim or disfavor of brutal guards, drawing her last breath, perhaps, while he had to wait in that dreadful amphitheater without knowing what torture was prepared for her, or what he would witness in a moment. Finally, as as a man falling over a precipice grasps at everything that grows on the edge of it, so he grasped at the thought that faith itself could save her. That one method remained! Peter had said that faith could move the earth to its foundations.

So he rallied and suppressed doubt. He poured his whole being into the statement "I believe," and he looked for a miracle.

He thought, then, that his prayer had been heard, for he felt as if he were dying. It seemed to him that Lygia must surely die too, and that Christ would take them to Himself soon. The arena, the white togas, the countless spectators, the light of thousands of lamps and torches—all vanished from his vision.

"You seem ill," Petronius said. "Do you wish to go home?"

And without regard to what Caesar would say, he rose to support Vinicius and go out with him. His heart was filled with pity, and, moreover, he was irritated beyond endurance because Caesar was looking through the emerald at Vinicius, studying his pain with satisfaction, to describe it afterwards, perhaps, in pathetic verses, and win the applause of hearers.

Vinicius shook his head. He might die in that amphitheater, but he could not leave it.

At that instant almost, the prefect of the city waved a red handkerchief, the hinges opposite Caesar's podium creaked, and out of the dark recess Ursus came into the brightly lighted arena.

The giant blinked, dazed evidently by the glitter of the arena; then he walked into the center, gazing around as if to see what he had to meet. It was known to all the Augustians and to most of the spectators that he was the man who had crushed Croton; so at the sight of him a murmur rose along every bench. In Rome there was no lack of gladiators larger by far than the common man, but Roman eyes had never seen the like of Ursus. Cassius, standing in Caesar's podium, seemed puny compared with that Lygian. Senators, vestals, Caesar, the Augustians, and the people gazed with the delight of experts at his mighty limbs as large as tree trunks, at his breast as large as two shields joined together, and his arms like Hercules. For those multitudes there could be no higher pleasure than to look at those muscles in the exertion of a struggle. The murmur rose to shouts, and eager questions were put: "Where do the people live who can produce such a giant?" He stood there, in the middle of the amphitheater, naked, more like a stone colossus than a man, with a composed expression and at the same time the sad look of a barbarian. While surveying the empty arena, he gazed wonderingly with his blue, childlike eyes, now at the spectators, now at Caesar, now at the grating of the prison, where, he thought, his executioners would come.

He hoped that perhaps a cross was waiting for him, but when he saw neither the cross nor the hole in which it might be put, he thought that he was unworthy of such favor—that he would find death in another way, probably from wild beasts. He was unarmed and had determined to die as worthy of a confessor of the Lamb, peacefully and patiently. Meanwhile, he wished to pray one last time, so he knelt in the arena, joined his hands, and raised his eyes toward the stars that were glittering in the lofty opening of the amphitheater.

That act displeased the crowds. They had had enough of those Christians who died like sheep. They understood that if the giant would not defend himself the spectacle would be a failure. Here and there hisses were heard. Some began to cry for scourgers, whose duty it was to lash combatants unwilling to fight. But soon they grew silent, for no one knew what was waiting for the giant, nor whether he would not be ready to struggle when he met death face-to-face.

Suddenly the shrill sound of trumpets was heard. At that signal a grating opposite Caesar's podium was opened and into the arena rushed, amid shouts of beast-keepers, an enormous German bull, bearing on his head the body of a woman.

"Lygia! Lygia!" Vinicius cried.

Then he seized his hair near the temples, squirmed like a man who felt a sharp dart in his body, and began to repeat in hoarse groans, "I believe! I believe! I believe!"

This time the amphitheater was silent. The Augustians rose in their places, for in the arena something unusual had happened.

That Lygian, obedient and ready to die, when he saw his queen on the horns of the wild beast, sprang up, as if touched by living fire, and, bending forward, he ran at the raging animal.

The Lygian sprang on the raging bull in an instant and seized him by the horns.

"Look!" Petronius cried, snatching away the toga he had placed on the head of Vinicius.

The latter rose and bent back his head; his face was as pale as linen, and he looked into the arena with a glassy, vacant stare.

In the amphitheater a fly might be heard on the wing. People could not believe their own eyes. Since Rome's beginning, no one had seen such a spectacle.

The Lygian held the wild beast by the horns. The man's feet sank in the sand to his ankles, his back was bent like a drawn bow, his head was hidden between his shoulders, on his arms the muscles came out so that the skin almost burst from the pressure; but he had stopped the bull in his tracks. And the man and the beast remained so still that the spectators thought they were looking at a picture showing a deed of Hercules or Theseus, or a group hewn from stone. But in that apparent repose there was a tremendous exertion of two struggling forces. The bull sank his feet as well as did the man in the sand, and his dark, shaggy body was curved so that it seemed a gigantic ball. Which of the two would fail first—that was the question for those spectators who loved such struggles; a question that at that moment meant more for them than their own fate, than all Rome and its lordship over the world. That Lygian was in their eyes then a demigod worthy of honor and statues. Caesar himself stood up as well as others. He and Tigellinus, hearing of the man's strength, had arranged this spectacle purposely, and said to each other with a jeer, "Let that slayer of Croton kill the bull we choose for him"; so they looked now with amazement at the picture, as if not believing that it could be real.

In the amphitheater men raised their arms and remained in that posture. Sweat covered the faces of others, as if they themselves were struggling with the beast. In the Circus nothing was heard except the sound of flame in the lamps and the crackling of bits of coal as they dropped from the torches. Their words died on the lips of the spectators, but their hearts were beating in their breasts as if to split them. It seemed to all that the struggle was lasting for ages. But the man and the beast continued on in their monstrous exertion; they seemed to be planted in the earth.

People thought themselves dreaming until the enormous head of the bull began to turn in the iron hands of the barbarian. The face, neck, and arms of the Lygian grew purple; his back bent still more. It was clear that he was rallying the remnant of his superhuman strength, but that he could not last long.

One could hear the painful groan of the bull as it mingled with the whistling breath from the giant. The head of the beast turned more and more, and from his jaws crept forth a long, foaming tongue.

A moment more, and to the ears of spectators sitting nearest came the crack of breaking bones; then the beast rolled on the earth with his neck twisted in death.

The giant removed in a flash the ropes from the horns of the bull and, raising Lygia, began to breathe hurriedly. His face became pale, his hair stuck together from sweat, his shoulders and arms seemed flooded with water. For a moment he stood as if only half conscious; then he raised his eyes and looked at the spectators.

The amphitheater had gone wild.

The walls of the building were trembling from the roar of tens of thousands of people. Since the beginning of spectacles there was no memory of such excitement. Those who were sitting on the highest rows came down, crowding in the passages between benches to look more closely at the strongman. Everywhere cries for mercy were heard, passionate and persistent, that soon turned into unbroken thunder. That giant had become dear to those people worshiping physical strength. He was the greatest hero in Rome.

He understood that the multitude were striving to grant him his life and restore him his freedom, but clearly his thought was not on himself alone. He looked around a while; then, approached Caesar's podium and holding the body of the maiden on his outstretched arms, he raised his eyes and pleaded, as if to say, "Have mercy on her! Save the girl. I did that for her sake!"

The spectators understood perfectly what he wanted. At sight of the unconscious maiden, who near the enormous Lygian seemed a child, emotion filled the multitude of nobles and senators. Her slender form, as white as if chiseled from alabaster, her fainting, the dreadful danger from which the giant had freed her, and finally her beauty and attachment had moved every heart. Some thought the man a father begging mercy for his child. Pity burst forth suddenly, like a flame. They had had too much blood, death, and torture. Voices choked with tears began to entreat mercy for both.

Meanwhile, Ursus, holding the girl in his arms, moved around the arena, and with his eyes and with motions begged for her life. Vinicius started up from his seat, sprang over the barrier that separated the front places from the arena and, running to Lygia, covered her naked body with his toga.

Then he tore apart his tunic, laid bare the scars left by wounds received in the Armenian war, and stretched out his hands to the audience.

At this the enthusiasm of the multitude passed everything seen in the Circus before. The crown stamped and howled. Voices calling for mercy grew simply terrible. People not only took the part of the athlete, but rose in defense of the soldier, the maiden, and their love. Thousands of spectators turned to Caesar with flashes of anger in their eyes and with clinched fists.

But Caesar halted and hesitated. He had no hatred against Vinicius, and the death of Lygia did not concern him; but he preferred to see the body of the maiden rent by the horns of the bull or torn by the claws of beasts. His cruelty, his perverted imagination and desires, found a kind of delight in such spectacles. And now the people wanted to rob him. So anger appeared on his bloated face. Self-love also would not let him yield to the wish of the multitude, and still he did not dare to oppose it, through his inborn cowardice.

So he gazed around to see if among the Augustians, at least, he could not find fingers turned down in sigh of death. But Petronius held up his hand and looked into Nero's face almost challengingly. Vestinius, superstitious, and a man who feared ghosts but not the living, gave a sign for mercy also. So did Scevinus, the senator; so did Nerva, so did Tullius Senecio, so did the famous leader Ostoriuis Scapula, and Antistius, and Piso, and Vetus, and Crispinus, and Minucius Thermus, and Pontius Telesinus, and the most important of all, one honored by the people, Thrasea.

In view of this, Caesar took the emerald from his eye with an expression of contempt and offense, when Tigellinus, whose desire was to spite Petronius, turned to him and said, "Yield not, divinity; we have the praetorians."

Then Nero turned to the place where command over the praetorians was held by the stern Subrius Flavius, so far devoted with whole soul to him, and saw something unusual. The face of the old tribune was stern but covered with tears, and he was holding his hand up in the sign of mercy.

Now rage began to possess the multitude. Dust rose from beneath the stamping feet and filled the amphitheater. In the midst of shouts were heard cries: "Ahenobarbus! Matricide! Traitor!"

Nero was alarmed. Romans were absolute lords in the Circus. Former Caesars, and especially Caligula, had permitted themselves sometimes to act against the will of the people. This, however, brought disturbance always, sometimes leading to bloodshed. But Nero was in a different position. First, as an actor and a singer he needed the people's favor. Second, he wanted them on his side against the Senate and the patricians, and especially after the burning of Rome he strove by all means to win it and turn their anger against the Christians. He understood, besides, that to oppose longer was simply dangerous. A disturbance begun in the Circus might seize the whole city and have incalculable results.

He looked once more at Subrius Flavius, at Scevinus the centurion, a relative of the senator, at the soldiers; and seeing everywhere frowning brows, excited faces, and eyes fixed on him, he gave the sign for mercy.

Then a thunder of applause was heard from the highest seats to the lowest. The people were sure of the lives of the condemned, for from that moment they went under their protection, and even Caesar would not have dared to pursue them any longer with his vengeance.

66

Four Bithynians carried Lygia carefully to the house of Petronius. Vinicius and Ursus walked at her side, hurrying so as to give her to the Greek physician as quickly as possible. They walked in silence, for after the events of the day they did not have the power to speak. Vinicius kept repeating to himself that Lygia was saved; that she was threatened no longer by imprisonment, or death in the Circus; that their misfortunes had ended forever; that he would take her home and not separate again from her. This seemed to him the beginning of some other life rather than his own. He bent over the open litter frequently to look on his beloved, who in the moonlight seemed sleeping, and he repeated, "This is she! Christ has saved her!" He remembered also that while he and Ursus were carrying her an unknown physician had assured him that she was living and would recover. At this thought delight so filled him that at moments he grew weak and, being unable to walk with his own strength, leaned on the arm of Ursus. Ursus, meanwhile, was looking into the sky filled with stars, and was praying.

They advanced hurriedly along streets where newly erected white buildings shone brightly in the moonlight. The city was empty, except here and there where crowds of people crowned with ivy sang and danced before porticos to the song of flutes, taking advantage of the wonderful night and the festive season. Only when they were near the house did Ursus stop praying and say, "Lord, it was the Savior who rescued her from death. When I saw her on the horns of the bull, I heard a voice in my soul saying, 'Defend her!' and that was the voice of the Lamb. The prison took strength from me, but He gave it back in that moment and inspired that cruel people to take her part. Let His will be done!"

And Vinicius answered, "Magnified be His name!"

He did not have the power to continue, for all at once he felt that a mighty weeping was swelling up within him. He was seized by an overpowering wish to throw himself on the ground and thank the Savior for His miracles and His mercy.

The servants, informed by a slave dispatched in advance, crowded out to meet them. Paul of Tarsus had sent back from Antium the greater part of these people. The misfortune of Vinicius was known to them perfectly; so their delight at seeing those victims that had been snatched from the malice of Nero was immense and increased still more when the physician Theocles said that Lygia had not suffered serious injury, and that when the weakness caused by prison fever had passed, she would regain health.

Consciousness returned to her that night. Waking in the splendid chamber lighted by Corinthian lamps, amid the odor of verbena and nard, she did not know where she was, or what was taking place within her. She remembered the moment in which she had been lashed to the horns of the chained bull; and now, seeing the face of Vinicius, lighted by the mild rays of the lamp, she thought she was no longer on earth. Her thoughts were confused; it seemed to her natural to be detained somewhere on the way to heaven, because of her tortures and weakness. Feeling no pain, however, she smiled at Vinicius and wanted to ask where they were; but from her lips came merely a low whisper in which he could barely hear his own name.

Then he knelt near her, and, placing his hand lightly on her forehead, he said, "Christ saved you and returned you to me!"

Her lips moved again with a meaningless whisper; her lids closed then, her breast rose with a light sigh, and she fell into a deep sleep, for which the physician had been waiting, and after which she would return to health, he said.

Vinicius remained kneeling near her, however, sunk in prayer. His soul was melting with a love so immense that he utterly forgot himself. Theocles returned often to the chamber, and the golden-haired Eunice appeared behind the raised curtain a number of times; finally cranes, reared in the gardens, began to call, heralding the coming day, but Vinicius was still in his mind embracing the feet of Christ, neither seeing nor hearing what was passing around him, with a heart turned into a thanksgiving, sacrificial flame, sunk in ecstasy, and though alive, half-taken into heaven.

67

Petronius, after the liberation of Lygia, not wishing to irritate Caesar, went to the Palatine with other Augustians. He wanted to hear what they were saying and especially to learn if Tigellinus was devising something new to destroy Lygia. Both she and Ursus had passed under the protection of the people, it is true, and no one could place a hand on them without raising a riot. Still, Petronius, knowing the hatred toward him of the all-powerful praetorian prefect, considered that very likely Tigellinus, although unable to strike him directly, would strive to find some means of revenge against his nephew.

Nero was angry and irritated, since the spectacle had ended quite differently from what he had planned. At first he did not wish even to look at Petronius; but the latter, without losing his composure, approached him, with all freedom, and said, "Do you know, divinity, what occurs to me? Write a poem on the maiden who, at the command of the lord of the world, was freed from the horns of the wild bull and given to her lover. The Greeks are sensitive, and I am sure that the poem will enchant them."

This thought pleased Nero in spite of all his irritation, and it pleased him doubly, first, as a subject for a poem, and second, because in it he could glorify himself as the magnanimous lord of the earth; so he looked for a while at Petronius and then said, "Yes! Perhaps you are right. But is it right for me to celebrate my own goodness?"

"There is no need to give names. In Rome all will know who you mean, and from Rome reports go through the whole world."

"But are you sure that this will please the people in Achaea?"

"By Pollux, it will!" Petronius said.

And he went away satisfied, for he was certain that Nero, whose whole life was an arrangement of reality to literary plans, would not spoil the subject, and by this alone he would tie the hands of Tigellinus. This, however, did not change his plan of sending Vinicius out of Rome as soon as Lygia's health should permit. So when he saw him the next day, he said, "Take her to Sicily. As things have happened, on Caesar's part you are threat-

468

ened by nothing, but Tigellinus is ready to use even poison—if not out of hatred to you both, out of hatred to me."

Vinicius smiled at him and said, "She was on the horns of the wild bull; still Christ saved her."

"Then honor Him with a sacrifice," Petronius replied with an tone of impatience, "but do not beg Him to save her a second time. Do you remember how Eolus received Ulysses when he returned to ask a second time for favoring winds? Deities do not like to repeat themselves."

"When her health returns, I will take her to Pomponia Graecina," Vinicius said.

"And you will do that all the better since Pomponia is ill. Antistius, a relative of Aulus, told me so. Meanwhile, things will happen here to make people forget you, and in these times the forgotten are the happiest. May Fortune be your sun in winter and your shade in summer."

Then he left Vinicius to his happiness, but went himself to ask Theocles concerning the life and health of Lygia.

Danger threatened her no longer. Emaciated as she was after suffering prison fever, foul air and discomfort would have killed her; but now she had the most tender care and not only plenty, but luxury. At the command of Theocles they took her to the gardens of the villa after two days; in these gardens she remained for hours. Vinicius decked her litter with anemones, and especially with irises, to remind her of the atrium of the house of Aulus. More than once, hidden in the shade of spreading trees, they spoke of past sufferings and fears, each holding the other's hand. Lygia said that Christ had led him through suffering purposely to change his soul and raise it to Himself. Vinicius felt that this was true and that there was in him nothing of the former patrician, who knew no law but his own desire.

In those memories there was nothing bitter, however. It seemed to both that whole years had gone over their heads, and that the dreadful past lay far behind. At the same time such a calmness possessed them as they had never known before. A new life of immense happiness had come and taken them into itself. In Rome Caesar might rage and fill the world with terror, but they felt above them a guardianship a hundred times mightier than his

469

power and had no further fear of his rage or his malice, just as if for them he had ceased to be the lord of life or death.

Once, about sunset, the roar of lions and other beasts reached them from the distance. Formerly those sounds filled Vinicius with fear because they were ominous; now he and Lygia merely looked at each other and raised their eyes to the evening twilight. At times, Lygia, still very weak and unable to walk alone, fell asleep in the quiet of the garden. He watched over her and, looking at her sleeping face, thought that she was not the Lygia whom he had met at the house of Aulus. In fact, imprisonment and disease had to some extent quenched her beauty. When he saw her at the house of Aulus, and later, when he went to Miriam's house to seize her, she was as wonderful as a statue and also as a flower; now her face had become almost transparent, her hands thin, her body reduced by disease, her lips pale, and even her eyes seemed less blue than before. The golden-haired Eunice, who brought her flowers to cover her feet, was a divinity of Cyprus in comparison. Petronius tried in vain to find the former charms in her and, shrugging his shoulders, thought that that shadow from Elysian fields was not worth those struggles, those pains, and those tortures that had almost sucked the life out of Vinicius. But Vinicius, in love now with her spirit, loved it all the more.

68

News of the miraculous rescue of Lygia was circulated quickly among those scattered Christians who had escaped destruction. Believers came to look at the one Christ had favored. First came Nazarius and Miriam, with whom Peter the apostle was hiding. Vinicius, Lygia, and the Christian slaves of Petronius listened with attention to the story of Ursus regarding the voice he had heard in his soul and that had commanded him to struggle with the wild bull. Everyone went away consoled, hoping that Christ would not let His followers be exterminated on earth before His coming at the day of judgment. And hope sustained their hearts, for persecution had not yet ceased. Whoever was declared a Christian by public report was thrown into prison at once by the city magistrates. The victims were fewer, for the majority of confessors had been seized and tortured to death. The Christians who remained had either left Rome to wait out the storm in distant provinces or had hidden very carefully, not daring to assemble in common prayer except in sandpits outside the city. Though the games were at an end, the newly arrested were reserved for future games or specially punished. Though it was no longer believed in Rome that Christians had caused the fire, they were declared enemies of humanity and the state, and the edict against them remained in force.

The apostle Peter did not attempt for a long time to appear in the house of Petronius, but at last on a certain evening Nazarius announced his arrival. Lygia, who was able to walk alone now, and Vinicius ran out to meet him and fell at his feet. He greeted them with great emotion, for not many sheep in that flock over which Christ had given him authority remained with him. So when Vinicius said, "Lord, because of you the Redeemer returned her to me," he answered, "He returned her because of your faith and so that not all the lips that confess His name should grow silent." And evidently Peter was thinking then of those thousands of his children torn by wild beasts, of those crosses filling the arena, and those fiery pillars in the gardens of the "Beast"; for he spoke with great sadness. Vinicius and Lygia noticed, also, that his hair had grown entirely white, that his whole frame was bent, and that in his face there was as much sadness and suffering as if he himself had passed through all those pains and torments the victims of Nero's rage and madness had endured. But both understood that since Christ surrendered to torture and to death, no one was permitted to avoid it. Still, their hearts were grieved at the sight of the apostle, bent by years, toil, and pain. So Vinicius, who intended to take Lygia soon to Naples, where they would meet Pomponia and go to Sicily, implored him to leave Rome in their company.

But the apostle placed his hand on the tribune's head and

471

answered, "In my soul I hear these words of the Lord, which He spoke to me on the Lake of Tiberias: 'When you were young, you girded yourself, and walked wherever you would; but when you are old, you shall stretch out your hands, and another shall lead you, and carry you where you would not.' It is proper that I remain with my flock."

He added, "My work is nearing its end; I shall find entertainment and rest only in the house of the Lord."

Then he turned to them, saying, "Remember me, for I have loved you as a father loves his children; and whatever you do in life, do it all for the glory of God."

Then he raised his aged, trembling hands and blessed them.

They were destined to see him only once more. A few days later Petronius brought terrible news from the Palatine. It was disclosed there that one of Caesar's freedmen was a Christian; and on this man were found letters of the apostles Peter and Paul, with letters of James, John, and Judas. Peter's presence in Rome was known formerly to Tigellinus, but he thought that the apostle had perished with thousands of other confessors. Now they realized that the two leaders of the new faith were alive and in the capital. They were determined to seize them at all costs, for it was hoped that with their deaths the last root of the hated sect would be plucked out. Petronius heard from Vestinius that Caesar himself had issued an order to put Peter and Paul in the Mamertine prison within three days, and that whole detachments of praetorians had been sent to search every house in the Trans-Tiber.

When he heard this, Vinicius decided to warn the apostle. In the evening he and Ursus put on Gallic cloaks and went to the house of Miriam, where Peter was living. The house was at the very edge of the Trans-Tiber division of the city. On the road they saw houses surrounded by soldiers, who were guided by informers. This division of the city was alarmed, and in places crowds of curious people had assembled. Here and there centurions interrogated prisoners about Simon Peter and Paul of Tarsus.

Ursus and Vinicius were ahead of the soldiers and went safely to Miriam's house, in which they found Peter surrounded by a handful of the faithful. Timothy, Paul's assistant, and Linus were at the side of the apostle.

At news of the approaching danger, Nazarius led them by a hidden passage to the garden gate and then on to deserted stone quarries a few hundred yards distant from the Janiculum Gate. Ursus had to carry Linus, whose bones, broken by torture, had not grown together. But once in the quarry, they felt safe; and by the light of a torch ignited by Nazarius they began to discuss, in whispers, how to save the life of the apostle who was so dear to them.

"Lord," Vinicius said, "let Nazarius guide you at daybreak to the Alban Hills. There I will find you, and we will take you to Antium, where a ship is ready to take us to Naples and Sicily. Blessed will be the day in which you shall enter my house and bless my hearth."

The others heard this with delight and urged the apostle, saying, "Hide yourself, sacred leader; do not remain in Rome. Preserve the living truth, so that it does not perish with us and you. Hear us, who entreat you as a father."

"Do this in Christ's name!" others cried, grasping at his robes.

"My children," Peter answered, "who knows the time when the Lord will mark the end of his life?"

But he did not say that he would not leave Rome; and he hesitated, for uncertainty, and even fear, had been creeping into his soul for some time. His flock was scattered; his work was harmed. That church, which before the burning of the city had been flourishing like a splendid tree, was turned into dust by the power of the "Beast." Nothing remained except tears, nothing except memories of torture and death. The sowing had yielded rich fruit, but Satan had trampled it into the earth. Legions of angels had not come to aid the perishing—and Nero was extending in glory over the earth. He was terrible, mightier than ever, the lord of all seas and all lands. More than once had that fisherman of the Lord stretched his hands heavenward in loneliness and asked, "Lord, what must I do? How must I act? And how am I, a feeble old man, to fight with this invincible power of Evil, which You have permitted to rule and have victory?

"What do You wish me to do now? Am I to stay here, or to lead the remnant of the flock to glorify Your name in secret somewhere beyond the sea?"

He believed that the living truth would not perish, that it must conquer; but at moments he thought that the hour had not come yet, that it would come only when the Lord would descend to the earth in the day of judgment in glory and power much greater than the might of Nero.

An increasing desire for peace and rest, and for the lake and Galilee, filled the heart of the fisherman.

But sudden fear came on him. How was he to leave that city, in which so much martyr's blood had been spilled and where so many lips had given the testimony of the Lord Jesus Christ? Was he alone going to give up? And what would he answer the Lord on hearing the words "These have died for the faith, but you fled"?

Others had been torn by lions, fastened to crosses, burned in the gardens of Caesar, and fallen asleep in the Lord after moments of torture. He could not sleep, and he felt greater tortures than any of those invented by executioners for victims.

For thirty-three years after the death of his Master he knew no rest. Staff in hand, he had gone through the world and declared the "good tidings." His strength had been exhausted in journeys and labor, until at last, when in that city that was the leader of the world, he had established the work of his Master. One bloody breath of wrath had burned it, and he saw that there was a need to take up the struggle again. And what a struggle! On one side Caesar, the Senate, the people, the legions holding the world with an iron grip, countless cities and lands. On the other side a man so bent with age and toil that his trembling hand was hardly able to carry his staff.

Finally Linus aid to him, "My lord, the Redeemer commanded you to feed His sheep, but they are here no longer, or tomorrow they will not be here; go where you may still find them. The word of God is living still in Jerusalem, in Antioch, in Ephesus, and in other cities. What will you do by remaining in Rome? If you fall, you will merely increase the triumph of the 'Beast.' The Lord has not revealed the limit of John's life; Paul is a Roman citizen, and they cannot condemn him without trial. But if the power of hell shall rise up against you, O teacher, those whose hearts are dejected will ask, 'Who is above Nero?' Let us die, but do not permit the victory of Antichrist over our leaders, and do not return until the Lord has crushed the one who shed innocent blood."

Tears flowed over Peter's face and those of his flock. After a while he rose and, stretching his hands over the kneeling figures, said, "May the name of the Lord be magnified, and may His will be done!"

69

About dawn of the following day two dark figures were moving along the Appian Way toward the Campania.

One of them was Nazarius; the other the apostle Peter, who was leaving Rome and his martyred brethren.

The sky was assuming a light tinge of green, bordered gradually with a saffron color. Silver-leafed trees, the white marble of villas, and the arches of aqueducts, stretching through the plain toward the city, were emerging from shade. Then the east began to grow rosy and illuminate the Alban Hills, which seemed marvelously beautiful, lily-colored, as if formed only of rays of light.

The light was reflected in the trembling leaves of trees and in the dewdrops. The haze grew thinner, opening wider views on the plain and the houses dotting it.

The road was empty. The villagers who took vegetables to the city had not yet succeeded in harnessing beasts to their vehicles. From the stone blocks that paved the road as far as the mountains, there came a soft sound from the bark shoes on the feet of the two travelers.

The sun appeared over the line of hills; but at once a wonderful vision struck the apostle's eyes. It seemed to him that the golden circle, instead of rising in the sky, moved down from the heights and was advancing on the road. Peter stopped, and asked, "Do you see that brightness approaching us?"

"I see nothing," Nazarius replied.

But Peter shaded his eyes and said after a while, "Some figure is coming in the gleam of the sun."

But not the slightest sound of steps reached their ears. It was perfectly still all around. Nazarius saw only that the trees were quivering in the distance, as if someone were shaking them, and the light was spreading more broadly over the plain. He looked with wonder at the apostle.

"Rabbi! What ails you?" he cried with alarm.

The pilgrim's staff fell from Peter's hands to the earth; his eyes were looking forward, motionless; his mouth was open in awe.

Then he fell on his knees, his arms stretched forward, and he cried, "O Christ! O Christ!"

He fell with his face to the earth, as if kissing someone's feet.

The silence continued; then the aged man spoke, broken by sobs, *"Quo vadis, Domine?"*

Nazarius did not hear the answer, but a sad and sweet voice came to Peter's ears, which said, "If you desert my people, I am going to Rome to be crucified a second time."

The apostle lay on the ground, his face in the dust, without motion or speech. It seemed to Nazarius that he had fainted or was dead; but he rose at last, seized the staff with trembling hands, and turned without a word toward the seven hills of the city.

The boy, seeing this, repeated as an echo, *"Quo vadis, Domine?"*

"To Rome," the apostle said quietly.

And he returned.

Paul, John, Linus, and all the faithful received him with amazement; and the alarm was the greater, since at daybreak, just after his departure, praetorian guards had surrounded Miriam's house and searched it for the apostle. But to every question he answered only with delight and peace, "I have seen the Lord!"

And that same evening he went to the Ostian cemetery to teach and baptize those who wished to bathe in the water of life.

And after that he went there daily, and after him went increasing numbers. It seemed that out of the blood of martyrs new confessors were born, and that every groan in the arena found an echo in thousands of hearts. Caesar was swimming in blood,

Rome and the whole pagan world went mad. But those who had had enough of wickedness, those who were trampled upon, the sad, the unfortunate, came to hear the wonderful tidings of God, who out of love for men had given Himself to be crucified and redeem them from their sins.

When they found a God whom they could love, they had found what the society of the time could not give anyone—happiness and love.

And Peter understood that neither Caesar nor all his legions could overcome the living truth—that they could not overwhelm it with tears or blood, and that now its victory was beginning. He understood with equal force why the Lord had turned him back on the road. That city of pride, crime, wickedness, and power was beginning to be His city, a dual capital, but the Christians would overcome.

70

At last the hour came for both apostles. But, as if to complete his service, the fisherman of the Lord won two souls even in confinement. The soldiers, Processus and Martinianus, who guarded him in the Mamertine prison, received baptism. Then came the hour of torture. Nero was not in Rome at that time. Sentence was passed by Helius and Polythetes, two freedmen to whom Caesar had entrusted the government of Rome during his absence.

The stripes prescribed by law had been inflicted on the aged apostle; the next day he was led forth beyond the walls of the city, toward the Vatican Hill, where he was to suffer the punishment of the cross assigned to him. Soldiers were astonished by the crowd that had gathered in front of the prison, for in their minds the death of a common man, and besides a foreigner, should not rouse such interest. They did not understand that that retinue was composed not of sightseers, but confessors, anxious to escort the

477

great apostle to the place of execution. In the afternoon the gates of the prison were thrown open at last, and Peter appeared in the midst of praetorian guards. The sun had inclined somewhat toward the Ostia already. The day was clear and calm. Because of his advanced age, Peter was not required to carry the cross; they believed that he could not carry it. He walked without hindrance, and the faithful could see him perfectly.

At moments when his white head was seen among the iron helmets of the soldiers, weeping was heard in the crowd. But it was restrained immediately, for the face of the old man had so much calmness, and was so bright with joy, that all understood him to be not a victim going to destruction, but a victor celebrating his triumph.

The fisherman, usually humble and stooping, walked erect, seemingly taller than the soldiers and full of dignity. Never had men seen such majesty in his bearing. It might have seemed that he was a monarch attended by people and armies. From every side voices proclaimed, "There is Peter going to the Lord!"

All forgot that torture and death were waiting for him.

Along the road people halted from wonder at the sight of that old man, but believers, laying hands on their shoulders, said with calm voices, "See how a just man goes to death—one who knew Christ and proclaimed love to the world."

These people became thoughtful and walked away, saying to themselves, *He cannot, indeed, be unjust!*

Along the road noise and the cries of the street were hushed. The retinue moved on before newly reared houses and before the white columns of temples, over whose summits hung the deep sky, calm and blue. Only at times the weapons of the soldiers clattered, or the murmur of prayer rose. Peter heard the last, and his face grew bright with increasing joy, for his glance could hardly take in those thousands of confessors. He felt that he had done his work, and he knew now that that truth he had been declaring all his life would overwhelm everything like a sea, and that nothing would have power to restrain it. And he raised his eyes and said: "O Lord, You commanded us to conquer this world-ruling city; so we have conquered it. This is Your city now, O Lord, and I go to You, for I have toiled greatly."

478

As he walked before temples, he said to them, "You will be temples of Christ." Looking at throngs of people moving before his eyes, he said to them, "Your children will be servants of Christ"; and he advanced with the feeling that he had conquered. The soldiers conducted him over the Pons Triumphalis, as if giving involuntary testimony to his triumph, and they led him farther toward the Naumachia and the Circus. The faithful from beyond the Tiber joined the procession; and such a throng of people was formed that the centurion commanding the praetorian guards understood at last that he was leading a high priest surrounded by believers and grew alarmed because of the small number of soldiers. But no cry of indignation or rage was given out in the throng. Men's faces were filled with the greatness of the moment, solemn and full of expectation. Some believers, remembering that when the Lord died the earth opened from fright and the dead rose from their graves, thought that now some evident signs would appear, after which the death of the apostle would not be forgotten for ages. Others said to themselves, "Perhaps the Lord will select the hour of Peter's death to come from heaven as He promised and judge the world." With this idea they committed themselves to the mercy of the Redeemer.

The procession stopped at last between the Circus and the Vatican Hill. Soldiers began to dig a hole; others placed the cross, hammers, and nails on the ground, waiting until all preparations were finished. The crowd, continuing to be quiet and attentive, knelt all round.

The apostle, with his head in the sun-rays and golden light, turned for the last time toward the city. At a distance lower down was seen the gleaming Tiber; beyond was the Campus Martius; higher up, the Mausoleum of Augustus; below that, the gigantic baths just begun by Nero; still lower, Pompey's theater; and beyond them were visible in places, and in places hidden by other buildings, the Septa Julia, a multitude of porticos, temples, columns, great edifices; and, finally, far in the distance, hills covered with houses, a gigantic resort of people, the borders of which vanished in the blue haze—an abode of crime, but of power; of madness, but of order—which had become the head of the world, its oppressor, but its law and its peace, almighty, invincible, eternal.

But Peter, surrounded by soldiers, looked at the city as a ruler and king looks at his inheritance. And he said to it, "You are redeemed!" And no one, not merely among the soldiers digging the hole for the cross, but even among believers, realized that standing there among them was a leader of the new city. Caesar's rule would pass away, waves of barbarians go by, and ages vanish, but Christianity would remain.

The sun had sunk still more toward Ostia and had become large and red. The whole western side of the sky had begun to glow with immense brightness. The soldiers approached Peter to strip him.

But he, while praying, straightened himself all at once and stretched his right hand high. The executioners stopped; the faithful held their breath, thinking that he wished to say something, and silence followed.

But he, standing on the height, with his extended right hand made the sign of the cross, blessing in the hour of death the city and the world.

In that same wonderful evening another detachment of soldiers conducted Paul of Tarsus along the Ostian Way toward a place called Aquae Salviae. And behind him also advanced a crowd of the faithful whom he had converted; but when he recognized acquaintances, he halted and spoke with them, for, being a Roman citizen, the guards showed more respect to him.

Beyond the gate called Tergemina he met Plautilla, the daughter of the prefect Flavius Sabinus, and, seeing her youthful face covered with tears, he said, "Plautilla, daughter of eternal salvation, depart in peace. Only give me a veil to bind my eyes when I am going to the Lord." And taking it, he advanced with a face as full of delight as that of a laborer who, when he has toiled the whole day successfully, is returning home. His thoughts, like those of Peter, were as calm and quiet as that evening sky. His eyes gazed with thoughtfulness upon the plain that stretched out before him, and to the Alban Hills, immersed in light. He remembered his journeys, his toils, his labor, the struggles in which he had conquered, the churches he had founded in all lands and beyond all seas; and he thought that he had earned his rest honestly, that he had finished his work. He felt now that the seed he had planted would not be blown away by the wind of evil. He was leaving this life with the certainty that in the battle truth had conquered the world; and a mighty peace settled down on his soul.

The road to the place of execution was long, and evening was coming. The mountains became purple, and the bases of them went gradually into the shade. Flocks were returning home. Here and there groups of slaves were walking with their tools on their shoulders. Children, playing on the road before houses, looked with curiosity at the passing soldiers. But in that evening, in that transparent golden air, there were not only peace and lovingness, but a certain harmony. Paul felt this; and his heart was filled with delight at the thought that to that harmony of the world he had added one note that had not been in it up to now, but without which the whole earth was like sounding brass or a tinkling cymbal.

He remembered how he had taught people love—how he had told them that though they were to give their property to the poor, though they knew all languages, all secrets, and all sciences, they would be nothing without love. Love is kind and enduring and does not return evil. It does not desire honor, it suffers all things, believes all things, hopes all things, and is patient in all things.

And so his life had been spent in teaching people this truth. And now he said in spirit, *What power can equal it, what can conquer it? Could Caesar stop it, though he had twice as many legions and twice as many cities?*

And he went to his reward like a conqueror.

The detachment left the main road at last and turned toward the east on a narrow path leading to the Aquae Salviae. The red sun was lying now on the heather. The centurion stopped the soldiers at the fountain, for the moment had come.

Paul placed Plautilla's veil on his arm, intending to bind his eyes with it; for the last time he raised those eyes, full of unspeakable peace, toward the eternal light of the evening, and prayed. Yes, the moment had come; but he saw before him a great road in the light, leading to heaven; and in his soul he repeated the same words that formerly he had written regarding his own finished service: "I have fought a good fight, I have finished my course, I have kept the faith. There is laid up for me a crown of righteousness."

71

Rome had gone mad for a long time, so that the world-conquering city seemed ready at last to tear itself to pieces for lack of leadership. Even before the last hour of the apostles had struck, Piso's conspiracy appeared, and then such merciless reaping of Rome's highest heads that even to those who saw divinity in Nero, he seemed at last a divinity of death. Mourning fell on the city, terror lodged in houses and in hearts, but porticos were crowned with ivy and flowers, for it was not permitted to show sorrow for the dead. People waking in the morning asked themselves whose turn would come next. The retinue of ghosts following Caesar increased every day.

Piso paid for the conspiracy with his head; then followed Seneca, and Lucan, Fenius Rufus, and Plautius Lateranus, and Flavius Scevinus, and Afranius Quinetianus, and Proculus, and Araricus, and Tugurinus, and Gratus, and Silanus, and Proximus —once devoted with his whole soul to Nero. Some were destroyed by their own insignificance, some by fear, some by wealth, others by bravery. Caesar, astonished at the very number of conspirators, covered the walls with soldiers and held the city as if by siege, sending out daily centurions with sentences of death to suspected houses. The condemned humiliated themselves in letters filled with flattery, thanking Caesar for his sentences and leaving him a part of their property, so as to save the rest for their children. It seemed, at last, that Nero was exceeding every measure on purpose to convince himself of the degree in which men had grown rebellious, and to find out how long they would endure bloody rule. After the conspirators, their relatives were executed, then their friends, and even simple acquaintances. When dwellers in lordly mansions built after the fire went out on the street they felt sure of seeing a whole row of funerals. Rufius Crispus was deprived of the right of fire and water because once he had been the husband of Poppaea. The great Thrasea was ruined by his virtue; many paid with their lives for noble origin; even Poppaea fell a victim to the momentary rage of Nero.

The Senate crouched before the dreadful ruler; it raised a temple in his honor, made an offering in favor of his voice, crowned his statues, appointed priests to him as to a divinity. Senators, trembling in their souls, went to the Palatine to magnify his songs and to go wild with him amid orgies of wine and flowers.

But meanwhile, from below, in the field soaked in blood and tears, rose the sowing of Peter, stronger and stronger every moment.

72

Vinicius to Petronius:

"We know, carissime, most of what is happening in Rome, and what we do not know is told to us in your letters. When one casts a stone in the water, the wave goes farther and farther in a circle; so the wave of madness and malice has come from the Palatine to us. On the road to Greece, Carinas was sent by Caesar, who plundered cities and temples to fill the empty treasury. At the price of the sweat and tears of people, he is building the 'golden house' in Rome. It is possible that the world has not seen such a house, but it has not seen such injustice. You know Carinas. Chilo was like him until he redeemed his life with death. But his men have not come to the towns lying nearer to us, perhaps because there are no temples or treasures in them.

"You ask if we are out of danger. I answer that we are out of mind, and let that be an answer. At this moment, from the portico under which I write, I see our calm bay, and on it is Ursus in a boat, letting down a net in the clear water. My wife is spinning red wool near me, and in the gardens, under the shade of almond trees, our slaves are singing. Oh, what calm, carissime, and what a forgetfulness of former fear and suffering! But it is Christ our beloved God and Savior who is blessing us. We know tears and sorrow, for our religion teaches us to weep over the misfortunes of others; but in those tears is a consolation unknown to you; for whenever our life ends, we shall find all those dear ones who perished and who are perishing still for God's truth. For us Peter and Paul are not dead; they are merely born into glory. Our souls see them, and when our eyes weep our hearts are glad with their joy. Oh, yes, my dear friend, we are happy with a happiness that nothing can destroy, since death, which for you is the end of everything, is for us only a passage into eternal life.

"Frequently, when the sun has gone down, or when the moon is shining in the water, Lygia and I talk of past times, which seem a dream to us; but when I think how that dear head was near torture and death, I magnify my Lord with my whole soul, for He alone could save her and return her to me forever. Petronius, you have seen what endurance and comfort that religion gives in misfortune; so come and see how much happiness it gives in the ordinary days of life. People did not know a God whom man could love, so they did not love one another; for as light comes from the sun, so happiness come from love. Neither lawgivers nor philosophers taught this truth, and it did not exist in Greece or Rome.

"You were acquainted with Paul of Tarsus and spoke with him; so you know better if in comparison with the truth he taught all the teachings of philosophers are only an empty rattling of words without meaning. You remember the question he asked you: 'But if Caesar were a Christian, would you not all feel safer, free from alarm, and sure of tomorrow?' You said to me that our teaching was an enemy of life; and I tell you now, that, if from the beginning of this letter I had been repeating only the three words, 'I am happy!' I could not have expressed my happiness to you. Before my eyes were open to the light I was ready to burn my own house, even, for Lygia's sake; but I did not love her, for it was Christ who first taught me to love. Compare your own luxury, my friend—lined with sorrow, the delights not sure of a new day, and the orgies—with the lives of Christians, and you will find a ready answer. Come to our mountains with the odor of thyme, to our shady olive groves on our shores lined with ivy. Peace is waiting for you, such as you have not known for a long time, and hearts that love you sincerely. You, having a noble soul, should be happy. Your quick mind can recognize the truth, and, knowing it, you will love it. Oh my Petronius, Lygia and I are comforting ourselves with the hope of seeing you soon. Be well, be happy, and come to us."

Petronius received this letter in Cumae, where he had gone with other Augustians who were following Caesar. His long struggle with Tigellinus was nearing its end. Petronius knew already that he would fall in that struggle, and he understood why. As Caesar sank lower each day to the role of a comedian and buffoon, as he sank deeper in a sickly and foul decadence, the exquisite arbiter became a mere burden to him. Even when Petronius was silent, Nero saw blame in his silence; when the arbiter praised, he saw ridicule. The brilliant patrician annoyed his self-love and roused his envy.

Petronius was spared so far in light of the journey to Achaea, in which his taste, his knowledge of everything Greek, might be useful. But gradually Tigellinus convinced Caesar that Carinas surpassed him in taste and knowledge and would be better able in Achaea to arrange games, receptions, and triumphs. From that moment Petronius was lost. There was no courage to send him his sentence in Rome. Caesar and Tigellinus remembered that this aesthetic person, who was occupied only in luxury, art, and feasts, had shown amazing industry and energy when he was proconsul in Bithynia and later when he was consul in the capital. They considered him capable of anything, and it was known that in Rome he possessed not only the love of the people, but even of the praetorians. None of Caesar's confidants could foresee how Petronius might act in a given case. It seemed wiser, therefore, to entice him out of the city and reach him in a province.

With this as the object, Petronius received an invitation to go to Cumae with other Augustians. He went, though suspecting the ambush, perhaps not to appear in open opposition, perhaps to show once more a joyful face to Caesar and the Augustians and to gain a last victory over Tigellinus before death.

Meanwhile, the latter accused him of friendship with the senator Scevinus, who was the soul of Piso's conspiracy. The friends of Petronius, left in Rome, were imprisoned; his house was surrounded by praetorian guards. When he learned this, he showed neither alarm nor concern and with a smile said to Augustians whom he received in his own splendid villa in Cumae, "Ahenobarbus does not like direct questions; so you will see his confusion when I ask him if it was he who gave command to imprison my household in the capital."

Then he invited them to a feast, and he had just made preparations for it when the letter from Vinicius came.

When he received this letter, Petronius grew somewhat thoughtful, but he regained his usual composure, and that same evening he answered as follows:

"I rejoice at your happiness and admire your hearts, for I had not thought that two lovers could remember a third person who was far away. You have not forgotten me, and you wish to persuade me to go to Sicily, so that you may share with me your bread and your Christ, who, as you write, has given you happiness so bountifully.

"If that be true, honor Him. To my thinking, however, Ursus had something to do with saving Lygia, and the Roman people also had a little to do with it. But since your belief is that Christ did the work, I will not contradict you. Spare no offerings to Him. Prometheus also sacrificed himself for man; but alas! Prometheus is an invention of the poets apparently, whereas people worthy of credit have told me that they saw Christ with their own eyes. I agree with you that He is the most worthy of the gods.

"I remember the question by Paul of Tarsus, and I think that if Ahenobarbus lived according to Christ's teaching I might have time to visit you in Sicily. In that case we could talk, in the shade of trees and near fountains, of all the gods and all the truths discussed by Greek philosophers at any time. Today I must give you a brief answer.

"Truth, Vinicius, dwells somewhere so high that the gods

themselves cannot see it from the top of Olympus. To you, carissime, your Olympus seems higher still, and, standing there, you
call to me, 'Come, you will see such sights as you have not seen
yet!' I might. But I answer, 'I do not have feet for the journey.' And
if you read this letter to the end, you will acknowledge, I think,
that I am right.

"No, happy husband of the aurora princess! Your religion is
not for me. Am I to love the Bithynians who carry my litter, the
Egyptians who heat my bath? Am I to love Ahenobarbus and Tigellinus? I swear by the white knees of the Graces, that even if I
wished to love them I could not. In Rome there are a hundred
thousand persons at least who have either crooked shoulders, or
big knees, or heads that are too large. Do you command me to
love these too? Where am I to find the love, since it is not in my
heart? And if your God desires me to love such persons, why in
His might did He not give them the forms of Niobe's children, for
example, which you have seen on the Palatine? Whoever loves
beauty is unable for that very reason to love deformity. One may
not believe in our gods, but it is possible to love them.

"Should I wish to go where you would lead me, I could not.
But since I do not wish, I am doubly unable. You believe, like Paul
of Tarsus, that on the other side of the Styx you will see your
Christ in certain Elysian fields. Let Him tell you then Himself
whether He would receive me with my gems, my Myrrhene vase,
my books published by Sozius, and my golden-haired Eunice. I
laugh at this thought; for Paul of Tarsus told me that for Christ's
sake one must give up wreaths of roses, feasts, and luxury. It is
true that he promised me other happiness, but I answered that I
was too old for new happiness, that my eyes would be delighted
always with roses, and that the odor of violets is dearer to me than
stench from my foul neighbor of the Subura.

"These are reasons why your happiness is not for me. But
there is one reason more, which I have reserved for the last: Thanatos, the god of death, summons me. For you the light of life is
beginning; but my sun has set, and twilight is embracing me. In
other words, I must die, carissime.

"It is not worthwhile to talk of this. It had to end this way.
You, who know Ahenobarbus, will understand the position easily.

Tigellinus has conquered, or rather my victories have reached their end. I have lived as I wished, and I will die as pleases me.

"Do not take this to heart. No god has promised me immortality; so no surprise meets me. At the same time you are mistaken, Vinicius, in asserting that only your God teaches man to die calmly. Our world knew, before you were born, that when the last cup was drained, it was time to go—time to rest—and it knows yet how to do that with calmness. Plato declares that virtue is music, that the life of a sage is harmony. If that be true, I shall die as I have lived—virtuously.

"I should like to take farewell of your godlike wife in the words with which I once greeted her in the house of Aulus: 'Very many persons have I seen, but your equal I do not know.'

"If the soul is more than Pyrrho thinks, mine will fly to you and Lygia, on its way to the edge of the ocean, and will alight at your house in the form of a butterfly or, as the Egyptians believe, in the form of a sparrow hawk. Otherwise, I cannot come.

"Meanwhile, let Sicily replace for you the gardens of Hesperides; may the goddesses of the fields, woods, and fountains scatter flowers on your path, and may white doves build their nests on the columns of your house."

73

Petronius was not mistaken. Two days later young Nerva, who had always been friendly and devoted, sent his freedmen to Cumae with news of what was happening at the court of Caesar.

The death of Petronius had been determined. On the morning of the following day they intended to send him a centurion with the order to stop at Cumae and wait there for further instructions; the next messenger, to follow a few days later, was to bring the death sentence.

Petronius heard the news with unruffled calmness.

"You will take to your lord," he said, "one of my vases; say from me that I thank him with my whole soul, for now I am able to anticipate the sentence."

And all at once he began to laugh, like a man who has come upon a perfect thought and rejoices in advance at its fulfillment.

That same afternoon his slaves rushed about, inviting the Augustians, who were staying in Cumae, and all the ladies, to a magnificent banquet at the villa of the arbiter.

He wrote that afternoon in the library; next he took a bath, after which he commanded the slaves to arrange his wardrobe. Brilliant and stately as one of the gods, he went to cast the eye of a critic on the preparations, and then to the gardens, where youths and Grecian maidens from the islands were weaving wreaths of roses for the evening.

Not the least care was visible on his face. The servants only knew that the feast would be something uncommon, for he had given a command to give unusual rewards to those with whom he was satisfied. To the cithara players and the singers he had ordered generous pay beforehand. At last, sitting in the garden under a beech, through whose leaves the sun-rays marked the earth with bright spots, he called Eunice.

She came, dressed in white, with a sprig of myrtle in her hair, beautiful as one of the Graces. He seated her at his side, and, touching her temple gently with his fingers, he gazed at her with that admiration with which a critic gazes at a statue from the chisel of a master.

"Eunice," he asked, "do you know that you have not been a slave for a long time?"

She raised to him her calm eyes, as blue as the sky, and denied with a motion of her head.

"I am yours always," she said.

"But perhaps you do not know," Petronius continued, "that the villa, and those slaves twining wreaths here, and all that is in the villa, with the fields and the herds, are yours from now on."

Eunice, when she heard this, drew away from him quickly and asked in a voice filled with sudden fear, "Why do you tell me this?"

Then she approached again and looked at him with curiosity.

After a while her face became as pale as linen. He smiled, and said only one word, "So!"

A moment of silence followed; merely a slight breeze moved the leaves of the beech.

"Eunice," he said, "I wish to die calmly."

And the maiden, looking at him with a heart-rending smile, whispered, "I hear you."

In the evening, the guests, who had been at feasts given by Petronius previously and knew that in comparison with them even Caesar's banquets seemed tiresome and barbarous, began to arrive in numbers. To no one did it occur, even, that that was to be the last festivity. Many knew, it is true, that the clouds of Caesar's anger were hanging over the exquisite arbiter; but that had happened so often, and Petronius had been able so often to scatter them by some skillful act or by a single word, that no one thought that serious danger threatened him.

His glad face and usual smile, free of care, confirmed this. The beautiful Eunice, to whom he had declared his wish to die calmly, and for whom every word of his was like an utterance of fate, had in her features a perfect calmness and in her eyes a kind of wonderful radiance that might have been considered delight. At the door, young people with hair in golden nets put wreaths of roses on the heads of guests, warning them, as was the custom, to pass the threshold right foot foremost. In the hall there was a slight odor of violets; the lamps burned in Alexandrian glass of various colors. At the couches stood Grecian maidens who moistened the feet of guests with perfumes. At the walls cithara players and Athenian choristers were waiting for the signal from their leader.

The table service gleamed with beauty, but that beauty did not oppress; it seemed to be a natural development. Joyfulness and freedom spread through the hall as did the odor of violets. The guests felt neither threat nor pressure hanging over them, as in Caesar's house, where a man might forfeit his life for lack of praising Nero. At the sight of the lamps, the goblets entwined with ivy, the wine cooling on banks of snow, and the exquisite dishes, the hearts of the guests were lifted. Conversation buzzed, as bees buzz on an apple tree in blossom. At moments it was interrupted by an outburst of glad laughter or murmurs of applause, at moments by a kiss placed too loudly on some white shoulder.

The guests, while drinking wine, spilled a few drops from their goblets to the immortal gods, to gain their protection, and their favor for the host. It did not matter that many of them had no belief in the gods. Custom and superstition called for it. Petronius, reclining near Eunice, talked of Rome, of the latest divorces, love affairs, races, and books in the shops in Atractus and the Sozii. When he spilled wine, he said that he spilled it only in honor of the Lady of Cyprus, the most ancient and the greatest divinity.

His conversation was like the sunlight that lights up some new object every instant, or like the summer breeze that stirs flowers in a garden. At last he gave a signal to the leader of the music, and at that signal the citharae began to sound lightly and youthful voices accompanied them. Then maidens from Kos, the birthplace of Eunice, danced, and showed their rosy forms through robes of gauze. Finally, an Egyptian fortune-teller told the guests their future from the movement of rainbow colors in a vessel of crystal.

When they had enough of these amusements, Petronius rose on his Syrian cushion and said with hesitation, "Pardon me, friends, for asking a favor at a feast. Will each man accept as a gift that goblet from which he first shook wine in honor of the gods and to my prosperity?"

The goblets of Petronius were gleaming in gold, precious stones, and the carving of artists; so although though gift-giving was common in Rome, delight filled every heart. Some thanked him loudly; others said that Jove had never honored gods with such gifts in Olympus. Finally, there were some who refused to accept, since the gifts were priceless.

But he raised aloft the Myrrhene vase, which resembled a rainbow in brilliancy, and was simply beyond price.

"This," he said, "is the one out of which I poured in honor of the Lady of Cyprus. The lips of no man may touch it from now on, and no hand may ever pour from it in honor of another divinity."

He threw the precious vessel to the pavement, which was covered with lily-colored saffron flowers; and when it was broken into small pieces, he said, seeing around him perplexed faces, "My dear friends, be glad. Old age and weakness are sad attendants in the last years of life. But I will give you a good example and good advice. You have the power, as you see, not to wait for old age; yet you can depart before it comes, as I do."

"What do you wish?" asked a number of voices, with alarm.

"I wish to rejoice, to drink wine, to hear music, to look on those divine forms you see around me, and fall asleep with garlands on my head. I have taken farewell of Caesar, and do you wish to hear what I wrote him at parting?"

He took from beneath the purple cushion a paper and read as follows.

"I know, O Caesar, that you are awaiting my arrival with impatience, that your true heart of a friend is yearning day and night for me. I know that you are ready to cover me with gifts, make me prefect of the praetorian guards, and command Tigellinus to be that which the gods made him, a mule-driver in those lands you inherited after poisoning Domitius. Pardon me, however, for I swear to you by hades, and by the ghosts of your mother, your wife, your brother, and Seneca, that I cannot go to you. Life is a great treasure. I have taken the most precious jewels from that treasure, but in life there are many things that I cannot endure any longer.

"Do not suppose, I pray, that I am offended because you killed your mother, your wife, and your brother; that you burned Rome and sent to Erebus all the honest men in your dominions. No, grandson of Chronos. Death is the inheritance of man; from you other deeds could not have been expected. But to destroy my ears for whole years with your poetry, to see your belly of a Domitius on slim legs whirled about in Pyrrhic dance; to hear your music, your speeches, your cheap verses, wretched poet of the suburbs—is a thing surpassing my power, and it has given me the wish to die. Rome stuffs its ears when it hears you; the world reviles you. I can blush for you no longer, and I have no wish to do so. The howls of Cerberus, though resembling your music, will be less offensive to me, for I have never been the friend of Cerberus, and I need not be ashamed of his howling. Farewell, but make no music; commit murder, but write no verses; poison people, but do not dance; be a traitor, but do not play on a cithara. This is the wish and last friendly counsel sent you by the—Arbiter Elegantiae."

The guests were terrified, for they knew that the loss of his rule would have been less cruel to Nero than this blow. They understood, too, that the man who had written that paper must die; and at the same time fear consumed them because they had heard the contents of such a letter.

But Petronius laughed with sincere and gladsome joy, as if it were a question of the most innocent joke; then he said to all present, "Be joyous, and drive away fear. No one should boast that he heard this letter. I will boast of it only to Charon when I am crossing in the boat with him."

He summoned the Greek physician and stretched out his arm. The skilled Greek in the twinkle of an eye opened the vein at the bend of the arm. Blood spurted on the cushion and covered Eunice, who, supporting the head of Petronius, bent over him and said, "Did you think that I would leave you? If the gods gave me immortality, and Caesar gave me power over the earth, I would still follow you."

Petronius smiled, raised himself a little, touched her lips to his, and said, "Come with me."

She stretched her rosy arm to the physician, and after a while her blood began to mingle and be lost in his blood.

Then he gave a signal to the leader of the music, and again the voices and citharae were heard.

Petronius and Eunice, resting against each other, beautiful as two divinities, listened, smiling and growing pale. At the end of the song Petronius gave directions to serve more wine and food; then he conversed with the guests sitting near him of trifling but pleasant things, such as are mentioned usually at feasts. Finally, he called to the Greek to bind his arm for a moment; for he said that sleep was tormenting him, and he wanted to yield himself to sleep before death put him to sleep forever.

In fact, he fell asleep. When he woke, the head of Eunice was lying on his breast like a white flower. He placed it on the pillow to look at it once more. After that his veins were opened again.

At his signal the singers began anew, and the citharae accompanied them so softly as not to drown a word. Petronius grew paler and paler; but when the last sound had ceased, he turned to his guests again and said, "Friends, confess that with us perishes—"

But he did not have power to finish; his arm with its last movement embraced Eunice, his head fell on the pillow, and he died.

The guests looking at those two white forms, which resembled two wonderful statues, understanding that with them perished all that was left to their world at that time—poetry and beauty.

Epilogue

At first the revolt of the Gallic legions under Vindex did not seem very serious. Caesar was only in his thirty-first year, and no one was bold enough to hope that the world could be freed so soon from the nightmare that was stifling it. Men remembered that revolts had occurred more than once among the legions—they had occurred in previous reigns—revolts, however, that were finished without involving a change of government, as during the reign of Tiberius, when Drusus put down the revolt of the Pannonian legions. "Who," said the people, "can take the government after Nero, since all the descendants of the divine Augustus have perished?" Others, looking at the Colossus, imagined him a Hercules and thought that no force could break such power. There were those, even, who, after he went to Achaea, were sorry for him, because Helius and Polythetes, to whom he left the government of Rome and Italy, governed more murderously than he had.

No one was sure of life or property. Law ceased to protect anyone. Human dignity and virtue had perished, family bonds existed no longer, and degraded hearts did not even dare to admit hope. From Greece came accounts of the incomparable triumphs of Caesar, of the thousands of crowns he had won, the thousands of competitors he had vanquished. The world seemed to be one orgy of buffoonery and blood; but at the same time it was believed that virtue and deeds of dignity had ceased, that the time of dancing and music, of lust and blood, had come, and that life must flow on for the future in that same way. Caesar himself, to whom rebellion opened the road to new robberies, was not concerned much about the revolt of the legions and Vindex; he even expressed his delight on that subject frequently. He did not wish to leave Achaea; and only when Helius informed him that further delay might cause the loss of rule did he move to Naples.

There he played and sang, neglecting news of events of growing danger. Tigellinus explain to him in vain that former rebellions of legions had no leaders, whereas at the head of affairs this time was a man descended from the ancient kings of Gaul and Aquitania, a famous and tried soldier. "Here," Nero answered, "the Greeks listen to me—the Greeks, who alone know how to listen, and who alone are worthy of my song." He said that his first duty was art and glory. But when at last the news came that Vindex had proclaimed him a wretched artist, he moved toward Rome. The wounds inflicted by Petronius, and healed by his stay in Greece, opened in his heart again, and he wished to seek retribution from the Senate for such unheard-of injustice.

On the road he saw a group cast in bronze, representing a Gallic warrior as overcome by a Roman knight; he considered that a good omen, and from them on, if he mentioned the rebellious legions and Vindex, it was only to ridicule them. His entrance to the city surpassed all that had been witnessed earlier. He entered in the chariot used by Augustus in his triumph. One arch of the Circus was destroyed to give a road to the procession. The Senate, nobles, and innumerable throngs of people went out to meet him. The walls trembled from shouts of "Hail, Augustus! Hail, Hercules! Hail, divinity, the incomparable, the Olympian, the immortal!" Behind him they carried the crowns, the names of cities in which he had triumphed; and on tablets were inscribed the names of the masters whom he had vanquished. Nero himself was intoxicated with delight, and with emotion he asked the Augustians who stood around him, "What was the triumph of Julius compared with this?" The idea that any mortal should dare to raise a hand on such a demigod did not enter his head. He felt himself truly an Olympian, and therefore safe. The excitement and the madness of the crowd increased his own madness. In fact, it might seem in the day of that triumph that not merely Caesar and the city, but the world, had lost its senses.

Through the flowers and the piles of wreaths no one could see the fatal precipice. Still, that same evening columns and walls of temples were covered with inscriptions describing Nero's crimes, threatening him with coming vengeance and ridiculing him as an artist. From mouth to mouth went the phrase "He sang until he roused the Gauls." Alarming news made the rounds of the city and reached enormous measures. Alarm filled the Augustians. People, uncertain of the future, dared not express hopes or wishes; they hardly dared to feel or think.

But he went on living only in the theater and music. Newly invented instruments occupied him, and a new water-organ, of which trials were made on the Palatine. With a childish mind, incapable of plan or action, he imagined that he could ward off danger by promises of spectacles and theatrical exhibitions reaching far into the future. Persons nearest him, seeing that instead of providing means and an army, he was merely searching for expressions to depict the danger graphically, began to lose their heads. Others thought that he was simply deafening himself and others in quotations, while in his soul he was alarmed and terrified.

In fact, his acts became feverish. Every day a thousand new plans flew through his head. At times he sprang up to rush out against danger, ordering them to pack up his lutes and citharae, to arm the young slave women as Amazons and lead the legions to the East. Again he thought to finish the rebellion of the Gallic legions, not with war, but with song; and he laughed at the spectacle that would follow his conquest of the soldiers by song. The legionaries would surround him with tears in their eyes; he would sing to them, after which the golden epoch would begin for him and for Rome. At one time he called for blood; at another he declared that he would be satisfied with governing in Egypt. He recalled the prediction that promised him lordship in Jerusalem, and he was moved by the thought that as a wandering minstrel he would earn his daily bread—that cities and countries would honor in him not Caesar, the lord of the earth, but a poet whose like the world had not produced before.

And so he struggled, raged, sang, changed his plans, his life, and the world into an absurd dream, fantastic and dreadful. It became an uproarious farce composed of unnatural expressions, bad verses, groans, tears, and blood. But meanwhile, the cloud in the west was increasing and thickening every day. The insane comedy was nearing its end.

When news that Galba and Spain had joined the uprising came to his ears, he fell into rage and madness. He broke goblets, overturned the table at a feast, and issued orders that neither Helius nor Tigellinus dared himself to execute. To kill Gauls resident in Rome, burn the city a second time, let out the wild beasts, and transfer the capital to Alexandria seemed to him reasonable and easy. But the days of his dominion had passed, and even those who shared in his former crimes began to look on him as a madman.

On a certain night a messenger rushed up on a foaming horse, with the news that in the city itself the soldiers had raised the standard of revolt and proclaimed Galba Caesar.

Nero was asleep when the messenger came; but when he woke he called in vain for the night guard, who watched at the entrance to his chambers. The palace was empty. Slaves were plundering in the most distant corners. But the sight of Nero frightened them; he wandered alone through the palace, filling it with cries of despair and fear.

At last his freedmen, Phaon, Sporus, and Epaphroditus, came to his rescue. They wanted him to flee and said that there was no time to be lost; but he still deceived himself. If he should dress in mourning and speak to the Senate, would it resist his prayers and eloquence? If he should use all his rhetoric and skill of an actor, would anyone on earth have power to resist him?

The freedmen, accustomed to flatter, did not have the boldness to refuse him directly; they only warned him that before he could reach the Forum the people would tear him to pieces and declared that if he did not mount his horse immediately, they too would desert him.

Phaon offered refuge in his villa outside the Nomentan Gate. After a while they mounted horses, and, covering Nero's head with a mantle, they galloped off toward the edge of the city. The night was growing pale. But on the streets there was a movement that showed the exceptional nature of the time. Soldiers, now singly and now in small groups, were scattered through the city. Not far from the camp Caesar's horse sprang aside suddenly at the sight of a corpse. The mantle slipped from his head; a soldier recognized Nero and, confused by the unexpected meeting, gave the military salute.

While passing the praetorian camp, they heard thundering shouts in honor of Galba. Nero understood at last that the hour of death was near. Terror and guilt filled him. He said that he saw darkness in front of him in the form of a black cloud. From that cloud came faces in which he saw his mother, his wife, and his brother. His teeth were chattering from fright; still, his soul of an actor found a kind of charm in the horror of the moment. To be absolute lord of the earth and lose all things seemed to him the height of tragedy; and, faithful to himself, he played the first role to the end. A fever for quotations took possession of him, and a passionate wish that those present should preserve them for posterity. At moments he said that he wished to die and called for Spiculus, the most skilled of all gladiators in killing. At moments he declaimed, "Mother, wife, father, call me to death!" Flashes of hope rose in him, however, from time to time—hope vain and childish. He knew that he was going to death, and still he did not believe it.

They found the Nomentan Gate open. Going farther, they passed Ostrianum, where Peter had taught and baptized. At daybreak they reached Phaon's villa.

There the freedmen told him that it was time to die. He asked them to dig a grave, then lay on the ground so that they might take accurate measurement. At the sight of the earth thrown up, however, terror filled him. His fat face became pale, and on his forehead sweat stood like drops of dew in the morning. He delayed. In a theatrical voice he declared that the hour had yet not come; then he began again to quote. At last he begged them to burn his body. "What an artist is perishing!" he repeated, as if in amazement.

Meanwhile, Phaon's messenger arrived with the announcement that the Senate had issued the sentence that the "parricide" was to be punished according to ancient custom.

"What is the ancient custom?" Nero asked, with a whitened face.

"They will put your neck in a fork, flog you to death, and hurl your body into the Tiber," answered Epaphroditus, abruptly.

Nero drew aside the robe from his breast.

"It is time, then!" he said, looking into the sky. And he repeated once more, "What an artist is perishing!"

At that moment the tramp of a horse was heard. That was the centurion coming with soldiers for the head of Ahenobarbus.

"Hurry!" the freedman cried.

Nero placed the knife to his neck, but pushed it only timidly. It was clear that he would never have the courage to thrust it in. Epaphroditus pushed his hand suddenly—the knife sank to the handle. Nero's eyes turned in his head, terrible, immense, and frightened.

"I bring you life!" the centurion cried, entering.

"Too late!" Nero said, with a hoarse voice; then he added, "Here is faithfulness!"

In an instant death arrived. Blood from his heavy neck gushed in a dark stream on the flowers of the garden. His legs kicked the ground, and he died.

The following day the faithful Acte wrapped his body in costly material and burned him on a pile filled with perfumes.

And so Nero passed, as a whirlwind, as a storm, as a fire, as war or death passes; but the church of Jesus Christ rules until now, from that city, every city, and throughout the world, for all eternity.

Near the ancient Porta Capena there stands to this day a little chapel with the inscription, somewhat worn: *Quo vadis, Domine?*

About the Author

Polish novelist **Henryk Sienkiewicz** served for a time as a news correspondent in the United States. He was awarded the Nobel Prize for Literature in 1905.

James S. Bell, Jr. (B.A., College of the Holy Cross; M.A., University College, Dublin) is editorial director at Moody Press. He is the former director of religious publishing at Doubleday and the former executive director of Bridge Publishing. He and his wife live in West Chicago, Illinois.